OUT OF THE DEPTHS

OUT OF THE DEPTHS

by

WILLIAM L. BIERSACH

Arcadia
MMVII

Nihil Obstat: *Huh?*

✤   Imprimatur: *Are you kidding!?!?*

ISBN: 978-0-9791600-1-1
0-9791600-1-4

Cover art by B. G. Callahan
Drawings signed "M.F." by the author
All other illustrations by Julia Ulano

All the characters and events in this novel are fictitious.
Any similarity to any actual persons,
living or dead, is purely coincidental.

©2007 by William L. Biersach

OUT OF THE DEPTHS

*The fourth book in the continuing saga of
Fr. John Baptist, the cop-turned-priest, and
Martin Feeney, his gardener-turned-chronicler.*

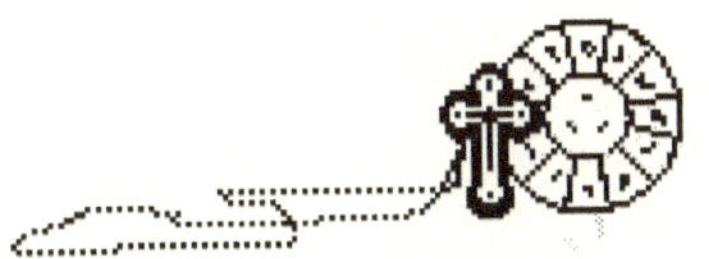

Other books by

William L. Biersach

∞

Published by Tumblar House

Fiction

The Endless Knot
The Darkness Did Not
The Search for Saint Valeria

Nonfiction

While the Eyes of the Great are Elsewhere

∞

Published by Catholic Treasures

Nonfiction

Of Mary There Is Never Enough

This book is dedicated to
My dear Friend

Anne Hale

Who believed in and promoted
My work from the beginning
And never ceased praying.

Stay with us, Lord, for evening is coming
and the day is now far spent …

—From Saint Luke XXIV: 29

Good Saint Anne,
Mother of She Who is Our Life,
Our Sweetness, and Our Hope, pray for us.

—Prayer to Saint Anne

Mark this well, for this we know with total certainty: that old and young, man and woman, rich and poor, prince and page, all the while we live in this world we are but prisoners and are in a secure prison out of which no one can escape ... we know with absolute certainty that we are already condemned to death, some by one way, some by another. None of us can tell what kind of death we are doomed to die, but definitely we can tell that we will die. And we know clearly that of this death we will get no kind of pardon. For the King by whose high sentence we are condemned to die would not of this death pardon his own Son. And as for escaping, no one can hope for that.

—St. Thomas More
The Four Last Things,
an unfinished treatise on a verse from Ecclesiasticus VII:40:
"In all thy works remember thy last end, and thou shalt never sin."

∞∞∞

It's hard to describe the passing of time when you're in a room without windows, clock, or watch ... Life slows to an over-cranked crawl and races with clenched talons all at once, and through a glass darkly to boot.

—Martin Feeney
Out of the Depths

∞∞∞

We must certainly be in a novel; what I like about this novelist is that he takes such time with his minor characters.

—G. K. Chesterton
Orthodoxy

∞∞∞

Nobody would do anything if they knew what they were in for.
—Amarante Cordova to Coyote Angel in the movie
The Milagro Beanfield War

Vuela, pequeño gorrión, de la cabeza extraña

En tu camino hacia la casa de oro

Que tu curso cruce sobre el arroyo de la vida

Que fluye de la fuente a la vid

Ahí donde y cuando son dichas las palabras sagradas

Mientras que tres veintenas y quince manos debajo

El tesoro sangra para rescatar almas

en la oscuridad.

0

AUTHOR'S NOTE: Unlike *The Search for Saint Valeria,* this present work is taking considerably longer than eleven days to write. In fact, I commenced on the Feast of the Assumption, 2002, and I'm still working on it as the same Feast approaches two years hence. Though the lion's share of this novel was and will be hammered out at Rock Haven, my home in Southern California, the words you are reading are being typed while I'm on vacation—my first in over ten years —overlooking the ocean on the coast of Oregon. I hope my readers won't mind if I take this opportunity to prattle more than usual before we get to our story.

Mission San Carlos Borromeo de Carmelo
Founded on June 3, 1770 by Padre Junipero Serra,
it became his resting place when he died in 1784.

On the way here by car, I made a point of visiting the grave of Blessed Junipero Serra at the Mission San Carlos Borromeo at Carmel-by-the-Sea. Since my writing is in some sense evangelical, I thought it fitting to acknowledge this great and humble missionary whose memory has been dragged through the mire lately by enemies outside the Catholic Church as well as by misguided souls within. Across his unassuming resting place in the sanctuary I mentally handed the outcome of my verbose literary efforts to Jesus Christ in the tabernacle. I found it touching that the wooden planks of Father Serra's original coffin were preserved lovingly in a glass case off to the side in that charming little church. ("No, my Mentor, you are not forgotten. While admitting that I have fabricated, in the course of my novels, certain historical details tangential to your courageous efforts among the indigenous pagans in what is now California, I trust my readers will discern where the Truth ends and the Biersachian deviations begin. If they don't … hoo-boy!")

The following day I visited the Mission San Juan Bautista, named for the Last of the Old Prophets and the namesake of my principal character. There I lit a candle and apologized if I have sullied his name with my verbal shenanigans, and again I gave my work and whatever may result from it back to God. This is something I must do continuously in hopes that my offering, emanating from my resistant Will, will some day radiate from my mutinous heart as well.

Half Dome
This picture of the famous rock formation in Yosemite National Park
was taken in the course of another trip entirely. I include it because
it is mentioned in our story and may be unfamiliar to some of my readers.

At present, the first book in this series, *The Endless Knot,* has entered its second printing, two years after its release. Just how remarkable that is depends on what impresses you and why. The fact that the entire stock of Mr. Frankini's first printing sold out speaks for itself. The detail that the first run consisted of 525 copies can turn the tale on its tail. Meanwhile, the camera-ready pages for the second book in the series have been finalized. Bonnie Callahan is working on the cover art as I write. Mark Alessio is composing a synopsis/blurb for the back. *The Darkness Did Not,* in other words, is about to see the light of day.

It's all a meager start, I'll grant you, but it's nonetheless a start. Momentum, as it relates to the projected progress of these books and their successors, is hovering out there in the same quadrant as chaos theory. Let us hope it doesn't become an argument for uniformitarianism, but all according to God's Will. In this respect I have had far more success than poor Martin Feeney, and my heart bleeds for him in his unpublished frustration.

As I tackle this fourth book, it occurs to me that I may not live to see my works flourish much beyond the high marks already reached. Is it vain to hope that after my passing my books might enjoy more widespread recognition? If such turns out to be the case, I would like to tell my readers and potential writers in the post-me future the following:

I wrote these books because they were in me to write. I have yet to make a penny from their publication, but money was never the point anyway. I am grateful that I have been granted the opportunity to say what I wish without concern for corporate policy and agenda-driven editing. I harbor a strange sense that these stories may give some Catholics out there the happy courage to deal with the dreadful mess in which we find ourselves. I'm also a believer in hanging our dirty linen in the breeze rather than pretending, for the benefit of wayfarers seeking entry, that all is well. It is only fair to tell those coming aboard our ship that "leaks are sprouting on all decks and most of the crew seems to be maniacally attempting to alleviate the situation by drilling more holes."[1] If nothing else, the titters from the pews might just shame some of our clergy back into sanctity. In any case, the bottom line remains the same, and was expressed best by our First Pope:

> Lord, to whom shall we go? Thou hast the words of eternal life.
> —The Gospel of Saint John VI:69

---

[1] This is a quote from a non-fiction work of mine entitled *While the Eyes of the Great are Elsewhere,* published by Tumblar House.

All that being said, it is not hubris, I think, to say that I enjoy my books immensely. They are my legacy, and I do so hope they become popular—or at least widely read—after I am gone, if not before. They make me laugh as I write them, and I so need to laugh. Moreover, Father Baptist and Martin Feeney and the rest are constantly reminding me not just to believe and accept, but also to practice the True Faith that comes to us from the Apostles with diligence, patience, perseverance, and a cheerful heart.

To those who don't get it, who are repulsed by merriment, who think that laughter in the face of adversity is aberrant, sinful, or out of place, may I suggest that they turn to Ecclesiasticus XXX: 22-27:

> Give not up thy soul to sadness, and afflict not thyself in thy own counsel. The joyfulness of the heart is the life of a man, and a never failing treasure of holiness: and the joy of a man is length of life. Have pity on thy own soul, pleasing God, and contain thyself: gather up thy heart in His holiness, and drive away sadness far from thee. For sadness hath killed many, and there is no profit in it. Envy and anger shorten a man's days, and pensiveness will bring old age before the time. A cheerful and good heart is always feasting, for his banquets are prepared with diligence.

Speaking of a cheerful heart, there are few things more gratifying than receiving responses from readers who have, in fact, gotten it. While not denying the pleasure a writer draws from praise, it is nothing compared to the delight derived from connecting with other human beings who share the same Faith, who experience life through the same lens, and who are fighting the same fight. My friendship with Mark Alessio, who writes splendid Marian articles for several Catholic publications[2], began when he wrote me a heartfelt letter after reading my little tome, *Of Mary There Is Never Enough*[3]. There is now a group of animated enthusiasts who discuss my books on the internet. I call them the Bapsters, and I'm waving to them as I write. The shocker-of-a-lifetime award goes to my seventh grade English teacher, Mother Mary Bernadine of the Sisters of the Holy Child Jesus, who phoned me regarding *The Endless Knot* a few months ago. It was this sweet though disciplinary nun who gave me my first set of J. R. R. Tolkien's *The Lord of the Rings* when I was yea high because she thought I

---

[2] Since this writing, Mr. Alessio's masterpiece on the Blessed Virgin Mary, *The Beauty of Thy House,* has seen the light of day. Loreto Publications. A must read.

[3] Published by Catholic Treasures, 1995.

might enjoy it. I told her recently that when I send her a copy of *The Darkness Did Not,* hot off the press, it would be inscribed, "This is all your fault!" (Alas, she is no longer a nun. She left the convent just as they were about to drop the habit and now ministers with her husband to the needs of the homeless in Bakersfield. God bless Mitchell and Diane Miller.)

Now, as to the present tale.

I have often been asked, "Just where is Saint Philomena's located?" In this story it, is finally pinpointed. My perspicacious readers will discover, however, should they procure a map of the real state of California, and further if they draw a line from Lompoc to San Juan Capistrano (why anyone should bother will become apparent later on), that said line will, except for a brief brush with the Palos Verdes Peninsula, float merrily in the Pacific Ocean several miles from shore. This provides further proof, should any still be necessary, that Cardinal Fulbright's archdiocese has no connection with the City of Los Angeles to be found on standard maps.

Ah yes, there are still those who insist, so let me call my reader's attention to another pair of anomalies that substantiate the mythical nature of the archdiocese in which my stories take place. Padre Alonso Miranda and Father Jean Pierre de Chantal never established the Del Agua Mission in what is now downtown Los Angeles. It is a complete fabrication. For that matter, Blessed Junipero Serra did not found a mission in Los Angeles, either, nor did anyone else. These historical inconsistencies, first mentioned in *The Endless Knot,* are now expanded upon in the present work. I therefore repeat: there never was a Misión del Agua de la Vida nor a Misión Nuestra Señora Reina de los Angeles de Porciuncula. There was a pueblo by the latter name, and a church called Our Lady Queen of Angels, but it was always just a parish and was originally served by the priests at the Mission San Gabriel. Now, back to my introduction.

One of the plot elements presented itself years ago when I visited Mission La Purisima in Santa Barbara County. I was disappointed to discover that this historic place was maintained and controlled by the State of California, not the Church of Salvation; hence the Blessed Sacrament was not reserved in the tabernacle. Having prowled the grounds and explored the restored buildings with all their rusty accoutrements, I was informed by an old codger outside the gift shop that the site of the original mission, which had been destroyed by an earthquake almost two centuries before, was actually several miles away. His directions were impeccable, and the photograph below reveals what is left of the grandest of all the California missions. Houses have been constructed over most of the site, and a railroad track plows right through, too. How sad. As disenchanting as the experience was for me, it gave me an idea, a notion that fermented over time and finally dripped out of the distillery onto these pages.

The "Lost" Mission
The original site of Mission de la Purisima Conception de Maria Santisima, which was destroyed by an earthquake on December 21st, 1812.

So, as my readers will find, the mythic tendrils reach out in new directions, both in space and in time. We have, among other things, some unfinished business from the *Darkness Did Not* and *The Search for Saint Valeria*. There is also the new matter of a fabulous artifact left in Cardinal Fulbright's care by the Holy Pontiff and guarded by the watchful eye of the papal nuncio. Most poignant of all is the problem faced by devout Catholics around the world who have been so let down by their clergy and deprived of the traditional Latin Mass. While I categorically disapprove of the solution proposed by some in the course of my story, I fully understand their desperation and would not be surprised if others have taken such radical steps to ensure their reception of valid Sacraments. So you see, I may laugh my way through the confusion, but I regard the chaos to be not only serious but devastating. Beware, oh ravening wolves in shepherd's clothing!

I sincerely hope this tale will remind all who read it that God is in control, that miracles are real, that laughter is good for the soul ... oh, and that Hope is a virtue well worth nurturing. Thank-you, and thanks again.

—WLB3
The Beachfront Inn
Brookings, Oregon
Summer Solstice, 2004

N.B.: The above introduction was written twenty-seven months before the manuscript was finished. I have chosen to leave it as is. I had a great time in Brookings. Since then *The Search for Saint Valeria* was published, as well as *While the Eyes of the Great are Elsewhere*, a theological work I wrote before I ever thought of Father Baptist. All things in their good time.

P.N.B.: I would like to take this opportunity to thank Stephen Frankini, my publisher, for his courage, generosity, patience, and forbearance with respect to me and my work; also congratulations on his marriage to Armida. Special thanks are also due to Charles A. Coulombe for helping me to navigate the complexities of the Roundhead familial tree, as well as the intricacies of California history, both actual and mythical; also to Julia Ulano for her invaluable assistance with the graphics and eleventh-hour proofing; Bonnie Callahan for another great cover; Joseph Treviño, the rising journalist, who hablas Español; Sgt. Anthony Futia of the Glendale Police Department for his investigative input; Tim Widman of USC for his geometric insights; Scott Sedillo and Beno May of Bernie Grundman Mastering for their suggestions regarding improvised electrical torture devices; Mark Alessio for his friendship, encouragement, and roiling blurbs, as well as his suggestions, in conjunction with his mother, Angela, regarding the papal nuncio; Margaret Dykes for suggesting a visit to La Purisma some years ago; Clare Buck for a curious turn of phrase with which I ran; Jeannette Coyne for inspiring a perplexing subplot that won't be resolved in this installment, as well as her manuscript scrutinizing; Connie Korte for her generous and enthusiastic moral support as well as her meticulous verbiage perusal; Annette F. Wilcox for setting me straight about transitives and intransitives; Christopher J. Waddell, my oldest friend, whose courage in the face of Parkinson's affects more people than he realizes; Dr. Ignacio Acosta, MD, for the *"¿Donde está el amor?"* on his office wall; Prof. William Dehning of the Thornton School of Music for the *"du vap, du vap, du vap"*; Caroline Beshenich of the Plains for

the inspiring pluck and dogged faith she exhibited during her recent illness; Christopher, Margaret, Isabella, and George Summit, for being
precisely who they are; Christopher Zehnder of the *Los Angeles Lay
Catholic Mission* who graciously granted permission for me to lift
Charles A. Coulombe's infamous article, "Fettuccini Cardinal Mahony"
from his newspaper, albeit with a few minor alterations to provide continuity with my story; Dena Suarez, Syler Womack, Ænola Koob,
Brendan King and all the Bapsters for their loyalty and encouragement;
Annie Witz, Jim O'Conner, and all those friends who will find comments they made along the way smiling up at them from the pages of
this book. Wink wink. Through it all, Anne Hale badgered St. Anthony of Padua with a seamless stream of novenas offered for the success of my work. "Badgered" would be her word. "Pummeled" would
be mine. I sometimes got discouraged, but she never wavered, not for
an instant.

P.P.N.B.: Please pray for Profirio, a homeless man who sat down on
the tracks near Bakersfield and was run over by a train while this book
was being written. A reminder that our woes and difficulties pale next
to those of so many others.

Wednesday, November Fifteenth

**Feast Day of Saint Albertus Magnus,
scientist and theologian, some say magician,
mentor of Saint Thomas Aquinas,
Doctor of the Church (1280 AD)**

1

"THAT'S THE LAST OF IT," SAID FATHER BAPTIST, emptying the bottle between our two crystal glasses. Even though it was nearly midnight and very dark, he didn't spill a drop. I would have heard it patter on the leathery ivy leaves at our feet.

"Very well," I sighed, pondering the dim starlight dancing upon the wavering surface of my wine. I gathered he was waiting for me to propose the final toast, but I wasn't about to cut the moment short. "One final aside, Father. About that lawyer."

"What lawyer?"

"Father."

"Oh, the one in St. Luke's Gospel?"

"The same. You brought him up last Saturday—"

"On this very spot, as I recall."

"—and earlier this evening, but you still haven't resolved the matter."

"What matter?"

We were in the garden between St. Philomena's Church and the rectory. Father was sitting on a wooden bench facing the statue of St. Thérèse the Little Flower, and I was resting against the pockmarked rim of the cement birdbath. Beside me huddled a little bird, a vague lump of stone really, which had broken off long before and had never been satisfactorily repaired. It had a tendency to fall off the edge into the ivy, but this night even it was too tired to take a tumble.

"What matter, you ask?" exclaimed yours truly. "Why, the crux, of course. The point of the exercise. Whatever it was you brought him up for."

"Oh, that," said he, rubbing his eyes wearily. "Well, if you must—Hold on."

A car was pulling up to the curb beyond the front gates. Even in broad daylight the trees, hedges, and the front wall would have blocked our view of its arrival. Either by design or happenstance, however, the shape of our little garden acted as a sort of acoustic collector of sound sources beyond our ramparts. We listened as the car door squawked slowly open, creaked back and forth several times, presumably during strained passenger extraction, held its peace during some muffled good-byes, then shut with a prolonged groan and an oxidized clang. Footsteps ascended the steps at the front of the rectory as the vehicle sputtered off on its gear-grinding way. Mumbles and curses erupted on the threshold as an annoyed hand probed the depths of a bottomless purse beneath the burned-out porch light. A grunt of triumph, and keys jiggled in the lock. The front door opened with a wooden moan and slammed with a hollow thud.

"Millie's home," commented Father. "I knew she was going out, but I don't know where."

"The Cladusky's," said I, knowingly.

"Is Bennie in the hospital again? Did Millie go to keep Muriel company?"

"No and yes. Bennie's fine. The Cladusky's have a television, don't forget."

"Millie never lets me forget."

Our housekeeper's footsteps pounded through the rectory like an ominous carnivore in a wooded thicket. They stomped down the hallway, paused at Father's study door, then continued on to Millie's quarters beyond the pantry.

"In any case," said Father, "it gives her an excuse to go out a few nights a week."

"And us to have some peace and quiet around here."

"Indeed, Martin." He seemed amused by the notion. "Indeed."

"And how, Father. Now, about that lawyer."

"I think I've had enough of lawyers for the nonce. The same thing goes for crime detection, ecclesial politics, and any further errands for our beloved cardinal."

"I can't argue with you there," said I, absently tapping the leather toe of my shoe with the rubber foot of my cane. "Do you sometimes feel like a 'son of a forgotten king, walking in loneliness, guarding from evil things folks that are heedless?'"

"No, Martin, but then I'm not a character in a Tolkien novel. Instead, I find myself trapped inside yet another of yours."

"How so?"

"I'm too tired, Martin. Let's finish and turn in."

"Very well." I looked down wistfully at my glass. Heaven knew when I'd get an opportunity to partake of the grape again.

> GARDENING TIPS: Having taken "the pledge" years
> ago, I do not imbibe alcoholic beverages. I know,
> I know. I often ask myself the same question, and
> the answer is always: "I gave up a good for a
> higher good in order to gain Grace." And boy, do
> I need Grace. On certain occasions, however, Fa-
> ther Baptist grants me a temporary dispensation.
> Hence this scene in the garden, and my reluctance
> to bring it to an end.
>
>   --M.F.

Deep within the bowels of the rectory, the door to Millie's bedroom opened, and the predatory footsteps, now muffled by slippers, made their way toward the kitchen. I peered at the illuminated clock on the stove through the window. 11:56. The numbers winked out momentarily as Millie passed by on her way to the sink for a glass of water. Her silhouette glared at us disapprovingly through the window as the time changed to 11:57.

Yes, the flesh being weak, it was time to down the last precious tears and hit the sack.

"Very well," I said again, clearing my throat and holding up my glass. "Here's to— Hold on."

Another car was pulling up to the curb, this one more expensive, or at least better maintained, than the last. The deep rumble of the motor ceased abruptly without prolonged, spluttering, mechanical protraction. The door opened with a lubricated sigh and closed with confident solidity.

"I wonder who that could be," said Father.

"Whoever it is," said I as the latch on the front gate squeaked, "he's not going to the rectory."

"You're right. He's coming this way."

Footsteps approached. Their rhythm was energetic, accented with spry clicks and scrapes of leather soles on the uneven brick path. I squinted to see their owner but could only perceive an indistinct glob of blackness against a backdrop of unresolved darkness. Just as the bolt on Millie's bedroom door clicked shut within, the advancing shadow resolved, much to my relief, into none other than Pierre Bontemps. The dim amber light of the stove clock illumined the outline of his opera hat and tailcoat. My knowledge of his habits filled in the details of his white bow tie and waistcoat, gray spats, and the regal monocle wedged in the socket of his left eye.

"Ah," he said cheerfully, clopping to a halt. "Father Baptist, Mister Feeney, I thought you might be here."

"I'd keep my voice down," I whispered. "Millie's just turned in."

"Quite right," said Pierre, shushing himself with a white-gloved hand. With a flourish he removed his monocle and began polishing it against his waistcoat.

"I see you got that repaired," I observed.

"Can't be without it," said he, expelling his breath upon it and giving it another circular rub.

"Why out here and not inside?" asked Father.

"I beg your pardon?" said Pierre.

"You came directly to the garden rather than the front door."

Pierre wedged the lens back into place between his eyebrow and up-thrust cheek. "I've had the privilege of reading Mr. Feeney's account of the Farnsworth affair. I am therefore aware of your, shall we say, tradition at the denouement of a case."

> GARDENING TIPS: Pierre figured prominently in the
> "Farnsworth affair," a series of events involving
> Father John Baptist and his faithful gardener,
> yours truly Martin Feeney, which had occurred the
> previous June, and which I had chronicled during
> the wee hours at my typewriter under the title of
> The Endless Knot. All my efforts to get it pub-
> lished had been unsuccessful. More on that in a
> moment.
>
> —M.F.

"And you've come to join us?" asked Father Baptist. He tried to sound enthusiastic, but the unmistakable sag of weariness hampered his vowels.

"After all," said Pierre with a self-involved sniff, "I was intimately involved in the case of Saint Valeria, may she rest in peace."

"We've been toasting that very thing," admitted Father.

"Alas, you're late," said the gardener, holding up his glass. "We've come to the dregs."

"Is that a fact?" said Pierre. "Surely you know that when it comes to a good time, a Bontemps always comes prepared."

Before we could protest—well, before Father could protest—our young friend produced a bottle of *Lacrimae Christi* from behind his back and proceeded to uncork it with a flourish.

"Of course, Sir Martin," added Pierre as I felt my own glass grow suddenly heavy as he graced it with a lavish continuance, "I consider the name you gave my character a mite contrived, but who am I to complain?"

"What about the name he gave me?" asked Father as his glass was similarly enhanced.

"Everyone's a critic," sighed the gardener, positioning his glass under his nose and inhaling deeply. "At the moment, I'm insensitive to the barbs of my detractors."

"At the moment," said Father, "you're on the verge of inebriation."

"I repeat," said I just before taking two extended sips. Then I rubbed the back of my neck to forestall an onset of stiffness. "I wonder why I let my friends read my drivel in the first place."

"In my case," said Pierre, "you were hoping I would use my influence as a journalist to persuade a couple of publishers to look at your opus with an open mind."

"And did you?"

"Did I what?"

"Give it to a couple of open-minded publishers?"

"A couple of publishers, yes. The openness of their minds remains to be seen. I haven't heard back from them yet."

"Let me know when you do. I can add their rejection letters to my collection. It's impressive."

"I don't suppose Joel is around?" asked Pierre, peering at the upstairs windows. They were all dark. "The lads and I were having quite a celebration, but he left early."

"He and his grandfather went to Barkinbay Beach," said Father.

"One of his sisters is celebrating her birthday tomorrow," I added.

"Not to be outdone," said Pierre, producing a glass for himself as if by magic. "We'll just have to have a party of our own."

GARDENING TIPS: Joel Maruppa was an ex-seminarian who, with the help of his ninety-three year-old grandfather, Josef, was in the process of rewiring and remodeling the upstairs rooms in the rectory. The original arrangement was work in exchange for room and board, but along the way the two of them had become absorbed into our household, though they missed a lot of meals, much to Millie's consternation.

--M.F.

"To Saint Valeria," said Pierre, "may she rest undisturbed."

"Bathed in the Blood of the Lamb," added Father, "and the Tears of Christ."

"Amen," agreed yours truly, knocking rims with theirs and hefting the nourishing liquid to my benumbing lips.

"If you gentlemen don't mind," said Father, setting his glass down on the bench, "I will take my leave."

"But the night," protested Pierre, "it is so young, Father."

"But this dumb ox," said Father, rising to his feet, "he is not. Please, finish your wine. You, too, Martin. No doubt you'll want to probe Pierre's mind for zingers for your next novel."

"Heavens," laughed Pierre, turning to me. "Are you? Writing another one, I mean?"

"Trying to," I said, grateful that my radiant blush was hidden by the night. "You remember the trouble at the 'House of Illusions' and how it came knocking at our rectory door."

"Oh, I say! Bravo!"

"Shhh," said Father, pointing toward the rectory.

"Bravo!" repeated Pierre in an exaggerated whisper. "Martin, dear chap, I would be only too happy to share my insights with you on that grisly matter."

"As I thought," said Father. "So if you two will excuse me, I'm going to—"

"Hold on," said a voice that didn't belong to any of us three.

"We hate to interrupt," said yet another voice.

"Is that you, Lieutenant Taper, Sergeant Wickes?" I asked, turning to peer through the gloom at the portentous shapes marching toward us from the direction of the rear gate. "Father, don't look now but I think we're surrounded."

"Saint Pope Gregory the Great," sighed Father, almost but not quite inaudibly, "give me strength."

"Taper and Wickes," whispered Pierre into my ear. "Talk about contrived names!" He was trying to be funny, but there was edge in his tone. This was understandable seeing as how these two officers of the law had arrested him on Monday. True, he had been released the following day, but these things can leave their mark.

"We know it's late," said Wickes.

"Indeed it is," said I, agreeing with the sergeant while shrugging at Pierre, "and Millie's just turned in so I'd advise keeping it down."

"Yipes," hissed Wickes, glancing at the kitchen window.

```
GARDENING TIPS: Pierre was referring to the names
    I had given our friends from the police department
    in The Endless Knot.  Like so many things in my
```

```
manuscripts, they had seemed ingenious in the wee
hours when I wrote them.
```
--M.F.

"We've got a problem," said Taper, his volume subdued but not his tone.

"As do I," said Father, taking a deep breath and letting it out slowly. He pressed his palms against the small of his back and leaned backwards. His spine responded with a chorus of joyful pops, an osseous symphony this arthritic gardener regarded with barely restrained envy. "Gentlemen," he yawned, "good as it is to see you, I'm tired."

"You said it yourself," said Wickes, quoting one of Father's recent sermons. "'A true Catholic never has the luxury of pleading weariness, not when duty calls.'"

"My duty," said Father, straightening, "is to my flock. I've spent far too much time lately, if I may be frank among friends, helping the police do their job."

"I understand, Jack," said Lt. Taper. "You know I do. But I'm sure you'll want to know about this, and I can guarantee the cardinal will be phoning you any minute."

"I hardly see—" began Father, but his protest was cut short by the shrill stereo ringing of the telephone in his study and the extension in the kitchen.

An ominous rumble of protest emanated from Millie's bedroom.

11:59 glowed the clock on the stove.

"That's probably him now," said Taper.

"*Laissez les Bontemps Rouler!*" beamed Pierre, downing his wine.

"Let the good times roll," sighed the gardener, doing likewise, but in several prolonged gulps.

"*Bona tempora volvant,*" said Father, heading for the kitchen door. "My eye."

Thursday, November Sixteenth

**Feast Day of Saint Gertrude,
often called the Great.
On the Feast day of St. John the Evangelist
she was taken by him
to rest her head upon the Sacred Heart of Jesus.
St. Teresa of Avila and St. Francis de Sales
were especially devoted to her.
She was forty-six when she died (1302 AD)**

2

"OF COURSE, YOUR EMINENCE," Father Baptist was saying into the telephone between suppressed yawns, just as I closed the kitchen door behind me. "If that is what you wish, I will meet you there."

"There and back again," I panted between gasps, leaning my cane against the wall and easing myself into my usual chair in the breakfast nook. A handful of aspirin would have hit the spot right about then. "What'd I miss?"

"A close brush with death!" grumbled Millie, our beloved housekeep-trix and sweetest of den mothers, slamming down five mismatched mugs on the tiny table. She was attired in wobbling green plastic rollers, frayed orange-and-pink plaid housecoat, sagging white socks, and a pair of those furry machine-washable scuff-along slippers, one faded yellow and the other very faded yellow. She shuffled over to the stove and returned with a fresh pot of six-molar caffeine which she dive-bombed into our cups without any collateral damage to two paper plates piled with teetering columns of her irresistible homemade oatmeal-molasses cookies. "How's a woman supposed to sleep around here with all this racket?"

"Can't imagine," said I, watching the murky brew rolling around the inside of the closest mug as if a shark was circling beneath the surface. The thought of aspirin suddenly lost its appeal. "I certainly couldn't."

"Nor could I," said Pierre, stepping aside so she could invade the chugging refrigerator in search of cream. His opera hat rested inverted in the crook of his left elbow with his white gloves lolling over the rim like the tongue of a thirsty dog. He was the only male in the room who was upstanding, and the only one of us all who looked fresh and presentable. "One can only wonder, Madam, how you put up with it."

"Can it, Good Times," she snarled, shoving foodstuffs this way and that on the creaking wire shelves within the fridge. The light bulb was missing or dead, so it took her a while to grope her way through the dark recesses. "No cream," she announced over her shoulder, "just 'blue moo juice.'" That was her term for "fat-free milk," and she didn't bother bringing it out because no one was going to ruin their coffee with it anyway.

"Deo gratias," said Father, handing me the receiver for cradling and sinking back into his chair like a sack of cement. He eyed the coffee in his mug. "Bless you, Millie."

"It's called 'working off your Purgatory time,'" said she, shutting the refrigerator door with a sideways thrust of her hip and trundling over to the sink to wash her hands. "Lord knows I've accumulated my share."

"I gather Cardinal Fulbright filled you in," said Lieutenant Taper who, along with his partner, was already seated at the table, glaring at the cookies ravenously. "Here Sergeant, try one of these. Jack, if I could afford it, and if my wife wouldn't object, I'd hire Millie away from you."

Father glanced at his friend from the force with drooping eyes, a look that seemed to whisper, drained and exhaustedly, "Considering how much Purgatory time I've racked up myself, Larry, there is no amount of money that could compensate for the Graces supplied through our angelic Millie. Furthermore, God bless her, she works here gratis." But all he actually said was, "Martin, did you talk to Monsignor Havermeyer?"

"I did indeed," said I, gazing upon Millie for the first time as a walking, talking plenary indulgence.

"And he's amenable?"

"Five hundred marauding dwarves with chainsaws couldn't dissuade him."

"That, at least, is good news."

I'd just returned from a laborious trek—for my spinal arthritis and me any trek is laborious—to our resident monsignor's top-heavy RV in the back parking lot. Michael K. Havermeyer, a product of the modernist revolution in the Church, had, as recently as the previous June, thought better of it all, resigned his sinecure at St. Philip's, and joined our parish family. Then, on the Sunday prior to the present conversation, November twelfth to be exact, after weeks of studious preparation, he had celebrated his first Tridentine Mass. This privilege he had repeated every morning since, Father Baptist having been otherwise engaged in "helping the police do their job." The monsignor had received the news of yet another opportunity to offer Solemn Sacrifice according to the Old Rite with fervent, childlike eagerness, which said much about him. I suspected that a great part of Father Baptist's present weariness stemmed from his own forced abstinence from that which meant more to him than life itself.

"So," I asked, "did His Elegance the Cardinal clarify the matter, Father?"

"Not entirely," said he. "We're to meet him at the archdiocesan seminary at 6:30."

"You and me? This morning? In Camarillo? Why there?"

"Because that's where he's going to be. In the meantime, we're to accompany Lt. Taper and Sgt. Wickes to New Golgotha Cemetery to look into the situation there."

"Good Heavens," exclaimed Pierre, setting his opera hat on the edge of the table dramatically and assuming an alert, almost military posture. He didn't seem to mind that all the chairs were taken, preferring as he did room to gesticulate with panache. "I should think we've had enough of *that* place. Er, what situation is that?"

"The one these gentlemen are going to tell us about," said Father, gripping his coffee mug with both hands.

"Keeping me up at this hour," said Millie, approaching menacingly, spatula in sinewy hand, "this had better be good."

The policemen looked cornered, even though they were armed.

"Well, it's this way," ahemed Taper after a brief stare-down with Millie, which he lost. "Jack, you cleared up the Galloway case less than forty-eight hours ago."

"Not to mention," added Wickes, taking a cookie from the pile, "somehow making the issue of the theft of Saint Valeria ... well, vaporize." He stuffed the thing whole into his mouth, no doubt for Millie's sake.

"Tell us something we don't know," said Pierre who, after all, had been arrested for both the night watchman's murder and the theft of the body of the Patron Saint of the archdiocese. He had a right to be a bit testy.

"Last night around ten," said Taper, who I gathered felt no obligation to apologize to Pierre whatsoever, "after filing all our reports, we decided to swing by the mausoleum and release the crime scene. We arranged for one of the watchmen, Duggo, to meet us there to seal up the crypt so we could remove our tape and barriers and pull out."

"Is this going to be a two-egg story or three?" growled Millie.

"Oh," said Father, "you needn't—"

It was only then that I realized how truly exhausted he was. Having been deprived of her sleep, and having surmised from this fragmented conversation that breakfast was not going to be served at its usual time, Millie had decided to make breakfast *now,* and no force above, upon, or below the earth could sway her from her raging course. For Father to miss this, clearly some of his cylinders were misfiring.

"—you needn't restrict yourself to eggs, Millie," said Father, making a shaky recovery. As they say, any landing you walk away from is a good one. "Do break out the bacon and hash browns, and how about some of your marvelous biscuits?"

She gave him a withering look as if to say, "Don't push it, Bub—excuse me, *Father* Bub," then grinned impishly as she whirled around and charged at the stove, a culinary banshee unleashed.

"Continue," said Father as Millie heaved a gob of butter into her second-largest frying pan and cranked the gas.

"Curiously," said Taper, "when we arrived at the mausoleum, we found the crypt in the wall resealed."

"Duggo got there ahead of you?" asked Pierre.

Taper shook his head. "Duggo showed up ten minutes after we did. Someone else had cemented a marble slab into place over the opening."

"Rethenthly, thoo," sputtered Wickes, snatching up a mug to wash down his half-chewed cookie. His first attempt at a swig scalded his lips, so he resorted to a noisy little sip. "Recently, too," he repeated after a loud, excruciating swallow. "The plaster was still wet."

"This was all the more puzzling," added Taper, "because we'd brought the original facing stone in the back of our car. You'll remember it was held as evidence in the Galloway death. You can imagine our surprise when we lugged that thing into the mausoleum and found the niche already sealed."

"Any idea," asked Father, "where the fresh facing stone came from?"

"There's a storage yard behind the mausoleum," said Wickes. "We found a stack of more than a dozen spare slabs there, along with sacks of plaster, and a shed full of internment implements—buckets and trowels and such."

"One of the buckets had been recently rinsed out," said Taper.

"Was this service area locked?" asked the gardener.

"No," said Wickes with an amused shrug. "The outer cemetery gates are chained shut at night, and it's not as though there's much call for funerary accoutrements on the black market."

"You're sure of that?"

Wickes' smile faded. His eyes looked tired. "I guess not."

Millie turned her attention to hacking up a couple of potatoes with a meat cleaver. The glint of metal, the rapid chops, the bits of flailing potato flesh—somehow it wasn't a pretty sight. Performed by any normal housewife it would have seemed comfy-cozy, but not when executed by our Millie. Somehow she turned meal preparation into something sado-prickly.

"So you opened it, of course," said Father. "The crypt."

"Yes," said Taper and Wickes together, though Wickes had to splutter the word around another cookie he had just inserted into his mouth.

"And?" asked the priest, the gardener, and the journalist in stunning unison.

"There was a body inside," said Taper. "A man."

"A very elderly man," said Wickes, tucking the wad of partially masticated cookie into his right cheek with his tongue so his words could get out, rendering his face comically lopsided. "My guess is he'd been dead for some hours, say eighteen to twenty-four, perhaps longer. His skin was cold to the touch and the rigors were wearing off."

"I take it," said Father, "he wasn't in a coffin."

"Right." Taper paused, searching for the right words. "He was probably pushed in while he was—um, sorry to be graphic in front of you, Millie—"

"No problem," she called, spinning her spatula like a six-shooter. "Around here you get used to it!"

"What you're trying to say, Larry," said Father, "is that *rigor mortis* had set in while the man was supine, and that the body was shoved feet first into the narrow burial compartment in that stiffened state, otherwise the limbs and torso would have buckled in the process."

"Something like that," said Taper. "How did you know it was feet first?"

"It would be a breach of procedure for you to pull the body out," said Father. "Sgt. Wickes exceeded his bounds by touching it at all, save to check for signs of life, unless the rules have changed. That privilege is reserved for the coroner's investigators."

Wickes paused his chewing long enough to heave an embarrassed shrug.

"Aside from that," continued Father, "you said the man was elderly, and I doubt you could have determined that by examining his shoes. Therefore, his head must have been nearest the opening. Since we all know that post-mortem rigidity is an unreliable indicator, we'll have to wait for the coroner's report for the time of death."

Well, I thought as I blew the layer of low-hovering steam from my coffee, at least some of his cylinders are combusting merrily away.

"Apparent cause of death?" asked Father.

"Unknown," said Wickes after an excruciating swallow and another surge of coffee. "There were no obvious indications. Rather than disturb the evidence—ahem—we left the body in place for the crime scene crew. We looked inside the niche with a flashlight but there was only so much we could see."

"He was dressed in a black cassock," said Taper. "Much like yours, Jack. Complete with a Roman collar and what looked like a pectoral Cross."

"A priest," said Father.

"We think so," said Taper.

"You *think* so?"

"The lab crew went to work as we were leaving. They shooed us out of there, but they did tell us that, at least on initial examination, there was no identification on his person."

"Shooed you away? From a crime scene?"

"Well, not exactly. Billowack ordered us to come here."

"I'm not following you."

"Pardon me, gentlemen, but neither am I," said Pierre, who had produced a small notebook in a silver case with a matching fountain pen. "You're saying someone put a corpse dressed in traditional clerical garb inside the same crypt that had previously housed the body of Saint Valeria?"

"That's right," said Taper. "And you won't print a word of this until I say so."

"Of course, Lieutenant," said Pierre stiffly. "Of course."

"This is intriguing," said Father after a long sip of coffee, "but I don't see how it has anything to do with me."

"Jack," said Taper, "I should think—"

"How many times do I have to tell you," said Father, setting his mug down hard. "I gave up crime detection when I took my vows. It's a part of my life I wish to bury once and for all. I have other duties now—"

"One of which is obedience to your lawful superior," said Taper. "You heard what the cardinal said—"

"He said nothing substantial," said Father angrily. "He huffed and he puffed and he ordered me to cooperate with you and then to come scampering all the way up to Camarillo to meet with him just before dawn. I've yet to see why any of this involves me in the least."

"The dead man's a priest," said Taper. "You're a priest—"

"And you're the police," snapped Father. "Homicide is your department, not mine. There is no reason—"

"Monsignor Aspic," said Pierre with a snap of his fingers. "Could the cardinal's summons have something to do with him?"

"Wawps thop ew pthayb?" said Wickes around another cookie—his third, I think. His eyes were wide as he spoke, but whether that was from surprise or just stretching his face to accommodate his mouthful I couldn't say. In any case, I believe the translation was, "What's that you said?"

"I beg your pardon, Sergeant," said Pierre, furrowing his eyebrows for a moment of doughy mental deciphering. "I was commenting that Conrad J. Aspic, Morley Fulbright's faithful watchdog and snake oil peddler, has been extraordinarily active in the campaign to downplay the whole Saint Valeria affair. Why, he held not one but two press conferences yesterday morning just to question her authenticity and thereby erase her memory. As a representative of the press, I was present at both events."

"So?" asked the gardener.

"It gets better," said Pierre, adjusting his cufflinks. "A few hours ago I was out celebrating my liberation from wrongful incarceration at Darby's with the lads." He emphasized mention of his arrest with a meaningful glance at Taper and Wickes. "You all know Father's friend, Alan Ross, the proprietor. Well, throughout the festivities he repeatedly threatened to tune the big-screen television to that horrid talk show, 'Religion Revisited.' Mr. Ross was joking, of course, just being cruel in a fun sort of way—or is it funny in a cruel sort of way? All my friends seem to have a cruel streak, have you noticed? Anyway, Monsignor Aspic was going to be the honored guest on the show for the second time in four days—some sort of confetti-proliferating triumph, apparently. It was to be a media event, an eruption of hoopla, a moment of moment, *et cetera*. In any case, Mr. Ross went so far as to turn to the channel a half-hour before the show to catch the promos. The station was really playing it up, running bits from the previous broadcast in which the monsignor thrashed the Catholic Faith and thereby won their hearts."

"So how was it?" asked Taper. "Last night's show, I mean."

Pierre shrugged. "Mr. Ross had us going right up until air time, but at the last second he switched to the Brewery Channel and we all got to see how they make lager in Bavaria."

"That was close," said Taper, smiling.

"Too close for comfort," agreed Pierre, wiping his brow for effect. "The lads and I were actually calling for our hats and coats when Mr. Ross finally relented."

"I think Millie can do you one better," said the gardener.

"Oh?" asked Pierre, unused to being outdone.

"Millie, didn't you go over to the Cladusky's to watch that show?"

"Indeed I did," she snapped, flipping the contents of her skillet in midair for effect. "I had to, seeing as how we don't have a TV here."

"And?"

"What business he has wearing a Roman collar is beyond me," she said, punctuating all sixteen syllables with whacks of her spatula applied to said skillet as she set it down on the back burner. That being settled, she began threatening something in the frying pan with a straining spoon. "Last Saturday he 'spoke in tongues' on the air. Can you believe it? Gobbledygook, plain and simple, but he called it 'praying in the spirit.' More like 'braying under the influence' if you ask me. When he was done embarrassing himself, they announced that due to popular demand—the phones were jammed with viewers actually *raving!*—they were inviting him back on Wednesday."

"Last evening, you mean," said Pierre.

"Why do you think I'm still up?" she huffed. "I went over to Muriel's again to watch the horror continue."

"So?" asked the gardener. "How was it?

She grabbed dangerous utensils, two to a fist, and started attacking everything atop the stove. "It was going to be worse, I just knew it! Muriel and I got our popcorn ready a good twenty minutes ahead of time so we wouldn't miss a second. At a quarter to the station was showing excerpts from his press conferences yesterday morning." As she continued, her voice grew more and more vociferous until she was shouting louder than her own metallic percussion section. "There he was, standing in front of the Chancery, and again at that beautiful Del Agua Mission, claiming that Saint Valeria was never really here in Los Angeles, that she'd been in Rome the whole time if at all, which was doubtful, that we silly, gullible believers had been praying to a hoax! 'So sorry,' he said, 'mistakes will happen!' Mistakes! Why, that charlatan wouldn't know a Saint if one came up and hit him on the head with a pressure cooker. And to think, Father, that you gave the weasel that beautiful, beautiful Crucifix not two weeks ago. He was wearing it right there in front of the cameras as he questioned our Dogmas and denied our own sweet Valeria!"

I'm guessing at her last sentence. Her voice had grown so shrill and fierce that it overloaded my eardrums. Fortunately her wrath was diverted just then to something gooey hiding under the rim of a saucepan lid.

"So, how was the show?" asked Taper, Wickes, and yours truly together.

Suddenly, there was silence.

The clang and clatter of steel against aluminum abruptly ceased. Even the bacon seemed to cease its sizzling. With perilous implements still clutched in her fists, Millie turned to us, eyelids fluttering with rage.

"The—louse—didn't—show," she said in a low, quavering voice.

"Excuse me?" asked the gardener.

"After all that brouhaha," said Millie, "all that building us up, and Muriel and me sitting there like teenagers with these bowls of popcorn in our laps, after all that: the little—grrrrrrrr!—he didn't even show up!"

"What ho!" laughed Pierre. "Surely you're jok—" His levity was cut short by an ominous sideways glare from our sweet housekeeper.

"There sat Sheldon and Eira—they're the hosts," said she, her agitated lips dancing around the edges of her clenched teeth. "There they sat—sickening snots, both of them—but even so! Lights, cameras, but no action. It was embarrassing. The monsignor didn't even phone the station to explain or apologize or anything. What could they say?"

"Therein lies the hazard of live television," said Father, detached and sensibly. "A simple thing like a traffic jam can render the whole affair pointless."

"Come to think of it," said Taper, "it might have been exactly that. Sergeant, didn't a report come over the radio a little before eight that there was a major tie-up in Hollywood?"

"Hm-hm," said Wickes, eyeing another cookie. Then he considered the feast sputtering and crackling on the stove and decided against it. "Five-car collision at Hollywood Boulevard and Highland. Quite a mess."

"Even so," said Father, "you'd think he would have phoned."

"These two hosts guys," ventured the gardener. "Sheldon and Ira?"

"Sheldon and E—I—R—A," said Millie with a distasteful sneer. "He's a him, and she's a her, and they're married. Levant's their last name. No wait, they're divorced—or remarried but still partners or something. It's hard to keep these things straight."

"Straight indeed," said Pierre. "Sheldon Levant has a certain, shall we say, reputation as a philanderer. His beloved wife, too."

"Why am I not surprised?" asked yours truly. "They host a talk show on religious deterioration, after all. So what did the snickering snots do?"

"After ten minutes of hemming and hawing," said Millie, gripping her utensils for another attack upon our breakfast, "they started running film clips of the press conferences again, and bits of last Saturday's show. They took some callers, most of them denouncing it as another Catholic plot to do something or other. Sheldon and Eira did their best, but it all fell apart."

"Whatever else he is," said Father, "Monsignor Aspic strikes me as a punctual fellow, assiduously so. I wonder what happened."

"How should I know?" called Millie over her shoulder. "To top it all off, Bennie, Muriel's husband, got chest pains. It was just gas—Saints in Heaven, hasn't he figured that out by now? So it was off to the hospital and back. We took him in Muriel's car. After all that, she brought me home and I didn't have time to get snoozing properly when all this new commotion exploded in my kitchen."

She paused to glare at Taper and Wickes, who weren't about to point out that she was making the rhinoceros's share of the clamor.

"I see," said Father, clearing his throat as he assessed the pertinence of this entire derailment of the conversation. "Pierre, you're the one who brought up Monsignor Aspic in the first place. What was your point?"

"Ah," said Pierre, pretending to change the channel knob on the side of his head. "As to a possible connection with this new development at New Golgotha, I was thinking that, with all the energy Fulbright has expended via Monsignor Aspic to downplay Saint Valeria, perhaps he's afraid that this new murder in the mausoleum—"

"We don't know that it's murder," said Taper.

"Quite right," said the gardener, regarding Pierre. "Best to be sure whether it is, in fact, a murder. Yes, indeed. I repeat: whether it is, indeed, a homicide and not death from natural causes. Wouldn't want history to *repeat* or anything like that—"

"Okay, Martin," said Taper. "We get the message."

"You were saying, Pierre?" said Father.

"This unidentified body, then," said Pierre, giving me an appreciative nod and a wink. "Perhaps His Eminence fears that a spotlight aimed by the media at New Golgotha will bring some of his recent indiscretions regarding the sale of relics to light."

"Possibly," said Father. "Sergeant Wickes, tell us the real reason."

Wickes tried to look professionally blank, but it came off as oblivious. "Huh?"

"No games," said Father, turning back to Taper. "What's the connection between Monsignor Aspic and the body in the mausoleum?"

"We didn't say there was any," said the lieutenant.

"Sergeant Wickes reacted to Pierre's comment a few minutes ago as though there were."

"I wasn't reacting," said Wickes. "I was talking with a mouth full of Millie's cookies."

Okay, thought the gardener, so some of Father's cylinders *are* misfiring.

"When I called in our discovery at New Golgotha to Chief Billowack," explained Taper, "he put me on hold and phoned Cardinal Fulbright. It's funny how those two have gotten so close since you Baptized his daughter, and I don't think it's because Billowack is considering converting."

"I doubt that very much," agreed Father, "and I didn't perform the Baptism."

"No, but you prepared her for it, which in his mind amounts to the same thing. Anyway, when the chief came back on the line, he was all worked up. Wouldn't say why. He told me to contact you immediately, that there was a new development."

"Such as?" asked Father.

Taper shrugged and picked up his mug. "I honestly don't know, Jack. But the cardinal is in an uproar; and when he's upset, Chief Billowack makes a point of making himself even more upset."

"And when the chief's upset," said Wickes, giving into his hunger by snatching another cookie, "we get—"

"Okay, okay, I got it," said Father, exasperated. He pressed his hands palms down on the table and spread his fingers as wide as they would go. Then he balled his hands into fists and pounded the table with both of them. "Lord, grant me *strength!*" His coffee mug heaved, reeled, and emptied most of its contents onto the tabletop.

Father Baptist so rarely lost his cool that even Millie ceased her clanging and battering. Pierre halted his scribbling, Taper ceased sipping, and Sergeant Wickes dropped his cookie and stopped breathing. I said a Hail Mary under my breath while turning mental pages in my head to Saint Paul's Epistle to the Romans.

Father pressed the palms of his hands to his forehead, then slowly plowed his hair back out of the way with his fingers. He locked his fingers behind his neck and twisted his head producing a loud crack. With eyes closed he took a deep breath, held it, then exhaled slowly, his lips writhing to a silent prayer, doubtless in Latin.

"Forgive me, Millie, Gentlemen," he finally said, opening his eyes. They were already aimed right at mine before his lids went up. A chill went through me as our stares collided. I could almost hear him say, disconcerting but reassuringly, "You're right of course, Martin: Romans chapter eight, verse twenty-eight—what was I thinking?" But what he actually said aloud, and apparently not to me, was, "I've allowed my fatigue to get the better of me. Do continue, Larry."

Millie signaled the passing of tension by three loud slams of her spatula against whatever was whimpering for mercy in the frying pan. Taper set down his mug, Wickes resumed respiring—in fact, he celebrated his relief by snatching up two cookies and inserting them whole into his mouth—and I said another Hail Mary in thanksgiving.

"That's all there is," said the lieutenant, gingerly mopping up Father's spill with his napkin. "The crime scene team took over just before we came here to see you. They'll be a while, so we can enjoy an early breakfast before we head back to the mausoleum. Chief Billowack said he'd meet us there, and he agreed not to transport the body until we return with you. Maybe you can identify him."

"Martin and I will come in our own car," said Father. "From there we'll head up to Camarillo to meet His Eminence. Pierre, would you care to join us?"

"Indeed! May I?" said Monsieur Bontemps, twirling his pen in the air like a sparkler. Then, as if an ember from that whimsical firework stuck him on the forehead, he winced. "Ah, but rumor has it—"

"I'm sorry, Pierre," said Lieutenant Taper, shaking his head. "Even with a press card—*especially* with a press card—the chief isn't going to let you anywhere near that mausoleum."

"Expected and understood," said Pierre. "Father, as for my accompanying you and Martin to Camarillo, I was about to say rumor has it that the cardinal is a bit miffed at me."

"You?" asked Taper.

"Burthunolly?" sputtered Wickes.

"Don't shake your head like that, Sergeant," said Pierre. "One of my anonymous contacts has assured me of this."

"I can imagine what contacts you'd have," said Wickes after another excruciating swallow.

"Actually, it's true, Sergeant," said Father. "I also have so heard, and my sources would not want their names connected with the information, either."

"Because of Saint Valeria?" asked Taper. "Is that why the Fulbright's ticked at Pierre?"

"No," said Father. "Because Pierre wrote an article for the *L. A. Artsy* about the cardinal's favorite restaurant."

"So?" asked Wickes.

"So," said Father, "that little bit of pointless journalistic voyeurism has put 'Paneno's' on the map. I understand the article was picked up by several major newspapers. Now His Eminence's lunches there are punctuated by the oohs and ahs of the inanely curious. Believe it or not, Cardinal Fulbright does have his adoring fans."

"Not to mention process servers," said I.

"I assume, Pierre," said Father, ignoring me, "that the article was accompanied by a photo of your august self?"

"At Madam Hummingbird's insistence," said Pierre. "As my editrix, she's got this plan to make me known in this town."

"An icon, even," said the gardener. "One who has written a number of articles that—how do I put this?—run counter to the flow of His Arrogance's desultory counter-religious quasi-cultural avalanche."

"His what-a-what?" asked Taper, Wickes, and Millie together. It sounded to me like a double-flatted diminished chord, but I'd have to check with Danielle Parks, our choir director—or better yet, Wanda Hemmingway, our first soprano who always smells of patchouli—to be sure. But that would have to wait.

"Exactly," said Pierre triumphantly. "Even if the cardinal reads my pieces, I doubt he'll understand them."

"Oh, he'd never bother himself," said Father. "He relies on clerks to render down to an index card everything said about him in the media each day. Even so, knowing the ways of restaurants that cater to the vain and their admirers, I'd wager that the offending article and accompanying photograph now reside in a glass frame above the cardinal's favorite booth. Yes, it's safe to say that His Eminence is only too aware of you—"

"Wait a minute," groaned Pierre, slapping his forehead. "This is Thursday now, isn't it?"

"Has been," said I, "for almost fifteen minutes. Why?"

"Madam Hummingbird has to put the *Artsy* to bed by ten this morning in order to go to press and be distributed throughout the city tomorrow."

"And a gentleman never leaves a woman in the lurch," said the gardener.

"Alas, that is so," said Pierre, shoulders subsiding, "especially if he wishes to allay any disruption in the continuity of his income. I'm afraid I can't accompany you, Father, even if I were welcome. In fact, I really should return her car before long."

"So that's what you're driving," said the gardener. "The ultimate pink Cadillac."

"Perhaps it's for the best," said Father. "I've no idea what the cardinal wants or where we may have to go to accomplish it. If I'm indisposed—Heaven forbid, but you never know—you'll have to rally the Tumblars tonight without me."

```
GARDENING TIPS: "The Knights of the Tumblar": an-
other facet of our parish family that will be ex-
plained in due time.
                                        --M.F.
```

"Quite right," said Pierre, accepting the situation with dignified style. "I can count on you to fill me in when Lieutenant Taper lifts the veil of silence."

"Of course," said Father after downing his coffee. "Now, that being settled, I suggest we enjoy Millie's—"

"Breakfast!" she yelled, tossing five platters piled with food onto the table.

Yes, she was a plenary indulgence, but also a great cook.

3

"IT'S ABOUT TIME YOU GOT HERE," bellowed Chief Montgomery "Bulldog" Billowack, spittle running down his wobbling jowls. His massive derriere was stuffed into a wheelchair two sizes too small, with crooked wheels that squeaked in agony every time he jiggled around, which was constantly. His left leg was out straight, supported by some sort of steel attachment apparatus, and his extended foot was wrapped in stained, frayed bandages like a bloated mummy. "I was hopin' you could ID this carcass, so I told the crime scene boys to hold off transportin' it."

"Kind of you, Monty," said Father, who was probably the only human being who got away with calling him that. "I'm sorry to see your ankle hasn't healed."

"You should know. I sprained it on your property."

"In the line of duty, don't forget."

"Oh, I don't forget. That's why I can't sue you out of church and cassock."

GARDENING TIPS: It had been two weeks since that
fateful Halloween when our beloved Bulldog tripped
over the birdbath in the garden, the one favored
as a roost by both myself and my little friend,
the porous stone bird. The chief had been chasing
Jonathan, his potential son-in-law, at the time,
which kind of negates the "line of duty" angle,
and would prove problematic in an official police
report. But all that's another story, one for
which I would have been probing Pierre's mind for
zingers in the garden if all this other rigmarole
hadn't come up.

                                        --M.F.

We were standing in a vaulted room in the mausoleum at New Golgotha Cemetery. The place was ablaze with the blistering glare of portable incandescent lamps. Policemen and technicians were milling all around. Through an archway I could see the crypt which had been the center of so much activity and controversy only five days before. The empty rectangular hole in the lower wall had been the short-lived resting place of Saint Valeria—no hoax, the real enchilada. It was still there, along with the blank facing stone that had apparently been cemented back in place and removed yet again, now leaning beside it.

"Don't let me keep you, Padre," said the bulldog, indicating a dark shape on the coroner's gurney. With a series of porky grunts, rubbery groans, and metallic rattles he managed to maneuver his wheelchair into a better position to watch. "Help yourself. See what you can see."

I know of no one who gets queasier around dead bodies than yours truly, Martin Feeney. The fact that this one was ensconced in a black body bag only made it worse because the flabby plastic folds and bulges served to fuel my morbid imagination. I felt my teeth grow soft as Father reached for the tab of the cold steel zipper and pulled it down as far as the dead man's collarbone.

No, I howled inside. No, no, noooooooooo—

But my revulsion vanished at the sight of the kindly face that came into view, like a flower blossoming on a warm spring day. The man was old, terribly old, but the latticework of cracks and crevasses garnishing his face seemed to be an integral part of his serenity, like the seams and joints of a fine stained-glass window that become interwoven with the sacred image depicted. His hair was as white as the silk veil of the tabernacle on the high altar back at Saint Philomena's, and it seemed to have golden rather than silver highlights. Like Saint Valeria who had rested in the same tomb, his face aroused no fear, no bile, no cold sweats in this necrophobic gardener. There was wisdom in that visage, charity, lively faith, heroic patience, and profound humility—qualities gained, no doubt, through prolonged mortification. I'd be tempted to use the word "angelic," except for fear that for some of my modern readers—should I ever have any—the term might evoke the warm-fuzzy image of a fluttering, chubby cherub rather than the Godly, penetrating, unswerving countenance of Saint Uriel, Archangel of the North, silently standing guard at the Gate of Eden after the Fall, citrine robes flapping and flaming sword held high. Here was a man I wished I'd met in life, and hoped to meet in Eternity.

"Well?" demanded Billowack, shattering the moment. Echoes of his grating bark went bouncing around the mausoleum, assuming the auditory texture of a pack of hungry wolves.

Ignoring him, Father Baptist gently brushed back a tangle of glistening white hair, then reverently traced the Sign of the Cross upon the dead man's forehead with his thumb.

"Lombard!" snapped the bulldog. "Just tell me—"

Father silenced him with a simple wave of his index finger. He bent nearer, noticing something. A tingle went down my rickety spine as he glanced up at me with those piercing eyes of his that gripped mine and by some invisible force drew my attention down to something around the dead man's neck. I inched slightly forward, as inconspicuously as I could, and followed Father's fingers as they traced the course of a metal chain. With hardly any motion of his arm, he pulled the zipper tab down a few more inches.

I gasped. I couldn't help it.

"What is it?" shouted Billowack, his wheelchair creaking under the force of his constricting belly.

"Ulp!" I gagged, clasping a hand over my mouth. I had to think fast, and it was the best I could come up with. Like a man on the verge of explosive regurgitation, I ran for the door—well, lurched and lumbered according to my nature. Whatever, I certainly drew a lot of attention to myself as I charged from the room, waving my cane frantically. "Urrrrggghhhh!!"

"Whatsamaddah with him?" I heard Billowack hollering as I shoved investigators aside, huffing and hobbling though several chambers until I felt a draft of crisp night air. Lieutenant Taper and Sergeant Wickes were standing on the threshold of the open door at the entrance, conferring with a uniformed officer about some point of procedural tedium. I knocked them every which way in my melodramatic lunge for privacy.

Outside, whirling gumball machines atop several police vehicles cast wild and phantasmagoric shadows among the asymmetrical array of tombstones and monuments that spread out in all directions like an army of ogres and trolls.

"Hey!" called Taper. "Martin, is that you?"

"What's wrong?" asked Wickes. "Hey, Feeney!"

I removed my hand from my mouth long enough to blurt, "You don't wanna know!" over my shoulder. Then, suppressing my inherent necropoliphobia, I swaggered and limped my way into the sea of silent headstones.

"Maybe he ate too fast," I heard Wickes chuckle, the expert on food inhalation.

"Let's leave him be," said Taper, the wiser of the two. "Now officer, let me see if I got this straight ..."

Imagining Father's saccharine improvisation within—"You'll have to forgive Martin, Monty, he gets that away around corpses; oh you should see him at funerals!"—I saw my ploy through by staggering up a hill, diving behind a large burial marker, and proceeding to make such convincing retching noises I almost started vomiting for real. Several cops outside the mausoleum chortled gleefully. They gave me a round of hearty applause as I emerged from my makeshift vomitorium, wiping my chin with the back of my sleeve. One big fellow kindly pointed to a nearby drinking fountain, to which I gratefully stumbled and proceeded to wash my face.

Rather than face Billowack and his merry Myrmidons, or Taper and Wickes who were considerate enough to go back inside the mausoleum without further comment, I opted to wait by our Jeep Cherokee some fifty yards distant. It was creepy out there, alone among the granite gnomes, listening to the inaudible rattle of long-dead bones. I tilted myself back against the warm hood—with my locked vertebrae it's the only way I can look straight up—to peer wistfully at the sky. So many stars that had been clearly visible in my youth were overwhelmed these days by the electrical effervescence of the vast metropolis around me. Even the Milky Way, once a stunning band of radiance across the heavens, was simply not there any more. I straightened again, not wanting to draw parallels to the present state of the Holy Mother Church, analogies that would only be depressing.

A flurry of fluttering lights and shadows drew my attention back to the mausoleum. The gaggle of cops parted as Father Baptist and Chief Billowack emerged from the large, gaping doorway. The bulldog did not look pleased, and he looked even less as two wet-behind-the-ears rookies pried him out of that flimsy wheelchair and deposited him in the back of a law enforcement version of a stretch limousine, all black-and-white with *"To protect and to serve"* italicized on the side. The big fellow who'd directed me to the water fountain pointed Father in my direction as Chief Billowack's incessant barking was cut short by the slam of his car door.

The gumball lights and high beams blazing behind him, I could see Father's face as he approached. His movements seemed grim and stilted, so naturally I assumed things had not gone well. My heart sank when he silently motioned me into the car as he circled around to the passenger side. I cringed as he pulled the door closed, bracing myself for a reprimand.

Suddenly, the most unexpected sound filled the Cherokee.

Father was laughing, guffawing uproariously, so much so that the heavy-duty suspension twittered along with him.

"Oh, Martin," he managed at last, holding his sides and gasping for air. "That—that—shivaree you just put on—it was—positively—brilliant!"

"It was?" I said, starting the motor so the cops wouldn't wonder why the car was shaking. "I mean—ahem—of *course* it was."

"You—you had Monty—so flustered—he hardly cared—that I didn't know—that man's identity." I felt his hand gripping my right shoulder as I eased the car into motion. "My Friend, more than anything, I needed a good laugh."

"Glad to oblige, Father. Anytime."

He continued chuckling as we wound our way through the foreboding maze of tombstones and statues. By the time we reached the front gate, which was opened for us by yet another cop, Father had himself under control.

"Where to now?" I asked, pulling out onto the street.

"Let's go west to the coast, then take a leisurely drive north to Camarillo."

"Sounds good to me."

We drove a while in silence. Since we had plenty of time, I decided to take Wilshire Boulevard rather than the freeway. Traffic was sparse and the lights were with us most of the way.

"So," he said presently.

"So," I agreed.

"You obviously saw the old man's chest."

"I saw a Crucifix, if that's what you mean."

"I do, Martin. You recognized it, of course."

"I'd know it anywhere. You told me it was one of a kind."

"I bought it for my wife from an artisan in Cambria." His voice grew momentarily sad. "Christine and I were on our honeymoon, and we found this hole-in-the-wall shop off the beaten track. We watched the fellow add the finishing touches to the Corpus. He was Romanian, I think, and we could hardly understand him. In those days I was just a nominal Catholic. She was the devout one, and like a lot of men I lazily relied on my wife's prayers to see me through the rough spots while postponing my own devotional commitment. A few months later, knowing how much it would mean to her, I gave the Crucifix to a friend who was traveling to Italy, and he managed to get it blessed by Padre Pio." His voice shifted down the better part of an octave. "After her illness, I almost buried it with her."

"I'll bet Christine was one fine lady."

"Ah, Martin," he sighed, settling back in his seat. His tone became thoughtful, distant, almost prayerful. "I've been blessed with the Graces of two vocations in one lifetime. That's more than most men can say. Though I miss her deeply, I can't say that I'm unhappy. In fact, I sometimes sense her presence when I'm saying Mass. Do you believe that?"

"A lot of people have friends who play the piano, Father, but none like my Elza."

"Quite right," he said, clapping his hands and rubbing his palms together. "We've both had our adventures, haven't we?"

We fell into silence for a while as the sounds of the city gave way to the crashing of ocean waves. The air grew cold and damp as I maneuvered onto the Pacific Coast Highway and headed northward.

"So," I said after a few miles of pounding surf.

"So," he said, suppressing a yawn.

"So Monsignor Aspic is linked to the body in the mausoleum."

"Obviously. Why?"

"When you asked Lieutenant Taper back at the rectory if there was a connection, he said, and I quote: 'We didn't say there was any.'"

"He didn't know."

"Are you going to tell him?"

"I don't know."

"How do you suppose it got there?"

"The Crucifix?"

"You gave it to Monsignor Aspic on Halloween night for protection against—well, we won't go into that. At first he refused to wear it. Then, after it saved his life, well, I'll never forget his parting words: 'I didn't know I had it in me'—as though he had somehow empowered the Cross and not the other way around! Since then, he's had it on every time I've seen him."

"Except in the cardinal's presence," added Father.

"Right," I agreed. "Around the Chancery he keeps it tucked inside his shirt pocket. It's doubtful Cardinal Fulbright ever saw it or knew he had it. Or maybe he did, got upset about it, and that's why Aspic keeps it out of sight."

Father rubbed his chin thoughtfully for several long seconds. "Millie said Monsignor Aspic wore it at the press conferences."

"That's right. Do you suppose Morley Fulbright was watching?"

"'Religion Revisited'? I suppose it's possible. I haven't a notion what our cardinal does with his evenings. But at least we know that Christine's Crucifix was in Monsignor Aspic's possession yesterday morning."

"Yet somehow it wound up on an anonymous corpse."

"Sealed in a crypt no less."

"Saint Valeria's yet. What are the odds?"

"Astronomical. Still, it did happen."

"Speaking of the cardinal, did Pierre's little article on his favorite restaurant really upset him?"

"That's what I'm told."

"Hm."

We fell into silence as we wound our way up the irregular coastline.

"I'm surprised," I said presently, "that Larry Taper didn't recognize—or didn't mention recognizing—Christine's Crucifix when he found the body. He knew her, didn't he? Surely he would remember it. You've often said he's almost as attentive to details as yourself."

"At that awkward angle, so close to the floor," said Father thoughtfully, "the body still in the narrow crypt, the small opening, with just a flashlight ... Back in the kitchen Larry only said that it *looked* like a pectoral Cross. He just made out the general shape. Under those conditions I'd hardly expect him to make a connection between it and my wife's sacramental."

"Then why is Morley Fulbright all hot and bothered about the body in the crypt? And why are we driving up this highway to Camarillo?"

"He was certainly upset when I spoke to him, but he never specified what about. As for Camarillo, your guess is as good as mine."

"I doubt it."

"I do know this," said Father. "I said earlier that I didn't see how any of this could involve me."

"And now?"

"Regardless of why His Eminence has summoned us, and no matter how that intriguing corpse made its way into Saint Valeria's crypt, Martin, from the moment I saw Christine's Crucifix—"

"Yes, Father?"

"—I became certainly, inexorably, inextricably involved."

4

"A BODY IN THE CRYPT, YOU SAY," said Morley Psalmellus Cardinal Fulbright, the noticeably agitated Archbishop of Los Angeles. The yellow-orange radiance of the rising sun revealed a few spots he'd missed while shaving. His crimson robes were disheveled and his red zucchetto slightly askew. Contrary to protocol, His Insistence forgot all about making us osculate his precious sapphire ring. "Oh, yes, Billowack," he sputtered inattentively. "He was jabbering something about that in the middle of the night. I'm afraid my mind was on something entirely different at the time. Still is."

"Indeed, Your Eminence," said Father Baptist.

"Something a thousand times more important, and a million times more horrendous!"

A thousand times? A million times? From what this gardener knew of Morley Fulbright's priorities that meant we had been summoned on an errand of ineffectual futility. Of course, life was always fraught with surprises. If His Impudence hadn't sent us on our last domesticated goose chase, Father Baptist wouldn't have a first-century Chalice that had once graced the table at the Last Supper secreted behind a loose stone in the church, and Pierre Bontemps might still be in jail for murder. I paused for a moment to consider a loftier perspective, like that expressed in Isaias fifty-five, eight and nine:

> For my thoughts are not your thoughts:
> nor your ways my ways, saith the Lord.
> For as the heavens are exalted above the earth,
> so are my ways exalted above your ways,
> and my thoughts above your thoughts.

"Then why, if I may ask," Father was saying with well-tempered obsequiousness, "did you suggest to the police that I visit the crypt at New Golgotha Cemetery?"

I held Father Baptist in such high esteem it was unsettling to see him deferring so to his awful, if lawful, superior.

"The what?" The cardinal began rubbing the prominent crimson bump on his forehead. "I said no such thing."

"But I was told—"

"In light of new developments, I recommended to Chief Billowack that in any and all matters dealing with the tomb of—I mean, you know, that *hoax*—he should get in touch with you."

"New developments, Your Eminence?"

"It was your idea after all, Father Baptist, that I deny the whole thing."

"I beg your pardon. I advised *silence,* not denial—"

"So I denied it. I did deny it. Boy, did I deny it! Ask anyone. Conrad did the talking, but he was speaking for me and don't you forget it!"

"I certainly won't, Your Eminence. Now, how may I—?"

"Something has happened, Father." Morley Fulbright stopped rubbing his bump and commenced wringing his hands. "Do you hear me? More appalling than anything and everything that's gone wrong thus far. I'm talking calamity here. Hell, it's a catastrophe!"

"I'm afraid I'm lost, Your Eminence. You just said that Monsignor Aspic was defusing the situation—"

"Damn it, man," shouted the cardinal. His bump was positively glowing. "Don't you see? He's the problem!"

"Monsignor Aspic? But I thought—"

"Him and his degrees. Conrad had me fooled. You, too, didn't he? Him with all his aplomb and expensive cologne!"

"I don't understand," said Father. "What did he—?"

"The iniquitous little twit has disappeared. Do you hear me? Disappeared! And he's taken it with him!"

We were standing on a plaza at the apex of a lofty outdoor staircase on the grounds of Saint Joseph of Copertino Seminary, built on a steep hill in 1957 at the direction of Francis James Cardinal McInery, one of Morley Fulbright's more worthy predecessors. Behind us loomed a high wall overlaid with a stunning depiction of a Trefoil made of white gold and metallic red tiles against a background of ocean blue with black grout in between. The pattern had an arresting three-dimensional quality about it, and was designed in such a way that the last rays of the setting sun would strike it and flare out in a dazzling blaze just before nightfall. It was mentioned in travel brochures, as the fleeting display was clearly visible from Interstate 101, several miles away. A "vista point" turnout had been constructed so motorists could pull to a stop safely and savor the moment.

As the sun was just in the process of rising above the hilly horizon in the east, the effect was entirely different. The Trefoil glistened wetly against an oily blue background of gently rippled tiles. The result was tranquil yet strangely charged; but whatever the artisan's intent, the mood was disrupted by the cardinal's pervasive angst.

Here is a classic
Martin Feeney crayon rendering
of this classic symbol
for the Blessed Trinity:

"I beg your pardon?" asked Father.

"No way," huffed the cardinal. "No way is he going to get away with it!"

At this very moment, I thought to myself, Monsignor Havermeyer is saying the Prayers at the Foot of the Altar back at Saint Philomena's. I'd say he's definitely chosen the better part.

Some fifty feet below us at the base of the stairs, a bronze statue of the institution's namesake was slowly emerging from the darkness. Saint Joseph of Copertino was a holy friar whose daily Mass had often lasted several hours while he, in a state of ecstasy, levitated several yards above the ground—an attribute the sculptor didn't attempt to commemorate in metal. Cardinal McInery wrote in his autobiography that he had hoped this seventeenth-century Franciscan, renowned as much in his day for his profound Charity as for his well-documented aerial abilities, would serve as an inspiration for the future priests of Los Angeles. I assume Cardinal McInery meant inspiration in terms of purity and sanctity, but over time the principle as far as the seminary was concerned had degenerated into a matter of moral and doctrinal flightiness.

> GARDENING TIPS: The town of Camarillo, by the bye,
> in addition to the archdiocesan seminary, is also
> home to the famous Camarillo State Mental Hospi-
> tal. The joke among the Tradosauri is that it is
> hard to tell apart the students of one institution
> from the inmates of the other ... or is it the
> faculty of one from the staff of the other ... or
> maybe the graduates of one ... Well, that's the
> joke. Boom cheesh!
>
> —M.F.

"What has the monsignor taken?" asked Father, calm but alert.

"It!" screamed His Explicitness, Cardinal Fulbright.

"Your Eminence, you're overwrought. That much I understand. But I'm clueless as to what 'it' is or why you've brought me all the way up here."

Notice how involved I was in this lively discussion. Actually, I was enjoying detesting the view of the mental hospital across the way as the dawn gradually illuminated its disordered, angular facades. It was an octagonal building with lots of randomly shaped windows, angular bal-conies, and a buttressed front entrance illuminated by subdued but clash-ing floodlights. It had much in common with most Catholic churches constructed in the last couple of decades: ugliness exacerbated by disproportion and imbalance. Perhaps the architect was an "ex" and designing this building was some sort of purge. Perhaps he was an inmate of his own artifice.

"You're here because I'm here," explained the cardinal, accenting his words with downward thrusts of his index finger. "You come when and where I tell you to."

"Of course."

"And tomorrow, should I be in Santa Barbara, or San Pedro, or Redondo Beach or—"

"I shall come when you call, wherever you call," agreed Father, nodding dutifully. "So tell me, Your Eminence, who are you avoiding?"

The cardinal's bump dimmed from fire engine red to broken-knee purple. "What's that?"

Father Baptist folded his arms, subservient still but subtlety assured. "For a prelate who rarely leaves the Chancery, it does seem odd that you're suddenly everywhere but there."

"Watch it, Father."

"I meant no offense, Your Eminence. Perhaps then you'll be so kind as to tell me why you are so uncharacteristically desirous of my company, and at all these far-flung locales."

Cardinal Fulbright cleared his throat. It sounded like a sediment-clogged water heater on a cold morning. "I have need of you."

Father cleared his throat, too, but the effect was entirely different. "To do what?"

"To find Conrad."

"And?"

"More so, to find the, um, *artifact* he took with him."

"Artifact?"

The cardinal jiggled his head angrily, yes.

Father took a step back. "Not Your Eminence's chalice again."

The vertical jiggling continued, yes, and then rotated sideways to the negative. My own heart sank down into my intestines at the thought of all we'd just been through to return that ugly chalice to His Annoyance's private display case, only to have it stolen again. But by Monsignor Aspic? That didn't make sense. And why was the cardinal now shaking his head no?

"Not just my chalice," said the cardinal through gritted teeth. The words came out like pasta through a strainer. It really pained him. "My chalice, yes, but also … the artifact."

"Both of them," said Father.

The cardinal pumped his head affirmatively again.

"Ah," said Father. "Tell me about this … artifact."

"Very well." The cardinal proceeded to pace back and forth, forth and back across the plaza in front of the glistening Trefoil, shooting his words at Father like a gladiator throwing spears from a zigzagging chariot. "You remember some years ago when the Pope visited Los Angeles."

"Indeed," said Father, bowing his head reverentially. "I was still on the police force. Though I was in Homicide, I volunteered to assist with security when the Holy Father celebrated Mass in the Coliseum."

```
GARDENING TIPS: I should probably interject here
that the Pope, the Vicar of Christ and Supreme
Pontiff of the Universal Church, is formally ad-
dressed as "Your Holiness," and is properly re-
ferred to as "His Holiness" or "the Holy Father."
Other titles include "Supreme Pontiff" and "Vicar
of Christ."

                                        --M.F.


N.B. You have doubtless surmised that one properly
refers to a cardinal as "His Eminence," but when
it comes to Morley Fulbright, well, this gardener
finds it problematical if not impossible to apply
the concept, let alone the terminology, of "re-
spect."  Purgatory looms.
```

"Yes, well," snorted Fulbright, his cheeks wiggling in cadence with his stride, "amidst all the ruckus, His Holiness stayed the night at my residence. We spoke—or rather he spoke—of many things. He seemed to have a keen interest in California history, and I had recently lured Jeremiah Ravenshorst away from the Diocese of San Francisco. Jerry was a monsignor back then, a historian and something of an archeologist. He joined His Holiness and myself for dinner."

"If memory serves," said Father, tossing me one of those "Pay attention!" glances, "the Pope's visit came shortly after Themolina Hubbard, heiress to the Roundhead Manhole Cover fortune, changed her will on her deathbed, leaving the Cordova Homestead Estate on Chapel Hill to the Archdiocese of Los Angeles."

"The Del Agua Mission!" exclaimed the gardener, making his one and only contribution to the conversation. Immediately, he wanted to stuff a handkerchief into his mouth and shove it down with his cane like wadding into the barrel of a front-loading cannon, but alas he had no hankie. Instead, he fixed his eyes on the sanitarium and pretended he could project himself into one of its inviting padded cells.

"Your memory serves you well, Father," grunted the cardinal, wishing me someplace worse with his eyes.

```
GARDENING TIPS: La Misio/n* del Agua de la Vida:
"The Mission of the Water of Life."  Some more of
that disjecta membra I mentioned earlier, and more
is yet to come. "And the Endless Knot goes on in-
terweaving within itself forever."
                                            --M.F.


*Sorry, this Underwood typewriter doesn't have any
diacritical keys, so "/" will have to suffice for
an acute accent over the preceding letter.
```

"In fact," added His Perambulance, "the deed of transfer signed by Mrs. Hubbard and executed by her attorney, Cecil B. Wexlack, was still on my desk. The Holy Father asked to see it, and even had one of his own secretaries photograph it while we dined."

"Did His Holiness explain the nature of his interest in the Chapel Hill property?"

The cardinal ceased his pacing for a moment. "I think so, but I can't recall. He and Jerry got on like old pals, going on and on about ancient ruins, abandoned shrines, and who knows what else. Somewhere during the main course they segued into Spanish."

"Do you?" asked Father. *"¿Habla español?"*

"No," said Fulbright, resuming his nervous strutting. "It was rude of them, leaving me out of the conversation in my own dining room."

"I can understand. So what happened next?"

"Jerry excused himself just before dessert to accept a phone call or something, and while he was out of the room the Pope all but *ordered* me to make him my auxiliary bishop."

Perhaps that explains the *tête-à-tête*—or rather the *cabeza-a-cabeza*—in Spanish, thought yours truly, admiring a flock of pigeons erupting from the roof of the sanitarium. Maybe Jerry had been doing some political pleading with the Vicar of Christ.

"And ... the artifact?" asked Father.

"Jerry returned and dessert was served. I tried but failed to nudge the subject onto the possibility of building a new cathedral here in Los Angeles. Suddenly, His Holiness signals to one of his assistants, and—bingo!—this, this—"

"Artifact?"

"Yes, this artifact was brought to the table. It was in a leather pouch about the size of a man's hand—" He held up his own hand and spread his fingers as wide as they would go. "—and it was tied with a yellow cord. There were two tassels, one on each end of the cord, and His Holiness made a point of spreading the strands to reveal a tiny golden medal in the middle of each."

"Medal, Your Eminence?"

"Maybe the size of a lentil—so small and close to the knot you'd never see it unless you knew to look—each engraved with the letters I-H-S."

Father gave the gardener another "Pay attention!" glance but he, the gardener, was busy softly humming *disjecta membra* to the tune of "Row, Row, Row Your Boat" and kept coming up three syllables short.

"I take it," said Father, "that the pouch contained something significant?"

"The Pope certainly thought so, and Jerry naturally agreed."

"So what was it?"

"The artifact?"

Father looked at his lawful superior with those unnerving eyes that seemed to whisper, imperative but patiently, "Considering that you've dragged Martin and me all the way up here to your modernist heresy factory precisely to deal with this all-important object of yours, why do I need a set of dental tools to pry it out of you?" But, exhaling slowly, all he actually said was, "Yes, Your Eminence."

"A disk," whispered the cardinal looking suspiciously at me of all people. "Solid gold, maybe six, seven inches in diameter." He stopped to make a circle with his thumbs and index fingers, then resumed his marching. "There's an inscription in Spanish etched on the underside, but otherwise the bottom is smooth and flat."

"I don't suppose you know what the inscription says?"

"Something about a bird flying from someplace to somewhere else. They didn't tell me that night, and Jerry was always a bit coy about it afterwards."

"Okay. What about the top side of the disk?"

His Avarice halted. Though panting from exertion, his face became momentarily serene, almost wistful. "The rim is beveled. There are symbols all around, insignias, like an astrological chart—but not. It's hard to describe."

"You say the rim is beveled," said Father. "By this do you mean the disk is thicker in the center?"

"Not exactly," said the cardinal. "I mean, yes, it gets thicker toward the middle, but then it doesn't."

Father closed his eyes for a moment and opened them again. "What is in the center?"

"Nothing."

"Nothing? You mean a hole? Like a doughnut?"

"No, a round indentation. A recessed circular area with three small notches—slots, sort of like an electrical socket. Jerry suggested that there was a missing part, a smaller disk that fit into the middle, with corresponding projections on its underside that matched the notches."

"A smaller disk," said Father, "that plugged into the center of the larger disk? A wheel within a wheel?"

The cardinal shrugged. "Something like that. Jerry researched the thing. Even traveled to the Vatican Library and the British Museum. So far as I know he never found any clue as to what the smaller disk was supposed to look like."

"Do you have any photographs of the larger disk?"

"No. Before he retired for the evening, the Holy Father entrusted the disk and pouch into my keeping. He said that it held special significance for him that he would explain, perhaps, during a subsequent visit. He made it clear that it was not to be photographed, and that its existence was not to be made public."

Just then, across the way, a score of inmates emerged from the tranquil grounds of dirt paths and manicured shrubbery and converged on the entrance of the sanitarium. A team of nurses with clipboards took an accounting as patients filed inside the door. It seemed a tad early for an institutional breakfast, but for all I knew they had a tiny cafeteria and meals were conducted in shifts. Perhaps this bunch was from the sleep-deprived ward. Maybe they were just passive-aggressives who drew the short straw.

"So," said Father. "What became of this fascinating golden artifact?"

His Avoidance started pacing again, this time not just back and forth, but crosswise and countermarch, tracing an erratic assortment of cutbacks, dodecagons, and stellar alignments.

"Your Eminence?" prodded Father. "Surely you realize that I can't help you if you withhold information from me."

"You've no idea," said the cardinal between huffs, puffs, and snorts.

"That's the problem," agreed Father.

"Very well," said the cardinal, slowing his pace to a gallop. "Initially, against my better judgment, the artifact resided in a wall safe at Jerry's residence at Saint Barbara's Chapel. Something about the inscription on the back piqued his academic curiosity—or so he intimated. He made detailed drawings of the thing in hopes of deciphering the symbols around the rim. Jerry prowled many a library in search of clues as to the thing's origin and purpose. From what I can tell, he never acquired an assistant, never took anyone else into his confidence."

"He didn't report his findings to you?" asked Father.

"Hah!" scoffed the cardinal, accelerating to Mach II. "Oh, he'd drop occasional hints, a hastily-scribbled memo, weave his vague innuendoes about the missing piece into the conversation, but he was cagey about the whole thing. From his behavior I gathered he thought the missing piece to be extremely important—essential to the purpose of the artifact, whatever that was."

"Could it have been a jewel?" asked Father.

"He didn't think so," grimaced Fulbright, groping for words. "More like a key to … well, he was never specific. He was ambitious, our Jerry, don't kid yourself. Whatever it was, he wasn't going to tell me, not after his wink-wink session with the Pope. So after a couple of weeks of his hemming and hawing I ordered the disk transferred to the wall safe in my own residence."

"Why there and not, say, a safe deposit box?"

Fulbright came to a full and complete stop. "You know the papal nuncio, Sylvio Bonsignore?"

"Not personally, but by reputation, of course." Father paused as his mental gears engaged. "Ah, now I understand your sudden predilection for travel. I've heard that His Excellency likes to move about his nunciature. He's not one to wither away at his residence in Washington DC."

GARDENING TIPS: A "nuncio" is a representative of
the Holy Father who is assigned to a sovereign
government or territory, and whose duty is to
safeguard the interests of the Holy See. His
province is called his "nunciature," and in it he
must reside until he is withdrawn and a successor
is appointed.

The nuncio in our story happens to be a
bishop. In most countries where the leveling myth
of democracy isn't held with such ferocity as in
our own, he would be addressed as "Your Lordship"
or "My Lord." In the U. S. of A., however, he is
called "Your Excellency" -- the same as the president at formal affairs.

--M.F.

N.B.: A "See" is a seat of power, and the "Holy
See" denotes the Chair of Peter, the Papal Authority of the Roman Catholic Church.

"Hardly," said the cardinal. "The man's a snoop, and he doesn't have the decency to send word when he's coming. You never know when he's going to show up. Next week, next month—"

"Sometime today, perhaps?" asked Father.

The cardinal's bump glowed like a neon ruby. His chest and belly swelled as though he was preparing to give Father a verbal thrashing he'd never forget. Instead, he apparently turned his attention on a less hazardous target. I could feel his eyes boring into the back of my skull, but I kept my attention on the patients marching into the maw of the sanitarium. I noticed the inmates were all men, and their keepers all female. Wherever the ladies pointed, the men dutifully marched. It wasn't the crisp "snap to" of a military operation, but the nurses were definitely in charge. I wondered if the cooperation of the men was drug-induced or the result of electric-shock conditioning.

"He was just here last week," said the cardinal. "Wednesday it was. He flew away the next morning. I thought I was rid of him for a while. But no."

"Your Eminence?" said Father.

"A friend of mine was attending a soirée in Washington yesterday," explained Fulbright, gathering his ire into a semblance of control. "He overheard a conversation in which the nuncio promised the French ambassador that he'd be sure to send him a postcard from Knott's Berry Farm on the Feast of Saint Gertrude. That's today. My friend phoned me yesterday afternoon to warn me."

"A curious choice in amusement parks," commented Father. "But I guess if one likes an old western theme—"

"Apparently His Excellency prefers it to Disneyland."

"And you came up here to avoid Bishop Bonsignore because …?"

"Every single time he shows his face, immediately upon kissing my ring and before he parks himself in a chair or accepts a glass of sherry, he always, absolutely predictably, invariably, without fail, asks—which is to say, demands—to see the disk! He feigns historical interest, artistic fascination, mystical wonderment, but I don't buy it. He's obsessed with it, or rather what it represents, or what he thinks it represents."

"Which is?" asked Father.

"He never says," said Fulbright, throwing up his hands. "Ever since the, um, problems we had back in June, he's been coming more and more frequently, but even before that he always had to see the disk, see the disk, see that infernal disk!"

Between the words "Every single time" and the last "see that infernal disk" in the above outflow from the drama of the cardinal's conflicted inner self, the amplitude of his voice quadrupled. Some of the straggling patients across the way looked up and pointed in this direction. Their keepers rushed to shush them.

"And now the disk is gone," said Father, clearing his ear with a wiggle of his pinkie. "And you think Monsignor Aspic took it."

"I *know* he took it!" Fulbright was still shouting. Something convulsed behind his third chin. His next line came out tight and raspy. "I handed it to him myself."

Father absorbed that for several seconds. "He came to your residence?"

"Yes."

"How recently?"

"Yesterday. He met me in my bedchambers. I removed the leather pouch from the wall safe and handed it to him."

"What time was this?"

"Noon on the dot."

"Were you alone?"

"My acting assistant, a seminarian named Axel, announced Conrad and saw him in, but left us immediately."

"Did the monsignor stay long?"

"Only a minute. He was bubbling with enthusiasm because he was going to be on that television show yet again. He jabbered about the hosts—what are their names? Sheldon and Moira Truant or something—how wonderfully open and ecumenical they are, something of the sort."

"He gave you no indication that anything was wrong?"

The cardinal clenched his teeth. "He was his insufferably usual, frisky self. Had I sensed anything out of the ordinary, would I have let him prance off with the Pope's whatever-it-is?"

"I'm trying to get events clear in my mind," said Father, tapping his temple with his index finger. "Why did you entrust this artifact, this center of so much ecclesiastical attention, into the monsignor's keeping?"

The cardinal paused, swallowed audibly, and reduced his output to a hoarse whisper. "After my Murkenstein chalice was stolen a few days ago right out of the display case in my private chapel—you know all about it, seeing as how you arranged its return—I decided that I'd better get the damn thing insured. Then I thought of the disk. What if something were to happen to it? I didn't think it seemly to take it to an appraiser myself."

"Naturally not," agreed Father.

Actually, I kind of enjoyed the image, but kept silent.

The cardinal winced, wiggled his jowls, and continued. "Conrad seemed the logical choice for the errand. The Murkenstein chalice was in dire need of a professional cleaning, considering the state it was in when you recovered it. I asked one of my acquaintances who knows about such things if he could suggest a jeweler who was also a reliable appraiser. He got back to me with a recommendation for a man on Sunset—Zinger or Ringer or whatever. I gave the information to Conrad, along with the chalice and the artifact."

"So Monsignor Aspic definitely left your residence with both items in his possession."

"That's right. The one hitch was that the monsignor's afternoon schedule was log-jammed with appointments. He assured me, on his honor, that he would safeguard the disk with his life, keep it on his person through the day, sleep with it under his pillow overnight, and take it to the appraiser first thing the following morning."

"Today," said Father.

"That's right—today. I didn't like it, but what was I to do? I gave it to him. Three hours later I get a phone call from a friend in Washington, warning me of the nuncio's imminent incursion. I couldn't have picked a worse time to let the disk out of my keeping. I tried to phone Conrad on his cell phone, but apparently it wasn't on. The housekeeper at his residence didn't know his itinerary."

"And when did your concern turn to alarm?" asked Father.

"The one place I knew he'd be was that television studio, KLIE in Hollywood." Fulbright pronounced it "Kay—Ell—Eye—Eee" and punctuated it with finger quotes. "The show airs live at eight o'clock. I called there and left word for him to phone me as soon as he arrived. At quarter to eight I phoned a second time but was told that he still wasn't there. At five after eight I turned on the TV and there were the hosts, hemming and hawing because their guest hadn't shown up. That was the moment, as you put it, when my concern became alarm."

"Why do you assume he absconded with it?" asked Father. "Surely you should first explore the possibility that he met with foul play."

"I'm not dense, Father Baptist. At my request Chief Billowack made a discreet check of all police reports from last evening, as well as the hospitals and urgent care facilities. Conrad was not run over by a truck or shot in an alley. He disappeared, and he had the artifact with him. Which reminds me—"

"Yes, Your Eminence?"

"I told Chief Billowack nothing regarding Conrad's errand. That he is missing is public knowledge, but the detail that he was carrying the papal artifact and my chalice I kept to myself."

"Might I ask why?"

"Too much possibility of leaks. You know as well as I do that the police department is like a sieve that way. I can't emphasize enough: the nuncio must not learn that the artifact is missing."

"But, Your Eminence, my resources are limited. The police have the means to—"

"No."

"At least allow me to utilize my trusted contacts within the department. They are better equipped—"

"You're friendly with a couple of cops, aren't you? What are their names, Candle and Wax or something?"

"Or something, Your Eminence."

"See that you don't take them into your confidence."

"Your Eminence, please don't limit me this way."

"Holy Obedience, Father. Holy Obedience!"

"Yes, Your Eminence. But inquiries must be made. I can't look for something without asking about it."

"Then be very careful who you question, who you take into your confidence." The cardinal looked as though he was about to add, "Or else."

Father shrugged, perplexed. "And what about the man in the mausoleum?"

"What man in the mausoleum?"

"The one they found in Saint Valeria's crypt."

"Who cares about him? Get your priorities straight, Father!"

Father Baptist fell silent, no doubt processing all this information in that intricate marvel God had placed between his ears. A distant bell tolled seven times, the sound of each clang ricocheting from hill to surrounding hill until the woodsy valley was aflutter with joyous, jingling tinkles. After what seemed the better part of a minute the echoing chimes died away, and Father said, "Monsignor Aspic is many things, Your Eminence, but I've never doubted his loyalty to you. I can't imagine him stealing something, the theft of which would damage not only your reputation, but your rapport with the Holy Father."

"Father Baptist," said the cardinal, jabbing at Father's sternum with his puffy index finger, "you will bring that disk back to me. I can only avoid the nuncio so long, so do so before I find myself in a position where I must face him without it."

"And Monsignor Aspic?"

The cardinal glared at Father for several long seconds. Then he spun around on his heels, squared his shoulders, aligned his paunch and chins, inhaled deeply, and headed down those stairs toward the statue of Saint Joseph of Copertino.

5

"SO," ASKED FATHER AS I PUNCHED the accelerator, launching the Jeep up the onramp to merge with the southbound morning traffic on Interstate 101, "at least you enjoyed the view?"

"I hadn't realized the mental hospital was so close to the seminary."

"It isn't, Martin."

"Are you sure?"

"I should be. I attended Saint Joseph's, don't forget. The mental hospital is at the other end of town, some ten miles distant."

"Then what was that building across the way? The one with the patients and nurses?"

"That was the Pope John XXIII Chapel. Surely you've heard of it, one of Cardinal Fulbright's most ambitious hideous building projects. He dedicated it back in April or May."

"Part of the seminary."

"A prominent part, I'd say."

"And the bell that rang at the conclusion of your conversation?"

"The call to morning Mass, which the cardinal was no doubt going to celebrate for the seminarians."

"Oh. That explains it."

"Explains what, Martin?"

"I wondered about the behavior of the men being herded into the building. Now I understand. Since Vatican II every seminarian undergoes a lobotomy as part of his preparation for the priesthood."

"Luckily," laughed Father, "that was one change they brought in *after* my ordination."

"Are you sure? How would you remember?"

"Martin."

"Right. So where to now?"

"First to visit a sick friend, then off to Monsignor Aspic's residence. We have to retrace his movements, and that's a likely place to start."

"Sure, if you say so. By the way, I was impressed by the cardinal's shift in priorities."

"Oh? To what shift are you referring?"

"He's actually more concerned about the Pope's disk than his own ugly chalice."

"Loss of the chalice again is embarrassing, but to misplace the Pope's artifact could severely damage his relationship with the Holy See."

"I guess I spoke out of turn. His priorities haven't changed at all. His only concern is himself." I thought that one over. "I shouldn't have said that, either."

Father cleared his throat but didn't respond.

"Frankly," said I, after changing lanes to get around a slow-moving cement truck, "I'm surprised His Obsequiousness gives a hoot what the Pope may think. Morley certainly ignores all the Holy Father's directives regarding liturgical abuses, annulments, and, well, just about everything else."

"I know that some writers," said Father, "our friend Pierre among them, have accused the cardinal of setting up his own church, independent of Rome; but I don't see it that way."

"How so?"

"As important as Morley Fulbright thinks himself to be—or really is, for that matter—he derives his power and authority from that picture of the Holy Father hanging over every doorway in the Chancery. The cardinal is forever stretching his credibility to the elastic limit, but there is a fine line he is loath to cross—at least, not yet. The Pope still has the power, if not the inclination or the nerve, to send our cardinal to another diocese."

"Like New Bangor."

"Or even Baghdad."

"We should be so blessed. In any case, Father, we now have irrefutable proof that we live in a fallen universe. The hideous Murkenmug has actually been stolen twice in one week."

"Both times in connection with something truly precious, which gives us hope. Perhaps we should turn our vocal energies to something more constructive."

"I feel a Rosary coming on."

"An excellent idea, Martin. And may Saint Gertrude guide us on our quest today. 'In the name of the Father, and of the Son, and of the Holy Ghost.'"

"'Amen.'"

"'I believe in God, the Father Almighty, Creator of Heaven and Earth…'"

6

"EXCUSE ME, SIR," SAID THE NURSE. "It's before visiting hours, and the patients haven't even had breakfast yet—oh!"

"I understand," said Father, smiling at her reaction to his Roman collar as he turned to face her. "I wouldn't intrude on Monsieur du Crane Cristal if it wasn't vitally important."

"Messyoower du what?" She looked puzzled.

"This is room 304, isn't it? I visited Guillaume only two days ago. It was more than an hour earlier, in fact, just at dawn."

"Guillaume? You don't mean Willie, do you?"

"He does go by that name as well."

There was a very good reason that Father wanted to see Willie "Skull" Kapps, also known as Guillaume du Crane Cristal, before embarking on the hunt for Monsignor Aspic and the missing accoutrements. Those "Pay attention!" glances up at the seminary were not mere eye exercises.

The previous Saturday, Willie had summoned Father and myself to his shop of bizarre merchandise on a street whose name I never seem to remember. Willie was scared that day, plain and simple, and he had entrusted something to Father's keeping, binding him with a promise not to ask any questions, not even about the nature of the thing itself. It was such a tense moment that I had since tried to capture its essence at my typewriter in one of my wee-hour key-clacking sessions. As we stood there in the corridor at Good Samaritan Hospital, I could still see the words, spotlighted by my little table lamp, creeping up the carriage of Dad's old Underwood:

```
   "Willie need to ask dah favor," said Willie,
slinking around behind a rickety wooden counter.
"No one else can Ah ask."  He stooped down out of
sight and started rummaging.  "No one else Willie
can trust."  Finding whatever it was he was look-
ing for, he raised himself to his narrow height
and set something on the countertop.  "Trust wit'
dis."
   I took a wary step closer to have a look.  It
was a stained leather pouch about the size of a
tuna sandwich, tied at the throat with a soiled
yellow cord.
   "And what is 'this'?" asked Father, examining
the tassel of the cord with the index finger of
his right hand.
   "Dah trust dat Ah ask," said Willie.  He set his
hands palms down, fingers spread like dry twigs,
on each side of the pouch.  "Willie won you keep
dis safe."
   "I repeat," said Father, moving his fingers over
the leather.  "What is it?"
   "Ah won you keep dis," whispered Willie, "but
promise not open, not look inside.  An' above all,
tell no one."
   Father took his hand away.  "You ask much, my
Friend."
```

Father and Willie went back some years before Father became a priest and I his gardener. It puzzled me at the time that Father accepted the pouch without further question; but I saw it as a measure of the depths of his capacity to trust his friends when they were in need. I questioned his judgment again on Tuesday when he returned the mysterious pouch to Willie in this very hospital room. At this point I had more questions than a contemporary "priest-presider" casting his endless stream of demoralizing doubts upon the sea of perplexed faces beneath childish felt banners in the average post-conciliar parish. But whatever my confusion, of this much I was absolutely sure: Holy Mother Church would be in far better shape these days if there were more priests like Father John Baptist tending the needs of Her children.

"Well," said the nurse, "as you can see—um, Father—Mr. Kapps checked out yesterday afternoon."

In fact, Room 304 was now occupied by an obese woman who insisted on wearing a black leather jacket, spiked choker, and mirrored glasses in bed.

"Excuse me," said Father to the hellish angel, then to the nurse, "I'm heartened that Guillaume made such a full and complete recovery."

"Whether he did or not," said the nurse, her face suddenly flushed, "his insurance company only paid for so many days. After that—"

"I understand," said Father. "Lately I, too, have been ashamed of those who share my profession."

In silence I followed Father to the elevator.

7

"D-D-DUH-DUH-DO YOU HAVE ANY IDEA what time it is?" sputtered a voice as the door to the "Presiders' Residence" at Saint Philip's was pulled open at precisely 8:14 a.m.

"More than a hunch," said Father. "I'm Father John Baptist, and this is my associate, Martin Feeney. We're here on behalf of Cardinal Fulbright. Say, aren't you—?"

Before Father could validate his memory for names and faces, the twitchy young fellow at the door, in an involuntary, paroxysmal fit of recognition, inadvertently managed to knock the door with elbow or knee with enough force to slam it loudly shut in Father's face. He yanked it open again immediately, but the unfortunate reflexive blunder had been made. He peered around the edge, glaring at us with haunted eyes that pleaded in an almost audible, horrid, whiny whimper, "C-c-cuh-cake! Must—have—chocolate—cake! Five-strata, triple-rich, double-fudge, sprinkles-are-for- sissies, chock—oh—lot—lay—or—cake!"

"Smoley, isn't it?" said Father casually, as though the lad's behavior was perfectly normal. "David Smoley?"

"Y-y-yuh-yes-ss-ss-ssss?"

"May we come in?"

Father and I had last visited this place the previous June while investigating the death of Bishop Eugene Brassorie. If I were to write that
Saint Philip's was the ugliest example of post-sanity architecture in
Southern California I would doubtless draw fire from those broadminded
expellers—I use the word ambiguously—who claim that human anatomy is perpetually, from any angle and under all circumstances, beautiful.

> GARDENING TIPS: My description of the anterior of
> the church building in my manuscript, The Endless
> Knot, is going to come up later in this story.
> Suffice it to say that Saint Philip's was designed
> by an architect who underwent some sort of trauma
> back in high school biology class. The structure
> gave a whole new connotation to the words "Holy
> Mother Church." As a result, you couldn't pay me
> to enter the nave by the front door, not in de-
> scription or in person. I was surprised there
> weren't more car accidents in front of the place.
> —M.F.

Fortunately, or at least less unfortunately, our present errand took us
to the hideous protuberance off to the left where the clergy holed up. I
would have called it a "wrecktory," but nobody asked me. It was
reached by climbing cement steps embedded with rainbow sparkles,
passing a ten-foot quartzite obelisk skewered with a spear entitled
THOUGHT, and following a serpentine path to the entrance recessed under a lopsided triangular arch. I marveled that anyone could make the
trek without arriving at the door with at least some psychological damage.

"May we?" asked Father again.

"Oh, um, uh," said the jumpy lad, standing aside, revealing an entry
space from which several hallways went off in search of disorientation.
"Sh-sh-sh-shoo-who do you want to see?"

"Whoever can tell us about Monsignor Aspic's itinerary yesterday."

The lad's eyes, already wide, almost popped out of the moonscape of
his face. "I—I—I guess that would be—be—be me—sort of. I'm sort
of, you know, his, um, his chauffeur."

"Indeed," said Father, gently. "Is there someplace we could talk?"

"I guess so. What about?"

"Monsignor Aspic's office, perhaps?"

"Uh-huh, um," said David reluctantly. "It's this way." As he led us down hallway number three, he said over his shoulder, "I'm sorry, um, Father, I—about the door."

"Don't mention it," said Father, glancing at me with a twinkle in his eye. "Martin here does that sort of thing all the time."

"That's right," I said under my breath as I lumbered behind, accenting each lurch with a thrust of my cane into the deep pile carpet. "Of course, our Millie's approach is so much more colorful, answering the door as she does with a meat cleaver in her hand." It's probably best that David didn't hear that.

The tubular hallway expanded like a funnel at the end, opening into a huge indoor arboretum some four stories high. There were tropical trees and crawling vines, multi-tentacled bushes with pulsing gills for leaves, Technicolor shrubs with hungry-looking blossoms, all resplendent under an immense aquamarine skylight. The air was heavy with humidity, and unseen jets of nutrient-rich water kept all the foliage wet and glistening. It was reassuring to see how all those hard-earned collection dollars had been put to use.

Our nervous guide led us down a meandering path of crunchy black Hawaiian sand. We crossed over a babbling brook by way of an arched Japanese bridge, and traversed the very clearing where Father and I had first met Monsignor Havermeyer. Yes, hard as it was to believe, before our own Michael K. Havermeyer came to join us at Saint Philomena's, this had been the place where he hung his biretta. I could still picture him standing there in a sagging sweatshirt, baggy faded jeans, and Tijuana sandals with tire treads for soles. These days he wore a cassock, of course, but he'd never been able to shed the sandals. They had once saved his life, after all, which was why I had nicknamed him "Ol' Lucky Soles."

"Hih—hih—here we are," said David Smoley, ushering us through an angular door into Monsignor Aspic's place of business.

"Ah," said Father, taking it all in, "this will do nicely."

"Erg," said the gardener, my stomach lacking Father's tact.

During his investigation into the death of Bishop Brassorie, whose murder had occurred in His Grace's private chapel upstairs, Father Baptist had questioned members of the household and staff in this very room. At the time it had been Monsignor Havermeyer's office. Monsignor Conrad J. Aspic had made a few changes since then. The walls, which had once been desert beige with burnt umber trim, were now gray with gray trim. The rubber plant in a pot of ferns that used to draw one's attention to the window was now a fiber optic splay of plastic tubing and morphing pinhead lights set before stark black drapes. The mahogany desk had been replaced with an inch-thick sheet of Plexiglas resting atop four aluminum posts. The walnut bookcase, once filled with leather-bound sets of Gore Vidal, Joseph Heller, David Stern, and Kurt Vonnegut, Jr.—whether actually devoured or not, I could not say—had been supplanted by a glass-and-wire assemblage of feeble shelves designed for dainty porcelain souvenirs of the monsignor's travels rather than the ponderous weight of words. The library had been reduced to a pile of impeccably stacked paperbacks on the corner of the desk unit.

The bright colors of the covers against the stark colorlessness of the room induced strobe-like effects in my eyeballs as I bent to examine the titles on the spines. There was *Love, Charismatic Style* by Sister Rosalind Gauze—smoldering red letters against a burning pink background, almost painful to look at. Picture this in purple letters against phosphorescent abalone: *Your Healing Hands: Setting Your Soul Afire* by Lillith Llorallyn Lyllyth. With the flickering and all, I may have missed a few L's. One for the self-consciously loquacious self-righteous: *Living Your Personal Liturgy by Sanctifying Your Patterns of Speech.* My favorite, but by no means the last in the pile, was *Praying in Tongues, or How to Transcend Meaning* by Anonymousky. Swirled orange and red letters over a counter-swirled peacock blue and turquoise background, a visual effect that could be described as thrillingly nauseating. And so on.

What swill this man absorbs, thought the gardener with a condescending sneer, then twisted his face into an unconvincing half-yawn to cover it up.

"Have a seat if you like, David," said Father, maneuvering himself around the desk thing.

"If—if you—if you don't mind," said David, eyeing the uncomfortable-looking crisscross of steel pipes that served as a guest seat, "I'll just stand."

"Good idea," said Father, noting the molded plastic eyecup on a spring-loaded pillar into which our missing monsignor apparently chose to squeeze his perky derriere. Father, too, remained on his feet.

Me, I sauntered over to a cylindrical aluminum post that had no apparent function and looked at myself in its polished surface. I was tempted to stick my tongue out and make faces, but decided against it. David Smoley craved positive reinforcement, not comedy relief.

"Are you, you know, sure it's okay for us to be in here?" asked David.

"I should think so," said Father, lacing his voice with kindly assurance. "Cardinal Fulbright is understandably concerned about Monsignor Aspic's disappearance. I thought this would be a good place to start."

"Here? B-buh-but it—it happened up in—it—in Hollywood."

"So I understand. You said you are his chauffeur. Did you drive him to the studio last night?"

"Uh-huh."

"He was going to be the guest on a talk show, is that right?"

"Um—uh, yes."

"It started at eight o'clock?"

"Uh-huh, but he wanted to get there a half-hour early."

"For make-up and such? I would imagine a television studio would be an exciting place to visit—all those cameras and spotlights, people running around behind the scenes."

"I—I, I, I wouldn't, I wouldn'—t!—know," said David with a dejected shrug. "It's not like, like he invited me in with him."

"He didn't?" said Father. "I'm surprised. I would have thought—"

"He told me to wait—wait in the car—so I did."

"In the car? The whole time? That hardly seems fair."

David fixed his eyes on the stack of paperbacks on the desk unit and withheld comment.

Father clasped his hands behind his back. "Did you drop him off at the entrance and then look for a parking space, or—?"

"Nuh, nuh, no. He didn't get out until after I parked."

"Really," said Father. "Did you park close to the building?"

"Couldn't. I was lucky to, um, to find an empty space at the far end of the lot."

"Is it very big, the parking lot?"

"Yeah, sort of, I guess."

"I don't suppose you accompanied the monsignor to the studio entrance?"

David shot Father a glare that practically screamed negation.

"So you remained in the car," said Father.

"He got—he got out," said David, wagging his head emphatically. "That's, um, that's the last, the last I saw him."

"How did you pass the time after he exited the car?"

"I listened—to the radio."

"Any particular station?"

David looked at him quizzically. "Um—no, not really. There's a SCAN button."

"So I gather you listened to a wide variety of programs."

David nodded, puzzled as to where this was leading. I was a bit puzzled myself.

"I wish our radio did that," said Father, glancing at me.

I could have mentioned that our recently-replaced car radio actually did indeed have that feature, but decided it wasn't important.

"So," said Father, stepping toward the window and peering outside. "When did you begin to think something was amiss?"

The kid thought long and hard. "It was—I guess it—I mean, it was around quarter after, um, eight. I was just channel surfing—you know?—and, and I heard his name—"

"Monsignor Aspic's?"

"Yeah, his. So I hit the button—you know?—to stop on that station. It was KLIE." He pronounced KLIE as "Kly—Eee," which took Father a second to figure out. It took me a second longer to realize how to figure it out.

"You mean," asked Father when he had, "they have a radio station as well as a TV station? They simulcast their TV shows on the radio?"

David looked appalled that Father didn't know that. Gathering resolve, he shrugged, then nodded more or less affirmatively. "The guy and the lady whose show it is, they were all excited because Monsignor never showed up."

"I'll bet that gave you quite a start."

"It was, um—you know?—kind of, um—you know."

"So what did you do?"

"I got out of the car," said David, swallowing loudly, "and went up to the door, the one marked CELEBRITY ENTRANCE. There's a guy behind a bulletproof window. He thought I was crazy, but he finally phoned some producer lady. She came and let me in. I told her what happened, and she told the guard guy to call the police. When they came they didn't seem too interested. One cop said he'd seen the monsignor on the show last Saturday and thought he was a flake."

"So they questioned you, and that was that?"

"I guess. I got home after midnight, but I was all, um—you know."

"Did you get any sleep?"

"Uh-uh. That's why, um—you know?—the uh—when you came—at the front door."

"I figured. Don't give it a second thought."

"I stayed up hoping he'd—you know?—call—or somebody."

"Did somebody—call, I mean?"

"On the rectory phone, yeah. Reporters—five or six. On his private line, only, um, well—the message is still there."

"He has an answering machine?" asked Father, glancing at the Plexiglas desktop.

"It's there behind the stack of books."

"This? I thought it was an ashtray."

"The monsignor doesn't smoke."

"No, of course not," smiled Father, still looking around. "Ah, now I see the wires. So that's an answering machine. You say the caller left a message. You didn't speak to him?"

David strafed Father with some rapid-fire blinking. "I, no, I wouldn't—don't—answer his phone."

Father considered that for a moment, then said, "I don't see an appointment book. Do you know if he kept one?"

"No."

"No, you don't know, or no he didn't?"

"Monsignor Aspic was a *genius,*" said David, his lips curling peculiarly on that last word a bit. "He kept everything in his head."

Father glanced at me, then thoughtfully tapped the table with his fingertips.

"That's what he said once," said David, shoving his hands deep into his pockets. "Not that he said much—to me, I mean. I was just—um—well, sort of like—"

"Wallpaper?" asked Father.

David shrugged, or shuddered, or something.

"I know the feeling," said Father. "I really do. So tell me, David, did you drive the monsignor any other places yesterday? Earlier in the day?"

"Oh yeah," said the lad, extricating his hands from his pockets and wiping his brow for effect. "Except for lunch, it was nonstop."

"Could you reconstruct your movements?"

"Yeah, I got it here," said David, pulling a small notebook from his shirt pocket. It was bound with a spiral wire at the top. He flipped it open and riffled through the pages. "Here it is. First there was the press conference at the Chancery—"

"Hold on," said Father. "That notebook."

"It's mine."

"May I see it?"

"Yeah, but you won't understand it," said the lad, handing it across the desk. "It's just notes I make to myself."

"You don't keep dates and times," said Father, flipping the pages. "These entries are mostly addresses. Addresses and—what is this?"

"Monsignor usually calls me in here the night before. He dictates a list of addresses where he needs to go the next day. I write them down, one to a page. Then I go get a map and figure out how to get to each one before we leave. That way I can prop my notebook in the cup holder on the dashboard and, well, that's it."

"So this last entry, 'KLIE,' with an address on Hollywood Boulevard." Father pronounced it "Kay—Lie," which had been my inclination all along.

"Uh-huh," answered David after he figured it out.

"The notation under it: 'N on HL to HWB, R, CH plus 5.'"

"'North on Highland to Hollywood Blvd.'," explained David, drawing the path in the air with his index finger. "'Turn right, five blocks past Cahuenga.' I just jot down what I need to get there. 'H' could mean different streets, depending where I'm going, but—"

"These notes are just to refresh your memory," said Father, "not a comprehensive record, otherwise you'd just take the map. That makes sense. Now, you said your first destination yesterday was the Chancery?"

"Uh-huh."

"Ah, that would be this entry a few pages back: 'CHAN,' right? No address or directions needed because you take the monsignor there frequently."

"Right." The lad seemed genuinely proud, or perhaps relieved.

"Do you remember what time that was?" asked Father.

"I think it was seven in the morning. He wanted to be there by six thirty."

"So it is his pattern to arrive at his destinations early."

"It sure is."

"The next entry, 'DAM,' also without an address or directions?"

"The Del Agua Mission. I don't know if it even has an address. I just know where it is."

"Technically it's on the Chapel Hill Estate."

David shrugged again. "There was a press conference there, too. Eight thirty. I got him there at eight on the dot, and then I just parked in the shade and—"

"Listened to the radio," said Father at the same time. "Now let me see: after 'DAM' there are two addresses with directions but no names, then 'CHAN' again. Chancery, right? Cardinal Fulbright mentioned their meeting at noon."

"Right. I mean, I took him there. I don't know who he saw."

"You stayed in the car?"

"Yeah."

"There follows one, two, three, four addresses between 'CHAN' and the last entry, 'KLIE.' The monsignor did have a busy day."

"Uh-huh."

"Busier than usual?"

"Not really."

"His last commitment yesterday was at the television station. Do you know if he anticipated going out afterwards with the hosts of the show?"

"No. I mean, he didn't say anything about it."

"He'd done the show before. Last Saturday, wasn't it? Was he invited out afterwards then?"

David thought that one over. "No."

"Odd," said Father. "Show people, in my experience, love to congratulate themselves long into the night after a good performance."

David Smoley looked at him blankly.

"Okay," said Father, clearing his throat. "Did the monsignor make any mention of appointments for today?"

"No. I was expecting him to do that when we got home, but, well, you know."

"Think, David. You were with him a good part of yesterday. He didn't say anything to you about what he was planning to do today?"

"No," said David, contorting his face. "He doesn't say much to me. Oh, but—"

"But what?"

"I heard him say nine o'clock."

"To whom?"

"He made a call on his cell phone. It was in the car, just as I was parking at the TV station. Last night. He said something like, 'See you at nine, but don't expect me to be very sharp after tonight.'"

"What do you suppose he meant by not being 'sharp'?"

David Smoley shrugged a bit impatiently.

"You've no idea who he was talking to?" asked Father.

David's shoulders hunched an inflated ditto.

"Hm," said Father. "Did Monsignor Aspic leave his cell phone on all the time, or did he just turn it on when he was making outgoing calls?"

"I don't know. Why?"

"The cardinal tried to phone him several times but got no answer."

"Then it must've been off. He had it with him."

"Well, then," said Father, "did anything unusual happen at any of these previous stops?"

David's eyes went wide again. "I, um, I don't know what you mean."

Father flipped the pages back and forth, noting the various addresses. "I'm just wondering if anything out of the ordinary occurred, anything that caught your attention or gave you pause. For example, after your second visit to the Chancery, did Monsignor Aspic exhibit any signs of excitement, agitation, perhaps? Did he maybe ... show you something?"

"What do you mean?"

"Was he maybe carrying something, something given to him by the cardinal?"

"He carried a briefcase in and out. That's all I saw."

"And he said nothing about his conversation—?"

The lad closed his eyes and slowly opened them. "It's like I said. He doesn't say much of anything to me."

"He never even asks the time—?"

"He wears a Rolex."

"Or whether the traffic is going to make him late for his next ?"

"That's why he goes everywhere early."

"In other words," said Father, shaking his head slightly, "the man never speaks to you."

"Only when—when—when he absolutely has to."

"So when you were driving him places, what did he do between destinations?"

Smoley scratched his head. "He has this briefcase. I sometimes see it in the mirror, open on the seat next to him. I think I heard him going through some papers a couple times. He sometimes has a laptop computer with him. I didn't pay much attention."

"You him and he you, apparently," said Father, running his fingers through his hair wearily. "I must confess this surprises me, his treatment of you. He certainly doesn't act like that around anyone else, not that I've seen. He's generally considered, well ..."

"Perky," interjected the gardener, knowing Father didn't much favor the word.

"Yes," said Father, thanking me with a not-so-thankful nod.

"I know," said David, smiling in spite of himself, "and when—when he first came here a little over a month ago, he was—he was different—you know?—friendly, really nice—nice to me."

"By 'when he first came here' do you mean to Los Angeles when Cardinal Fulbright procured his services as a consultant?"

"Uh-huh."

"Perhaps it's none of my business," said Father, "but you'll understand that in an investigation of this sort, one never knows what is and isn't pertinent at this stage of the game. Would you mind telling me if something in particular, some specific event, perhaps something you inadvertently did or said, changed his opinion of you?"

"Awk!" said David. A torrent of emotions rippled all over his face. For a second I thought he was imitating a crow. "Awk ... awk ... October," he finally managed to say. "Tuh-twuh-twuh—twenty— twenty-seventh. Buh-buh-buh—but I really don't want to t-tuh-tuh-talk about it!"

Father gave me one of those "Pay attention!" glances.

"Sounds pretty bad," said Father while David trembled all over.

"For a couple days," said David, "he even drove himself. Didn't want anything to do with me. I thought he was gonna fire me, and then what was I gonna do?" The words came slowly at first, then faster and faster. "Then—I think it was the day after Halloween—yeah, the next day, or the day after—he told me to drive him to the Chancery, but he didn't look at me, and he wasn't ever friendly after that. I really don't want to talk—to talk—talk about—about—"

"Very well," said Father, his voice soothing. "I'm not here to embarrass you, David. We'll let it go. Okay?"

David looked as though he was going to discombobulate any second, but Father changed gears as if nothing untoward had happened.

"You mentioned Monsignor's valise," said Father.

David apparently didn't know the word.

"Briefcase," explained Father.

"Oh," said David, regaining some control over his twitches. "Yes, he has a briefcase."

"He takes it everywhere?"

"Yes."

"Into every place you took him yesterday?"

"Yes."

"Focusing on yesterday, were all these stops at businesses?"

David thought that over for a moment before answering. "Mostly. Two of them were houses, though, creepy old houses with—" Suddenly David started twitching again. He started rubbing his arms as if he was standing in a freezer, and sweat started popping out of his forehead as if he were in an oven. "I d-duh-duh-don't wanna t-taw-taw-talk about it anymore."

"I think I've got enough to go on," said Father nonchalantly. "Would you mind if I took this notebook with me?"

"No," said David, then he choked. "I mean, no—I'd, um—I'd rather you didn't. There's some personal stuff in there."

"Oh," said Father.

"You can use the photocopier," said David helpfully. "There in the closet, to duplicate the last few pages."

"Splendid," said Father. "While I'm doing that, if it isn't too much trouble, would you mind getting me some coffee? Black and strong. Martin, perhaps you'd like some, too. We've been on the go all night and haven't slept, and this promises to be a long day."

"Sure, I don't mind," said David, teetering on feeling useful or something.

"You don't need me, do you Father?" I asked. "I'd kind of like to tag along with David here. This rectory is one ... *interesting* ... place." It was hard to find a neutral word that wouldn't give my true opinion away.

"Sure," said Father with a sideways wink so David wouldn't see it. "This is truly one of the most unusual ... *architectural statements* ... in the city."

"Well," said David, expanding perceptibly. "Right this way, um—what did you say your name was?"

"Martin Feeney," said I.

"Take your time," said Father, reaching for a button on the answering machine.

*"Con*rad," I heard an electronic voice say as I lurched down the hall behind David Smoley. Either the caller had a lisp or the line was noisy. The connection, or the speaker, certainly sounded erratic. "Con*rad,* are you *there? Please* pick *up* if you *are.* This is *D.K.* You didn't *leave* a *mes*sage. I really *must* speak *with* you. ... *Please* call *me* back, *hm? ...* Con*rad? ..."*

I made sure that David showed me copious weird structural anomalies and extraterrestrial flora on the way to the kitchen and back, enough to give Father time to photocopy the entirety of Smoley's spiral notebook. When we returned, Father was again playing the recorded message.

The line, I decided, was not noisy.

"...Please call *me* back, *hm? ...* Con*rad? ..."*

8

"THIS WILL INTEREST YOU," said Solomon Yung-sul Wong, snapping another x-ray into place on the blazing light box. His nametag said that he was the chief coroner, but his demeanor sometimes convinced me that he was Boris Karloff playing a mystical, serene, penetrating Oriental character in an old black-and-white movie. "You see?" he said, tracing the ghostly tendrils and globules on the film with his long, slender fingers. "I count four, no five the size of kiwis, and this one here approaches a grapefruit."

"I would assume," said Father, gingerly touching the images with his own outstretched fingers, "that kidney stones of those dimensions would be painful."

"Excruciating," agreed Solomon. "Unimaginably so. Now, notice the distorted, degenerative structure of the shoulders, the vertebrae, the pelvis."

"What would explain that?"

"Long-term calcium deficiency. I've seen evidence of nutritional neglect before, but never as severe as this."

"I have," said the assistant coroner, unfolding his arms and slipping off the stool from which he had been keeping watch. John Holtsclaw, being full-blooded Gabrielino Indian, couldn't help looking like he was perpetually charging out of a John Wayne movie. "Both in South America and on my own reservation. Impoverished people often live on severely restricted diets. Here in the city even the garbage dumpsters provide a wide variety of choices. But in some parts of the world they have one and only one staple, and that's it. Imagine living on cornmeal and water, day after day, all your life. The sensory tedium alone, let alone the lack of a full spectrum of vitamins and minerals, would drive most civilized folk to distraction. But there are people who live precisely like that."

Having quitted the architectural insanity of Saint Philip's, Father Baptist and I were now in another of my least favorite places: the morgue. It was a modern chamber of horrors, as far as I was concerned—all those stainless steel tables, the glistening sharp tools of the trade, the specimen jars, the disinfectant ambiance, the harsh tubular lights, the sentinel microscopes, the computer-driven analyzers, and the cloying smells. I couldn't imagine how anyone would aspire to working in such a place, but in this respect we were in the company of giants.

"Are you saying," said Father, indicating a body on a nearby slab draped with a bleached white sheet, "this man is from some such part of the world?"

"No," said Solomon, easing himself onto a tall, uncomfortable stool identical to the one John Holtsclaw had just vacated. "I'm saying his diet was detrimentally limited, probably to a regimen as simple as bread and water. His stomach contents confirm that his last meal consisted of bread—just ordinary wheat bread."

"Not even any butter," added Holtsclaw.

"Any idea where he did come from?" asked Father.

"Probably right here," said Wong, taking up a clipboard. "Tissue sample from his lungs indicate he spent his life breathing the exhaust of modern industry."

"Hydrocarbon deposits," explained Holtsclaw. He started to take a Dunhill cigarette out of the red box in his shirt pocket, thought better of it, and stuffed it back into place. "Synthetic compounds, plastics—big city air."

"Smog," summarized Father.

"Yes," said Solomon, "and something else: asbestos fibers. His advanced age certainly puts him back in the decades when it was used indiscriminately, but—"

"But?" asked Father.

"But," answered Holtsclaw, "as evidenced by the sheer concentration and dissemination of the contaminant throughout the lungs, it is far more likely that he's been inhaling asbestos all the while he was living on bread and water."

"Years and years," summarized Solomon. "It's a miracle he didn't develop lung cancer."

"A prison, maybe?" asked the gardener, who by this time was boasting green coloration in parts of his anatomy other than his thumb. He was trying to distract himself from his discomfiture, albeit unsuccessfully, by gazing out the blue-tinted windows at the meticulously manicured lawns of Pomeroy Police Plaza. "Maybe he was confined in one of the older, outdated facilities?"

"There'd be a record of him in the Correctional Services databank," said Holtsclaw, shaking his head. "That drew a blank, so we initiated the broadband fingerprint search an hour and a half ago. Something may turn up in the next twenty-four hours. The Department of Motor Vehicles came up zilch, but their fingerprint records only go back so far."

"We asked Sybil Wexler to give it a whirl at her terminal," said Solomon. "If anybody can find anything on this man—"

"But she's assigned to Burglary," said Father, "the task force investigating stolen religious articles."

"Until yesterday," corrected Solomon. "She's in Records Division now."

"What happened?" asked the gardener, whose middle-aged heart had performed an earnest if not agile flip-flop at the mention of her name.

"The department chatter," said Holtsclaw, "is that she decked her partner."

"Tragg Halcomb?" said Father and I together.

Solomon Yung-sul Wong and John Holtsclaw answered with a synchronized grin.

"You can find her in the basement of Building C," said Holtsclaw, pointing past me to a modest sandstone structure on the far side of the courtyard.

"Perhaps we will pay her a visit," said Father, smiling. "Now, back to the matter at hand." He strolled over to a wall-mounted hook from which hung a cassock sealed in a large, clear plastic evidence bag. Also visible, draped around the hanger, was the Crucifix which inexorably sealed his involvement in this case. "Have you considered the obvious: that this man was dressed like a priest, therefore he was, in fact, a priest?"

"We contacted the Chancery," said Holtsclaw, "but they said there was little they could do without a name, or at least more information. Their fingerprint files go back farther than DMV's, but they haven't been scanned into computers so there's no practical way to access them. To tell you the truth, I didn't think the clerk I talked to gave much of a damn. Perhaps, Father, you could ask your Cardinal Fulbright to nudge his troops."

"If the opportunity presents itself, I will," said Father. "But I suspect His Eminence would likewise not consider this a priority, at least not at the present juncture."

"If I may backtrack a moment," said Solomon, "to something Mr. Feeney asked a moment ago."

"Hrhm?" blinked yours truly, the mention of my name snapping me out of a hopeless daydream about Sybil Wexler. Just then, as the room came into focus, I noticed a finely-executed pen-and-ink drawing framed on the wall. In the upper left corner there was an awkwardly-scrawled inscription: "To Solomon and John, all in all, Wink Wink." It depicted a body on an autopsy table draped with a sheet slipped just enough to reveal that the deceased was a woman. In the foreground stood a nine-teenth-century surgeon holding the woman's heart up to the light. Beneath was the caption: "¿DONDE ESTÁ EL AMOR?" Where is the love? I said again, "Hrhm?"

"Though it was unlikely that our John Doe was incarcerated in our penal system," continued Solomon, "there are indications that he was, nevertheless, a prisoner."

"Come again?" said Father, peeling his attention away from the hanging cassock.

"See for yourself," said Holtsclaw, striding over to the form on the slab and lifting a corner of the sheet. "The scarring around the left ankle denotes continuous abrasion resulting in the buildup of a considerable layer of callus."

"A shackle of some kind," surmised Father, leaning close.

"More than likely," said Holtsclaw.

"But those are all long-range problems," said Solomon solemnly. "There is something in the immediate that defies explanation. The stomach, for example."

"Yes," agreed Holtsclaw. "And more so the matter of the liver, and by extension, the heart."

"Or vice versa," said Solomon.

Father looked at them with those incisive eyes that seemed to whisper, knowing yet inscrutably, "Considering what happens when I say Mass, or perform a Baptism, or absolve a penitent in the confessional, gentlemen, what is one more mystery?" But all he actually said was, "Do tell."

"Excuse me," I ventured to say. Though my first impression of this corpse in the mausoleum had been a departure from my usual necrophobic reaction, I had no desire to view him again under these sterile, methodical conditions, especially if his insides were on the outside. Besides, one good daydream deserved another, and there was another matter, an errand of personal import, that begged my attention. "Father, I just realized it's Thursday. I take it you're going to be a while. Would you mind if I—?"

Father looked at me with sleep-deprived eyes that seemed to whisper, compassionate but analytically, "Martin, Martin, Martin, why do you torture yourself even in your acts of Charity?" But all he actually said was, "Of course. Better get a move on. Pick me up across the way. I'll most likely be in Building C by the time you return."

"Good day, gentlemen," sighed I, hobbling toward the door.

"Now," I heard Father say as the heavy door swung shut on its silent hinges, "tell me about the stomach, the liver, and by extension, the—"

9

"THIS IS THE LAST TIME I'M ALLOWING THIS," said Gladys Tracy, commander and chief administrator of the California Penitentiary for Women at Vernon, tucking a file folder under her pudgy arm as she led me down a long concrete corridor at a brisk, military clip. "It was necessary a few weeks ago, but Ms. Farnsworth—"

"Miss," I corrected her, huffing and hobbling behind. "Cheryl prefers—"

"Frankly, Mr. Feeney, I don't much care. Do you have any idea what a nightmare she's been for me? No, of course not."

"Excuse me, Miss Tracy—"

"Ms.," she corrected me. "I prefer Ms., but that's outside. In here I'm *Warden* Tracy."

"My apologies, Ma'am," said I as she and her spongy, undulating posterior preceded me up a steep metal stairway. I was panting deeply by the time we had ascended halfway. "I meant no … offense, and I didn't … expect or request the privilege … of visiting Miss Farnsworth … in her cell. That … was … your idea." I pressed my eyelids tightly closed to squeeze away a wave of dizziness. When I opened them the scenery hadn't improved. "The visitor's room would be fine with me, not to mention it being situated on the ground floor. Warden Tracy, if you don't mind my saying so, I seem to be detecting a bit of an edge in your tone—"

She halted and whirled around abruptly.

"—since the last time I was here, I mean." I returned her savage glare with my most charming smile. It hurt. "Forgive my impertinence, but you see, I've grown accustomed to your kindness and it pains me—truly—that Cheryl has been the source of such annoyance to you."

She softened slightly, like a slab of granite sprinkled with meat tenderizer. "You've no idea, Mr. Feeney."

"Then please explain, Warden Tracy. I want to help."

"I know you do," she said, a barest hint of benevolence in her voice. Catching herself, she spun around and continued up the stairs. "You had a calming effect three weeks ago. Perhaps it will work again. I was considering phoning you when the guard buzzed me that you were at the front gate."

"I'll do what I can," I gasped as we gained the summit. She motioned me on, but I planted the tip of my cane between my toes, stacked my hands atop the handle, and refused to go further until I caught my breath, meanwhile allowing the ache in my bones to settle down to an endurable screech. "A nightmare, you said."

With a thrust of her middle finger, Warden Tracy pushed her batwing eyeglasses to the precipice of her mucilaginous nose. "WOPOPs are always a challenge, Mr. Feeney. A life sentence 'With Out Possibility Of Parole' is a daunting prospect, like a diagnosis of pancreatic cancer or Parkinson's disease. I know *I'd* have a hard time accepting it." She paused a moment, I supposed, so I could acknowledge her magnanimousness.

"Do go on," I panted, though my legs had no intention of doing so.

"When she first arrived she kept pretty much to herself," said she, glaring at me under eyelids that seemed to flap like a predatory bird. "You're probably aware of that. Most of the inmates avoided her because of all the weirdness that came out at her trial. I suspect she fueled the fires, intimidating some of the girls with cold stares and cryptic comments—nothing provable and certainly not punishable, but disruptive nonetheless. Then, a few days before Halloween, she worked herself into a frenzy and, well, you know about that."

"I'll never forget," said I with a nod and a loud gulp. "You summoned me to see if I could reason with her. The Crosses she painted, hundreds of them, all over every inch of her cell. It was quite a sight."

"And one big administrative headache," said she, removing the file folder from her armpit and flipping it open with clerical authority. Her eyes followed her index finger down to a bit of information preserved in broad-stroked squiggles. "That was October twenty-sixth. You came again a week later, on November second."

"The Feast of All Souls," I agreed. "That was the last time I was here. The Crosses were still there, but she seemed to have calmed down considerably."

"I agree." She snapped the folder closed, reinserted it under her arm, and bored into me with glacial eyes. "What I find unnerving is that she came to some sort of calming realization on November first, the day *before* your visit."

"The Feast of All Saints," I noted for the record.

"Whatever. On that day she confided to me that the danger had passed. Furthermore, Mister Feeney, she said you had something to do with the downfall—that was her word—the downfall of whatever it was she was so afraid of."

"She told you this," I said, just to be sure I had the sequence of events straight, "the day before my last visit."

"That's what I'm saying. It was as if your presence the following day, November second—"

"The Feast of All Souls."

"—only confirmed what she already knew."

"That is interesting, Warden Tracy," I assured her. "Very interesting."

"The day after your visit, November third, she agreed to paint out the Crosses. It took her most of the day—two coats. When I came to inspect her work, she told me that it was the Feast of Saint—" The warden whipped out the file again and squinted at her own ragged penmanship. "—Malachy O'More, apparently some sort of visionary."

"His predictions regarding the papacy are famous," said the gardener, visualizing the copy of *The Prophecies of Saint Malachy* on the top shelf of Father Baptist's bookcase.

As she snapped the file closed again, her eyes did a little somersault. I assumed she was reacting to the apparent logjam of Catholic Feasts at the onset of November. I didn't have the heart to tell her that we have Feasts on every single day of the year.

"In any case," she said after a long expulsion of breath, "I would say that you had a hand in her temporary recovery. I don't believe any of it, of course—the downfall of some evil force, I mean—but Miss Farnsworth can be persuasive." Ms. Tracy paused for a couple of seconds, as if rehearsing her next words before uttering them. "You know, Mr. Feeney, sometimes she can draw you in, into her world, in spite of yourself." The warden then stepped a little closer so I could smell what she'd had for breakfast and whispered, "Did you? Do something, I mean? And if you did, how did she know?"

"I'm not sure how to answer that," I admitted honestly, pulling my head back slightly. "I don't know if I can. Cheryl Farnsworth is an extraordinary woman. Whatever she's done in the past, however she acts here in prison, I … Well, let me put it this way: Cheryl has the ability to see things that the rest of us do not."

"You mean she's—" Warden Tracy's lips constricted with fascinated contempt. "—psychic."

"Not exactly."

"Spiritual, then."

I shook my head. "I mean she has a wider range of perception than most. I, for example, can't tell the difference between black and navy blue. I'm colorblind in that region of the optical spectrum. You can probably tell them apart, but that doesn't make you more 'spiritual,' just more 'perceptive.'"

She looked disappointed or disgusted, I'm not sure which. "I'm surprised to hear you say that. From what Cheryl has told me, you are a profoundly spiritual man."

"Devotional," I corrected her. "I wouldn't presume to apply the word 'spiritual' to myself, and you, Madam, if you'll permit my candor, shouldn't use it so frivolously. To the average person the word has come to connote something ethereal and therefore insubstantial. 'Spirituality' is generally considered these days to be something inherent, congenital, a given, a cinch—something attained without exertion. 'Devotion,' on the other hand, denotes diligence, repetition, tedium, self-examination—effort, in other words. That is the realm in which I reside, or rather strive to dwell. I am a profoundly maladroit, undisciplined man, Warden Tracy, struggling to pull together some semblance of a rickety devotional life—"

My voice trailed off because her eyelids were fluttering. She crept several millimeters closer, removed her glasses, and purred, "Call me Gladys."

Call me AARRGGHH!! screamed the gardener silently.

I'm sure my cry was inaudible because I suddenly realized I had swallowed my tongue, my tonsils, and my larynx all in one excruciating gulp. As if to prove just how rickety and maladroit I could be, I made a big, clumsy show of pointing the way with my cane, urging her into unwilling perambulation. I felt like a ranch hand nudging a lazy cow toward another part of the pasture.

Oh, the look she gave me!

"Temporary," I suddenly managed to utter after burping my speech apparatus back into place. "That's how you described Cheryl's recovery a moment ago."

"Right," she snapped, reverting to Warden. Her officiousness clutch re-engaged, the pistons in her rear engine went into high gear, leaving me hobbling behind in her frosty wake. "Miss Farnsworth appeared to stabilize emotionally for the next week or so, but then her *spiritual* delusions returned to the fore."

"Do tell," I called as she increased her distance.

"She's become withdrawn. Hardly eats. Spends most of her time in her cell, avoids the other inmates, declines to use the exercise facility at her appointed times."

"Have you spoken to her about it?"

"No, I've been busy. The staff shrink visited her yesterday and reported that she didn't say a word to her, not a single word. Just sat there on her cot with her head in her hands."

"That hardly seems like Cheryl."

"See for yourself," she huffed, coming to a sudden stop before a large metal door. "Visitor," she barked into a small square hole in the center as I came hobbling up.

No sound came from within.

"Sergeant Lugg," she growled at the female sequoia tree standing across the hallway, "Mister Feeney may have fifteen minutes. When he's done, escort him to the front gate. I'll be in my office if you need me."

"Sure thing," said the guard, lethargically unhooking a ring of keys from her belt.

"Sergeant!"

"Um, yes, Warden Tracy."

I watched, my heart pounding, as the key was turned and the latch lifted. A moment later I felt the surge of air as the door swung shut behind me with a thunderous boom.

The first thing I noticed, even before the total whiteness of the walls, was the faint but sickening stench of recently dried industrial paint. The walls bore the lumpy, globular texture of water-based acrylic thickly and repeatedly applied to obliterate what was underneath.

Ah well, I thought to myself, just as in the world outside, obscured it may be but the Truth is still there.

Cheryl was sitting on the cot, face buried in her hands, silent and motionless as a lump of rock salt. Her denim uniform, faded to a barely perceptible hint of blue, hung loosely from her shoulders and knees. She had lost weight. Late morning sunlight poured steeply through the window, igniting golden highlights all over her long red hair as it hung limply around her forearms. The effect was mesmerizing.

It took me a moment to remember where I'd seen that same effect before, that very day, in fact. Golden highlights ... golden highlights ... Of course: the old man in the crypt! But here the glow imparted a sense of tension rather than tranquility, as if the air itself was tightened like a string about to break.

"Cheryl?" I said softly, creeping toward her.

She made no movement, no sound whatsoever. She didn't even appear to be breathing.

"Cheryl?" I said a little louder.

"You've been busy again," she said, her voice muffled behind her hands.

"Pardon?" I asked, stopping my advance. As creepy as the crypt had been, and the mortuary upsetting, this was by far the most unnerving moment of my day. "What did you say?"

"I said, you've been busy again."

"I have? I mean, I *have*."

"Martin, my Friend, you are about to become a whole lot busier."

I swallowed loudly. "How so?"

"A trial approaches."

I thought for a second she meant for herself—new evidence come to light, perhaps?—but then my skin chilled as she said, "You will be swallowed by darkness."

"Excuse me? What are you saying?"

"Engulfed by the intensity of their need, drawn into the void left by those who knew better. It's all so sad, and ultimately avoidable, but that is the way of things in these times."

What had I said to the warden? *Cheryl has the ability to see things that the rest of us do not.* Her premonitions had proved true before: *Spiders and flies, spiders and flies ... What's an 'earwig'? Is that a bug, too?* What dire events was she seeing in my future this time around? What dark need was going to engulf me?

"And when it's over," she said after a protracted silence, "I want you to do me a favor."

"Anything, Cheryl, you know that."

"Bring Father Baptist."

"Oh?"

"To hear my Confession."

The unsettling moment had just transmogrified into the most shocking—shocking not just in the sense of unanticipated, but more so astonishing, bewildering, exhilarating ... downright *electrifying*.

"Cheryl," I said, dropping to my knees before her, my cane clattering somewhere on the floor. As I peered up at her face, still hidden in her hands, the vertebrae in my neck crackled and ground in protest, but the pain seemed far away. My center of gravity thus compromised, my torso wanted to topple, but some unseen hand held me upright, albeit quivering precariously on trembling knees. I actually felt something akin to heat radiating from her, but it wasn't anything like the emanations of the sun or an open vent. I extended my furtive fingers to touch her hands, to brush her hair aside, but withdrew for fear of overstepping.

"You were right," she said softly.

"Me? About what?"

"You are a devotional man."

"How—?" A shiver crackled through me. It wasn't pleasant. "I try—I wish I could say, 'my best'—but—"

"You've been praying for an increase of Faith."

"Yes, I have. And—?"

"Your prayers will be answered shortly."

"Oh?"

"As will mine." Her hands still clamped to her face, she began rocking her head slowly, almost imperceptibly, from side to side. Her shifting hair sent out golden flashes of light, piercing as flashbulbs yet subtle as a rainbow hovering over a waterfall. "Martin, it's so, so … *beautiful!*"

"What is?"

"It bleeds."

"Did you say bleeds? What bleeds?"

Her head became still, and I shivered as I sensed that she could see me right through her fingers. After several seconds she whispered a single word. *"It."*

"Cheryl," I said, daring to reach out my fingers and enclose them gingerly around her emaciated wrists. I gave them the gentlest of tugs, and her hands came slowly away from her face. "Oh my God!" I gasped. "Oh … oh … O Mother of Mercy!"

Her features were much the same as I remembered them, though perhaps a bit pale. Her skin was like pliable ivory, soft and serene; and though there were more lines than before, they didn't make her seem older, but rather deeper. Her lips were drawn back into the sweetest smile I have ever seen, and her nostrils did a little involuntary twitch for my benefit. Around her eyes the tissues were puffy and translucent. As she blinked, tiny blue veins rolled beneath the surface of her lids, waving playfully at me. But also as she blinked, pools of welling tears surged over the rims of her lower eyelids and went cascading down her cheeks.

I gasped again.

The color, the fluidity, the viscosity—there was no mistaking it.

She was crying tears of blood.

10

"OVER HERE, MARTIN," CALLED THE WOMAN sitting across from Father Baptist in the booth next to the gurgling fountain. Sybil Wexler was the only woman I've ever met who could wear a red outfit and make it look demurely feminine instead of daringly sexy. The effect was partly due to the luscious shade of her thick hair, the look of unaffected modesty in her eyes, her delicate yet deliberate womanly mannerisms, but mostly it was simply that red was her color. She looked good in it.

"So it's 'Martin' now," said the gardener, lumbering toward them. "Two days ago it was 'Mister Feeney.'"

"Two days ago I was in Burglary with Lieutenant Tragg for a partner," said Sybil, scooting over so I could sit beside her. "Hope you like Italian."

"Two days ago Tragg Holcomb had a full set of teeth," said Father Baptist, smiling in spite of himself. "I take it the desk sergeant in Building C told you we'd be here."

There was so much I wanted to tell him then and there, but not in the presence of Sybil Wexler. I had spent several minutes in the restroom before seeking their table, washing and rewashing my face with cold water while taking deep, slow breaths to calm the uproar within. I'm usually not very good at hiding my feelings, so I just concentrated on how long it had been since Millie's wee-hours breakfast. It helped. Father Baptist no doubt realized something was amiss the moment he looked up at me, but being who he was he set all questions aside until a more propitious moment.

"Welcome back to the human race," I said to her, hooking my cane on the edge of the table. "I prefer 'Martin,' by the way, at least from beautiful women. Yes, the grump at the front desk told me you'd be here at 'Paneno's.' Yes, I love Italian—Father, I hope you phoned the rectory to inform you-know-who that we'd be you-know-whating out—and, yes, I'll gladly contribute to the 'Let's-Reconstruct-that-Irritating-Smirk-on-Tragg's-Puss Dental Fund.'"

"Looks like you got into a tiff yourself," said Sybil, pointing to the bloodstains on my shirtsleeve cuffs.

"No, Ma'am, " I said, ravenously snatching up a menu, "I'm a 'dab the wounds of others' kind of guy. So this is the place that Pierre wrote up in the *Artsy.*"

"The article's framed on the wall, as I predicted it would be," said Father, glancing at it for my benefit.

I shifted slightly and—yipes!—there on the wall, centered in a gaudy frame was a glossy photograph of Cardinal Morley Fulbright, smiling as if his reputation depended on it. Beneath it, in a simpler frame, was Pierre Bontemps' innocuous though curiously intriguing article. Pierre's million-dollar smile was so wide it protruded into the text. I practically knew the article by heart, since Pierre had graciously read it to me several times when he was in the process of writing it:

Fettuccini Cardinal Fulbright

by Pierre Bontemps
Artsy Contributing Editor

Los Angeles has many fine restaurants: Cole's P. E. Buffet and Phillipe's, for example (both dating back to 1908), Hollywood's Musso and Frank (which opened in 1919) and of course Darby's on Sycamore Drive (much more recent, but you won't realize it once you're inside). Chancery personnel patronize some of these establishments. Taylor's Steak House in the Wilshire district often boasts monsignori, flush with martinis and prime rib, at lunch, and let us not forget Clifton's Cafeteria for supper.

But perhaps most closely identified with Cardinal Fulbright is an Italian restaurant downtown called Paneno's. Located at the corner of Ninth and Charivari, the establishment often hosts government and police officials, along with executives from many local corporations. Italian style steaks, veal dishes, pasta of every description, and a selection of gourmet pizzas highlight a bill of fare crowned by a wine list featuring Italian and California vintages.

Our cardinal is very much at home at Paneno's. Marking his devotion to it, the restaurant has named their signature dish, "Fettuccini Cardinal Fulbright"—pasta topped with chunks of ham and crab in a creamy tomato-cognac sauce. Questioned on the origin of the dish's name, the waiter replied, "We used to just call it 'Fettuccine with Ham and Crab,' but Cardinal Fulbright kept ordering it, so we named it in his honor. It was popular before, but after the new name, it became very popular indeed." Asked about the cardinal's choice in wine, the waiter replied, "I can't remember anything specific, but he is definitely a red-wine man." How is he to wait on? "You're printing this? Very nice, very nice, oh yes, very nice! And generous! Let me tell you about generous!"

Cardinal Fulbright's picture hangs about midway through to the rear entrance of the restaurant. It overlooks his favorite booth, which is next to a delightful, gurgling fountain.

"I especially like Pierre's whimsical reference to 'monsignori,'" said I, assessing the clientele at the nearby tables, "'flush with martinis and prime rib.'"

"Pierre Bontemps?" asked Sybil. "Your friend with the, uh—" She made a monocle with her thumb and index finger and placed it over her left eye.

"The same," said Father. "He followed the cardinal for several days and discovered not only that this is his favorite place to eat, but that they had named a recipe after him."

"And that put this place on the map?"

"It certainly gave it a boost. The press is more powerful than the facts, my dear woman. Surely your tenure with the police department has convinced you of that."

"So," I said, "there's the picture, the fountain, and we're midway to the rear entrance. I'd say we're sitting in His Corpulence's favorite booth. What could be more uncomfortable?"

"You should try Chief Billowack's favorite eatery," giggled Sybil, then groaned at the thought.

"I don't think I want to know," said the gardener.

"I do know," said Father, "and I agree: you don't want to know."

"Fettuccini Cardinal Fulbright," said Sybil, pointing to the specialty section on the fifth page of her menu. "'Homemade pasta with chunks of ham and crab.' Hmm. Sounds good to me."

"I'm leaning toward the veal scaloppini," said Father. "Martin?"

"I judge an Italian restaurant by one dish and one dish alone," said I.

"Spaghetti and meatballs," said the three of us in unison, the sound of which attracted a standoffish waiter who introduced himself as "Hal." With a sniff and a tick, he tossed a wicker basket loaded with gnarled breadsticks into our midst, whipped out his pad, and began scribbling impatiently as we repeated our desires for his edgy benefit.

"And to drink?" bleated Hal, fidgeting as though the very thought made him want to dash to the men's room.

"House red," said Sybil.

"A rye highball," said Father.

"And you, Sir?" said Hal, pouring his gaze upon me like a bucket of dishwater upon a campfire.

"Saint Thomas, Salisbury," said I. "'Blue label' if you have it."

"Is that an obscure brand of beer?" he said with a snort.

"Hardly, Sir," snorted I right back. I do believe mine was the more sophisticated. "It's a superior brew of discriminatory ginger ale. I take it that it's news to you."

"We carry only the best," sniffed Hal, "and I've certainly never heard of it."

"Look at you: all of twenty-four, and such an expert."

"Do you wish for me to call the manager, Sir?"

"Call him what you like. This overrated establishment's just dropped ten points in my book, and I'll have you know that Pierre Bontemps had breakfast with us this very morning. The chef at 'Millie's' prepared it tableside, do you hear? Tableside! Now there's a lost concept for you. You've heard of 'Millie's,' of course, you being an expert and all. Is Monsieur Bontemps going to get an earful after this!"

Hal's eyes locked with Cardinal Fulbright's on the wall, then fell to Pierre's byline, then widened with apprehension. "No Sir, no Sir," he stammered pitifully. "I meant no offense. I've only been here three weeks. I'll see what I can do." With that he went scurrying between the tables, his knees rubbing together and his ankles waddling widely apart.

"So where is this 'Millie's'?" asked Sybil. "I've never heard of it."

"It's right in our rectory," I explained, watching Hal gesticulating at an obese man in a tailcoat at the host's podium. "Millie's our house-keeper."

"Oh yes, I believe I met her," she said with a wry smile, "and you are cruel and devious."

"Only when the situation requires."

"Speaking of which," said Father. "Sybil, you're now in Records Division. At least this demotion wasn't my fault."

"Don't be too sure," said Sybil, taking a sip of water. "Lieutenant Tragg Holcomb is missing three teeth right now precisely because of a remark he made about you."

"What remark was that?" asked the gardener.

"Nothing I'm going to repeat until the disciplinary review," said Sybil. "Don't worry about it. I'm seriously thinking of going into private practice anyway."

"A private eye?" asked Father. "Won't that be interesting."

"More like an intrusive and very expensive nose," said she, tapping hers gaily. "So, if you want to use me before I start costing big bucks, now's your chance."

"Indeed, now that you mention it," said Father, pulling a hefty wad of folded photostats from the mysterious folds of his cassock. "You did bring your laptop, didn't you?"

"Right here," she said, reaching into her pocketbook and producing a sleek cigarette case, or so I at first thought. It was a little larger than that, but not much. Actually it was a little computer, the tiniest one I'd ever seen. She touched a purple spot on the otherwise smooth silver surface and the screen flipped up automatically, flickering instantly to electric blue life. The screaming yellow words "SEARCHING FOR SATELLITE UPLINK" appeared, then morphed into "COMMUNICATING WITH HOST," then "SHE'S ALL YOURS!"

"Wow," I said, peering at the widgets and symbols that started popping up all over the flat, liquid screen. "All of that from this little thing."

"You only see part of it," she winked, setting a printer the size of a paperback murder mystery beside the main unit, "and the rest you're better off not knowing." There were no connecting wires. The units communicated by just being near each other. Such marvels of technology, though mundane to most people, continue to be wonders to me.

"Okay," said Father, flattening out the stiff pages and handing them across to her. "This will be child's play for you. I have these addresses. I need to know the names and telephone numbers that go with them."

"Oh," said she, her fingernails flickering over the noiseless keys. They weren't keys at all, just illuminated dots on a glossy, flat surface. "You just want a 'reverse directory.' I'll have the info in no time. I take it these are directions underneath."

"One fellow's shorthand," said Father, "is another's confusion."

"I think I can fix you up with something comprehensible."

"I don't know what we'd do without you."

"Don't even consider it."

"Excuse me, Sir," said a deep voice about two feet above my head.

I looked up—*yeow!* did my neck crack—into a pair of porcine eyes sunk deep amidst rolls of greasy flab. The man with whom Hal had been frantically gesturing was now here at our table, supporting a serving tray on his upturned left hand. He exuded courtesy, expertise, authority, and a whole lot of garlic.

"I understand you requested Saint Thomas," he boomed, the sound coming from somewhere deep inside his bulk. "A thousand pardons, but I'm afraid we only have 'Yellow label.'"

"Barbados?" I said, crestfallen. "Not even 'Red label'?"

"Key West," he agreed, the sinews under his adipose facial tissues quivering with astringent distaste. "It's been many a year, if I may say so, Sir, since I've encountered anyone so knowledgeable and discerning—"

"You mean picky," quipped a plumpish fellow in black at the next table, flush with martinis and prime rib.

"—about quality ginger ale. Rest assured that next time we will be able to accommodate you." With that he set down two bottles of Saint Thomas, Barbados, before me with two tall glasses piled with crushed ice. "Until then, please accept these on the house," said he, then strutted purposefully away.

"What do you make of this one?" Sybil was asking Father. "Does that look like 456 Cuthbert Drive to you?"

"Your guess is as good as mine," said he, eyeing the page.

"The only Cuthbert Drive I know of," said the gardener who doubled as Father's chauffeur, "is in Pacific Palisades. Remember the time we drove by Mr. Turnbuckle's house, just to see what kind of place he lived in? We couldn't even see the house from the street."

"Bingo," said Sybil, tapping the EXECUTE key with a swipe of her adroit pinky. "Thurgood T. Turnbuckle it is."

"One of our most outspoken parishioners," said Father.

"Judging from the neighborhood," said Sybil, "he's probably one of your richest. I hope he's proportionately generous."

"He's definitely one of our most proportionately outspoken parishioners," said the gardener, pouring himself a glass of inferior amber bubbles. Well, inferior to Salisbury, but miles above Schweppes or Canada Dry. I reminded myself to be grateful for everything, bar nothing, Romans eight twenty-eight and all. "So Monsignor Aspic visited him yesterday."

"As will we today," said Father, "or, perhaps tomorrow."

I watched, amazed, as that tiny printer noiselessly spewed an index card onto the starched white tablecloth. There, in tiny but sharply resolved print, was not only Mr. Turnbuckle's name, address, and phone number, but a summary of his professional résumé and a map to his house with the most energy-efficient routes indicated in green. This Sybil scooped up and added to a stack of similar destinations, which she in turn handed to Father Baptist.

"Can you access phone records with that thing?" I asked.

"Sure," said Sybil. "Whose?"

"Monsignor Aspic's cell phone." The moment I said his name her fingers started dancing. "That's Conrad Jonas Aspic. David Smoley said his boss made a phone call as he was parking the car at the television station."

"Very good, Martin," said Father. "I'd almost forgotten. The monsignor made an appointment to see someone today at nine in the morning. It may be significant."

"This will take a while," said Sybil, frowning at the gibberish on her screen. "I see no listing for a mobile unit in his name. He probably uses one of the—let's see—twelve hundred thirty-seven phones on the archdiocesan account. If you don't know his number—"

"Sorry," said I.

"—I'll have to do some digging. Wait a minute. He called from KLIE, right? I have the address right here. I can pinpoint it on the mobile grid."

"Wow. You can do that?"

"This equipment can, in conjunction with the supercomputers it's talking to." Her fingers did a quick Irish jig. "Whoops, I'm experiencing a time-share interruption."

"What's that?"

"Someone else just dumped one whopper of a problem into the system, probably JPL or Caltech."

"How long will that take?"

"I'm getting a 'LESS THAN 10 MINUTES' message, but that's the computer guessing how long it will take to solve a problem it's only just started processing. Computers have enormous egos, you know. They always underestimate. Most delay messages are under three seconds, so your guess is as good as mine. It could be two minutes, could be two hours."

"I gather that precludes anything else I'd like you to check," said Father.

"All it means is that we're waiting in line," said Sybil. "What else do you need?"

"Bishop Jeremiah Ravenshorst."

"That name sounds familiar. Is he important?"

"Was," said I. "He died last June."

"What would be involved in researching his activities?" asked Father. She winked confidently. "Financial, social, clerical, what?"

"All of the above, and add archeological."

"You're joking."

"He was the official archdiocesan historian. I can't tell you what to look for, but I have a hunch there's something to find."

"After lunch, Father. It may take some time, and I want to enjoy my meal. Is that okay with you?"

"Soon thereafter, please."

"Count on it."

"Incredible," said Father, turning his attention to the deck of addresses and directions in his hands. "I really don't know what I'll do without you when you go private."

"Let me in on this one," she said, touching a button that collapsed her laptop into a featureless silver box again, "and I'll do the next one gratis."

"I don't follow you," said Father, tucking the cards into the mysterious folds of his cassock. "You've already been a big help."

"I *want* to help you," said she, slipping the computer and printer back into her pocketbook.

"But you can't very well desert your post, even if it is in Records."

"Not for some frivolous reason, no. But you're involved in another investigation for the cardinal, right? You may need me in the next few days: my expertise with computers, my knowledge of new police procedures, my sidearm even. Chief Billowack doesn't realize this, but I still have access to a squad car, and I can be wherever you need me with sirens wailing."

"You'd do that?" said Father, shifting in his seat. "But surely you're in enough trouble as it is."

"I want to leave the Force with a bang," said she, pounding the table gently with her balled fist. "Everywhere *you* go, things happen."

"Oh, I wouldn't say—"

"Not just ordinary things, decidedly extraordinary things."

"She's got a point, Father," interjected the gardener.

"Furthermore—how do I put this?" she said, folding the photocopies of David Smoley's notebook and pushing them to the far corner of the table. "I don't know if this will make sense—I mean, of course it will make sense to you, but it doesn't to me. You remember the other day when Lieutenant Holcomb and I were taking inventory in Willie Kapps' store after it was burglarized?"

"I do indeed," said Father, taking up the photocopies and tucking them into those seemingly bottomless mysterious folds of his.

"You rightly pointed out that I didn't know what I was doing." She made a little twirling motion next to her head with her finger. "I wrote down 'five medallions bearing star-shaped mystic symbols,' but you said, and I'll never forget this: 'This is a pentagram, this a hexagram, a dodecagram, a Seal of Solomon, and a medal of Our Lady of Guadalupe.'" She paused to take a long sip of water. "Well, after you left, I … I was drawn back to that medal of, um, you know, Guadalupe. I hadn't given it more than a glance before, obviously, since I had inaccurately lumped it in with 'star-shaped medallions.' I picked it up, and put it back, oh, several times. It was old and tarnished. It had a five-dollar price tag stuck on the back, and the glue had sort of become one with the corrosion." She finished the water in her glass.

"Go on," said Father, keenly interested.

"I don't know why, but, well, I grew up in this town. That image of, of—"

"Her name is Mary," said Father kindly.

"Yes," she said. "I've seen that picture on walls, on shop windows, on taco stands, just about everywhere. It's like a cultural icon or something. The Latinos seem to be obsessed with it—Her." She picked up her glass but found it empty. "I told you when we first met that my father was a 'fallen-away Unitarian,' and my mother was the vaguest of Christians. Then came my assignment to that task force to investigate the theft of Catholic Relics, and that brought me into contact with … well, you. No, not just you, but Martin here, those Tumblar guys, and all that you believe and represent." She set the glass down hard. "Listen to me. I'm all flutters."

"Don't let that stop you," said Father.

She took a deep breath and let it out. Then she squared her shoulders and said, "The real reason I knocked Tragg's lights out was that he caught me putting money into Mr. Kapps' cash register."

"You bought the medal," said I.

She nodded conspiratorially and continued. "It was irregular, but I wasn't stealing. I put in the exact change plus tax. I even wrote out a receipt and stuck it in the register drawer, but Tragg wouldn't let it alone. He harped on it and harped on it, all through the day, all the next morning. Finally I told him where he could get off and, well, he said what I won't repeat, and now I'm in Records Division."

"And the medal?" asked Father.

"Right here," she said, pulling on a delicate chain hanging around her neck. An oval of coppery gold came into view. "I dipped it in cleaner—it took some scrubbing—and I had this chain from a locket I used to wear in high school."

"It's lovely," said Father. "Not just the medal, but your attraction to Our Blessed Mother."

"Our …" The words stuck in her throat. "You call her … Mary."

"That's her name," said Father. "Why is it so hard for you to say it?"

"I don't know. Something just goes all haywire inside."

"I understand."

"Do you? I mean, really?"

"Red wine for the lady," barged in Hal, leaning over the table to distribute the drinks. "Julio already brought the ginger ale I see; and here's a rye cocktail for you, Sir—er, Monsignor."

"It's Father," corrected Father, "and I ordered a rye highball."

"There's a difference?" Then Hal glanced at Cardinal Fulbright in his gold-leaf frame. "I mean, of course—(cough! cough!)—of course, my mistake. I'll correct it immediately." He snatched back Father's drink and was off, waddling frenetically toward the bar.

Just then a group of five plump, breathless tourists came shuffling by, four chatty gals and one wide-eyed husband that somehow got caught in the flow. The females sported sweatshirts that bragged of visitations to various public shrines in Southern California: Disneyland, of course, Griffith Park Observatory, Universal Studios Tour, and the Queen Mary. In addition to his Hollywood Bowl nylon jacket, the man was wearing a Day-Glo cap that said, KNIGHTS OF COLUMBUS, ST. APOLLINARUS PARISH, MEDFORD, OREGON.

"Oh, lookie!" squeaked Disneyland, pointing to the cardinal's picture above us.

"His favorite table!" marveled Griffith Park.

"We must try his fettuccini," said Universal Studios. "It sounds yummy!"

The four ladies clasped their hands and heaved their torsos in a coordinated, prolonged sigh.

"I must get a shot of this for Grampa Cutter," said the man, producing a disposable camera. He peered intently through the viewfinder for several prolonged seconds, then said, "You folks won't mind will you?"

"By all means," said Father, shifting back to get out of the shot.

Sybil did likewise.

Me, bend this spine of mine backwards? My rheumatologist and chiropractor should be so unlucky! Instead, I set my forearms on the table and wearily rested my forehead upon them. That seemed to satisfy our intrusive photographer. He let loose a flash.

"Gramps will be so impressed!" said the Queen Mary as they waddled away.

"You can come up now," said Father, touching my arm.

"Whew," said I, raising my head and opening my eyes warily.

"Where were we?" asked Sybil, drawing closer to the table.

"Something going haywire," said I, pointing to my heart and nodding encouragingly, "inside."

"Our human nature is fallen, Sybil," said Father, leaning forward on his elbows. "It's corrupt, corroded, as tarnished as that medal when you found it in Willie's display case. Something inside us, the core of our being—the thing we call 'the soul'—though damaged and broken, it nonetheless cries out to God. The created soul yearns to be with its Creator. But there's a problem: God, unlike us, is sheer Perfection. His nature is Divine, Transcendent, Omnipotent, Pure—completely and devastatingly incompatible with our poor human nature, which is foul and loathsome."

"You don't talk like anyone else I know," said Sybil, a tear—an ordinary drop of organic saltwater—meandering down her cheek. "Most people say that God loves us just the way we are."

"I don't know how to tell you this," said the gardener, "but God can't *stand* us the way we are! That was the whole point of the Crucifixion."

"And we can't stand Him, either," said Sybil thoughtfully, staring at the medal in her hand, "or the things that draw us to Him."

"You might call it a clash of natures," said Father. "Even when we yearn for God, our human nature squirms at the approach of the Divine."

"I would say mine squeals," said I.

"Your hesitation," said Father softly and intently, "to speak the name of the Mother of God. Why do you suppose that is?"

"Ah! Here we are!" chirped Hal, invading the moment with a battery of rattling dishes balanced precariously on his spindly arms. "First: your drink, um, Father, Sir. Let me know if it meets with your approval. Second: Julio, the manager, told the chef to give you all double portions. So here we go, Geronimo—hah, hah. Veal scaloppini, spaghetti and meatballs, and Fettuccini Cardinal Fulbright!" With a lot of clatter and surprisingly little splatter, our plates landed in front of us, twirling impressively. Hal attempted one of those "maitre d' pops" with the flat of his hand against his open mouth, but all he succeeded in doing was whacking himself in the face. With that, he charged off to get us some garlic bread even though we didn't need it.

"I guess he gave me yours," said Sybil to Father, gripping her plate to hand it across the table.

"And I got Martin's," said Father, doing likewise. "Martin?"

"Oh my," said the gardener, gazing at the smoldering pile of ham and crab chunks before him. Believe it or not, there was a little plastic figurine of Cardinal Fulbright, complete with miter, crook, and comic book smile, stuck in the middle of the heap like a birthday candle. A little book lay at his feet, opened to the words, "LET US PRAY," but a tiny bit of pasta had lapped itself over the "R."

"Martin?" prodded Father, holding my plate of spaghetti in his outstretched hand.

"I'm sorry," said I, hefting the platter of fettuccini and handing it to Sybil. "I was distracted by—"

"Eek!" laughed Sybil, glaring at the statuette waving at her from the center of her lunch.

"—another one of our local cultural icons."

"There you have another impediment to the soul's search for the Truth," sighed Father, smiling sadly. "Evangelization is difficult when one must first explain the devastated vineyard to the thirsty seeker. It's not peculiar to our time, but it's certainly rampant within it."

"You mean—?" said Sybil, plucking His Imminence's figurine from her meal, dripping with pinkish, viscous sauce.

"The tackiness of our shepherds," said Father, shaking his head, "I fear it's enough to keep some self-respecting souls from boarding the Barque of Peter in which they so long to sail."

"Well, he won't stand in my way," said she, dropping the silly thing unceremoniously into her empty water glass.

"Bravo," said Father, folding his hands. "And now we'll say Grace."

"Here?" said Sybil, blushing slightly and looking around. "Won't people be, you know—offended?"

"I doubt it occurs to them," said Father, dropping his voice a minor second, "how much it offends me when they eat their fill without thanking the One Who provided it."

"Arrrrr, Lassie," said the gardener, adopting his swashbuckling ersatz pirate's persona, "when ye hook up with Capt'n Bappy here, arrrrr, an' sail the Seven Seas with the likes o' him, arrrr, ye must secure lanyards, splice the mainbrace, reef yer main'sls—"

"Martin," said Father.

"Father," said I. "Arrrrr."

"Please proceed," said Sybil, paying me no mind.

"In the name of the Father," said Father, "and of the Son, and of the Holy Ghost."

"Arrrrmen," said the gardener.

"Amen," whispered Sybil Wexler, glancing from side to side sheepishly.

11

"BLOOD, YOU SAY," SAID FATHER as I turned left onto Highland and headed north toward Hollywood.

"I didn't have time to do a hemoglobin test," said I, changing lanes to avoid a couple of rotund gentlemen emerging from a car parked at an obtuse angle to the curb. "But all indications—feel, taste, how quickly it clotted on my hands—yes, I'd say it was probably blood."

"Taste?"

"It wasn't a yummy moment, if that's what you're implying. But yes, I had some on my fingertips so, yeah, why not? I touched my tongue. At a moment like that, I don't know, I somehow felt ..."

"Protected?"

"Something like that. You'd've had to've been there."

"Did you notify the warden?"

"Her? No way. She's upset with me."

"How come?"

"I wouldn't call her Gladys. I only had fifteen minutes, and if Cheryl was experiencing a real you-know-what, well, I decided to let her enjoy the peace of the moment. If she wasn't, then the less attention called to it the better. Besides, I figured they'd find out soon enough when they pick up her laundry. Which reminds me." I hoisted the sleeves of my jacket up to reveal the extent of the blood on my shirtsleeves. "I'm glad Sybil didn't see all this. I don't suppose we'll have time to drop by the rectory for a change of clothes this afternoon."

"I think not."

"Figures. Remind me to roll them up. Someone will think—heck, who knows what they'll think."

"Martin," said Father, tapping his temple thoughtfully with his index finger, "Cheryl Farnsworth was a nun once, wasn't she?"

"Yes," said I, returning to the outside lane, "or at least a novice. I forget if she took final vows."

"Then whatever else she's done, she's still a Baptized Catholic."

"As far as I know, yes. They would have checked before allowing her to enter the convent. So what are you thinking?"

"'And when it's over, bring Father Baptist.'"

"Her very words. So?"

"Quite a movement of Grace. Whatever 'it' is, I hope it's over soon."

"Sure took me by surprise."

"Today, I suspect, is going to be full of surprises."

"I'd say we passed our quota hours ago."

Seeing roadwork up ahead, accompanied by the usual flurry of flashing yellow lights and detour signs, I made a right and started zigzagging my way through a densely cluttered neighborhood of narrow, aging, two-story houses.

"Why are we starting at KLIE?" I asked, glancing at the card provided by Sybil Wexler's computer. Not having a cup holder like David Smoley, I had wedged the bottom left corner into the ashtray.

"I thought we'd retrace Monsignor's steps in reverse order," said Father. "Backtrack through his day, so to speak. Apparently whatever happened to him occurred in the parking lot at the television studio, and that may have been instigated by an earlier encounter in the day."

"Happened to him? So you don't think he ran off to the Kasbah?"

"Stealing the object, leaving his superior in the lurch—no, that would be out of character."

"You think he was kidnapped for the gold thingy?"

"It's possible, but why would a perpetrator not just steal it and be done with it? A simple pointing of a gun and a terse 'Hand it over!' would have sufficed. Why take a hostage? And who besides the cardinal knew he was carrying it?"

"David Smoley, you think? I don't trust him."

"Neither do I. He's nervous, severely bruised, and probably dishonest. On the other hand, he lacks the stuff of overt criminal action."

"You mean he'd more likely cover for an indiscretion than perform one."

"Something like that."

"As I recall, Father, back in June he and our Joel were both seminarians assigned to assist Bishop Brassorie at Saint Philip's while they reconsidered their vocations."

"That's true."

"Joel left and joined us, settling the matter for himself. David is still there, presumably reconsidering. I wonder if he's going to remain, return to the program—you know, see it through, become a priest."

"These days, considering the caliber of man they routinely approve for Ordination, I wouldn't be surprised."

"Ah," I said, as we came to a signal. "This is Cahuenga. Should I turn left here and go up to Hollywood Boulevard?"

"Let's go straight for five blocks and then turn up. I'm rather enjoying these side streets."

"Fine with me."

Naturally, the street we were on did not go straight. Instead, after two blocks we came to a Y. Figuring the left fork would bring us closer to our goal than the right, I went that way. That was a mistake. Suddenly I was steering through a tangle of narrow lanes that veered in every direction except the one in which I wished to go. The buildings were four- and five-story apartment hives that had once housed the upper echelons, but now swarmed with the mediocre in the middle.

"Meanwhile," said the inept gardener turned incompetent navigator, "what did you and our friends at the morgue discover about Father John Doe?"

"I forget exactly where we were in the discussion when you left," said Father, lowering his head so he could see further up the facades of the buildings towering over us like the walls of a treacherous canyon. "His health had been severely neglected over a long period of time. In addition to sizeable kidney stones and signs of malnutrition, he had several mature tumors in his—well, we needn't go into that. No barbiturates or painkillers in his system. He must have been suffering terribly."

"But his face, Father."

"Yes, wasn't that something? My Ordination was relatively recent, so I haven't assisted that many people at their deaths. My experience in that crucial area is admittedly limited. But this man—in spite of severe health complications, and the evidence that he'd been shackled for a long, long time, he seemed to have the uncanny serenity of Sanctity about him."

"Chained and neglected in a dungeon of some kind? That hardly suggests an American prison."

"Our official institutions, at least. But prisoner he was, and for many years. There was something else that really threw Wong and Holtsclaw."

"Do tell."

"As you probably know, the waxing and waning of *rigor mortis* is a decidedly unreliable means of determining time of death."

"Yes, I've read Erle Stanley Gardner. Examining the digestive tract is far more accurate."

"That's usually the case. Father John Doe, as you call him, did eat bread and water for his last meal, but he had a tumor in his stomach—one of a dozen maladies that were working in concert toward his demise. I don't understand all the jargon, but apparently this malignant growth caused the stomach to secrete an enzyme which rendered their usual analysis ineffective."

"What about the temperature of the liver?"

"You are up on your detective novels. The liver is the largest internal organ, and it holds heat longer than the others at a rate of—"

"I know, I know. Perry Mason derailed Hamilton Burger with that one more than once."

"The trouble here is that our man had obviously been dead for hours, long enough for the rigors to come and go. Nonetheless, when they checked his liver, it was two degrees higher than it should have been at the moment of death. Upon further examination in my presence, they discovered that this anomaly was due to the temperature of his heart, which was still registering five point eight degrees higher than normal in life."

"His heart was … *hot?* You're joking."

"No, I'm not."

"I don't suppose it was enlarged, so much that he also had two ribs broken, the ends thrust outward, having never rejoined or healed."

"Like Saint Philip Neri, you mean. You've been reading other books as well. No, not quite. The heart was of normal size, but Wong and Holtsclaw were nonetheless dumbfounded. Martin, I could feel the warmth of the dead man's heart through the gloves. It was uncanny."

"You mean you actually had your hands in—? No, spare me the details."

Coming to a cul-de-sac, I hit the brakes and performed a swift but smooth U-turn.

GARDENING TIPS: When he was twenty-nine years of age, Saint Philip Neri was praying in the Catacombs of Saint Sebastian on the Appian Way when a ball of heavenly fire appeared. It entered his mouth and descended into his heart. From that moment on he felt heat radiating from his chest. It became so intense that he was known to walk through the freezing snow with his cassock unbuttoned and to sleep with his windows open. He also experienced palpitations that were audible to others and often described as the beating of a hammer or the shaking of the room.

Many penitents, when pressed to his bosom, felt consolation for their sinfulness and relief from temptations. It's a fascinating story, and ends with his autopsy during which it was discovered

that his heart was so enlarged that two ribs had
been broken outward and never healed.

As for me, the hottest thing to enter my mouth
and burn on the way down was an appetizer I once
ordered at a long-gone Indian restaurant called
"Gypsy's" in Santa Monica. All those peculiar
sounds emanating from my body are due to arthritic
joints, profound indigestion, or an uncontrollable
larynx. I can only imagine the level of sanctity
practiced and enjoyed by the likes of Saint Philip
Neri, but I'm grateful for his example and patron-
age.

--M.F.

"So what's going to happen to your Crucifix?" I asked, peering down
the cross-streets for some hint of the main boulevard. "It was hanging
there with his cassock. Did you tell them about it?"

"No," said Father, also peering to see where the narrow avenues
might lead. "I suppose I should have, but somehow this matter has
become personal, more so to me as priest than detective. I'm trusting
my instincts in a way I never have before, and I hope to God that's the
right course to take. By strange and circuitous circumstances, and I
suspect by way of detours we've yet to encounter—much like the meandering route you are navigating as we speak—the Crucifix is probably coming back to me."

"How so?"

"If no one claims him by the weekend—there's always that possibility, I suppose, but barring that—I've offered to take the body and personal effects off their hands and provide a proper burial in our own
cemetery."

"Does that mean you'll bury the Crucifix with him?"

"Naturally, I'd rather not. I need more information before I can make
that decision. As yet, I've no clue as to how it came into his possession, or at least, to be on his person. I'd sure like to know if he was,
in fact, a priest. Or even a Catholic. If so, he deserves a Requiem."

"What about undertaking?"

"Excuse me?"

"Wong and Holtsclaw are coroners, not morticians. Embalming isn't
on their list of tax-supported services."

"I don't think that will be necessary."

"No?"

"There's no law requiring it, and I have a feeling he won't need it."

I thought that one over, from several directions, before I said, "You
may be right."

From the street numbers, I realized I was closing in on my destination, albeit several blocks south of the main boulevard. Spying a signal at the end of a long, slender street to the right, I turned and went barreling toward what I hoped would be the intersection "five blocks past Cahuenga."

"This has been an amazing day all around," I noted. "Even Sybil Wexler was full of surprises."

"There is definitely Grace at work," agreed Father.

"Do you get the feeling we're like a bowling ball in a gutter, headed inevitably toward a specific end?"

"Not in those terms, Martin, but yes. In a sense, we're all in that predicament."

"Heading for death, you mean."

"Of course."

"We'll, I'm thinking more along the lines of a prophecy that's drawing inexorably to a preordained conclusion, except we haven't been told the signs to look for. We're stumbling over them as we go, heading toward a crisis beyond our experience. In the end we'll find ourselves at a sumptuous feast, flasks and flagons colliding, celebrating a marvelous denouement—"

"Martin."

"Yes, Father?"

"Isn't that a transmission tower coming into view?"

"Shiver me timbers! Look ye to the mainmast! It's the bonnie 'Kay Lie!'"

"Martin, pull into the lot, park at the far end."

"Right ch'ar, Capt'n Ba—"

"Don't you dare call me Capt'n Bappy, Matey."

"Arrrr."

12

"TELANGIECTASIA!" CRIED THE WOMAN in the chartreuse leather jumpsuit with the stringy puce fringe. "The world ends yet again!"

Her name was Napolia Krackershak, and she was the producer-slash-director of the show, "Religion Revisited." She was the second person Father talked to at KLIE. The first was a receptionist-slash-guard named Mick Troger.

Mr. Troger's job was to stand behind an inch-thick window next to an imposing security door marked, CELEBRITY ENTRANCE: GUESTS, PARTICIPANTS, AND NON-TECHNICAL PERSONNEL, and decide who would and wouldn't enter the building. He could either punch a big brown button on a control panel, in which case the aforementioned door opened with a prolonged hydraulic hiss, or not. If he wasn't sure, he could pick up a burgundy-tinted phone and ask someone who was. His air of authority was somewhat undermined by the mobile hanging from the air conditioning vent above his head. Dangling from its rocking horizontals were cheap, goofy-looking plastic fish whose amazed eyes, jiggling fins, and incessant buoyant bobbing suggested that he was just a heavy artifact placed in the bottom of an aquarium to hide the air-pumping apparatus.

"My name is Father John Baptist," said Father into an imposing chromium microphone mounted in the glass. It looked like a cross between a stainless steel jet engine and an aluminum roulette wheel. "Cardinal Fulbright sent me to—"

"The opportunity is already blown," came back Mr. Troger's voice infused with non-whole-number harmonics added by the shiny transducer. "The Levants say they'll never allow another one of you guys on the show ever again."

"I don't follow you," said Father. "What 'opportunity' was 'blown,' and to what 'guys' are you referring?"

"Last night's show is what," said Troger, pointing to Father with an eight-inch stick of black licorice before inserting it whole into his mouth. "You priests is who. Understand?"

"I'm afraid it is you who doesn't understand. I've no wish to be a guest on your show. I am investigating the disappearance of Monsignor Aspic."

"The cops was here last night."

"I am aware of that."

"They're doing everything they can."

"I don't doubt it, but as I said a moment ago, I'm here on behalf of Cardinal Fulbright."

"And what's that supposed to mean to me?"

"If you don't know, then perhaps you would be so good as to call someone in authority."

"I oughta do just that."

"By all means."

While Mick Troger carried on a muffled conversation with his higher power on the burgundy phone, Father turned to me and said, "Martin, are you okay?"

"Excuse me?"

"You were grimacing."

"I'm a champion grimacer, Father. Just ask Mrs. Magillicuddy."

"You were shifting on your feet."

"I'm shifty by nature."

"Martin."

"Father."

"Is something wrong? You look as though you're in pain."

"I've ... well ..."

"Yes?"

"I've been experiencing tingles."

"Where?"

"The soles of my feet, and sometimes the toes. Nothing to worry about."

"Describe them."

"My feet?"

"The tingles."

"You've got enough on your mind, Father."

"Nothing on my mind at the moment is more important than my responsibility to my trusted friend."

"Really. Have I met him?"

"Martin."

"Okay, okay. Sometimes it's almost imperceptible. Other times it's prickly, like when your leg gets numb from sitting the wrong way and then the circulation comes back when you stand up."

"And just a moment ago?"

"Sort of like walking barefoot on hot asphalt."

"How long has this been going on?"

"Oh, off and on, now and then. I think I first noticed it a few months ago. More frequent now. Not to worry. It's nothing."

"Perhaps we should have Dr. Yomtov take a look at you."

"Nickolai the Nerve Guy? I'd rather not."

"Dr. Yomtov, the neurologist, who frequents our Masses on Sundays."

"I repeat, and I'd rather not."

GARDENING TIPS: A certain police sergeant who
shall remain nameless told me, after reading the
manuscript of The Endless Knot, that he thought I
complained too much throughout about my aches and
pains. He'd be right if it was his story or if I
were a noble Saint.

    I am writing about my experiences, both as Father Baptist's observant sidekick and as the stridently candid, albeit catawampus -brained observer, of my unreliable self. I cannot hide the
fact that I'm in pain from my friends and acquaintances. I'm not that good an actor. As I write
my memoirs, I'm certainly not going to pretend

that I'm comfortable as I go lurching about my
life. I describe my pain because it is the lens
through which I sample my experiences. I hope
that I do not come across as a whiner. Com-
plainer, yes; grumbler, okay; whiner, no. I've
called pain my Friend, and that sentiment is sincere. Not being the heroic sort who is likely to
do battle in the public forum for the Faith, I
have been provided by Providence with an infirmity
that I can carry around in my jacket, and now my
shoes. This new disorder conveniently makes every
step I take a potential pain offering, an opportunity to gain Grace and thereby achieve Heaven,
which is, after all, the whole point of my existence. If you don't know that yet, then I have
failed in my attempt to draw you into my world.

I have said all that in order to say this:

When one's body has worked so earnestly against
one, one may be excused for wishing to ignore the
signs of further deterioration. I can pinpoint
when these strange sensations in my feet began. I
described it in <u>The</u> <u>Endless</u> <u>Knot</u>:

* * *

The big-bellied guard, having abandoned
the attempt to capture Monsignor Goolgol in
favor of less slippery prey, tightened his
grip on my knotted arms and pushed me in
the direction of the platform.

"But Officer," I protested.

"But nuthin'," he answered, giving me an
angry shake. "Get movin'."

The phone rang again. Fulbright's eyes
darted defensively this way and that. His
gaze fell upon the pair of approaching cassocks. "Father Baptist?!?! What in
heaven's name--?"

"Indeed," said Father Baptist, "in
Heaven's name."

"Stop your dab gum struggling," ordered
the guard, bringing his knee up into the
small of my back and propelling me sav-
agely.

"Awrk." I tripped over something--my own
feet or his--and teetered forward, stumbling to my knees near the cascade of gaily
gurgling vodka.

* * *

```
     The following day I removed my shoe to rearrange
my sock which had apparently bunched up under my
toes, only to find my sock tight and smooth around
my whole foot.  The day after that I thought I had
pebbles in my shoe that weren't there.  Other
times the soles of my feet grew numb, the other
end of the spectrum.  These sensations have been
growing more intense and frequent over the past
few months.  This, I admit, I kept from my reader-
-as well as myself--until Father Baptist called me
on it.  Now the cat is out of the bag and merrily
clawing it to shreds.  This has been a self-
serving public service announcement.  Thank-you.
                                        --M.F.
```

"Hey, I'm just doing my job." Mr. Troger's garbled voice came leaking through the shiny transducer. He sounded like he was gargling, which added to the impression that he was talking under water. "He says he was sent by the cardinal. How am I supposed to know? You wanna see him or not?"

"Were you on duty here last night?" asked Father after Mr. Troger slammed the phone down with an inappropriate expletive.

"You can ask her majesty," said the guard, brushing back his oily hair with a meaty hand. He accidentally jarred the mobile, sending the plastic fish into a twirling, ogling frenzy.

"Of course I can," said Father. "I also have access to police reports. It would save time, however, if you'd answer a simple question. David Smoley, the monsignor's chauffeur, said he came to this window a little after eight fifteen to express his concerns. If you were on duty, you could corroborate that."

"Yeah, sure," said the guard, punching the button on his panel. "I was, he did, and the rest you'll have to get from Crackerjack."

"Is that Sheldon Levant or Eira?"

"Hah! That's the boss!"

There was a burst of pressurized air around the rim of the door as it opened smoothly on invisible bearings. As we stepped through I felt like we were boarding a spaceship. With slow-motion grace, the hatch sealed behind us with a deep, subterranean thump.

We found ourselves in a peculiar room. It was strange in that it seemed cavernous with hints of a ceiling way above, but it was also very dark so it was hard to tell. I had no sense of whether the walls were black and close or shadowed and distant. In the immediate, more or less surrounding us, there were horizontal shelves and vertical panels of clear plastic arranged in complex geometric patterns, with hidden lamps highlighting the edges with an ultraviolet shimmer. The shelves were cluttered with the mandatory plethora of awards, most of them issued by organizations about which I'd never heard. The panels were devoted to immense translucent posters of the station's prominent personalities. This was my first glimpse of Sheldon and Eira Levant, their bloated faces smiling down upon us as we ventured between them toward a zone of deeper murkiness beyond. We were nearing the end of the displays when a woman in a tight leather outfit came bounding out of the gloom, clipboard wedged in armpit and miniature headset fastened to her face.

"I didn't get your name, Father," she said, sticking out a freckled hand. Her teeth seemed to take up sixty-five percent of her face, and her lips another twenty. She had a fingernails-against-chalkboard voice like Judy Holliday in *Born Yesterday*. Her hair was coarse, frizzed, and dyed electrocution yellow. It did not coordinate well with the ochre hue of her leather jumpsuit. Her outfit was as shiny as polished shoes, with stringy, dull red fringes dangling mop-like from every seam. She exceeded the capacity of her clothing by at least thirty pounds, which probably accounted for her breathlessness, not to mention the reflectivity of the precariously stretched cowhide. All in all she was the kind of person who desperately needed advice on apparel and deportment, but alas was also the kind of person who would annihilate anyone who dared give it. Hence, she was uniquely, uncompromisingly, unconditionally, and absolutely: "Napolia Krackershak."

"Father John Baptist," said Father, enveloping her stippled hand in his and giving it a reassuring shake. "This is my associate, Martin Feeney."

"Charmed, I'm sure." Oh great, she was chewing gum, too. She did this funny thing with her eyes—sort of a wide open stare followed by several rapid blinks, then quickly looking away. "Mick said you were sent by the cardinal. What can I do for you?"

"I'm investigating Monsignor Aspic's disappearance."

"Whoopee!" she said, whirling her finger in the air like a lariat. "Oh, don't look at me like that. I hope he's okay, sure. But what he did for our ratings, you would not believe."

"Excuse me," blinked Father. "I'm not sure I understand. I got the impression from the guard that the broadcast was a disaster."

"That shows you whose shoes he licks. Sheldon makes a point of tipping Mick as he and Eira leave each night. Sheldon goes by belly laughs. If he gets five or more in an evening, Mick gets a bar of imported white chocolate wrapped in a twenty. If he scores between one and four, a Snickers wrapped in a fiver. If Shel bombs completely, it's a stick of licorice and loose change."

"I saw the licorice," said Father, tossing me a wink and then returning his attention to her. "Does Mrs. Levant tip Mr. Troger, too?"

"She measures the audience in 'oohs,' 'ahs,' and rounds of applause. She positively thrives on oral flattery. When she's had her fill, she kisses everyone on the way out, even me, on the mouth. It's not exactly the highpoint of my day, but I've gotta get along with these people."

"And if she doesn't?—receive her positive affirmation, I mean."

"She extends a frigid finger."

"Even to you?"

"Especially to me."

"So I take it Sheldon and Eira Levant were unhappy about the turn of events last evening."

"Sheldon and Eira wouldn't know happiness if it reached up and bit them on the ... well, excuse me, Father. They're personalities, you see, not producers. They get egg on their faces, they scream 'Aaarhhhhhhhrrrrrrggggg!'" She demonstrated the principle with the back of her hand pressed to her forehead. "But if it's driving the ratings up, I grab a gopher and say, 'Quick, off to the supermarket and fetch another three dozen—make 'em jumbos!'"

"And I take it the ratings went up last night?"

"Right through the freaking ceiling."

"Indeed."

On that note pregnant with implications, all of them spinning obliviously off into space as far as she was concerned, Napolia Krackershak spun around on her four-inch heels and proceeded to lead us back into the nebulous gloom from which she had come. I wondered if she had rehearsed that walk in front of a mirror.

"So what happens tonight?" asked Father as the darkness around us resolved into a ceilingless corridor between two high walls of soundproof material.

"Tonight we milk the mystery," winked Napolia over her angular shoulder, her fringes swaying erratically like seaweed in a riptide. "Sheldon will wring his hands as if he really cares, Eira will beg viewers who know something—anything!—to phone the station, and I will make sure there's plenty of tissues on the set."

"Amazing," said Father, tossing me a knowing glance, then clasping his hands behind and nodding in affectation of a myopic college professor, "the way you can manipulate the situation to your advantage."

"It was a Godsend, let me tell you. At the execs' meeting on Monday there was talk of canceling the show. Not any more."

We passed a large double fire door bearing a sign, STUDIO A: "RELIGION REVISITED." NO UNAUTHORIZED PERSONNEL, and headed instead for a smaller doorway through which creamy pink light was shining brightly. PREPARATION. I thought for a second it was a beauty parlor as we entered, and in a sense it was. There were four gyratory salon chairs set in the floor before four opulent mirrors with track lighting all around. Two of the chairs were occupied, and surrounding each was a hive of frenetic beauticians, clippers and combs and brushes and powder puffs blurring in their speedy hands.

"Excuse me," said Napolia Krackershak to the seated form at the center of the nearest frenzy. "Excuse me, Eira, this is—"

"Will you look at this!" shrieked the woman in the chair. She had a tiny oval face tapering to a dagger for a chin. Small as her features were, they had all been exaggerated by the magic of powder and paste. Her thin lips were swollen with paint, her wispy eyebrows and lashes fattened with ink, and her sunken cheeks inflated with eye-bamboozling powders. This little unhappy visage was framed in a tangled, enameled explosion of strawberry blonde hair. "Napolia, you're here! Good! Fire this little snit immediately! Look what she's done to my nose!"

The "little snit" was a six-foot, two-twenty female weightlifter with a flat line for a mouth, black marble eyes, a camel hair applicator in her meaty fist, and a nametag announcing SUGAR on her ample bosom. Buzzing close at hand were BOBBIE, FRAPPÉ, CELESTE, ARGYLE, and TWISTER, but in this hive SUGAR was definitely the queen bee of applied beauty. "Ms. Krackershak," she acknowledged through gritted teeth.

"What seems to be the problem?" asked Napolia, her words pouring soothingly out of her mouth like corn huskers' lotion. "Why Eira, you look sensational."

"Sensationally hideous, you mean!" whined the gal in the chair, trying but failing to lift her hands under the plastic tarp engulfing her. "Can't you see what she's done to me?"

"I've only applied the foundation," said Sugar. "I haven't even gotten to the shading yet."

"But it's too thick," said Eira, resorting to a pathetic whimper. "With a schnoz like this, they'll think my husband beats me or something.

"Sweetheart," cooed Napolia, ignoring the death wish in Sugar's eyes and crouching down before the quivering bundle that was Mrs. Levant. "I'm right here. See? Now listen to Crackerjack. No one—no one at all—could ever think that of Shel. Trust me on this. And everyone knows you're the best ex-wife a man could grovel for. Eira, sweetie—not over there, look right here. I know this is way early in the day for you, but Honey, you've got to get a grip! The moment must be milked, remember? You and Shel have a ream of promos to do this afternoon. We'll be inserting them every ten minutes into our regular programming. The crew's in the studio waiting for you. Yes,

yes, I know it's all so ... *so* ... but you're the star, and it's time for you to shine. Now, one more thing: Sugar here admires you almost as much as I do. She would never do you wrong. Trust me on this, Sweetiekins, it's what you pay me for: your—nose—looks—just—fine!"

"Then, then, w-wuh-wuh-why did you bring him?" asked Eira, nudging her plastic shroud in Father's direction.

"Him?" asked Napolia, momentarily confused, glancing at Father Baptist via the mirror. "Why, he's just—" She turned and whispered, "I'm sorry, your name again—?"

"Father John Baptist, Mrs. Levant," said Father, stepping forward. "I'm looking into Monsignor Aspic's disappearance on behalf of—"

"Oh no," cried Eira, "not another one! I'm being punished for telling that pope joke on the air last summer. Don't let him hex me, Napolia! Keep him away!"

"Of course, Dearie, whatever you say," said Crackerjack, rising to her full height and facing Father. Silly as it was, she was protecting her pathetic star from Capt'n Bappy's evil eye. Arrrr. It's what she was paid for, after all. "Mrs. Levant is understandably overwrought," she said coolly.

"Yes, I can see that," said Father, turning his attention to the other focus of cosmetic commotion two chairs over.

"Don't pay attention to the gal behind the curtain," called a voice from within a billowing cloud of powder surrounded by ROGER, CLIFF, WINKIE, THITHERO, and ANABETH. This pruned-lipped gaggle of prim cosmetologists parted to reveal Eira's partner in slime. "So you're Father Baptist! That stunt you pulled on TCN last June, right? Brilliant piece of work! I'm truly pleased—no, I'm positively ecstatic—to meet you!"

"You must be Sheldon Levant," said Father, sidestepping that particular issue.

GARDENING TIPS: Things got a bit out of hand the night Father Baptist and the Tumblars concocted a fake TV show for the purpose of breaking a certain alibi. One of our parishioners, Steve Lambert, in a burst of uninvited initiative, used his technical expertise to splice the video into the main feed of TCN, the "Totally Christian Network" -- a.k.a. "the Rapture Channel." Father had never been comfortable with the result, though personally I thought it was a hoot.

--M.F.

"So, Crackers," smiled Sheldon gleefully, a web of crevices erupting around his powdery lips. Under all that camouflage he had a mouth made explicitly for a cheap cigar. "How'd you snag this guy? Hey, Father, if you're in on this you'd better park yourself in the next chair. Sugar'll dull your shine just as soon as she gets through making the former missus presentable."

"You misunderstand, Mr. Levant," said Father evenly. "I'm not here to 'milk the moment.' Cardinal Fulbright has asked me to investigate Monsignor Aspic's disappearance."

"Sure he has," said the joyful host, giving Father an exaggerated wink that buckled his makeup further. "His Worship's *gluteus maximus* must be covered, and covered it shall be. But seriously, I'm sure Crackerjacker here could compensate you for your time if you'd care to join us for a promo or two." His plastic tarp squeaked as he tried unsuccessfully to lift his hands under it. "Just think of it—"

"I would prefer not to," said Father.

"The least we could do is get you a new—whatchacallit—cassock. Nice touch, by the way, the one you're wearing. Frayed just enough to tug the ol' purse strings—"

"Mr. Levant," persisted Father, "am I correct that you never saw Monsignor Aspic last evening?"

"What can I say?" said Sheldon, his eyebrows sliding down the sides of his forehead in a rehearsed display of simulated dismay. "He never showed."

"And he didn't call ahead to say there was a problem?"

"Nope."

"Mrs. Levant?"

"No," sniveled Eira.

"Miss Krackershak?" asked Father.

"Not a peep," said she with a shake of her head. "His Eminence the Cardinal called once around four in the afternoon, all in a huff, looking for him. I think he called again a little before we went on the air. I thought it odd that they'd be out of touch with each other, but I'm a producer, not a babysitter."

The gardener stifled a sarcastic cough.

"Hm," said Father, rubbing his chin thoughtfully. "Did any of you speak with Monsignor Aspic during the week, since the show last Saturday?"

"Twice," said Napolia. "Once on Monday, then again yesterday morning. Just little odds and ends about his coming back on the show."

"Was he to be compensated for his time?" asked Father.

"Oh yes. He demanded and got twice what we offered him."

"Tell him the rest, Crackers," said Sheldon.

"Yeah," added Eira, squirming beneath her tarp as Sugar tried to fix her nose.

"It's just that, well," sighed Napolia with an affected cringe, "we agreed that he could plug his unpublished book on the air."

"And that's over the top!" cackled Sheldon. "Normally we won't allow plugs unless the work is published and available in major outlets. We're not here to promote wannabes and vanity presses!"

"He's written a book?" asked Father. "What about?"

"His personal pilgrimage," sneered Sheldon, his fingers making quotation bumps under his tarp, "from skepticism to faith, or to faith in faith, or something like that."

"The nerve," said Eira, writhing as Sugar closed in with an implement that looked like one of Millie's spatulas. "All that, and still he pooped out on us!"

"A book," mused Father, peering into every face in the salon. "And he wanted to talk about it on the air?"

"He, like a million other geniuses," said Sheldon, "was shopping for a publisher."

At this moment the gardener cringed.

"So far he hadn't found one," said Napolia. "He was hoping someone within range of our signal would offer to make it happen."

"You'd think with all his connections in the Chancery," said Sheldon, "he could strong-arm someone into handling his drivel. You know: deny absolution to some mealy-mouthed exec who'd been unfaithful to his wife."

"Even *my* book got published last year," said Eira, "and I didn't have to deny anybody anything."

"And how," mouthed Bobbie, Frappé, Celeste, Argyle, Twister, Roger, Cliff, Winkie, Thithero, Anabeth, and Sugar silently but as one.

"Maybe the monsignor knew too many of the cardinal's secrets," speculated Sheldon. "He was brought in, after all, to clean up the mess from last June. Maybe he stuck his nose under one rug too many and the cardinal had him bagged to keep him quiet."

"Down boy," said Napolia. She silenced her garrulous star with a withering glare while speaking out of the side of her mouth at Father. "You must forgive Sheldon. He's under a terrific strain."

Like that udder of the moment you're milking, thought the gardener.

"So why," asked Father, "all things considered, did you ask Monsignor Aspic back?"

"When he started glossolaliating on Saturday's show," said Shel, his voice on the verge of a hilarious howl, "the phones started ringing off the hook."

"The ratings took off like a fiery chariot," said Napolia.

"When he was glosso-what-ing?" asked Eira, shedding a little powder herself.

"Speaking in tongues, Honey," explained Napolia.

"Oh, that."

"He was maketh intercessioning for us," expounded Frappé with a knowing lisp, "with groanings which cannot be uttered."

"Romans eight twenty-six," uttered the gardener, groaning silently to himself. He was "maketh grimacing" not so much at the prissy beautician's awkward participial rendering as the fact that it came from the King James translation.

"Gloobala glabbida," demonstrated Sheldon. *"Ergwing zerff blomma dwamma hargiddy har har* hah hah HAH!"

"Mr. Lavant!" groaned Winkie and Anabeth, scrambling to keep his face together.

"Gobbledy goobidy zooblemum mummizum," blathered Sheldon, relentlessly. *"Blobbidy bloobidy hork*—hork!—HACK!"

"Oh pooh!" whined Cliff and Roger, pathetically snatching up aerosol cylinders to contain the catastrophe, but it was too late. Makeup cascaded from their master's cheeks like an avalanche of new-fallen snow.

"Which made as much sense as most of our guests," wheezed Sheldon as the rest of his beauty team threw up their hands in fitful dismay. "Crackers here was flashing us the 'ratings rising' sign—also known as 'Yippee!'—so, against all better judgment, right there on the air we begged the guy to come back for a follow-up."

"Mr. Levant!" groaned Anabeth, "look what you've done!"

"Your facial veins are showing again!" whined Roger and Winkie.

"His dermatologist calls it 'telangiectasia,'" said Eira with a couple of knowing tuts. "Now they'll have to start all over. I could've slept another hour."

"Telangiectasia!" cried Napolia Krackershak, her chartreuse leather jumpsuit almost bursting at the fringy seams. Her eyes did that wide-eyed stare followed by quick blinking thing again. Perhaps it was nerves. "The world ends yet again!"

"Oh heck!" gasped Sheldon Levant, gazing at the horror that was himself in the mirror. "Eira, my dear, you may have to do the first promo without me."

"Eek!" was his ex-wife's reply.

Perhaps it wasn't in her contract to do promos without her hilarious former hubby. More likely, though, she was reacting to the dozen full-figured gals who suddenly came bounding into the salon, all tights, heels, glitter, giggles and jiggles. They weren't wearing much, and the little that was covered was hardly concealed. "Here we are!" they announced in seductive dodecaphonic disharmony.

"It's about time," said Napolia with "Yippee!" in her eyes.

"Crackerjack!" said Sheldon, his licentious eyes popping right out of his telangiectastic face. "You're a genius! Hey, Father, you sure you don't want to be in the promo?"

"Ulp!" I gagged, hand over mouth. I suppose I could say it was a reaction to all the facial powder swirling in the air, or that it certainly wasn't in *my* contract to do promos with Sheldon and Eira Levant. Actually, it was a matter of propriety. Just driving Father about town, I find myself saying the following prayer by Saint Alphonsus di Liguori an average of once per minute:

> By Thine Immaculate Conception, O Mary, make my body pure, and make my soul holy. My Mother, preserve me this day from mortal sin. Amen.

But this, this was simply too much. Father Baptist, a priest whose fortitude towered above the pathetic moral weakness of his gardener, had mastered the monastic art of "looking without seeing." At that moment, however, try as I might, I couldn't see anything else. So, encoring my performance of the wee hours at the cemetery, I lurched and lumbered for the door like a man on the verge of explosive regurgitation. The delectable pool of temptation parted, oblivious to my true plight. I heard their wondrous twitters fading as I charged through the award display on my way to the hermetically sealed entrance. "Urrrrggghhhh!!"

"Whatsamaddah witchoo?" scoffed Mick Troger as I banged on his inside window with the handle of my cane. His eyes went wide as I pantomimed my plight. The threat of impending "ups and overs" rarely fails. In a moment the spaceship door swung smoothly wide accompanied by an explosive hiss of compressed air. Mr. Troger's plastic fish bobbed and ogled as I stumbled by his outside window, lumbering my way toward the Jeep at the far end of the parking lot.

"You okay?" asked Father a few minutes later as he settled himself in the passenger seat. He wasn't laughing this time. He looked serious.

"Sorry about embarrassing you like that," said I. "You know, well, you know how I—"

"I certainly do, Martin," he said reassuringly. "You responded correctly, albeit over-dramatically. Commendation, not reprimand, is in order."

"Okay, if you put it that way."

"I do."

"Thank-you."

"Besides, you provided me with the perfect excuse to extricate myself from a preposterous situation."

"You mean this was a dead end?" said I, turning the key and pumping the gas.

"Not necessarily. We may have been among the minds that conceived whatever befell Monsignor Aspic."

"*Those* minds? I hardly think so."

"Ravenous as they are for ratings, who knows? Fools with money can always hire others to formulate and carry out their plans. They were getting on my nerves, however, and I'm glad to be away from them."

"You have powder on your sleeve, Father. So where to now?"

13

"SEVENTEEN," SAID AN INDIFFERENT ELECTRONIC VOICE as the elevator doors parted. There was no need for us to search for a suite number because one firm occupied the entire floor. Before us stood a double-wide archway with words carved into the simulated marble lintel above the mahogany doors:

BENDLEBRAIN, CRUISER & WEDGE
CONSULTANTS
PUBLIC PERCEPTION, CRISIS MANAGEMENT,
AND TERGIVERSATION

Father pushed on through as I heaved and hobbled behind. The day kept stretching longer and longer before us, and my arthritis was waxing more and more insistent. The electric rock tune in my feet wasn't abating in the least, either. The dried blood on my shirt chafed against my skin under my jacket sleeves, enlivening the image of Cheryl's haunting face against the backdrop of my imagination. I was getting twitchy from sleep deprivation, and considering Father's weary condition back in the wee hours, I could only imagine what was going on beneath that veneer of attentive calm which he continued to exude as he approached the receptionist.

"Good afternoon, gentlemen," honked the woman seated behind a massive oak desk. She had vertical nostrils reminiscent of the cardinal's own receptionist's at the Chancery. In fact, I suspected they were related. Cousins, perhaps. After a long moment apparently assessing

Father's Roman collar and cassock, not to mention his gardener's crooked posture and cane, she glanced skeptically at a complicated three-dimensional multicolored chart on her flat computer screen. I could see it reflected in her oversized glasses. "Do you have an appointment?"

"I'm afraid not," said Father. "My name is Father John Baptist, and this is my associate, Martin Feeney. At the behest of Cardinal Morley Fulbright I am investigating the disappearance of Monsignor Conrad J. Aspic. I understand that he came to this office yesterday afternoon."

"Disappearance?" said she, amused. "You're referring to that TV show last night."

Father nodded meaningfully.

"You're not taking that seriously," she said, interlocking her fingers and leaning forward on her elbows.

"The cardinal certainly is," said Father. "Are you suggesting it's a publicity stunt?"

"I—" She caught herself. Then she rolled her eyes, tugged one of her earrings, and adjusted the pearl hanging around her neck on a thin silver chain. "I guess in this business you just come to expect—" She caught herself again. "Ummmmum," she mumbled, examining the chart again. She scowled, jabbed at the keyboard built into her desktop, and watched as the chart rotated to display yesterday's complexities. "Oh yes," she said, suddenly businesslike, "Monsignor Aspic had an appointment with Mr. Wedge at four o'clock yesterday afternoon. As I recall, he arrived about a half hour early." She looked at a digital clock on the corner of her desk. "Now isn't that a coincidence? It's three-thirty now."

"Did Mr. Wedge see him immediately upon his arrival?"

She shook her head. "Mr. Wedge sees his clients on time."

"So Monsignor Aspic remained in this reception area for while. Tell me, Miss—" Father glanced at the plaque on her desk. "—Dunton, how did he seem to you?"

"What do you mean?"

"I'm curious how the monsignor spent his time as he waited. Did he appear to be agitated, preoccupied, serenely reflective? Did he say anything to you?"

"Let me think." She adjusted the collar of her blouse, checked her watch, and rechecked her earrings. "First he sat over there next to the lamp. He had a briefcase opened on his lap, and he was shuffling papers for a while. I offered him some coffee, but he said no. Oh, and he did mention something to me about a book he had written."

"A book?" asked Father.

"Yes. He wondered if I might know of any local publishers who, you know, might be interested in his insights on religion. I thought it odd, me being a receptionist and him being an important man in the

Church. He reminded me of my brother when he wrote a book and didn't know what to do with it, where to take it, you know?"

"I wouldn't know," said Father. "I've never written a book. Now Martin here—"

I was so absorbed in some of the framed objects on the wall that I almost didn't catch my name being mentioned. There was an ad I'd seen on many a billboard, a pristine tropical scene with a man and a woman walking on a black sand beach with their toddler between them. "PROTECTING THE ENVIRONMENT FOR OUR CHILDREN," said the caption. Emblazoned on the setting sun was a stylized "HZ" surmounted with a crown, a familiar insignia to motorists in Southern California. Three out of ten gasoline stations in Los Angeles are owned and operated by the HoxZy Petroleum Company. More interesting, however, was the fact that recently HoxZy's refinery in San Pedro had been shut down for pollution violations. If that wasn't protecting the environment enough, one of their supertankers had somehow discharged a million gallons of crude less than a hundred miles from the shores of Hawaii, and two of their offshore platforms had spouted major leaks in the Santa Barbara Channel.

Next was a picture of an old-fashioned family seated in front of a turn-of-the-previous-century farmhouse. Papa was cranking the familiar ice cream maker as the kids looked on in wonder and hankering. "KLOTZINGER EISCREME," said the caption, "PURE, NATURAL, AND DELICIOUS." It was all so heartwarming, except I recalled something about this German purveyor of frozen confections having to recall three consecutive batches of their popular Neapolitan. Significant levels of a fifteen-syllable toxin usually found in industrial rat poison had somehow made its way into their pure, natural, and delicious product. This startling ingredient had sent several dozen consumers, most of them children, puking all the way to the hospital.

There was Lylvilya Pharmaceuticals, whose pain pills had caused liver failure in seven arthritic patients, now portrayed as the champion of trustworthy allopathy; Mama Luiza's Italian Kitchen, whose *puttanesca* sauce contained more botulism than anchovies, now touted as an undisputed exemplar of culinary excellence; Yoshisan Motors, manufacturer of low-riding motorcycles whose rear wheels sometimes fell off at high speeds, now conscientiously sponsoring traffic hazard awareness courses in public schools; and the Bongo's Hamburger chain, famous for the greasiest fries in town, now displaying diagrams of nutritional pyramids at all their drive-throughs.

Most significant and disconcerting was the largest of them all: a picture of Manly D. Mann, Archbishop of New Bangor. His Grace was notorious for hiding pedophile priests from the law by transferring them from parish to parish under assumed names while offering damaged families huge sums gleaned from diocesan funds as hush money. Back in September the Diocese of New Bangor filed for bankruptcy, but somehow this Manly Mann had squirreled away enough acorns to hire an elite PR firm like B, C & W to sweeten his vinegary image. There he was, standing tall before a statue of Our Lady of Ransom, his arms outstretched in a magnanimous gesture of uninhibited love, an air-brushed halo emanating from his shiny, bulbous head. The caption beneath made my bile rise: "Come to me, and I will give you rest."

"The rest of what?" I said aloud.

"Now Martin here," Father was just saying, "has written several."

"Several what?" asked yours truly. "Oh, excuse me. I was just, um—"

"Indeed." I watched as Father's glance settled on the image of Manly D. Man. His eyes stayed there for all of a moment, perhaps two, and widened no more than a millimeter before he turned his attention back to the receptionist. "Miss Dunton, do you suppose I might have five minutes of Mr. Wedge's time?"

"I'd have to ask him," she said, rubbing her neck uncertainly. "I know he'll need to see some authorization from his client before he'll discuss any business with you."

"What client is that?" asked Father.

"Why, Cardinal Fulbright. I thought you said he sent you."

So, thought the gardener, Monsignor Aspic, too, had been here on behalf of Cardinal Fulbright.

"Yes, but there you have me," said Father. "In times past the cardinal has always given me a letter of introduction for contingencies such as this, but alas the matter was overlooked this morning. I don't suppose you could phone the Chancery yourself?"

"Normally no, but seeing as how you're the one who makes life interesting for my cousin who works there, I'll make an exception in your case. Yes, I've heard of you."

Bingo, smiled the gardener. So they *were* related.

"I am Wedge," said the man behind the desk as we were escorted into his office about ten minutes later. He rose from his chair, his movements smooth, confident, and well-oiled. "Willis P. Wedge."

"Father John Baptist," replied Father, "and this is my associate, Martin Feeney. Thank-you for squeezing us in."

"I can only spare a few minutes, you understand," said Mr. Wedge, motioning us to a couple of corpulent leather chairs. Everything in his office was fancy, bloated, and expensive. "Ms. Dunton informs me you're here on behalf of Cardinal Fulbright."

"That is correct."

"This surprises me because your name has come up on numerous occasions in connection with some of his difficulties."

"Indeed."

"Yes. In fact, when His Eminence first entered this office back in July—he was still just an archbishop, as I recall—your name was among the first words out of his mouth."

"I'm surprised, Mr. Wedge. I wouldn't have thought that my small role in archdiocesan affairs would loom large in his mind."

"You don't have to play humble with me, Father. Morley Fulbright had a first-class crisis on his hands. All his auxiliary bishops and their support staff had been murdered, and by someone he himself trusted. Between charges of personal and administrative incompetence, suspicions of witchcraft and pedophilia in connection with his auxiliaries, the spectacles at Saint Barbara's Chapel and the Del Agua Mission, a certain photograph taken by one Ziggie Svelte of the *Times* that made the rounds—yes, the press were eating him alive. He sought our help to control the damage to his image."

No doubt his parishioners took comfort in that, thought the gardener, looking casually around the room. After all, what could be more important to them than His Incompetence's precious image? What had Father said? *Fools with money can always hire others to formulate and carry out their plans.*

On the wood-paneled wall behind Mr. Wedge's desk, there was an impressive oil painting of three men against a turbulent blue-and-black background. I recognized the one on the right as our very own Willis P. Wedge, so I assumed the others were his partners, Bendlebrain and Cruiser, whose first names I had yet to learn. The storm at their backs, the sun in their faces, they looked like heroes in a three-and-a-half-hour epic movie.

Closer at hand, on the corner of the desk, was a tilted Plexiglas slab in which a copy of *Image* magazine had been sealed against the ravages of time. WILLIS P. WEDGE: THE WIZARD OF SPIN, read the caption beside his confidently smiling face on the cover. A graphics artist had airbrushed little stars and dollar signs swirling around his head.

Well, thought the gardener as he attempted and failed to cross his rickety legs, it's also reassuring to know that His Manipulance, Morley Fulbright, only bought the best for himself.

There were also two file folders on the desk, one with a yellow tab, the other orange. I almost sprained my eyes trying to read the labels upside down. DEMOGRAPHICS AND PSYCHOGRAPHICS, said the yellow one, I'm pretty sure. AUDIENCE ANALYTICS, said the orange. How uplifting that Mr. Wedge was such a "people person."

My attention was then drawn to an assortment of framed portraits, mostly ten-by-twelves, on the wall to my right. They were arranged in a sunburst pattern, and after a moment's consideration I realized they were organized chronologically. The outermost visages were the most recent, preserved in color and printed on simulated canvas. These were businessmen—B, C & W among them—decked in crisp, modern apparel and smart hairstyles. The black-and-white faces closer to the center wore cravats with ornate tiepins, had monocles or wire rim spectacles, and sported walrus moustaches or topiary beards. The oldest portrait in the center was a centuries-old woodcut, doubtless a genuine museum piece, of a sinister-looking man, presumably the father of the line or the founder of the guiding principle of their business. The look in his eyes, roughly-hewn as they were, sent chills down my convoluted spine.

Fools with money, I thought to myself. Heaven help us if they sought out a scoundrel like that!

"It hasn't been easy," Mr. Wedge was saying as I emerged from my reverie. "The cardinal has been plagued with one problem after another. Each time we get one situation properly understood in the public mind, another pops up requiring more media manipulation."

"When did Monsignor Aspic come into the picture?" asked Father.

"About a month ago. The cardinal originally hired him as a sort of 'head hunter.' His job was to seek out bishops and experienced staff to fill all the vacancies. His task hasn't been easy. A lot of qualified people are understandably leery of filling positions vacated by violence. We've been working with him on a campaign to give the Archdiocese of Los Angeles a new corporate image. By the time we're done, every ambitious bishop and motivated ecclesiastical bureaucrat across America will want to transfer here, I assure you."

Oh joy, moaned yours truly, sinking dishearteningly in my soft, spongy chair.

"May I ask how this will be accomplished?" said Father.

"Ah, that would take hours to answer," said Mr. Wedge. "Suffice it to say that our goal is to make perceptions match the reality of the situation."

"As you did with HoxZy Petroleum and Klotzinger Eiscreme?"

"Two of our most successful campaigns," nodded Mr. Wedge. He looked for a moment toward the wall covered with framed portraits. Was it my imagination, or did he seem to draw approval, perhaps even raw power, from the woodcut at the center? "I'm not a Catholic, Father, but that doesn't stop me from wanting to help the Church work through this difficult time. That's what we do here."

"'Crisis management,'" said Father. "You make perceptions match the reality."

"Precisely."

"And the reality is ...?"

"Really, Father, I shouldn't have to explain that to you. As I said, I only have a few minutes. Is there something pertinent you wish to ask me?"

"As you probably know, Monsignor Aspic has disappeared."

"Yes, so I understand."

"He had an appointment with you at four o'clock yesterday afternoon."

"That is correct."

"How long was he here?"

"Two hours. It was my last appointment of the day."

Father Baptist made a steeple with his fingers and rested his chin upon it. "Yesterday morning the Monsignor held two press conferences regarding the discovery of Saint Valeria's body in Rome."

"Against my advice, I assure you," said Mr. Wedge. "It's another one of those situations that keep popping up. I advised silence on the matter. Sometimes the best way to let smoke clear is to leave it to disperse on its own. Cardinal Fulbright was impatient, however."

"Mr. Wedge, how do I put this—?"

"Ah, Father Baptist. I can see your wheels turning. You want to know if Monsignor Aspic's disappearance is a ploy to distract the media away from this Saint Valeria business, as well as from some other controversial matters that plague our client." Mr. Wedge shook his head from side to side, but his meticulously controlled smile seemed to stay in the same place. "Bendlebrain, Cruiser, and Wedge doesn't manipulate events, just the public assessment of them. You notice our placard says, 'Public Perception,' not 'Public Relations.' We use the media to alter opinion, but we would never advise a client to resort to that kind of subterfuge. The chance of exposure and further damage to the client's reputation is far too risky, and the legal ramifications onerous besides." He looked long and hard at the woodcut on the wall while making a motion with his hand as if he were rolling a hundred-dollar cigar between his thumb and fingers. "That's not to say we won't take advantage of the situation. To be sure, Monsignor Aspic vanishing under suspicious circumstances may be a fortuitous development from our perspective, but I can assure you that this firm had no hand in it."

"I have your word on that," said Father Baptist.

"My word is Reality," said Willis P. Wedge. He touched the face of the wristwatch on his left wrist with the index finger of his right hand, but did not look at it. "I'm afraid time is pressing and I must react in kind."

As we rose to leave—well, Father rose, I strained, heaved, and kind of burst out of my chair. As soon as I regained my balance I managed to say, "Excuse me, Mr. Wedge. I was admiring the pictures on your wall. The fellow in the middle—might I ask who that is?"

"Of course," said Mr. Wedge proudly. "That's Antonio del Corro."

"An ancestor of yours?"

"Not by blood, no. By intention, philosophy, and objective, indubitably. You might say he's my mentor of mentors. That portrait is genuine sixteenth century, the work of one of his contemporaries."

"Interesting," said I, completely unaware who Señor del Corro might be.

"Isn't it," agreed Mr. Wedge. "And now, gentlemen, if you will excuse me—"

"I have a message for you, Father," said Miss Dunton as we passed by her desk on the way out.

"How would anyone know I'm here?" asked Father, surprised.

"My cousin, Darlene," smiled Miss Dunton. "I phoned her a little while ago at the Chancery to verify your credentials, remember? Well, she just called to tell you that Cardinal Fulbright wants you to meet him in Malibu tomorrow morning at seven sharp."

"Where in Malibu?"

"Our Lady of the Waves. And you're to tell no one of his whereabouts."

"His will be done," sighed Father. "Martin, it would seem ... Martin?"

I was lost in thought, staring up at the sign above her desk:

BENDLEBRAIN, CRUISER & WEDGE
CONSULTANTS
PUBLIC PERCEPTION, CRISIS MANAGEMENT,
AND TERGIVERSATION

"Martin?"

"Oh, excuse me, Father. Nice meeting you Miss Dunton."

> GARDENING TIPS: I wasn't familiar with the word,
> but after our conversation with Mr. Wedge I had a
> hunch which proved to be pretty close when I
> looked it up later:

> ter´gi•ver•sa´tion *n.* 1. Desertion of a cause, party,
>   faith, etc.; apostasy; also, a shifting; equivocation.
>   2. A shift, subterfuge, or evasion.

—M.F.

14

WARM YOURSELF BY THE FIRE OF HIS LOVE. That's what the sign on the door said. It also said that the business hours when the establishment opened its door to share the warmth were different every day of the week:.

Monday:	**10 – 3**
Tuesday:	**11 – 4**
Wednesday:	**9 – 5**
Thursday:	**CLOSED**
Friday:	**10 – 7**
Saturday:	**12 – 6**
Sunday:	**CLOSED**

It was located at one of those three-and-a-half story geometrical amazements where a crafty developer figured out how to cram twenty-seven small businesses onto the footprint of what had once been a corner gas station. The shop a few feet to our left was 1014F, MCKINLEY & BREUSTER: HARD-TO-FIND PARTS FOR VINTAGE PHONOGRAPHS. I wished Messrs. Breuster and McKinley well in their obdurate but futile venture. The enterprise to the right and up three steps at 1014H was called FREEMAN'S POSTERS: B-MOVIES OUR SPECIALTY. I made a note of the location and promised myself I'd return to browse if I ever had a day off. Our immediate concern was 1014G, WAY TRUE LIFE PUBLISHING, INC. I could see a sign hanging behind an office desk within. The letters were blue and gold against a yellow background, swirls and wings aplenty, within a frame of polished aluminum:

> *The only letter I need is you yourselves! By looking at the good change in your hearts, everyone can see that we have done a good work among you.*
> *They can see that you are a letter from Christ, written by us. It is not a letter written with pen and ink, but by the Spirit of the living God; not one carved on stone, but in human hearts.*
> —2 Corinthians 3:2-3
> *The Living Bible*

"So Monsignor Aspic came here before seeing Mr. Wedge," said I, having knocked uselessly on the glass door. If there's one thing I dislike more than the King James Bible, it's one of the more recent, imprecise, emotionally adolescent versions.

"Apparently," said Father. "We'll have to come back tomorrow."

"I never thought I'd have something in common with Monsignor Aspic," I panted as I wedged myself back into the Jeep after descending many zigzagging stairs to the street.

"Oh?" said Father, buckling his seatbelt.

"Rejection. The poor guy was desperate to get his book published. I know the feeling."

A few minutes later we were barreling westward on Franklin. Picturesque storefronts, quaint cafés, and deteriorating apartment buildings went whizzing by.

"Right," said the priest-slash-copilot a few minutes later.

"Right?" asked the gardener-slash-chauffeur-slash-rejected author. "You mean left. The next stop on our reverse itinerary is on Sunset, and that's south, not north."

"Our next destination is five or six blocks up Beechwood, then left on Lawnridge," said Father.

"Excuse me?"

"An unscheduled stop, but as it turns out, necessary."

"Care to let me in on it?"

"You'll see. Wanda Hemmingway stumbled upon it by accident when she was up this way looking for a girlfriend's new apartment. She told me about it after choir practice the other day."

> GARDENING TIPS: Wanda Hemmingway is the first soprano in our "in lieu of" choir. In this gardener's opinion she has five heartwarming things going for her: 1) she was once the vocalist in a rock band called Salvador Dolly, 2) she had the good sense to move on, 3) she had enough Good Will to rediscover the Catholic Faith in her early thirties, 4) she has the most endearing smile, not to mention the most striking fulcra, in the choir loft, and 5) she always smells of patchouli.
>
> —M.F.
>
> N.B.: Virtually everyone who works in any capacity around Saint Philomena's parish, with the exception of Father Baptist, does so "in lieu of" cash in the plate. He works for less.

"You haven't been to choir practice in weeks," I observed.

"Okay, so it was the other week. After where we've been, and where I suspect our quest is going to take us, we need a respite."

"Respite? I need a vacation."

"You'd better slow down, Wanda said the street sign is partially obscured by an overgrown oleander bush."

"Sure thing. And while I'm applying my foot to the deceleration pedal, might I point out, Father, that whatever happened to Monsignor Aspic might have its roots in events that happened days or weeks ago? What makes you so sure his disappearance hinges on where he went yesterday?"

"It's not so much a matter of surety as of reach, Martin. Cardinal Fulbright has pressed Chief Billowack to instigate a discreet investigation into Monsignor Aspic's disappearance. He apparently didn't tell Monty what he's really after, but even so, the authorities have the manpower and resources to backtrack the monsignor's movements for months if necessary."

"Then why don't you just sit back and let them do all the work?"

"My Vow of Obedience."

"Oh. There is that."

"The cardinal has ordered me to investigate, so investigate I shall for the greater glory of God; but I can only do so within the scope of the means at my disposal."

"Meaning me."

"You, and of course, the Knights Tumblar, if I need them. But there is something else."

"What's that?"

"I have a hunch."

"Oh, well if you've got one of those, hey, lead the way. You are the driver, I am the car. You are the capt'n, Capt'n, and I am—"

"Martin."

"Father. I *said* I need a vacation."

"And you shall have one, albeit brief. There it is. Now turn left, and watch for a stucco wall on the right up ahead. She said the entrance is narrow."

"Matthew seven fourteen, paraphrased."

The driveway was indeed narrow, and the gate more so, but I managed to maneuver the car into a red brick parking lot surrounded by a tall stone wall covered with ivy. Three vehicles were parked there at odd angles: a rusty Volkswagen Bug with dented fenders and no rear bumper, a clean but road-weary Harley Davidson motorcycle with an impressive array of intertwining exhaust pipes, and an immaculate Rolls Royce with whitewall tires and the glaze of paste wax all over. I nosed the Jeep Cherokee up to a gurgling fountain surmounted by a weathered cement statue of Saint Michael the Archangel towering over the defeated dragon, Satan. Above and beyond the wall rose arches and buttresses, tiled roofs and turrets. Hushed and serene, this was a place set apart from the frenetic city all around. The sun being low in the sky, everything was bathed in a heartwarming orange hue. A simple wooden sign beside a stucco archway announced:

MONASTERY OF THE ARCHANGELS
THE SISTERS OF THE APPARITION OF MOUNT GARGANO
CLOISTER

"What a find!" I exclaimed as I heaved myself out of the car. "Just look at this place."

"It gets better," said Father, indicating another sign just inside the portico. BLESSED SACRAMENT CHAPEL, it said, PUBLIC WELCOME, with a stylized hand pointing to the right. A little old man in baggy pants, tattered flannel shirt, and extra large gloves was trimming the branch of a spindly rose bush away from the word BLESSED with a pair of squeaky clippers. He paused to present us a toothy smile with some jarring gaps in it, doffed his ratty straw hat, and then cheerfully returned to his chore.

We followed a mossy path around the side of the monastery to a large wooden door with medieval studs and a humongous iron latch. The hinges groaned deeply and invitingly as I pulled it open and motioned for Father to enter first.

It was a simple place, about fifty feet long and thirty wide, illumined only by sunlight streaming through stained-glass windows and the bobbing flames of several dozen votive candles in an ornate wrought-iron rack. The floor and ceiling were made of wood, the walls of sandstone blocks. Instead of pews there were twenty or so wooden chairs, each with its own *prie-dieu,* all facing east. In that direction there was an archway perhaps twenty-five feet at the apex. The lower third of this portico was blocked by a wall of ornately carved marble about eight feet high. Above the wall we could see the vaulted ceiling of a larger chapel beyond, no doubt where the Sisters of the Apparition attended Mass. Against this wall was set a stone altar adorned with a tabernacle flanked by Angels with majestic wings. Above this rose a pillar of bronze ascending to a height of about ten feet. It was crowned by an immense golden monstrance, in the center of which the Blessed Sacrament was exposed.

It took me a moment to figure out the layout. This room was behind the high altar of the sisters' chapel. Being cloistered, they were hidden from us beyond the stone wall. Their religious life revolved around perpetual adoration of the Holy Eucharist, and in their generosity they had provided a means for lay folk to join them. The monstrance had glass apertures in front and behind, allowing the Sacred Host to be viewed from both directions.

The one sad and jarring concession the sisters had to make to the realities of modern life was the installation of a steel grate a few feet in front of the altar, ornate but utilitarian, from floor to ceiling. We visitors could see the Blessed Sacrament, but no vandal could possibly reach it.

As we entered the chapel, it only took a second to take all this in. Every line and angle drew our attention to the incredible, mind-melting Reality exposed for the consideration of those who dared to approach and believe: the *Immaculatam Hostiam*, the Spotless Victim, the Bread of Life.

> <u>GARDENING</u> <u>TIPS</u>: The traditional Catholic practice
> is to genuflect on one knee (from the Latin <u>genu</u>
> <u>flexio</u>, "the knee I bend") before the Real Pres-
> ence when It resides within the Tabernacle. When
> the Blessed Sacrament is exhibited, however, the
> custom is to get down on both knees and then bow.
> Perhaps I should underline "traditional" because
> the modern practice is to ignore, if not deny, the
> Real Presence altogether.
>
>   --M.F.

I tried to make the appropriate obsecration with as little huffing and grunting as possible, then stole myself to a kneeler in the back. Father Baptist, on the other hand, chose to kneel on the bare floor directly before the Tabernacle. Between him and me were five other worshippers, who in my distraction I tried to match with the vehicles outside. The muscular dude in the leather pants and jacket no doubt belonged to the Harley. I wondered if his biking pals were aware of his devotional side. The haggard woman with the polka-dot bandana probably went with the VW, but so could the twenty-ish gal in jeans and T-shirt with no head covering. There was a middle-aged man in a cheap suite and tie, and an elderly woman with a flowery hat. No one obviously went with the Rolls, and any of them could have come on foot for all I knew.

Scolding myself for forgetting where I was and where my mind should be, I set about the task of gathering the tattered strings of my meandering imagination into a momentary ball of focus. When that didn't work, at least not in second person, I tried taking stock in the third person—I'm talking point-of-view here, not the Triune nature of

God. I pondered how, to the uninformed observer, it might seem strange, perhaps even appalling, to find such a mismatched group of people worshipping what appears to be a mere piece of bread. It's not hard to explain, however, once one gets beyond the hurdle of Faith. Saint Peter Julian Eymard wrote one of the most superb books on the subject entitled *The Real Presence*, in which he said it best:

```
   In order to abase Himself thus, our Lord has to
display all His power.  He sustains the accidents
by a miracle.  He contradicts all the laws of na-
ture in order to humble and abase Himself.  Who
could envelope the sun in a cloud thick enough to
intercept its light and heat?  That would be a
very great miracle.  Our Lord performs it in His
own person; beneath the Eucharistic Species, which
in themselves are so frail and common, He is glo-
rious and luminous; He is God.
```

These words came to me clearly because I had just copied them for the parish newsletter a few days before. I could visualize them creeping up the page as I typed them on Dad's old Underwood. In the Holy Eucharist we have the ultimate irony. God's might is displayed, not in thunderbolts and colliding planets, but in the suppression of all semblance of power and might. As appalling as the notion may be, this is the heart and soul of the Catholic Faith, the Catholic walk, the Catholic worldview, and the Catholic Conscience: Jesus Christ not only died horribly in our behalf, but elected to stay with us, helpless yet ever available, under the appearance of mere bread. If I may belabor the point—if only to give some future editor something to cross out and draw question marks on both sides—Saint Eymard explained in the same book:

```
   He has chained Himself to the Sacred Spe-
cies to which the sacramental words bind
Him inseparably.  In the Eucharist as on
the Cross or in the Tomb He has no move-
ment, no action of His own, although He
possesses within Himself the fullness of
the risen life.
   He is fully dependant on man like a Pris-
oner of love.  He cannot break His bonds,
or leave His Eucharistic prison; He is our
Prisoner to the end of time.  He pledged
```

Himself to this; His contract of love goes
as far as that.

"And to think that This is right here in the middle of it all," I marveled as we returned to the car some twenty minutes later.

"Sometimes we get so involved in rankling with the horror," said Father, "we forget that there are still believers all around us, and shelters
like this for them to come in from the storm."

Just then three newcomers arrived. One was a black kid on a wobbly
bicycle who screeched to a halt beside the Harley Davidson. Since his
vehicle had no kickstand, he leaned it against the building and trotted on
by us without a word. The other two were a young couple, probably
recently or soon to be married from the way they held hands as they
strolled up the driveway. They nodded as they walked by us, demurely
releasing their grip as they passed under the monastery arch and headed
around the side toward the chapel.

The Rolls was gone, as was the little old man in the baggy pants.

Martin, I thought to myself, you are no judge of people.

"Thanks, Father," I said aloud as I unlocked the Jeep. "I needed that."

"Don't we all?" said he, climbing into the passenger seat. "Now for
that shop on Sunset."

"They might be closing right about now."

"I suspect they'll just be opening for business—real business."

"Oh."

15

"I'M CLOSING," GOBBLED THE MAN with the hyperactive Adam's apple
without so much as an "Excuse me, Sir," or a "Sorry."

"Of course you are," agreed Father, pushing past him.

The stencil on the door glass said, E. WINGER'S FINE JEWELS AND
SETTINGS, now reversed since we were inside, and the sign swinging
just under it said YES, WE'RE OPEN! except of course its opposite was
now facing out. It's all a matter of perspective. In more ways than
one, actually. First impressions aren't always reliable, as I had just
been reminded at the Monastery of the Archangels, but I had a hard time
imagining one of the cardinal's "affluent acquaintances" recommending
this dump for something as important as an appraisal of a historical
artifact. I thought I caught the same reaction in Father's eye, but it
could have been a speck of lint. The place was certainly dusty.

"Hey, hey, Bub," said the proprietor, slipping ahead of Father and poking him in the chest with his twitching index finger. "You can't just—"

"The name is Father John Baptist," said Father firmly, "and this is my ... *gardener* ... Mister Feeney." He made my occupation seem ominous indeed. "He's looking for Aspic."

The man's eyes widened and then narrowed. "Who?"

"Monsignor Conrad J. Aspic."

"Monsignor?" pondered the man, trying while failing to act tough. His oily eyes darted at me and then back to Father. "You're in the wrong place, Mack. Try a church."

"And *I'm* looking for ... the *artifact* ... the one he brought here yesterday afternoon."

"I don't know what you're talking about."

"Oh, I think you do, Mr. Winger."

All the while Father kept advancing slowly but inexorably, while the nervous jeweler retreated in short, erratic stumbles. Meanwhile I did my best to look ominous in the horticultural sense while mulling over another incongruity. Morley Fulbright had distinctly said, only this morning:

> *"The one hitch was that the monsignor's afternoon schedule was log-jammed with appointments. He assured me, on his honor, that he would safeguard the disk with his life, keep it on his person through the day, sleep with it under his pillow overnight, and take it to the appraiser first thing the following morning."*

The following morning would have been today, and the monsignor disappeared last night, so how was it that he had come here yesterday afternoon instead? Ah, perhaps Father was playing out a hunch within the scope of the means at his disposal. Or something like that.

"We know he came here," continued Father, seeming to loom larger and larger.

"Says who?" countered the proprietor, if not getting smaller, certainly not any bigger.

"We know he had it with him."

"I told you I don't know this Aspic guy. He hasn't been here, and he didn't bring any artifact with him."

The proprietor's heel banged against a wastebasket wedged in the corner at the intersection of two display cases. Father looked down as the metal mesh receptacle tipped to one side, rolled around its bottom rim twice, and rattled noisily to an upstanding standstill on the mottled hardwood floor. Waxy papers shuffled themselves into a new cluster of disorder within. Father considered the contents for several long seconds before he spoke again:

"One of the unexpected benefits of my profession, Mr. Winger, gleaned from long hours in the confessional, is the ability to discern—to hear, to sense, to smell even—when a penitent is being dishonest with himself and with me."

"But—"

"Yes, yes, I realize you're not repentant, but nonetheless there are ranks and grades of prevarication. Did you know that? To the average sinner it may all seem a blurred continuum, but to the trained confessor the muddle resolves into distinct strata: evasion, equivocation, and rationalization, to name but a few; deceit, pretense, duplicity, guile and just plain lying. Mr. Winger, *you are lying.*"

"I—"

"Not a good trait in someone who deals in precious merchandise," said Father, indicating the plethora of gems, rings, earrings, tiaras, necklaces, and metal vessels all around. "People trust you to tell them the worth of what they bring you, the value of what you sell them."

"What—?"

"That metal chalice on the worktable," said Father, pointing to an ugly vessel if there ever was one sitting amidst an assortment of less ugly ewers and goblets, all in need of a jolly good polishing. "Shall I tell you its sordid history?"

I realized with a start that the object Father was indicating was none other than the cardinal's own Murkenstein chalice, that hideous quasi-liturgical schooner I had nicknamed the Murkenmug, and which had been the focus of our last investigation for His Malevolence, Cardinal Fulbright. The outside, despite its disruptive angularity of design, was actually fairly clean. The inside, however, looked as though it had been used as a rich man's ashtray—precisely because it had. Our missing monsignor had in fact brought the accursed thing to Mr. Winger the previous afternoon for a colonic cleansing—that was *so* LA! Father must have spotted it the moment we entered the shop.

"Is, is, is that the artifact you're interested in?" asked the proprietor.

"No," said Father. "I have better taste than that. But it confirms my suspicion. It, too, was in Monsignor Aspic's possession. He brought them both here, the chalice for cleaning, the other item for appraisal."

Mr. Winger's mouth opened and closed several times but no words came out. He looked at me, cleared his throat, and turned back to Father. "I can't tell you anything."

"You know something else?" persisted Father, nudging the wastebasket with his shoe. "Martin was just saying on the way here how much he's got a hankering for a hotdog—one of Ernie Corben's 'world famous' hotdogs, to be precise."

"I was*?*" blinked the gardener who, having drifted in and out of day-dreams about going home shortly to indulge in one of Millie's slaver-worthy dinners, had most certainly *not* been thinking any such thing. Being a regular visitor to Father's confessional, I had contributed a fair share of his extensive knowledge of the intricacies of dishonesty. Ironically, he had become more adept at appearing to stretch the truth than his humble test subject. Not to be outdone, summoning my own vast store of horticultural ominousness, I cleared my throat and corrected myself with an exaggerated nod of assurance. "I mean, I *was.*"

"Y-y-yuh-you know er-er-er-Ernie Corben?" gasped Mr. Winger.

"You'd be surprised who I know." Father looked around with a severe, critical stare. Above the old-fashioned cash register was a crusted mirror in a splitting wooden frame. The words *EDISON G. WINGER, PROPRIETOR* were etched in the glass amidst a tangle of ornate curlicues. Father returned his glare to the man shrinking before him. "It's been a long day, Edison, longer than you can possibly know. Mr. Feeney and I have another stop to make. I will make a point of mentioning you to Mr. Corben—"

"Now wait a minute."

"—unless you'd care to speak to him first. Martin?"

"Huh?" said I, snapping out of my reverie. The mention of Ernie Corben of hotdog fame had sent me mentally singing *"disjecta membra"* to the tune of "Auld Lang Syne." It actually worked in an odd three-to-two sort of way. "Of course, Father. Anything you say."

"Wait, wait just a minute," said Edison Winger, his voice shrill. "You come barging in here out of nowhere, making demands, and now you—"

"Good day to you, Sir," said Father, ushering me out the door before he slammed it solidly behind us.

"You're not serious," I complained as we headed for the Jeep. It was parked three shops down and the sidewalk there was commodiously wide.

"About what?" asked Father.

"About going to Ernie Corben's for dinner."

"Who said anything about—"

We were interrupted by a young woman in a long brown skirt with a yellow sweater who handed me a couple of bright-colored photocopied pages stapled in the upper left corner. Before I could say, "No thank-you," she had moved on to pester another pedestrian headed in the opposite direction.

"You did," said I, glancing at the flyer.

The words *"Our Lady of* IRWINDALE*, pray for us!"* rippled across the top of the first page above a line drawing of the Blessed Virgin standing upon what looked like a pile of rocks. There was an opened scroll beneath her feet proclaiming: BYENGI EGNYUK AND SONS, QUARRIED STONE AND GRAVEL, EST. 1929, IRWINDALE, CALIFORNIA. At the bottom of the page was a bio of one Quintana Morbo of New Orleans. Apparently a woman of French and African descent who made a mean gumbo, Miss Morbo had at twenty-six applied for a secretarial position in the business offices of said quarry. Shortly thereafter she underwent a "stupendous conversion experience" after which she called herself the "Little Taper." I doubted she was related to Lieutenant Taper, but I made a mental note to ask him. Miss Morbo's spiritual adventures apparently continued on the second page, but I folded and stuffed it into my jacket pocket.

"I said no such thing," said Father, resting his hand on the door handle while waiting for me to lumber to the driver's side and unlock the vehicle. "I simply noticed Ernie's distinctive wrappers in the wastebasket, still wet with mustard and relish."

"But," said I, unlocking my door with a double-twist that also unlocked his side, "you said—"

"I said we have a stop to make. I also said I would mention Mr. Winger to Ernie Corben. I did not say the two intents were connected."

"Oh," said I, easing my sore bones into the driver's seat, wondering who taught him that level of finesse in the confessional. It certainly hadn't been me. "That's what I get for allowing my attention to wander."

"There was something else of interest in the wastebasket."

"Oh? Such as?"

"Mr. Winger's enterprise, it would seem, is located in a building that has been flagged by the Department of Health for mandatory asbestos removal. Part of the notice was smeared with catsup, but I gather the city is holding him responsible."

"I imagine that could be expensive. Asbestos, you say. Are you thinking what I'm thinking?"

"The fibers found in the lungs of our mysterious clergyman? I imagine there are many old buildings in Los Angeles that are insulated with asbestos. Too early to tell if there's a connection. Speaking of mysteries, what about the flyer that girl handed you?"

"An invitation to a vision in Irwindale. Some of our parishioners have been talking about it. You want to go?"

"Oh, the quarry. Yes, actually, I do want to check out the Little Taper, but only in disguise, and not till we've got this other business settled."

"Disguise, did you say?"

"I wouldn't want my presence to give the thing credence. Some incredible claims have been made, and someone with a level head—"

"In this archdiocese?"

"—should check them out. So, we'll save that investigation for another day. In the immediate, we have another stop to make."

"Oh, that. The next stop in our retroactive itinerary is in Pacific Palisades. I don't think we can make it there and get home in time for dinner."

"I agree. No, I wish to make a quick visit to the library. There's a detail from today's cache of information that I want to check out before we go home. It will only take a moment."

"Sure thing."

"It also occurs to me that we should have made an inspection of the monsignor's car. It shows you how tired I am. We'll see to it tomorrow. Now I have a question for you."

"Such as?"

"Why are you humming 'Auld Lang Syne'?"

16

"MAYBE WE SHOULD REVIVE THIS in your honor," said Edward Strypes Wyndham, patting me on the back with one hand while holding up a small copper picture frame. It contained one of Father Baptist's examples of amateur calligraphy-slash-self-incrimination-slash-precipitous-profundity that had been bouncing around various drawers and closets at the rectory for months:

> As a dog that returneth to his vomit, so is the fool that repeateth his folly.
>
> —Proverbs XXVI: 11

"You must admit," laughed Jonathan Clubb, swirling the champagne in his fluted glass, "you have a unique way of extricating yourself from awkward situations."

"Albeit awkwardly," added Pierre, tapping his cigar over the ashtray on Father's desk. "What, ho! A dozen damsels in skimpy dancing apparel, eh? An attack of acute nausea was the best you could come up with?"

"What can I say?" said I, sinking into my favorite chair. "I had to think fast. It hurt."

"Your pride?" asked Edward.

"No, my back," retorted the gardener. "My pride was already shattered by the earlier incident at the mausoleum."

"Hey, it worked, didn't it?" said Joel Maruppa, returned from his sister's birthday celebration in time for the regular Thursday evening Knights' meeting.

"Indeed it did," said Father, who was seated in his chair behind the desk. He exhaled smoke through his nostrils as he spoke in that accent peculiar to men who talk around a pipe clenched in their teeth. His hands were occupied holding a fragile, dried-out old book. "Don't be hard on Martin. He did the right thing, and there are precedents. Gentlemen, if I may read a few lines from Father V. J. Matthews' biography of Saint Philip Neri:

> An abandoned woman, who lived in the via Giulia, boasted that the virtue of this priest who was so much talked of would not be proof against her charms. She therefore gave it out that she was ill and wished to change her life, if Philip would come and hear her confession. When he arrived, however, she advanced to meet him wearing only a transparent veil, and he turned and fled. So furious was the woman that she caught up the first thing to hand—it happened to be a heavy stool—and flung it after Philip. He came away unharmed; but it was a maxim that he was fond of impressing on others afterwards that, in the battle with the temptations of the flesh, it is cowards—those who run away, that is—who are the victors.

"Very well," said Pierre. "We agree that fleeing temptation is the best course. Of the emetic overtones, however, well, what can be said?"

"You'll think of something," said I, reaching painfully for the nearby poker to nudge the logs crackling on the hearth. The evening wasn't particularly chilly, but the impressive fireplace in Father's study simply demanded a cozy blaze, especially during a meeting of the Knights of the Tumblar.

Briefly, these formally attired fellows were—believe it or not—Knights, as true, authentic, and perhaps fated to be as legendary some day as the gallant warriors who once sat at King Arthur's illustrious Round Table. Well, "legendary" is stretching it, but not unduly. After weeks of exhaustive preparation, having taken oaths that certainly curled my toes, these gentlemen had been duly and authentically knighted by His Lordship, Bishop Xandaronolopolis of Lebanon. The ceremony in which all this was accomplished had occurred only a month before the events in this story.

Joel, the youngest of the troupe and latest to join, was intense and impassioned, his veins boiling with the blood of his Slovakian ancestors. He was dark, almost swarthy, and prone to perpetual five o'clock shadow.	Until the previous June he had been considering the priesthood, but he was rescued from the archdiocesan seminary machinery by suspicion of murder, and he was acquitted of the charge by the efforts of none other than Father John Baptist. He then followed his own father's footsteps in that he was an electrician, but he was also quite a handyman, proficient in all sorts of woodworking and construction.

Next in ascending age was Jonathan Clubb: thin, tall, and twenty-six. His prominent forehead was his second most obvious feature. The lads often kidded him about what a huge monstrosity his brain must be to dent his skull outward like that. They were exaggerating, of course. His first most obvious physical characteristic was not evident this evening. I'm referring to his straggly excuse for a beard. He had to shave twice daily, once at dawn to rid himself of the overnight growth, and again in the afternoon to eradicate the daytime damage, so quick were his follicles to develop. If he didn't get the chance for that second mowing, or if he perchance ran out of razor blades, the consequences were startling. I'd only seen it once, and that was enough. Left unchecked, his beard hairs, which matched the mustard-brown crop atop his head in color but not texture, emerged like crazed, carnivorous stop-motion vine-creatures in a low-budget science fiction movie, the result of a maniacal radioactive experiment gone awry. Some of his whiskers grew ferociously, others more so. Some were thick, others thin. Some were straight, some grew crooked, many were corkscrewed, others curlicued. The end result was an uneven, unkempt, impossible to keep kempt, disheveled excuse for a jaw mop. Knowing his sensitivity regarding this bizarre malformation of what should have been his manly pride, his friends chose to harp on his forehead while ignoring his face. I haven't reported it previously in my chronicles for this very reason. However, it will play a part in coming events, so it had to be mentioned. Aside from this anomaly—that is, when he was clean-shaven as he presently and usually was—he was certainly handsome, as evidenced by the fact that he, as we shall see, was madly in love with a gorgeous young woman, and she with him. Of course, she had never seen him in his altered state. More on that when the time comes.

Next came Edward Strypes Wyndham, the fellow who taunted me with Proverbs twenty-six eleven at the beginning of this chapter. At twenty-eight, his intense eyes gleamed like pearls of obsidianite. He had a pair of bushy black eyebrows that had merged into a bird-of-prey crest above the bridge of his long, playground-slide nose. Though all the Tumblars were serious about the Faith, he was perhaps serious about everything. This didn't dim his sense of humor, not at all, but it gave it an edge that was sometimes unsettling in its brutal honesty.

Pierre Bontemps was, well, Pierre Bontemps. He has already been in and out of this story, and will continue to come and go, as will they. Pierre was so involved in being Pierre that he was truly an entity unto himself. No one could be fascinated with the tiny details of his average day, nor enjoy perusing his essays and articles, more than he. His vocabulary was immense, his memory daunting, and his sense of humor relentless, hilarious, and extremely catching. The last of his long and courageous lineage, Pierre deemed it his duty to live up to the family motto which had guided their steps since the reign of Pope Urban II at the turn of the twelfth century AD: *"Laissez les Bontemps Rouler!"* Translation: "Let the good times roll!" Pierre's humor was sometimes more brutal than Edward's, not because Pierre was more serious than Edward, but precisely because he was so much less. Rarely did he seem bothered by circumstance. He once told me that he viewed all the information coming in through his senses, no matter what, no matter how seemingly positive or negative, as God's Face smiling upon him. Father Baptist had often said something similar about himself, but the effect was not the same.

Lastly, there was Arthur von Derschmidt, the oldest, widest, and perhaps wisest of the Tumblars. Somewhere in his forties, he looked like a character out of *The Moonstone* by Wilkie Collins. He was attached, whether consciously or not, to some aspects of the long-gone decade known as the Sixties. Of all the Tumblars, he was the only one with long hair, so long it was pulled back into a brown-and-gray ponytail. He had an imposing paunch, and rather than worry about it, he accentuated it with vests that wouldn't quite close and suspenders that were creaking against their elastic limit. One never knows what a fellow traveler sees when he looks in the mirror, but Arthur seemed the most comfortable with his age, his shape, his demeanor, and indeed, his very self. He was also the only Knight who was not present this evening. The reason will become apparent shortly.

GARDENING TIPS: Whoops, I almost forgot. Yours truly, Martin Feeney, without benefit of all that rigorous preparation, but at the behest of Bishop Xandaronolopolis, was also knighted that fateful evening in the church along with the Tumblars. When I asked His Lordship why he had insisted, he told me:

"Funny it is that you should ask. Just as I finished with Pierre Bontemps, a voice like a

```
mouse seemed to whisper in my ear: 'Remember Par-
cifal.'  I looked around, and there you were."
   I didn't know how to take that then, nor do I
now.  But there it is.
```

—M.F.

Okay, back into the thicket.

"Explain again about the mausoleum," said Joel. "You say you saw Father's Crucifix, the one he gave to Monsignor Aspic, on the body of the dead priest?"

"There it was," I sighed, weary of the tale. "The Cross that couldn't be there, but was. From Father's demeanor I knew I wasn't to spill the beans, but the only way I could think not to was to act as though I was about to."

"It was effective," said Father, noticing that the cinders in his bowl had gone out. He gently closed the book, set it aside, and removed that gnarly burl pipe from his mouth. His speech normalized instantly. "Better than anything I could have come up with, and one of the high points of my day."

"One ever-so-long day," said I, glancing at my watch wearily. It was just creeping past eight-thirty. "Anyone interested in coffee?"

"Hardly," said Pierre, holding his champagne glass up to the light. "Caffeine has an unsavory way of undermining the bubbles, so to speak."

"What about Irish coffee?" asked Edward.

"Hm," said Pierre. "Perhaps that is an exception, but I prefer to be a purist in these matters."

"Any ideas?" said Jonathan, offering to pour Father a glass of bubbly. "How it got there, I mean?"

"None," said Father, declining. "Somehow, somewhere, Monsignor Aspic's path crossed that of a malnourished, interminably constrained, intriguing old man in a cassock. The one thing we know they exchanged, though by no means how or why, directly or indirectly, is the Crucifix. I tell you nothing has presented itself as a possible connection thus far. Oh, and Gentlemen, I stress that the matter must not leave this room."

"You mean for the present," said Pierre.

"For the present I mean for the present," said Father. "In the future I may mean for all time. I can't say until I know what I'm talking about."

"That never stopped Pierre," said Edward.

"Hah hah *hah*," responded Pierre in a detached monotone. Then his voice descended to a serious G flat. "Father, surely when you crack this case you will lift this restriction." That last syllable wobbled between imperative and interrogatory just a wee bit.

"As far as the Crucifix goes, no," said Father. "I want no attention whatsoever called to it. Ever. No, don't look at me with 'human interest' eyes. You write for the *L. A. Artsy,* Pierre—the *Artsy* for Heaven's sake."

"There you have it," said Pierre, waving his hand in an ascending swirl. "I am not appreciated in my own time."

"No," said the others severally, "you write for the *Artsy!*"

"As for the rest," said Father, smiling, "I have no idea where this is leading. I can't make promises when I do not yet grasp the premises. I have only revealed part of the situation to you—a small part, in fact. Cardinal Fulbright is adamant that certain other matters must never receive a public hearing. No, Monsieur Bontemps, that 'freedom of the press' pout is not going to unlock any doors, either."

"Is there any way we can be of service?" asked Joel.

"Not this time," said Father. "At least, not as far as I can see. Just having you fellows here this evening helps in ways I can't explain."

"It's the Tumblar charm," said Jonathan.

"I'd say it's the Tumblar booze," said Edward, "except Father hasn't had any."

"I'm too tired to chance it," said Father. "Martin and I didn't get any sleep last night."

"Nor did I," said Pierre.

"Ah," said Father, "but you have the advantage of youth."

"Coffee," mumbled the gardener, rubbing his gritty eyes.

"Gentlemen," said Father. "My brain needs to turn the page, as it were."

"He wants to change the subject," said Edward knowingly to Joel, who nodded meaningfully.

"Our investigation today took Martin and myself to another strange place," said Father, thoughtfully tapping the ashes of his pipe and plunging it into his tobacco pouch for a refill. "The office of one Willis P. Wedge, of Bendlebrain, Cruiser and Wedge."

"The spin doctors?" asked Pierre. "I've heard of them. There's a rumor that Cardinal Fulbright hired them to clean up his image."

"The perception of his image," corrected the gardener.

"What were you doing there?" asked Edward and Jonathan.

"Retracing Monsignor Aspic's footsteps," said I.

"So Morley did hire them," said Pierre. "I've heard they charge a thousand an hour."

Father heaved his shoulders, settled back in his chair, and continued. "Mr. Wedge had a sixteenth century woodcut on the wall of his office.

He said it was a portrait of Antonio del Corro. The name rang a bell so I looked it up in the library on my way home, just to be sure."

"And?" asked the Tumblars in disorganized unison.

"Del Corro was an Isidoren monk who apostatized," said Father. "He had a hand in the production of the Reina-Valera Bible, which became a popular Spanish translation."

"Watch out, Mister Feeney," said Pierre, raising his glass to me. "That's the Hispanic equivalent of the King James Bible."

The others made to duck as if I were going to explode or something. I rolled my eyes for their benefit, but all I could get excited about was the thought of the smell of a steaming cup of coffee.

"Whew," said Joel as they relaxed. "That was close."

"Not even remotely," I mumbled, crossing my arms.

"Aha! Of course!" popped Pierre. "Antonio del Corro, also known as Reginaldus Gonsalvius Montanus." The words rolled out of his mouth like dice out of a confident gambler's hand. "In 1567 he wrote *A Discovery and Plain Declaration of the Sundry and Subtle Practices of the Holy Inquisition of Spain.*"

"Most impressive, Monsieur Bontemps," said Father, striking a match and drawing the flame into the bowl of his pipe. Between puffs he added, "I had to look it up."

"Do tell," said Edward.

"Montanus," explained Pierre, basking pleasantly in Father's praise, "wrote a diatribe about the Spanish Inquisition, masquerading as a victim. It was drivel, of course, but within a year it had been translated into English, French, German, and Dutch. It was welcomed wholeheartedly by Protestants because it described unspeakable horrors in detail, atrocities that never actually happened, but which became widely accepted in the public mind."

"He brought to the world an image," said Father, "a gross falsehood which has persisted ever since."

Pierre took an authoritative sip of bubbly. "It's only been in the last few years that the actual court records were opened and scholars have been able to evaluate the situation fairly. Naturally the truth has not made any headlines."

"In any case," said Father, "the portrait of Antonio del Corro hanging in a place of prominence in the offices of Bendlebrain, Cruiser and Wedge says volumes."

"The wizards of spin," said Edward.

"You fellows have been borrowing a lot of my books of late," said Father. "We all got caught up in the results of that research a few days ago. What a romp that was. I'm curious as to where your studies are leading you now."

"In other words," whispered Edward loudly behind a cupped hand, "Father wants to know from what direction the next wallop is coming."

"A wise precaution," commented Pierre. "Profoundly so. As to direction, I'd have to say there are several."

"Where to begin?" said Joel.

"Coffee," I whispered.

"Arthur," said Edward.

"Yes, Arthur," said Pierre, saluting the glass set on the corner of Father's desk in honor of their absent comrade. It was full, of course, and would eventually be downed by them all before they departed. Such was the Tumblar tradition. "Herr von Derschmidt came across a delightful account in one of his books—"

"A particularly crumbly, moldy old book," added Jonathan.

"Not that shabby," said Joel, "but definitely used."

"—while we were all planning his trip to Rome," said Pierre.

"It's about the Church of the Virgin Mother of Good Counsel," said Edward, "built near Rome in the fourth century on the site of a shrine to Venus."

"Another example of Catholic triumphalism," said Pierre, "from a time when we used to triumph."

"We still do, Gentlemen," said Father.

"Of course," said Pierre, "we've just grown subtle about it."

"We hide it better now," said Joel. "Even we don't see it anymore."

"It's called humility," said Jonathan.

"And there ain't no humility without humiliation," said the Tumblars together, bowing to Father Baptist whom they were quoting.

"In any case," said Pierre, "come the fifteenth century, this ancient church had fallen into disrepair. A widow by the name of—now what was it?"

"Noteria," said Joel. "Petruccia Noteria."

"The very one," said Pierre. "Shows you the wiles of the old gray matter. Reginaldus Gonsalvius Montanus, I can remember. Petruccia Noteria—" He fluttered his fingers next to his forehead.

"It's the champagne," suggested Joel.

"Never," said Pierre, straightening to his full height. "Champagne is fuel for the brain. Anyway, spurred by a vision she received from Our Blessed Mother, the good woman risked the ire of her family and the townspeople when she committed all her money to its restoration. Their ridicule escalated when her funds ran out and the work was barely begun."

"The townspeople did not share her enthusiasm for the project," said Jonathan.

"Rumors spread," said Joel. "Stories that she was pretending to be another Saint Francis."

"Steadfast children of the Renaissance," said Edward. "You gotta love 'em."

"Meanwhile," said Pierre, "across the Adriatic Sea, the Turkish Army was invading Albania. Two devout men were praying in the capital city of Scutari before a fresco of the Virgin and Christ Child said to date back to the time of the Apostles. They knew the Moslems would desecrate their churches and massacre those who refused to convert to their stifling religion."

"Ah," said Edward, "our own investigative reporter is on the verge of using the word 'synergy.'"

"Perhaps," said Pierre, peering at Edward through his glass. "Then again, perhaps not."

"De Sclavis and Giorgio were their names," said Joel, then wistfully, "and Our Lady appeared to them and told them to prepare for a journey, that they were to follow the painting wherever it would go."

"I'll bet they were surprised," said Edward, "when the fresco miraculously detached itself from the wall, floated out the door, and proceeded toward the beach."

"Better still," said Jonathan, "when it continued right out over the water."

"I wonder if I would have the Faith and courage," said Joel, "to accompany a painting out to sea."

"Imagine walking on water," said Jonathan. "I mean, I can't imagine it. It's so sloppy and swishy—"

"Not to mention wet," said Pierre.

"That's what I mean," said Jonathan. "It's not solid, it's fluid, constantly moving, yet they walked upon it without losing their balance or getting tossed by the surge."

"We don't know if they got seasick," admitted Edward. "But they did accompany the painting all the way to Italy. But then it vanished from their sight."

"To appear fabulously," said Pierre, his voice grown lofty, "in the Church of the Virgin Mother of Good Counsel, where they caught up with it shortly thereafter."

"It's a fresco," said Joel, "paper thin, and it's floating inches from the wall to this day."

"As it has been for more than five centuries," said Pierre. "Many Popes have been devoted to Our Lady of Good Counsel. Pius IX made a pilgrimage there in 1864."

"I hope Arthur takes some pictures," said Joel.

Somehow this discussion reminded me of Cheryl Farnsworth's bloody tears on my shirtsleeves. I glanced at my cuffs, but saw no blood. It took me a moment to realize I had changed my shirt when

Father and I arrived home. Shows how tired I was. Ah, for some coffee. Just one, steaming, scalding cup of—

The phone rang.

Glancing at the time, Father snatched up the receiver before I could reach it. "Arthur!" he said without waiting to see who was on the line. He smiled at us all and made an "okay" sign with his thumb and fingers. "I knew you wouldn't miss a Knights' meeting, even when you're in Rome."

"Hurrah!" said the Tumblars, loud enough for their companion to hear them. They raised their glasses and cheered, "To Our Lady, Empress of All the Americas!"

A tiny voice hailed them from the other side of the world.

"Yes, we're all here," said Father. "What time is it there? Ouch. I admire your spunk."

To Pierre's questioning gesticulations Father replied, "Four thirty-two in the morning."

"Yikes," said Jonathan and Joel.

"My word," said Pierre.

"What did you say?" said Father loudly into the phone. "You'll have to speak up. What's that racket? Where are you?" He relayed the information to us: "The bar of the Hotel Flora on the Via Veneto."

"Is that good?" asked Joel.

"That's perfect," said Pierre. "To Arthur!"

"Arthur!" said the Tumblars, clinking their glasses.

"To coffee," said the gardener, struggling out of his favorite chair. "If you fellows will excuse me, I'm going to the kitchen." Before I left I pitched my voice toward the phone. "Ahoy, Sir Arthur! Enjoy it while you can!"

"So how is your 'sister' doing?" asked Father as I exited the room. "Resting peacefully, eh? Splendid, and how about Father Nicanor's uncle ...?"

I headed down the hall.

17

STRANGELY, AS I APPROACHED THE KITCHEN a new set of voices, feminine to be sure, interposed themselves upon the male blather behind me. First I thought it was a symptom of sleep deprivation, but it sounded so convincing. Then I thought that perhaps Millie had her transistor radio going, but the voices sounded full and present, not tiny and distant, and they lacked the electronic sizzle that Millie's radio imparted to pauses and fricatives. The voices grew louder as I approached. Finally, as I entered the cozy warmth and amber glow of the kitchen, I discovered an invasion of sorts—or at least something I had never encountered before at Saint Philomena's rectory.

"*'Do you not fear, I ask—'*" said Millie gruffly.

I almost said, "Who, me?" but then realized she was reading aloud from a book—a very old, stained, dilapidated book. She had a smoldering cigarette poised in her right hand, and a glass of red wine near her left. I have italicized her words in order to convey the high-voltage intensity of her delivery.

"*'—being such as you are,'*" she continued, "*'that when the day of Resurrection comes, your Maker may not recognize you, that He may set you aside when you come for His rewards and promises, and may exclude you and, reproving you with the severity of a censor and judge, may say: "This work is not mine nor is this our image."'*"

"What do you think he means by that?" asked Danielle Parks, our choir director, who was seated across from Millie, a glass of white wine in her hand.

"I hate to tell you this—" said Stella Billowack, daughter of Chief Montgomery "Bulldog" Billowack, the fellow in the wheelchair who had phlegmed up the mausoleum in the wee hours of the morning. Stella, who showed no signs so far of inheriting her papa's wobbling jowls, was Jonathan Clubb's sweetheart, and Jonathan was the guy who'd put his potential future father-in-law in the wheelchair. I had the feeling their situation was just going to get better and better, but in the immediate, Estelle finished her sentence, "—but I think he means us."

"Do you really think so?" asked Wanda Hemmingway, our first soprano with the endearing smile, striking fulcra, and the predilection for patchouli. She didn't seem very happy about what Millie was reading to them. None of them did.

"*'You have defiled your skin with lying cosmetics,'*" growled Millie after taking a long drag on her cigarette. She expelled the smoke through her mouth, punctuating her delivery with billowing gray bursts. "*'You have changed your hair with an adulterous color. Your face is overcome by falsehood; your appearance corrupted; your countenance is that of another.'*"

Danielle's hands shot up to her cheeks and Stella's to her hair. Wanda lifted her glass of rosé, thought better of it, and put it down again.

"*'You cannot see God,'*" frothed Millie, tapping the dry pages for additional emphasis, "*'since your eyes are not those which God has made, but which the devil has infected. Him you have followed; the red and painted eyes of the serpent have you imitated; adorned like your enemy, with him you shall likewise burn.'*" Millie seemed to take delight in prolonging the final five syllables. Suddenly she noticed me and snarled, "What do *you* want?"

"Coffee," I muttered, pointing to the pot on the stove. "Don't mind me."

"Do you think only *men* can read and drink and smoke?" dared Millie, glaring at me with defiant eyes.

"Heavens, no," I assured her. "You ladies go right ahead and carouse all you want."

Danielle was trying not to cover her face, Stella was attempting not to draw attention to her hair, and Wanda, who had been fidgeting with the chain around her neck, let it go and reached for a cigarette.

"Oh my," I said under my breath as I fumbled a cup from the cupboard shelf. "Oh me, oh my." Out of the corner of my eye I noticed Wanda and Stella shifting their fulcra every which way under the table. Danielle did likewise, but the effect was somewhat concealed by the jeans she was wearing.

"Just ignore *him,*" said Millie with a snort. Her knees were immovable. She sucked the life out of her cigarette, stamped out the butt in the ashtray, and continued. "*'Listen, therefore, virgins, as to a father; listen, I pray you, to one who is faithfully watching over your advantages and interests. Be such as God, the Creator, has made you; be such as the hand of the Father has fashioned you.'*"

I felt Millie's disciples' eyes boring into me as I poured murky stimulant into my cup with nervous hands. I got the distinct impression that somehow their discomfiture was *my* fault.

"*'Let your countenance remain uncorrupted,'*" read Millie, "*'your neck pure, your beauty genuine. Let no wounds be inflicted on your ears—'*"

Six hands shot up to fiddle uneasily with earrings.

"*'—nor let a costly chain of bracelets and necklaces confine your arms or your neck—'*"

A half dozen hands attempted to cover said accoutrements.

"*'—let your feet be free from golden fetters, your hair colored with no dye—'*"

The kitchen chairs creaked with every shift, wiggle, and surreptitious adjustment.

"*'—your eyes worthy to behold God.'*"

Hoo-boy, thought the gardener, tensing to make his escape. Hoooooo-boy!

"*'It is written: "All things are lawful, but all things do not edify."'*"

First Corinthians ten twenty-three, I thought to myself. I tried—oh, how I tried—not to glance at them as I lumbered toward the doorway; and how I wished I hadn't when I did. Yes, undeniably, incontrovertibly, and no doubt eternally, I was five thousand one hundred and ninety-nine percent to blame. All I had done was fetch myself a cup of coffee;

but all the while, by the Grace of God, I was irritatingly, gallingly, infuriatingly *male.*

"'*But if you adorn yourself too elaborately and appear conspicuous in public,*'" continued Millie, pretending not to notice my departure, "'*if you attract to yourself the eyes of the youth, draw after you the sighs of young men, foster the desire of concupiscence, enkindle the fire of hope, so that, without perhaps losing your own soul, you nevertheless ruin others and offer yourself a sword and poison, as it were, to those who behold you, you cannot be excused on the ground that your mind is chaste and pure.*'"

At last I was lurching down the hallway, Millie's resonant voice receding behind me:

"'*Your shameless apparel and your immodest attire belie you, and you can no longer be numbered among maidens and virgins of Christ, you who so live as to become the object of sensual love ...*'"

Much to my relief, a different kind of verbiage grew in volume as I approached Father's study:

"Jolly good timing," Pierre was saying.

"It will be good to have him back," said Edward.

"Yes," said Joel. "It's almost like we're not all here when he's not here."

"Brilliant observation," said Edward. "Irrefutable, inimitable, all the way to—"

"But nonetheless true," said Jonathan.

"Oh, drat," said Pierre. "I forgot to ask if he got to see Genazzano."

"Who?" I asked as I lumbered into their midst, "or should I ask what or where is Genazzano?"

The phone was resting in its cradle. The levels of champagne in the bottles and glasses had gone down appreciably during my brief absence. The smoke in the air seemed a bit thicker, too.

"That's the town where the fresco is still floating," said Joel.

"Oh," said I. "Our Lady of Good Counsel. I should like to see that some day."

"Hey, Martin," said Edward as I sank into my chair by the fireplace. "Is something going on in the kitchen?"

"Millie, Danielle, Wanda, and Stella," I said after a long sip of coffee. It tasted all the richer because it had been obtained at such a cost.

"Stella?" said Jonathan, brightening. "She's here?"

"Down, boy," said I. "They're proving that men aren't the only ones who can read, drink, and smoke at the same time."

Patronizing masculine chuckles chortled around the room.

"What're they reading?" asked Joel.

"Millie's doing the actual reading," said I. "Danielle, Wanda, and Stella are listening attentively."

"To what?" asked Pierre.

"Saint Cyprian," said I. *"Treatises."*

For a moment, a disturbing, glacial silence descended upon our manly gathering.

"Oh," said Jonathan, gulping audibly.

"'Oh' is right," said Pierre, patting Jonathan on the shoulder. "Dear Chap."

Millie's indistinct recitation reverberated ominously down the hallway.

"You're sure—?" asked Jonathan.

"'Fraid so," said I.

The silent curtain came down again and remained for close to a minute until Pierre shook himself, poured himself another fizzing libation, and changed the subject.

"When I travel to Europe some day, God willing," said he, "I hope to visit Seefeld."

"Along with a couple of hundred other places you've mentioned," said Jonathan, his tone and expression bordering on gloom.

"Is that where champagne was invented?" asked Edward.

"Hardly," said Pierre. "Don Pérignon, whose cause for canonization I wholeheartedly endorse, was the viticulteur and cellarmaster at the Abbey of Hautvillers. That's in France, my Friend: Gallia, the Cradle of the Church. I hope some day to pay homage there on my way to Seefeld, which is in Austria."

"Forgive me," said Edward, adding an inch of foam to his glass. "It's the bubbles, you see. They scramble my sense of geography."

"And you our designated driver," laughed Joel.

"Be that as it may," said Pierre, "in 1384 there lived a certain knight by the name of Oswald Milser. He was the guardian of Schlossberg Castle."

"So what heroic miracles were performed by Sir Oswald?" asked Jonathan, who was trying to appear interested but his apprehensive attention was obviously down the hall in the kitchen.

"Alas," said Pierre, "I regret to report that our man Milser was a sinfully arrogant man. One day he barged into the parish church with his soldiers during Mass and marched right up big as you please to the side of the altar. There he demanded that the priest give him the large Host used during the Consecration. The small ones distributed to the commoners were insufficient, in his augustly prideful opinion, for one such as he."

"Are you editorializing?" asked Edward. "Or did he grant an interview?"

"I'm reporting the facts as I remember reading them," said Pierre.

"The nerve," said Joel, thereby saying aloud what I would have probably inserted as a Gardening Tip when I got around to writing this part. "Any-sized host, or particle thereof, contains the entirety of the Body, Blood, Soul, and Divinity of Christ."

"Yes, well," said Pierre, adjusting his monocle, "such considerations neither impressed nor deterred our not-so-valiant knight. The priest, fearing for his life, placed the Host on Sir Oswald's insistent tongue, whereupon the stone floor gave way beneath Milser's feet. Terrified, the knight grabbed the edge of the altar."

"I can see how that would shake one up," said Jonathan.

"A wee bit," agreed Edward.

"So there was Sir Oswald," said Pierre, "hanging onto the altar for dear life. He gesticulated for the priest to remove the Host from his mouth."

"At least he had the good sense not to remove it with his own fingers," said Edward.

"The knight's grip was so intense that he actually left indentations in the altar," said Pierre. "They, as well as the depression in the floor, have been preserved to this day. So affected was he by the turn of events that he fled to a monastery where he confessed his sin, and died a holy death several years later. There's more to the story—"

"Too bad Cardinal Fulbright doesn't follow suit," interrupted the gardener, "instead of resorting to Bendlebrain, Cruiser and Wedge, the wizards of spin."

"While we, on the other hand," announced Pierre, checking his watch and taking up Arthur's honorary glass, "are the wizards of grins! Father, by your leave."

One by one they took the glass, toasted their absent comrade, and passed it on. Pierre, being leader and spokesman, enjoyed the first and last libation.

"Adjourning early this evening," noted Father.

"You look exhausted," said Pierre.

"And Sir Martin looks comatose," laughed Joel.

"I resemble that remark," said I, grateful for a warm cup in my hands. "Where are you fellows headed?"

"There's a new place that's come to our attention," said Edward. "Or rather, a very old place that we've only just learned about."

"No bar is worth going to unless it's older than we are," said Pierre.

"Combined," added Joel.

"Do tell," said Father. "As a policeman I used to know every hangout in town."

"We'll report all when next we see you," said Pierre. "And now, lads, we must be off!"

"Hurrah!" said they all. Well, all but Jonathan. As they pulled him along with them his eyes, as well as his heart, reached toward the kitchen.

18

I FOUND MYSELF SITTING ALONE in Father's study. The cozy fire was now a settling clump of smoldering coals. Echoes from opposite ends of the rectory were drifting in through the hallway door. The ladies were chatting in subdued tones as they washed their glasses and tidied up the kitchen. The lads were guffawing on the front porch, prolonging their good-byes, casually leaving a mess behind them. Overflowing ashtrays, empty fluted glasses and bottles balanced on precipitous edges, books left on chairs—yes, it was a mess worthy of the Knights Tumblar.

Just as I set my empty coffee cup beside Saint Anthony of Padua who, being a hand-carved statue, ignored it with practiced male thoughtlessness, the phone rang. No, not the rotary phone with its grating mechanical clang—the cell phone with its shrill, electronic, methodological bleat. It took me a couple of seconds to recognize the trilling sound for what it was, then to figure out where it was coming from—the middle drawer of Father's desk, as it turned out. I had to hobble around, yank the drawer open, and rummage through the assorted contents within.

"Hey, Feeney," said a deep voice once I figured out which button to press. SEND, of all things! "That you?"

"Last I looked," said I, easing myself into Father's chair. "Who's this?"

"Ah, c'mon. You remember your old pal, Some Guy. It's only been a couple o' days."

"About sixty-eight hours," I agreed. "How time flies."

"That it does, Li'l Buddy. That it does."

Yes, the last time I saw Some Guy was when he dropped Father and me off in the back parking lot just before zooming off in the longest of limousines. He worked for Roderick Roundhead, one of the richest men in the city, the very man who had befouled Morley Fulbright's precious Murkenmug with cigar ash—a little detail of which His Obliviousness was unaware. Furthermore, he was somehow connected with Ernie Corben, proprietor of "Ernie's 'World Famous' Hotdogs" on Figueroa. Father had once described Corben to me as, and I quote, "one of the most dangerous men I know—I don't believe he's ever committed murder, but he's connected with a lot of people who do." Father did Ernie's sister a favor once, and Ernie had reciprocated just three nights before. "Auld Lang Syne" comes to mind.

"So," I ventured, wishing my coffee cup full again. From the distant sounds in the kitchen I gathered the gals were letting themselves out the back door. Chances were that the percolator had been washed, dried, and put away. Sigh. "What can I do for you?"

"Just sit tight. Ernie and me will be visitin' you just as soon as them penguins stop joshin' on your front porch."

"You're watching the place?"

"Parked down the block."

"You and Ernie?"

"Yup."

"Swell."

"We'll drop by when the coast is clear."

"Can't wait," said I as the thing beeped in my ear. I guessed that meant the big, big man at the other end had hung up. I set the phone down on the blotter. Not wanting to be found obstructing Father's chair, I heaved myself onto my feet and trudged around to my own favorite seat. I barely remember sinking into it.

Somewhere, on the fringe of consciousness, I heard Millie snap off the lights at the kitchen end of the rectory. From the front I heard the doors of Edward's van slamming, final farewells as the motor rumbled to life and took off, and the deep thump of the front door closing. Floorboards creaked as footsteps approached from both directions and met at the door to the study.

"Father," said Millie.

"Ah, Millie," said Father. "I understand you girls had a meeting of your own. I trust it went well."

With great effort I raised my eyelids and nudged my eyeballs toward the doorway. Through strands of cold cigar smoke hanging in the air I beheld Millie, arms folded and lips tightened to a straight line, glaring at the carnage, the disgusting filth, the manly residue of the Knights' meeting.

"I quit," said she.

"I'm sorry to hear that," said Father. "See you at breakfast."

"Hrmph."

Father looked at me, and I at him, as Millie's footsteps pounded down the hall. He waited for the slam of her bedroom door before venturing into the masculine wake.

"Don't get too comfortable," said I, blinking dry flakes from my eyes. "The night's not over yet."

"Oh?" said he, picking up the cell phone from the desk. "Did Ernie call?"

"Some Guy. He and Ernie are parked down the block."

"The limo."

"You spotted it."

"Hard not to. It was a bit conspicuous in this neighborhood. I figured I'd hear from Ernie, but I didn't expect a personal appearance."

Large knuckles rapped on the front door.

"I'll get it," said Father.

"I'm glad," said I.

I heard Father's footfalls in the hall, the rusty squeak of the peek hole latch, the exchange of amenities as the door was pulled open, and the approach of multiple feet of various weights and strides. Father stood aside politely to allow Ernie Corben to enter first. The humongous shape of Some Guy paused just outside for nearly a minute, then in he came. Father followed and went casually but directly to his chair behind the desk.

Ernie was a wiry beanpole who stored every calorie in his overhanging gut, with a nose that looked like a gourd drooping on an overloaded vine, and eyes that reminded me of snail shells. He stood there in his jeans and long-sleeved denim shirt for a long moment, scratching his sagging belly with dirty fingernails. He looked from Father to me, then back to Father.

"You shook down one of my guys," he said. "I thought we was square."

"Even, yes," said Father. "Square, perhaps. I'm not sure."

Ernie's molluscoidal eyes shifted back to me and glowered. "This your ... *gardener*, Jack?"

"My one and only."

"Hah!" He clutched his tummy as though it might fall off and guffawed away. "Hah! Hah! Ho-ho! HAH!" His humor thus expressed, and after assuring himself that his gut hadn't slipped, he relaxed and wiped his greasy eyes. "You shoulda heard Edison wailin' on the phone. I thought maybe someone was hornin' in on my territory. But when he said it was a priest and some *gardener*, well, who else could it be?"

"Indeed," agreed Father. "Who else?"

"Hey, Martin," said Some Guy. Even though he towered over Ernie Corben, he seemed to peer around him to look at me. What am I saying? His knuckles almost scraped the ceiling as he pointed back over his shoulder. "You wasn't kiddin', were ya? I mean about that sign."

He was referring to the framed message Father had posted just outside his study door. It was a quotation from Saint John Eudes about the state of the Church today and the reason why. Funny, it had been penned in the seventeenth century. I had recited it by heart for Some Guy just the other night:

The most evident mark of God's anger, and the most terrible castigation He can inflict upon the world, is manifest when He permits His people to fall into the hands of a clergy who are more in name than in deed, priests who practice the cruelty of ravening wolves rather than the charity and affection of devoted shepherds. They abandon the things of God to devote themselves to the things of the world and, in their saintly calling of holiness, they spend their time in profane and worldly pursuits. When God permits such things, it is a very positive proof that He is thoroughly angry with His people, and is visiting His most dreadful wrath upon them.

"Say," Mr. Guy had said at the time, "I kinda like that."

"Good," had said I, sweating bullets.

"Hot stuff," he said in the present.

"If you only knew," said I, too weary to sweat this time around.

<u>GARDENING</u> <u>TIPS</u>: For some reason the significance of Saint John's last sentence seems to elude most people, especially Trads, but it was perfectly obvious to this . . . <u>gardener</u> (ominous emphasis, mine). The present chaos in the Church is 1) a punishment, 2) inflicted by Almighty God, 3) because He is furious at <u>us</u>. Yes, <u>US</u>! It's easy to blame the clergy and the hierarchy, but they are only fulfilling the role God has carved out for them, namely, to castigate us for our lack of Faith, lax living, and our abandonment of the Doctrines and Dogmas of the Catholic Religion.
   'Nuff said.

                         --M.F.

"If you two lovebirds is finished," said Ernie, "Father Jack and I got business to discuss."

"Why don't you take Mr. Guy to the kitchen?" said Father to me. "I think Millie made a pitcher of lemonade. It's probably in the fridge if the gals didn't finish it."

"How about some coffee?" I said, brightening. "I could put on a pot."

"Naw," said Some Guy. "I'm goin' home after this, an' I need my beeyooty sleep."

"I don't like repeatin' myself," said Ernie sternly.

"This way," said I, struggling to my tingling feet.

"What is it you're after?" Ernie asked Father as I lumbered past.

"A golden disk about so big," said Father. "I know the cardinal told Monsignor Aspic to have it appraised. He also wanted his favorite chalice cleaned, and I saw it in Mr. Winger's shop, so I know Monsignor Aspic had been there. I know you've got connections with Roderick Roundhead, whose interest in such things is well known to me, so it follows ..."

Their voices receded as I led my pet giant down the hall to the kitchen. Along the way I could feel the floorboards subsiding under his weight. Some Guy was one guy I wouldn't want to provoke to anger. I didn't want him to find me cuddly, either. A manly hug from him would be, without question, death by compression of one's entire skeletal assemblage.

"Nice place you got here," said Mister Guy. "The ceilin's could be higher."

"As could the water pressure," said I, lumbering to the refrigerator and yanking the door. "Nope, no lemonade. Wait a minute, the percolator's still on the stove."

"I don't need nuthin, Li'l Fella. I'm fine."

"Maybe you don't," said I, hefting the vessel to see if there was any left. Much to my surprise, there was. "I certainly do. Now where does Millie keep those matches?"

"Ain't your stove, whatchacallit, automatic? Don't it have a pilot light?"

"Around here, my humongous friend," said I, scrounging through the drawers nearest the stove, "modern technology has yet to make inroads. We're lucky to have hot and cold running water."

"HAR! HAR! HAR!" he boomed good-naturedly. It rattled the silverware in the drawer I had just pulled open. "Hey, is that a, um—? What's that called?"

I noted where the log he called a finger was pointing. It gave a whole new meaning to Saint Matthew seven three: "And why seest thou the mote that is in thy brother's eye; and seest not the beam that is in thy own eye?" All I can say is, what a beam!

"Me mudder had one just like that," he was reminiscing, a burst of sadness shifting the rolling landscape of his face.

"She had a telephone?" I asked as I found the matches in the bottom drawer under the dishrags. Stooping so low wasn't the problem. It was getting back up. Yikes. "Oh," I grunted, "you mean a rotary phone."

"Yeah," he said, waxing maudlin. His cheeks swelled and his eyes glistened. "I had trouble learnin' how to use it when I was liddle because my fingers wouldn't fit in the holes—except my pinkie, but I kept breaking the dial off. Mumma got so mad." He rubbed his forehead thoughtfully, as if that's where she whacked him with a pickaxe. She must have been one brave woman.

"Those little buttons on cell phones," said I, striking a match against the side of the coffeepot and cranking the gas. "They must be murder."

"Ah, Mr. Roundhead had one made special just for me." He reached into the pouch he called a coat pocket and produced a custom communicator about the size of a cigar box. The buttons were the size of silver dollars. In fact, I think they were silver dollars.

"Wow," said I, tossing the spent match into the flowerpot on the windowsill. I wasn't being thoughtlessly masculine. That's where Millie threw all her matches. She said the burnt part was good for her prickly cactus plant. I wasn't one to argue. "That was darn nice of him."

"Mr. Roundhead is okay. He's double okay."

"How did you two link up?"

"My fadder used to work for his fadder."

"Your father was his father's chauffeur?"

"Naw, his accountant. Dad wasn't, you know, like me. As soon as I was old enuff to drive, Grampa Roundhead had a car made just for me. You know, the pedals far enough away so I didn't bend them. The roof higher, the knobs bigger."

"Grampa?"

"That's what I called him. The Roundheads are good people."

"Loyalty, I'll grant you, is rare these days." I tried to imagine a steering wheel built tough enough to withstand Mister Guy's grip without buckling in traffic.

"You said it," said he.

"You sure you wouldn't like some of this?"

"Nope. I'm okay. Thanks."

It didn't take long for the sludge in the pot to start burbling. I questioned my judgment when I poured some into a cup. It looked like the stuff they use to resurface streets. The fumes alone were blistering the paint on the ceiling.

"You're going to drink that?" asked Some Guy.

"I've had worse." I took a tentative sip. I think my blood pressure doubled before I even swallowed. I looked at him, then at the chairs around the tiny table in the dining nook. "I'd offer you a seat, but I doubt anything here would hold you."

"That's okay," he said, smiling appreciatively. "You go ahead. You look tired."

"I'm beyond tired. I'd better stand. If I sit down you'll be talking to yourself in no time."

"You're funny, Martin. I think that's why I like you."

Ah, shucks, thought I.

As I took a second sip, something seemed to be going on behind his eyeballs, back in the brain section. His smile widened and he took a step closer. If he hadn't been so huge and potentially dangerous, I would describe his expression as "childlike eagerness" or "ingenuous enthusiasm." I was frankly touched. Apprehensive, but touched. I reminded myself that he had come here in the questionable company of Ernie Corben.

"Martin," he whispered, glancing back over his shoulder to make sure no one overheard. "Would you put me in one of your stories?"

"Excuse me?"

"You know, your books."

"How do you know about that?" I asked, taken completely aback.

He held his beam up to his lips and shushed me. The blast of wind practically knocked me back against the stove. "I'm not supposed to," he hissed. "I overheard."

"Overheard who?"

"Mr. Roundhead."

"You mean Grampa?"

"No, he died when I was fifteen. I mean Mr. Roundhead."

"Roderick? Who was he talking to?"

"His aunt." Endearingly, he pronounced it like "on" with a "t."

"I didn't know he had an aunt," said I, pronouncing it to rhyme with the insect.

"Well, he does," said he.

"And what were they saying about my book? How would they even know about it? It hasn't been published."

There was a spurt of mental commotion behind those eyes. His face registered puzzlement, concern, realization, and then apprehension. "Maybe I'm not s'posed to know. Maybe I shouldn't be tellin' you. I just thought, if you ever write about the other night—you know, when you and Father, and I, you know—you'll include me, won't you?"

"If you mean the trip in the limousine, you were an integral part of the story line. As far as writing about it, I have certainly thought about it. I'm in the middle of another story that took place a few weeks ago, but hope to get to the other night eventually. To answer your question, of course I'll include you. But I'd still like to know—"

"You change everyone's name, right?"

"How do you know that?"

"It's in the introduction or something. I haven't read it. I just—"

"Heard them talking about it."

"That's right."

This was all too strange, but hey, when opportunity knocks. This discussion paved the way for me to ask about something that had been gnawing at me. "Tell me something: where did you get a name like 'Some Guy'?"

"Hah!" laughed the giant. The cups rattled in the cupboard. "My real name is hard to say. Back in school the teachers didn't like me because they always botched my name the first day so I had to correct them."

"Might I ask what it is?"

He looked around the kitchen, for what I don't know. "Just because we're pals," he said with a flap of his eyelids. They came down and up like an automatic garage door. "My real name is Slurth Zabzdyr." It sounded like a complicated belch, but then he spelled it out for me. No wonder his teachers had resented him. Not only was he taller than they even when he was seated—imagine what his bulk, even then, must have done to an average classroom desk with attached chair—but a name with five unrelated consonants in a row. Wow.

"Don't use it in your book," he said, scowling slightly. "I wouldn't like that, and needer would Mr. Roundhead." Then his face became grossly cherubic again. "I'm just tellin' you 'cause we're friends."

"I appreciate that, um, Some. I really do."

His smile widened at my avoidance of his real name. "Me, too, Li'l Buddy. So, just remember, as far as you're concerned, my name is—"

"Some Guy! Hey!" Ernie Corben's summons reverberated down the hallway. "Where are you?"

"Be sure you get it right," said the chauffeur, patting me with his paw. I think he dislocated my shoulder in the process. "S-o-m-e—G-u-y. Gottit?"

"Hey, no problem. Of course you realize in keeping with my established policy, I would have to change that to something else."

"Something else? Like what?"

"Well, I'd have to give it some thought. Maybe something along the lines of—"

"Hey!" shouted Ernie. "Time to go!"

"Be seein' ya," said Mister Guy with a wink. Then he huffed over his shoulder, "Comin', Ernie!"

As his house-rattling footsteps pounded down the hallway, I poured the rest of my coffee down the sink. Something sizzled down in the drainpipe. The thought of sleep became overwhelming.

I wondered, as I made my weary, blurry way outside and headed for my quarters, if my last thought for the day after my muddled examination of conscience as I hit the pillow would be the rivulets of blood pouring from Cheryl Farnsworth's eyes.

It was.

Friday, November Seventeenth

**Feast Day of Saint Hugh of Lincoln,
a Carthusian monk whose coffin was
carried to his grave by kings and nobles,
so great was his holiness (1200)**

∞ Day of Abstinence ∞

19

"FATHER BAPTIST," I whispered as I opened my door. It was five past two in the morning. "What are you doing up? Is there something wrong?"

"Not really," said he, likewise subdued. "May I come in?"

"Of course. Here, let me move those books so you can sit down."

"No need. I'll just be a minute. I saw your light and heard you typing. I was surprised to find you up, considering how exhausted you looked during the Knights' meeting."

"I shouldn't't've had that coffee. I slept for an hour and a half, and then—bing!—I was wide awake. It's okay. You know me. If the coffee doesn't keep me up in the wee hours, my arthritis will. And now this weird tingling in my feet. Not a problem. It's when I get my writing done. No interruptions."

"Until now."

"You know what I mean. Some artists do their best work late at night, or in the heat of the afternoon. What I do may not be art, but whatever it is, my creative zenith is between two and five in the morning."

"I do understand. It's an inexplicable, tantalizing time, and I truly am sorry to intrude, but you left without saying anything about your conversation with Some Guy in the kitchen."

"I barely remember it. There was something he said I wanted to mention to you, but I can't seem to dredge it up now. It'll come back. Did you learn anything from Ernie Corben?"

"Pretty much what I expected."

"Which was?"

"That he resented me intimidating one of his underlings, and he'll have to get permission from higher up his food chain to tell me more."

He glanced around my room, taking in my dark little world. There was my bed, nightstand, dresser, bookcases, and cozy armchair. The only illumination came from the nightlight in the bathroom and the lamp next to the typewriter on the roll-top desk. Like the masterful detective that he was, Father was drawn to the stack of typewritten pages next to Dad's old Underwood.

"Working on your next masterpiece, I see."

"Erg," I mumbled, my face flushing. "Well, that is ..."

"Could I ask you something?"

"Surely."

"Why do you place your stories in Los Angeles? There, if you don't mind my saying, goes your credibility—right out the window."

"I don't know. I guess I've always liked the name: 'El Pueblo de Nuestra Señora Reina de los Angeles de Porciuncula.' My pronunciation is deplorable, but I still like the way it rolls off the tongue. What other city's moniker includes Our Blessed Mother, the Angels, and the Crucifix that spoke to Saint Francis of Assisi?"

"You may have a point there."

"Besides, no one would believe it all really happened *here.*"

"Well, there is that."

All the while he'd been eyeing the pages beside the typewriter. Now he ratcheted up the sheet that was still in the carriage and examined it carefully. Oh, the embarrassment.

"Martin."

"Father."

"Is there some reason you happen to be working on the events of Friday, October twenty-seventh?"

"David Smoley said that things went sour between himself and Monsignor Aspic that day. I had already written that part, but it needed a rewrite. Why?"

"Because it occurred to me to ask if you'd gotten that far in your story." He peeled several pages off the top of the pile, cradled them in his hands, and looked at them one by one. "You are my chronicler, as you've so often said. I want to see how well you're doing your job."

"Be my guest, Father." I snatched up the books that I'd offered to move before and set them on the bed.

"Thank-you." He eased himself into the armchair and clicked on the reading light. He rested the pages on his lap and moved his lips as he read. I knew every word by heart, so it was easy to follow where he was.

"Please be seated," said Father to Conrad Jonas
Aspic.

"Sure," said the monsignor, settling into my favorite chair's twin. He didn't acknowledge my
presence, and I returned the compliment. "But I'm
afraid I haven't given the matter of your bill a
thought in days."

"Neither have I," said Father Baptist. "I have
asked you to come because there is something I
want you to do for me."

"What could I possibly do for you?"

"I would like you to perform a priestly function."

"What's that?"

"A priestly function?" asked Father.

"No," scowled Aspic. "I mean: what's the
priestly function you want me to perform?"

Father made his fingers into a steeple. "I want
you to pay a visit to Mr. Thurgood T. Turnbuckle."

"What?"

"I took the liberty of having Sybil Wexler make
an appointment for you to see him and his son,
Biltmore, at their home at eleven-thirty."

"Who's Sybil Wexler?"

"A voice Mr. Turnbuckle wouldn't recognize."

"And why do you want me to go there?"

"Well," said Father, "I could say it's because
Thurgood and Biltmore could use some attention
right now, spiritual guidance, that sort of thing,
but after some of what you've said to me recently,
you're hardly the man for that job."

"I didn't come here to be insulted," said Aspic.

"That wasn't intended as an insult," said Father. "It was a simple statement of fact. For a
priest who doesn't believe in the Resurrection--"

"I was being philosophical," snapped the monsignor.

"One of the great problems of our day," countered Father, "has been the divorce of philosophy
from metaphysics, and theology from sanctity--but
that discussion will have to wait for another
time."

"Insufferable," said Aspic.

"Yes it is," said Father.

"So what do you want me to do?"

```
     Father's finger steeple collapsed.  "I want you
to make sure that Mr. Turnbuckle and his son stay
at their home until, say, two o'clock."
     "What the devil for?"
     "'What the devil' is right.  I simply have to be
sure where they are, that's all."
     "Why?"
     "That I can't tell you.  Not now, anyway.  It is
better that you don't know."
     The monsignor scowled at the last bit.  "And how
am I supposed to keep them there?"
     "Heavens," said Father, "you ask that?  Talking
is your business, Monsignor.  Cajoling, winking,
nudging, tasting expensive wines, sampling the
private chef's favorite dishes, even begging for
donations for some fund no one's ever heard of--
these should come easy for a man of your talents."
     "And what if they have other plans?"
     "See that they don't."
     "And what if they leave anyway?"
     "You won't let that happen."
     "Why not?"
     "Because, my dear Monsignor ..."
```

"You used the word 'scowled' twice within this section," said Father, examining the pages closely. "You told me you try to use different verbs if possible. You might substitute 'frowned' for one of them."

"It's a rough draft," said I. "Thanks for the input. How's my job performance?"

"As a gardener? Questionable."

"No, as a chronicler."

"I would say excellent. Do I really make steeples with my fingers?"

"Sometimes. Yes, just like that."

He randomized his fingers with a snap of his wrists, then shuffled the typewritten sheets back into alignment. "Friday, October twenty-seventh. Was that the day we took care of the gruesome business in our cemetery?"

"Yes," said I, accepting the pages from him and returning them to the pile on the desk. "It was wise of you to make sure that Mr. Turnbuckle didn't happen upon what we had to do."

"To be sure. But somehow, sending Monsignor Aspic on that errand brought about his alienation from David Smoley. Or so it seems."

"Any ideas how that might have happened?"

"Not a clue. However, we'll be paying a visit to 456 Cuthbert Drive later today. Perhaps we'll find out." With the kind of painful slowness usually exhibited by me, he worked his way out of the chair and got to his feet. "I think I need to spend a little time in the church."

"Perhaps I'll join you in a few minutes."

"That would be fine. I was just thinking that I told Millie I'd see her at breakfast, but the secretary at Bendlebrain, Cruiser & Wedge relayed Cardinal Fulbright's summons to meet him in Malibu. In addition, I haven't said Mass in days. Would you—?"

"Serve as altar boy? I'd love to. I've been missing it as well."

"Good. I'm going to be reciting my Breviary. Come join me in a half-hour or so."

"Great."

"If only you knew."

With that he let himself out of my little world. I spent a little time rearranging the clutter. Before I left I ratcheted the page I'd been working on back down the carriage.

20

SAINT PHILOMENA'S CHURCH is one of the most satisfying places I know. By that I mean it reflects a time when Catholics actually believed and applied the Doctrines and Dogmas of the Faith to their daily lives, when the Mass of the Latin Rite was celebrated all over the world in one tongue with the same meticulous reverence, when Heaven was the hope of the steadfast instead of a presupposition of the riffraff, and when Saints were venerated instead of dismissed like distant relatives who didn't leave any cash when they croaked.

Around the nave—the section where the congregation sits—the builders of this beautiful stone church incorporated alcoves and side altars, recesses, all sorts of nooks where the statues of Saints could be venerated, where candles could extend prayers, where sinners could seek out the consolation of those who had gone before and achieved Eternal Life. Saint Jude, the Patron of Things Despaired Of, resided in a side chapel across from Saint Rita, the Patroness of the Impossible. They were perhaps the busiest of the bunch. Good Saint Anne, Mother of She Who is Our Life, Our Sweetness, and Our Hope, stood proudly in her niche, her hands resting maternally on the shoulders of the Virgin Mary as a little girl. Saint Scholastica and her brother, Saint Benedict, smiled down from adjacent archways near the vestibule. Saint Mary Magdalene, the greatest of penitents, waited beside the Epistle-side confessional, ready to help those with guilty consciences, while Saint John Marie Vianney prayed for the priests on the Gospel side, aiding them in the mystery and miracle of Absolution.   All in all, it was a wonderful place to think, to pray, to meditate, to just plain be.

The place had its architectural curiosities. Most notable was a grotto near the front of the nave on the Epistle side. Tucked behind a pillar and curving around out of sight behind the side altar dedicated to Our Mother of Sorrows, it was not readily visible to the casual visitor, yet having discovered it, said observer couldn't help but realize that it threw off the symmetry of the building. The walls and ceiling of the grotto were constructed of rough, unfinished granite stones set in thick, chalky mortar — a stylistic departure from the rest of the church. There was no rack for votive candles within, though some parishioners left five-day candles in glass jars on the irregular floor before the four-foot statue that was set atop a large, gray boulder. The conical shape of the boulder suggested that most of it was buried beneath the stone floor, that it was here first, and this part of the church was built around it. The figure itself was cast in dark metal, executed with angry coarseness. Yet the face conveyed a sense of power, serenity, and confidence. Though the statue's origin was a mystery, Father and I and everyone had always assumed it to be a representation of Jesus Christ. The wounds in the hands and feet were a dead giveaway, unless it was supposed to be a stigmatist like Saint Francis, but he wasn't wearing a habit. No, it was definitely Jesus, but the Son of God as we'd never seen Him depicted elsewhere. Whenever I looked upon that commanding yet composed countenance, I was reminded of the incident at the end of the fourth chapter of the Gospel of Saint Mark. Our Lord was sleeping in the boat when a fierce storm arose. His disciples, fearing for their lives, awakened Him saying:

> Master, doth it not concern thee that we perish?
> And rising up, he rebuked the wind, and said to the sea: Peace, be still. And the wind ceased: and there was made a great calm.
> And he said to them: Why are you fearful? Have you not faith yet?
> And they feared exceedingly: and they said one to another: Who is this (thinkest thou) that both wind and sea obey him?

It was here in this curious cavern that I found Father Baptist, having looked for him everywhere else in the church.

"Ah, Martin," he whispered.

"Father, " I mumbled back.

"I needed strength, so I sought it here."

"I was looking for you, and here you aahhhHH!" Talk about fearing exceedingly (thinkest thou). The floor was made of erratically shaped flat stones. The one upon which I had just shifted my weight and forward momentum seesawed under my foot. I was no stranger to this hideaway. I often came in here to enjoy the gloom, conceal myself within the quiet, to ponder the chasms in my makeup. That rock had never shifted in its cozy mortar bed before that moment. With a back like mine, in which every vertebra is arguing with every other, an unexpected shift like that not only hurts—an understatement—but can instigate a skeletal squabble that will go on all day. If today was going to be as long as yesterday—groan! "Pardon me, Father. I was thrown off balance."

"How so?" He reached out and steadied me.

"That stone shifted under my weight."

"Which one?" It was hard to see, the only source of light being the flames bobbing in the tinted candle jars. Tapping around with his right foot, he quickly discovered the culprit. But then he found another, and another. "Hm, strange." Crouching, he surveyed the uneven topography. "Martin, I think the floor is subsiding."

"That's odd."

"There are no records, unfortunately, but I suspect this archway, wall, and floor were part of an earlier structure."

"I thought this building replaced a wooden chapel."

"Yes, but the chapel was built on the site of a shrine. You can see the difference in the masonry here, the size and shape of the stones, the chunky mortar."

"Reminiscent of the fireplace in your study, don't you think?"

"You may be right, my Friend. Perhaps the rectory, too, was built over a previous edifice. Or maybe the fireplace was built out of stones that were originally part of this structure. In any case, I'm concerned about this floor, this many stones suddenly coming loose. I'll ask Roberto Guadalupe to check it out. He's been talking about repairing some of the cracks in the walls of the nave."

"Not everyone is as klutzy as I am, but an older person with weak ankles or poor balance could hurt themselves in here."

"There's some masking tape in the sacristy. I'll stretch some across the entrance."

"Just like a crime scene."

"This place has a history. Who's to say the story is pleasant, the characters benign? Maybe this is fortuitous."

"An opportunity to learn more about what we have here, you mean."

"Well, Martin, surely there is that. Perhaps we'll find some clue about the origin of this statue while we're at it."

I looked up at the roughly cast face. "Talk about mysteries."

"I'm reminded of Saint Candidus."

"That rings a bell. Oh yes, you mentioned him to Sybil Wexler when she was nosing around here with Lieutenant Holcomb last Saturday. Something about his relics being in our altar."

"Surely you know of him."

"Um, I must have fallen asleep during that sermon."

"Not a sermon. A curious bit of Los Angeles history. Not being 'one of the gang' when I was a preparing for the priesthood, I spent many an evening behind the seminary library—which is to say, meeting the Saints through their own words."

"Did you say behind the library?"

"Father Carver, the librarian, was in the process of purging the shelves of some of the more traditional books. Discarded volumes I salvaged from the dumpster formed the nucleus of my own personal library."

"Come to think of it, I've noticed the seminary stamp on the inside cover of some of the books in your study."

"In any case, Saint Candidus was the second in command in the Theban Legion under Saint Maurice."

"Hang on. Saint Maurice." I rubbed my forehead, coaxing information out of the ol' resistant gray matter. "He lived in the third century, right? The Roman Emperor at the time was Maximillian—"

"Maximian."

"That's right. Maximian wanted to squash a rebellion in what is now France. He ordered all his troops to sacrifice to the gods for success. There was a problem, however. The Theban Legion was composed of recruits from Egypt, and they were all Catholics. Hard to imagine Egypt as a Catholic country, but those were the days. As good soldiers, they were ready and willing to obey their emperor in all things military, but they weren't about to renounce their Faith for him. The end result was that all six thousand plus were martyred. If I remember correctly, their relics are to be found in altars throughout Switzerland where the massacre took place."

"Very good, Martin. You have been reading the *Roman Martyrology.*"

"The old, unrevised version. I'm glad some of it is sticking."

"Those were the days indeed. There was a time when Saint Maurice was almost as popular as Saint George among military men."

"So Saint Candidus served under him?"

"That's right. It was Saint Candidus who spoke eloquently in defiance of the emperor's order. After the slaughter, his relics were placed in a wax figure of a Roman soldier. Eventually the statue made its way to Rome where it was venerated for centuries."

"I thought you said this was a bit of Los Angeles history."

"It gets there. A few years before Pope Pius IX sent the body of Saint Valeria to California he presented the statue to Thaddeus Amat, Bishop of Los Angeles. The bishop in turn bestowed it to the Lazarists who were running Saint Vincent's College at the time."

"Isn't that where the Saint Vincent Jewelry Merchants Building stands today?"

"Very good again, Martin."

"Oh? That was about as lame a guess as I've ever tossed off."

"I repeat. Bishop Amat had a bone taken from the waxen reliquary divided into tiny fragments. Something like ninety percent of the altar stones in the diocese contained one of those chips."

"Unfortunately, most churches don't even have altar stones anymore."

"Sad but true. In 1887, the statue was moved to the new Saint Vincent's Church, which was run by the same order. In 1925 it was moved again to a new church of the same name, which is arguably one of the most beautiful in the archdiocese."

"Not counting Saint Philomena's."

"Fair enough."

"Father, how can you possibly remember all these details?"

"I refreshed my memory while I was in the public library yesterday. As it turned out, the authentication papers were thrown out with old baptismal records, and the reliquary stood in the sacristy for years, its significance completely forgotten. Then, in 1991, the truth came to light—I'm not clear just how—and the statue was moved to Serra Chapel at the San Fernando Mission. If we get the chance we'll drop by and pray to Saint Candidus for help in our current campaign."

"Okay, so that explains our altar stone," said I. "Are you saying there's a connection between Saint Candidus and our grotto?"

"Not directly. A precedent, perhaps. Many such relics and holy objects, once famous and widely venerated, have been misplaced, lost and ignored over time. Some are slowly forgotten in plain sight. I have a hunch that this statue in our grotto is significant, but I can't guess how."

"Could it be a reliquary?"

"If we are meant to know, we'll find out. In the immediate, I'm going to get this place taped off until Roberto and his men can look it over."

"Or rather, under."

"Then, thanks be to God, I'm going to celebrate Mass."

And so he did, Martin Feeney assisting. As the Consecration of the Bread approached, I was reminded of a passage from the *Imitation of Christ* by Thomas à Kempis:

Trusting in Your great goodness and mercy, Lord, I come as one sick to the Physician, as one thirsty to the Fountain of Life, as one in need to the King of Heaven; I come as a servant to my Master, as a creature to my Creator, as a dejected soul to my loving Comforter.

But why should You come to me? Who am I that You should give Yourself to me? How can a sinner dare to show his face in Your presence? And why do You condescend to visit a sinner? You know Your servant; You know he has no good in him, and, therefore, You have no reason to grant him this great Grace. Thus I confess my unworthiness; and I acknowledge Your goodness. I praise Your mercy, and I give thanks for Your boundless love.

I got so involved in my thoughts I almost forgot to ring the bells during the Elevation. Fortunately I did not fail. It was good that we started the day thus.

A couple of curious footnotes regarding that Mass deserve mention, as they connect to later events in this story. The first involved something that happened during the Fracture, that is, when Father broke the Consecrated Host into three pieces, then dropped the smallest particle into the Chalice of Consecrated Wine while saying the words:

Hæc commixtio et consecratio Corporis et Sanguinis Domini nostri Jesu Christi, fiat accipientibus nobis in vitam æternam. Amen.

That is:

May this mingling and hallowing of the Body and Blood of our Lord Jesus Christ avail us that receive it unto life everlasting. Amen.

As Father whispered these words, I felt a peculiar burning sensation in my left hip. I thought for a moment that perhaps a book of matches had somehow ignited in my pants pocket. This didn't make sense since I don't carry matches. I couldn't get to my pocket through the cassock and surplice I was wearing at the time. I resisted the impulse to swat myself, and fortunately the searing heat subsided during the *Agnus Dei* and was all but gone by the *Domine non sum dignus*.

GARDENING TIPS: The Agnus Dei, for those who only
know it as a cha-cha song in the Novus Ordo, is a
thrice intoned appeal to Jesus as Sacrificial Victim that was inserted into the Latin Mass by Pope
Sergius in the seventh century. "Lamb of God, who
takest away the sins of the world, have mercy on
us." For the third utterance the last phrase
changes to "grant us peace."
    The Domine non sum dignus, which immediately
precedes the reception of Holy Communion, is a
poignant rephrasing of the words of the centurion
in the eighth chapter of Saint Matthew's Gospel:
"Lord, I am not worthy that Thou shouldst enter
under my roof; but only say the word, and my soul
will be healed."

                                          --M.F.

Afterward, as Father divested himself in the sacristy, I changed
quickly and checked my pocket. The only thing in it was a bundle
wrapped in black cloth, the gift given to me by Bishop Xandaronolopolis the night he returned to Lebanon. Reverently, I unfolded the velvety
material until there emerged a small round golden case with a tiny viewing window. Mounted in the center of a circle of red satin was a tiny,
insignificant wooden splinter. Along with the reliquary was a folded
piece of parchment, the certificate of authentication. Neither showed
any ill effects from the momentary rise in temperature, if indeed that
hadn't been a figment of my imagination.

So, I thought to myself as I rewrapped the precious bundle, maybe
I'm doing the right thing keeping these together. Heaven forbid, if I
should ever lose this chip from the Crown of Thorns, at least the finder
will know what he has in his hands ... providing, of course, he understands Latin.

Dennis Goodman, the owner of a local pawnshop, had graciously
given me a larger, more elegant reliquary for this incredible memento of
Christ's Passion a few days before. It was sitting on the nightstand in
my room. Perhaps, I told myself, I should leave Bishop Xandaronolopolis' more-than-generous gift there. "Later," I said aloud. I so
liked carrying it in my pocket, a constant reminder of God's unwavering
love for weak, wretched sinners like me. "Maybe later."

Then, just before leaving the church, I decided to go back to the
grotto with a five-day candle of my own. As I traversed the nave, I
happened to notice a dark shape halfway down the center aisle. It was
huddled close to the floor, and I thought I glimpsed silver buttons on a
dark coat. It took me a moment to realize that it was a Hispanic man,

hat in hands and lips forming silent prayers, making his way slowly up the center of the nave on his knees.

I said a Hail Mary for him as I dipped my fingers in the holy water font as I exited the side door.

21

OUR LADY OF THE WAVES may strike some as a peculiarly "So L.A.!" name for a church. The Blessed Mother's association with ocean waves, however, is not unique to the West Coast, not by a long shot. In Ecclesiasticus twenty-four eight we read: "I alone have compassed the circuit of Heaven, and have penetrated into the bottom of the deep, and have walked in the waves of the sea ..."

GARDENING TIPS: Saints have attributed these words to the Blessed Virgin Mary, as prefigured in the Mind of the Holy Ghost, written down two centuries before the Birth of Her Son (and, of course, Ecclesiasticus was one of the books of the Bible rejected by Martin Luther, so you know it has to be good). St. Bernadine of Siena believed that the "waves" in this passage represent the fires of Purgatory:

* * *

The pains of purgatory are called waves, because they are transitory, unlike the pains of hell, which never end; and they are called waves of the sea, because they are so bitter. The clients of Mary, thus suffering, are often visited and relieved by her.

* * *

This was quoted by St. Alphonsus di Liguori in his book, The Glories of Mary. St. Alphonsus further wrote:

* * *

Fortunate, indeed, are the clients of this most compassionate Mother; for not only does she succor them in this world,

```
but even in purgatory they are helped and
comforted by her protection.  And as in
that prison souls are in the greatest need
of assistance, since in their torments they
cannot help themselves, our Mother of mercy
does proportionately more to relieve them.
                   *  *  *


    Having, as I do, a number of relatives and
friends whom I hope got as far as Purgatory -- and
indeed one friend named Elza who definitely made
it -- and mindful that I myself pray daily that I
will join them, I take great consolation in the
words of Ecclesiasticus and try fervently to be
the Blessed Virgin's good servant.
                                   --M.F.
```

All that being said, I'm sorry to report that Our Lady of the Waves in Malibu was, in fact, "So L.A.!" it made me nauseous. No artistic or structural reference to the Holy Souls in Purgatory was evident. Built on a superb location, a hill overlooking the beach, buffeted by the sea breeze and designed with the wealthy surfing community in mind, it was one of those hideous "worship spaces" that integrated the elusive Spirit of Vatican II with some contrived form of nature veneration. The main edifice looked like a set left over from some campy caveman movie—roughly hewn slabs of sedimentary rock leaning against each other at catastrophic angles. Benches along the paths outside were hewn of the same type of stone. The grounds were indistinguishable from a seafront resort: mounds of sand, waving grass, swaying palms, at least three luau barbecue pits, and a noisy waterfall forever emptying into a wading lagoon that apparently doubled as a Baptismal font.

We found His Impatience, Cardinal Fulbright, pacing near the deep end. The look of the casual beachcomber was not upon him. The pallor of his face matched the crimson of his royal gown. He did not look pleased to see us.

"Well?" he grumbled angrily.

"Your Eminence?" asked Father Baptist. He bowed to kiss the cardinal's sapphire ring but Morley yanked his hand away.

I enjoyed a brief moment of relief. Imagine, the second time in as many days, unt no kizzing der ringer finger. It doesn't get better than this in one of my tales. Something unspeakable and horrible just had to be lurking around the next turn, poised and furious, raring for me to roll a seven. Well, don't ask me why, but I was feeling lucky, and I don't even believe in luck.

```
    GARDENING TIPS: I really, really detest the ring
thing, not in concept, but in immediate applica-
tion.  I've met the cardinal's staff, I've encoun-
tered many of his priests, and I've seen pictures
of him in the papers schmoozing with the darlings
of Hollywood and the mechanics at City Hall.  I
know how much His Inconsistence relishes the gleam
of saliva on his precious sapphire.  Considering
where it's been, and to whom it's attached, I'd
rather not kiss the damn thing, thank-you very
much.

                                        --M.F.
```

Despite this glitch on the cardinal's behavioral graph, he did look more himself in some other respects. He seemed less agitated, but more angry; less nervous, but a lot more furious. The reason became instantly obvious as he barked, "Bawntemps!" (That's how he pronounced it, so that's how I'll spell it.)

"Your Eminence?"

"Bawntemps! A friend of yours."

"Are you referring to Pierre Bontemps?" asked Father. (That's not how it sounds, but that's how it's spelled.)

"What do you think?" rumbled Fulbright. "I've been aware of his sanctimonious diatribes for some time. But this beats all. Because of him, I don't dare go anywhere near—" He caught himself and looked around suspiciously.

"Your Eminence?" said Father innocently.

"The nuncio reads the papers." The cardinal stamped and snorted like a peeved rhinoceros. "Now he knows my favorite—" He took a deep breath and held it.

"Let us p'ay," murmured the gardener, feigning interest in a nearby volleyball net. He almost sneezed "Fettuccini!" but controlled himself.

Father glanced at me and shrugged. "I hardly see how—"

"He's ruined everything," said the cardinal.

"If Your Eminence would be more specific."

"You know precisely what I mean, Father."

"I wouldn't presume—"

"Don't be evasive. You want specific? Here it is: get him off my back."

"Because he wrote a favorable review about your favorite restaurant?"

"You know then."

"I ate there myself only yesterday because of his recommendation."

"He's a pest, a meddlesome one. He's one of yours, and I don't appreciate him publishing his nefarious opinions."

"About restaurants?"

The cardinal nodded furiously, then shook his head equally so. His jowls flopped menacingly. "Don't be circuitous. You know what I mean."

"Your Eminence," said Father, "I assure you, Pierre Bontemps is as staunch in his convictions as any man I've met. I know from experience he's not going to be swayed from any course he chooses to take, certainly not by me, not if he believes he's in the right."

"I suggest that you try."

"I'll do what I can, but I make no promises."

"I will if we have to repeat this conversation."

"Excuse me, Your Eminence, but I don't appreciate threats."

"Then don't precipitate them. As to other matters, what about the artifact?"

Father Baptist took a moment to compose himself, then he said, "We have been tracing Monsignor Aspic's movements. So far, I've nothing substantial to report."

"Nothing substantial. What am I supposed to tell Sylvio Bonsignore?"

"Why, the truth of course."

"You're serious."

"Truth has the advantage of verity. Once stated, it cannot be shown to be false."

"Once stated, I may as well resign."

"Does Your Eminence really think it's that serious?"

The cardinal surveyed the grounds of Our Lady of the Waves. "Would I be meeting you here if I didn't?"

"I suppose not, Your Eminence. But while we are here, I request your permission to examine Bishop Ravenshorst's files at his residence at Saint Barbara's Chapel."

"What for? You were just there a few days ago. The housekeeper called my office and said you were ransacking his library."

"That was her interpretation, Your Eminence. I was reviewing the late bishop's papers in search of information regarding the Murkenstein chalice."

The dreadful Murkenmug, thought the gardener, visualizing the ugly thing in Edison Winger's jewelry shop. It would take more than a clean and a polish to rid that thing of its inherent hideousness.

"And now you want to mess up Jerry's files further," said the cardinal.

"I wish to tap into his expertise as a historian," said Father. "You said he made an extensive study of the artifact. I have always found that knowing what I'm seeking makes it easier to find. The recent return of the Murkenstein chalice to Your Eminence's worthy possession was the direct result of my perusal of Bishop Ravenshorst's files at Saint Barbara's."

"At tremendous cost to the archdiocese."

"The chalice was returned," repeated Father, folding his arms.

"Oh, very well. Permission granted, but nothing in writing. Anyone asks, have them phone me. If they don't know how to reach me, they're not important enough in the first place."

"Your Eminence." Father bowed his head. He might have been making sure his shoelace was properly tied, but the gesture appeared to express gratitude and acceptance.

I coughed. Apparently Bishop Ravenshorst's housekeeper was an important woman indeed.

Morley Fulbright crinkled his nose. "Speaking of which, what the devil were you doing at Bendlebrain, Cruiser and Wedge?"

"Retracing Monsignor Aspic's movements, Your Eminence. Since he had the artifact in his possession, it stands to reason that where he went—"

"Yes, yes. You spoke with Willis."

"I did."

Fulbright looked as though he had just swallowed a bug. "How did it go?"

"Go, Your Eminence?"

Morley gyrated his hands in impatient, desultory loops. "What did he tell you?"

"Not much, other than to confirm that Monsignor Aspic visited him about four hours before he disappeared."

"How did you find out about him?"

"The monsignor?"

"No, you id—" The cardinal caught himself, suppressing his agitation rather than insult his clerical facsimile of Perry Mason, Nero Wolfe and Father Brown all rolled into one.

Note that I, being the literary equivalent of Paul Drake, Archie Goodwin, and an old umbrella, was contributing even less to this conversation than to the one the previous morning.

Morley Fulbright huffed, then he puffed, then he gathered up all his tension like a spider whose web has just been snapped out from under it, and uttered evenly, "About Willis P. Wedge."

"As I said, Your Eminence," said Father, face stern but eyes amused, "I was retracing Monsignor Aspic's movements. He saw Mr. Wedge, so I saw Mr. Wedge. Is there a problem?"

"I suppose not," said the cardinal, puffing his cheeks in and out like a fish I once saw at the Long Beach Aquarium. "Anything else?"

"I have confirmed that Monsignor Aspic did indeed see Edison G. Winger."

Morley's eyes widened a tad. "And?"

"Your chalice, the gift from Professor Murkenstein, was at his shop, awaiting cleaning. At least we know that it is safe."

A tad more. "And?"

"Unfortunately, the artifact was not there. Mr. Winger denied any knowledge of it. I believe you said a friend of yours recommended him."

Several notches wider. "An acquaintance."

"Might I ask who?"

The cardinal's eyelids slammed shut, then sprung halfway open again. "It's not important."

"How can you be so sure? Clearly it's—"

"I said it's not important, Father. Leave it alone."

"As you wish."

"Good."

"There is still the question of the body in the crypt." Father unfolded and refolded his arms. "The police have been unable to establish the man's identity."

"The body in the crypt, you say."

"Yes, Your Eminence, just as I did yesterday. I would appreciate it if you could initiate inquiries in the archdiocesan archives."

"Whatever for?"

"The man was apparently a priest, and he's been missing for years. Surely that concerns you."

"Marginally. We've managed to muddle along without him, whoever he is. Chief Billowack told me he couldn't be sure the man was, in fact, a priest. For all we know this could be some sort of prank."

"A prank, Your Eminence?"

"He could be some medical fraternity's idea of a daring homecoming stunt. Did it occur to you to check the hospitals and medical schools to see if there are any missing cadavers?"

"I assumed the police would do that as a matter of routine—"

"Father Baptist," huffed our very own Prince of the Church, his robes billowing with impatience. "I will hardly dedicate secretarial hours to an extensive records quest with such vague search parameters. At least, not until all other avenues of inquiry are exhausted. Besides, I don't see any connection between him and the artifact."

"I suspect there is," said Father. "The explanation is complicated, and it would take valuable time which we both can ill afford. I ask you to consider my résumé and trust me. Please initiate an investigation."

"Will you rein in Peeyair Bawntemps?"

"I'm afraid it is now I who doesn't see the connection."

The cardinal made a big show of rolling his eyes and twitching his nostrils. "And you the big detective."

Father smiled humbly. "It pains me to think how disappointed you must be in me. If Your Eminence is giving me notice, I shall be glad to be about the affairs of my parish."

There are limits. I won't report what His Discourteousness replied. Immediately afterward, however, he snapped, "You will do as you're told, Father Baptist. Find the artifact." With that, His Insolence turned and strutted away. On the third angry footfall he spun around, the hem of his red gown swirling dramatically. "And I'll brook no further interference from Peeyair Bawntemps. See to it."

Father and I watched in silence as Morley Fulbright ambled away, around the lagoon, between the kumquats, over the sand dune and under the date palms. Only when he was beyond hearing and out of sight did we turn and say to each other, "Fettuccini Cardinal Fulbright!"

22

456 CUTHBERT DRIVE said the sign hanging beneath the enormous mailbox. An eight-foot wall of gray-green stones and cascading mortar surrounded the property. The elaborate wrought-iron gate across the driveway was adorned with a black-and-gold "T" with a lion and a unicorn poised on each side and a stylized belt buckle around its middle. The driveway beyond, itself a mosaic of gray-brown cobblestones laid out in complicated hourglass patterns, curved to the right as it ascended the grade, then swerved to the left out of sight behind a forest of ancient Royal oaks, Australian eucalypti, Deodar cedars, Ponderosa pines, and thick, prickly British holly. It was an unusual horticultural blend, and apparently planted more than a century before. All we could see of the house from the gate were the tops of five ornate brick chimneys above the treetops. A rock guardhouse squatted just inside the entrance, but it looked unoccupied. Of course the gate was locked. The padlock must have weighed several pounds, and the chain considerably more. There was a call box mounted on a wooden rail that had probably been used to tether horses long, long ago.

"Perhaps we should have phoned ahead," said the gardener after reaching through his open window and pushing the red button. The digital clock on the dashboard said 8:38. "We're a wee bit on the inconveniently early side."

"What is the world coming to," said Father calmly beside me, "when a pastor can't pay a visit to one of his most outspoken parishioners without an appointment?"

"I'm reminded of a joke."

"Do tell."

"A new pastor went about his parish visiting his parishioners. At one house in particular he knocked and knocked, but there was no answer. He was sure he heard movement within, but no one came to the door. So he left a note that said, 'Apocalypse three twenty.'"

"Something tells me I've heard this one."

"The following Sunday, the pastor received a note in the collection basket. He laughed and laughed—as you will, too, in just a moment—because he knew precisely who wrote it, even though it wasn't signed. The note said, 'Genesis three ten.'"

Father did not laugh. He did not even smile. I was impressed by his self-control.

```
GARDENING TIPS:  Sigh.  Okay, for the reader too
lazy to look them up, here are those verses:
   Apoc. III.20: "Behold, I stand at the gate and
knock . . ."
   Gen. III.10: "And he said: I heard thy voice in
paradise; and I was afraid, because I was naked,
and I hid myself."
   Boom cheesh.
                                         --M.F.
```

"Try again," said Father. "The button, not another joke."

I complied. Still no response.

A peacock was perched on the windowsill of the gatehouse. He eyed us with disdain as his harem of peahens pecked the manicured grass beneath him.

"We can come back," said I.

"Give it one more try," said Father.

"Sure, why not."

This time an electric crackle erupted from the speaker. The voice was breathy, raspy, and weak. "Yes ... yes ... (wheeze) ... What is it?"

"Father John Baptist to see Mr. Turnbuckle," said Father across me.

"Ah ... yes ... Well, the Master is not in."

"When do you expect him?" asked Father.

"I do not know ... when he's due ... (wheeze) ... back ... Maybe you ... could try ... another time."

"Perhaps I shall."

"An appointment would be ... appropriate."

"Indeed. To whom am I speaking?"

"Greeley, Sir ... the butler."

"Please tell Mr. Turnbuckle that I will be by later. I cannot make an appointment because the nature of my business requires that I remain flexible."

"Flexible, Sir?"

"That's right. Did you get my name?"

"Father John Baptist ... Now, if you will excuse me ... I will be sure to give the Master your message."

"Thank-you, Greeley."

"Good-b—(click!)"

"Well," said I, rolling up the window. "That was enlightening, or not. He acted as though you're a stranger."

"You've never met him, have you, Martin?"

"I guess not. I don't think he's ever accompanied Mr. Turnbuckle to Mass."

"I seem to recall that he's a Unitarian."

"Oh. Where to now?"

"Ecclesiasticus."

"That's not on any of these high-tech address cards."

"Thirty-eight sixteen."

"Wait a minute." I thumbed through the pages of the Bible in my head. "Yes, I've got it: 'My son, shed tears over the dead and begin to lament as if thou hadst suffered some great harm, and according to judgment cover his body, and neglect not his burial.' Whose funeral are we going to?"

"Roger Galloway."

"Of course, the guard who died in the mausoleum last week." I started the car, checked the mirrors, and backed away from the Turnbuckle gate. "The man Pierre was picked up for murdering."

"The very one."

"To New Golgotha, then, to shed tears over the dead."

23

"'JOY! JOY! JOY!' Let me hear you sing! 'Joy! Joy! Joy!'"

Yes, it was the burial service for Roger Galloway, whose untimely death had thrown such a terrible wrench into the plans of the Knights Tumblar a few days before. It was a little past nine in the morning. The sun was shining and a brisk breeze was herding the yellowing leaves on the grass under the sycamore trees. This being one of the newer sections of New Golgotha Catholic Cemetery, the markers around us were plaques set flat in the ground rather than the upstanding headstones so prominent in the older areas. The ground into which the ponderous hole had been dug sloped gently to the south, and the distant but insistent sound of gridlocked traffic buffeted us from all directions.

Roger's round little widow, Penelope, was veiled and draped in black. She had a tissue in one hand and a bouquet of blood-red roses in the other. Her face was grim and a tad perplexed. I had a hard time imagining that what was going on was her idea. I suspected the credit went to her plum-cheeked eldest daughter, the late-twenties gal wearing the cheerful floral bandana and turquoise sweatpants. No doubt it was she who had arranged for Furmelda Furkin and the Music Ministry from Saint Cyprian's in Burbank to supply the—ahem—music. Yes, a church named after the same Saint Cyprian so poignantly quoted by Millie the night before, which shows you how much the pastor there adhered to the ideals of the parish namesake. Among some people I won't mention by name the ensemble was known as "The Ever-Twangin' Mostly-Saggin' Steel Pluckers." Freddie Furkin, Furmelda's cigar-sucking ice-chomping husband had defected from the joy-joy zone at Saint Cyprian's to burrow his foxhole in the fifth pew at our beloved Saint Philomena's. Nothing Freddie had said could have prepared me for such an unprecedented defalcation of the basic principles of melody, harmony, and rhythm—not to mention the absence of the merest conceivable notion of good taste.

"'Joy! Joy! Joy!'" chimed the piercing sopranos.

"Let me hear you sing!" brayed Furmelda, directing everyone with her twirling tambourine and flabby arms.

"'Joy! Joy! Joy!'" trumpeted the altos, adding their husky jangle to the sopranos' corny jingle.

With the exception of Mrs. Furkin, all of them were playing fretted instruments. From left to right: banjo, guitar, autoharp, mandolin, ukulele and sitar. In this gardener's opinion, they all needed some advice about what to do with their tongues when they mouthed their open vowels. I wasn't about to be the one to give it to them, but they nonetheless needed it desperately.

Apart from the entertainment, there was a handful of friends and relatives, most of them in sweatshirts and tank tops, all of them consulting their watches frequently. No doubt they were hoping to move on to the reception at Penelope Galloway's house as quickly as possible. I heard one of them mention that Mrs. G. was a dynamite cook. Why else would anyone attend a funeral, even with all the joy, joy, joy?

The torturous singing finally abated to an ooey-gooey hum. If only they could have agreed on a note on which to drone. If I had any input, I would have named them "The Joyful Noise." That's not half as insulting as it sounds, considering it's from Psalm Ninety-Four:

> Come let us praise the Lord with joy: let us joyfully sing to God
> our savior.
> Let us come before his presence with thanksgiving; and make a
> joyful noise to him with psalms.

Funny they should take it so literally.

Father Spindle, the MC for the occasion, was a priest I had not ever had the discomfiture to meet. He stepped forward, hands clasped fervently, to announce, "And now, my friends, at the request of the family"—oh, how that plum of a daughter beamed—"Roger's children are going to present him with their memorial offerings."

This was a curious innovation. The discordant hum swelled as one by one Roger and Penelope's progeny approached the ominous coffin, deposited their tribute on the lid, explained why, and scampered hurriedly away. Debbie, the youngest, went first. She waddled up with her dolly's body in one hand and the head in the other, whining pathetically that her daddy had never been able to fix it right. From where I was standing, I could see that she left out the part about how the beheading had been accomplished by the application of an implement with irregular, jagged teeth. Debbie had some issues, apparently. She was so little Father Spindle had to lift her up to set the evidence atop "Daddy's cozy new bedroom."

Next in order of age came pouting Darlene with a video game her papa had forbidden her to play. It was out-of-date now so apparently she didn't mind leaving it with him forever. Ricky, a sulking lad of twelve, added Boomer's leash to the pile. Boomer was the family mutt, the dog Dad had returned to the pound. I suspected it was that or watch the poor animal starve from neglect. Earl, bent with the weight of an enormous chip on his shoulder, left the football Dumb Old Dad had ruptured when he ran the car over it in the driveway. Patricia, who was in charge of the garden behind the garage, deposited several unrecognizable withered vegetables, the fruit of her half-hearted labors. Roger Junior, his left cheek embossed with a tattoo of a snarling skull, tossed the keys to the car he had totaled on his eighteenth birthday. Last but not least, Erica, the plum who had so proudly orchestrated all of the above, placed a framed photograph of Daddy on the heap. She had snapped the picture herself with a cheap, disposable camera, since Pops neglected to buy her the expensive self-focusing digital model she would have preferred.

"We miss you, Daddy!" chimed the children unconvincingly as they regained their folded metal chairs around Mom. What made this weirder still was that they were all wearing T-shirts with their papa's face silkscreened on the front. It was the same image as the one in the frame.

Erica's cruel lens had captured Mr. Galloway looking as though he had just been caught with his hand in an embarrassing, perhaps even prosecutable jar. "So long! G'bye!"

"How touching," cooed Father Spindle, rolling his eyes and pointing skyward. "I can almost hear Roger up in the clouds singing with Frank Sinatra and Dean Martin in the Celestial Lounge."

"Oh, brother," groaned one disgusted gardener.

Standing apart from the friends and relatives, yet very much present, were Edward Strypes Windham and Pierre Bontemps. Edward was apparently representing the Knights Tumblar, while Monsieur Bontemps, pen and notebook in hand, was there on behalf of the *L. A. Artsy*. The attendees gave Pierre a wide berth because, prior to his exoneration, he had been the prime suspect in the death of Roger Galloway. Obviously he must have done *something* wrong, or the police wouldn't have arrested him.

"I don't get it," said Edward with a frustrated sigh. "Mr. Galloway wouldn't have wanted this kind of funeral."

"Agreed," said Pierre, adjusting his monocle. "Like so many, he became a Trad while his family remained attached to the silliness. He didn't make prior provisions, so the services are entirely in their hands."

"There ought to be a law," agreed yours truly.

"This isn't a funeral," said Edward, "it's a 'fun-for-all.'"

"And nobody's laughing," added Pierre.

"Except the funeral directors," said I, noticing two skeletally gaunt men in wrinkled charcoal suits and crooked ties leaning against the hearse, leering gleefully at the bizarre assembly. They got paid no matter how idiotic the ceremony.

"If you will excuse me," said Father Baptist, "I must have a word with the Interment Ministry."

"The what?" asked Edward.

"Them," said Father, pointing to three men standing about thirty yards away under a gnarled tea tree.

We watched as Father approached Roberto, Duggo and Spade. They were gravediggers, not to mention groundskeepers and part-time guards. Most of all, they were friends of Father Baptist and regular "in lieu of" contributors at St. Philomena's.

"Ah, Pierre," said I as Father engaged the Entombment Specialists in muted conversation. "Or should I call you Morley's Bane?"

"What are you talking about, Sir Martin?"

"We have confirmed that the cardinal is avoiding 'Paneno's' because of your article in the *Artsy*."

"Who told you that?" asked Edward.

"His very self, and he's not pleased about it," said I. "Actually, His Prominence told Father Baptist within my hearing, but that's still technically first-hand. Father has been ordered to tell you to lay off."

"I'm flattered," said Pierre with a slight bow. "When was this?"

"Earlier today."

"So why did His Eminence summon you and Father all the way up to Camarillo yesterday?"

"The same reason he's avoiding 'Paneno's,'" said I. "The same reason we had to meet him in Malibu this morning. He's avoiding the nuncio."

"Sylvio Bonsignore is in town?" piped Pierre, his monocle popping right out of his eye socket. "Where is he staying?"

"I wouldn't know," said I. "But I have it on good authority that he's fond of Knott's Berry Farm."

"You're serious."

"In addition to crotchety and dour."

"Thank-you," said Pierre, clasping my hand. *"Merci beaucoup!"*

"Don't mention it, and it's impolite to talk in a foreign language around someone you know doesn't speak it. Be advised, in any case, that the cardinal is furious with you."

"That means Pierre's being effective," said Edward, elbowing his partner.

"Very," I agreed. "Fulbright ordered Father Baptist to get Pierre off his case. I've never seen him so ... the word escapes me."

"Then I must redouble my efforts," said Pierre, smiling so widely the corners of his mouth met behind his neck. "Notice that none of my critiques of his silly sermons caught his attention. My calling him out on dogmatic discrepancies in his pastoral letters didn't spark his ire, nor did my bringing to light that fact that *Hola!,* the Spanish edition of the archdiocesan newspaper, accepts ads from clinics that provide birth control paraphernalia and abortion referrals to teenage girls. None of those articles riled him in the least. But when I write some ludicrous column-filler about where he dines—where he dines, do you hear me?—that ruffles the old bat's wings."

"Hey," said Edward, "don't go raggin' on our friends in the order *Chiroptera.*"

"Anything else we should know?" asked Pierre of me while glancing quizzically at Edward.

"Still strictly off the record," said I, "Father and Sybil Wexler and I lunched at 'Paneno's' yesterday. Miss Wexler had the Fettuccini Cardinal Fulbright. She said the ham and crab were interesting, but the plastic figurine of Morley the Beneficent was over the top."

"Ah, 'Let us pray,'" said Pierre. "Kahlúa struck that tidbit out of my article for length—and perhaps out of prudence. What did you think of the place?"

"'Paneno's'? They didn't have blue label."

"What?" said Edward. "No Salisbury?"

"Just yellow," said I.

"Key West?"

"Barbados."

"Well, at least it was St. Thomas'," said Pierre.

"My dear friend," said I, "that's like saying Emmett's Backyard Vineyard is akin to Chateauneuf-du-Pape because it also goes by the name 'red wine.' By the way, keep Sybil Wexler in your prayers. She may be heading Romeward, as they say."

"I say," said Edward.

"Cheerio," said Pierre.

"I also forgot to mention last night," said I, "that Cheryl Farnsworth has requested that Father come to the prison and hear her confession."

"What ho!" said Edward.

"Blessed be God," said Pierre, "in His Angels and in His Saints."

"They have been active," agreed the gardener.

"'Daddy Loved Life,'" announced Erica Galloway, who was now standing front and center with a gold-edged scroll unrolled in her hands. The Music Mince-istry persisted in their subdued disharmonious humming. "Daddy loved life so much, it makes me glad to think, that though he's gone I can go on, that life is sweet and pink ..."

"Erg," said Edward, turning away and motioning with his index finger as if he were attempting to induce a gag reaction. "This is definitely not what Mr. Galloway would have wanted."

"Insufferable," grumbled Pierre, capping his pen and putting away his notebook. "Keep your eye on the coffin. Any moment now he's going to start turning over."

"If only Arthur were here."

"Just the one," agreed Pierre, snapping his fingers and turning his previous snarl of revulsion into a fiendish smile. "He loves hating foofy funerals."

"'Foofy?'" said I. "Is that a word?"

"It is now," said Pierre. "One writer to another, what word would you use?"

"Hmm," said I thoughtfully. "Perhaps 'jejune.'"

"'Jejune'? Is that a word?"

"Arthur's plane is arriving tomorrow afternoon," interjected Edward, who was not a writer and wanted to change the subject so we'd be speaking a language he could understand.

"And to think he just phoned us from the Hotel Flora last night," said I.

"He did indeed," said Pierre. "He told us his trip has been cut short."

"Oh, that's too bad," said I. "I was in the kitchen during most of his phone call. It's a shame Arthur has to come back so soon."

"Something came up at his work," said Edward. "His employer was civilized and charitable enough to give him a day or two to take his 'sister' to Rome, but since he was supposedly delivering her to a hospital she was, after all, in good hands …"

My attention was distracted by a fountain of giggles that bubbled through the assemblage around the coffin. Some element in the eldest daughter's poem apparently struck a note.

"Life is a yummy cream pie," emoted Erica, eyes closed, reciting by heart, "and death is the full tummy after, and just 'cause we die's no reason to cry, so lets bake another with laughter."

"Excuse me, Noble Knights," said I. "It occurs to me that I would like to hear Father's conversation with the Hole-in-the-Ground Society."

"Very well," said Edward. "Don't leave without saying good-bye."

"Wouldn't dream of it." With that I huffed and hobbled over to where Father was having a serious discussion with Roberto, Duggo, and Spade. The deep, springy grass made perambulating all the more difficult for me, but considering the surroundings, hey, at least I was still walking. Furthermore, I wasn't in a coffin being goo-gooed into the grave, thank God!

"My uncle, Pablo," Roberto Guadalupe was saying as I approached. "I took him to visit beautiful St. Philomena's once when he was up here visiting. Tío Pablo, he knows these things, and he say that part of the church, the grotto with the metal statue, it remind him of shrines he has seen down in Mexico—very old, not reinforced. You say the floor, it is sinking. That could be very bad, Padre. Oh—hola, Señor Feeney."

"Buenos dias," said I. "Roberto, Spade, Duggo."

"I would appreciate it if you could look at it as soon as possible," said Father.

"We are, how you say, swamped today," said Roberto. "But we will see to it tomorrow. Right, muchachos?"

Duggo and Spade nodded enthusiastically.

Roberto Guadalupe was a powerful man with a huge moustache, broad shoulders, and a pouch of chewing tobacco swinging from his belt. He claimed linear descent from Pancho Villa, and was not the least bit ashamed of his job. Duggo and Spade were skinny, swarthy, and devout. The three of them were dependably hard workers, and we were deeply grateful to them for the labors they had donated to our crumbling little parish. Rumors that they did it for thirst-quenching pitchers of Millie's magical lemonade were not entirely without foundation.

"With your permission, Padre," said Roberto, "we will bring our tools and pry up the floor. If the foundation, it is in trouble, we find out right away."

"I can't thank you enough," said Father. "Oh, and there's the matter of the body at the county coroner's. You did say—"

"Of course, Padre," said Duggo. "We are on top of it."

"You can count on us," said Spade.

"Thank-you," said Father, "and thanks again. Well, Martin and I must press on."

"Another case for His Eminence?" asked Roberto.

"Partly," said Father.

"Please, Padre, your blessing," said Spade, sinking to his knees. Duggo and Roberto did likewise. I bowed my head.

"Of course," said Father, motioning with a flat hand. *"Benedicat vos omnipotens Deus: Pater, et Filius, et Spiritus Sanctus. Amen."*

"Deo gratias," they replied.

I noticed a couple of the Galloway kids pointing at us and snickering, them and their video games, ruptured footballs, and erudite poetry.

"Do you wish to leave now, Father," I asked as we trudged back toward the funerary funfest, "or do you want to stick around and give Mr. Galloway a real blessing after the—was I about to say 'mourners'?—have left?"

"We must press on," said he, motioning to Pierre and Edward to join us. "Perhaps we'll come back in a day or two and pay our respects under more favorable conditions."

We paused as the two Knights of the Tumblar approached.

"Pierre," said Father, "the cardinal has ordered me to tell you to get off his case."

"So Sir Martin has told me," said Pierre. "In return, do you think His Eminence will honor the oath he took upon his elevation to the College of Cardinals, his pledge to see to the spiritual welfare of the souls in his charge, to defend the Holy Catholic Faith to the death?"

"Say what?" laughed Edward.

"You were talking about His Irreverence, Cardinal Fulbright?" asked the gardener.

"He made no promises to me," said Father sternly, "other than to make some serious ones if you don't cease and desist."

"Then neither will I," said Pierre, "other than to say I will not falter."

Father replied by putting a hand solidly on Pierre's shoulder. Then he turned to me and said, "Shall we go? We have much to do today."

"So do we," said Edward. "Be seeing you."

As we headed for the car, I was reminded of one of my favorite passages from Robert Bolt's *A Man for All Seasons,* an insightful, though at times inaccurate, dramatization of the struggles and martyrdom of Saint Thomas More, Lord Chancellor of England under King Henry VIII:

> Now listen, Will. And Meg, you listen, too, you know I know you well. God made the angels to show him splendor—as he made animals for innocence and plants for their simplicity. But man he made to serve him wittily, in the tangle of his mind! If he suffers us to fall to such a case that there is no escaping, then we may stand to our tackle as best we can, and yes, Will, then we may clamor like champions, if we have the spittle for it. And no doubt it delights God to see splendor where he only looked for complexity. But it's God's part, not our own, to bring ourselves to that extremity! Our natural business lies in escaping ...

I wondered, looking back at Pierre as he and Edward went their way, if I was witness to the commencement of a parallel martyrdom in the making. Time would tell.

Luckily I had managed to find a parking place close to the burial site. Father and I were seating ourselves in the Jeep when the moment came for the widow to give her eulogy. My window rolled down, I held off turning the key in the ignition to hear what she had to say. Even Furmelda Furkin and the Ever-Twangin' Mostly-Saggin' Steel-Pluckers held their peace for the first time that morning.

Penelope Galloway stood where Father Spindle had been jabbering about the fairytale wonders of death, a bouquet of red roses in her gloved hands. She surveyed her family and friends, then the pile of "memorial offerings" displayed on the coffin. It took her a few moments to make her mind up about something. Grief gave way to determination. With finality she tossed the flowers on the ground and said, "Roger, you were a rat to leave me stranded with these people. I'll never forgive you for this!" With that, she stomped on the flowers, turned on her heels, and strutted away.

Father and I looked at each other, then straight ahead, then out our respective windows, then forward again.

"Hmm," said we as I cranked the key and prodded the accelerator. "HRRRrrmmmmm."

24

WIDE EYE DO DAT? said the sign shaped like a huge, glaring eyeball. It creaked as the wind rocked it on its rusted metal hanger. There was another sign nailed crookedly on the door beneath it:

FORTUNES UNTOLD
∞ BONES READ ∞
POTIONS FOR ALL OCCASIONS
GUILLAUME DU CRANE CRISTAL, PROPRIETOR.

I'd found the establishment yet again, though I can never seem to remember the way till I get there. The place belonged to Willie "Skull" Kapps, AKA Guillaume du Crane Cristal, Los Angeles' only purveyor of mweemuck root tea and vendor of extraordinarily hard-to-find and why-would-you esoteric stuff. Through the grimy window, Willie's wares looked vaguely bizarre and dimly ominous, shapes and forms that beckoned and repelled at the same time—well, repulsed and then winked at you. It's hard to explain.

Father stood beside me at the door, examining the lock. "Uh-oh," said he.

The deadbolt, or rather its anchor plate, which had been broken when the door was vandalized the previous Saturday evening, had not yet been repaired. The slightest pressure on the handle and the latch simply gave way accompanied by the scratch of scraping splinters. Bits of police crime scene tape still adhered uselessly to the shattered doorframe.

"Willie!" called Father into the murkiness.

Silence echoed back.

"It's been left like this all week," said Father. "I should have seen to repairs while Willie was in the hospital, but it completely slipped my mind. A lot has been going on, but that's no excuse."

"I can't believe he didn't fix this the moment he got home yesterday," said I as we entered. I cringed slightly as I stepped across the threshold in anticipation of the little bell above the door. The uncanny thing defied the laws of acoustics by being flesh-crawlingly out of tune with itself. It did not disappoint me. "Erg! That is, if he's even been here."

"Oh, he's been here, but perhaps whatever is in that pouch of his is more important than all this."

All this. Right. The place was eerily deserted. Well, that needs clarification. Willie's shop was never really empty, nor still. It was crammed with weird and withered things, many of which had been alive at one time. Everything in the display cases and hanging on the walls wiggled and writhed on the periphery of my vision until I looked directly at them, when of course they naturally—if the word applied—proved to be deathly still. Between the irksome bell and the slithery merchandise, the place never failed to give me the creeps. And let's not forget the stench of stale mweemuck root tea.

Still, Willie was Father's friend from back when, and sort of mine now, too, and of course we were concerned for his welfare. The man had been beaten and robbed by intruders, then hospitalized until the previous morning when Father found the fat lady in the black leather jacket in what had been Willie's bed.

"How can you be sure he's been here?" I asked, fumbling for the light switch.

"Little things," said Father, groping his way to the counter on which sat the ancient cash register.

"What things?"

"Objects out of place."

"In here? Objects move around on their own, and you know it."

"Martin."

"Father." Darned if even the light switch hadn't moved from where I remembered it. "And how can you be positive even if something didn't relocate itself—I maintain everything does, incessantly, but I'll concede your skepticism—how can you be sure it wasn't moved by an intruder? The place has been virtually wide open for days."

"I pity the person," said Father, "who violates one of Willie's hexes."

"Considering that we're intruding, I hope Mr. Kapps' spells aren't blind."

"Nearsighted, perhaps, but that's not my main worry at the moment."

"Really. It's one of mine."

"That being the case, do you prefer facing it in the dark?"

"Here we go," said I as my fingers found the switch and threw it. The lights did not come on. "Uh-oh."

"Perhaps a fuse."

"Perhaps an unpaid bill."

"Would that we had come yesterday," said Father, running his fingers along the countertop. "Martin, would you please check the back room?"

"Sure, why not?" said I. A thousand reasons why not skittered on the fringe of my imagination as I plodded through the gloom, using my cane as a feeler. As many a time as I'd been in this place, it never felt familiar to me. Why was I afraid? Suddenly I bumped something—or it bumped me—and whatever it was, and whatever its purpose, it was heavy and metallic and it fell to the floor with a resounding crash and clatter.

"You okay?" asked Father.

"Sure, sure." I almost added, "Just take it out of my pay," but then he would have said, "What pay?" so I left it alone.

As I inched further through the murkiness, my nerves still resonating with that jarring metallic uproar, the words of Psalm Ninety-Four replayed in my head. This time I didn't stop at verse two.

> Come let us praise the Lord with joy: let us joyfully sing to God our savior.
>
> Let us come before his presence with thanksgiving; and make a joyful noise to him with psalms.
>
> For the Lord is a great God, and a great King above all gods.
>
> For in his hands are all the ends of the earth: and the heights of the mountains are his.

For the Lord is a great God, and a great King above all gods. Yes, in moments of fear, surrounded by pagan talismans, casting quilts, and things that leer and wiggle at you till you look directly at them, it is good to remind oneself who is really in charge, after all.

I reminded myself a hundredfold as my cane encountered the strings of beads hanging in the doorway to Willie's quarters in the back. It was silly of me, really. I knew perfectly well that they were just plastic beads, not black widow spiders. Black widows don't hang in ordered rows on strings, and they don't make those clickety-clacking noises … unless they're really riled or just plain hungry.

The midmorning sun was hitting the back window, and though the pane had been painted over eons ago, enough light penetrated to give Willie's bedroom-slash-kitchen a modicum of visual definition. Just enough, as it turned out, for me to realize it was his lumpy cot that I had just bumped into—that, or a giant gardener-eating Caribbean mollusk, one of Willie's more dangerous pets that hadn't been fed for a week. The stove I recognized from the faint blue glow of the pilot light emanating from the cavity beneath the front burner. A stagnant pot of half-evaporated mweemuck root tea festered on the idle back burner, which accounted for the stench throughout the place.

After looking around in the relative radiance of the back area, I returned to the front room, blind as before. Suddenly the darkness was pierced by a flash of brilliant orange. Father had just struck a wooden match along the edge of the countertop. He held it high, peering into the glass case.

"Why don't you light a candle?" I asked.

"I don't think so," said he, indicating the ritual wax cylinders and figurines used in esoteric ceremonies, behind the cash register. "Not those, anyway."

"Right," I agreed. "Better to curse the darkness than to inadvertently set off one of Willie's myopic spells."

"Hello, what's this?" Father pulled a small envelope from a declivity between the cash register and the display case.

"Do tell."

"One moment," said he, tossing the spent match into something that might have been an ashtray. He fished around in the mysterious folds of his cassock and produced another, which burst courageously into flame as he scraped it along the edge of the display case. He examined the envelope. "From the bit of adhesive tape on the top edge, I deduce that this might have been left attached to the front door."

"Or anywhere," said I, helpfully.

"Yes, but I noticed a small clean spot, just about eye level when we came in. In any case, this certainly isn't Willie's stationery."

"I'd never seen Willie stationary until he was laid out in that hospital bed."

"Martin."

"Father. So is there anything inside?"

"Yes." He tossed the match into the ashtray. "It would be easier if we went outside."

"No argument here."

A moment later we were standing in the morning blaze. While my eyes were adjusting I heard him open the envelope, pull out a card, and read aloud, "'The Saranac Lounge, Saturday afternoon, 5 o'clock.' No signature." I could hear his thumb rubbing the card. "There's an insignia embossed in the lower left corner. An 'A' in a circle—actually, there are raised circles all around the edge. This stationery is a bit overdone, in my opinion, overstated, cluttered, and perhaps even gaudy." He held the card up in the brilliant sunlight. "Elegant stock, though."

"Elegant is not something you'd expect to find in Willie's place."

"Guillaume du Crane Cristal is full of surprises, or so I've found."

"The Saranac Lounge," said I as I pulled the door shut and gave the handle an extra tug, as if that would make the broken lock more secure. "That has a vaguely familiar ring."

"Does it?"

"Yes. It will come to me if I don't think about it. Where to next?"

"We have a little unfinished business with David Smoley."

"Sounds ominous. Maybe we should stop at a bakery on the way."

"Whatever for?"

"To get the kid some chocolate cake."

"Martin."

"Never mind, never mind."

25

"PERMIT ME TO APOLOGIZE AGAIN," said Father as David led us to Monsignor Aspic's car.

David aimed the remote on his key ring and pressed a button. The car chirped as if to say, "Yippee! I'm open!"

With his hand placed on the rear door handle, Father looked calmly yet penetratingly at the lad. "David, have you used this vehicle since the night the monsignor disappeared?"

"What?" David gulped audibly. "N-n-nuh-no."

"Are you sure?"

"Y-y-yuh-yes." The uncertain sort-of-seminarian shifted back and forth from one foot to the other. It wasn't the wild, wide waddling of the hapless five-year-old, but rather the slow, involuntary rolling of a war-wracked vessel floundering at sea, bound for the salvaging yard years before its time. This kid, I realized, all joking aside, was one tangled-up young man. He was playing secretary and chauffeur to a managerial consultant-slash-psychoanalytic monsignor while reconsidering his vocation. Such a generous privilege required the granting thereof, which meant someone in charge actually considered him priestly material. The implications were unsettling. My good opinion he did not earn, but he had my full and complete sympathy. He looked at me as though he perceived my thoughts, then as though he didn't. He said to Father, "I—I'm—I'm sure."

"Not for any errand whatsoever, say a run to the store?"

"No."

"Or a quick dash for a hamburger?"

"If there's any trash in the back it's his, not mine." The lad's eyes went wide. "What do you want me to say?"

"David, I'm not trying to pin something on you, nor to catch you in a lie. I am attempting to reconstruct Monsignor Aspic's movements on the day he disappeared. I need to know for certain if this car was used since then so I don't misinterpret what I may find inside."

"Yeah, right," said David sullenly. "You're a big detective."

I blinked. For David Smoley, that comment, especially the way he lowered his voice and rolled his eyes on the last two words, was practically an act of defiance.

"Unfortunately, that has become the general perception," said Father with a protracted sigh, apparently choosing to play along with rather than react to the young man's impertinence. "So, honestly now. Did you take this car out since Monsignor Aspic disappeared? I will believe you."

"No!" snapped David. Then, startled, he whispered, "I didn't."

"Fine, and thank-you," said Father, opening the rear door. "This shouldn't take long."

I watched through the window as Father ran his hands along the flat of the bench seat, exploring the cracks and crevices with his fingers. He paid special attention to where the seatbelts and buckles were anchored. He then turned his attention to the carpeted floor, probing the dusty recesses under the rear seat and stooping to look under the back of the driver's seat. All the while David stood, or rather swayed, from foot to foot, like a sailor on a rocking ship. It took all my self-control not to go into my pirate routine just then.

"Well," said Father, backing out of the door and turning to face us. He held up a greasy paper wrapper with a pair of drums printed on the ickiest side. "Bongo Burgers. How about that?"

"But that was days ago," protested the lad, adding a bit of forth-and-back to his side-to-side.

"How many days ago, David?" Father stood placidly still, which made the contrast almost cinematic.

"Tuh—tuh—two or three."

"Think hard."

"It was the day, the day of the … *the!* …" (pronounced *thuh!*) "… after we left the Chancery, on the way to his next appointment."

"You mean the day of his disappearance."

"Uh-huh."

"And the day before that?"

"Tuesday? He had lunch at 'Paneno's,' I think. I'd have to check my notebook. It's inside."

"No, that's all right. I'm not concerned with what he did that far back. So, he grabbed a quick lunch at Bongo Burgers on Wednesday."

"Right."

"And what about you?"

"Me?"

"What did you get to eat?"

"What I always get to eat: whatever I bring with me. That day was, um, bologna and jack on whole wheat."

"Did the cook make it?"

David glanced at the rectory. "You mean here? Her? No. I did."

"Are you telling me that Monsignor Aspic never bought you any meals?"

"Not since, um, you know, that—that day."

"You mean October twenty-sev—"

"I said I don't want to t-tuh-tuh-talk about that!"

"Easy, David. We won't go there. But as for the day he ate something from Bongo's in the back seat, as evidenced by this wrapper, you were on your own as far as lunch was concerned?"

"That's right."

"How inconsiderate of him. I can imagine how that must weigh upon you. Okay, so this hamburger wrapper has been here for a couple of days. Was it not one of your responsibilities to keep the car clean?"

David scratched the side of his nose, his ear, then his nose again. "Every Friday he has me take the car to the Long Wow Carwash. It's up on Beverly. They only do limos and expensive cars. He told me to never stick my nose in the back of his precious car, not ever, or he'd see me removed from 'consideration.'" The lad suddenly blushed a deeply self-revealing shade of red. "He reminds me of that a lot."

"I understand," said Father. "You're under the gun."

More like a cannon, thought the gardener. Do they make them double-barreled?

"Were you planning to do that today?" asked Father. "Have the car washed, I mean."

"I guess so. Maybe this afternoon."

"I'll ask you to forego that," said Father. "In fact, I'd prefer that you lock it up and not open it again until this whole matter is cleared up. You might want to move it to the garage. Will that be all right with you?"

David shrugged vaguely.

"So much for Bongo's," said Father, tossing the wrapper onto the back seat. Then he held up a tiny vial of clear glass with a black cap. "Actually, I'm far more interested in this."

"What is it?" asked David, eyes wide.

"You don't recognize it?"

He shook his head. Then he shook it some more. "No."

"Do you, Martin?"

I limped closer and peered at the thing he held lengthwise between his thumb and forefinger. It was all of three inches long. Filled with clear fluid, a pocket of air wriggled around inside. Then I saw the tiny Cross etched on the side of the glass. "Could that be Holy Water?" I asked.

"Likely," said Father. "I believe this is from a sick call kit."

"What's that?" asked David, rubbing the side of his nose.

"A small leather case containing the items necessary to administer the Last Rites," said Father. "Mine has two vials very much like this one, one for holy water, the other for blessed oil—also a pyx, a Crucifix, blessed candles, a stole, and a book containing the necessary prayers."

"Oh."

<u>GARDENING</u> <u>TIPS</u>: A <u>pyx</u> is a small golden vessel for carrying the Holy Eucharist. A <u>stole</u> is a strip of cloth designed to hang around the priest's neck. It is the symbol of his office and is worn whenever he administers the Sacraments.

  Father's own sick call kit was impressively compact, about the size of a cigar box. He kept it in the bottom drawer of his desk in the study.

                                 --M.F.

"The question presents itself," said Father. "Has the monsignor visited a hospital, or a sick person at home recently?"

David looked ill himself. "No, no hospital. If anyone was sick in one of those old houses, he never told me."

"You mean the two residences he visited on Wednesday."

"Yeah, or any other day."

"Monsignor Aspic doesn't strike me," interjected the gardener, "as the kind of priest who makes many sick calls."

"But he is a man who caters to the rich," said Father. "'Death comes for us all, my lords. Yes, even for Kings he comes.' Who said that?"

"The character of Sir Thomas More," said I, "during his trial in *A Man for All Seasons.*"

"Ah, yes," said Father. "The point being that even the wealthy face their appointed ends, and fearing difficulty driving their camels through the eye of a needle—"

"Matthew nineteen twenty-four," said I.

"—often send for a priest as the event draws nigh."

"Ca-ca-camels?" said David with an amplified shrug. "I don't know what you're talking about."

"So you think maybe Monsignor Aspic made a sick call the day he disappeared?" asked yours truly, barely concealing my angst that a seminarian wouldn't know the reference.

"David?" queried Father.

"I don't know," said the kid. "I don't know. I don't know. How many times do I have to tell you—?"

"Easy, son," said Father. "We'll leave it at that. Martin and I are still following up the addresses to which you delivered Monsignor Aspic on Wednesday, as well as some other possibilities."

"Can I go now?"

"Of course," said Father. "Oh, one more thing."

David winced. I think he bit his tongue.

"A trivial detail, really," said Father. "Nothing important. Last Halloween I gave Monsignor Aspic a Crucifix. It was about so big—black enamel, a golden Corpus, on a silver chain."

"I didn't drive him on Halloween," said David. "He gave me that night off."

"Oh?"

"He was still really mad."

"You mean about the events of October twenty-seventh."

David's eyes went wide, then crossed just before his lids came down. He managed to shut Father out for a few seconds, but then, perhaps realizing the futility, he reluctantly opened them again. "I know the Cross you mean," he whispered. "He wears it a lot."

"Ah," said Father. "Do you remember if he was wearing it on Wednesday?"

David mulled it over, then he mulled it over some more. "I think so. Probably. I'm not sure."

"Very good," said Father. "If anything should occur to you that you think might help us find him, anything at all no matter how insignificant or far-fetched it may seem, would you be so kind as to let me know?"

"Okay."

"Otherwise, I hope this will be the last time we'll be troubling you."

"I doubt it," said David under his breath as he turned and hustled stiffly away.

We watched as he climbed some stairs and entered the rectory through a not-exactly-rectangular doorway.

"Next time maybe you'll listen to me," said I.

"Oh?" said Father. "About what?"

"I told you we should have brought some chocolate cake."

26

"AH, SAINT BARBARA'S CHAPEL," said I as I steered the Jeep into a diagonal slot in the parking lot. I couldn't park as close as I would have liked because of the plethora of trucks and machinery hogging the area nearest the church. An assortment of muscular men, biceps bulging, hard hats teetering and utility belts jingling, were marching in and out of the front door. The front steps were covered with piles of scorched beams, soot-crusted plaster, burnt clutter, and gray ash.

"I see they're finally getting around to cleaning up the mess from last June," said Father.

"This is all kind of sudden, isn't it?" asked the gardener. "I mean, none of this was going on when we were here a few days ago."

"Didn't I point it out to you in the newspaper the other day?"

"Point what out? When have you had time to read a newspaper?"

"I must have found some, because I remember an article in the *Times* about some movie star—I forget who—who suddenly got religion when something exploded on the set during the shooting of a scene."

"I hadn't heard."

"Well, apparently the archdiocese did. Money from Hollywood has a way of getting noticed."

"Do you think they'll restore it to the original décor," said I, emerging stiffly from the car, "or will they redo with froo-froo?"

"One guess."

"Yeah, right."

```
GARDENING TIPS: Saint Barbara is the Patroness of
Lightning, Explosives, and Artillery.  She grew up
in the northern Egyptian city of Heliopolis in the
third century.  Much to her pagan father's ire,
she became a baptized Catholic.  He went com-
pletely ballistic, however, when she destroyed all
the idols in his house.  He had his daughter tor-
tured and finally beheaded with his own sword.
Imagine that.  Then imagine papa's surprise when
he was subsequently incinerated by a lightning
bolt!
   Curiously, the chapel named in her honor had
suffered its own parallel history of violence.
Altogether now, to the tune of "Auld Lang Syne"  .
. .
                                        --M.F.
```

"You again," complained the cantankerous woman who answered the rectory door. "I phoned the Chancery about you messing up Jerry's library."

"So I heard," said Father graciously. "The situation is such that we need to intrude again."

"It's lunchtime."

"We're sorry to disturb you."

"But not enough to go away." It was heartwarming to know that other rectories, too, had their own walking, talking plenary indulgences. Too bad belief in Purgatory was at an all time low. "I told you before he wouldn't like it."

"Madam, we're hardly competent to know what Bishop Ravenshorst—may he rest in peace—would or wouldn't like. At the moment it's more a matter of what the cardinal requires. You're free to phone him again, but in the meantime we know our way to the library."

"Well, of all the—!"

That's one of those sentences often left unfinished. She didn't, and we did find our way to the library.

The late Bishop Jeremiah Ravenshorst, erstwhile official historian for the archdiocese, had amassed and enjoyed one humdinger of a library in his lifetime. At least twenty of Father Baptist's studies could have easily fit within these walls of fine, polished shelves brimming with leather-bound books. Hanging from the ceiling was a ballroom-size crystal chandelier, which filled the room with cheerful light when I threw the switch. The fireplace set in the east wall was big enough for a lumberjack to dump a tree trunk on the andirons and stand up, slapping his hands, without bumping his head. There were more than a dozen wooden file cabinets that matched the bookshelves, and an impressive card file like you used to find in public libraries before the computer revolution. In one corner stood a large cork display board to which were tacked all sorts of diagrams, drawings, and photographs. Dominating the room was a thirty-five foot mahogany table piled with stacks of books, manuscripts, scrolls, legal tablets, and writing utensils.

"Someone has been here since our last visit," said I, eyeing the cluttered table.

"I believe you're right," said Father. "All these piles have been rearranged slightly, as if hastily perused, and the dust on the tabletop disturbed in places we didn't touch."

"I wonder what they were looking for."

"Good question. I wonder what we're looking for."

"And you the big detective."

"So everyone reminds me," said Father with a weary shrug. "Ah, where to begin?"

"Well, Father, as our very own Mrs. Magillicuddy has reminded us more than once." I paused to get into character. "'No distance is too great once you start a 'puttin' one foot in fronts of the other'n.'"

"Mrs. Magillicuddy," smiled Father, "thanks for reminding me. She'll be dropping by the rectory this evening. And, with respect to starting out, she's right as usual." He turned his attention to the filing cabinets, pulled open the third drawer from the top of the second one from the right, and began riffling the folders. "Prayers to Saint Anthony would be in order."

"You got it," said I, lumbering over to the hearth, imagining the crackling, toasty blazes that once roared within. I reached into my jacket pocket and started fingering my Rosary. Because of the inevitable flights of my wandering imagination, my recitation is invariably slow, erratic, and no doubt tedious at the reception end in Heaven. But at Fatima Our Lady asked that faithful Catholics pray the Rosary, and part of my Oath of Chivalry was the promise to say this marvelous string of prayers daily, so say it I did—awkwardly, inelegantly, and peripatetically—offering my tiresome pleas to Mary, Queen of All Hearts—and in this case, a special nudge to Saint Anthony, who faithfully helps us find that which is hidden.

Throughout the first and second decades, "The Agony in the Garden" and "The Scourging at the Pillar," while I concurrently pondered the significance of the year-old gray ashes in the hearth—*Remember, Man, that thou art dust, and unto dust thou shalt return*—I heard Father rummaging through the files, then rustling some papers on the table, then fluttering the index cards in their little gruff drawers.

During "The Crowning with Thorns" and "Jesus Carries His Cross," he attacked the bookshelves, pulling out various volumes, peeling them open, slamming them shut, and stuffing them back. About every tenth one ended on the table, added to one of several stacks. Then he headed back to the cabinets for some intensive file shuffling.

I was in the middle of the Fifth Sorrowful Mystery, "The Crucifixion," when I heard a triumphant "Aha!" I glanced over my left shoulder. Well, actually, my neck doesn't rotate that far. I had to turn my whole arthritic carcass to see what he was up to. He was at the corkboard examining the charts, drawings, maps, and paper scraps held there with pins. He lifted up a sheet to read the one behind, shifted others out of the way, and let them all fall back into place. "Aha!" he exclaimed again.

By the time I finished the concluding prayer, the Hail Holy Queen—to which I sometimes add several favorites in my personal recitation of the Rosary, including the Memorare, Pope Leo XIII's prayer to St. Michael (the long version), St. Anselm's Prayer to his Guardian Angel, and an appeal to the Four Archangels of the Compass (an ejaculation Father Baptist taught me once in the Confessional)—Father was scribbling furiously on a pad of foolscap with a dull pencil.

"Amen!" said he and I together.

Note what a team we make. I think that's why he keeps me—that, and my charming personality.

"So," said I, hobbling over to where he stood. Just then he underlined something several times and jabbed an exclamation point after.

"So," said he, absently stowing the pencil over his right ear. I suspected the gesture was a mannerism subconsciously revived from his homicide detective days. He was, after all, the big detective whether he cared to admit it or not. "Martin, we're in the middle of a grand mystery—no, more than that. We're standing, you and I, at the intersection of several mysteries."

"Sort of the Hollywood and Vine of mysteries," said I.

"More like all roads leading to Rome, only in this case, some make a detour and converge here in Los Angeles."

"Well," said I, scratching my forehead with the handle of my cane. "There goes your credibility."

"I'm going to strain it a good deal further, my Friend. Not to mention your amenability."

"Oh? Do tell."

"I must be sure to appropriate what I'll need."

"You're going to remove Jerry's precious stuff?"

"No, you are." He indicated three teetering piles of books, ledgers, and file folders that he had assembled during my Rosary. There were also several parchments rolled up into loose tubes and tied with faded ribbons. "I've got some more digging to do while you're carting this out to the car."

"Ulp."

"I hate to impose, Martin, I know it's a difficult chore for you; but I sense that our access to the marvelous information in this library is not going to continue indefinitely. In the immediate, please get a move on. Time is precious."

"Of course," I said, summoning my strength and courage while suppressing an overwhelming urge to whine. "I am always at your service, Father."

Hooking my cane on my left arm, I gathered up the first pile with both hands. The irregular sizes of the binders and ledgers made it hard to grasp, and the smell of decayed leather and dry parchment made it hard to breathe. Still, I grunted my way to the door, lurched down the hallway, made the necessary turns beyond that, and finally gained the front porch.

More than ever, I wished I'd been able to park the Jeep Cherokee closer. My trek was made all the longer by the pickup trucks and cement mixers I had to stagger around to get to it. Rather than uncouple the rear-mounted tire to get to the luggage compartment in the stern, I opted to dump the materials onto the back seat. Then, as I summoned my resolve to tackle the next round, I espied the hodgepodge of tools and equipment lying around in front of the chapel. I'll admit I exaggerated my limp a wee bit as I approached one of the workers and asked if I might borrow a wheelbarrow for a couple of minutes.

"I'm just bringing some books out to the car," I explained. "This would condense several trips into one and reduce my aspirin bill considerably."

"Sure, Mack," said the guy, construction dust snowing from his eyebrows as he talked. "It's not mine anyway."

With a grateful wave I grabbed the handles and heaved. The thing was heavier than it looked, caked as it was with dried concrete. I thanked my Guardian Angel that the housekeeper was not around as I pushed the thing through the front door of the rectory and onto the clean carpet. To make matters worse, the lopsided wheel made a horrendous "Skree-skree-skree-*thunk!* Skree-skree-skree-*thunk!*" sound as it wobbled on its dry, rusty axel.

"Ah, Martin," said Father, looking up as I pushed the noisy thing into the library.

"Who else?"

"I had no idea what that horrible noise was coming down the hall."

"Just me and my ingenuity."

"Excellent. I applaud your resourcefulness."

"So do my vertebrae."

He had added another pile in my absence, and several more scrolls. These I started transferring to the wheelbarrow. Some of the volumes were darn heavy. In no time at all I was not looking forward to the trip back to the car. In a few minutes the one-wheeled wagon was loaded and ready to roll.

It was then that I spied the telephone books atop one of the filing cabinets. Los Angeles, with all its adjacent and interlocking municipalities, fills a dozen directories, and that's just the white pages. While Father continued his rummaging, I did some minor investigating of my own. "Sera ... Saran ... Sarancik ... Nope." The second and third volumes weren't much help either. I found a Saranac Mining Company in South Central, which specialized in metal detectors and panning equipment. There was a Saranac Organic Grooming Products in Redondo Beach, which catered to vegan veterinarians. There was a Bubbie Saranack in North Hollywood, who was anybody's guess. But as for a Saranac Lounge, nothing. Of course, these phone books were over a year old. Perhaps it was a new place that just opened. Something kept tugging at the drawstring of my mind, however. I was sure I'd heard of the place somewhere, sometime.

"How's it coming?" asked Father as I nudged the last phone book back into place.

"It's not," said I, scowling.

"Not to worry."

"I take it you found something."

"Not exactly. Sometimes St. Anthony can be subtle."

Curious, I followed him to the corkboard. He pointed to a sketch tacked amidst various charts and diagrams. About twelve by fourteen inches, it was executed in dark pencil on translucent tracing paper—the kind Dad used to call "onionskin." It had apparently been handled a lot, resulting in a lot of smudging and smearing of the graphite.

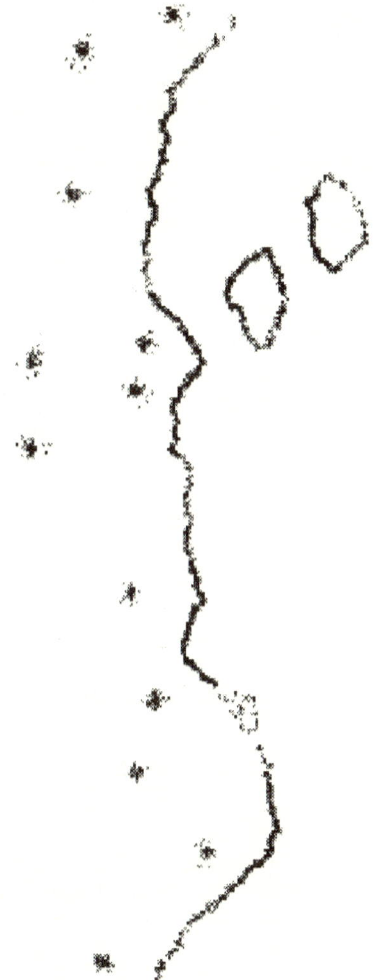

"Any idea what that is?" asked Father.

"Hmm," I said, scrunching my eyebrows. I've never been good at Rorschach tests. I stalled for a minute, trying to discern something significant. But hey, all sorts of off-the-wall things presented themselves: a teenage kid with acne looking amazedly at a couple of corn-flakes, or a ghost looking at some fireflies. Figuring that this wasn't what he wanted to hear, I ventured: "Other than a poorly drawn map, no.   Maybe it's an eastward-facing coastline—Lower Slobobia, maybe—with two islands offshore, or it's a westward-facing coastline with two lakes inshore. Depending on your orientation, these splotches could be meteor craters, cities, volcanoes, exploding depth charges, or even squashed spiders. There isn't even a compass to show which direction is north. What do you think it represents? Is it important?"

"Don't know," said he, removing the tack that held the map to the corkboard.

"Right," said I. "St. Anthony's being subtle."

As he gripped the map a photograph that had been pinned behind slipped and fell to the floor.

"I'll get it," said I, bending my knees to lower myself to my unique approximation of a crouch. With difficultly I managed to grab the photograph, which I examined as I drew myself to a more-or-less standing position—I can't say "to my full height" because I haven't had one in years. "Hey," said I, drawing the photo close. "This looks familiar. In fact, hey, would you believe—"

"*What* do you *think* you're *doing*!?!"

Father and I turned to see the source of the shrill voice. Funny, but somehow the jarring tone agitated the color green in my visual spectrum. Everything in the room flashed verdant for a moment and then subsided back to its original color.

"My name is Father John Baptist," said Father evenly. "This is my associate, Martin Feeney. And you are ...?"

"*De*Quet," warbled the tall cucumber of a man coming toward us. "I am *Bish*op Mor*ell* de*Quet.*"

*D.*K.? thought the gardener, blinking the emerald shimmer to the periphery of his vision. D.*K.* ... D.K. ... D ...

> *Con*rad ... "*Con*rad, are you *there? Please* pick *up* if you *are.* This is *D.K.* You didn't *leave* a *mes*sage. I really *must* speak *with* you. ... *Please* call *me* back*, hm? ... Con*rad? ...*"

Aha, I thought as the synapses engaged, the voice on Monsignor Aspic's answering machine. Hearing it in person I confirmed that the lisp was not electronically induced. It was a lifestyle choice—and a bishop, to boot. The irksome sibilance, however, did seem psycho-acoustically amplified there in the library.

"I re*peat*," he screeched, "*what* do you *two* think you're *doing*?"

"We're here at the cardinal's behest," explained Father, falling to one knee in the presence of a bishop.

"*Be*ing here is *one* thing," said the bishop, his long finger pointing at the loaded wheelbarrow. "*Steal*ing is *quite* a*noth*er."

"Borrowing, My Lord," corrected Father, reaching for the bishop's hand to osculate his ring. The bishop snatched it away, disgusted rather than charmed. Father rose gracefully. "My research on behalf of Cardinal Fulbright requires that I utilize these materials, and the nature of my errand demands that I take them with me."

```
GARDENING TIPS: In countries where democracy is
not the nationally enforced religion, Catholic
bishops are addressed as "Your Lordship" or "My
Lord."  In the United States, where everyone who
isn't part of the plutocracy is leveled flat by
the weight of popular opinion, the appellation has
become "Your Excellency" -- even though most bish-
ops shun the designation in actual practice, fear-
ing its un-populist ring.
   Father Baptist, God bless him, preferred Tradi-
tion over fashion, deferring to the theory of
authority over the whim of trends.
                                        --M.F.


N.B.: Prior to Vatican II, the stone worn by bish-
ops was amethyst.  Nowadays most of them tend to-
ward cubic zirconium nose rings.  Just kidding,
but not much.
```

"Well," tisked His Lordship, hands flapping. "*I* certainly don't *think* so. You will *cease* what you're doing im*med*iately, do you hear? This *in*stant!"

"Begging Your Lordship's pardon," said Father with a slight bow. "Have you been appointed auxiliary bishop under the cardinal archbishop of Los Angeles?"

"*I'm* ... con*sid*ering *it*. Monsignor Aspic *has* been *most* persuasive, *but* I haven't yet *made* up my *mind*. *Cur*rently I'm au*xil*iary under Archbishop *Mann*."

"Ah," said Father, glancing at me. "New Bangor."

Come to me, thought the gardener, and I will take the rest.

"Pre*cise*ly," said His Greenship. "So you *will* cease im*med*iately and *ret*urn those items *to* their *prop*er places."

"I answer to His Eminence, Morley Fulbright," said Father, his voice still even as the horizon in Death Valley. "You have no jurisdiction over me, nor any control over the late Bishop Ravenshorst's property."

"Don't you *dare* speak to *me* that way!" shrieked His Screechship.

"I am simply stating the facts, My Lord."

"Here, *you*," gobbled the truculent prelate, turning his withering eyes on me. With his leathery olive skin, the streaks of white in his dark jade hair, his overall oblong stature, not to mention the ivy smock he was wearing, small wonder he reminded me of a hothouse cucumber. I was getting a headache from the green sparkles I kept seeing every time he exercised his larynx. Another irksome thing I noticed as he bore down on me: there was a smudge of mustard clinging to the left edge of his upper lip. From the grey-yellow color with dots of brown, I took it to be Dijon. We had interrupted his lunch, after all. Food on one's face is rarely realized by the one, but it is nonetheless distracting to the other. The smudge was now inches away as he hissed, *"Yes,* you."

"Excuse me?" said I, descending awkwardly to one knee. That's what faithful Catholics historically do in the presence of a bishop, even if he is a cucumber. The practice no doubt originated before arthritis. Repulsed as I was by his demeanor, I reached out to take his hand and osculate his ring. Third time lucky! He pulled it away, so I was freed from the task. Relieved, I heaved myself back up onto both feet with the help of my trusty cane, gripping the edge of the table for support. I almost creased the photograph in my hand as I did so.

"You've *no* right to *take* that," said he, grabbing for the glossy.

"Oh?" said I, whisking it out of his reach. I'm usually not that quick, but there was no time to be proud of myself. "I beg your pardon, My Lord, but I am merely a Traditionalist. Ask Manly D. Mann, Archbishop of New Bangor. At a recent press conference, when asked what he thought of the Traditionalists in the Church, he said there are no such persons, and I quote: 'only pitiable, hapless laymen, barstool theologians with chips on their shoulders who think they know more than their priests.' Tell me, My Lord Bishop of Moral Decay"—don't worry, I inhaled as I pronounced "of" rendering it inaudible—"do you agree with your lawful superior's assessment?"

"It is *the* policy of *the* Arch*di*ocese of *New* Bang*or*, that *all* auxiliaries support their arch*bish*op *at* all times and *in* every way." I tell you, his bizarre zigzagging syllabic emphases were almost as teeth-grittingly grating as the green-inducing emanations of his voice. He also had this revolting habit of keeping his lower jaw rock steady as he talked while his cranium went up and down. This provided recipients of his verbiage with rapid glimpses of his hairy nasal passages.

For a moment I imagined him as a dummy poised on Manly D. Mann's manly knee, his wooden jaw squeaking and his eyeballs wiggling. It helped to put this quirky situation into perspective.

"Okay," I said, relaxing my stance, but still keeping the photo out of his reach. "So we agree on one thing. But I take orders from Father Baptist, and he gets his from His Dominance the Cardinal. I don't see that yours matter much, but then I'm just a barstool theologian with chips."

"Are *you* going to let *him* talk to *me* that way?" said Bishop D.K., turning to Father.

"Why not?" said he, smiling. "I think he described the situation succinctly. Besides, he recently accused me of prolixity."

"If you will excuse me," said I, inserting the photograph into the top file folder on the wheelbarrow. Grabbing both handles and heaving, I managed to coax a couple of audible cracks from my spine as well as to aim the cart right at His Lordship's cucumbery form. "I have an uncontrollable urge to seek out a priest and challenge him to a doctrinal bee. Forgive me if I run over your foot, My Lord, but after all, I am hapless."

"Be *care*ful with that *thing*," he squealed as he jumped aside, "you—you luna*tic*!"

"Not insane, just no such person," said I as I veered the single-axle vehicle through the door and down the hall.

"*You* are *deplorable*," said he, scurrying behind. I could hear the "Shickuh-shick-shick" of his garments as he scurried behind, but it was no match for the "Skree-skree-skree-*thunk!*" of my mighty wheelbarrow.

"Pitiable," I corrected him. "The word is 'pitiable.' Support your lawful superior."

"*Father* Bap*tist,* I insist *that* you *rein* in your ac*comp*lice."

"Martin," called Father from somewhere behind.

"Father," I replied, struggling through the front door and out into the fresh air. "A little bit of truth making its getaway."

"Bravo," said Father, catching up to me in the light of day.

"*Well!*" tisked Bishop deQuet from the doorway. "I *never*! *Hmph!* You haven't *heard* the *last* of this! Is *Mor*ley go*ing* to get *an* ear*ful,* you, you—"

"You know, Father," said I between grunts and puffs, "women like that give feminism a bad name."

27

"HOW DID YOU KNOW?" asked the gardener between gasps as he let go of the handles of the wheelbarrow. It settled with a heavy thump beside the Cherokee.

"Know what?" asked Father, scooping up some books and setting them on the back seat. Between us we made short work of the transfer.

"You said the spigot to Ravenshorst's library was going to be shut off, or words to that effect. Were you just showing off in spite of being in denial about your detective chops, or did you already know about Bishop deQuet?"

"Before I answer that, Martin, you were about to say something about that photograph as he interrupted us."

"Oh? Oh yes. I know the location of the Saranac Lounge."

"Really. Do tell."

"Just a minute. I have to return this wheelbarrow." Two can play the "before I answer that" game. I couldn't find the man who permitted me to borrow it even though it wasn't his, but I left it in plain sight.

"Where to from here?" I asked as I grunted my way into the driver's seat and fastened my seatbelt. "Back to Turnbuckle's?"

"No. I want to ponder some of what I've just discovered before I deal with him."

"Would you care to share?"

"Not just yet. I want to look at some of these books and files more closely, especially Bishop Ravenshorst's sketches of the artifact."

"Father, you're dangling a carrot bigger than this car and you know it."

"I am and I do.

"Excuse me?"

"I'm agreeing with you, and I know I'm being irksome—"

"Exactly, and you don't even have mustard on your mouth, which is why you really need to explain about the 'Hollywood and Vine of mysteries'—sorry, I prefer my simile to yours—or I'm going to yank this steering wheel off its column, throw it out the window, fold my arms, hold my breath, cross my eyes, and floor the accelerator until you do."

"I'd like to see you try."

"Hey, I'm nearly there. Just irk me a teensy bit more and I'm liable to at least hold my breath. C'mon, Father. You want me to get on my knees and beg? Me kneeling on the accelerator isn't going to improve the situation."

He laughed. "I suppose not. Let me put it this way. I'm beginning to form a theory as to the nature of the golden artifact that so concerns Cardinal Fulbright. His Eminence is alarmed by the fact of its disappearance because the Holy Father entrusted it to him, and the papal nuncio is its watchdog. He doesn't want to appear irresponsible."

"Heavens no." I turned the key in the ignition. "The man has his priorities. Whatever else may be said about His Negligence—his heretical teachings, his lack of regard for the souls in his charge, his penchant for hideous church architecture, his misappropriation of archdiocesan funds, his shielding of pedophile priests from criminal prosecution—he certainly wouldn't want to appear careless in the eyes of his keepers."

"On the other hand," said Father, giving me a "down boy" hand sign, "according to Cardinal Fulbright, and confirmed by evidence I've just gathered from his library, it would appear that the late Bishop Jeremiah Ravenshorst had an intense interest in the thing itself."

"The artifact, you mean."

"Yes."

"No doubt it's worth a lot of money."

"Yes, but I doubt that's the point. The cardinal said it was covered with symbols. Bishop Ravenshorst made copies of those symbols. I didn't have time to study them closely, but surely they mean something. Something important."

"Such as?"

"I don't know."

"But you have an idea."

"I intend to find out. For whatever reason, God has seen fit to set this puzzle before me. It would seem fitting that I exercise the talents He gave me to decipher the riddle."

"So you do admit to having detecting chops."

"Of course, Martin. I've never denied that. I object to being called away from my priestly duties to serve as the cardinal's private eye—an as yet *unpaid* private eye—but ultimately it is God, not Morley Fulbright, who is setting the conundrum before me."

"So what are we doing here? Why aren't we somewhere else?"

"Because we haven't left yet."

I looked at the speedometer. It was pointing to zero. "Okay, let's remedy that at least. Where do you want to go if not Thurgood T. Turnbuckle's?"

"Hmm. I think it's time we pay a visit to the Doily Sisters."

"Oh?" said I, sifting through the cards propped in the ashtray. "Here we are. Hortense and Mehitabelle—is that a name?—Doily. 7214 Villanova Terrace." I put the car in DRIVE and headed out of the parking lot. "Why there?"

"If I have my chronology straight, Monsignor Aspic held two press conferences in the morning, the first at seven o'clock at the Chancery, and the second at eight-thirty at the Del Agua Mission. He visited Mr.

Turnbuckle at ten, then went to a copy shop, Glen's Photocopies, which we've yet to visit. You're a writer. Three guesses why he went there."

"Glen's? Probably to make a copy of his manuscript."

"We'll check, of course, but that's the likely explanation. From there he went back to the Chancery to accept the artifact from Cardinal Fulbright. His first stop after that was 7214 Villanova, where we're now headed. From there he went to Edison Winger's Fine Jewels and Settings, where he left the Murkenstein chalice."

"Interesting," said I, turning left onto Sepulveda.

"First to Villanova, then to the jeweler," said Father. "So, in the monsignor's mind, his visit to our next stop took precedence over the cardinal's errand."

"Maybe he just had a prior appointment."

"The cardinal did say something about Monsignor Aspic's afternoon being full ..." His voice trailed off. Then he sighed in frustration. "What am I thinking?"

"I wouldn't know, Father."

"How did His Eminence put it?"

"Put what?"

"Yesterday morning up at the seminary, he said he asked someone he knew for a recommendation for an appraiser. He gave the information to Monsignor Aspic, but the monsignor's afternoon was full of appointments."

"I believe the term His Utterance used was 'log-jammed.'"

"Right. Because his afternoon was log-jammed with commitments, the monsignor promised to keep the artifact safe until the next day when he would take it to the appraiser first thing."

"That sounds right," I acknowledged.

"But in fact," said Father, "the monsignor went to the appraiser that very afternoon."

I considered mentioning that I had noted the same discrepancy but decided against it. Let the big detective have his moment. "So," I said, "you're assuming that, along with His Tastelessness' hideous goblet, Monsignor Aspic also took the Pope's artifact to Edison Winger?"

"Ernie Corben is checking out that very detail as we speak."

"Right," said I, veering into a left turn lane. "I feel so relieved. Okay, so from Winger's the monsignor went to see Willis P. Wedge of Bendlebrain, Cruiser & Wedge."

"'Public perception, crisis management, and tergiversation.'" Father rubbed the bridge of his nose with his thumb and forefinger, as though soothing a headache. "One has to wonder about a man who keeps a portrait of Antonio del Corro on his office wall, regarding him as his 'mentor of mentors.'"

"One also has to wonder about a monsignor who would then scurry to a television station to participate in a show called 'Religion Revisited' with the likes of Sheldon and Eira Levant."

"Not to mention their ratings-hungry producer, Napolia Krackershak. But the monsignor had his own agenda, don't forget."

"His manuscript."

"Right. On several occasions throughout the afternoon he mentioned his unpublished book. It was even a stipulation for his going on the air with Sheldon and Eira Levant. This makes our visit to 7214 Villanova Terrace all the more intriguing."

"How so?"

"You read the names. Mehitabelle and Hortense Doily. Don't they mean anything to you?"

"Mehitabelle and Hortense ... Mehitabelle and Hortense Doily ... Doily. Wait a minute. The Doily Sisters. Of course. They're publishers!"

"Of a sort. By that I mean they print tracts, devotional pamphlets, missals, exuberant hagiographies, all of them elegantly done. A little on the fluffy side for my taste, but—"

"Little old ladies need their prayer books, too." I made another left and headed up a road that wound its way up a densely wooded hill. "So you think the monsignor might have gone there to shop his book?"

"That's what we're going to find out. In the interim, while we're en route, would you care to tell me about the Saranac Lounge?"

"Can you get that top folder in back? That's where I put the photo, the one Bishop deQuet tried to grab."

"Yes," said he, straining to reach it. "Ah, here we go." He slipped out the black-and-white glossy and scrutinized it. "It looks like a large and very old hotel."

"Not just any old hotel, Father. That's the Adirondack. I recognize it because that's where my high school held our senior prom."

"The Adirondack," said he, thoughtfully.

"Yes. Our events committee reserved the Ticonderoga Ballroom for the occasion, and boy was that a grand idea. It was like dancing at the Hofburg."

"The Imperial Palace in Vienna? What would you know about dancing there?"

"Not a thing, but I had dreams. I had coordination back then, not to mention looks and charm. Well, coordination, sort of. Anyway, the Adirondack had not one but two bars."

"Indeed."

"Yes, the Champlain Room and the Saranac Lounge. I didn't visit the Champlain, but I remember the Saranac well because the bartender refused to accept my word that I was twenty-one."

"You and a hundred other lads that night."

"Hey, it was worth a try. The place had such a cool vibe. There were autographed glossies in prominent places: Humphrey Bogart, Lauren Bacall, Clark Gable with Carole Lombard, Craig Stevens and Lola Albright, Crispin the Psychic, Jack Webb—"

"Crispin?"

"Surely you remember 'Crispin Predicts!'"

"Oh yes, of course. He foretold wild and crazy things that couldn't possibly happen."

"But with panache, and wild white hair, and on national television."

"He certainly had a flair for ..." His voice trailed off as he examined the photograph of the Hotel Adirondack. Then he fished around inside his cassock and produced the elegant card from Willie Kapp's shop. He held them side-by-side. "The 'A' insignia on the card, it's the same as the one over the entrance. This stationery came from that hotel."

"Am I a valuable sidekick or what?"

"Priceless, Martin. But don't let it go to your head."

"Never higher than my shins."

Father slowly brought the photograph so close to his face it almost touched his nose. "What are these dots?"

"Excuse me?"

"All over the façade of the building there's a motif of black dots. They're tiny in this picture, but they must be a foot or two in diameter. Maybe they're emblems—shields or something."

"That rings a bell, but I was just a kid the last time I was there. My mind was on other things."

"The architect certainly made a point of using them. See? They accentuate every window, archway, turret, and rain gutter." He compared the photo to the card again. "I wonder if there's any connection between them and the raised circles around the edge of this invitation."

"This is where my value as a sidekick wanes," said I with a protracted sigh. "Um, by the way, do you think it was wise to rile a potential auxiliary bishop?"

"You mean His Lordship, Bishop deQuet?"

"The very one."

He set the photograph and card on his lap and folded his hands upon them. "Martin, you and I, just like Jesus, Mary, the Apostles, and all the Saints have been in harm's way since our Baptism, and don't you forget it."

"Never," I assured him as I turned off Treviño Avenue onto Villanova Terrace. "But I would like to point out that we've discovered who left that message on Monsignor Aspic's answering machine the night he disappeared."

"You mean Bishop deQuet?"

"'*Con*rad,' lisped I in my most cucumbery voice, "'are you *there*? Please pick *up* if you *are*. This is *D.K.*!'"

"Ah," said Father. "You caught that. Keep it up, Martin, you'll be a fine detective yet."

"This is it," announced the gardener as he pulled the Jeep to the curb in front of a stately old early-California house with a statue of the Blessed Virgin gracing the roses in the front with Her august presence.

"This should prove interesting," said Father, unbuckling his seatbelt.

The great detective strikes again.

28

"OH MERCY, MERCY ME!," gasped the white-haired woman in the high-backed, antique chair as Keating, the butler, showed us into the living room. "Darling, look what we have here!"

"Indeed, indeedy do, Sweetheart," agreed the gray-haired woman standing by the fireplace. "How often does a priest come to visit us these days?"

"Why Darling, you know good and well this is two days in a row. No, I mean, two in three days. Well, you know what I mean."

"But before that, Sweetheart. Before that! They used to love to come here to beg, now didn't they?" Her expression dropped. "Before the rot set in."

"Don't be vulgar, Darling. And don't let us be rude. Good afternoon, Father."

"But you know it did, Sweetheart. You know they did, and it did. Indeedy it did." The gray-haired lady, whom the other called Darling, approached Father the way she might examine a fine piece of furniture. "Why, I'll bet you my Miraculous Medal, the one Archbishop McInery blessed at that luncheon on the first anniversary of his appointment to the archbishopric, which you know I wouldn't part with without one whiz-bang of a fight, that this man who fills a cassock so handsomely, a cassock which could use some attention, if you don't mind my saying so, Father, but you don't begrudge a little tease from an admirer, do you? You must be Father John Baptist. There. You see, Sweetheart? I was right." She turned her gaze upon me, and for a moment I felt very out-of-place indeed. "And this must be his, um, yes, well, whatever you are, young man, you are most certainly Marvin Spleeny."

"His name is Feeney, Madam," said Father, taking Darling's right hand respectfully, perhaps a tad gallantly. "Martin Feeney. I am afraid you have me at a loss."

"Oh, we've never met, good gracious no," said she, fluttering her eye-lashes. "But you have been the subject of many a conversation around our family's dinner tables."

"You mean you're the one?" said Sweetheart, the seated lady with white hair, offering Father her hand, limp-like, as if hinting for him to kiss it.

"If I'm the one she means," said Father, accepting her appendage and obliging with the barest of pecks.

"I pictured you so much differently," said she, looking at the back of her hand as if it tingled.

"That's because you never read the papers, Sweetheart," said Darling, returning to her place by the fireplace. "You were quite the rage last June, Father, as if you didn't know. Why, Roddy and Threety were placing bets on whether you'd crack that awful, awful case." She eyed her white-haired companion meaningfully. "Would you believe it? Some people I know were rooting for the perpetrator."

"Vulgar, vulgar, vulgar," chided Sweetheart in ascending minor thirds, smiling disarmingly up at Father. "My sister gets nervous around priests."

"Don't mind her, Father, mine gets giddy."

"Everyone is guilty of something," said Father kindly yet philosophically. "The reaction is to be expected, and indeed hoped for."

"Imagine that, Darling."

"Indeedy do, Sweetheart."

"Excuse me, Mesdames, Father, Sir," said Keating the butler, who had been waiting patiently for a moment to intrude. "Allow me the honor." He indicated the white-haired lady in the high-backed chair thus far known only as Sweetheart and nodded. "Mrs. Mehitabelle Doily." He shifted his deference to the gray-haired woman who'd been answering to Darling. "Mrs. Hortense Doily." He smiled encouragingly at Father, but as his gaze fell on me, I felt more out-of-place than ever. "Father John Baptist, and his associate, Martin Feeney."

"You're such a dear, Keating," said Mehitabelle, adjusting the fluffy pink boa draped around her shoulders, "but you know, I think we were on the verge of getting all that straight ourselves."

"Of course, Ma'am." Keating bowed deeply and withdrew a few paces.

"Sweetheart, don't be so hard on Keating." Hortense played with one end of her identical feathery boa, then let it fall. "I'm not at all sure we would have figured it out, I'm really not."

"Oh bosh, Darling," said Mehitabelle, bracing to hoist herself up onto her high-buttoned shoes, "of course we would."

"And now we'll never know, will we?" asked Father, smiling play-fully. He extended a helping hand to the seated Doily Sister and assisted her to her feet. I admired his skill at fitting into their world rather than expecting them to force themselves into his. Why should they, after all? He and I were intruders into their space, specks on the lens of their point of view, as it were.

"Why, thank-you young man," tittered Mehitabelle, once she had established herself in the upright position. It took a few moments to confirm her balance. "I mean, Father John, is it?"

"You are quite welcome," said Father. "Would you ladies think ill of me if I were to presume to ask a personal question?"

"Oh, do," said the gals together, their wrinkled mouths forming tight little O's.

"How is it that you are sisters and yet are both 'Mrs. Doily'?"

That had been my question, too, but since I was just whatever I am, and Marvin Spleeny to boot, I held my peace.

"Me oh my," said Hortense, her expression shifting from pain to joy to severe distress. She produced a handkerchief and dabbed the corner of her eye. "You would have to ask that, Father."

"Technically we're sisters-in-law," sniffed Mehitabelle, producing an identical hankie and applying it daintily to her nose. "We married twin brothers, you see. Fillmore Doily was my dear husband, and—"

"Roscoe Doily, God rest his soul, was mine," added Hortense with a shuddering heave. "We were married on the same day, you know. A double wedding at Saint Valeria's Cathedral, no less."

"Really," said Father, making an encompassing circular gesture with his hands before clasping them passionately in front of his chest. In any other context I would have assumed him to be overplaying, but in this case he seemed to be right on par with them. "That must have been grand."

"Beyond grand," said Hortense. "So far beyond, you wouldn't believe how far. Would he, Sweetheart?"

"Oh no, Darling," said Mehitabelle. "It was way, way beyond. I believe the colloquialism is 'out of sight.'"

"Indeed," said Father, enjoying himself immensely. "You must tell me all about it."

The ladies could have been blood sisters. Mehitabelle had aged whitely and Hortense grayly, but other than that they had the same witty yet clueless eyes, matching delicate but crinkly complexions, similar fidgety yet refined gestures, and identical whimsical yet cynical smiles. Mehitabelle sported an electric-blue silk blouse with a rippled collar and long sleeves with ruffled cuffs, and Hortense a green-and-gold paisley jacket. Other than that, they wore identical long black skirts and had matching pink feather boas draped around their shoulders. Perhaps they had lived together for so long that they had merged into one entity. They were obviously inseparable.

The house itself was like the moldering mansion in *Sunset Boulevard* starring William Holden and Gloria Swanson, crossed with the creepy house in *The Addams Family,* starring John Astin and Carolyn Jones. It was gaudy yet classy, cluttered below yet high-vaulted above, a curious juxtaposition of memories clung to and absentmindedness exalted, of time standing still and time fallen off the train and laying broken beside the track. One could not help but notice old, yellowed newspapers laying about the place. KENNEDY ASSASSINATED! cried the headline nearest to me, and that appeared to be the most recent. MICKEY COHEN ARRESTED! shouted another; BUDDY HOLLY DIES IN PLANE CRASH; and the most telling of all: EDSEL: FORD'S NEW TRIUMPH!

Also evident about the place was a musty air of regal, ancestral, and staunchly professed Catholicism. A luscious oil painting I presumed to portray Fillmore and Roscoe Doily as young men, faces severe and magisterial, hung above the fireplace. In the background of that painting towered a statue of St. Michael the Archangel standing triumphant upon the carcass of Satan, the defeated Serpent. The walls on both sides of the mantel were draped with tapestries depicting the Raising of Lazarus on the left, and the Resurrection of Christ on the right. Statues of various Saints poked their halos above various chairs and couches, most of them strewn with Rosaries and Scapulars. One end table in particular seemed to be the designated Traditional Catholic periodical receptacle, stacked as it was with worn, faded copies of *The Rambler, The Remainder,* and *The Tridentine Tribune.*

"I have a wonderful idea," said Hortense, motioning Father toward a huge leather chair. "Why doesn't your valet accompany our manservant to the kitchen and help him prepare a tray?"

Father glanced at me to see if I objected. For a moment I thought of protesting, but then decided she had got it about right, although "valet" was reaching a bit. Besides, I wasn't fitting into the conversation anyway.

"This way, Sir," said Keating, smiling conspiratorially. He seemed used to the old gals' ways, and wouldn't want to change anything for the world.

"If you will excuse me," said I, attempting to bow deferentially.

"Do sit down, Father," said Hortense sweetly as I followed Keating from the room. "It's so good of you to come for a visit. Isn't it, Sweetheart?"

"Oh, yes, Darling," agreed Mehitabelle. "Father John, do make yourself at home."

Keating had the ruddy jowls, balding crown, widely bowed legs, and billowing paunch of many a leprechaun who had grown into a full-blown Irishman. All of these endearing characteristics were sagging and splotching with age, which I guessed to be approaching seventy—a spry seventy, to be sure, but there are limits. His swollen knuckles belied the advance of arthritis, and he favored his left leg slightly. He sported an attractive red vest, striped pants, and gray spats on his glassy black shoes, but oddly no tailcoat. The studs and cufflinks on this dress shirt were golden shamrocks, and he wore a red garter high on his left arm. He kept winking at me over his shoulder as he led me down a narrow hallway with creaking floorboards.

As we entered the kitchen I was engulfed by a corona of cozy heat. It was like something out of a nineteenth century novel. There was a wood-burning stove, all black cast iron, with a large, tin vent pipe rising from the back and disappearing at an angle through the wall to the outside. There were four lacquered sixteen-inch wooden square doors set in one pine-paneled wall, each with a refrigerator latch. It took me a minute to realize they were genuine iceboxes, the kind probably used by my great-grandmother. The topper was the spigot in the sink, which actually had a hand-pump attached. This was one really, really old house, and it was inhabited by people with Luddite tendencies. The truth be told, I was fascinated by the place's anachronistic simplicity. It made the rectory at Saint Philomena's seem like the House of the Future.

"Fire and brimwater!" exclaimed Keating, hanging a copper kettle on the spigot and giving the lever a couple of solid yanks. "So you're Martin Feeney." Water gurgled noisily from the faucet and drummed inside the metal vessel. "I was hoping to meet you one of these days."

"Oh?" said I, never having been told such a thing by anybody in my life.

"You know, Sir, one Irishman to another."

"Sorry to disappoint you, but I'm not Irish."

"G'wan, with a good old Irish moniker like Feeney, what else could you be?"

"Things are not always as they seem. The family name was Fényi, actually. Some clerk at Ellis Island misspelled my grandfather's name when he came to this country. He was Hungarian—my grandfather, not the clerk."

"Well, I'll be." With a playful pretense of clenched teeth and muscles, Keating heaved the kettle onto the stove. There was no need to turn on the heat. Energetic flames were visible through a narrow grate in the side. The wet base of the kettle sizzled as it made contact with the radiantly hot stovetop. "I happened to attend Mass at St. Philomena's—Heavens, was it only yesterday? Goodness me, yes, it was."

I was about to inquire what had brought him to our poor but rich parish, but he added, "What was his name, the monsignor who celebrated Mass? Hammer-Wire or something—"

"Havermeyer," said I.

"Thank-you, Sir. Monsignor Havermeyer."

Again, I was about to inquire, but then he said:

"He mentioned you in his sermon."

Now that took me completely by surprise.

"No," said I.

"Yes, indeed," said he. "Honestly, he went on at some length."

"Did he? I don't know what to say."

> GARDENING TIPS: I was speechless on two counts.
> First, that Monsignor Havermeyer would have men-
> tioned me of all people in a sermon. Second, that
> the monsignor would have given a sermon on a week-
> day. It was Father Baptist's policy to preach
> only on Sundays, Holy Days, and special Feast
> Days, but never on regular weekdays. Perhaps he
> had not made this clear to his prote/ge/, Monsi-
> gnor "Hammer-Wire."
>
>   --M.F.

"As me sweet, gray-haired grandmother used to say," said Keating, retrieving a massive silver tray from one of the cherry wood cupboards,
"'If you don't know what to say, Lad, don't bother.' You weren't there,
as the good monsignor pointed out, or I would have sought you at the
time. He said that the reason he was able to fill in for Father Baptist in
his regrettable but unavoidable absence was that you had painstakingly
rehearsed him in the language and rubrics of the Latin Mass. Is that so,
Mr. Feeney?"

"Well, yes," said I, blushing furiously. "I suppose I did give him a
few pointers, but—"

"You don't have to play humble with me," said he, winking and
blinking, "even if you're not Irish. Monsignor made it eminently clear
that any parishioners who have maligned you for your deportment or
demeanor should be ashamed of themselves—that you are a treasure,
albeit a crotchety, limping one."

"He said that?"

"I'm condensing it considerably to be sure, and freely substituting me
own terms, but that was essentially his drift."

"Oh dear." Out of sheer embarrassment I went over to the window
and gazed out into the yard. The pane itself was actually an impressive
window box, an extended glassed-in mini-garden of little potted herbs.
Beyond the immediate greenery was a beautiful rose garden out back.

No, more than a rose garden. It was also a fruit, vegetable, and herb farm, with everything planted in the eye-pleasing arrangement of a flower garden.

The driveway meandered alongside the house, past the garden, and swung around to a four-car garage beyond that had probably once been a horse stable. The family automobile was parked in plain sight before the garage, one of those classic vehicles that came and went ages ago, the product of some obscure company that only manufactured a few cars by hand before going under. But what cars! The glossy black auto had chromium spoke wheels, whitewall tires, an enormous hood roomy enough to accommodate at least fourteen cylinders, and a commodious passenger compartment with red and gold curtains. On the driver's door was an insignia that I knew I'd seen before, but couldn't quite place. It was executed in molded chrome, and represented a famous mountain, the name of which fluttered just out of reach of my memory. The hood ornament was patterned along the same lines.

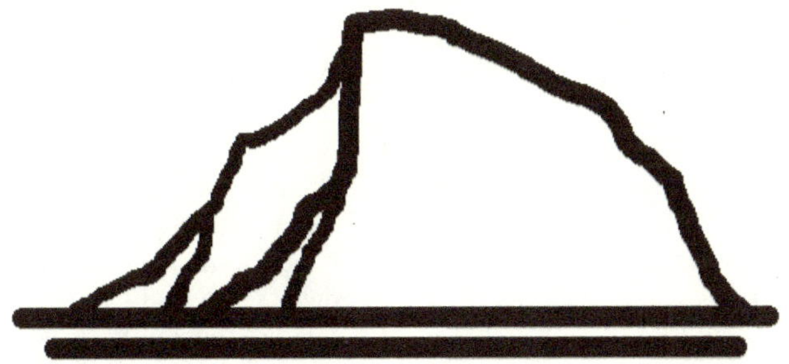

GARDENING TIPS: It took some serious searching in the library, but I finally found a facsimile of the company logo in an old magazine. I copied it as best I could with my trusty crayon. Imagine it executed in polished chrome against a shiny, antique black background. I provide it here for my readers who like out-dated stuff.

                                    --M.F.

"Excuse me," said I, craning my neck painfully to see the logo better. "That's a fine car you have out there. I've never seen anything quite like it. May I ask what make it is?"

"Ah, the old clunker. Mesdames call it Doilybelle, but I call it Beelzebub. Fire and brimwater! It may be a classic, but it's also a pain in the camshaft." Keating began filling the tray with saucers and cups from another cupboard. "It's a miracle of ingenious engineering, no argument there, but all the parts are worn out. They were all made by hand, wouldn't you know? There are no replacements. The company was called Harrigan Doily Motors, owned by a gentleman of the same name who was also the eldest brother of Roscoe and Fillmore. They all went to God together, I'm afraid."

"Excuse me," said I, detaching my attention from the car out back. "What did you say?"

Keating paused filling the sugar bowl to shrug and say, "A long story, Sir."

"You're saying all three brothers died at the same time?"

"I'm afraid so, Sir."

"How terrible. I don't suppose Harrigan left a widow, too."

"No, Sir. His wife accompanied him and the rest of them on the train that never made it to its destination. The western branch of the Doily clan was on its way to St. Louis to celebrate Easter Sunday with their eastern relatives, you see. They had exclusively reserved five railcars on the Southern Pacific: two sleepers, a dining car, a bar of course, and the caboose. Who would have thought? I ask you, in a million years, who would have thought? Mesdames were both down with measles at the time, poor dears, though it proved to be fortuitous that they stayed behind."

He paused, eyebrows raised and jaw half lowered, expecting me to respond. When I didn't he continued his tale. "Mesdames lost most of their in-laws in one horrendous accident, but remained unscathed themselves—physically, anyway." He pointed knowingly at his temple. "The truth be told, the ordeal kind of unhinged their wits, if you get me meaning. I don't mean it hurtfully, not at all. Honestly, they are the kindliest pair of ladies you or I are ever likely to meet. The Jalopy from Hell out there reminds them of their brother-in-law, Harrigan. That's why they wouldn't part with that rolling disaster if you gave them a Bentley or a Rolls Royce Phantom II. It's rumored he was more than just thoughtful to them in a brother-in-lawyerly way, but don't you believe it, Sir. Those two are the most devout souls I've met in all me travels. They took me parents in when me father got laid off and couldn't find work. Mother died shortly thereafter of diphtheria, and Mesdames paid me tuition—at Notre Dame, no less, Sir. Small wonder Dad stuck with them through thick and thin, he did. He was caring for them here when the great train disaster killed their kin. When Dad got too old and feeble, I left me job and assumed his duties. I was six months shy of retirement me self, Sir, and they were about to downsize me out anyway. I had no family so I didn't need to worry about insurance packages and all that rot. Mesdames insisted that Dad retire in his quarters, right here in their home, where he lived rent-free until he succumbed two years ago next March—thank God, just minutes after receiving the Last Rites. But as to what you asked."

"I'm sorry, I completely forget what I asked."

"You inquired, Sir, about the make of the family rattletrap, and if Harrigan Doily left a widow. I already answered the second part in the negative, but back to the first. Harrigan was an inventor, and a clever one. But as is the way with some geniuses, he couldn't balance his checkbook let alone make a profit on his own bright ideas. That fell to his brother, Fillmore, and Fillmore's twin, Roscoe, who were both capable businessmen. I trust you're getting this all straight."

"Uh, yeah, pretty much. That is to say I'm keeping up with you but I can't imagine what's coming next."

"Among other things, Harrigan invented a revolutionary internal combustion engine. It had to do with the shape of the pistons and the orientation of the valves, and he claimed he got the idea while visiting Yosemite National Park. He called his car the 'Half Dome' and used a stylized representation of the mountain of that name as his logo. You'll notice the sharp drop-off of the roof of the passenger compartment, and the commodious trunk behind. That aerodynamic design is borrowed from the mountain as well."

"Ah, of course. I thought that insignia looked familiar. Something very like it was on a travel brochure I ordered from the National Park Service when I was planning a vacation I never took. You said you left your job just shy of retirement. What career had you pursued, if I may ask?"

"I'd rather let the dead bury their bygones, if you don't mind, Sir. I had to see to Dad's needs. I promised him I'd never put him in one of 'those places.' This was his home, and he lived to a ripe old age and died in his bed with the Sacraments. For that I am grateful, for I have a father who is also a Friend in Heaven, in addition to Our Father Who art in Heaven. Antoinette, the maid, was a great help, too. You'll like her when you meet her. I wonder where she's got off to. She's been having foot trouble of late, and may well be soaking them up in her room."

"Have you ever thought of retiring?" I asked. "I mean, from here?"

"Good Heavens, Sir, what would Mesdames do without me? For that matter, what would I do without them?"

At first it surprised me, this continuous string of personal information about his employers. Then it hit me. Mehitabelle and Hortense Doily were more than mere employers. They were his family. His attachment to them was more than servile, but somewhat less than peerage. Ironically, he really did consider me Father's valet, a servant like himself. Servants are notorious gossipers, at least, so I've read in many a novel less cheesy than this one.

"But as to the 'Half Dome' engine," he was saying, "which was your original question, if Mister Harrigan's design had caught on, Sir, it would have drastically reduced the nation's petroleum requirements. Ford and Chrysler wouldn't listen to him, figured him for a crackpot, or so I understand—it was before me association with the family. But it worked. I should know. I only fill that bucket up every other month, if that. Fillmore and Roscoe were his very first customers in addition to being his partners, and now the only mechanic who knows how to service the dang contraption properly is one of their former employees. Old Rudyard is in his nineties and keeps threatening to retire. I don't know what I'll do when he finally does because Mesdames are so used to that old heap, I can't imagine them buying, let alone riding in, another."

All the while Keating carefully set the tray. In the center was a towering teapot unlike any I'd ever seen before. It had the usual spout and handle, but between had three different round lids with grips insulated with ornate steel coils. Around the pot he placed cups and saucers, as well as plates of scones, wafers, cranberries, and grapes. There were also little silver serving boats containing what appeared to be different varieties of tea leaves, each with its own little spoon. The handle of each was formed in the shape of a graceful capital "A."

"Excuse me," said I, picking up one of the boats. "I can't help but notice that this says Hotel Adirondack on the side."

"Ah," said Keating, shaking his head. "It is Mesdames' custom to dine there on Tuesday and Saturday evenings. Those are the quietest and noisiest nights respectively, customer-wise. The way they tip, Sir, well—

"They get a lot of attention."

"Precisely, Sir. The Blue Mountain Grill still serves an exquisite chateaubriand, carved tableside. The mushroom sauce comes in those little boats. You can imagine how the ladies raved about them, as ladies do. Several years ago the maitre d' presented Mesdames with an engraved set on behalf of the staff. There's an inscription on the bottom."

I held the vessel high so I could see the base without spilling the tealeaves. "'To our most beloved patrons, Hortense R. Doily & Mehitabelle T. Doily,'" I read aloud. "That must have tickled them."

"Indeed it did, Sir. Indeed it did. Are you familiar with the Adirondack?"

"My high school held our prom there, but I haven't been since. By sheer happenstance, Father and I are going to be meeting someone there tomorrow evening in the Saranac Lounge."

"Ah, the Saranac. That's where I sometimes retire while Mesdames dine. It's a lovely place to drink and think. It's like something out of an old, familiar movie. Tomorrow evening, you say. Well, perhaps our paths will cross. Um, excuse me, Sir."

"Of course."

With a mighty heave-ho he hefted the copper kettle from the stove, brushed past me, and proceeded to pour the steaming hot water slowly into one of the open lids of the teapot. The pot's metal tummy rumbled its approval.

"By the way," said he, "speaking of coincidences, I wanted to mention earlier what a great one it is, you showing up on our doorstep today, if you don't mind me saying so. Like I said, after Monsignor Hammer-Wire—"

"Havermeyer."

"Right. After Monsignor Havermeyer's sermon I wanted to meet you then and there."

"I can't say I believe in coincidences."

"Hm. No believing Catholic would, I suppose. Still, it's interesting you being here like this."

"Father Baptist is retracing Monsignor Aspic's movements on the day of his disappearance."

"My stars, that's right. I heard about that on the radio, the monsignor vanishing just outside that TV station, I mean. To think he was here earlier that very day."

"Wednesday."

"That's right. Yes, that's when it was."

"Do you know why he came to visit Mrs. and Mrs. Doily?"

"Why does anybody come to visit them anymore? He had a manuscript, or so I assume. I was out running an errand for the ladies at the time—royal blue ink for their fountain pens, they never 'blue-line' with ballpoints, not them—so I'm not sure. But that would be me guess."

"So you didn't meet him?"

"No, Sir, I didn't. He had departed by the time I returned."

"Did he have an appointment?"

"Of course. Mesdames were expecting him. Antoinette went with me because she had an appointment with her podiatrist. When she and I departed I only locked one of the five bolts on the front door for Mesdames' convenience when the monsignor arrived."

"Isn't that a bit unusual?" I asked. "Leaving the ladies to see to company themselves?"

"Hardly," said Keating. "As long as the teakettle is hot and full and left in the sitting room, they can handle anything and anybody. Excuse me for saying so, Sir, but I imagine your Father John is asking these same questions in the living room."

"Could be. He's the detective. I'm just the gardener."

"Oh? I thought you were his valet."

"I'm whatever he needs me to be, which is usually a chauffeur."

"Sounds like me." He set the empty kettle on the counter by the sink. The steam within sighed through the spout. Then he snapped his fingers, spun around, and opened a breadbox on the opposite counter. "Pumpernickel," he explained, detaching a red plastic clip from the cellophane bag enfolding the loaf of hard, dark bread. "Madam Mehitabelle's favorite. I bought it for her just the other day. Evening, actually, come to think of it."

"Fresh?" I asked.

"Of course, fresh. It would mean me head if I bought it even a day old." He drew a finger across his throat by way of illustration. "What she doesn't eat by the end of the second day she crumbles and gives to the birds in the garden on the third. This loaf is slated for birdfeed tomorrow morning."

"That wrapper looks familiar. Is that from the 'Tory Hill Bakery' on Melrose?"

"You know bread, I see."

"I know where Millie sends me to buy it. She's our housekeeper. So if that bread is two days old, you bought it the same day Monsignor Aspic was here. Not that it's a coincidence since we don't believe in them. Was the bakery part of your stationery run?"

"Let me think," said Keating. Having placed several slices of the aromatic bread on the serving tray, he twisted the wrapper closed and replaced the red clip. "Wednesday," he said, closing the breadbox. "By the time Antoinette and I returned home, as I've already said, Monsignor Aspic was gone. Antoinette went to her room to rest her feet. Mesdames had an appointment at the beauty parlor at three. While they were thus occupied, I picked up a few supplies at the grocery and hardware stores. I brought Mesdames home around seven-thirty, and then at Madam Mehitabelle's request, I went back out for the pumpernickel. Why do you ask?"

"No particular reason. I've been around Father Baptist so long I've picked up some of his habits."

"I know what you mean." He surveyed the tray with approval. "Well, that's as far as I take it. Mesdames insist on blending and steeping their tea themselves, as you will see shortly."

"Right behind you," said I as he hefted the huge tray and carried it, rattling vigorously, down the creaking hallway. This time the trek was much slower, and I had time to look into two different spacious bathrooms, one on each side, as we walked past. Both had water tanks mounted near the ceiling with a pull chain as a flusher. I wondered whether the elevated bathtubs had hot running water or Keating had to fetch it from the kitchen in buckets. Lamely I said, "I don't feel as though I've been much help."

"Sure you have," said he over his shoulder. "Surely you will be."

29

"FIRE AND BRIMWATER!" said Keating through gritted teeth as we returned to the living room. "They're not here. Would you mind moving those magazines from the coffee table, Sir?"

"Sure thing," said I, finally feeling a wee bit useful. I whisked away three ancient copies of *Vogue*, issues published while Jacqueline Kennedy was the First Lady. "Where could they be?"

"Ugh!" he grunted, setting the tray down none too gracefully. He straightened, pressing his palms against the small of his back. "One of these days that thing is going to dislocate me whole spine. Let's see. Perhaps they're in Mesdames' reading room, or as Madam Mehitabelle sometimes calls it, 'The Sunroom of Postponed Hopes.' This way."

I followed him through a couple of small rooms into a bright, cheerful octagonal room in the southeast corner of the house. Four of the walls featured windows, each with a window box brimming with brightly colored herbs and spices. The smell gave the room a timbered scent. In the center was one of those wooden desks designed in such a way that two people would sit at it facing each other.

```
GARDENING TIPS: The thought of trying to
think, to ponder content, to consider allit-
eration versus clarity, to read the dialogue
aloud, in short, the notion of writing, or
trying to write with some person inches away
staring at me, or worse, himself going through
his own hilarious writing contortions, simply
put, makes my teeth soft.  The cluttered page
emerging from the carriage of my Underwood, I
can handle.  My own reflection in my bathroom
mirror is pushing it.  But another person?
   This went through my mind as I stood looking
at the place where Mehitabelle and Hortense
Doily apparently performed their publishing
functions.
   Am I self-absorbed or what?
                                      --M.F.


N.B.: As I reread the above passage I realized
I neglected to consider my Guardian Angel, who
```

> has always been my best audience. I read all
> my ramblings to him aloud. Of course, he is
> but a Messenger of God Who is also watching,
> as well as the clouds of witnesses Saint Paul
> mentioned in passing in his Epistle to the He-
> brews . . . My mouth goes bone dry at the
> thought!

The room was ringed with manuscripts, some thick, some thin, all of them whiningly awaiting the judgment of the Doily Sisters. Some were typed, some handwritten; all of them earnest, all of them hopeful. They were arranged, not on tenterhooks, but on bookshelves, piled on several antique tables, and stacked on the loveseat. Against one of the four solid walls stood a mahogany barrister's case with glass panels inside which were preserved an assortment of books with the most elegant leather binding I have ever seen. Many of them were white, though some were velvety pastel hues, the titles rendered in gold with curlicued frills.

"I don't understand," said I, eyeing the titles in the display case. "I see the sermons of Saints Alphonsus di Liguori, Francis de Sales, John Marie Vianney, a deluxe edition of Saint Cyprian, and the complete works of Anne Catherine Emmerich. Here's a Latin-English missal, a book of Litanies, a compendium of prayers by and to the Saints, and a volume called *The Devout Woman's Garden of Prayers and Meditations*." I indicated the unpublished clutter around the room with a wave of my arm. "Are all these submissions devotional works? I had no idea there were so many still writing that sort of thing."

"No, Sir," said Keating, surveying the shambles. "What you see there in that case is what they currently publish, which is pretty much what they've always published. This other material is mostly novels."

"Novels? Why would writers send fiction to the Doily Sisters?"

"Because Mesdames are listed as publishers, and there are a lot of authors out there who don't bother to query first. Mesdames actually do peruse all of it. It takes them a while, but they fastidiously return each and every one with a lengthy letter of explanation and criticism. They take the time, unlike most publishers, to read what they reject. They reject everything, but they do it kindly."

"Then they are, without doubt, a refreshing exception to the rule," said I, drawing from my own experience. "Speaking of whom, where might they be?"

"Ah," said Keating, pointing toward a crooked bookcase. "They're showing Father John the chapel."

It took me a long moment to realize the bookcase was itself a door left slightly ajar. Keating gripped one of the shelves, gave it a tug, and the whole thing swung easily a foot or so outward. I tested it with my hand and found its mechanism silent, precisely balanced, and meticulously lubricated.

"Whoever installed this," said I, "had a flair for cloak and dagger."

"Not precisely, Sir. This house—or at least this part of it—dates back to the days when the American Army seized California. Some of the wealthy Catholic families, understandably concerned, installed hideaways like this to conceal their valuables, to protect their religious articles, and as potential refuges for their priests. As it turned out, unnecessarily, but who knows, Sir, if some day it will be needed indeed."

"Hmm," said I, regarding the bookcase. "I wouldn't want to get trapped in there."

"Can't, Sir. There's no lock. The slightest push from within and it opens." He swung it shut. "But see, when it's closed, there's nary a trace." As he pulled it open again there was no grinding or squeaking, just a gentle whisper of displaced air. "Now that's craftsmanship, Sir. Saint Nicholas Owen would be proud."

"Indeed he would."

```
GARDENING TIPS:  During the days of the Reforma-
tion, Nicholas Owen devoted his talents to the in-
stallation of ingenious hiding places for priests
who were ministering to the persecuted Catholics
of jolly old England.  This courageous carpenter
died under torture in the Tower of London in 1606,
taking his secrets with him.
                                            --M.F.
```

Behind the bookcase was a chamber about the size of a large walk-in closet. The walls, floor, and ceiling were paneled in pale wood, probably oak. Three coarse shelves on the left-hand wall contained several old books stacked on their sides, tattered ribbon markers lolling from their withered pages. An uncomfortable-looking bunk was mounted on the right-hand wall. The far wall, oddly, seemed to be painted black. It took me a moment to realize that it was in fact a doorless doorway into dark nothingness. As I stepped closer the edges of descending stairs came into view.

"Perhaps I should go first, Sir," said Keating, sensing my hesitation.

"Perhaps," I agreed as he descended into the gloom.

The stairwell seemed to be hewn from solid stone. It was a steep staircase indeed, and treacherously dark. The handrail felt cold, rough, and metallic. Fortunately I had my cane, so each descending step held no surprises. Still, for a man who expends as much energy as I do protecting my spine from jolts and jiggles, it was a tentative effort. A slight impact can leave me shaking, and though I'm the first to admit my sins deserve worse, I'm not one to provoke the process.

"Those two old—" I began to say. "I mean, they actually—?"

"Indeed they do, Sir. Being prayerful, and having their own chapel—and a beauty, as you will shortly see, Sir—Mesdames use these stairs several times a day. They say climbing the stairs keeps them young. It's not my place to argue. There's no light until the first landing, so be careful."

"Right."

The first landing was down seven steps, and if he'd implied that there would be light there, I didn't perceive it. I did hear voices, distant and indistinguishable, emanating from somewhere below and to my left. We descended seven more steps in that direction. At the next turn, this time to the right, a faint, yellow, undulating glow dabbed at the darkness, and the voices became less reverberant, though still unintelligible. The third and final landing ended in a peaked archway with another set of stairs descending in a sharp curve to the right, the amber light growing vibrant and the voices resolving into the tones and inflections of our hostesses and Father Baptist. One, two, three, four, five steps more, and we were deposited at the rear of a chapel perhaps thirty feet wide and fifty long. There was no way not to make a dramatic, panting entrance after all that.

The floor was made of irregular not-so-flat stones, reminiscent of the primitive masonry in the mysterious grotto at Saint Philomena's. The walls, on the other hand, as well as the vaulted ceiling were covered in intricately carved rectangles of waxed mahogany two-foot square. Each segment was a bas-relief rendering of an incident from the Bible or the lives of the Saints. I caught glimpses of Moses and the Burning Bush, Abraham about to slaughter Isaac, Jesus giving the Sermon on the Mount, Saint Thomas More at the chopping block, Saint George slaying his dragon, Saint Martha defeating hers, Saint Simon Stock receiving the brown scapular, Saint Cecilia standing trial before the Prefect of Rome, and Saint Catherine facing the torture wheel. These all became a blur of detail as I espied Father and the Doily ladies standing off to the left beneath the Sixth Station of the Cross, Saint Veronica compassionately wiping the Face of Jesus, her piety rewarded by the imprinting of the Sacred Image upon the cloth. The craftsman had managed to convincingly depict this miraculous transference in nothing but etches in the wood, without the use of any stains, inks or paints whatsoever. This scene, like the rest of the Stations, was convincingly rendered in golden oak and mounted in a walnut frame just above eyelevel.

"Marvelous," marveled a voice, not mine. It was Father Baptist's. "Simply marvelous."

"We knew you'd think so, didn't we, Sweetheart?"

"Oh, yes, Darling. We certainly did."

There were ten rows of pews with kneelers divided by a center aisle leading up to a knee-high wrought-iron gate mounted in the center of the wooden Communion rail. Beyond that was the Sanctuary, like a dream from my childhood, complete with a traditional altar fashioned out of a single block of fine, polished redwood, perhaps from a giant Sequoia tree, surmounted with a tabernacle that could have adorned a high altar in a cathedral or monastery, at least, in centuries past. In fact, all of the sacred accoutrements—from the cruets on the little table at the Epistle side to the ponderous altar missal left closed on the Gospel side, from the Gothic Crucifix above the altar to the regal candlesticks upon it, from the intricate tapestries on both sides to the sumptuous though tread-worn once-royal-red rugs tumbling down the altar steps—all had that mismatched Old World quality, like the castellated hodgepodge of artwork and structure William Randolph Hearst had assembled a few hundred miles up the California coast overlooking San Simeon.

"This is wonderful, if I may say so," said I, lumbering into their midst. "Why, I haven't seen anything like this since—"

"Young man," said Hortense abruptly, eyeing me up and down as though there was something seriously wrong with me.

"Yes, Ma'am?" I blundered further. "I beg your pardon. I was just saying—"

"Young man," she said again, pointing significantly over her shoulder. I think you'll agree that when one points with a finger at the end of an extended arm, the arm establishes the direction and the finger draws the eye to the intended item. When the finger in question is at the end of an arm doubled up upon itself, and the finger itself is curved like a crescent moon, the target becomes harder to determine. I looked beyond her, but there was so much to take in, so many beautiful works of art and craftsmanship all around, I didn't know where to focus.

"Martin," whispered Father, drawing my eyes with his to the Sanctuary lamp. It was an ornate affair made of gleaming gold and ruby red glass with a candle flame burning moodily within. There must have been a hundred other candles bobbing in various holders and fixtures around the chapel, but this one suspended from the ceiling betokened the presence of the Blessed Sacrament in the Tabernacle, which was God's incomprehensible response to the eternal plight of all humanity.

"Oh, I see—" I said, then caught myself. A graceful genuflection is beyond me, especially after descending all those stairs, but with my cane I was able to perform the act without wobbling too erratically. Keating, I noticed, with all his years, was managing as genteel an obeisance as I've ever witnessed. My heroic effort seemed to appease our hostesses, at least until I righted myself awkwardly and whispered to them, "Do please forgive me, Ladies. There is so much here to see, I didn't realize—"

Hortense cut me off with a stern look.

Mehitabelle eyed me more sternly still.

I looked at Father, confused.

He made a gesture around his ear that either meant I was crazy or the ladies were hard of hearing—two equally plausible propositions. "Isn't it amazing?" said he, but he said it in a peculiar way. He extended his neck and animated his face as though he were whispering, but his actual tone of voice was louder than normal. It was a pretense of speaking in hushed tones for the ladies' sake before the Real Presence. As usual, I was left feeling like a klutz. "Who would have thought," he continued in this conflicted, stylized manner, "that all this could possibly be secreted away in the heart of this house?"

"I'm speechless," I attempted, then decided it was best to leave it at that. To avoid the stabbing glares of the Doily Sisters I fell silent and allowed my eyes to drift where they would. They chose the chandelier suspended from the pinnacle of the vaulted ceiling. It was made from an old wagon wheel, centered over the spot where the priest would say the Prayers at the Foot of the Altar at the commencement of Mass. I counted nine kerosene lamps burning around its perimeter, each crowned with a reflecting lid of polished chrome, collectively showering the chapel with pleasing, vibrant light.

On impulse, I turned around to see something equally remarkable. On the rear wall, set on each side of the entrance and one above, were three gorgeous stained-glass windows. They were cleverly backlit, probably with similar kerosene flames, giving the impression of late afternoon sunlight penetrating the latticework of lead and colored crystal.

The window above the entrance was round unlike the others, which were rectangular. In it stood a man holding a saw, a hammer, and a T-square. At first I thought it might be St. Joseph, the husband of the Blessed Virgin and the foster-father of the Christ Child, but then I noticed the rack and other implements of torture behind him and realized he was the same Saint Nicholas Owen I had mentioned minutes before.

In the window on the left, that is, on the Epistle side as I faced the back of the chapel, stood a trio of men in seventeenth century everyman's garb, one of them clutching a satchel of books, and all three standing beneath hangman nooses. In the opposite window stood three men dressed royally, two of them with miters and crooks, the third with a chain of office around his neck, along with two executioner's axes and a pair of swords awaiting their deadly purpose at their feet. I recognized the latter as Saint Thomas More, Lord Chancellor of the Realm, whose hand-carved statue stands guard on the desk in Father Baptist's study, and who was beheaded by order of King Henry VIII on Tower Hill in 1535. I so wanted to inquire as to the identity of the other five I couldn't identify offhand, their faces so noble and steadfast, but I didn't want to break the flow that Father had going with these two interesting old gals.

"So you two are responsible for this?" said Father, blaring his vowels while acting as though he was barely pronouncing them. I wished I had a video camera with a microphone to capture the effect—not that I'd know how to operate such equipment, but the moment deserved preserving.

"Oh, Father John," sighed Mehitabelle, enthralled by his approval. "It's taken us years and years, hasn't it, Darling?"

"It was always here, Sweetheart, long before we married into the family," explained Hortense, "but it had fallen into disrepair and had been sorrowfully neglected. But when the rot set in—"

"Temper, Dear. We decided to restore this chapel so we could worship Our Lord as we always had, didn't we Darling?"

"Indeed, indeedy do, we did, Sweetheart. We didn't like the New Mass at all. It was so, so—"

"Don't be vulgar, Darling."

"Not me, Sweetheart. It!"

"So you know a priest who is willing to come and say Mass for you here?" said Father, moving slowly but surely up the side aisle toward the Sanctuary.

"How do you know that?" asked Mehitabelle, unwrapping and rewrapping her feathery boa.

"By the presence of the Real Presence, Silly," said Hortense, playfully swiping her sister with the end of her own. "The Sanctuary lamp!"

"That, of course," said Father, "but also the wear of the rug in front of the altar."

"He's so observant, isn't he Darling?"

"He's a great detective, don't forget, Sweetheart. Yes, Father John. Father Albert has been coming here for years and years."

"Father Albert?" asked Father Baptist. "What is his parish, or is he in one of the orders?"

"We promised never to tell," said Mehitabelle and Hortense together. They looked at each other, winked, then stifled a shared giggle.

"We don't mean to be coy," said Hortense. "Do we, Sweetheart?"

"Of course not, Father," said Mehitabelle. "It's just that we made a promise, didn't we, Darling? It would be a sin to break it."

"Am I mistaken, or is that a sacristy?" said Father, pointing to an iron-studded door facing the altar from the wall at the Gospel side of the Sanctuary.

"Indeedy deedy do, it is," said Hortense. "Mehitabelle and I can't go in there, of course, because the only entrance is through the Sanctuary."

"Might I have a look inside?" asked Father. "I find this all so fascinating."

Both old ladies looked at Keating, who blinked, sniffed, and cleared his throat. "I believe, Mesdames, Father Albert inadvertently left with the key the last time he was here. Lord knows I should have a copy, but I'm afraid I don't."

"I certainly hope you have a key to the Tabernacle," said Father. "If ever there should be a fire or an earthquake—"

"Oh yes," said Keating, patting the pocket of his vest. "In that event I am of course prepared to take the Holy Eucharist to safety."

"I should hope so," said Father, a wee bit sternly. "To keep the Blessed Sacrament reserved in one's home is an awesome responsibility."

GARDENING TIPS: Having the Blessed Sacrament, the most Precious Thing on earth, under one's roof is no small matter. Indeed, it is an awesome burden. One must be prepared to protect It against any and all mishaps and calamities. Remember the words of Saint Peter Julian Eymard: "He has chained Himself to the Sacred Species to which the sacramental words bind Him inseparably. In the Eucharist as on the Cross or in the Tomb He has no movement, no action of His own . . ."

I remember reading about one Paul Comtois, who was the Lieutenant Governor in Quebec, which meant he represented the Queen of England. He resided in the Government House in Sillery, known as "Bois-de-Coulonge." Within the house there was a private chapel in which the Blessed Sacrament was reserved. One fateful evening the house caught fire. After ushering his guests out, Monsieur Comtois courageously went back to save the Blessed Sacrament from the flames. As he attempted his escape from the inferno with the Body of Christ, the stairs gave way under him. He perished, but the Blessed Sacrament, which he had gathered to his chest, was saved.

        These events did not take place in some century
    long past. Elizabeth II was the Queen, and the
    year was 1966.

                                            --M.F.

"It was the only thing we could think to do, Sweetheart. We shed so many tears, don't you know? You wouldn't believe, Father, how many."

"But we kept them, Darling, right there at Our Blessed Mother's feet."

"Go on, show Father, Sweetheart."

"Keating," said Mehitabelle. "Please."

With a nod and a bow, their manservant strode to the center of the chapel, genuflected, then opened the iron gates in the center of the Communion rail. Gingerly, as if entering a minefield, he penetrated the Sacred Space and crossed over to a statue of the Blessed Virgin Mary at the Gospel side of the marble altar. Arranged around Her sweet feet stood a dozen small glass vials, each about four inches tall, bulbous at the bottom and tapering to a corked mouth at the top. Hesitantly he picked up one and strode toward us, handing it over the rail to Mehitabelle.

"Here they are," said she, holding it up and wiggling the contents, "our copious tears."

"This is our latest lachrymatory," said Hortense. "Each one holds one thousand one hundred and eleven little proofs of our sorrow."

"There is much to be sad about," agreed Father, politely declining to handle the bottle, "and no better depository for our woes than Our Lady of Sorrows."

"You're so right," said Mehitabelle, reluctantly handing the vial back to Keating, who carefully put it back in its place with its lachrymal companions.

"It's hard for me to tell in this candlelight," said Father, "but your floor is similar to the stonework in part of our church. Don't you think so, Martin?"

"I do indeed," said I, no doubt sounding less than knowledgeable. I was also uncomfortable with loudly spoken whispering—it just wasn't natural. "It might have been laid by the same stonemason."

"These pews, wouldn't you know," said Keating, somewhat proudly. "As old as they look, they are really quite new. Well, that is to say, they are as old as they look, truly they are, but their assemblage here is recent."

"Our distant cousin by marriage," explained Hortense. "Isn't he the one?"

"Clifford," said Mehitabelle. "Clifford Hubbard, he's such a dear, isn't he Darling?"

"Indeed he is, Sweetheart, even if he is from the eastern branch of the family. They're generally so … *you know*. He has prayed in this very chapel, Father, and knowing our interests, he, um—what's the word for what he did to get these wonderful pews, Sweetheart?"

"I believe it's 'brokered the deal,' Darling," said Mehitabelle sweetly.

"That's right, thank-you Sweetheart. Until a few months ago these pews resided in a monastery in San Marino. Not San Marino, California, of course, but the quaint little mountain republic in Italy."

"Their chapel was undergoing renovation, Father."

"And he knows what *that* means, doesn't he, Sweetheart?"

"I'm sure he does, Darling."

"Not that I minded kneeling on a *prie-dieu,* Father."

"Nor I, Father. But these pews are so—what's the word I'm looking for, Darling?"

"I wouldn't know, Sweetheart, but I think they're just, just—"

"They certainly are distinctive," said Father, running his hand along the wood. "And you put these together, Keating?"

"Me dear old dad was the more skilled with his hands, Father," said Keating, shyly. "Me talent was in, well, it wasn't in anything practical. He was responsible for the restoration of all these beautiful panels on the walls."

"Some of the candles need replacing, don't you think so Darling?" said Mehitabelle.

"You know, Sweetheart," said Hortense. "I think you may be right."

"We must tell Antoinette, Darling," said Mehitabelle.

"Antoinette?" asked Father.

"Our maid, you know," said Hortense. "I think she's out in the garden tending my new valerian plants."

"I don't think so, Madam," said Keating. "She certainly wasn't there when I prepared the tea tray. Speaking of tea, if I may say so, it's going to get cold if we don't—"

"Of course, of course," said Hortense. "We shan't let our tea get cold. The world may decline all around us, but we mustn't let the basics slide, mustn't we, Sweetheart?"

"Absolutely, Darling, absolutely. Father, Mister—Feeney is it? Oh, yes, good gracious me. Of course it's Mister Feeney."

"Marvin is his name, Sweetheart. You haven't forgotten have you?"

"No, indeed not, Darling. Do please let us return upstairs to the living room."

"As you please," said Father.

"As God wills," mumbled Marvin the gardener, dreading the ascent up all those steep steps.

All of us being Catholics, albeit from different eras, we made our genuflections to the Real Presence in the Tabernacle. Some obeisances were more awkward than others. One gardener was particularly shamed by a couple of elderly ladies in this regard. While Keating repeated his genteel genuflection beside me, I made a violent pretzel contortion which had to suffice.

"This way, if you please," said Keating, indicating the doorway at the rear of the chapel.

It was as disconcerting ascending the stairs in the dark as it had been descending them, and far, far, far, far, far more laborious besides. Echoes of my gasps flapped about the stairwell like bleary bats beating themselves to death against the walls. Eventually the afternoon sunshine beckoned from the open bookcase above.

Wouldn't you know, upon achieving "The Sunroom of Postponed Hopes" I managed to lose my balance and fall flat on my face on the floor. My cane knocked against the two-way desk on its way down, and even my keys managed to leap from my pocket and skitter across the carpet.

"Martin," said Father, stooping to help me up.

"Fire and brimwater, Sir," said Keating, hefting me from the other side. "That was a nasty fall."

"Clumsy of me," mumbled yours truly, embarrassed to be set on my feet like a lopsided toy soldier. "Fortunately your carpet is thick."

"Oh dear, dear me, Mister Spleeny."

"Feeney is his name, Darling."

"I thought you said it was Marvin, Sweetheart."

"Better now?" asked Father, handing me my cane.

"Sure," said I.

"You're quite sure, Sir," said Keating, slipping me my keys.

"Sure I'm sure," I assured him.

"You wouldn't sue us, would you, Mister Spleeny?" warbled Hortense. "Would he, Sweetheart?"

"It's Feeney, Darling," said Mehitabelle. "And he wouldn't, would you, Mister Feeney?"

"For my own clumsiness?" said I, trying but failing to act gallant. That was Father's department. "Dear Ladies, hardly. If I have lost any loose change in my display of gaucherie, consider it a small donation to the candle fund."

"Sweet of him, isn't it Darling?" said Mehitabelle, unconvincingly.

"He's the deary-weariest, Sweetheart," said Hortense, equally unimpressed.

"You can say that again," said Father, patting me on the shoulder.

I gave him a look that seemed to say, irked and pained, "I dare you, Father, indeedy-doo I double dare you, to say 'deary-weariest'!" But all I actually said was, "Thank-you, thank-you, I'm fine. Sorry to be so much trouble."

"It's the exertion," said Hortense. "It brings on the dizzies. Mister Spleeny, you should go for walks more often, shouldn't he, Sweetheart?"

"I should think so, the way he's gasping, Darling."

"Ah, but he does have a cane, Sweetheart."

"That he does, Darling. He suffers from arthritis, after all. So does dear Clifford, and you know how he heaves and gasps whenever he makes the ascent."

"Even Roddy, the dear boy, Sweetheart. For all his hard work, it's all sitting at a desk. He doesn't get enough physical activity. And let's not forget Threety. He practically exploded the last time he came up from below."

"That he did, Darling. That he really did."

"So Father," said Hortense gaily, "you will join us in a spot of tea?"

"Of course," said he, master of graciousness that he was.

"Of course," agreed I, albeit under my heaving breath and somewhat less graciously. I couldn't see the point of lingering in this house any longer. Charming as it was, it was obviously another dead end. Not that we had anything pressing, save the ire of His Petulance Cardinal Fulbright, but it was well past one and this gardener's stomach was not going to be satisfied by anything on that tray waiting for us in the living room.

Sometimes I hate being right.

30

"MOST PEOPLE BREW TEA, Father," said Hortense sweetly, "much the way they percolate coffee. Don't they, Sweetheart?"

"It's simply dreadful, Darling," agreed Mehitabelle, hovering over the large teapot with the various lids. She picked up each of the silver boats, care of the staff at the Adirondack, and sniffed the contents, then set them back on the tray. "You know how they measure it: One for me, one for thee—"

"One for the pot," said Father, smiling broadly, "and one for luck."

"Well," said Hortense, beaming with pride, "my sister has elevated the preparation of tea to an art, haven't you, Sweetheart?"

"Oh, I wouldn't know," said Mehitabelle. "I just do it the way Fillmore liked it, God rest his soul."

"Fillmore was—how do I put this delicately, Father?—particular, wasn't he, Sweetheart?"

"Don't speak unpleasantly of the dead, Darling," said Mehitabelle, lifting one of the lids and holding her free palm over the opening to check the steam rising from within. "Ah, it's still hot enough, and Roscoe was no less demanding than Fillmore, Father, I assure you."

"They were brothers, after all, Sweetheart. Peas in a pod, as it were. Finicky peas they were."

"'Persnickety,' Darling. I think that's the word we're avoiding. Now where is the oolong? Here it is."

"Oooh, Sweetheart. Do your magic!"

"I hate to return to an uncomfortable topic," said Father as Mehitabelle shoveled various strains of tea into the diverse openings in the teapot. "I wish this were a purely social call, but I *am* investigating the disappearance of Monsignor Aspic. You did say that he visited you within the last few days."

"A monsignor, you say?" asked Mehitabelle, absently.

"An exuberant fellow," said Father. He glanced at me. "Some have described him as 'perky.'"

"The one with the manuscript," said Hortense. "Remember him, Sweetheart?"

"Father John is the first visitor we've had in ages," sighed Mehitabelle, still scooping, "who didn't come with a manuscript under his arm."

"What day was the perky fellow here, Sweetheart?"

"You know me and the calendar, Darling." Mehitabelle inserted a foot-long spoon into one of the openings and jiggled it around inside. "Somewhere along the way, Father, years ago, I lost all track of days. You're not a writer, I take it."

"No," said Father. "Martin here is the one with that talent."

"Is that so?" said Mehitabelle and Hortense, both turning their eyes on me. At first I thought it was with appreciation, but there was something vaguely discomforting in their gaze. Perhaps they had had their charming fill of writers. I could understand that, certainly, though I hadn't come with a manuscript tucked under my arm. Oh, how I wished Father and I were saying our goodbyes to these old biddies on the front porch. The moment would come, I told myself. Surely the moment would come. It took an act of Will not to blurt out that I'd already covered the whole Monsignor Aspic business with Keating just to shorten the time.

"Father flatters me," said I, shrugging as humbly as I could. "I've seen the kind of material you ladies publish. Mine is nothing like that."

"No doubt," said Hortense with a sniff. "No one writes like Saint Cyprian anymore."

"Too true," I agreed.

"Martin, like your Keating here," said Father, "is a man of many talents."

"Oh, no, Father," said Keating, who was standing attentively near the fireplace. "Talent is something I lack entirely."

"False humility isn't really humility at all, is it, Darling?" asked Mehitabelle, setting down her implements and rapping the teapot thrice with her knuckles. "There, it's done."

"I should think not, Sweetheart," said Hortense. "I'm referring to humility, of course, the false kind, not the tea. Keating, will you do the honors?"

"Are you sure, Madam?" asked Keating, hesitantly.

"You are the man of the house," said Mehitabelle, standing upright and handing him the first empty cup rattling in its delicate china saucer. "The first for Father, of course, our honored guest."

"Ladies first," said Father, turning on the charm.

"Thank-you, no, Father," said Mehitabelle. "We insist."

"Each cup is different," said Keating, pouring the steaming brew and handing it to Father. He then turned a lever or something on the side of the teapot that caused a metallic clank within the bowels of the vessel. "Don't ask me the particulars, Father, but Madam Mehitabelle blends her teas to match personality. She adds herbs from her garden, too. All I know is that every time I partake of a cup of Madam's tea it's different, yet it's somehow just what I need."

"That wonderful pot was a gift from my Fillmore," sighed Mehitabelle. "He always said it was invented by his older brother, Harrigan, but I'm convinced he had a hand in it. It actually brews several blends at once. I put a sweet pinch of one of my secret formulas in yours, Father."

"Which mixture did you give him, Sweetheart?" asked Hortense, accepting a cup from Keating.

"One part number twelve, and two parts number seventy-eight, Darling."

"That will put hair on your chest, Father, if you don't mind me saying so, won't it Sweetheart?"

"Don't be vulgar, Darling. What would Father want with hair on his chest?"

"Here you are, Madam," said Keating, handing a cup to Mehitabelle.

The combination of pungent aromas permeated the room.

"Would you care for some bread, Father?" asked Hortense. "Keating, the Pumpernickel is fresh?"

"The clip was red, Madam," said Keating, most assuredly.

"You do keep on top of things, doesn't he, Sweetheart?"

"I aim to please," said Keating with a bow.

"Now yours, Keating," said Hortense.

Keating complied, setting his cup aside for the moment.

"Mister Spleeny gets the last," said Mehitabelle. "I hope your man isn't offended, Father, but I gave him number ninety-six. It must steep the longest."

"Here you go, Sir," said Keating, handing me the final cup and saucer.

"I thank you," said I, peering into the delicate cup. It looked and smelled to this gardener's eyes and nose no different than plain old Lipton, just as I sometimes order at "Peanuts," the coffee shop across the street from St. Philomena's. Even Willie "Skull" Kapps had brewed that very brand in the back of his shop for me on occasion, knowing as he did my aversion to his specialty, mweemuck root tea. All he needed was a pan of boiling water and a strainer. Perhaps this Doily rigmarole held some hidden significance that escaped me. I just kept picturing Father and myself on the front porch saying our farewells. The moment would come, surely it would, eventually—please!

"Tea is not usually a toasting beverage," said Hortense. "Is it, Sweetheart?"

"But Father won't mind indulging two obliging widows," said Mehitabelle, "now will he, Darling?"

"I would be delighted," said Father, hefting his cup. "First, to Our Lady, Empress of All the Americas."

"To Our Lady," said we all, severally.

"Second, to our hostesses," said Father. "Mehitabelle and Hortense Doily, whose acquaintance has marked the highpoint of my day."

"To Mesdames," said Keating.

"To the ladies," said I.

To wringing hands and sopping wet handkerchiefs, thought the gardener to himself, vividly imagining Father and himself descending the front steps as they made their way to their getaway vehicle.

"Well," said Hortense, scrunching up her lips to take a tentative sip. "Bottoms up."

"Don't be vulgar, Darling," said Mehitabelle.

"Excellent," said Father after a long, silent sip. "My compliments."

"You're too kind, Father," said Hortense. "Isn't he, Sweetheart?"

Ah, thought I as my first swallow landed warmly in my empty stomach. I was right. It tasted very close to Lipton, but there was something else there, some indistinct hint of a suggestion of—

Suddenly my gut clenched itself into a tight fist. A wave of shivering cold rippled through my body, wringing frigid sweat from every pore. My spine popped in several places, and a jolt of searing pain detonated at the base of my skull. A scorching fireball ignited in my throat as a second spasm gripped my stomach. Even Willie's mwee-muck root tea had never affected me like this.

"What is it, Sir?" asked Keating as I lunged past him.

"Martin?" called Father as I stumbled down the hall with the squeaky floorboards.

"I don't understand, Darling," said Mehitabelle somewhere behind me as I turned into one of the bathrooms. "Perhaps I confused sixty-nine for ninety-six."

"Perish the thought, Sweetheart. Oh dear. Antoinette has been off her feed of late—or should I say her feet? I do hope the *twa-twa* is clean."

"Don't be vulgar, Darling. Of course it is—"

Kicking the bathroom door shut, I lunged for the *twa-twa*. It was clean indeed, but not for long.

"Saint Aegidus," I managed to utter before the first eruption roared up my esophagus. "Saint Acacius," I managed between the first and second. "… Saint Erasmus … Saint Blaise … Saint Vitus …"

<blockquote>
GARDENING TIPS: There are fourteen Holy Helpers, Saints that are invoked for certain needs. Saint Aegidus, known in Italy as Saint Egidio and in England as Saint Giles, is the patron of cripples, so I call upon him often. Saint Acacius is invoked against headaches, Saint Erasmus against diseases of the stomach, Saint Blaise for maladies of the throat, and Saint Vitus, also known as Saint Guy, protects against nervous diseases, epilepsy, and paralysis. The list goes on, and I figured it was worth calling on the lot, seeing as how my sudden affliction seemed to merit all their attentions.

—M.F.
</blockquote>

" … Saint Barbara," I coughed as the fit passed. She is the protectress against lightning, and I sure felt as though I had just been struck by some.

"Good Heavens, man," said Father, helping me to straighten. He must have let himself in between Saint Cyriacus and Saint Denis. "You look terrible."

"Thanks for the assessment," said I, glaring at myself in the mirror as I clutched the edge of the sink. "It fits me to a tea."

31

"FEELING ANY BETTER?" asked Father as he came out of Glen's Photocopies and sat down next to me in the Jeep. I hadn't accompanied him into the place because the thought of that chemical smell and the blowing heat of those copying machines made my stomach convulse. "I say, Martin. Are you feeling any better?"

"Do I look any better?"

"No."

"Well, for once appearances aren't deceiving." Without effort—it was only making my stomach tilt—I tore my attention away from the sheet of paper I had been trying to focus on, the strange onionskin tracing with all the splotches and smears from Bishop Ravenshorst's library, placed it back in its folder, and stretched to place it on the pile of stuff in the back seat. "Did you find out anything?"

"Just that Monsignor Aspic did come here Wednesday morning. The cash register in there makes a record of all transactions along with the time. It shows that the monsignor paid for one reproduction of his manuscript with a credit card at eleven seventeen, to be precise. He had left the original the day before. The register recorded thirty-seven transactions between eleven and noon; Monsignor Aspic's being the twenty-third. Mr. Glen has no specific memory of Monsignor Aspic or his manuscript. There's a parish church with an attached grammar school within walking distance, so the monsignor's black clericals didn't stand out. The copying was done by one of the employees, and she doesn't remember the job. Her function is to set the customer's materials on a tray and the machine does the rest."

"Was this the first time he'd availed himself of their services?"

"The register didn't request an ID when the monsignor used the credit card, which means he was already in their computer. As to how many copies he made before, Mr. Glen doesn't know how to access the information, but his accountant might, but I doubt he'll remember to call her. I was surprised at how cooperative he was with me, considering how busy he was, and the fact that I have no legal authority to ask for the information."

"If there weren't a church nearby I'd say it was your Roman collar. A few people do still respect such things. Or perhaps it's your supersleuth personality."

"How many copies of your own book have you sent out?"

"The same number as the rejection letters I've gotten back, and you've seen my collection. I don't want to think about it, let alone admit it. Does any of what you learned in there help, Father?"

"Well, it does confirm what the Doilys and others have told us: that the monsignor had an actual, physical manuscript to sell."

"Wow." I'll admit my tone was sarcastic.

"What's eating you, Martin?"

"I can't believe you just asked that question. You're the one who blessed me three times with the holy water in that vial from the backseat of Aspic's limo so you could empty it and gather an actual sample of what's doing precisely that."

"Is that what I did?"

"You know it's what you did."

"I was curious," said he, admitting the deed with a nod of his head while folding his arms, "and the Doily Sisters didn't have a spare lachrymatory."

"Curious, you say."

"Your attack came immediately upon swallowing. Few agents act that quickly in the stomach."

"I feel like my insides still want to be on my outside."

"It's also possible you have a case of the flu. You're acting as though you were deliberately poisoned. Do you really think that?"

"Who knows what that lady grows in her window boxes? Keating said Mehitabelle mixes her homegrown herbs into her personal tea blends."

"Yes, I caught a glimpse of her garden through the kitchen window when I went looking for a container." Father folded his arms. "Okay, so you believe you were deliberately poisoned. Several questions come to mind then. Mehitabelle Doily brewed the tea. Keating served it. Who administered the toxin, she or he? If she did, did Keating know? If he knew, why would he go along with it? Why would he, she, or they want to poison you—you specifically—anyway?"

"You're the legendary cop-turned-priest-turned-cop. You seem detached and practical now, but you were concerned enough at the time to destroy one potentially vital piece of evidence to carry away a sample of what I regurgitated. You tell me."

"Speaking of which," said he, "might I suggest we swing by Wong and Holtsclaw's to drop it off for analysis?"

"Do you think they'll do it?"

"They ran a blood alcohol test as a favor to you, once."

"True, but that was because I knew you. Hey, I just answered my own question."

"That reminds me."

"What reminds you?"

"The holy water vial. It's a good thing I brought the cell phone." From within the mysterious folds of his cassock he produced the device that Ernie Corben had given him a couple nights before in connection with another case—the same phone for which I had rummaged around in Father's desk when Some Guy phoned from down the block the previous night. It beeped merrily as he tapped in a phone number.

"Who are you calling, Father?"

"St. Philip's."

"What on earth for?"

"Hello? I'd like to speak with David Smoley, please." He looked at me and said, "You know, if you turn the key and press the pedal we could start making progress."

"Sorry, my stomach was enjoying the positional stability."

"Let's see what happens if—excuse me. Hello, David? Father Baptist here. Something I meant to ask earlier. I'm interested in knowing: of the stops you made with Monsignor Aspic on Wednesday, which ones were repeaters? Yes, which destinations had he visited before, to the best of your knowledge? What's that? Well, let's see. We know you took him to the Turnbuckle residence back in October—don't worry, I'll leave that one alone. KLIE goes without saying, we know he'd been on the show several times. I assume his visits to that consulting firm, Bendlebrain, Cruiser & Wedge—"

"And del Corro," said the gardener, gathering the resolve to turn that key in the ignition. Somehow the world seemed a steadier, less dizzying place when I wasn't steering a moving vehicle across it. "By intention, philosophy, and objective."

"—were semi-regular? Well, occasional, then. Let's see, who else? Ah, the photocopier. Glen's ... How many times? Really."

"How many times?" asked I, flexing my wrist to prepare the muscles for the stress of turning that key.

"Really," said he again, winking at me and glancing at my key-turning hand, which had still to turn the key.

"Ask him about the Doily Sisters," said I, resting my key-turning hand on my steady, non-twistable knee.

"What's that?" asked he of me.

"Mehitabelle and Hortense and Keating, oh my!" I stretched my face diagonally, as if that imparted additional information. "Ask him."

"The Doily Sisters," said he, his eyebrows colliding over the bridge of his nose. Was it something I said? "Excuse me, David? Two old ladies—oh, that's right, you didn't go in so you wouldn't know. What if I gave you the address? 7214 Villanova Terrace. That's right: a really, really old house. Had Monsignor Aspic ever been there before? ... You're sure."

"He's sure, what?" I asked.

"Tell me, David, did you notice whether he took the manuscript he had copied at Glen's into the Villanova address? ... Oh, right. The briefcase. What did you say? ... Coincidentally, that's where we're

going next. 'Way True Life Publishing,' 1014G Myrtle at Sycamore.
You've been very helpful, David. Thank-you."

His cell phone played a descending arpeggio as he turned it off.

"Well?" said I, clutching the key and finally turning it, my stomach
cowering behind my liver at the thought of forward momentum.

"Martin, I'm curious. I was getting around to asking young Smoley
about the Doily Sisters, but you insisted. Why?"

"Let's just say, like you, I'm curious."

"Because of the possibly-poisoned tea?"

"No, something else. I feel strange telling you because I don't like
being a snitch.   On the other hand, knowing the folks at St.
Philomena's, it's only a matter of time before you find out anyway."

"Martin, I've no idea what you're talking about. If it's pertinent to
the case, then you have an obligation to tell me."

"It's only pertinent in so far as I find it embarrassing, and since I'm
your chauffeur-slash-chronicler, it may color my perception and presen-
tation of events should this wild, romping tale ever become one of my
summarily rejected manuscripts."

Father sighed long and hard. "Martin, snitch or not, published or
not, you've come this far."

I sighed even longer and harder. "Okay, for what it's worth, Keating
said he attended Mass at St. Philomena's yesterday morning—I don't
think he had his Tweety Bird employers with him—and apparently
Monsignor Havermeyer mentioned me in his sermon, something about
how I tutored him in the rubrics of the Traditional Mass."

"Really, in a sermon, you say."

"Keating said our beloved resident monsignor told everyone that I was
a treasure, albeit a crotchety, limping one. Naturally when he told me
this I was caught off guard. 'Mortified' may be too strong a word,
but—"

"I can understand that, as well as your reluctance to snitch on Monsignor Havermeyer."

"You see? Everyone hates a snitch, and now I'm branded."

"I'll try to keep you out of it, and I'd rather know than not."

"After all," said I, gripping the steering wheel, "Ol' Lucky Soles was
just being gracious, even if it was at my expense."

"He's come a long way, Martin, and no small thanks to you."

"Whatever. Now, back to toxic tea and those who brew it. Father,
you said a moment ago that you were going to ask David Smoley about
Monsignor Aspic's prior visits to the Doily Sisters even before I insisted. Why was that?"

He shifted in his seat. "I could say I was just being thorough."

"But—?" prodded the gardener.

"Remember when we returned to the living room after seeing the underground chapel? Mehitabelle stated that you had arthritis. There are many reasons why a man might use a cane, many maladies that make a man a mite cranky. Arthritis is only one of them. Yet she stated it as a fact, not as a question. Perhaps Monsignor Havermeyer mentioned your malady by name in his sermon, and Keating repeated it to the ladies. There is also the possibility that Monsignor Aspic told them, though I can't imagine why. It's one of those little dangling details that I find irksome."

"Perhaps our reputation is beginning to precede us," said I, then shook my head. "So how many times had the monsignor visited the photocopier?"

"Not as many as you, my Friend, but copiously."

"And the Doilys?"

"Once before, perhaps a week ago. David didn't remember the date, but I do have a copy of his notebook. I can check when we get back to the rectory. For now—"

"It's time for 'Way True Life Publishing.'"

"First the coroners, then the publisher."

"Oh, joy."

32

"IPECAC? DID YOU SAY IPECAC?"

"I did."

"But you haven't even run any tests yet."

"I can tell by the smell."

"And how would you know such a smell, especially if it, you know, came from, you know—"

This was one of those conversations I'd just as soon not report, but there it is. Father and I had arrived at the morgue while Solomon Yung-sul Wong was off appearing in court somewhere. John Holtsclaw, the assistant coroner, was holding down the fort, which was an ironic choice of words considering he was of Native American—he himself preferred the word "Indian"—descent. You'd think he'd be circling the building with his bow and arrow or something. As it was, Holtsclaw was sniffing the glass vial Father had found in Monsignor Aspic's limo and which he later filled with, well, with what he filled it with.

"Don't forget," said the assistant coroner, pouring the contents into a small beaker, "I did some volunteer work when I was interning in

South America.   Would it make you feel any better if I called it *Cephaelis ipecacuanha?* The smell of it once reacted with the secretions of the stomach is unmistakable.   Down there nature provides many poisons, and ipecac is one that is excellent for getting other more virulent poisons out of the stomach quickly."

"I thought it was something your mother gave you if you swallowed a mothball," said I, grimacing as he held up the beaker to the light and swirled around the contents.

"Exactly," said he, setting the beaker down on a countertop. "I can run more exacting tests, Father, but not right away. I'm behind as it is."

"When you can, then," said Father, who was standing by the cadaver drawer marked FR. JOHN DOE. "While I'm here, I should finalize arrangements for our mysterious boarder here."

"The forms are on the clipboard on top of the filing cabinet." Holtsclaw took up a test tube with a bottom tapered to a point, poured a portion of the gardener's stewed stomach into it, then inserted it into a slot in a centrifuge. With the click of a switch he sent it spinning into a whirring blur. "It must be nice having friends like Roberto Guadalupe."

"In more ways than you may imagine," said Father, producing a pen and clicking it. "So it will be all right for him and his men to come for the body Saturday afternoon?"

"I'll tell the duty officer personally. I don't mean to pry, is he making the coffin, too?"

"Roberto?" said Father. "No. I keep one on hand in a storeroom all the time in case one of our poor families should need it.   There's a Trappist monastery in Iowa that makes them. Simple, basic, no frills, but what else does a coffin have to be?"

Holtsclaw cleared his throat. "I … that is … I'd kind of like to … Would you mind if I attended the funeral?"

Father smiled kindly as he reached for the clipboard. "Your presence will be most welcome, John. Barring unforeseen complications, I plan to say the Requiem at the six-thirty Mass on Monday."

"That's AM?" asked Holtsclaw, hunching his shoulders and cracking his neck. The gesture made it hard to perceive the precise inflection he gave the question. "Monday. Oh, right. No funerals on Sundays. But as for Monday, is it customary to do them at dawn?"

"In small parishes, it happens. When there is no family to consider, I will often say the Requiem at the morning Mass. The few people who regularly attend are almost like family, in a way."

"But if your men pick up the body on Saturday, where will you put it until Monday? And what about embalming?"

"There is a gated chamber off the vestibule for that purpose. As for the other, I think we shall forego any preservatives. I have a hunch he won't be needing them."

"I don't understand."

"Perhaps better left for a later conversation. In any case, he's going to be buried at St. Philomena's so the interment will follow immediately after Mass."

"With all that's been going on, I'm surprised you have the time."

"Don't remind me. Monsignor Havermeyer, of course, is more than willing to fill in for me, but he's unfamiliar with the specifics of the Latin Requiem."

"As am I," said Holtsclaw.

"Come to think of it, though, with the way my time is getting gobbled up on these inquiries for the cardinal—Martin, remind me to warn the monsignor he might have to do it after all."

"Gladly," said I. "But you know, Father, it's not as though there are going to be any mourners to inconvenience, other than Mr. Holtsclaw here. You could say the Requiem whenever you do find the time."

"We'll see how it plays out," said Father.

"Well," said Holtsclaw with another shrug and neck crack. "If it's going to be iffy, perhaps I'll pass. By the way, you should know that your boss, Cardinal Fulbright, has pulled some impressive strings. The Aspic case has been shoved up the ladder to Chief Farley's division. Those boys usually only handle high-profile cases. I understand Billowack has offered to loan them some of his men to assist in the investigation, too."

"That is impressive," agreed Father absently, scribbling information on the form.

"With all that manpower involved, what can you do that they can't?"

"That's a good question, John, but I've committed myself to the pursuit."

"Why? I thought you didn't want to do detective work anymore."

GARDENING TIPS: With that, John Holtsclaw, mild-mannered coroner for a large metropolitan police department, clicked himself up a few blinking dots on the zany "Just what I was beginning to wonder about!" scale. My poor, quivering stomach was beginning to question the whole point of this meandering investigation that had so far led us everywhere but a solution, and me in particular to an undignified consequence in the bathroom.

Perhaps I was losing hope that this business would culminate with Father and me toasting his

<blockquote>
solving of the case in the garden late one eve-
ning. In the shape my stomach was in, even that
thought had lost its savor.

--M.F.
</blockquote>

Father signed his name on the dotted line with three squiggles, two slashes and a jab. As he returned the clipboard to its nest atop the filing cabinet, I heard him whisper, "'Out of the depths I have cried to Thee, O Lord: Lord hear my voice.'"

Psalm 129, the sixth penitential Psalm, was also known among Trads with tattered missals as the *De Profundis*. Ah, but did Father quote the first verse out of context as an erudite way of calling attention to his predicament, or was it to suggest a subsequent verse further down like, "If Thou, O Lord, shalt observe iniquities: Lord, who shall endure it?"?

"I suppose I could give you something to help your stomach," said Holtsclaw, turning his attention back to me. "How did you get this stuff inside of you again?"

"A little old lady made me some tea that was supposedly matched to my personality," said I.

"Oh," said he.

33

IT WAS SHORTLY AFTER FOUR when we pushed our way past the door with the WARM YOURSELF BY THE FIRE OF HIS LOVE sign on it, well within the limits of the proprietor's erratic scheduling requirements. There was a fire burning all right at WAY TRUE LIFE PUBLISHING, INC. Its manifestation went by the name of Mercedes Sinclair. The mother-of-pearl plaque on his desk said so. Mr. Sinclair wore a button in his lapel that said MY GOD LOVES YOUR GOD. Really. He wore a buffed tangerine suede suit—I kid you not, it hurt my eyes—a silvery pink shirt and a turquoise silk tie with a diamond pin. Ruffles protruded from the ends of his sleeves and his glistening black hair huddled in tight, shivering curls all over his head. He was seated behind his desk beneath that diluted quotation in fancy blue and gold letters from the *Living Bible*. There was a cloying sweet smell hanging in the air. Some sort of aerosol room freshener, I imagined. That, or Sinclair's idea of cologne.

"May I help you?" said he, rising flamboyantly. Underneath all that gaudy silk and suede he was stretched-to-snapping skinny, narrow-boned and high-cheeked, with angular, protruding elbows. "I do so hope you're responding to my ad."

"Not that I'm aware," said Father, shaking his head just a tad for emphasis. "I'm here on archdiocesan business at the behest of Cardinal Fulbright."

"You don't say."

"My name is Father John Baptist, and this is my associate, Martin Feeney."

"Pleasure, pleasure."

Mercedes took Father's hand in both of his and pumped it earnestly while glancing at me dismissively. He dipped into his seat, waving Father into a chair opposite him with a generous scoop of his hand. His courtesy tapered off there, and since there were no other chairs, I was apparently left to my own devices. My stomach was still perturbed, in spite of the gooey white stuff John Holtsclaw had given me to swallow. He said it would coat my lining and alleviate the queasies. I wished. Be it contrived or genuine, nausea seemed to be my secret word for the week.

The office was small and sparse, void of furniture, potted plants, and bookshelves. The walls were covered with wallpaper that was supposed to look like wood. It wasn't convincing. There was a calendar tacked on the wall sporting a gal in choir robes hefting a humongous wrench. The symbolism escaped me. Between the acoustic paneled ceiling and the rubbery outdoor carpeting, the atmosphere was detached and sterile. It wasn't what you'd call an open-arms sort of business office.

"Father Baptist," said Mr. Sinclair, doing a little dance on his temples with his index fingers. "That rings a bell. Sure it does. It will come to me, just watch." He snapped his slender fingers while simultaneously winking his waxy eyes. "Say, you wouldn't happen to be the priest they're looking for in South Central, are you?"

"I certainly hope not," said Father. "I'm retracing the movements of Monsignor Conrad J. Aspic two days ago."

"The one who disappeared outside the television station?" He pulled open his middle desk drawer and dug around and around in the clutter within. "Hang on. Wait a second."

"You've heard about it then."

"It was on the news. I didn't connect him to *him* until just this second. He didn't call himself 'Monsignor.'" Unable to find what he was looking for, the narrow fellow pushed the drawer shut with his concave tummy, flapping his fingers like a butterfly itching to flutter, and then slapped his hands palms down on the desktop. "He said he was an ordained minister within a major Christian sect."

"Oh, brother," grumbled the gardener, grinding his cane into the industrial carpet.

"Did he have an appointment to see you?" asked Father, glancing at me.

"One moment." Mercedes Sinclair crinkled his lips into a tight little "w" as he thought about that one. "He phoned the day before and said he'd be in sometime in the afternoon, if you want to call that an appointment."

"May I ask the nature of his business with you?"

"Certainly not. I mean, I'm not at liberty to discuss a client's affairs."

"Then he is your client."

"Um, no, not exactly."

"Did he not bring you a manuscript for consideration?"

"Why would he do that?"

"You are a publisher, aren't you?"

"You have me there." Mercedes Sinclair shrugged dramatically, inhaled with a whistling hiss, then allowed the weight of his bony shoulders to push the air out through his narrow arrow nose. "Okay. Yes, I'm a publisher. Yes, he brought me a manuscript. No, I don't think I want to publish it, though I haven't yet told Mr. Aspic. You can understand my reluctance to tell someone else first."

"Do you have the manuscript here?"

"Here? No. He took it with him." Sinclair turned in his chair and blinked at a door set in the wall behind him. It was marked KEEP OUT. There was also a smaller door off to the right marked WASHROOM. He blinked at that one, too, then he looked back at Father. "I'm thinking of offering him something for the title, though. I could do something with that. In fact, I know I could make a killing with it, on the right book, of course. It's called 'Three Days of Brightness.'"

"Erg," grunted the gardener, grinding his cane further into the carpet.

"Really," said Father.

"In fact," said Sinclair, rubbing his hands together, "I'm thinking of enlarging it into 'Three *Golden* Days of Brightness,' or perhaps 'Three Days of *Golden* Brightness,' and dispensing with the problematic subtitle—"

"That does it—ulp!" I winced under my breath. I re-swallowed a gob of John Holtsclaw's stomach-soothing goo, gripped my cane tightly, and said audibly, "Father, Mr. Sinclair, you must excuse me. I need some air."

"By all means, Martin," said Father. "I'm sorry you're not feeling well. Wait outside or in the car. I shouldn't be long."

It felt so good to yank that door open and brush past that WARM YOURSELF sign. The air outside, thick with motor emissions and carcinogens aplenty, was healthier for my soul than whatever-it-was within that establishment.

"No, not to worry, Mr. Sinclair, it's not the flu," I heard Father say before the door whispered shut behind me. "Food poisoning, poor fellow. A most unfortunate—"

I'll admit that tolerance in the face of self-possessed silliness is not one of my virtues. Normally, however, I have more endurance. Some of my gears were slipping. Perhaps it was an aftereffect of the ipecac, a consequence of too little sleep, that quotation from the so-called Living Bible hanging behind the desk, or maybe an accumulation of overall disgust with everything in general and anything connected with Cardinal Fulbright in particular. Whatever, it was good to be outside, to stroll past the various shops as I meandered my way down the tangle of stairs and walkways to where the trusty Jeep waited patiently at the curb. The normally inviting smell of Chinese takeout emanating from one shop called "Wang Wang's" mingled with the beefy aroma of "Bert's Burgers" as I dug in my pocket for my Rosary, leaned against the Jeep, and fingered my way through the Sorrowful Mysteries one more time, longing for the day when my stomach would feel normal again.

I was up to "The Crowning with Thorns" when my reverie was shattered by the sudden arrival of four black-and-white police cars. They came roaring down the street, sirens off, and hurled themselves into a screeching halt all around me. Eight uniformed officers emerged as an unmarked vehicle arrived last. I was surprised, momentarily delighted, and then alarmed to see Lieutenant Taper and Sergeant Wickes jump out and take charge.

"Now remember," barked Taper. "We'll converge on the front door from both sides. Campbell and Sanchez, you go around and scope out the back, see if there's a rear exit. No heroics. We just move in quickly and ... Martin, what are you doing here?"

"Um," said I, gathering up my Rosary and dribbling it reverently into my shirt pocket. "Why am I anywhere, Lieutenant?"

"He's not up at 1014G is he?"

"'Way True Life Publishing'? I'm afraid so."

"Great," he said dryly. "Men, listen up. There's a civilian in there. A priest. Some of you know him. Father John Baptist."

"What's going on, Lieutenant?" I asked. "Sergeant? Hey!"

"No time, Martin."

With that they all drew their guns and thundered up the stairs, swiftly winding their aggressive way up the tangle of walkways that I had just slowly descended. A cold chill gave me a good rag-doll shaking as the possibilities began multiplying in my head. Father Baptist was in danger, but so depleted were my reserves from my emetic convergence that it took me more than a minute to summon the resolve to go back up those formidable steps. I felt like James Stewart in *Vertigo* except, well, perhaps not. In any case, I gathered my resolve, took a deep breath, and started pumping my lopsided way up the stairs. When I reached 1014G I confronted a wall of dark blue backs. Two police-men—two very broad policemen—were blocking the open door.

"Excuse me, officers," I ventured between deep gasps, "may I be of any help?"

They turned their heads just enough so each could see me with one eye over his shoulder. It was quite an image, those eyeballs, one brown one blue, regarding me as the harbinger of asininity.

"Is that Mr. Feeney out there?" Sergeant Wickes' voice came from inside the office. "Let him in."

The barrier of blue parted with a grunt. I felt so very small, passing between those pillars of enormity. Once inside, my heart did a Fresno back-flip at the sight of Father Baptist, right hand resting on left wrist, leaning against the desk. That door marked KEEP OUT was open, re-vealing a storage room lined with metal shelves and tube lights sus-pended from the ceiling. Two officers were rummaging through rows and rows of corrugated cardboard boxes. Lieutenant Taper and Sergeant Wickes were very much in charge, and Mercedes Sinclair was warming himself by the fire of his love as he was handcuffed from behind by a couple of cops that were bigger than the ones at the door.

"I'm placing you under arrest," said Lieutenant Taper evenly yet se-verely, "for the murders of Monsignor Raymond Padgett of Washing-ton DC; Father Terrance Sumpff of St. Louis, Missouri; Father Chris-tian Zink, SJ of New Orleans, Louisiana; Father Brighton Drulesky of Prescott, Arizona; and Monsignor Miles Adolph Hoffman of Glendale, Utah—for starters."

"You're insane," protested Mr. Sinclair. "You've got me mixed up with someone else. I've never heard of any of them."

"I don't understand," said Father Baptist and his trusty gardener simul-taneously.

"Mr. Sinclair here likes to eradicate Catholic priests," explained the lieutenant.

"It's a damn lie!" said Mr. Sinclair.

"The kind who pass themselves as 'spiritual experts' on radio talk shows," said the sergeant.

"He's graduated up to popular television shows," said the lieutenant.

"Not so," said Mr. Sinclair.

"'Spiritual experts,'" said I as the excess of blood from the exertion of the ascent up the stairs caught up with my brain and almost over-whelmed it. Dizziness on top of nausea—it doesn't get wobblier than this. "Ah, you mean the liberal, whacky, magnanimously heretical, self-contradictory sort of priests."

"The kind who write syrupy, self-involved memoirs about their personal spiritual pilgrimages," said Father, giving me a "You okay?" look, which I answered with a nod and a momentary crossing of my eyes. "Or who resort to speculative drivel about the imminent end of the world."

"The kind who take their manuscripts to publishers like 'Way True Life,'" said Taper. "It's a chain outfit, you know, with offices spaced right along the line you get if you connect the dots on the map."

"What dots?" I asked.

"The towns where the priests I mentioned disappeared and were later found mutilated."

"Mutilated!"

"You don't want to know."

"You're right," said I, rubbing my stomach.

"Mr. Sinclair here is one of WTL's roving managers," said Sergeant Wickes. "He goes from office to office rallying the employees, encouraging authors, that sort of thing."

"That, at least, is true," said Mr. Sinclair.

"Washington DC, St. Louis, New Orleans, Prescott," read Wickes from the letterhead of a sheet of 'Way True Life' stationery on the desk. "I've never heard of Glendale, Utah, but there it is—and finally, Los Angeles. Those are the locations of your company's offices. Says so right here."

"Placing you in the perfect position to meet and mark your victims," said Lieutenant Taper.

"There you go again," said the roving manager. "I tell you you're mistaken. I've been here at this office for the last month. That, that *female* I hired last spring to run things got herself pregnant—confound her!—and I had to assume her responsibilities until I could find a replacement."

"Was the incident in Glendale, Utah, the most recent?" asked Father.

"Yes," said Sergeant Wickes. "Monsignor Padgett of DC was his first victim—that we know of, anyway. Padgett disappeared last June. Sumpff was in July, Zink in August, and Drulesky in September. Monsignor Hoffman disappeared on October second. His body was discovered two weeks later. Lieutenant Russell Byington of New Orleans solved the murder of Father Zink a few hours ago."

"That was the knot that, once untied, sent the whole tapestry unraveling," said Taper. "He phoned Chief Farley here in Los Angeles, bulletins went out to all concerned departments, Billowack included, and, well, here we are."

"You're not listening," said Mr. Sinclair, writhing within his handcuffs. "I didn't do these horrible things. My whole life is about finding peace, spreading understanding, encouraging aspiring writers to—"

"You'll get your say," said Taper to Sinclair, then to Father, "This does not bode well for Monsignor Aspic, I'm afraid. Why are you here, anyway, Jack? I thought you're working on that John Doe at the mausoleum."

"Father John Doe," corrected the gardener, but was ignored.

"We are," explained Father. "Tangentially, Martin and I have been backtracking the monsignor's movements based on information provided by David Smoley, his chauffeur."

"You, too," said Taper.

"Ah," said Father. "I'm surprised our paths haven't crossed already."

"Actually, they have. You've been working backwards, I take it."

Father shrugged his acknowledgement.

"We've been working forwards, except we haven't been able to see Cardinal Fulbright. For some strange reason he's been absent from the Chancery."

"He's been in touch with Chief Billowack, though," said Wickes. "Boy, has he."

"I know the cardinal's reach is long," said Father, "but I hadn't realized how effective."

"Oh, it's not just him," said Taper. "Once Byington of NOPD cracked the case the machinery kicked in. Christian Zink, a Jesuit stationed in Algiers—that's a town situated across the river from New Orleans—wrote a book about his alleged conversations with an Angel named Abaddon who appeared to him regularly when he went fishing along the Mississippi."

"Abaddon?" said the gardener. "That's the Angel from the Bottomless Pit in the Apocalypse."

"Sure," said Taper with a shrug. "Why not? It seems that 'Abby,' as the Angel preferred to be called, befriended Father Zink so he could fill him in on how and when the world is going to end. As you know, books about the End Times can be very profitable. So Sinclair here made sure there would be no complaints—"

"Via decapitation and mutilation," said Wickes.

"Erp," said I. Suddenly the air outside became appealing all over again.

"—then brokered the book as a third party," said Taper. "Said the author was a recluse. Everybody believed it. What Sinclair didn't know was that Father Zink, being a throwback who actually typed his whole manuscript on a typewriter—"

Sergeant Wickes and I exchanged knowing glances. He's keenly aware of my late-night activities on Dad's Underwood.

"—gave a set of carbons to his sister for safekeeping. She notified the police when she found her brother's work on sale at a bookstore with an imposter's name on the cover."

"Poppycock," said Mr. Sinclair, wincing against his restraints. "By-ington's had it in for me ever since I turned down his own memoirs. The man can't write a complete sentence."

"Lieutenant, you'll want to see this," said an officer from the storage room door. In his rubber-gloved hands was an open cardboard box with a green-and-orange GLEN'S PHOTOCOPIES sticker on the lid. The title page of the manuscript within read:

<u>Three</u> <u>Days</u> <u>of</u> <u>Brightness</u>

or

How to Survive the End of the World

by

C. Jonas Aspic

"No mention of his priesthood," said I, disgustedly. "I guess he's capitalizing on his middle name."

"The sign of Jonas," said Father.

"Saint Matthew sixteen four."

"I thought you said Monsignor Aspic didn't leave his manuscript with you," said Father to the proprietor.

"I'm dumbfounded," said Mr. Sinclair unconvincingly. "I honestly thought he took it with him."

"Sure," said Wickes.

"That just about cinches it," said Taper. "Sergeant, would you be so kind as to read Mr. Sinclair his constitutional rights?"

"Gladly," said the sergeant.

"Outside, will you?" said the lieutenant. "I want to talk to Jack for a minute. The rest of you men clear out now. Let's leave the science team to do their magic. They should be here in a few minutes. We've confirmed what we needed to establish."

"Sure, yeah, yessir," said the officers as they exited, dragging Mercedes Sinclair along in their intimidating deep blue current. "See ya, Father. 'Bye, Jack."

"This is an outrage, I tell you," whined Mercedes Sinclair as he was hauled past the WARM YOURSELF BY THE FIRE OF HIS LOVE sign. "I demand to see my solicitor. I insist upon—"

"What did you want to see me about?" asked Father when the room was empty save for him, Lieutenant Taper, and the gardener who was perfecting his imitation of wallpaper.

"I've known you a lot of years, Jack," said Taper. "I caught that flare in your eyes. You're not convinced."

"I'm not?"

"No."

"Perhaps you're right."

"I know I'm right, Jack."

"Okay, I'll concede the point. I'm not convinced."

Where am I now, thought the wallpaper, an episode of *Dragnet*?

"Halleluiah," said Taper as he made a big show of tucking his haggard shirttails into his waistband. "So, what makes you think Mr. Sinclair isn't the perp?"

"Regarding the crimes in DC through Glendale, Utah," said Father, "I'm incompetent to say, though for the nonce I am willing to accept Lieutenant Byington's conclusions. As for the disappearance of Monsignor Aspic, whatever Mr. Sinclair may have had planned, and whatever evidence you've found on these premises, I don't believe he committed the abduction."

"Why not?"

"There is another factor that I'm not at liberty to disclose."

"This is a police investigation."

"Nonetheless, I am not at liberty."

"Did you meet with Cardinal Fulbright yesterday morning?"

"Yes."

"Up in Camarillo, wasn't it?"

"At the seminary, yes."

"And again this morning in Malibu?"

"Am I being followed?"

"No, but we have our sources, too."

"Millie? Monsignor Havermeyer?"

Taper hesitated. "Of course. We dropped by Saint Philomena's but you were out. Fulbright wasn't at either of those places when we followed up on it. Does this 'other factor' have something to do with him?"

Father said nothing.

"Is it," said Taper, "perhaps something the cardinal doesn't want made public?"

Father remained silent.

"Surely it would seem so," said Taper.

"Surely I haven't said," said Father.

"Does Chief Billowack know about it?"

"Whatever you're talking about, you'll have to ask him."

"I may have to." Taper uselessly repeated the shirttail stuffing routine. He did not look pleased. "Is this all the help you're going to be?"

Father folded his arms firmly across his chest. "I can tell you this, Lieutenant, for what it's worth. Monsignor Aspic recently acquired a 'quality,' let us say, that may have incited the interest of certain parties, a quality for which some might resort to theft, kidnapping, torture, or even murder."

"That's some quality," said Taper.

"Indeed. I harbor genuine fears that the monsignor may have met with foul play, but not in connection with 'Way True Life Publishers.' In fact, I can state unequivocally that someone other than Mr. Sinclair is responsible. You'll have to trust me on this."

"And do what?"

"And go in another direction. Fortunate as the apprehension of Mr. Sinclair may be, he is not the one who nabbed Monsignor Aspic."

"Jack, I need more than your assertion. I need facts."

"You shall not get them from me."

"Do you have any idea what position you're placing yourself in?"

"Precisely the same position I've enjoyed in every case into which my services have ordered against my wishes. Permit me to expound. I answer to God first, Larry."

"So do I, Jack. I'm a Catholic too, don't forget."

"Good. Then as a Catholic you'll understand and respect the fact that the vows I took upon my Ordination outweigh all other considerations. They were clear on the point. After God my duty is to the Popes, starting with St. Peter the Apostle on down to the present Holy Father. Then comes the lawful ecclesiastical authority placed over me, namely His Eminence, Cardinal Morley Psalmellus Fulbright, Archbishop of Los Angeles. Then, of course, there is myself. Yes, myself. I have all of them to consider before you, I'm afraid."

"But Fulbright is a, a—"

"He is my lawful superior, like it or not. That is the crowning irony and challenge of my vocation, not to mention the position I'm in. Because of a strange combination of all of the above, I cannot tell you how it is that I know Mr. Sinclair is not responsible for whatever happened to Monsignor Aspic. I shouldn't have to prove my qualifications as an investigator to you. Based on all that you know of me, your experience when I was your commanding officer, the outcome of more recent events, you must trust me on this."

"Do you have any idea what position you're placing *me* in?" Taper rearranged his shirttails one last time. "You ask a lot, Jack."

"So do you, Larry. This goes beyond citizenship, beyond friendship. It goes to God. Ultimately that's Who we're both answering to. Take my word, as a man who answers to God assuring another man who does likewise, that you must turn your investigation elsewhere. Do so, and you may pick up the trail before it grows cold. Fail to do so, and the real culprit may get away. You have the resources of the police department, while I am out here on my own. Oh, I've got Martin here —" Father smiled. "—and it's becoming more than likely that once again I'll have to turn the Knights Tumblar loose on the unsuspecting citizenry of Los Angeles."

"Hold on, Jack. Don't you dare get those fellows mixed up in this. If what you say is true, you may be endangering their lives."

"Then don't make me do so."

"I'm powerless to help you."

"Then I'll use the tools provided," said Father. "As you are aware, Pierre and his comrades provided me some time ago with a list of who I should notify in the event any harm befalls them. They realize the dangers they face when they're evangelizing."

"Is that what you call what they do? Evangelizing?"

"You know better than that." Father Baptist, who had been leaning against the desk all this time, heaved himself upright. "I'll tell you something you don't know. Last June, before I was first summoned by the cardinal and ordered to work on the Brassorie case, seven young men and six women made inquiries regarding the feasibility of night classes on Catholicism at Saint Philomena's—not your typical RCIA non-sense, but Catechetics, Classical Metaphysics, Church History, Moral and Dogmatic Theology. Some were 'lukewarms' that had somehow got themselves boiling, others were 'fallen-aways' that yearned to return with a vengeance. All thirteen cited the Tumblars as the spark that had ignited their interest."

"Very well, I'll concede—"

Father gave Taper a look that stopped him in mid-sentence. A good five seconds passed before the next words came out of Father's mouth. "I was planning to accommodate them when I was suddenly ordered to instigate certain investigative duties by my lawful superior because someone with the weirdest power trip on record had decided to assassi-nate our auxiliary bishops, one by one. By the time I solved the case, all those seekers had gone elsewhere, wary of my notoriety. I don't blame them. But more continue to knock at my door—five so far this month—and I would much rather be seeing to their spiritual needs than trying to convince you where to take your investigation."

The gardener-slash-wallpaper refrained from applauding. Instead, he swallowed his goo for the third time and remained silent.

"Okay, okay," said Taper, running his fingers wearily through his hair. "I don't want to be misunderstood when I say this: we're not in a contest, but I've got a superior, too. He's as fit for his job as yours is for his, I'm sorry to say. He's the one I have to convince. You tell me to investigate elsewhere. Show me a clue that points me there."

"You have the same list of people the monsignor visited as I do," said Father. "Martin and I have managed to see most of them. You have more resources than I."

"Don't underestimate your resources, Jack. I certainly don't. In some respects your connections are better than mine."

"How so?"

"I have my badge to consider, so I don't mix with the likes of Ernie Corben and his watchdog, Some Guy—or are you going to try to convince me that they dropped by the rectory to be shriven?"

"How do you know about that?"

The lieutenant hesitated. "It was reported."

"Reported."

"Yes."

"Not by Millie or Havermeyer. They knew nothing of that meeting." Father stiffened ever so slightly. "So I am being watched. I can't see what you hope to gain by it, but be my guest."

"It's not my call, Jack. I'm under strict orders, too. That's why I asked if Billowack knows what's bugging Fulbright. Perhaps the bulldog knows what he's doing."

"By having me tailed? That sounds like sheer laziness to me, Larry. Or desperation."

"Like I said, it's not my call."

"Fine. Let's leave it at that. Martin and I have work to do. I'm afraid from here we're just going back to Saint Philomena's. You can inform your men. They can stop for coffee and doughnuts on the way."

"Jack, this isn't personal."

"Don't be too sure. Come on, Martin, we're going home."

Home? I thought, peeling myself from the wall. Hurrah! Yay! ... *Erp!*

34

"IPECAC? DID YOU SAY IPECAC?"

"Yes, Millie, that's what I said."

"But that stuff'll push your insides outside."

"That's a fair description of just what happened."

"You poor, poor man." Millie expressing compassion was almost as unnerving as ipecacuanha poisoning. "I know just the thing to soothe your stomach."

"Please don't go to any trouble," said I as she started prowling through the shelves in the chamber of mysteries just off the kitchen known as the pantry.

"Some weak tea might help," said Father.

"Weak tea?" said I distastefully.

"It tastes better than bile when it comes up," said he authoritatively.

I shuddered in response.

"Does warm milk sound good to you?" asked Sybil Wexler who, along with Father and myself, was seated at the table in the dining nook.

"It does not," said I, rubbing my tummy gingerly. "Nothing sounds good to me."

"If everything that's good for us tasted good," said Millie, shoving things this way and that on the wooden shelves, "we wouldn't need doctors."

"What good will a remedy do me," I asked, "if it won't stay down? I want things to stop coming up, thank-you very much. I therefore submit that the reasonable course of action is to do nothing."

"Never," said Millie. "Now where is that licorice root?"

"You're outnumbered," observed Sybil, smiling.

"I'm dying," said I weakly, "and you guys are trying to embalm me."

"Saves time before the funeral," said Father.

The phone rang.

"Are *you* telling *me?*" I chuckled sickly as I picked up the wall extension with the coiled cord. "Good afternoon, or is it evening? This is St. Philomena's Catholic Church."

"So formal," said Sybil.

"Feeney? Is that you, Feeney?" huffed a not-so-wee voice in my ear.

It took me a minute to recognize the source. "Oh, Mr. Turnbuckle."

"I understand that Father Baptist came by my house today and told Greeley he would come back."

"That he did, Sir."

"Without an appointment."

"That's correct."

"I repeat, without an appointment."

"You'd have to ask Father. Would you like to speak to him?"

"I would not. Please inform him that I will come by the rectory and see him this evening, say, around eight."

"Hold on, please." I cupped my hand over the mouthpiece. "Father, Mr. Turnbuckle wants to make an appointment to come see you this evening—eightish."

"Tell him I prefer that I come to his house," said Father. "That is, if you're up for another excursion."

"Hey, sure," said I, as if my stomach was all better. It was not. I removed my hand from the mouthpiece. "Mr. Turnbuckle, Father Baptist would prefer to visit you at your home."

"Why the blazes would he want to do that?"

"You'll have to ask him. Would you like to speak to—?"

"I would not. This is most inconvenient, but very well. Let us say eight-thirty."

"Eight-thirty?" I asked Father, who nodded. "Done and done," I said into the receiver.

Mr. Turnbuckle snorted into his before he hung up.

"The fun never stops," said I, cradling the phone.

Just then the backdoor opened. Monsignor Havermeyer came bustling in. "I hope I'm not late."

"Just in time," said Father. "Sybil, much as I want to speak with you, I must ask you to indulge me by going to my study for a few minutes."

"Excuse me?" said she.

"It would take too long to explain," said Father. "I'm going to be receiving a visitor shortly, and the nature of the situation is such that you shouldn't be present. This is no reflection on you whatsoever, but is rather a dynamic of the exercise."

"It's a pastoral thing," explained the gardener.

"Oh, of course," said Sybil, a mite flustered, gathering her briefcase and purse. "It's down this way, yes?"

"I'll go with you, Sweetie," said Millie, untying her apron and hanging it on the edge of the sink. "There's something I want to discuss with you, anyway."

"Really," said Sybil, smiling conspiratorially. "Let's."

"Your remedy will have to wait," said Millie to the gardener.

"I'll survive somehow," said he with a weak wave of his fingers, then under his breath, "Don't hurry back."

"You've allowed others to be present before," said the monsignor after the women had departed.

"Other than yourself," said Father, "only a select few, and only because they were already involved in some way. In this case, Sybil isn't a Baptized Catholic."

"Ah, right," said Havermeyer.

A moment later there came a tapping at the window. It was a very special stained-glass window, mostly executed in dark shades, featuring an elegant white Dove perched on the rim of a golden Chalice, a single drop of red blood dangling from its beak. Father Baptist turned the clasp and opened it, revealing the kindly, mildly-crazed visage of Mrs. Magillicuddy.

"There's you are's, Faddah," she sputtered through gaps once occupied by teeth. "It's always so nice it is when you're's actually here, it is. Not's like sometimes when you're's not's."

Father bowed his head. Only once had he missed Mrs. Magillicuddy's regular visit every Friday at six-fifteen. The case he had mentioned to Lieutenant Taper, the one the previous June that had derailed his plans to start classes in Catholic theology, had also interfered with his guardianship of this poor woman's soul. She had never forgotten, nor let him off the hook for his negligence.

"You're looking well," said Father.

"I wish I could's say I'm's feelin' that a'ways, I surely does, but alas, Faddah, I'm so very sad, I is."

"What's troubling you, my good woman?"

"Just that's, Faddah. I'm not's good, I'm not's—as you know all too wells. You's been a'shrivenin' me for a long, long times, you have's."

"True, but you don't despair, you keep returning for the Grace of the Sacraments. That is a good sign. The greatest temptation to the habitual sinner is to give up, to stop trying, to listen to that voice that says, 'Give it up, you'll never beat this thing.' To despair is to play into Satan's hands. Something that never ceases to amaze me is God's ceaseless ability to forgive. In spite of our countless failures and regressions, all He asks is that we repent and seek Absolution."

"Well, Faddah, if the Lord Jesus told Saint Peter he had to forgives his brother seventy times seven times, then He Hisself's must forgive's at least that much's, if not's even more's—even of the likes of me's."

Matthew eighteen, thought the gardener, twenty-one and twenty-two—expanded.

"I couldn't have said it better," said Father. "Shall we proceed?"

"Bless me Faddah, for I have sinned, I have's," said she, making a tremblingly reverent Sign of the Cross. "It's been a week's, methinks."

"Very well," said he, blessing her silently in return.

"It's so hard's," said she, bursting into tears. "Oh me, oh my. I promised me self, I did's, I promised I wouldn't make's a scene, and here I am's a'blubberin' away."

"Take your time," said Father reassuringly.

"He's after me, he is," said she, looking over her shoulder, then digging around inside her sleeve and producing a ratty handkerchief. "You remembers I went's to visit's me sister, Abigail, I did's. Last month's it was, when the wee folks went away."

"Have they returned?"

"Have they!" Mrs. Magillicuddy emptied her nasal passages noisily into her hankie, gave her bulbous nose a couple of hearty rubs with it, then stuffed the soggy thing back up her sleeve. "Why, Faddah, some of Abigail's wee folks came's back with me, they did's. They got kin, you know, kin in my woods. They brought their little harps and fiddles and—what do you calls 'em?—oh yes, hurdy-gurdies! Why, I's hardly gotten myself's any sleep in some nights, let me tell's you."

"Sounds grand," said Father as if this was all very normal in his parish. "So what seems to be the trouble?"

Again she looked over her shoulder, then side to side before continuing in a hushed tone. "Faddah, me thinks he's out's to gits me, he is."

"Get you? Who?"

"Lou Costello."

"Excuse me?"

"Shhhhhh, Faddah. Just the other morning there was watcha might's call's a commotion at the mission. A lots of people were there's—not wee people like's me friends, oh no, but reg'lar folkses. Lots of them cameras flashing and mikey-phones squeakin', they was. That plump little priest, the one who came's around here a few times a while's back, was talkin' to them, like he was tellin' 'em somethin' important, but it's was wrong what he said's, Faddah. He did said Sancta Valeria wasn't real! If I'd've had me Willum's 'noculars I'd've throwed 'em right at that awful man, I would's."

"Monsignor Aspic?" whispered Monsignor Havermeyer.

"The press conference at the Del Agua Mission," breathed yours truly. "She was there."

"Did she say Lou Costello?"

"I think so."


```
GARDENING TIPS: Mrs. Magillicuddy is what most
people would classify as "homeless."  In fact, she
has magnificent lodgings, albeit open to the ele-
ments, in the old oak forest on the grounds of La
Misio/n del Agua de la Vida, "The Mission of the
Water of Life," which I mentioned before.
  By the by, there is a causal connection between
the bump on Cardinal Fulbright's forehead and Wil-
lum's binoculars, but that's a long story.  An
"Auld Lang Syne" story.
                                         --M.F.


N.B.: I would advise my readers not to hastily
dismiss the "wee folk" she mentioned.  Long, long
story.
```


Father Baptist hushed Havermeyer and me with a blast of silencing flame from his eyes.

"I can't tells you, Faddah, how many times these sore old feets of mine has taken me to the old cathedral to pray to blessed Valeria. She's such a sweetheart, she is. And there was this, this—" She let out a groan to fill in the blank. "—sayin' that she never was, that she never, ever was at all's! And me, I should've run's up and socked him, I should's've." She paused and took a deep breath, glancing from side to side. "But then I saw's the hearse."

"Hearse?" asked Father.

"Parked with all the other cars, it was," said she, sniffing mightily. "Cold shivers, it gave's me, it did's. I thoughts to me self's, 'Uh-oh, he's a'comin' for you, you old crumpet.' I mean's, I asks you, Faddah, why would Lou Costello become a nun? And why would's he comes after me? So's I hidey-tailed it out of there."

"I beg your pardon?" asked Father.

"I was always so sad, I was, when Abbot 'n' Costello broke up, they did's. But I ask's you, would the nuns take's that cute li'l Lou into their convent? And why's was he's after me's?"

Father looked at me, perplexed. I returned the facial expression. Mrs. Magillicuddy took a little time to unravel, but oddly enough everything she said invariably made sense on some level, once you figured out what level that was.

"Lou Costello?" mouthed Monsignor Havermeyer silently.

"A nun," I mouthed back, nodding.

"That reminds me," said Mrs. Magillicuddy, gathering something up from beneath the windowsill. She produced a handful of gnarled things that looked like withered ferns. "I brought these daffydillies, I did's, all the ways from me sister Abigail's garden, for that cranky Mr. Feeney." She handed the things to Father, who plopped them in my drinking glass. The muck caked on the roots turned the water murky. "I didn't bring's 'em last week, I didn't, because I wants'd them to blooms first, I did's."

GARDENING TIPS: A curious feature of Mrs. Magillicuddy's Friday evening confessions, aside from the
confessions themselves, is that she doesn't appear
to see the rest of us at the table, just Father
Baptist.

Another notable feature, at least to me, is her
persistent perception of me as "grim," "dour," and
now "cranky." Hence the endless bouquets of
"periwinkies," "sunfloosies," and now "daffydillies." Indications are that I require a systems
check of my personality, seeing as how, according
to Keating, Monsignor Havermeyer considered me "a
treasure, albeit a crotchety, limping one."

As Father Baptist has so often pointed out,
"There ain't no humility without humiliation." I
choose to be touched that, with all else on her

mind, Mrs. Magillicuddy is concerned about me at all.

--M.F.

"But as for not defendin' blessed Saint Valeria to that, that—" Again she made an exasperated noise. "—I lost's me courage, I did's, an' for that I'm a'sure's sorrier than I can say, I am's. So's for these and all me sins, all's of them's, I repents."

There was a long silence while Father Baptist considered his words. After some preliminary chin rubbing and temple polishing, he began: "My dear Mrs. Magillicuddy, first let me assure you that Saint Valeria was and is as real as real can be. Of this I have personal, irrefutable knowledge, and you have meritorious conviction. Be glad of that, that you have the Catholic Faith, that you are a member of the Church, and therefore participate in the Communion of Saints. Saint Valeria is an exceptional friend to have, and surely she regards your loyalty to her with gratitude and generosity. As for your not speaking up, according to your account, you were distracted by something you found alarming. There was insufficient time to reflect, so your fault was mitigated. At the same time, I appreciate your candor, your lack of excuses, your sorrow over a missed opportunity to defend a great Saint. For your penance, say a Rosary before the Blessed Sacrament in honor of Saint Valeria. I'm sorry that we don't have a statue of her in the church, but she is certainly in our hearts. Now, make a good act of contrition."

As Father whispered the Absolution in Latin, Mrs. Magillicuddy pressed her forehead against her clenched knuckles and said: "Oh my God in the highest, and on earth in thought, word, and deed, where there is now and every shall be through my most grievous fault, but most of all because ever this day be at my side to avoid the near occasion of sin. Amen."

"Go in peace, beloved daughter," said he, making the Sign of the Cross over her.

"Thankee, Faddah. You're the greatest, you is, even if you didn't show's up once, you didn't."

"I'm only human."

"Me's too. And please don't forget to gives them daffydillies to that cranky Mr. Feeney. He needs his self a good lady, me thinks."

"He has Our Blessed Mother," said Father, smiling at me. "What man could ask for more?"

"Indeeds," said she, nodding and winking. "But then again's—well, good night's and good bye's."

"God bless you and Mary keep you."

"I never cease being amazed," said Monsignor Havermeyer as Father Baptist closed and latched the window. "That poor woman, that wreck of humanity, homeless and befuddled, probably illiterate—I can't imagine her perusing many books, even if she can read—yet the Faith she carries in her heart, it's enough to, to—"

"We are blessed to have her in our midst," agreed Father. "Who was it who said, 'Remember that our good Master prefers the poverty of our heart to the most sublime thoughts and affections borrowed from others'?"

"St. Peter Julian Eymard," said I, showing off. *The Real Presence.*

"Yes, of course, literacy is not a prerequisite for Salvation," said Monsignor Havermeyer. "But still, I am concerned about her."

"Mrs. Magillicuddy?" Father ran his fingers through his hair, then locked them behind his neck. "How so?"

"Well, I don't want to sound unkind, but you heard her rant this evening," said Havermeyer.

"You mean her description of me—me, mind you—as cranky?" asked the gardener. "An unnecessarily harsh portrayal perhaps, but hardly a rant."

"Be serious, Martin," said the monsignor, "if only for a moment."

"Martin," said Father, smiling, "are you actually suggesting you're not a crank?"

"Ex-key-*ooze* me," said I.

"This is not a laughing matter," insisted Havermeyer. "I know she lives in a world different from ours, at least some of the time."

"Scrambled though her wits may be," said Father, "she comes here to our church and prays daily, receives the Sacraments—including legitimate Penance, in her lucid moments—and makes sure that every Saint has flowers at their feet."

"Not to mention me," said I, nudging my tumbler full of "daffydillies."

"As strange as Mrs. Magillicuddy's observations may seem," said Father, "they have always proved to be based on fact."

"Wee folks with harps, fiddles, and now hurdy gurdies?" said Havermeyer.

"And the hearse," said I. "Don't forget the hearse."

"I can't explain those things yet," said Father. "But I'll wager a dinner at Darby's that her current *idée fixe,* no matter how muddled, will become clear. We know that she segues between lucidity and reverie as easily as we go in and out of prayer."

"Or as I drift from reality to daydreams and back," said I. "Her simple, unswerving devotion sure puts me to shame."

"That I'm not denying," said Havermeyer. "But Lou Costello as a nun—?"

"He's got a point," said I to Father.

The three of us looked at each other, pondering what could possibly leave Mrs. Magillicuddy with that particular visual impression. Wheels turned silently, wobbly, and uselessly.

"… impressive," said the voice of Sybil Wexler. She was approaching in the hallway.

"Yes," said Millie, also drawing near. "A bit lean on St. Cyprian and a few other books I could mention, but other than that, fairly comprehensive—oh, look: the *men.*" She placed a creepy emphasis on the last word. "Ah, Father. I was just showing Miss Wexler your library."

"Do please call me Sybil," said Miss Wexler to Millie, then to Father, "I've been in your study before, of course—just the other day. But I didn't really look at the titles. You have some fascinating reading material, Father. Perhaps some day—"

"Interested souls are always welcome," said Father, rising as the ladies entered the kitchen.

"Provided they promise to return what they borrow," said Monsignor Havermeyer, also rising. "Not that I'm suggesting—"

"I know what you mean," said Sybil. "I dread loaning books to friends. Books have a funny way of becoming absorbed into other peoples' collections."

"I once read," said I, likewise struggling to my feet, "that Saint Bonaventure was reluctant to lend books for that very reason."

"Many of the volumes in my library are out of print," said Father.

"I guessed as much," said Sybil, seating herself in the chair Monsignor Havermeyer pulled out for her. "Perhaps you could allow people to borrow books so long as they don't remove them from the premises. They could read them in your beautiful garden, or in the church."

"That's a thought,' said Father, freefalling into his chair. His weariness was showing. "What do you think, Martin?"

"Fine by me," said I, sinking into my own chair. "Of course, Monsignor Havermeyer has the best idea."

"I do?" asked the Monsignor.

"Yes. Just a few days ago you said you wanted to do a fundraiser for the parish library."

"A library?" asked Sybil. "Where would you put it?"

"Where it already is," said I. "In the room next to mine."

"Excuse me?"

"It's been sitting untouched since 1965 when then-pastor then-Monsignor now-deceased Auxiliary Bishop Eugene Brassorie forbade his flock to read any book whatsoever published prior to 1962, believing as he did that anything written before was unenlightened."

"Including the Bible?" she asked.

"Especially the Bible," said I, "except the most progressive translations."

"Then you already have books."

"Indeed we do," said Father, "but they are in sad shape. Most of them need rebinding, and some, I fear, are deteriorating from moisture, mold, and silverfish. When's the last time we looked in there, Martin?"

"Not since I had no clue that you were a retired homicide detective," said I. "It's had time to molder more since."

"I hate to think about it," said Father. "Unfortunately, funds are in short supply. Are you going to join us for dinner, Sybil?"

"Can't," said she.

There was a moment of stunned silence. Father, Monsignor, and I each glanced furtively toward Millie to glimpse the impending horror. No reasonably cognizant human being uttered the word "Can't" in relation to one of Millie's meals—although I admired the simple elegance of the offense.

"Maybe next time," said Millie sweetly, to our shock and surprise.

35

"OH, BUT BEFORE I GO," said Sybil, fishing around in her slim briefcase, "I mustn't forget what brought me here this evening." While we *men* adjusted to an inexplicable shift in the rationale of the universe—Millie's uncharacteristic acceptance of the word "Can't"—Sybil produced a sheet of paper. At first glance it looked to me like a horrid cross-section of a tissue sample out of an autopsy report. Lord knows I've seen enough of that sort of thing tagging alongside Father Baptist; and after all, she did used to work for Solomon Yung-sul Wong and John Holtsclaw. But then, upon closer inspection, I realized the veins and arteries looked familiar, in fact, I had traveled on some of them in the corpuscle we call the Jeep. It was a printout of a map of downtown Los Angeles. Arranged upon it were dark dots with white centers.

"You asked me yesterday to check into the late Bishop Ravenshorst's affairs," she explained. "It took longer than I thought because I had to do some deep probing, and once I got there, there was so much to find."

"Sounds ominous," said Father, accepting the map and examining it with furrowed brows. There were thirteen dots in all. "What do these marks represent?"

"Property," said Sybil. "Some vacant lots, some buildings, even a parking lot tucked away under a freeway overpass."

My neck cracked audibly as I strained for a closer look.

"I don't understand," said Father. "Are you saying Bishop Raven-shorst owned all these sites?"

"That's right," said she.

"Gives me a warm, gooey feeling," interjected the gardener, "seeing our donation dollars at work."

"Though not all at once," added Sybil. "Most of these parcels he re-sold within a few months after purchasing them."

"Did he employ a broker?" asked Father.

"No," said she. "He took courses at a city college to qualify for his own license."

"Wheeling and dealing, apparently," said Havermeyer, smiling amusedly. "I had no idea Jerry was into real estate."

"Not exactly," said Sybil. "In every case he obtained the property and immediately arranged for a geological survey. In some cases this in-volved drilling through basement floors to take core samples up to thirty feet down."

"Core samples," gasped Father. "That doesn't make sense. Did he have a degree in sedimentology, too?"

"If he did, he didn't enroll anywhere under his own name. He did have two degrees in archeology, though."

"But to what purpose?" asked Havermeyer. "These core samples, I mean. All the oil in the LA area was pinpointed decades ago."

"Thirty feet isn't deep enough for that," said Sybil. "I haven't been able to access the reports yet. The geologist he hired to do them is on the faculty at Cal State Long Beach, but he's on sabbatical—unless the name and contact information are bogus, which is possible. Bishop Ravenshorst was slippery. I've no idea what he was looking for. As far as I can tell, his latest and most ambitious acquisition, three months before his death, was a lot at the corner of El Barranco Drive and La Colina Avenue."

"Interesting," said Father. "That's just a couple of miles from here."

"In the Latino quarter," said the gardener.

"The property was one of those courts with seven little rundown cottages on it," said Sybil. "He actually evicted the tenants—poor families all—bulldozed the structures, then set the backhoes loose. I don't yet know where he got the funding, but he had a crew dig a thirty-foot hole as if to lay a subbasement. However, as far as I can tell, there were no plans on file with the city to build anything on the site. How he obtained the permit to excavate is beyond me."

"Is the pit still there?" asked Father.

"Yes. There is some dispute among his heirs as to just what to do with the property. The neighbors are upset because the barrier around the lot was thrown up in haste. Parents are afraid their kids might go exploring and fall in or worse. But there is something else."

"Do tell," said the gardener.

"I've been working on my own 'pattern recognition' program," said Sybil. "It scans all the documents and emails going through my computer looking for discernable relationships in complex configurations, be it verbal, graphic, topographic, whatever."

"And your brainchild software came up with something," said Father.

"I'll show you," said she, producing a ruler and a blue felt-tipped pen. "Watch."

With speed and precision she connected the dots without obliterating them. The result was seven lines criss-crossing the map. Three were roughly vertical, though slanted from the upper left toward the lower right—not precisely parallel to each other, fanning apart as they approached the bottom of the page. Four lines were more or less horizontal, the upper two fanned to the right, the lower two to the left, and the middle two intersecting near the right side of the page. I am so glad Sybil later gave me a copies of these printouts or nothing in this paragraph would make much sense:

"There's a pattern to his land purchases," said Sybil. "Note that not only are the sites arranged in straight, although askew, lines, but—"

"They occur where the lines intersect," said Father.

"Are you sure your program isn't making something out of nothing?" asked Havermeyer. "I mean, surely you could draw any number of lines connecting those dots."

"But not with several sites on each line, and only where the lines cross," said Sybil. "No, there's definitely a pattern here."

"I assume you've extended the lines to see where they go," said Father.

"I assume my name is Wexler," said Sybil with a disarming wink. "Of course I tried that. So far I haven't traced them to anything significant, at least to me. But then, I don't know what to look for."

"How about astral alignments," suggested Havermeyer, "or points on the horizon where the sun rises and sets on equinoxes and the solstices?"

"Ah, Stonehenge West," said I.

"I could find no such correlation," said Sybil. "Bear in mind that I probably haven't uncovered all the bishop's holdings. He was very clever at covering his tracks. He didn't want anyone to know what he was doing."

"Including His Insistence, the Cardinal," mused the gardener.

"Especially His Eminence," said Father.

"This wouldn't happen to be connected with an intersection of mysteries, would it?" I asked. "Sort of the Hollywood and Vine of mysteries?"

Father looked at me with those penetrating eyes, nodded imperceptibly, then shook his head a little more obviously. I shrank inside accordingly. Me and my big mouth.

"What's he talking about?" asked Sybil.

"Yes," said Havermeyer. "What's Martin saying?"

"He's reflecting my own words back at me," explained Father. "He does that all the time, and worse, he types it all up in the wee hours of the morning."

"Sheer prolixity," said I. "Father's, not mine. Well, the first part, anyway. I came up with the metaphor."

"What's this secret?" asked Sybil. "You know a girl can't have secrets floating around without being in on them."

"A secret," said the gardener sagaciously, "is defined as 'something you only tell one person at a time.' There are far too many present at the moment—"

"I'll say this much," said Father, by way of changing the subject. "We have two problems on our hands. The first is the plight of Monsignor Aspic. I have been following his footsteps in hopes of discovering what happened to him. Concurrently, he was running an errand for Cardinal Fulbright. I have been ordered not to discuss the nature and purpose of that errand, so I can and will not. Martin spoke out of turn."

"Erg," said I, shrinking dutifully.

"It's only a matter of time before I figure it out anyway," said Sybil, examining her elegant red fingernails.

"We shall see," said Father. "In any case, I thank you for this information about Bishop Ravenshorst's extra-ecclesial activities."

"Oh, I almost forgot," said Sybil, producing one of those marvelous printed cards. "Have you ever heard of the name 'W. Warren Shufeld'?"

"Can't say that I have," said Father.

"Rings a bell," said Monsignor Havermeyer, "but I can't place it."

"Don't look at me," said I.

"My pattern recognition program kicked it out," explained Sybil.

"Excuse me?" said Father.

"That's what it says," said she, pointing to the card. "'Cross-reference: W. Warren Shufeld; also see the Lizard People.'"

"Come again?" asked Havermeyer.

"Your computer suggests a connection," said I, "between Bishop Ravenshorst's drilling interests and a lost science fiction movie?"

"I'm not sure what it means," said she, not quite laughing. "I'll know next time I see you."

"No doubt," said Father.

"Oh," said Sybil, glancing at her watch. "I really do have to be going." She gave me a enigmatic look and fluttered her eyelashes. "Prolixity, eh?"

"By the ton," I assured her, interlacing my fingers and turning my palms out. "Too bad you can't stay for dinner."

"Not for her," said Millie, looming with frying pan in hand. "You don't know what I'm fixing."

I smiled as best I could under the circs, as did Father and Monsignor. Sybil giggled and pushed herself away from the table. "Oh, one more thing. That phone call Monsignor Aspic made from the parking lot at KLIE Wednesday evening shortly before eight. It only lasted seventeen seconds. It was made to—"

"7206 West Manchester," piped the gardener.

Sybil paused before straightening to her full, gorgeous height. "How did you know?"

"St. Barbara's Chapel," said I, perhaps a bit smugly. "The former residence of Bishop Jeremiah Ravenshorst, and now the temporary lodgings of one Bishop Morell deQuet."

"That confirms it, Martin," said Father.

"I may become a fine detective after all," I said to Sybil. "Father said so."

36

"W. WARREN SHUFELD," I REPEATED into the telephone receiver in the study. "That's right. No, I'm not sure about the spelling. I've never seen it in print. And don't forget the Lizard People."

"I'm not sure I'm following you," said Pierre on the other end.

"I'm not sure I'm following me," said I. "Call it a hunch. You're a journalist, you're always on the lookout for unusual stories. This sounded unusual to me. All I ask is that if you find out anything interesting you run it by Father Baptist before you go to print."

"Why?"

"I've already spoken out of turn once today."

"Excuse me?"

"And do yourself a favor. Look up Psalm Seventeen, thirty-seven and thirty-eight."

"Will do. Why?"

"No time. Father's waiting for me. We're going to the mouth from Hell."

"You mean *into* the mouth *of* Hell."

"I know precisely what I mean. See you around."

37

"BUSHWA!" HUFFED THURGOOD T. TURNBUCKLE, looking angrily at his pocket watch. "Your impertinence never ceases to amaze me."

"Nor does it change the facts," said Father Baptist evenly.

"You dare to bring your investigation into this, my house."

"I go where the trail leads me."

"You can go to Hell."

"Possibly, but hopefully not," said Father, glancing at me.

I was standing at the fireplace, seemingly absorbed in one of the Grecian urns displayed on the twenty-foot wide mantelpiece.

A mere quarter of an hour before this tense exchange, Father and I had arrived at the gate. A coastal fog had pushed its way inland for the night, obscuring the stars and blanketing the landscape in damp, gray darkness. If we hadn't been there earlier that day I would have had trouble finding it because there was no light in the gatehouse, and none on the post of the cavernous mailbox to illuminate the address dangling underneath.

"Here goes nothing," I had said as I reached for the red button I knew to be on the callbox.

"Yes?" wheezed a frail voice after a robust burst of static.

"Father Baptist to see Mr. Turnbuckle," said I. "Mr. Turnbuckle is expecting us."

"Us? ... Who, may I ask ... are you?"

"I'm Martin Feeney, Father Baptist's chauffeur." I thought that would impress him.

"Oh." It didn't. "The padlock is ... unlocked. You may ... ascend ... the driveway."

"Thank-you."

The padlock may have been open, but the gates certainly weren't. Good sport that he was, Father Baptist got out and saw to them.

"How is your energy level?" he asked as he got back in beside me.

"Depleted," said I, easing my foot onto the accelerator. There were no lights or even reflectors along the steeply ascending, serpentine roadway, so I crept up ever so slowly. "But not to worry, Father. A confrontation with Mr. Turnbuckle is just the thing to recharge my batteries."

"Why do you assume our conversation will be confrontational?"

"Why should tonight be any different than any other time?"

"Noted. Oh, and Martin, wherever the discussion may wander, please make no references to the missing artifact."

"Right. I'm sorry I said too much in front of Miss Wexler."

"Fortunately she's on our side, as of course are Monsignor Haver-meyer and Millie. But Mr. Turnbuckle is another matter. We already know that, even though he regularly attends Mass at Saint Philomena's, he has a direct channel to Morley Fulbright."

"Namely money."

"Exactly. We can assume that our conversation will be repeated at the Chancery in short order. Therefore we must be scrupulous about what is actually verbalized."

"Gotcha," said I, pretending to close my lips with a zipper. "Mmmrrmble mmlk mmmgrph."

"All I need," sighed Father, "is for the cardinal to learn that my gar-dener is an idiot."

"Mmmrrmble—" I unzipped my mouth. "I thought he already had that figured out."

"No doubt. But your readers, what will they think?"

"If I should ever have any, they'll figure it out, too."

I swung the car up around behind the forest, which in the passing glow of the headlights became a black-and-gray jungle of creeping, sneering shapes. To our right swelled an impressive wood and stone mansion, no doubt built by a wealthy, blind, Victorian gentleman who inadvertently hired a contractor with a subtle sense of humor and a flamboyant, perhaps clairvoyant prankster for an architect. Driving as carefully as I was, I didn't dare avert my attention to give the place a good stare, but that was my first impression as we came level with the front porch. The parking area was cramped and dark, originally intended for guests' horses.

"Whoa," said I as I locked and shut my door. I peered up at the jum-ble of hazy outlines and indefinite shadows, the only illumination being one sixty-watt bug light by the front door. Except for three on the ground floor, all the windows in the twisted house were dark, and the three exceptions emanated light dimly from sources deeper within the house. "I'd sure like to see this place in broad daylight."

"In order to see the details," suggested Father.

"That," said I, "and because what little I can see in this gloom gives me the willies. So what's the etiquettical thing to do, Father, knock or just wait for Greeley to open the door? It's not like they don't know we're here."

"Martin, Martin, you worry about so many things."

"Father, Father, and you don't."

"What happened to those zipped lips?"

"Mmmrrmble mmlk mmmgrph," I assured him.

The knocker on the door, bathed in the paranormal radiance of that yellow bug light, was something out of a Dickens' novel, a vehicle for a ghostly voice to call our names. It was a ferocious bronze lion with a ponderous ring hanging from its nostrils. No wonder it looked perturbed. Suddenly, lo and behold, the thing actually wheezed, or seemed to. I almost choked on my mumble, the effect was so convincing — until the latch rattled, the ornate knob turned, and Greeley's pained face peered around the edge of the door as he pulled it ever-so-slowly open.

"Good evening ... Father," he rasped, bowing with an audible crack. Straggles of white hair fell down upon his face as he straightened, like a conductor taking a bow after a splendid though draining performance of *Le Sacre du Printemps*. He beckoned us into a large foyer with arched doorways and an impressive stairway that swirled majestically up to the second floor. The air was motionless and musty. "And ... I'm afraid I didn't catch ... your name, Sir ... the call box being ... so noisy."

"Feeney," said Father before I could forget my mouth was zipped. "Martin Feeney."

"Your, ah ... chauffeur, Father ..."

It was a statement that was open-ended, a discreet question to determine whether or not I should spend the evening in the kitchen gossiping with the servants. My fate was in Father's hands.

"My associate who happened to drive this evening," corrected Father, relegating me to the living room with the grownups.

"Very ... well," said Greeley. "This way."

We followed the wheezing but stately Greeley down a long hallway. The carpeting was thick and springy, though I couldn't see the pattern clearly. The walls were cluttered with portraits in gaudy frames, but I could barely see them. There was an impressive chandelier suspended from the ceiling, but none of its dozens of flame-shaped bulbs were lit. As without so within, the economy of darkness prevailed. There was but one light source for the corridor, and that was a single floor lamp with a plain canvas shade at the far end. Halfway down, Greeley turned to his left and grasped the lever-style knobs of a gigantic double door.

The room we entered may well have been the living room, but there was nothing lively about it. It was almost as dark as the hallway, and the air was stale and still. The ceiling, a honeycomb of plaster crowns and grapevines, loomed in the gloom above us. There was a nine-foot piano in the corner draped with a frilled paisley throw and bristling with photographs in metal frames. A couch and two high-backed upholstered chairs were gathered around a coffee table, the entire ensemble facing the fireplace. I could have sworn I glimpsed spiderwebs attached to the knobby log on the hearth, but my eyes may have been playing tricks on me in the chilly murkiness.

Our host was standing at a barrister's cabinet, a rickety antique bookcase with glass panels reminiscent of the display case in the Doily Sisters' office. His profile was hawkish, and his fingers moved with the subtle intricacy of spider legs as he turned the pages of a book, searching for something. His forehead was furrowed, contorting his bushy white eyebrows into furry, writhing caterpillars. Red-rimmed eyes darted this way and that, scanning the printed words through a pair of semicircular lenses perched on the tip of his precipitous nose, and his lips were puckered into an angry snarl. His aged but meticulously preserved three-piece suit was charcoal gray, his cravat and matching kerchief silky silver, and his cufflinks and studs black opals. The toupee, as usual, was just enough off-center to reveal itself, and his barreled moustache was so immense it blocked his nostrils. Mr. Turnbuckle was bent, bowlegged, and his paunch protruded all the more because of his otherwise spindly physique. Without looking at us he said in a gruff, gravelly voice, "You misrepresented Thomas Aquinas again in your sermon last Sunday."

"Good evening, Mr. Turnbuckle," said Father. "Monsignor Havermeyer celebrated Mass last Sunday. The sermon was his, and it was about the Holy Eucharist."

"The previous Sunday then—"

"If I may," ahemed Greeley as only a gasping old butler could interrupt his master. "Would Your Reverence ... and the gentleman ... care for anything? Port? Brandy, perhaps?"

"Brandy would do nicely," said Father, rubbing his palms together against the penetrating chill of the house and its owner. "Martin?"

Whoops, so much for keeping my lips zipped. Figuring that a request for premium ginger ale was out of place, I shrugged, rattled the marbles in my head, and asked, "Would coffee be too much trouble?"

"Not at all," replied Greeley, almost insulted. "I anticipated the need ... and made a fresh—"

"Benedictine for me," sputtered Turnbuckle, shoving the book into its niche in the cabinet. "And tell Biltmore his presence is required."

"Very good, Sir," said Greeley with another dramatic bow. Diaphanous slow-motion strands of silky white hair trailed behind his head as he exited the room.

Mmmrrmble mmlk mmmgrph. Yes, safely zipped again.

"So tell me, Father," said Mr. T., wedging his crooked thumbs and forefingers into the straight, slim pockets of his waistcoat, "why did you come to my gate without an appointment earlier today?"

"Because, as I told Greeley, I am conducting an investigation and therefore must remain flexible. New information may emerge without notice and I must be ready to act upon it as it comes. I would rather offend by arriving unannounced than not at a time agreed upon. I can assure you that Martin and I have seen a great deal of the City and County of Los Angeles in the last two days."

"I can't abide such a disordered existence."

"I don't care for it much myself, to tell you the truth, but I am acting in accordance with the cardinal's orders."

"Him again," huffed the old man, producing a pocket watch by a sharp tug on a silver chain and snapping it open.

"He is my lawful superior, Mr. Turnbuckle. I've told you before I don't appreciate being ordered to perform detective work, but my vows compel obedience."

"When convenient, it would seem."

"Indeed. The convenience of my lawful superior, not mine."

"Bushwa!" Mr. Turnbuckle glowered at his pocket watch, then stuffed it back into his vest pocket. Somehow the chain got snagged on his finger, so as he lifted his hand away the watch popped out again. Mumbling something to himself, he jammed it back in. His jaw muscles knotted as he jeered, "Your impertinence never ceases to amaze me, Father Baptist."

"Nor does it change the facts," said Father Baptist evenly.


```
GARDENING TIPS: The term "bushwa" being one of Mr.
Turnbuckle's favorite expletives, I finally looked
it up in Webster's:
```

Bush´wa *n.* Bodewash; esp. *Low slang,* bosh; trash.

```
   No big surprise here, except that a man of Mr.
Turnbuckle's background and deportment would re-
sort to "low slang."
                                          --M.F.
```


"You dare to bring your investigation into this, my house."

"I go where the trail leads me."

"You can go to Hell."

"Possibly, but hopefully not," said Father, glancing at me.

I had meandered over to the fireplace and was studying an ornate Grecian urn on the mantelpiece. What a difference a crackling fire on the hearth would have made. As it was, I was beginning to long for my squeaky, rickety, lumpy, but ever so beckoning bed.

"What could possibly bring your investigation to my door?" Mr. Turnbuckle's distasteful facial expression and tone of voice made "investigation," although properly pronounced, sound more like "regurgitation." It was quite a trick. He cleared his throat and loudly swallowed the result. "How can I possibly be involved?"

"I'm retracing the movements of Msgr. Conrad J. Aspic prior to his disappearance two days ago. I understand he came to see you at ten o'clock Wednesday morning."

"He had an appointment."

"No doubt."

"Any conversation between the monsignor and myself would be privileged."

"He came to hear your Confession?"

"No, but I would still consider the matter confidential."

"I don't need to know the specifics, Mr. Turnbuckle, but it might be helpful to know in general terms the purpose of the meeting."

"What part of 'confidential' do you not understand, Father? You seem to think you can just—"

"Begging your pardons," said Greeley, who had reentered pushing a stainless steel serving cart. The wheels emitted an annoying, high-pitched, unevenly oscillating squeak as he guided them ever so painfully slowly across the Persian rug. It was such a relief when it ceased. "Your Benedictine, Sir, your brandy, Reverend Father, and your coffee, Sir." He gave me an impenetrable look as he handed me a dainty little china cup and saucer with about a jigger of asphalt-black coffee wiggling around inside. "Cream, Sir?"

I nodded.

He handed me a pitcher the size of a thimble.

I gave him a look that I hope conveyed, "You've got to be kidding."

He gave me an "I don't care enough to bother" blink in return.

"Greeley, did you locate Biltmore?" asked Mr. Turnbuckle as I overturned the pitcher above my darling little cup. The drop of velvety cream was instantly devoured by the caffeinated blackness and forgotten forever. Even if I had preferred sugar in my coffee, I would have declined. Seriously, the cup was so tiny the addition of a single cube would have caused an overflow.

"Yes, Sir," said Greeley after pausing and turning to face his master. "He will be ... here directly. May I ... be of further service?"

Mr. Turnbuckle made a weird denture-suction sound that Greeley took as a dismissal. ·

"By your leave, Sir, Reverend Father, and Sir." The wheels of his cart squealed their prolonged, piercing farewells as Greeley slowly but surely exited the room.

"I have no wish to penetrate your private affairs, Mr. Turnbuckle," said Father Baptist, picking up the conversation as though it hadn't been interrupted, "but Monsignor Aspic has disappeared. His Eminence is concerned for his welfare."

"Bosh," said Turnbuckle, swirling the amber liquor in his snifter. "Morley Fulbright is concerned about his own welfare or you wouldn't be involved."

Father shrugged indefinitely, then enjoyed a long whiff of his brandy.

"The conversation between Aspic and myself," said Turnbuckle, strolling to one of the high-backed chairs, "could have no possible bearing on his disappearance."

"How can you be sure of that?"

"I am, and that's enough."

"We found a vial from a sick call kit in the back of his Mercedes. Is it possible someone in your household has been ill?"

"Absolutely not," said Turnbuckle, eyeing the seat cushion as though it were a negative stock report.

"You're sure."

"You are impertinent, Sir," rumbled the old man, swatting the cushion. "I would certainly know if someone under my roof was sick enough to call for a priest!"

"Might the meeting have had something to do with his manuscript?"

Mr. Turnbuckle hesitated in the midst of seating himself, then completed his descent. Once settled, he set his glass on an elegant end table and adjusted his cufflinks. "It might have."

"Did he approach you, perhaps, for funding?"

"He did not, not this time."

"Then he had before?"

"I don't see the point of this."

"Had he before?"

The old man glared defiantly at Father, then turned his attention to making sure all the buttons on his vest were secured. "Yes, and I turned him down. I'm a businessman, not a resource for first-time authors."

"You saw his manuscript as a poor investment?"

"For starters. I also saw no reason to fuel the fires of the man's idiocy."

"Ah."

"I found his ideas hazy, his writing puerile, and his conclusions heretical. The slippery son of a—er—the Church had hoped to cash in on the clerical services he has recently provided for me and my household—"

"I beg your pardon," interrupted Father. "'Clerical' services?"

"All right then, 'spiritual,' 'sacramental,' 'priestly.' Whatever you want to call it. I set him straight, by Jove, straight away. I, Thurgood T. Turnbuckle, do not support nor profit from heresy."

Considering his considerable donations to Morley Fulbright, I almost coughed on that one, but it's hard to do when one's mouth is firmly sealed. Instead, I rolled my eyes exaggeratedly, and as I did so I noticed two significant things. The first was one of two large oil portraits hanging on the chimney wall above the mantel. It was a young woman, a regally impressive lady, in a shimmering lavender gown with a white mink wrap. Her hint of a smile didn't seem to say, "I'm happy," so much as, "I insist on making the best of things." The frame was draped with a black cloth, and though she had not aged gracefully by the time I had met her, I recognized Eleanor Turnbuckle, the deceased wife of Thurgood T. Turnbuckle, whose own handsome young tailcoated figure filled the adjoining painting. Even in his youth he had made no pretence of smiling. I wondered what kind of a marriage they had endured. It escaped me at that moment how long it had been since Mr. Turnbucke had come knocking at the rectory door one stormy evening, depleted, ashen, grief-stricken, and devastated. More on that, methinks, some other time.

The second thing I noticed, as my eyeballs came round the other way, was a recent photograph among the forest of picture frames on the piano. It caught my eye amidst all those glossy portraits of Thurgood and Eleanor at different stages of their marriage: she everlastingly steadfast and he perpetually grim, he in charge and she self-controlled, both standing straight and barely touching, unmoved by the famous places behind them. There went Rome, Venice, and the Riviera unnoticed and black-and-white. Their three sons and one daughter started joining them in color as whelps in Paris, adolescents in Cologne, and young adults in Istanbul. Buckminster came first, then Horatio, Clarice, and finally Biltmore. I remembered a time when they all used to come to Mass together—a time faded and worn like an old shirt. Occasionally they were joined by the more-or-less Turnbucklian faces of their relatives. The photograph that netted my interest was a shot of a group of mature-to-ancient folks taken amidst a wild and colorful assortment of exotic cactus plants. Thurgood was among them, though Eleanor was not. Prominent in the foreground were a couple of ostentatiously arrayed elderly females with fruit-crowned hats and matching pink boas. These two old gals were the only ones smiling radiantly on the whole piano. Perhaps that's why that picture stuck out so.

I almost coughed again. In the wee hours of the morning I had told Father that I had learned something significant from Some Guy the night before, but I couldn't remember what. Now it came back to me:

"Martin," the giant had whispered, looking around to make sure
he wasn't overheard. *"Would you put me in one of your stories?"*
"Excuse me?" I had said, taken by surprise.
"You know, your books."
"How do you know about that?"
"I'm not supposed to," he hissed, shushing me. *"I overhead."*
"Overheard who?"
"Mr. Roundhead."
"Roderick? Who was he talking to?"
"His aunt."
"I didn't know he had an aunt."
"Well, he does."

Somehow I needed to call Father's attention to the women in that
picture. I tried clearing my throat. Then I coughed. He didn't so much
as glance at me.

"Monsignor Aspic's a bearable enough chap—for a priest," Turnbuckle was saying. Then he shook his head gruffly. "No, let's face it.
He's a self-absorbed, annoying little buffoon."

"In other words," said Father, his attention riveted to the liquor rocking in his glass, thus missing my winking and blinking at him, "you
told the monsignor you would give him no help whatsoever."

The old man frowned. "I wish you hadn't put it that way. In order to
answer truthfully I'd have to say not exactly."

I tried stretching my face sideways, turning it into an admittedly
weird pointer. Father still didn't notice. I sawed the underside of my
nose with my index finger, pointing, pointing, pointing. The great
cop-turned-priest-turned-cop's attention remained absorbed in the surface
tension of his brandy.

"Come again?" asked Father.

Mmmrrmble mmlk mmmgrph! screamed the gardener silently.

The old man frowned even more. Then he snatched up the snifter and
brought it to his lips. His words sounded hollow and glassy as he said,
"You said 'whatsoever.'" He took a sizeable sip and swallowed it noisily. He set the snifter on the end table and folded his hands atop his
paunch. "After I turned him down financially, he asked if I would, shall
we say, put in a good word with my sister."

Inside I was dancing on one foot, a stunt I could only achieve in my
imagination. I was waving my hands and brandishing my cane. Oh
Mammy! Of course all I could do on the outside was swing my eyes
from right to left, right to left—over here, Father, over here!

"Your sister," said Father.

AARRGGHH!! screamed the gardener, trapped in a silent movie for which he didn't write the screenplay.

"Mehitabelle," said old man Turnbuckle. "She married into the Doily family and runs a modest publishing business with her sister by marriage, Hortense. Your gardener has been trying to draw your attention to that snapshot on the piano—a family outing last spring at the Huntington Library."

"Oh," said Father, finally looking at me with eyes that seemed to say, weary yet patiently, "What were we saying about my gardener being an idiot? Don't you realize, Martin, I saw that photograph the moment we entered the room?" But all he said, and not to me, was, "Sister by marriage?"

"Ah, why not 'sister-in-law,' eh? Well, Hortense is the widow of Mehitabelle's deceased husband's twin brother." He paused to think that through again, then proceeded. "Both of their marriages were arranged to seal the breach between the Turnbuckles and the Roundheads."

"Roundheads," said Father. "I had no idea your families were connected."

"Since the wedding we have been, and good riddance."

"May I ask what breach existed between—"

"You may not. Ah, here comes Biltmore."

38

THE MAN ENTERING THE ROOM shared some of his father's physical characteristics, though not as fully developed. He was well on the way to bowleggedness, but his paunch needed time yet to billow and overflow his pants. His hair was brown and thick with only a hint of gray around the sides, and was certainly his own. Unlike his papa, his eyes didn't have that commanding, penetrating, condescending sheen, and his lips tended to pout rather than scowl. All of this was certainly correctible with practice, but it remained to be seen just how much Biltmore would grow into his father's persona. A couple of glances between him and his mother's portrait over the fireplace confirmed that her genes had won in the struggle to shape and arrange his facial features. I wondered if his father appreciated or abhorred that in his son.

"I'm glad to see you, Biltmore," said Father, extending his hand.

Young Turnbuckle, who was attired in a brown flannel suit and vest, yellow shirt with a simple black tie, hesitated, swallowed audibly, and gingerly returned the shake. He made no motion toward me other than to rotate his squelchy eyes in my direction and then turn them away again. Taking that as a sign, I set down my empty coffee thimble and saucer and backed slowly, I hoped imperceptibly, into the shadows, thus shucking all pretence of being a participant in the ensuing conversation.

"It is actually fortuitous that you are here, Father," said Thurgood Turnbuckle, taking up his snifter again. "Biltmore and I have something to discuss with you."

"Indeed," said Father pleasantly. "Would you mind if I finished my inquiry before we turned to other matters?"

"Inquiry," said Biltmore, his voice sullen and disinterested.

"Yes," said Father. "I'm checking up on the activities of Monsignor Aspic. I understand he was here a couple of days ago. Were you present during his visit with your father?"

"He was not," said Mr. Turnbuckle.

Biltmore didn't seem to mind that his father had answered for him. In fact, he seemed almost as removed from the conversation as I was.

"Oh," said Father amiably. "How about several weeks ago, Friday, October twenty-seventh?"

"Here, now," huffed Daddy Turnbuckle. "What's this?"

"I understand that Monsignor Aspic came to see you on that day," said Father.

"The last week in October," said Biltmore distantly. "Right after Bucky, um—"

"Why are you bringing that up?" huffed Thurgood. "What could that possibly have to do with—"

"The monsignor came to pay his condolences," said Father.

"Oh yes," said Biltmore, a strange series of twitches rippling through the fabric of his countenance. "Aunt Hitty was here, Aunt Horty, too, and then the monsignor arrived just before lunch."

"By appointment," said Thurgood, no point too pounded to hammer further.

"Of course," agreed Father. "The monsignor is fastidious that way. I know it was a trying time, and it's probably not important, but do you remember if he had a seminarian named David Smoley with him that day?"

"Smoley," said Thurgood and Biltmore simultaneously, but in very different tones.

Father smiled as though their response confirmed what he already knew.

"Why do you ask?" asked Thurgood. "What possible significance can be placed on such a visit? My son, Buckminster, was dead. I would have thought that you, my pastor, might have come to the house to pay your respects. Instead this twerp from the Chancery, Fulbright's little henchman, comes bobbing in here, self-conscious and positively babbling, feigning sympathy, and, and—"

"I thought he was rather kind," said Biltmore vaguely, eyes not focused on anything in particular. "It was Aunt Hitty that let the cat out of the bag."

"Cat?" asked Father. "What cat was that?"

"Hush, Son," said Thurgood, sternly. "This involves family, and we never discuss family with outsiders."

"Your parish priest, an outsider?" asked Father.

"Hitty," snickered Biltmore, then he giggled and sniggered, enjoying a private joke as if we weren't there. "My, my, my. She's that way, and there's no helping it, and who would want to? No sooner did that nervous little Smoley fellow introduce himself right here in this room—or was it a little later, when Greeley served the cucumber sandwiches and tea?—oh, no matter, I guess."

"Biltmore!" barked Daddy Turnbuckle, rising from his chair on legs that cracked and snapped like old twigs. "Be still!"

Instead, Biltmore pulled off a fair imitation of his Aunt Mehitabelle. "'Did he say Smoley, Darling? Are you the David Smoley dear Roddy hired to spy on Morley's bowl of gelatin?'"

"Silence!"

"And then Horty made it all the worse!" continued Biltmore, pausing to snort grossly. His Aunt Hortense surpassed his Aunt Mehitabelle: "'Aspic is a gelatin, isn't it, Threety?'" For a moment he was Biltmore again, but he seemed to be addressing a floor lamp. "That's what my aunts call my father, you know. Thurgood T. Turnbuckle. Three T's. Threety, get it?" His chuckle became a self-gratifying guffaw. Then he continued his warbling impersonation of Aunt Mehitabelle. "'I believe the name is Aspic, Sweetheart. That's a sort of gelatin, isn't it, Threety? Oh, I say, Monsignor, I do suppose you are firmer than your name, at least a little bit!'"

"Son!" roared Threety—I mean, Mr. Turnbuckle. "Desist! This instant!"

The word "Son" did the trick. Suddenly Biltmore's hilarious expression snapped like an elastic band into its former morose, distant gaze. A large, lone, jiggling tear oozed from the corner of his right eye and meandered down the contours of his cheek.

"Father Baptist," harrumphed Daddy Three T's, his toupee slipping, "as you can see, Biltmore is not himself. He hasn't been since Buckminster's untimely death, compounded by your interference with the Requiem and burial." He dug inside his breast pocket and produced a formidable looking legal document, executed on parchment, and folded in thirds. "It is fortuitous that you are here because you are hereby given notice that I am going to have Buckminster's body exhumed from the cemetery at St. Philomena's. In fact, I'm having my whole family disinterred. We are taking our dead, ourselves, and our beneficence to Our Lady of Good Success."

"The SSPX chapel," said Father.

"That's correct. Right now they're located in Vernon, but I'm going to give them enough money to buy some property in Barkinbay Beach, build a new chapel, and even start their own cemetery. My family and I have suffered under your dictatorship long enough."

GARDENING TIPS: In 1984 Archbishop Marcel Lefebvre (I've heard it pronounced all sorts of ways) elevated four priests loyal to his cause to the rank of bishop against the orders of Pope John Paul II, creating what came to be called The Society of St. Pius X (commonly referred to as the "SSPX"). The archbishop did this to preserve the Tridentine Mass which had all but vanished in the whirlwind after Vatican II. Archbishop Lefebvre, believing a state of emergency existed, acted accordingly after negotiations with the Vatican broke down. It takes bishops to ordain priests, and this insured the continuance of a priesthood dedicated to the Old Rite. The Holy Father responded by issuing a *motu proprio* (a document written "in his own hand") entitled *Ecclesia Dei*, in which he, among other things, declared the archbishop and his four bishops to be in schism.

A little problem here: while ordaining four bishops without the Pope's permission is punishable by excommunication, it is not, according to Canon Law, a schismatic act. There is a difference. Long story short, the Society itself and many canon lawyers do not consider the SSPX to be in schism despite the Holy Father's declaration, and attempts to cast the shadow of schism onto laymen who attend their Masses have failed to pass the ecclesiastical courts. In other words, it is just one more mess within the One True Church whose leaders have forgotten its reason for being.

My own opinion of the SSPX will become clear over the course of time and events, perhaps in another story.

                                                                  --M.F.

"That is entirely up to you, of course," said Father Baptist. "However, I would strongly advise you not to disinter Buckminster's body."

"Give me one good reason why I shouldn't."

"Reluctantly, I will, but only to you. I don't think it would be good for Biltmore to hear."

Mr. Turnbuckle looked long and hard at the soft-shell taco with extra cheese that was his son, then said, "Mr. Feeney, you will accompany Biltmore to the billiard room."

"Behind the old eight ball, eh?" said the young man I was to accompany.

Startled as I was to be roused from my concealment in the shadows, I was glad to get out of the oppressive chill that so permeated the room. The thought of a bright green pool table dotted with multicolored balls actually raised my spirits a flutter or two—until Biltmore led me into said game room three doors further down the hall, which turned out to be just as dreary and cold as the living room. Perhaps worse.

39

I SIGHED AS I MADE A LEFT TURN and a lazy right as we made our getaway from the Casa de Buckle. Soon the quiet residential streets gave way to the clutter and glare of commercial blocks. We were halfway home when, much to my surprise, Father shifted in his seat, looked around as if awaking from a dream—or finding himself trapped in one.

"Martin, how far are we from the corner of El Barranco Drive and La Colina Avenue?"

"You want to visit Bishop Ravenshorst's last real estate project?"

"Well, it's not exactly on the way, but it's not far from home."

About twenty minutes later, after resorting to an examination of the map in the glove compartment, I drove the Jeep between a pair of weathered adobe brick obelisks, about ten feet tall, which had been constructed long ago on each side of El Barranco Drive. They seemed to define the boundary between the city we left behind and the barrio we were entering. On each pillar there was a proclamation executed in colorful tiles with skeletal figures dancing all around. The message on the left was in Spanish, and the one on the right in English. I found it interesting that someone had taken the trouble to make the message bilingual. I flicked on my high beams and slowed the car to a creep so I could give the statement my attention:

<table>
<tr><td>LA MUERTE</td><td>THE GREATEST</td></tr>
<tr><td>NO ES LA PERDIDA</td><td>LOSS IN LIFE</td></tr>
<tr><td>MAS GRANDE</td><td>IS NOT DEATH</td></tr>
<tr><td>EN LA VIDA SINO</td><td>RATHER</td></tr>
<tr><td>LO QUE MUERE</td><td>WHAT DIES</td></tr>
<tr><td>DENTRO DE NOSOTROS</td><td>WITHIN US</td></tr>
<tr><td>MIENTRAS VIVIMOS.</td><td>WHILE WE LIVE.</td></tr>
</table>

Beyond the pillars the street narrowed, the branches of the jacaranda trees on both sides met overhead, the asphalt buckled, the streetlamps were burned out, the houses and apartments were crammed tightly and erratically together, and the curbs were lined with battered pickup trucks and very small, very used autos. I dimmed my headlights and continued to inch us further into what seemed an unsavory neighborhood.

There were a number of people milling around on the neglected sidewalks, all of Mexican descent. The girls had puffy blouses, colorful skirts, gaudy earrings, and wide eyes made all the larger by the application of dark makeup around them. The guys wore faded jeans, tattered shirts with torn armpits, and solid gold Crucifixes on gleaming chains. Telltale red dots of smoldering cigarettes abounded on shadowy porches. Several boom box radios were playing garish modern Hispanic music on different channels simultaneously. The smells of simmering chilies, beer belches, and smoldering hemp permeated the air.

The second block was much the same, except the people thinned out and most of the houses looked boarded up. Perhaps the landlords had decided to tear them down and build who knows what in their place.

There was a post but no street sign at the corner where La Colina crossed El Barranco, but we figured we'd reached our goal because the lot on the southwest corner was vacant and surrounded by a sagging chain-link fence. There were metal signs every few feet warning everyone to KEEP OUT in bold, fluorescent red letters. There was no place to park on the street because the curb was painted red, so I nosed the car into the driveway entrance to the lot. Access was blocked by a chained gate, so the Jeep ended up obstructing the sidewalk with its rear portion jutting out into the street. I rationalized it was better than parking in a red zone, but not by much. The chain links looked stark white against a black background in the glare of my headlights before I turned off the ignition. A few feet beyond the gate the cement driveway had been chomped away by the teeth of a backhoe. The ground fell away after that into the hungry darkness of an excavated pit.

"So what are we looking for?" asked the gardener.

Father shrugged. "I think we just look. We find what we find. Then we think about it."

"Do you realize you just quoted Lieutenant Joe Leaphorn, the Navajo detective in *A Thief of Time*?"

"Hm-mm," mumbled Father as he got out of the car.

"I'll take that as a no," said I, heaving myself out on my side. "I don't think you've read any Tony Hillerman. Might I point out we don't even have a flashlight?"

No sooner had we shut our doors than a black-and-white police car came to a halt behind the Jeep. Cops don't worry about blocking traffic. The gumball machines on their cockpits give them immunity from all the rules in the California Vehicle Code. They also have spotlights with penetrating beams that blind you as they emerge from their cars. There must be special classes at the Police Academy on looming postures. They don't just walk up to you; they menace you with their humongousness.

"You can't park like that," said the voice of the ominous shape emerging from the driver's side.

"What are you doing here?" asked the matching voice of the shape exploding in slow motion from the passenger's side.

"Er ... er," stuttered the quivering gardener, even though he hadn't done anything seriously wrong. Suddenly he wished he wasn't holding a cane. Surely they would think it was a weapon.

"Chuck," said Father calmly, still peering through the fence at the emptiness beyond. Rather than blind himself as I had just done, he didn't bother to turn to face them. "Officer Charles Martel, and if I'm not mistaken, Fred Staplewhite."

"Jack Lombard?" asked the officers together.

"Ahem," said Father, revealing his profile.

"Oh, yes," sputtered Officer Martel. *"Father* ... um, what's your name now?"

"Baptist," said his partner, Staplewhite. "He's Father John Baptist."

"That must make you the Feeney," said Martel to me.

The Feeney? I wondered. "At the service," I said aloud, nodding but not offering to shake their hands.

"Fancy running into you two," said Father. "Martin, you remember these gentlemen. They were assigned to protect Chief Billowack's daughter in the hospital a few weeks back."

"A Saturday night I'd rather forget," said Staplewhite, rubbing the back of his head. "Why do you think we've been assigned to patrol this hellhole? Well, me anyway. Chuck here got nailed by association."

"Enough about that," said Martel, dismissing the distasteful subject with a gesture involving his face, neck, and left shoulder. "Jack, er, Father—whatever—what brings you to The Ravine of Darkness?"

"Excuse me?" asked Father.

"This street is El Barranco," explained Chuck Martel. "Apparently you're not aware that its full name used to be 'El Barranco de la Oscuridad,' 'The Ravine of Darkness.'"

"Sounds cheerful," said I.

"This cross street, if you follow it thataway, up the incline, takes you to 'La Colina de las Mantazas y Olores Asquerosos.'"

"'The Hill of Slaughter and Foul Smells,'" translated Fred Staplewhite.

"Nice neighborhood," remarked the gardener.

"We've asked some of the locals about the origin of these names," said Officer Chuck, "but either they don't know or, more likely, they don't trust us."

"Insidious names reflect sinister pasts," said Father. "It may be worth looking into."

"Or not," said Officer Fred. "What brings you here?"

"This property," said Father.

"Looking to build a church?" asked Officer Chuck.

"Have one," said Father. "No, I'm curious as to why the owner of this lot tore down the buildings on it just to dig a hole."

"Yeah," said Staplewhite. "Folks are not pleased. This junky part of town ain't much, but they call it home. Bad enough some nameless hotshot bought this lot and tore down the dilapidated bungalows on it. The cottages were about ready to topple on their own, but they provided shelter for several families with lots of kids."

"Then to dig it up and leave it like this," said Martel. He pointed with his chin at the gaggles of people scattered down the block, all of them looking at us. "That's criminal in their eyes. Mine, too."

"The owner is dead," said Father. "I don't know what he had in mind. I'm trying to find out."

"A big shot in a high-rise downtown?" asked Officer Fred.

"Something like that," said Father. "I guess I really didn't expect to find much here."

"Just a forgotten hole," said Officer Chuck, indicating a small but fuming group of locals who were inching toward us. "Uh, unless you want to explain yourselves to the neighbors, I suggest you move on—meaning no disrespect, um, Father, but—"

"No offense taken," said Father. "I've seen enough. Martin, let's go home."

"A splendid idea," said I, eyeing the approaching residents. "Somehow 'SLAUGHTER AT THE DARK CORNER OF FOUL SMELLS' isn't as memorable a headline as 'SHOOTOUT AT THE O. K. CORRAL.'"

As I eased the car back down the street between those adobe obelisks with the cryptic bilingual messages on them, a hundred distrusting barrio eyes boring into us all the while, a thought occurred to me.

Roberto, Spade, and Duggo would be examining the stone floor in the grotto within Saint Philomena's the following day. A snippet of an earlier conversation tickled the back of my brain:

"Martin," Father had said, *"I think the floor is subsiding."*
"That's odd," had been my comment.
"There are no records, unfortunately, but I suspect this archway, wall, and floor were part of an earlier structure."
"I thought this building replaced a wooden chapel."
"Yes, but the chapel was built on the site of a shrine. You can see the difference in the masonry here ..."

Who knew what might be under those subsiding stones? Something Bishop Ravenshorst might have gotten his backhoes into if he'd lived so long? The dots and crisscrossed lines on Sybil Wexler's computer-generated map flickered behind my eyes. I opened my mouth to voice my thought, but just then Father subsided in his seat, wrapped his arms around himself, and said, "Oh, for a little peace."

Figuring my thought could wait, and indeed, if it was worth thinking he'd probably think it sooner or later himself anyway, I let it go. It was good to be heading for home.

40

"WHAT COULD THAT BE?" I asked, with a face-ripping yawn between "could" and "that."

I had parked the Jeep in the back lot next to Monsignor Havermeyer's lopsided RV, and we were trudging up the brick path toward the rectory. My brittle bones ached, my dry joints creaked, and my strained brain was whimpering for sleep. The headstones in the churchyard glowered silently at us on the left, and the door to my own room beckoned cozily from the right. The ceaseless clamor of the city murmured oppressively all around us. In fact, as the amber glow of the kitchen window came into view, the sound seemed to transmogrify into a strangely rhythmic rumbling. At first I thought my weary senses were playing tricks. Then I realized a new sound had invaded our garden. It seemed to emanate from the bushes and trees, from the mossy bricks upon which we walked.

"Strange," whispered Father, drawing to a halt beside me.

"What *is* that?" I asked, this time yawn-free.

"I don't know."

"I have a bad feeling about this."

"You have a bad feeling about everything."

"I resemble that remark."

"Look, someone is moving around in there, and it doesn't look like Millie. We must check this out."

The sound clarified slightly as we approached the kitchen door, but into what I wasn't sure. It had a roiling, churning quality, like broken waves swirling around the rocks at Barkinbay Beach—but not. Whatever it was, I could feel it through my shoes, and it grew immensely louder as Father turned the knob and opened the door.

"Took you long enough," shouted Ernie Corben. His voice was almost inaudible, lost as it was in the ferocious, oceanic roar that permeated the kitchen.

"What did you say?" yelled Father.

"I said, 'Took you long enough!'"

"What?"

"Never mind!"

During this intellectual exchange I took my mental inventory. Millie was standing there, arms folded. I also recognized the refrigerator, the stove, the dining nook, the door to the pantry, the door to the hallway, the door to the laundry room, the phone with the long coiled cord hanging on the wall, and the silver Crucifix Bishop Xandaronolopolis had given Millie before his departure to a land devoid of hamburgers and French fries hanging above the sink. I took this inventory—the term "reality check" might actually apply—because in an almost hallucinogenic way, the kitchen had become a very different place since the last time I'd been in it.

There were five new things that hadn't been there before. One of them was Ernie Corben of hotdog fame. Slurth Zabzdyr, conveniently known as Some Guy, didn't count because he had shared his literary concerns with me in the kitchen the night before. Still, his being there now added a certain something extra to this bizarre scene. The second was a large cardboard shipping carton, collapsed into a corrugated rectangular bundle, leaning against the refrigerator.

The third was a boxlike object in the center of the kitchen floor. It was about two-and-a-half feet wide and deep, perhaps three-and-a-half feet tall. The thing was coated with the same kind of white enamel as our refrigerator, but the surface was brand new rather than scarred and stained with age. It had a door on the side facing me hinged at the bottom. The top of the box was flat except for a raised panel at the far end. The panel had a row of convex blue dots across it, each with a sky-blue label beneath and a tiny red light above. It took an effort to focus on the designations, so tired were my eyes. I knew the words must make sense, but they were all science fiction to me: AUTO CLEAN, DRAIN, DELAY/RESUME, RINSE ONLY, LIGHT WASH, NORMAL WASH, HEAVY WASH, SUPER-SCRUB, HEATED DRY, EXTRA RINSE, and PROGRAMMED CYCLE COMPLETED. The light above SUPER SCRUB was brightly on. With an effort, I pulled my attention from the unfamiliar words and focused on the stranger umbilicus that emerged from the back of the thing. It was a tangle of four black cables, or rather three industrial hoses and a heavy-duty electrical cord, which trailed across the kitchen floor and disappeared into the laundry room.

The fourth new thing, which I've already described, was the rumbling roar coming from this intimidating contraption. It actually shook the floor and rattled the dishes in the cupboards.

The fifth was the greatest marvel of all: the smile on Millie's face. Smiles were not beyond our Millie. In the years I'd known her she must have exercised those facial muscles at least a half dozen times. But this was different. I've tried and tried, but words fail to convey the intensity of the sheer satisfaction emanating from her countenance. No, not satisfaction: triumph. No, not mere triumph. As I said, words fail.

The light above SUPER SCRUB went off and DRAIN came on. Suddenly the roar stopped. As my ears adjusted I could hear the sound of water dripping, trickling, settling within the appliance.

"Well?" asked Ernie.

"Well," said Millie, eyes sparkling. "What can I—"

Her sentence was cut off by a new sound, as loud as the original clamor, but entirely different. It was an excruciating, protracted sucking noise, deep and eerie, accompanied by spasmodic twitches of the umbilicus. From the laundry room came the sound of sputtering air, then water gushing into the old enameled washbasin, followed by hollow gurgling as the outflow found its way down the drainpipe. It took two and a half minutes for the tirade to end. The cycle completed, the light above DRAIN went out. PROGRAMMED CYCLE COMPLETED dutifully came on.

Silence.

"Mr. Corben," said Millie at last. "How can I possibly—"

Her sentence was cut off again. This time by a piercing, grating, nerve-penetrating, eye-crossing buzz. It went on for about ten seconds, and then ceased with a final click and shudder within the white box. The light bulb in the ceiling, which had dimmed during the auditory carnage and electrical imbalance, revved back up to full brightness.

Silence.

Millie marched over to Ernie and landed a kiss on his right cheek.

"Aw," said Ernie, his eggplant nose positively glowing, "it was Some Guy's idea. He said you could use a dishwashin' machine."

Millie turned to the gentle giant and threw her arms around him. Well, not very far around him. Against his enormity her gesture looked like a bug flattened against a windshield. Nonetheless, Some Guy blushed beet red.

"You two men look as though you could do with a good breakfast," said she.

"*Could* we," said Some Guy, eyes wide, mouth sagging into an imbecilic smile.

"Never question a woman," said she, smiling mightily, her dominating maternal instincts rising to the occasion.

"Never *ever,*" agreed Mr. Guy.

"I didn't know they made stand-alone models," said Father. "Dishwashers, I mean."

Millie threw Father an "Oh, it's *you*" look and turned her attention to her new toy. "If you men will be so kind as to push this miracle out of the way, I'll fire up the stove."

Unlike Greeley's serving cart, Millie's new dishwasher made no sound whatsoever as Some Guy pushed it towards the laundry room on its brand new casters. Ernie Corben gathered up the umbilicus along the way. The hoses made obnoxious squealing sounds as he dragged them against the waxy floor. Father and I just stood there, useless. Father looked genuinely pleased for Millie, grateful to Ernie and Some for their generosity, and wary of Corben and Guy because of who they were and with whom they affiliated. My grin was not entirely heartfelt, considering as I was the inconvenience this contraption was going to cause in the kitchen down the line. The dishwasher wouldn't fit through the laundry room door, so it was relegated to the narrow wall space between the laundry room and the pantry—as if the kitchen weren't cramped enough already. Ernie dumped the hoses and power cord on the floor beside it, half-blocking the doorway. I smiled harder.

"You'll be eating, too," said Millie, searing Father and me with a glance.

"Oh?" asked Father, forgetting never to question a woman.

"Phone call from His Nibs," said she, choosing several frying pans from her arsenal. "You and Mr. Feeney are to meet him in Lompoc at sunrise."

"Cardinal Fulbright?" asked Father.

"Lompoc?" asked yours truly, also forgetting the rule.

"Sit," commanded Millie.

41

"MISTER ROUNDHEAD SAID SO," said Ernie Corben around a mouthful of Millie's most splendid omelet creation ever. Onions, spinach, mushrooms (the regular kind, not the fashionable, leathery portabella variety), black olives, red jalapeños, paper-sliced garlic—oh yes, eggs so fluffy you could stuff pillows with them—oozing with Swiss cheese, flanked with fried potatoes, and crowned with her own secret salsa. "I ain't makin' it up."

"But Monsignor Aspic did take the artifact to Edison Winger for appraisal," said Father, seated across from Ernie. "You've confirmed that."

"Like I said," said Ernie, who was seated next to me, "Eddy's instructions were to make a wax cast of the thing and give it back. He done the first but not the laddah 'cause Aspic never came back for it."

"So where is the disk now?"

"As far as Roundhead is concerned, Eddy still has it. Roundhead got what he wanted."

"A cast of the artifact, not the thing itself."

"Right."

"Indeed." Father scratched his ear. "How did Monsignor Aspic link up with a guy like Edison Winger in the first place?"

Corben sighed. "Fulbright phoned a rich crank he's been schmoozing—a gruff old bird named Turnbuckle—who he would recommend, and the old screw called Roundhead. They're related somehow. When I asked Mr. Roundhead about this disk thing for you, he joked about all the 'plants' he has inside the Chancery, and the best turns out to be old Bucklepants, who's actually on the outside, whatever that means. Eddy Winger's been in Roundhead's pocket for a long time. And that's how them bones is all connected."

"Really," said Father. "Those are some connections. So upon Mr. Turnbuckle's recommendation the cardinal sent Monsignor Aspic to Mr. Winger for an appraisal."

"Yeah, and as I understand it, even before Big Man Morley summoned Pipsqueak Aspic to send him on the errand, Mr. Turnbuckle had already phoned him—"

"Him, meaning Monsignor Aspic."

"Right. Mister T. already phoned Monsignor A. about where to take the disk when the cardinal gave it to him."

"I see," said Father, those wonderful gears twirling furiously behind his eyes. "From this we can surmise that Monsignor Aspic, being meticulous in his daily schedule, phoned Edison Winger to make an appointment before he himself took possession of the artifact from the cardinal. Winger, needing time to make a wax casting, told Aspic that to make a proper appraisal the artifact would have to be left with him overnight. Monsignor Aspic, doubtless uncomfortable knowing of the cardinal's errand before the cardinal has even told him about it, tells his superior a non-truth, that he will deliver the disk to the appraiser the following day rather than that afternoon."

"Do you really think that fits?" asked yours truly.

"For the moment it encompasses the known facts," said Father. "I'll gladly change it as new information comes in." He savored a long sip of steaming coffee and took his time swallowing. "I find it enormously interesting that Mr. Roundhead, a ravenous collector of authentic Catholic relics and artifacts, is not interested in the Pope's cherished golden disk itself. He just wanted an impression of it, a mere copy."

"That's the scoop," said Ernie. "Right, Some?"

"Yuh, right," said Mr. Guy who was standing at Millie's stove. Too large to sit in one of our kitchen chairs without crushing it into splinters, he contented himself by engorging at the source. The largest of Millie's frying pans had been used to make Some Guy his very own omelet. It served as his plate as well. Her largest serving spoon served as his only implement. He looked happy.

"Does Mr. Roundhead have the missing center?" asked Father.

"Missing center of what?" asked Ernie.

"You haven't seen the disk?"

"Nope. Winger delivered the thing to Mr. Roundhead himself. I never saw it."

"What are you going to tell the cardinal, Father?" asked the gardener after attempting to hide a long, gassy burp behind his napkin.

"The truth," said he, with an added glance that hinted, "although perhaps not all of it, not yet."

"Lompoc's a three-hour drive," said I.

"Not that long, I should think. We'll be traveling in the wee hours, thereby avoiding the traffic snarls that have become typical on the stretch through Santa Barbara."

"Whatever, it's almost to the end of the world."

"Cardinal Fulbright's, anyway. Los Angeles is the largest archdiocese on earth, and he's gone to the farthest outpost. I hope you don't mind if I use the cabin light in the car."

"There's probably a law against it—glare on the windshield or something."

Ernie grunted as he buttered one of Millie's cornflake muffins, amused at my concern for such technicalities.

"Nonetheless," said Father, "I've yet to give the materials we—ahem—borrowed from Bishop Ravenshorst's library a perusal, and that would provide me with an excellent opportunity."

"A better one would be to stay at home and peruse them in your study," said I.

"Perhaps, but His Eminence is avoiding the nuncio, and I must humor him."

"Where are we supposed to meet His Inconvenience exactly?" I asked Millie.

"La Purisima Mission," answered she, scooping more ground coffee into the percolator. "I was wondering, Father, would you mind if I went with you? I've heard of La Purisima, of course, but I can't imagine how I'll ever get to see it otherwise."

My heart stopped.

"Why, of course," said Father, looking at me over his cup. "I don't know what time the mission opens to the public. We're meeting the cardinal at sunrise—around six-thirty—and I doubt we'll be with him more than an hour. We'll probably head back right after that. I imagine all the buildings will be closed. Are you sure you want—?"

"You just try and stop me," said Millie. She cleared her throat. "Now all of you men listen up. I'm itching to give my brand-new dishwasher—care of Messrs. Corben and Guy—a trial run." She flashed Ernie a disarming smile and gave Some's paw an affectionate rub. "So be good boys and finish up so I can fill it with dishes and let 'er rip."

My heart started again.

"Yes, ma'am!" said all the masculine voices in the room together.

"I got a suggestion, Millie Dear," said Ernie as he mopped up the last bit of cheese and salsa from his plate with his muffin.

Millie Dear??????

"What's that, Ernest Sweet?" asked Millie.

Ernest Sweet????????

"Just stuff in all the dishes, put in the soap, and turn it on when you leave."

"Yeah," said Some Guy, his spoon paused between skillet and maw, "that way it'll all be done and dry when you get back."

"Dry?" squeaked Millie. "You mean it dries them, too?"

"Count on it," said Ernest Sweet with a wink. "It's a cinch. You can even set it to start a couple of hours after you leave. This is the same as the one I got at my digs. I'll show you how to set it up."

"Oh bless you!" sighed Millie.

Oh brother, thought the gardener.

Saturday, November Eighteenth

Feast Day of Saint Rose Philippine Duchesne, Missionary of the Madams of the Sacred Heart, known among the Indians as "She who prays always." Her relics are enshrined in St. Charles, Missouri (1852)

42

"WE SHOULD BE GOING," said Father over my shoulder.

"Sure, sure," said I, starting one more sentence. It was hard to write with my attention divided. "Not that I'm complaining, but all your helping the police do their jobs sure has been impinging on my wee-hour creativity the last couple of days."

"At least it's not interfering with your regular job."

"I beg to differ." I mouthed the letters of the last word as I typed them, then I said, "Have you seen me doing any gardening lately?"

"No, I can't say that I have."

"There," said I, punching the period key with finality. Then, realizing I wasn't quite done, I pressed the shift and typed the quotation mark. "I rest my case."

"Martin," said he, reaching around me and cranking the page up the carriage a couple of turns. "I don't mean to be critical, but don't you think your description here of Chief Billowack is a bit exaggerated?"

I reviewed the words carefully, shrugged, and said, "I don't understand what you mean."

```
    "Bah," bleated Billowack, turning away and
stomping elephantine footprints into the linoleum
all the way down the hallway.  "If I find out any-
thing's screwy around here, heads will roll.  Even
yours, Toots."
```

"You don't?" said Father.

"No," said I, folding my arms for emphasis.

"Just when did he bleat that, and to whom?"

"Halloween. It was in his daughter's hospital room, directed at Father Nicanor's housekeeper, Veronika."

"Really. I don't remember it quite like that, and good Heavens, he didn't leave footprints in the floor."

"You remember it your way, I'll remember it mine. It's called poetic license."

"You're not a poet."

"And I'm writing without a license."

"Isn't jumping from 'bah' and 'bleated,' which are clearly references to sheep, to stampeding elephants switching metaphors?"

"You exaggerate your way, I'll embellish in mine."

"What about this?" he asked, indicating one of several partially typed sheets nearby, some of my scattered ideas not yet incorporated into the main body of my story:

```
    "Hrmph," grunted Billowack, strings of wiggling
phlegm dangling from his jowls.  "Officer Fred
Staplewhite, you're on report.  Officer Martel,
you take his place.  Taper, Wickes, I want this
floor sealed off.  No one comes, no one goes."
```

"Yes," said I. "Bumping into Officers Staplewhite and Martel triggered my memory cells, such as they are. I'll insert it in the second draft."

"I admit Monty tends to spray a bit when he gets excited, but—"

"A bit? He's a phlegm geyser and you know it." I glanced at the piles of books that had been moved to my bed from various places around the room during the wee hours. The last two piles had come from the armchair to make room for Father when he first came in. Chances were that the next time I came through that door I'd be bushed, and the last thing I'd want to do is remove the books so I could hit the sack. On the other hand, the armchair had often served when the bed was so burdened. I looked up at Father. "I suppose you don't like the name 'Billowack' for his character, either."

"Now that you mention it—"

"I thought you said we should be going." What the hey. Anything to change the subject. I'd just have to deal with the books when we returned, whenever that would be. "Well, Father, don't just stand there. Do you have time to say Mass?"

He checked that battered thing he called a watch. "Barely. It being Saturday, I'll forego the sermon."

"Thank Heaven on two counts. Well, what are we waiting for?"

As much as I enjoy the grandeur of High Mass on Sundays, I must admit my favorite Masses are those Father says in the wee hours—just him with his understated gardener-slash-embellishing chronicler at his side, managing the cruets and ringing the bells. The word "privilege" comes to mind.

Oh, come to think of it, I shared the honor that morning with some-one else—the man I'd seen the day before, trudging up the center aisle on his knees, the fellow with silver buttons on his dark clothing. I caught sight of him as I poured the wine into Father's chalice during the Offertory. Not that I minded the presence of so respectful a fellow penitent, but I was curious as to how he had gained entry at that hour. Before I received Holy Communion I turned to see if he was going to approach, but he had slipped silently away.

I thought it strange, and meant to say something to Father about it, but like so many things, it fell between the cracks of my mind during the Last Gospel when Father uttered the words, *"his qui credunt in nomine ejus; qui non ex sanguinibus, neque ex voluntate carnis, neque ex voluntate viri, sed ex Deo nati sunt";* that is, "to them that believe in His name, who are born, not of blood, nor of the will of the flesh, nor of the will of man, but of God." Born not of blood was the Faith of Cheryl Farnsworth, and yet expressed and revealed in it. I couldn't shake the sight of Cheryl Farnsworth's eyes, the blood running down her face, the crimson stains swelling on my shirtsleeves.

I was shuddering at the final genuflection.

43

"THAT WAS IT?!?!" exclaimed Millie as we headed west on Route 246, having just exited Interstate 101 at Buellton, about thirty miles north of Santa Barbara.

"That was what?" asked the gardener-slash-driver.

"Some 'world famous' restaurant," sneered our housekeeper-slash-copilot. Even without her razor sharp cooking utensils she had a way of piercing the buffers of Reality. "We've been passing billboards for a hundred miles advertising their split pea soup."

"It's a bit early for pea soup, don't you think?"

"I wouldn't know. It just seems kind of ..."

"Anticlimactic?"

"Harebrained."

"Well, there is that." A sign announcing the distance to Vandenberg Air Force Base swelled and vanished on the rightmost fringe of my vision. It was too dark to see much of the scenery around us, but I was vaguely aware of barbed wire fences, haggard trees, and tilting mailboxes on both sides of the road. I glanced at Father Baptist in my rearview mirror, bathed as he was in the yellow-beige glow of the ceiling dome light. "Hey, back there. Haven't heard from you since Ventura County. You okay?"

"I've enjoyed the ride, I assure you," said he, looking up from the crumpled papers in his hands. "More so, I've appreciated the opportunity to read through Bishop Ravenshorst's notes."

"Care to share?"

"Don't mind me," said Millie. She seemed absorbed in the indistinct shapes rolling by, but I had the creepy feeling that she was scrutinizing my reflection in her side window. It was hard to tell because I was concentrating on the double-yellow line ahead. Maybe it was just me not being used to having her along on our manly excursions. Sideways glances in her direction produced less than useful results. She seemed to be chewing on something stuck between her jaw and her brain. "I should have known you two would talk shop eventually."

"We is what we is," I attempted to explain. "We does what we does, and—"

"Don't press it," said she, folding and refolding her arms. "I *said* you can get on with your business."

"You're sure."

"It can't be far now. I can keep still that long."

"We'll miss you till we get there." I peeped in the mirror, then concentrated on the road. "Father?"

"Martin?"

"Anything more on that intersection of mysteries?"

"Some—actually, a bit more than some. It's interesting that the Pope's visit to Los Angeles came just after Themolina Hubbard bequeathed the Cordova Homestead Estate on Chapel Hill to the Archdiocese."

"Yes. His Incessance said the deed of transfer was still on his desk when the Holy Father visited his residence, though of course back then our beloved Morley Fulbright was just an archbishop."

"That's right, Martin. The deed was on the desk, the Pope was in the room. A coincidence?"

"You don't believe in them."

"Of course not, and neither do you. From what I know of Vatican mechanics, the Pope's visit to Los Angeles was planned a year or more in advance. The bequeathal of the Chapel Hill Estate to the archdiocese could not have been foreseen. Although some of Christ's Vicars have exhibited astonishing abilities over the centuries, I'm not about to assume that this one possessed angelic sight. Still, always informed and invariably prepared, he had the deed photographed on the spot. Minutes later he presented the cardinal with the artifact. I can't help but think the two things—the property and the golden disk—were related, at least in the Holy Father's mind."

"The Seat of Peter has changed hands since then," said I. "I wonder if the current Holy Father is as interested in this business as his predecessor."

"The nuncio's continued scrutiny suggests that he is," said Father.

"It's not like you can phone the Pope and ask him."

"No, hardly. Even Morley Fulbright would have to go through stringently regulated channels. It's enough for now to note the inference. The property and the disk were and are of interest to Rome."

"Noted."

Millie grumbled something I didn't quite catch. I noticed that she was wearing her favorite hat. It featured two plastic pears and three artificial strawberries arranged in front with green ribbons dangling behind. Every time she moved her head I could hear the ribbons rustle. This really was a big event for her.

"You'll remember the Pope left orders that the artifact not be photographed," continued Father. "But that didn't prevent Jeremiah Ravenshorst from making a detailed sketch."

"You have it there?" I asked.

"I do." After a brief shuffle of papers, he held up a drawing so I could glance at it in the rearview mirror.

```
GARDENING TIPS:  I only got a glimpse of
the sketch in the mirror at the time.  I
didn't get a good look until later.  I'm
inserting it here for my reader's benefit.
                                  --M.F.
```

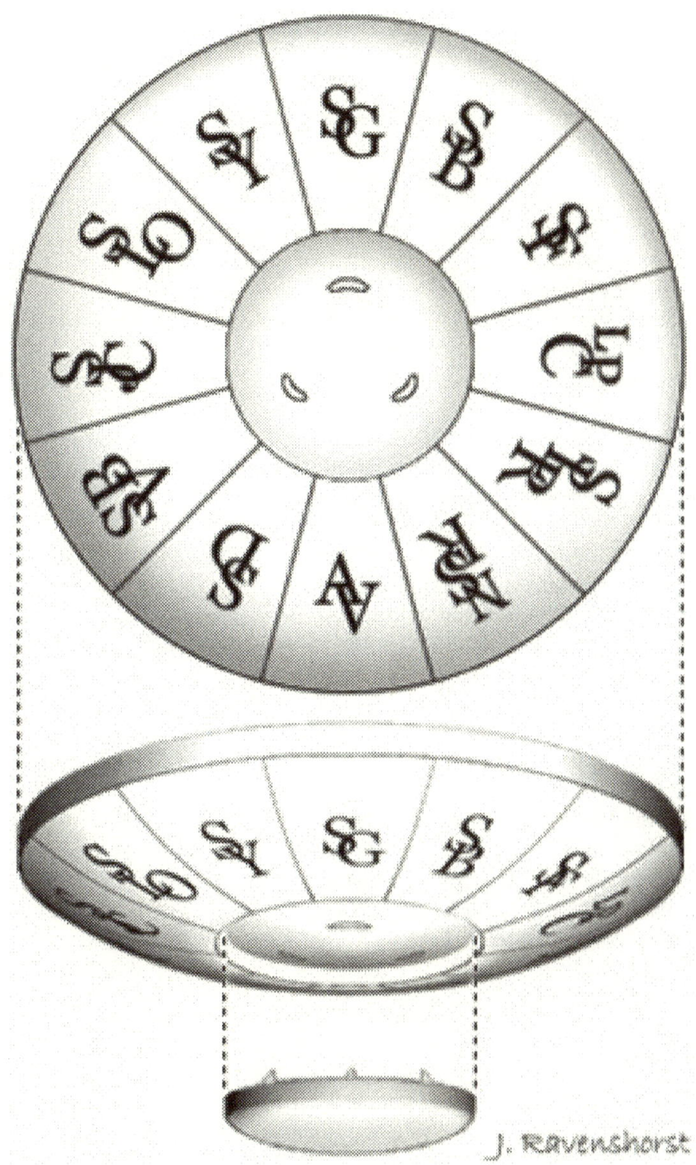

"Reminds me of a poster for a flying saucer movie," said I. "What's that little guy docking beneath the mother ship?"

"His educated guess as to the shape of the missing piece that plugs into the center," said Father.

"And what would that be for?"

"To complete the pattern, I would assume."

"And what pattern is that?"

"I don't know enough yet to hazard an opinion. Jerry Ravenshorst had been working on this for some time. Surely he had more information at his disposal than I do. What really intrigues me is that the Holy Father was so interested."

"I'm not following you."

"These symbols around the front of the artifact, the ones His Eminence suggested were reminiscent of the signs of the Zodiac. They are intertwined letters, probably initials: SG, SB, SF, LPC, SLR, NSR, AV, SD, SBV, SJC, SLO, and SY."

"Most of them begin with S," I observed.

"That's right," said Father. "All but three: NSR, LPC, and AV."

"Could you read them all again, please?"

"Certainly." He did.

"Did I count right?" said I. "Are there twelve whatever-they-are's?"

"Right. Not unlike the Zodiac."

"And what do you make of all that?" I tore my eyes from the road and looked for a second at him in the mirror. "The Salisbury Plain is a long way from here."

"Excuse me?"

"Stonehenge, remember? Do you think that disk is some sort of astral alignment puzzle, you know, like the dots Sybil was connecting yesterday?"

The angle of the overhead light rendered Father's eyes in shadow. They glistened like stars on a dark lake. "I don't believe so. It's certainly a puzzle, and I do believe there is a connection with Miss Wexler's lines and dots, but I doubt these designations are astral. Sybil already checked for that."

Dots, I thought to myself. Who else was talking about dots? Oh yes, it was Larry Taper:

"'Way True Life,'" he had explained as Mercedes Sinclair was being taken away. *"It's a chain outfit, you know, with offices spaced right along the line you get if you connect the dots on the map."*

"What dots?" I had asked.

"The towns where the priests I mentioned disappeared and were later found mutilated."

"Mutilated!"

"You don't want to know."

"Maybe they're geographical," said I aloud to shake a grisly image out of my mind, "like Lieutenant Taper was saying yesterday about connecting the dots of the towns where those priests were found."

"Any dots on a map can be said to be geographical," said Father. "What's your point?"

"Point? Me?" I fixed my eyes back on the road. Didn't I have some sort of insight last night? I should have spoken up at the time. It was gone now. "Okay, so what do you think they represent?"

"I don't know."

"They're more complicated than the 'casting quilt' from the Farnsworth case last June."

"Interesting that you should mention that, Martin. This, like that, is a puzzle. This, like that, will make perfect sense when we put it all together, but until then—"

"There's nothing like a good boggling. Right, Father?"

"Indeed."

Just then I thought I saw a cow wearing a cowboy hat standing on its hind hooves by the side of the road, clutching a pair of dice in its forehoof before rolling them bones onto a crap table. I shook my head. There really was a cow throwing dice by the side of the road, only it was enthusiastically losing its wages on a billboard advertising an Indian-run gambling casino somewhere up ahead. Two of the three bulb lights extended above the image to illuminate it were burned out. The thought of gambling casinos springing up on Indian reservations clashed in my mind with the hopes of the priests and nuns who had worked so hard to teach them the Faith before the inexorable changes wrought by the advancing white settlers would destroy their way of life. History was a waterfall of cascading ironies. Cows in cowboy hats indeed. Whatever happened to the buffalo?

"Speaking of puzzles," I said aloud, "couldn't the S's stand for *Sanctus*?"

"As in the name of a Saint? It certainly could, but it only precedes nine of them. Why the inconsistency? Or, to put it another way, what kind of list would contain nine canonized Saints and three non-Saints? Or three of something else entirely?"

"You're asking me? Hmm. Didn't the cardinal say there was an inscription on the back of the disk? Does it explain anything?"

"No doubt it does, but I don't *habla Español,* and unless you and Millie have been keeping secrets, neither do you." He unfolded and held up another page for my instant perusal in the mirror. Apparently it was Bishop Ravenshorst's hand copy of the inscription. Seven lines—perhaps a verse of a poem? Father refolded it and filed it within the mysterious folds of his cassock. "I know a few words, of course. I think *tesoro* means 'treasure,' but I'm not sure. I'll have to run it by Roberto Guadalupe later today."

"'Treasure,' huh? I begin to see why the nuncio has been keeping an unsubtle eye on it. Do you believe Fulbright's explanation as to why he gave the disk to Monsignor Aspic in the first place?"

"To have it appraised? Yes, actually. That makes sense. As creative as he has proven himself to be with respect to theology and liturgy, Morley Fulbright has never demonstrated much in the way of imagination when it comes to practical matters. His chalice had been stolen and returned ill-used, therefore in need of professional cleaning. Why not get the golden disk appraised at the same time? Monsignor Aspic was the logical errand boy. I don't find a problem with any of that."

"Hmm," said I, as a snippet of conversation from our last meeting with the cardinal whirred through my head:

> It began with Father Baptist saying: *"I have confirmed that Monsignor Aspic did indeed see Edison G. Winger."*
> Which caused Morley's lizardly eyes to widen a tad. *"And?"*
> *"Your chalice, the gift from Professor Murkenstein, was at his shop, awaiting cleaning,"* said Father. *"At least we know that it is safe."*
> Fulbright's reptilian eyelids opened further. *"And?"*
> *"Unfortunately, the artifact was not there. Mr. Winger denied any knowledge of it. I believe you said a friend of yours recommended him."*
> Several notches wider. *"An acquaintance."*
> *"Might I ask who?"*
> At that the cardinal's eyelids slammed shut, then sprang halfway open again. *"It's not important."*

"Hmm," I repeated, imagining the cardinal wearing an alligator cowboy hat. Shaking that image out of my head, I added: "But Conrad J. Aspic did lie to his keeper. He said he would safeguard the disk overnight and take it to the appraiser the next day, but in fact he took it to Edison G. Winger's that afternoon." I was about to point out that His Evasiveness the Cardinal had either missed or ignored the significance of this detail, but the wheels of my mind were derailed by Father's next comment:

"The price of being too plugged in."

"I beg your pardon?"

"I touched on this last night, but let me flesh it out a little. Martin, imagine the spot Monsignor Aspic was in. He received a phone call from Mr. Turnbuckle, a man whom he earnestly desired to impress. The monsignor had his manuscript to consider."

"That's right. Ernie Corben said that Fulbright asked Turnbuckle, who asked Roundhead, who told Turnbuckle to phone Monsignor Aspic—"

"To tell him that his boss, the cardinal," interrupted Father, "was going to be phoning him directly about an important errand. Imagine working for a powerful man like the cardinal, only to discover that on the side you've been schmoozing the man who pulls his strings, or who knows the man who does. Envision Conrad J. Aspic's position as he answers his master's call."

"Which master?"

"Both of them. Turnbuckle just told him what the errand would be, then Fulbright calls to summon him to give him the errand to run. Certainly Monsignor Aspic didn't want the cardinal to know that he already knew nor that the jeweler had already been contacted and wanted the artifact overnight. So he contrived that his schedule was packed—not that much of a contrivance, I'll grant you, considering all the running around we've been doing—anyway, he said his afternoon was packed, and that he'd guard the artifact with his life until the following day."

```
GARDENING TIPS:  Jesus Himself warned in the six-
teenth chapter of the Gospel of Saint Luke, verse
thirteen:  "No servant can serve two masters: for
either he will hate the one, and love the other;
or he will hold to the one, and despise the other.
You cannot serve God and mammon."  (Saint Matthew
likewise recorded this caveat in the sixth chapter
of his Gospel, verse twenty-four.)  How much more
imperiled is the man who tries to serve mammon and
mammon!
                                          --M.F.
```

"By that bit about the man who knew who knew who pulled the strings," said I, glancing in the mirror, "you're not suggesting that Roderick Roundhead controls Cardinal Fulbright are you?"

"I was overreaching," said Father. "But Mr. Turnbuckle is a major contributor to the cardinal's coffers, and Roundhead exerts influence on him."

"And Roundhead has spies planted in the Chancery. Strange, these rich and powerful Trads tangled up in the cardinal's clothesline."

"Doubtless we don't know the half of it. St. Paul was on target when he wrote: 'For the desire of money is the root of all evils; which some coveting have erred from the faith, and have entangled themselves in many sorrows.'"

"His First Epistle to Timothy, six ten," said I. "You don't usually hear the second half."

"It certainly hasn't been a temptation for us at St. Philomena's," grumbled Millie.

"And we should be glad of it," said Father, seriously.

"When Monsignor Aspic turned up missing," said I, desiring to change the subject, "you'd think Morley would've phoned Turnbuckle."

"He probably did," said Father.

"I can hear it now," said I, instantly sprouting a walrus moustache in my imagination. "Turnbuckle snorting and shrugging and saying, 'Harrumph, Morley. You asked me to recommend a jeweler. Now you're calling me to accuse me of something?'"

"I doubt it was as direct as that," said Father. "Men in power tend to talk in undertones with their peers."

"One thing's for sure: Morley's isn't about to tell you about his liaison with Turnbuckle."

"It's a good thing I didn't press him harder yesterday. I won't bring it up again with him. I'd rather not call attention to what I've learned about all the string-pulling in the background."

"And to think that the Doily Sisters are the familial glue that bind Turnbuckle and Roundhead together." I rubbed my stomach thoughtfully. "So what about Monsignor Aspic's call to Bishop deQuet from the parking lot at KLIE?"

"According to what David Smoley overheard and Miss Wexler's technical report, Monsignor Aspic made an appointment to see deQuet at nine the next morning. That's why Aspic was brought to Los Angeles in the first place: to find replacements for the auxiliaries who died last June. After our little difference of opinion with him yesterday, I doubt the bishop from New Bangor will be cooperative with us, but there's nothing particularly suspicious about Aspic phoning him. However, you do us the service of drawing us back to a serious crux, Martin, in redirecting our minds to the handful of seconds between that phone call in the car and his arrival at the studio entrance. During that very narrow window, Monsignor Aspic vanished."

I was watching in the mirror as a pair of pale blue headlights grew out of the darkness behind us. "Do you think his disappearance could boil down to Sheldon and Eira Levant, or maybe their producer, Napolia Crackerjack—"

"Krackershak."

"—whatever, boosting their ratings? They knew he was coming. They could have arranged for someone to snatch him."

"Of course it's possible, but—"

"For that matter, maybe he inadvertently uncovered something Cardinal Fulbright didn't want dragged into the light of day." The headlights from behind were almost upon us. "Sheldon Levant suggested as much. How did he put it? 'Maybe he stuck his nose under one rug too many and the cardinal had him bagged to keep him quiet.'"

"And then ordered me to find out what happened to him?" said Father. "Way too risky, even for Morley Fulbright. His tergiversator, Willis P. Wedge, in whom he apparently places considerable confidence, would surely have advised him against it. It occurs to me that all this would make for an interesting plot in your next novel."

"Hardly," said I as a paint-free pickup truck with a wailing transmission swerved angrily across the double-yellow line and passed us haphazardly on the left. I decelerated a little to give him room. "I don't know how to put this, Father, but this hasn't been that exciting a case."

"Excuse me? I have found this adventure to be most interesting."

"I'm the chronicler, remember? Who cares about interesting? Exhilarating, that's what I'm looking for. The Farnsworth case, that was full of tension, conflict, danger, occult undertones, and—dare I say it?—*pathos*. Bishops were dying, one by one, who would be next?"

Millie harrumphed and refolded her arms.

"Our subsequent adventure," I continued, "the situation at the 'House of Illusions,' was nothing short of terrifying. I earned most of the gray hairs you see on my head while that plot reached its conclusion—even if you were too prolix at the time. I understand, Father. You can't help yourself. It's the pulpit complex, an occupational hazard with priests. The larynx gets warmed by the Roman collar and verbiage ensues. Besides, the inherent verbosity was balanced by the love interest and other poignant factors. Then came the case of Saint Valeria. I'll never forget how close the Tumblars came to prison in the matters surrounding the theft of her body. I can't wait to get my Underwood smoking on that one. But this case ... um ..."

"Yes, Martin?" said Father.

"I don't know," said I, shifting uneasily in my seat. "I can't imagine bothering to expend a typewriter ribbon over this one."

"Do you really want to give your readers the impression that parish life is an endless war against witches, vampires, and grave robbers?"

"Isn't it? I suppose it depends on the parish. But seriously, look at what I'm dealing with here, me being an aspiring author. There's been a death, but of natural causes—an inordinate number of natural causes, to be sure, but natural all the same. The man in the crypt died of old age, in other words. Okay, so he was a prisoner of some sort, and we're entirely in the dark about that. I repeat, though, that he wasn't murdered. Concurrently, Monsignor Aspic has disappeared. No question about it, he's an obnoxious fellow whom everyone wishes would go away, but he's hardly so catastrophically annoying as to provoke his annoyees to murder. Wouldn't it be something if he showed up in Bermuda, having had enough of Morley Fulbright in all his magnanimousness? Nah, he wasn't the sort. He was entrusted with the papal artifact because he had earned a position of confidence, but he left the darn thing with that Edison fellow. He didn't have it on him when he went missing. He disappears in a parking lot somewhere between a car driven by a gravely conflicted young man he's been treating shabbily, and the entrance to the television station where lurk the Levants who need a ratings boost in the worst way, and who are herded around by that Krackershak dame who is just cheeky enough to make it happen for them. There's certainly a potential plot there, but hey: Sheldon and Eira Levant? At best they're red herrings; at worst they are, well, Sheldon and Eira Levant." I slapped the steering wheel. "I know: the real culprit is none other than the guy back at the car, David Smoley, the closet psychopath who finally snapped. C'mon, Father. That's just not an exciting enough resolution after so much effort in the ascent, if you'll pardon my candor for saying so. Not that I'm complaining, mind you. Well, okay, so I am. I will admit that I get annoyed whenever the name Roundhead comes up, and here it is coming up. Being a collector of sacred objects—collector, hoarder, not above hiring scoundrels nor below enlisting thieves, though his hands somehow remain squeakily clean—"

"Not to mention a friend of Pierre and the Tumblars," added Father.

"—being all that and more, he's keen on the papal artifact. He knows that stealing the thing outright and secreting it in his private vault would invite trouble all the way from Rome, so he arranges to have a wax cast made of it. Not sure what that means, but that's what Ernie Corben says he did. You tell me if that's reliable information. Let's see, have I left anyone out? Oh yes, it wasn't David Smoley who kidnapped our annoying monsignor. I take that back. It was the Doily Sisters."

"And what motive would they have for abducting him?" asked Father, who seemed mildly amused by my tirade.

"The same they had for poisoning me—*none!*" I swerved to avoid a trampled hubcap in the middle of the roadway.

"You left out a couple of things," said Father.

"No doubt," said I. "When your brain is a colander, details escape."

"Harrumph!" affirmed Millie, disentangling and re-entangling her arms.

"For example," said Father. "The holy water vial I found in Monsignor Aspic's car, obviously from a sick call kit. Who did the monsignor visit that was grievously ill?"

I shrugged exaggeratedly. "I haven't heard anyone so much as cough on this case. Well, I did after I was poisoned and while I was throwing up, but I didn't phone Monsignor Aspic. He's the last priest I'd call if I needed the Last Rites. Besides, that was after he disappeared."

"I'll give you another example," said Father patiently. "Why do you suppose Bishop Ravenshorst was purchasing plots of land in the downtown area? Why the core samples, and that barrio property excavated?"

"He was looking for something, obviously," said I, "but he didn't know exactly where to find it. You said the inscription on the back of the disk mentions treasure."

"I said that I think *tesoro* means 'treasure,' but I'm not sure."

"Come to think of it, somebody called me a treasure recently."

"Oh? Who was that?" growled Millie.

"Never mind," said I. "Never mind."

"Let's set treasure aside until we're sure that's what the word means," said Father. "In the mean time, let me remind you, Faithful Chronicler, of the truly interesting item amidst all the ruffling feathers."

"You're referring to Cheryl Farnsworth's, um—how do I put it?" said I.

"You're not still sneaking off to visit that, that ... woman!" spat Millie, making a tighter pretzel of her arms.

"Matthew twenty-five thirty-six," I said, a mite sheepishly. "'I was in prison, and you came to me—'"

"Yes, yes, I know, I know," she hissed. Then she heaved her shoulders, twisted her neck to make it crack, and settled down into her seat like a sack of loose gravel. She resumed peering out the side window. "Sometimes ... oh, never mind."

"Ahem," said Father. "That wasn't the interesting item I meant."

"Ah," said I to Father. "You're referring to Christine's Crucifix."

"The same," said he. "Committed as I am to obeying the direct orders of my lawful superior, my capitulation with respect to my own curiosity is the more powerful intention here, and that is a dangerous admission."

I flexed my fingers around the rim of the steering wheel. "So you're drawn in for personal reasons, Father. What's wrong with that? For once you and His Inadvertence happen to be marching, if not to the same drummer, at least in the same direction as the guys with the sounding brass and tinkling cymbals. It's nice to be flowing with the current for once. Come on, we can admit it in front of Millie. She'll never tell." I glanced at her reflection in her side window. Was it my imagination or was she dicing me to pieces with those cold, blue icicles radiating from her eyes? "Will you, on us, Millie?"

"Don't look at me," she snarled. It was a snarl with internal rhythm. "You stop and think how little I know about what you two are talking about. You take me for granted, that's what you do. It took a mean bean like that nice Mr. Corben to kick through with a basic necessity like a dishwasher. My convenience has never been high on your list of priorities, now has it?"

"Nor has mine, I assure you," said Father. "Words mean what they say. For what it's worth, we are taking you into our confidence, Millie. We're trusting to your discretion with respect to all that you've just heard. I'm certain that Mrs. Cladusky is never, I repeat *never* going to learn any of the details of the matters we've been discussing."

"You skewer me through the heart, Father, you do. How can you suggest it?"

"I know a bit about human nature. I also know that the cardinal's wrath would shower down upon us if any word of this—even a syllable—gets to the papal nuncio, and the nuncio's ears are everywhere. Let your embarrassment at being admonished go, Millie, and bask in the trust I am placing in you."

"Well," she sniffed, "when you put it that way."

"I do," said he with confidant finality. "Speaking of human nature, Martin, I used the word 'dangerous' with respect to my own position and I meant it. When the satiation of my curiosity propels me in the same direction as that commanded by my superior, the potential for peril escalates. What will I do should circumstances change and my own motivation again deviates from the course ordered by my cardinal?"

"Ultimately you answer to God, as I understand it," said the gardener helpfully.

"I repeat," said he, "the potential for peril escalates, and—"

"Wait a minute," interrupted Millie with a gasp. "Christine's—? That beautiful Cross? What does that have to do with anything?"

"It was found Thursday morning around the neck of an old man," explained Father, "probably a priest, whose body was discovered in the mausoleum at New Golgotha Cemetery."

"Not just in the mausoleum," added the gardener. "In the very crypt that had been St. Valeria's temporary resting place."

"Good Heavens!" said Millie. "You mean to tell me—? What on earth—? You never should have given such a precious thing to a heretic like Monsignor Aspic, Father. I told you that at the time."

"Yes you did, Millie," agreed Father, "emphatically."

"Some old man, you say." She rubbed her chin significantly. "How did he come by it?"

"That's the intriguing question," said Father. "Martin and I saw the Crucifix on Monsignor Aspic's person just a few days ago. You saw him wearing it on television the day he disappeared. Then it suddenly shows up on the corpse of an unknown priest who died of so many medical complications the coroners can't decide which was the primary cause of death."

"Then there's your connection," said Millie.

"What connection?" asked the gardener.

"You said something about a holy water vial," said she. "Maybe Monsignor Aspic went to give this sick old man the Last Rites."

"That thought occurred to me," said Father. "But there were indications that the old man had been kept a prisoner, complete with scars from shackles on his ankle. Where was the old man kept and why, and who would summon Monsignor Aspic to give him Extreme Unction?"

"Which reminds me, Father," said I. "The old man had asbestos in his lungs. Didn't that tie in with Edison Winger, the notice in his wastebasket?"

"Yes, but not compellingly."

"Oh, well, if not compellingly—"

"Well, I'm certainly lost," said Millie, as a brown sign with reflective letters whizzed by. "At least we're almost to the mission. It's only a mile now."

"I happen to have a compelling unifying element of my own, come to think of it." I said this as I eased up on the accelerator and watched for indications of the turnoff.

"Sure," grunted Millie.

"Do tell," said Father.

"Remember the other morning when you asked me what Some Guy had to tell me in the kitchen the first night he and Ernie dropped by? I couldn't remember, but I knew it was somehow significant? Well, it's coming back to me now. I think the affirming warmth of this cuddly time in the car with the two of you has thawed some of my frozen memory cells. Get this: Some Guy knew about my manuscript—you know: 'The Endless Knot.' He said he overheard Mr. Roundhead talking to his aunt about it."

"Really," said Father. "That's interesting."

"Very, at least to me. That familial glue again. Hortense Roundhead Doily, sister by marriage to Mehitabelle Turnbuckle Doily. I got too close and got poisoned."

"We don't know that it was intentional."

"Tell that to my stomach. But in any case, imagine my surprise when Mister Guy, a man who merely eclipses the sun every time he shrugs, suddenly out of the blue, shyly but certainly asks me to write him into one of my novels."

"So you asked him how he knew you were a writer."

"That's right. 'Maybe I'm not supposed to know,' he said. 'Maybe I shouldn't be telling you.' So now I ask you: how did Mr. Roundhead and his Aunt Hortense know about my manuscript? Some Guy overheard them talking about it."

"Mr. Guy didn't know?"

"Mr. Guy didn't say. Another thing: maybe I don't make good sense, but somehow the mention of Roderick Roundhead strikes me as kind of spooky right now."

"There it is," said Millie as the sign came into view. "The turnoff."

"Yes'm," said I, adjusting the steering wheel accordingly. "And if I may say so, Father, I liked the way you explained things so far, I mean, the parts you had explanations for. As for the gaping chasms, it will be interesting to see how you fill them in with unexpected information as you go."

"But interesting isn't intriguing enough for you."

"For my readers, Father, for my readers. It's all for them, you know. For me, hey, where you go, I go. But as for this current caper, I'll probably—"

"Caper?" snorted Millie.

"A *bona fide* term," said I, breaking at a stop sign, then following the brown placards with yellow arrows toward the mission. "I'll probably crank it all out, incident by incident, page by page, just to keep my fingers limber until something exciting, electrifying, *gripping* finally does occur. Yes, that will be the starting point of the next novel. I'll just throw these uninteresting pages away and move on."

"I'll try not to be so boring in the future," said Father. "As for *pathos*, well, we'll see. Dare I hope that my erudite though verbose explanations will survive intact when they finally do find themselves trapped in your next novel?"

"Hope away," said I with a wave of my hand. "That reminds me. I've been meaning to ask you something."

"Of course."

"Does my chronicling of your exploits bother you?"

"No, but your predilection for hyperbole does."

"This place looks closed," said Millie as I eased by the darkened guardhouse at the entrance. She peered at the sign under the window. "Say, they charge five bucks to park here. Is that Cardinal Fulbright's doing?"

"No," said Father. "Alas, he doesn't have anything to do with it. La Purisima has been maintained and operated by the State of California for some years."

"How did that happen?"

"It's a long story, and I'm not familiar with most of it."

"The State, huh? Does that mean the Blessed Sacrament won't be in the chapel?"

"I'm afraid so, Millie."

"The cardinal told you to meet him here?" said she. "How come he gets the run of the place if the State owns it?"

"Good question," said Father. "I imagine he is on friendly terms with whatever agency maintains this place. He may have contributed funds to the restoration or upkeep of the buildings. I wouldn't be surprised if there's talk of the State deeding the mission back to the Church."

Millie scowled. "But that, that's—"

"The cardinal's super-stretched limo," said I, indicating the obvious as I nudged the Jeep into a nearby parking space. "And you say *I* have a predilection for hyperbole."

44

"I AM NOT AT ALL PLEASED," said Morley Psalmellus Fulbright as he strutted along the dirt path amidst the mission buildings. It was dark: that quiet, brooding sort of gloom that precedes the rising sun in bucolic regions far away from the brazen lights of the big city. Venus, the Morning Star, was glowing hopefully above the distant, murky hills. "I send you out to locate the—er, well, the *thing*—and in return I receive a report of you ransacking Jerry Ravenshorst's library, while claiming you had my permission to do so!"

"I've done many other things in your service," answered Father. "Would that witnesses to those events had called you, but—"

"Oh, there have been other complaints, I assure you. Mr. Turnbuckle, for one."

"Really, Your Eminence."

"You seem to have gone out of your way to antagonize your largest contributor."

"Alas, Your Eminence—"

I held my tongue with a pair of pliers rather than correct him on the spot. Mr. Turnbuckle was our *loudest* contributor, but hardly the most generous. Millie, whose existence had not been so much as acknowledged by His Impoliteness the Cardinal, was walking beside me. The two of us were following a few steps behind our shepherd and our pastor.

"And let us not neglect Bishop Morell deQuet, who is here at my behest," continued Fulbright. "He and I are considering the possibility of his filling the void left by Jerry Ravenshorst. They were friends, you know."

"Indeed," said Father.

"Did their doctorates together in Minneapolis. Before his death, Jerry proposed Morell to fill the position left vacant when poor Gene Brassorie met his untimely end last June. There's irony for you: it's Jerry's seat he'll be filling. Monsignor Aspic has been schmoozing him—effectively, I think." Suddenly his eyes went wide and his bump neon pink. "Did you really wheel out Jerry's research in a wheelbarrow? What were you thinking?"

"It presented itself as the most time- and energy-efficient means at our disposal, so we took it."

"You admit it then. You and your gardener, or whatever he is."

"Excuse me, Your Eminence, but Mr. Feeney—"

"You really riled up deQuet." The cardinal puffed his flabby cheeks for emphasis. They deflated cacophonously. "My word, Father, did you rile that man up."

"His Lordship is an excitable fellow." Father was trying his career-on-the-line best to look innocent. Right, sure. "I think perhaps he is overreacting."

I had decelerated my pace considerably the moment the cardinal of the largest archdiocese on the planet designated me, Martin Feeney, as "whatever he is." My strategy was to reduce my speed so as to lag further and further behind. Relying on my inherent ambiguity, I figured in no time I'd not only be deleted from their conversation, but forgotten entirely. This daring plan in my noggin culminated with me strolling leisurely alone around the mission grounds in the near-dawn gloom. Much as I regretted not being able to include Father Baptist on my private tour, he was, after all, wrapped up in the very conversation from which I wished to extricate myself. How we'd hook up again I'd leave to our Guardian Angels.

Brilliant as the plan undoubtedly was, it was not unique to me, for as I slowed to a dawdling crawl, Millie did likewise. As I halted, so did she. Meanwhile, the cardinal strolled on his way like a royal peacock in spring plumage with Father Baptist deferentially at his side and one step behind. We watched as our betters shrank in the distance, turned right as they reached the largest of the mission buildings, and headed down a breezeway-slash-colonnade along the side. We lessers were left to bob in their wake, glad for the respite.

"I'm afraid there's not much to see this time of morning," I said lamely. The dark sky was just beginning to fade to welcoming blue, at least in the east. I rubbed a sudden chill out of my arms. "It's been a long, long time since I was here last—I was a freshman in college, come to think of it—but I seem to remember lots of rooms you can walk through—when the place is unlocked, of course—rooms where you can see the original living quarters, the kitchen complete with primitive stoves and cooking utensils, the places where the friars ate their meals and—"

"I wonder what they used for soap," said the woman beside me.

"No doubt something disgusting," said the gardener beside her.

"Life must've been hard."

"They certainly didn't have a brand-new dishwasher."

I'd meant that as a good thing, but Millie responded with a sound. I'm not sure if it was an indistinguishable word or a nonverbal snort. Whatever it was, it was emphatic.

It suddenly occurred to me that though we lived, worked, and sparred at the rectory on a daily basis, we rarely found ourselves alone together. Even then there was always cleaning in progress, a meal being prepared, some parishioner banging on the door, some new critter setting up residence in the walls, or some conundrum on the radio. Sometimes we found ourselves visiting the Blessed Sacrament in the church at the same time, but then we were talking to God, not to each other. Now, here we were, a hundred fifty miles from home, stranded together on a dirt path between two large patches of goat-mowed grass.

"So," said I.

"So," said she.

I began lumbering again, ploddingly, without purpose. She accompanied me, though a bit behind and to my left. Eventually we came alongside a nondescript building. The roof overhung the side, making a kind of covered walkway. I came to a stop, peering up at the rafters.

"When I was here before," I said, the sound of my voice startling me slightly, "I asked one of the groundskeepers if they'd had some sort of wasp infestation."

"Wasps?" said she.

"That's just what he said. I'd asked because, well, you can barely see them now, but the swallows build their nests up in these rafters. They make them out of mud, about so big, kind of round with a tiny entry hole, and affix them to the corners up in the eaves. I thought they looked like something wasps or hornets would make, but, shows you what I know about birds."

"Swallows?" said Millie. "I thought they nested down at that other mission. You know, San Juan Capistrano."

"There, too," said I, "or maybe they rest there when they're migrating up here. I don't know. I just thought I'd mention it."

Falling silent, we walked a little further. We came to a stop near something that looked like a well.

"Do you remember the night Bishop Pip ate at the rectory?" I asked, desperately searching for some common ground on which to tread with her. Pip was Bishop Xandaronolopolis' nickname, which he claimed was short for his first name, which was five syllables longer than his last.

"Do I ever," said she, pulling something from the deep pocket of her sweater that gleamed silvery in the bluing darkness. "He gave me this Crucifix that night."

"The one you keep above the kitchen sink."

"That's right."

"You brought it along, then."

"Yes. He said it contains a splinter from the True Cross. I know about the splinter he gave you."

"You mean from the Crown of Thorns," said I, retrieving the bundle from my hip pocket, the relic that had seemed to burn my skin during Mass the previous morning. I held the wrapped object in my hand for a moment. "There isn't enough light for you to see it very well, but here it is."

"You have shown me, at least a dozen times."

"Really? Well, what can I say? It's the most precious thing I own in the whole world. Did I say own? One can't own such a thing. One can only cherish and protect it, then pass it on to the next unworthy temporary guardian."

"Strange to think," said she, "that these two tiny bits of wood were there, you know, back then, when Our Lord, you know—"

"And after all these centuries and who knows how many changes of hands, they find their way all the way here, at the far end of the New World, at this mission, with us."

We had, after all, found common ground.

"It occurs to me," I found myself saying, "that I should make some sort of provision for this should anything happen to me. The worst thing would be for it to be forgotten or lost. Father was telling me how the relics of St. Candidus were lost in plain sight for years, right inside a church. Things get moved around, papers get mislaid, people forget."

"Sort of like dear Saint Valeria."

"Yes, isn't hers a sad tale? Here she reigned for a century as the patroness of the largest archdiocese on earth, yet only a handful will remember that she was here."

"At least now she's appreciated where she is."

"Millie, what I was starting to say, well, how do I put it? Something could happen to me. What am I saying? Of course something will happen to me eventually."

"You're talking about dying?"

"That, or an illness, or an accident, or who knows. Monsignor Aspic disappeared between his car and the entrance to the television station.

Things happen. I haven't said this to anyone, and I'll ask you not to repeat it, but since Father Baptist has been detecting for the cardinal, there have been moments when, well, when things might have gone awry."

"What are you getting at?"

I peered into her face in the dimness. "Millie, if anything untoward should happen to me, I'd like to ask you to make sure this chip from the Crown of Thorns worn by Jesus Christ Himself, doesn't get lost or forgotten. If I should wind up unconscious in a hospital, be sure to go through my clothes. Don't let some nurse's aide steal it and try to pawn it. And if it's not there in my pocket, check my room back at the rectory."

"You've asked me not to go in there."

"To clean, no. You've always had more than enough to do with the rest of the rectory, and my unique filing system is, well, my unique filing system."

"You mean your mess."

"It is not a mess. It's a continuum of free-flowing ideas." I paused to recollect the title of the movie in which Walter Matthau had said that, but couldn't place it. "In any case, if something should happen to me, I'd want you to go through my things until you find this. I want you to be sure it's safe."

"What would I do with it?"

"You're a devout woman. I'll leave that up to you. You might give it to Father Baptist, or Monsignor Havermeyer, or the Tumblars, or keep it yourself. Just don't let it be forgotten or lost due to neglect, not like sweet Saint Valeria."

There was a long moment of silence between us.

"Okay," she said at last. "If that's what you want."

"I do. This doesn't mean we're engaged or anything."

I paused to see if she'd found that funny. She hadn't. Maybe she was considering her own precious relic of the True Cross. Perhaps something else was on her mind.

"Um," said I after another long, painful silence. "Well, let's see. We've exhausted this section of the grounds. Would you like to see what's over there?"

"Not particularly, Mr. Feeney. Meaning no offense, but you don't have to play the chivalrous Knight around me. You don't even have to pretend to be a guide. In fact, if you don't mind, I think I'd rather wander a bit on my own."

"Oh, okay," said I, not sure what else to say. I waved my arms in a vague gesture that was supposed to mean I wasn't offended, even though I kind of was, strange as that may seem.

"Heaven knows," said she, fishing around for something in that frayed, dumpy thing she called a purse, "it took me this many years to get here once, and I don't know if I'll ever get up here again." She produced a cigarette, which she wedged between her lips, then continued digging for some matches. Hunched over as she was, I thought her hat would tumble off. But wiggle and pitch as it did, apparently it was pinned in place. "I'd like to take some private memories home with me."

I watched as she found a matchbook, peeled one off, struck it, and brought the flame up to her cigarette. Her face blazed yellow-orange as she drew the fire into the tip. For a brief moment her features took on a sly, pixie-like quality, but the effect only lasted for the first long puff. It vanished as she whirled out the match and tossed it aside.

> GARDENING TIPS: I wasn't about to remind Millie
> about her visit to Dr. Sarah Mathuson, her "in
> lieu of" physician, the previous August. I was
> just acting as chauffeur at the time, but I over-
> heard Dr. M.'s parting words as she ushered our
> housekeeper back into the reception room. Her
> little speech included key words like "systolic,"
> "diastolic," "elevated," and "STOP SMOKING!!!"
>
>   --M.F.

> N.B.: Dr. Sarah Naomi Mathuson (shortened from
> Mathusalason, in other words, "begotten of
> Mathusala") offers her services to our housekeeper
> gratis, not because she shares our theology or our
> cause, but because in her religion it is consid-
> ered a mitzvah to assist one's income-deficient
> neighbor. Need I say there is a long story there?

"I understand," I said presently as her exhaled smoke tickled my nostrils, "and I don't mind."

"Good," said she, drawing hard on her ciggie. Her face glowed red-orange as the tip brightened. "I'll meet you back at the car."

"Sure," said I as she turned and walked away. "Sure."

Not wanting to interfere in any way with Millie's private memories, I purposely headed the other way. After a short while I came upon an entrance to a large, flat, rectangular area of bare dirt surrounded by a tall wall at the south end of the mission complex. Since there was nothing else of interest in the strange courtyard, I drifted toward the large wooden Cross standing at the far end. Halfway there I bumped into a post that sported an explanatory sign. I could barely make out the gold letters against the pale turquoise background, but I caught enough to gather that I had meandered into a cemetery. Unlike the burial grounds at every other mission I had ever visited, where every grave had a tombstone or plaque and most were lovingly adorned with flower patches, small bushes or arrangements of stones, this one had no individual markers. It was a field of invisible, anonymous burial sites with one, big, blank, wooden Cross overseeing the lot.

I had two simultaneous reactions. First, my usual fit of the queasies upon finding myself surrounded by dead people. The second, a vague sense of anger at the apparent lack of diligence with respect to the friars and Indians who had built this place. Catholics have always honored their deceased relatives and friends, not just to keep them alive in their own hearts, or as reminders to pray for them should they be languishing in Purgatory, but because in life their bodies had been temples of the Holy Ghost and receptacles of the Holy Eucharist. God had resided in them, so their remains were precious. This principle had somehow been lost at La Purisima, and the thought rankled.

Of course, I reminded myself, La Purisima, unlike most of the missions, was currently owned and run by the State of California. That explained the finished quality to some of the buildings. To make them safe and presentable for tourists, the old mission buildings had been restored, honed to a modern sense of "rough." They were made to look old, but not convincingly so. But the flagrant dismissal of the respect due the dead in this yard, this was something else. No attempt had been made here to preserve the typical mission cemetery, despite the State's claims to authenticity.

I had just talked myself around a circle and back to "rankled."

A wave of nausea swept over me as I stumbled toward the silent Cross. The queasies and the angries collided. The Cross bore no Corpus nor inscription. Like the cemetery it overlooked, it was blank and out of character. In a surge of mental activity within my roiling mind, the thing suddenly became a symbol of the silent, distant hierarchy in the modern Church today, providing no answersnor solace for the nameless masses because it had abandoned, indeed forgotten all about Jesus. Meanwhile a carousel of disharmony twirled within my abdomen. Thousands of sharp, jabbing pricks of cold, angry sweat erupted all over the bag of bones and flesh that is my body. A sinking sensation in my gut along with a spasmodic surge of acrid saliva in my mouth alerted me that I was about to throw up. I was glad Millie had gone exploring on her own. I didn't want her to see and hear and smell this. Having staggered to the foot of the bare, silent Cross, I reached out my hand to steady myself.

"Here it comes," I moaned, hating as I did, every nuance of the process of regurgitation. And this was the second genuine time in two days! Would that this was one of my contrived performances. My eyelids scrunched tightly shut, I awaited the horrid commotion that was about to commence.

"Oh, my Guardian Angel, to whom God has entrusted me, I wonder what you, as a wondrous being fashioned from Subtle Matter, must think when you witness the indignities our coarse bodies put us through ... oh dear ..."

45

"PARDON, SEÑOR," INTRUDED A VOICE.

"Ulp!" gulped yours truly as the twitching muscles around my stomach prepared to constrict. I knew that voice couldn't belong to my Guardian Angel because he would never call me "Señor."

"¿Señor?" queried the voice.

"Not now," I gasped, squeezing my eyelids tighter. On second thought, convinced as I am that God has a sense of humor, I wouldn't put it past Him to give me a Guardian Angel who would. Still, now was not the time. "Please go away."

"But Señor—"

"Look, whoever you are, I'm about to be sick."

"I theenk not, Señor. Not on such a beeyooteeful day."

Suddenly everything changed. It was like waking up in a lovely dream, although my eyes were still closed. My stomach relaxed. No, more than relaxed. It sighed, smiled, snuggled up against my liver, and fell fast asleep. All my pores, erupting a moment before like miniature volcanoes all over my body, subsided into perspirative dormancy. Even the strange sensations in my feet, the nagging tingling and itching, abated. Strangely, my skin felt warm all over—not the dank, rippling warmth that sometimes accompanies upheavals of the stomach, but the healthy, dry, invigorating heat that comes from basking in midmorning sunlight. More remarkable still, the insides of my eyelids glowed bright red, just as if they were shuttered against dazzling sunshine. Most curious of all, the tangy smell of sage prickled my nostrils.

I opened my eyes and gasped.

The sun was shining brightly, the aromas of summer billowed all around me, and the mission was nowhere to be seen. I was standing in a charming dell, its gentle, grassy slopes dotted with clusters of pale green sagebrush. Behind me was a stand of grizzled oaks, and standing before me, big as you please, was a broad-shouldered, thin-hipped man with olive skin, large pearly teeth—except for the right front incisor, which was missing—and a humongous, drooping moustache. He was wearing an ornate jacket of fine black material that was cut high above his waist, and his middle was wrapped in a black sash like a cummerbund. His hat was black and flat-rimmed, with a garish band of silver all around. Speaking of silver, all his buttons were made of it, as were the two rings on each hand and the ostentatious medallion of Our Lady of Guadalupe hanging from his neck. His hair was jet-black, curled in ripples, and glistening like machine oil. The smell of sage poured off of him, as though he had spent long hours walking through the chaparral. In short, I was in the company of a Californio who had apparently strayed off the set of an old Zorro movie.

"Pleez forgeev my intrusion, Señor," he said again. His accent was peculiar. The inflection was Hispanic, but unlike anything I had heard before. "I can see that joo are lost."

"I am?" I shut my eyes and counted to ten. When I opened them the mission was still gone and he was still there. I looked him in the eye and said, "I mean: I *am*."

"Thee misión, eet ees over there." My eyes followed his pointed finger. Southwest, if my bearings were right. The ground in that direction ascended gradually toward the craggy mountains beyond. Far up the distant slope, several miles away, stood a magnificent edifice of pale adobe walls and stone archways. It was reminiscent of the structure that had just vanished around me, but it had a primitive roughness about it, the jagged edges of a building made of the raw materials at hand.

"That's the mission?" I asked.

"Do joo not theenk I would know where ees La Misión de la Purisima Concepcion?" He continued to point, drawing my attention down the length of his arm. "Joo see? Thee good friars, they beeld their misións where they can be seen for many miles so that travelers, like joo and me, we can find our way."

"S-suh-suh-so what happened to the m-muh-muh-mission that was right here?" I stammered, not at all sure what was happening or to whom I was speaking.

"Oh that," said my mysterious companion with a toss of his hand. "That came later, after thee beeg earthquake. Ai yi yi, eet was terrible, Amigo. Such a beeyooteeful misión, so much—¿Como se dice?—thee wreckage. Thee rubble. So thee padres, they rebeelt eet down here—a valley, not as good a place. Then, a leetle later, thee filthy greengos—pardon, Señor—took possession and turned eet eento a stopping place for thee tourists, not a haven for travelers."

"It came later, you say." I looked around, then I looked around the other way. My neck didn't crack. No doubt about it. It was summer, and there was no mission here. I had to be dreaming, or I was either going nuts or everything else was. Gathering my wits, scrambled as they were, I decided not to jump to conclusions. "Uh-huh. So tell me—"

"But was has become of my manners? Allow me to eentroduce myself." He patted himself grandly on the expanse of his chest. "I am Juan Pablo Gusto Adán Ezequiel Jeremías Mateo Marcos Lucas Jesús el Cordero de Dios Alverado y San Pasqual." He held out a meaty hand. "I am known by many names een many places, but joo, Amigo, joo may call me Gusto." (Pronounced "Goo´-sto.")

"Very well," said I hesitantly, not sure if I should extend my hand. "I'm—"

"Or rather *Don* Gusto," said he, stroking the tips of his moustache. Apparently he didn't mind foregoing the handshake. "Joo may not believe thees, my Friend, but I was Baptized there at thee misión—Sí, Señor, that very misión on thee hill."

It took me a moment to wade through his accent to realize what he had just said. Then I blinked. "But that would mean—"

"Sí, eet would, and that ees because I am. My older brother, Miguel, he eenherited my father's ranchero, and a grand place eet ees—or was. Joo must excuse me, Señor Fényi, but where I am, time, eet flows strangely."

"What did you call me?"

"Fényi Márton. Eet ees joor name, no? Ah, perdóneme. I should call joo *Caballero* Fényi Márton."

Caballero, I remembered from some Tyrone Power movie, was the Spanish equivalent of the French *Chevalier*, which in jolly old England would have been rendered *Sir Knight*. This mysterious stranger knew! My brain actually turned three hundred and sixty degrees around inside my skull. "How would you know—?"

"I was there, Señor."

"You—?"

"Joo'd be surprised how many were there." He took a deep breath and let it out slowly and noisily. "Ah. I have knelt een joor beeyooteeful leetle church many times as joo served Mass beside Padre Juan Bautista. I used to pray there long ago, too, when eet had another name."

"You're talking about St. Philomena's?"

"Sí, sí, when eet was an *asistencia* dedicated to El Señor de los Temblores."

"A what dedicated to whom?" A sudden ripple of recognition went through me. Of course: I had seen this fellow crawling down the center aisle on his knees! "Wait a minute. You were at Mass yesterday—whoa, and again this morning. This morning!? How did you get here so—?"

"But I was, een fact, Baptized at La Misión de la Purisima Concepcion," continued he, ignoring my turmoil, "and on thees very day! That ees why I am here."

"I'm afraid I'm not following you."

"No? I am not surprised. Do joo realize I never spoke a seengle word een Eengleesh een my life? But now I am here, and eet ees coming to me because—well, just because. Eet ees very strange, my Friend. Very strange."

"You're telling me!"

"Joo see, my brother Miguel, he settled down weeth a beeyooteeful wife and queeckly raised many bambinos, and many head of cattle, too. Me, when I was seexteen, I realized my brother, he was a bore. I like to dance. I like to seeng. I *love* to dreenk. So I wandered up and down thee Royal Road, veeseeting thee friars een their misións, and looking een on my relatives. At thee misións, joo see, they have a Franceescan notion of hospitality. They welcome travelers like me weeth open arms. They inseest that guests receive thee best food and dreenk their keetchens have to offer. Of course, eef joo stay three weeks they figure joo should start helping out weeth thee work. I stay two.   Then I veesit my cousins all over Caleefornia, from Sonoma to La Paz.   They love to see me coming, me on my trusty steed, Huracán, and my servant, Profirio—he ees small of stature, so he prefers to ride hees leetle burro, Poca Roca. I breeng news, and gossip, and I seeng like thee bird. I am very good at cards, and a fine horseman. Ah, thees ees—or was—thee life!"

"I may tend to agree with you there."

"Of course joo do, Señor, of course joo do. Now Profirio—where has he gone off to?" He drew me close and whispered, "Profirio ees slow, Señor, very slow, but hee ees as attenteeve as a doting uncle, and as faithful as a nephew who hopes to eenherit thee casa." He chuckled, straightened, and waved his hand as if to indicate the hills all around us. "Taking care of my house, eet ees so easy, he never complains."

Just then a cow lowed nearby. The animal wasn't in plain sight, but it was answered by the moos of several others, equally unapparent.

"Ah," said Don Gusto. "There was so much cattle een Caleefornia. Sometimes Profirio and I would lasso a cow, keel eet, eat eet, then stop by thee main casa of thee local ranchero to tell thee señor what we had done, and that Miguel, my brother, he would breeng heem a heifer een thee spreeng. He deedn't mind, Señor. Eet was cheaper than having me for a guest!"

"Stop," I said, raising my hand like a traffic cop. "I'm confused."

"Pardon me," said he, pursing his lips. Then he tapped the side of his head with one of his ringed fingers. "Joo are not loco, Amigo, eef that ees what joo fear. I am real, Señor. Purgatory, I'm afraid, eet ees also all too real."

"So you're a ghost?"

He shrugged. "Eef that ees thee term joo prefer, I do not mind eet. I do not understand why eet ees that joo are so surprised. Elza, she told me about what joo deed for her, and she for joo."

"Elza?!"

```
GARDENING TIPS: Dean Koontz wrote in a book enti-
tled The Face:


                        * * *
    If you reported having seen a ghost, you
    were a regular guy who'd had an uncanny ex-
    perience.  If you reported seeing another
    ghost at another place and time, you were
    at best an eccentric whose every statement
    would thereafter be taken with enough salt
    to crust the rims of a million margarita
    glasses.
                        * * *


Sigh.  There goes my credibility . . . Again.
                                          --M.F.

N.B.: Koontz, like Frank Capra, who produced that
Jimmy Stewart movie, It's a Wonderful Life, pro-
motes the metaphysical absurdity that dead people
eventually become Angels.  Sigh.
```

He sighed, his patience grand and laborious. "Elza Maplewood Roundhead. She tell me she likes you, by thee way."

I reacted to that bit of information in ways that are too hard to explain. So I just smiled and nodded, urging him to continue.

"Elza," he complied, "she ees thee granddaughter of Thomas Phineus Roundhead."

He pronounced "Phineus" as "Feeney-us," which I found momentarily amusing. The name Roundhead always jars me, even when connected with Elza Maplewood. But as for the point, I looked at him, not comprehending.

He sighed again. "Thees Roundhead, he was married to Doña Maria Consuela Sepulveda y Alverado."

My face was still blank.

"Doña Maria," he said, patting himself on the chest again, "she ees my cousin! That means that Elza ees my—let me theenk—oh, never mind. Eet ees too compleecated."

"You're telling me."

Don Gusto took a deep breath and let it out slowly. When next he spoke his tone was thoughtful and serious. "Sometimes, my Friend, we leave theengs unfeeneeshed when we die. I—well, eet ees not for me to discuss my seens—but part of my penance ees to retrace El Camino Real, thee Royal Road, to visit all thee misións over and over and over again. For many, many jeers, as I have approached thee magnificent beacon of Franceescan hospitality that ees La Purisima, I have been made to leave thee Royal Road to come down to thees *barranco*, thees valley where thee misión will be rebeelt, and here I must tell thee empty air that eet ees lost, that thee misión ees not here but over there."

"But this time I'm here," said I in a rare moment of insight.

"Sí." His face blossomed into a jovial, conspiratorial smirk. "Joo weel appreciate thees, Señor Fényi. More than once, when I have been standing here addressing thee empty air, people have chanced upon me, people not looking for La Purisima. Joo know: men hunting thee rabbits, thee occasional surveyor, once even a pair of lovers strolling by, taking een thee beeyootees of spreeng—ahhh! So, would joo believe eet? Thees place has a reputation for being—¿Como se dice?—*haunted*. That ees thee word. Haunted. Imagine that, my Friend, imagine that!"

I couldn't help smiling. In fact, the beginning of a guffaw welled up within me, but it was cut short as the sky suddenly dimmed. It was as if a black blanket had fallen from above and settled on Don Gusto and myself.

"Ah," he said, "my time, eet ees short."

As my eyes adjusted to the sudden gloom, the Morning Star's courageous emanation was the first light to penetrate. My skin tingled with the sudden drop in temperature. Gradually I began to see the pale blue of approaching dawn reaching upward from beyond the hills in the east. The smells of summer were replaced by the faint odor of raked earth and car exhaust. The tingling resumed in my feet with renewed insistence. An ache rolled down my spine like a bowling ball in the gutter. My strange companion was still standing before me, but he didn't seem as solid somehow. I could see the ersatz mission buildings resolving into solid forms behind him—no, through him, as if he were a dirty window.

"Bueno," he said, a bit of his indomitable good humor subsiding slightly, "I must be on my way. And joo, my Friend, joo must be on joors. Thee place joo seek, eet ees—¿Como se dice?—that-a-way."

"You mean it's still there?"

"Joo go and see," said he. Sort of like Lewis Carroll's Cheshire Cat, all of him had faded away except his eyes and, more strangely still, the gap of his missing incisor. He winked one of his eyes. Then he blinked them both—once, twice—and they were gone. The hole in his smile was the last to go.

"Martin," intruded a familiar voice.

"Yes, Father?" answered mine.

"What are you doing?"

"Good question." With Herculean effort, I opened my eyes. Yeow! Brilliant sabers of light from the rising sun lanced my optic nerves. "I must've fallen asleep."

"I can see that."

"Then why did you ask?"

"I'm the great detective, remember? Where's Millie?"

"She wandered off in search of some private memories."

"Excuse me?"

"Sure, be my guest." Taking stock of myself, I blurrily realized I was sitting on a coarse wooden bench just outside the tombstone-challenged cemetery. I was facing southwest. In the hazy distance, several miles away, the ground ascended gradually toward the rugged mountains beyond. The slope was dotted with homes and trees and streets and such. After rolling my tongue around inside the parched cave that was my mouth, I raised my right arm and asked, "What's over there?"

"Where? Ah, the town of Lompoc."

"Oh." It took me a moment to realize what I had expected him to answer: something about a marvelous edifice of adobe and stone, a great mission built high up the distant slope so as to be seen for many miles by travelers. Of course, it had been a dream. There was no mission across the valley, no Californio with a big moustache and silver buttons, no smell of sagebrush, no mooing cows—I felt the front of my jacket—and best of all, no vomit. Thank God, I hadn't thrown up after all. I gave the back of my head a good scratching as I asked, "So you are through with the cardinal?"

"Let us say he is finished with me for the nonce."

"So what now?"

"Let's find Millie and be on our way."

"Sure thing, Father," said I, heaving myself up onto my feet. "And what way is that?"

"South, or rather southeast, to the San Fernando Mission."

"Not La Purisima?"

"Wake up, Martin. That's where you've been sleeping."

"Oh, right."

46

"I THINK THIS IS IT," said the gardener-slash-driver as he turned south onto a little side street off of Locust Avenue. I was basing my calculations on a faded map of Lompoc that had been taped to a crusty window at the local gas station. "Are we on E Street or F?"

"I don't know," said Millie, scratching her head. Then she pointed to where the road ended about twenty yards ahead. "But isn't that one of those California Bear signs?"

"So it would seem," said Father, his head centered close behind ours. He patted the back of my car seat. "Martin, you still haven't told us why you wanted to come up here."

"For the moment, let's call it a hunch," said I, maneuvering the car around the cul-de-sac and parking facing the way we had come. I turned off the ignition, pushed my door open, and planted my cane on the warming asphalt. Heaving myself out of the car, I headed back to the bronze plaque set at a readable angle at the curb. The sun had been up for more than an hour and a couple of crows were pecking at something squashed on the pavement. They looked up from their breakfast at us, back at their meal, back at us, flapped their wings lazily, then settled down and resumed eating.

Millie and Father were close behind me. Together we halted and read the thick, metal, bas-relief plaque with the state mascot lumbering across the top.

ORIGINAL SITE OF MISSION DE LA PURISIMA CONCEPTION DE MARIA SANTISIMA

THE RUINS AT THIS SITE ARE PART OF THE ORIGINAL MISSION LA PURISIMA, FOUNDED BY PADRE FERMIN DE LASUEN ON DECEMBER 8, 1787, AS THE 11TH IN THE CHAIN OF SPANISH MISSIONS IN CALIFORNIA. THE MISSION WAS DESTROYED BY EARTHQUAKE ON DECEMBER 21ST, 1812: THE PRESENT MISSION LA PURISIMA WAS THEN ESTABLISHED SEVERAL MILES AWAY.

CALIFORNIA REGISTERED HISTORICAL LANDMARK NO. 928

PLAQUE PLACED BY THE STATE DEPARTMENT OF PARKS AND RECREATION IN COOPERATION WITH

THE LA PURISIMA PARLOR NO. 327, NATIVE
DAUGHTERS OF THE GOLDEN WEST.

SEPTEMBER 26, 1979

"So?" said Father to me.

"So?" said I to him.

"So tell us," said Millie and he together.

"Tell you what?" I said to them both.

"When I found you snoozing back at the cemetery," said Father, "I told you where I wanted to go."

"And arrive there you shall, Father," said I. "This will only delay the blessed moment by a matter of a few minutes."

"More like an hour, but I've no quarrel with your wishing to make a detour. I'm just surprised by your insistence."

"I didn't insist."

"We're here, aren't we?"

"It's a free country, you're welcome to go somewhere else."

"You've got the car keys."

"You're welcome to walk somewhere else."

"Nevertheless, we are here." He indicated the plaque with a thrust of his chin. "Is this what you expected to find at the end of your quest?"

"Why do you say 'quest'?"

"Because you made such a big deal out of it."

"You've brought it on yourself, Mr. Feeney," said Millie. "You've been acting queerly—I mean that in the way it used to mean, of course—but you have been, and that's a fact."

"I think you're exaggerating," said I.

"I never exaggerate," said Millie. "I don't have the imagination."

I held my breath, as did Father, waiting for her to add the sinister words, "Do I?"

The grassy, ascending landscape was hilly and irregular. Here and there were small mounds of weathered, mortared stones and coarse scraps of adobe, not much left of the original buildings at all. A deep, wide trench had been cut crosswise through the terrain to provide a roadbed for some old train tracks. The rails were brown from disuse. To the left and right of us were houses on both sides of the dead-ended street, but the second lot behind us to the left was vacant except for the eroded remains of several stone-and-mortar arches and a lot of weeds. In other words, a neighborhood and a right-of-way for a mining train had superimposed themselves on the site of what had once been the largest of all the California missions. It must have been grand in its day, but like the Church in modern times, it had fallen into decay while the encroaching, uncaring world had its way.

Several earnestly-squeezed Rosary beads later, Father and I relaxed as Millie dug a folded piece of sky-blue paper out of that purse of hers and changed the subject: "I found this stuck on a cactus back at the other place. I think it's what the gate guard gives people as they drive in, only we came before they opened. I thought you'd be interested in this, Father: 'In 1831, the California governors began taking over the missions and their land, a process called *secularization*.' The word 'secularization' is—uh, what do you call it when it's all squiggly?"

"Italicized," suggested yours truly.

"Italianized," she agreed. "Let's see … 'La Purisima, which had been relocated after the earthquake of 1812, passed from Church control in 1834 when the Franciscans left. By 1881 nothing was left but rubble. Reconstruction began in 1934. In 1935, over five hundred acres were designated as La Purisima Mission State Historical Monument. The dedication of the *restored* mission'—'restored' is Italianated—'dedication of the *restored* mission took place on December 7th, 1941.'"

"That's an interesting date," observed Father, saying exactly the words that had popped into my mind to say. "A very interesting date indeed."

"And it explains the not-so-convincing appearance of those buildings back at the other site," said I, eyeing Millie guardedly—guardedly should be Italianized. I really wasn't used to having her along on our manly adventures. I swallowed audibly and said, "Not to mention the Real Absence in the church. But what has that to do with this?"

"You're asking me?" said she, unfolding and refolding the sheet. "On the previous flap here, it says pretty much what's on this California Bear sign: that the *original* mission was founded on high ground overlooking what is now modern-day Lompoc in 1787, destroyed in 1812. It also says that the altar was at the west end of the church, and that the church was one hundred feet long, fifty-two feet wide, and thirty feet high."

"No minor feat," said Father, "considering the building materials at hand. These missions sure weren't made to last forever. The friars understood only too well that all material things decay. But in this seismologically active part of the continent, so many miles on the wrong side of a tectonic convergence, these magnificent buildings—these examples of Faith, courage, resolve, and action on the part of the Catholic missionaries—didn't stand a chance. That any of the missions, let alone most of them, are still standing and in public use is remarkable."

I got the impression he was working on his next sermon. Well, why not?

"Ah," said Millie, squinting at the flyer. "'Residential buildings and other structures have been built on part of the site. The "lost mission"—that's in quotation marks—'can be found five miles to the south and west by the inquisitive traveler between South E and F streets.'" She folded up the page and stuffed it back into her purse. "I noticed that before we left the other place, but I wasn't going to say anything because Father seemed set on where he wanted to go next. But when you insisted, Mr. Feeney, frankly, I was kind of glad, to tell you the truth. Begging your pardon, Father, not that any of us should be disobedient to a priest and invite the Wrath of God upon our heads."

"Absolutely not," agreed Father wholeheartedly.

"Your turn," said Millie to me.

"My turn to what?" asked me of her.

"To explain why you were so all-fired set on coming up here."

"I think you're exaggerating."

"We've been over that. You're fidgeting."

"Fidgeting?"

"Okay, stalling."

Meanwhile Father turned and made for the vacant lot behind us to the left. Millie and I followed like dutiful sheep. There was a dirt path through the weeds leading to the crumbling arches—no, not complete arches: stumps, just vague suggestions of them. We followed it, the gravelly earth crunching under our feet.

"Amazing, isn't it," said I as we paused at the first section of crumbling wall, "how such an important historical site could be treated so off-handedly."

"I guess it's only important to the likes of people like us," said Millie.

"For all we know," said Father, stooping to pick up a lemon-sized cluster of ordinary pebbles held together with chalky mortar, "the people living in these homes chose them precisely so they could raise their children on a piece of history, or on hallowed ground."

"Or because the price was right," said Millie, accepting the chunk from Father as he stood up. She turned it over in her sinewy fingers, then handed it to me. "You're still evading the question, Mr. Feeney."

"I am?" queried yours truly, hefting the thing. I couldn't help but imagine the calloused hands of Padre Fermin de Lasuen mixing this less-than-stable concoction from the raw materials *in situ*. No doubt his sweat permeated the mortar. Talk about an Act of Faith! "What question is that, Millie?"

"You know perfectly well," said she. "We're not going to let it go."

"You're not?"

"I'm certainly not, and I decide what ends up on your dinner table."

Now that was a serious threat. I looked to Father for support, but he was busy running his fingers down the jagged edge of the crumbling wall—as if he was an archeologist or something. Surely the fact that Millie also controlled what he would be eating had nothing whatsoever to do with his sudden interest in primitive masonry.

"Mr. Feeney," pressed Millie, sure of her leverage.

"Okay," I huffed, shifting the clump of stone and mortar from one hand to the other. I suppose it was intended as a dramatic gesture. It didn't work. "Okay," I said again. This time I rotated my shoulders as if preparing to do something strenuous. The very notion was so preposterous even I almost walked away right there. "Okay," I said a third time, this round inflected with what I hoped sounded like concession. All the while I was trying to come up with an honest yet credible answer to the question.

"Martin," said Father.

"Father." Oh well, when all else fails, the beans must be spilled. "That empty courtyard at the restored site is apparently a cemetery void of all grave markers. I didn't realize it until I read the sign near the big Cross at the far end, and you know about my necropoliphobia."

"I know nothing of the sort," snorted Millie. "And don't you go saying I do."

"I thought you did," said I.

"I have no notion whatever about whatever it was you said. You and your big writers' words."

"Necropoliphobia. It means 'fear of cemeteries.'"

"Everyone fears death," said she, but the tone conveyed, "Why don't you grow up?"

"I didn't say 'fear of death,' I said 'fear of cemeteries.' There's a difference. You try watching all the B movies I did when I was growing up and see how you turn out." I looked down and realized I still had that chunk of La Purisima in my hand. "Anyway, when I realized I had been walking all over who knows how many forgotten graves, I suddenly felt as though I was about to be violently sick. My stomach seized and I got the rippling chills. I mean, it was definitely a'comin' 'round the mountain, if you get my drift."

"We do," said Father.

"And thanks for all the details," said Millie.

"Well, you asked," said I. The moment had come. I could postpone it no longer. A deep breath packed under my belt, I marveled as the words rolled over my tongue and out my mouth. "Father, you say you found me napping, but I don't remember falling asleep, or how I ended up on that bench outside the cemetery. The way I remember it, I was leaning against the big Cross at the far end of the cemetery. I shut my eyes against the nausea. Then, would you believe it, I opened my eyes and found the sun shining, cows mooing, and the mission gone. No, not just gone: not yet there. I could see this place here from there, not as the ruin it is now, but as the marvel it was when it was whole."

"Really, Mr. Feeney?" said Millie, blinking skeptically, Italianizing the word "Really."

"I wouldn't lie to you," said I. "Somehow I lost two hundred years, and I distinctly remember winding my watch this morning before Mass."

Father whispered something as he wiped the dust from his hands. I think the last word was "original." He looked at me and smiled. "Go on."

I took a deep breath and let it out slowly. "Were either of you aware that the dell down there where they rebuilt the mission has a reputation for being haunted?"

"As a matter of fact," said Millie, again producing the blue flyer from the mysterious depths of her purse, "there's mention on the back about an apparition that's been seen in the cemetery. He accosts visitors in Spanish and points toward the south."

"Southwest, actually," said I.

Millie glared at me then squinted at the flyer.

"I saw him," I continued.

"The ghost," said Millie, lifting her squint at me.

"Yes," said I. "He introduced himself to me as Don Gusto. It was a warm summer's day, and he seemed to have lost track of his servant, Profirio."

"He spoke to you," said Father. "The apparition."

"On a warm summer's day?" added Millie, folding up the flyer and re-inserting it in her purse.

"He did," said I, "and it was."

There was a long silence. It went on and on as we strolled among the exposed bits of flotsam and jetsam that had once been La Purisima.

"Don Gusto said he rode a horse named Huracán," said I when I could endure the vacuum no longer, "and Profirio preferred a burro name Poca Roca—though I only have Señor Gusto's word for it. He's the only one I actually saw."

Father and Millie cleared their throats together. The effect was un-nerving.

"A ghost," said Millie.

"You mean another ghost," said I. "This one's my second."

"My Great-Aunt Carmella saw a ghost once," said Millie. "That's how all her hair turned white."

"I don't suppose the apparition asked to hold a Rosary," said Father, "or made any other attempt to prove its good faith and intention."

"No," said Millie, "nothing like that, and she said the ghost appeared to be a she."

"I was speaking to Martin, Millie," said Father.

"You go right ahead," said Millie, folding her arms. "Don't mind me."

"Martin?" asked Father.

"Father," I answered.

"Did your ghost leave a sign?"

"Not even a spent cigar," said I. "Though he did mention that Purgatory is all too real."

Silence fell again.

"You'll find this next bit interesting," said I, figuring that since my right foot was already sizzling in the fire, I might as well drag in ol' leftie for the sake of keeping my balance. "Don Gusto also told me that Elza Maplewood Roundhead was the granddaughter of one of his distant relatives, one Doña Maria ... something-or-other."

"He knows Elza?" asked Father.

Millie gave Father a look that said, "Don't encourage him!" but what she said to me was, "Who's Elza?"

"My first ghost," said I, wistfully. "She used to play the piano at the 'House of Illusions' in Hollyweird."

"Used to?" asked Millie.

"Used to what?" asked the gardener.

"Your ghost friend played the piano."

"That's what I said."

She sighed. "Used to."

"Oh, past tense. The last time I heard her play was her encore before she moved on."

"To where?"

I waved my hand skyward, then I pointed to indicate beyond all that. "To where souls go when they leave Purgatory."

"You mean Heaven."

"That's the place."

"Come to think of it, maybe I do remember you and Father talking about a ghostly flapper who was fond of blueberry brandy."

"That's the one."

"Excuse me, Martin," said Father, "but I should caution you against presumption. All you know is that Elza's no longer playing the piano at the club. No doubt she has advanced toward the Beatific Vision because of the aid she rendered to you, but we can't assume that incident brought to fulfillment all that is required of her."

"Oh," I said with an exaggerated shrug. "For a moment there I thought it was salvific to save my hide."

"Sorry to pop your bubble," said Millie. Maybe it was the angle of the sun, but her eyes seemed to glisten like stainless steel skewers.

"But in the immediate," said Father, turning to go back to the car, "you've had this 'experience,' for want of a better term. A dream, perhaps. A visitation, who's to say? Assuming for the moment this Don Gusto is what he claims to be and not some deceptive demon trying to foil some part of our investigation, why do you suppose he spoke to you?"

"You mean to me in particular?" I asked.

"Yes. Why you, and what was his message? What makes you sure this apparition was telling you the truth?"

"I wasn't at all sure," said I. "I've listened to your sermons and I know better than to jump to conclusions when it comes to apparitions. I've been around the block in the haunting department. That's precisely why I insisted we come up here: to at least verify what facts I could."

Somehow the walk back to the car seemed shorter than the stroll away from it. It wasn't until I was settled in the driver's seat that I realized I still had that chunk of pebbles and mortar in my hand. For a moment I thought of returning it to its place near the crumbled arches. Then I considered the railway track carved right through the mission site.

"You're coming with me," I mumbled, stuffing the thing into my jacket pocket and starting the car. I looked at Father in the rearview mirror. He was already examining another scrap of paper in the back. "So where to now?"

"Where I wanted to go all along," said he. "The San Fernando Mission. It won't take long, Millie."

"No rush," said she. "It's not like I've got a sink full of dishes waiting for me when we get home."

47

MUCH AS I WANT TO GET to what was in fact waiting for us back at the rectory, I must include our visit to the San Fernando Mission first because something significant happened there. We were in the gift shop. Visitors had to go through there to get access to the church and grounds. I wasn't entirely sure why Father wanted to be there in the first place. I mean, yes, he had mentioned it the previous morning in connection with the lost-and-found relics of St. Candidus—

"I refreshed my memory," Father had said, *"while I was in the public library yesterday. As it turned out, the authentication papers were thrown out with old baptismal records, and the reliquary stood in the sacristy, its significance completely forgotten for years. Then, in 1991, the truth came to light—I'm not clear just how—and the statue was moved to Serra Chapel at the San Fernando Mission. If we get the chance we'll drop by and pray to Saint Candidus for help in our current campaign."*

"Okay, so that explains our altar stone," I had responded. *"Are you saying there's a connection between Saint Candidus and our grotto?"*

"Not directly. A precedent, perhaps. Many such relics and holy objects, once famous and widely venerated, have been misplaced, lost and ignored over time."

—but with all else that was going on, why this diversion? While Father was certainly capable of making detours in order to pray—our side trip to the Monastery of the Archangels two days before being an example—and though the San Fernando Mission was only a few freeway miles deviation from our direct route home (maybe twenty minutes as the crow drives), somehow I had the feeling that something specific and immediate was playing on his mind.

```
GARDENING TIPS: For those who aren't familiar with
the layout of the mythical City of Angels (con-
sider: how can one be acquainted with a fictitious
place?) the San Fernando Mission is located
twenty-three miles northwest of downtown Los Ange-
les. Like all the original missions, it was built
so as to be seen from a long distance by travel-
ers. These days it overlooks the San Fernando
Valley -- Angelenos with their penchant for impre-
cision just call it "The Valley" -- which in mod-
ern times has become the pornography production
capital of the world. How sad the souls of the
good padres must be, looking down from Heaven (we
hope), watching the tide of swill rising around
what is left of their once-majestic mission.
                                        --M.F.
```

There were two young gals manning the counter and cash register in the gift shop, and the way the place was cordoned off, going through the shop was the only way to gain access to the mission grounds. They might have been sisters. Their Mexican heritage was evident in their black hair, dark eyes, the style of their clothes, and golden brown skin. They certainly had their "looks" down pat. A chunky lady in a metallic brown dress with feathers around the collar was complaining indignantly to one of them:

"What do you mean I have to pay five dollars to enter the church? I'm not a tourist. I'm driving from Bakersfield to San Diego because my sister is undergoing emergency surgery—I can't believe I have to explain all this to you—and I saw the sign on the freeway and thought I'd stop here to say a prayer for her. And you're telling me I have to pay just to go into the church to talk to God?"

The gal behind the counter responded with a lizard-lidded gaze that clearly conveyed, "My mind is a featureless, vacuous void. You don't seriously think your problem is somehow going to become mine, do you?"

Concurrently, Father Baptist was addressing the other woman in a soothing, deep voice. He was doing his affectation of Bing Crosby in *Going My Way* so effectively I thought he was going to break into a song. "I hope you can help me," he said gently. "I'm interested in the relics of St. Candidus. I understand they are preserved in a statue of a Roman soldier. Could you please tell me where it is?"

The gal he was talking to blinked. White frost fell like disturbed snow from her eyelashes. "You actually expect me to know something about this boring place?" her expression said. "Look, Pal, buy something, go on the self-guided tour, or better yet: go away. The sooner I don't have to look at you, the sooner I can withdraw back into my self-absorbed gelatinous inner world. And by the way, who the heck is Bing Crosby? No, scratch that. I don't want to know. My brain is empty, which is as full as it gets."

The talents for which these young ladies were hired were not limited to radiantly uninterested looks. As if on cue, they shrugged a full half centimeter and uttered together the standard anthem of Latino apathy in the presence of irksome gringos: "No lo sé."

Millie was over in the book section, glowering at the titles on the spines and making occasional harrumphing sounds.

Meanwhile, I busied myself with the examination of various objects for sale. I've never really liked effeminate depictions of Angels, especially the Archangels. Somehow St. Michael as a woman doesn't cut it for me, but there "she" was, all porcelain and pastels, slapping that wicked old Serpent silly. Somehow, in the artist's cosmology, Lucifer remained defeated and male, in a gloppy, ceramic sort of way. St. Uriel standing guard at the Gate of Eden with a flaming sword looked more like a frizzy-haired housewife brandishing a curling iron. Oh well. There was also a plethora of crucifixes—I won't bother to capitalize the word here because I don't consider wooden crosses worthy of the designation if the Corpus of Jesus Christ is waving, smiling, empowering, drawing energy from the earth, or doing anything other than hanging devastated and expired. They did have an impressive assortment of Rosaries, but next to them were even more impressive medallions depicting the signs of the Zodiac.

As Millie turned her ire to the rack of touristy postcards—she was probably wondering why happy-happy pictures of Disneyland, Forest Lawn Memorial Park, and the Santa Anita Racetrack were mingled with unappealing views of this mission and its grounds—a weathered wooden sign nailed to the wall caught my attention:

MISSION SAN FERNANDO REY DE ESPAÑA
FOUNDED ON SEPTEMBER 8, 1797
BY FATHER FERMIN DE LASUEN,
NAMED FOR ST. FERDINAND,
KING OF SPAIN (1217 - 1252)

I wondered just how many mission steeples the industrious padre had notched on the spine of his Breviary. I couldn't help smiling at the thought of the likelihood that a leader of a modern nation would ever be canonized. In that connection, I was just about to open my mouth to say something insightful, penetrating, and, the truth be told, downright hilarious, when suddenly—

"Father Bapteesta?" said a reedy voice. It came trailing behind a fingery hand. Yes, that could be said about most hands, but this hand had an excess of them—excess not of number, but of length. I can't speak for the metacarpals, but the distal, middle, and proximal phalanx segments were noticeably elongated—

GARDENING TIPS: Interested readers can find those
terms in an anatomy text (just as I did) under
"Bones of the Hand." Uninterested readers can
guess from context, or will more likely skip them
altogether.

                                            --M.F.

—while the knuckles seemed bulbous by comparison, and the connecting joists between them, sheathed as they were in tight, pale skin, were topped with shocks of wiry black hair. One finger sported an ostentatious amethyst gem mounted on a glistening platinum ring. I couldn't imagine how it had gotten past the globular knuckles. The nails were impeccably manicured and the way the articulated digits flexed, I'm tempted to describe the movement as "spider-like," but I hesitate to give them a repulsive association. Still, just as I've sometimes set aside my innate revulsion of arachnids in order to marvel at the hypnotic grace of one of them spinning its geometric intricacy of a web in the glare of morning sunlight, so too was I momentarily fascinated by the complexity of delicate movements in this deceptively simple gesture. The wrist, incidentally, disappeared into the sleeve of an immaculate black cassock. There was a purple sash with gold trim around the wearer's waist, and a matching biretta on his dolichocephalic head.

"Ah, My Lord," said Father, turning. Right there in the gift shop, he sank to one knee and reverently osculated the amethyst. "Imagine meeting you here."

"Where else?" asked the owner of the hand. "Knott's Berry Farm?"

"That is the prevailing theory," said Father.

"Upon my head, it is strange indeed."

"My Lord?"

"The prevailing theory."

"So I thought, My Lord."

"Who do you think would spread such a strange untruth?"

"I cannot say, My Lord," said Father, rising.

At the sight of Father's grand obeisance the mouths of several customers fell open, then shut with tinny clicks. The gals behind the counter countered with a rehearsed stare that said, "Small-bead Rosaries are ten dollars, the large-beads are twenty, and anything outside of that is beyond our closely-guarded, rigidly-maintained cognitive limit." A couple of children over by the magnetic figurine display giggled and pointed. Millie was too involved in scowling at the prices of the coffee mugs to notice.

The gardener looked on nonchalantly. Having associated with Father Baptist for so long, he had come to anticipate the unexpected. Or so he kept telling himself.

"Martin, Millie," said Father, signaling us to approach. "Come meet the papal nuncio."

When Millie saw the purple biretta and sash, she came hustling and bustling. Me, I did my usual limping and lurching routine. I wasn't sure who seemed more out of place at that moment, Millie and me, or the rack of glow-in-the-dark characters from the latest blockbuster animated movie we almost knocked over as we approached.

"My Lord," said Father with dignified aplomb, "permit me to introduce Millie, my indispensable housekeeper, and Martin Feeney, my—"

Father's explanation of my existence was drowned out by Millie's windy sighing and exaggerated curtseying as she gave the bishop's ring a noisy, prolonged, salivary suction treatment he would not soon forget.

"His Lordship, Sylvio Bonsignore," said Father, his face serious except for the telltale tick in the corner of his mouth. Millie really was overdoing it, and stridently so.

"I am honored," said I when Millie was finally done with her labial vacuuming. As she backed away, wiping her lips with the back of her hand, I bowed stiffly because that is the only way that I can. Figuring the bishop's ring was already as wet as could be, I brought my lips to within an inch of the thing and made a faint, inarticulate pecking sound. As I straightened, I could tell by the look in his eyes that he understood my subterfuge and didn't mind.

"Meester Finny," he said, folding his arms so as to surreptitiously wipe the ring in his armpit. "I understand dat you are, ah, Father Bapteesta's biographer."

"Hardly, Your Lordship. I would say I'm his fictionalizer."

Those overhanging shrubberies that served as his eyebrows shimmied up his forehead, brushed the golden fringe of his elegant biretta, and settled back down on the balustrade of his nose. His expressive shift of facial muscles was no doubt matched by a similar though less lofty contortion of the device that serves as my face. How did the papal nuncio, of all people, know I was a writer? Was there any possible connection between Some Guy and him? Implausible, far-fetched, too much of a stretch. Ah, but Some Guy did overhear Roderick Roundhead talking to his aunt, and a link between Roundhead and Longhead was not only conceivable but more than likely.

GARDENING TIPS: For those readers who didn't look
up "distal, middle, and proximal phalanx segments," "dolichocephalic" means "long-headed."

--M.F.

N.B.: Lest my future public mistakenly imagine I
was in a good mood on the day, some weeks later,
when I wrote this chapter--(Me? Looking up words
for lazy readers? What am I, in love or something?)--allow me to explain:
     The day before I typed these very words, I drove
Father Baptist to St. Basil's Maronite Catholic
Church to visit his confessor, Father Stephen Nicanor. When Father emerged from the confessional
I figured what the hey, Grace is Grace, and went
in myself. Father Nicanor knows me too well.
He's heard me fume about priests who have given me

```
"Go do something nice for someone" as a penance.
I hate that.  Give me a Rosary to say, on my knees
if it flips your sacerdotal pancake, but not some-
thing vague and open-ended to carry out if and
when an opportunity presents itself.  He is also
aware that I am Charity- and Humility-challenged,
so he gave me a penance that addresses both short-
falls.  Hence this gardening tip typed with teeth
clenched and lips stretched into a tortured smile.
"Go do something nice for someone" indeed!
```

Still, I was taken aback. I glanced at Father to see if he had reacted to this information, but being a former cop who had more than once stared down the barrel of a gun in the hand of a violent perpetrator, he didn't even blink.

"Your feection then," conceded the nuncio. "It is still based onna fact, yes?"

"Once facts are fictionalized, Your Lordship, they are no longer facts."

"An excellent point, my Son. Perhaps we can, ah, discuss dees further. But right now I must, ah, speak with da coppa-turnda-priesta-turnda-coppa."

"That wasn't mine," said I, index finger raised pedagogically. "That moniker was coined by Jacco Babs of the *Times*."

"Si, si, I know."

Wella, wella, wella, thought I as he aimed his finger-abundant hand at the automatons behind the counter, fluttered his digits like a paper fan, and led us through the door to the grounds beyond without further ado or exchange of cash. He was the nuncio, after all. I doubted that the "look at my look" gals had a clue what that meant. They probably just didn't know what to do to stop us and certainly didn't care enough to try anyway.

I was pleased to see the chunky lady in a metallic brown dress with the feathers and sick sister slip through the door with us. She made a beeline for the church, huffing and clucking all the way.

"So, Father Bapteesta," said the nuncio as he and Father Baptist took the lead as we strolled through the garden.

"Yes, My Lord," said Father, as Millie and I straggled behind.

"Were you, ah, expecting to find me here? Your skeels as a detective, though celebrated, are perhaps, ah, underrated."

"As in politics, My Lord, it isn't what one knows, it is who."

"Is it possible? Could it be dat you know somebody who knows, ah, my itinerary?"

Father shrugged. "I cannot say."

"Strange. Nor can you say where is your head, I mean, ah, your cardinal, I suppose?"

Father indicated himself with a twist of his hand. "Me, Your Lordship? How would I know the whereabouts of Cardinal Fulbright?"

"Da same way you knew I was coming here thissa morning."

"When the prevailing perception is that you prefer amusement parks."

"Perception may trump who you know, my Son." We were just passing a charming bowl-within-bowl stucco fountain when His Lordship said something almost but not quite under his breath: *"Non e curioso che hanno nominato la missione dopo uno santo non famoso?"*

```
GARDENING TIPS: Father surprised me some time
later when he repeated the nuncio's sentence back
to me, phoneme by phoneme.  I hope it's right.  He
doesn't speak Italian.  Repeating strings of for-
eign syllables after a single hearing without com-
prehension was a talent he developed when he was a
beat cop downtown.  He said the knack proved use-
ful in several criminal cases.

                                        --M.F.
```

"Excuse me, Your Lordship?" asked Father.

"I was thinking aloud, a tendency whicha comes from age. I sometimes amuse myself with da study of names. Take dees beautiful mission, so poorly made, so durable nonetheless. It was dedicated to da sainted thirteenth-century kinga of Spain."

"That seems most fitting, My Lord."

"Yet three days journey onna horseback to the southeast stands Mission San Juan Capistrano. A strange choice of patron, don't you think?"

"I confess I'm deficient in my knowledge of that particular Saint. In what way was he an odd choice?"

"Why, he was Italian," said the nuncio, pressing his enfolded hands to his sternum. "Not dat I object, mind you, but for Franciscans from Spain, I find it, ah, curious. I find it strange, very strange. My head, it almost aches. To think dat on every Feast of Saint Joseph da celebrated California swallows descend upon a mission built by Spaniards and named after an obscure Italian Saint."

"I am tempted to look into it, My Lord, now that you bring it to my attention."

"Yes, you should keep it in your head—I mean, in your mind."

I so wanted to mention that Saint Francis, the founder of the Franciscan Order, was himself Italian, but I got the distinct impression that more was going on in this conversation between Father Baptist and Bishop Bonsignore than the words I was hearing. It was almost as if they were sparring, yet without conflict. Gentlemen friends fencing—*en garde, touché,* and all that. I looked to see how Millie was reacting to it all, but she seemed to be mouthing something silently to herself. I got the impression she was rehearsing something she desperately wanted to say.

"An old saying comes to mind," said Bishop Bonsignore. "I believe it applies to your problem: *È una cosa strana quando il cuore regola le teste.*"

"My Lord?" asked Father Baptist.

"È una cosa strana quando il cuore regola le teste," repeated the nuncio. "'It is a strange thing when da heart rules da head.' It loses something when translated into English, I'm afraid. And what of your cardinal's assistant?

"I beg your pardon?" asked Father.

"Da monsignore, da consultant Aspic."

"My Lord?"

"He has vanished, no?" The nuncio shrugged. "It was on da news. Strangely, he is harder to find thanna Cardinal Fulbright."

"If I see him, I'll tell him you asked about him."

"Yes, if and when you find him, I'ma sure you will."

We arrived at a wooden gate that apparently led back to the parking lot.

"Dis has been brief," said the bishop, "but informative."

"Indeed," agreed Father.

Brief, yes, thought the gardener. Informative, *huh?*

"Bishop Bonsignore," said Millie, curtseying deeply. "Begging your pardon, Your Worship, but before you leave us, there's something I'd like to ask you."

"But of course, my good woman," said he.

"Do you have His Holiness's ear?"

"Excuse me, Madam?"

"The Pope. You're his ambassador, right? So you talk to him, don't you?"

His Lordship, Sylvio Bonsignore, paused to pick his words ever so carefully. "Through channels, mostly. Da Holy Father, he is, ah, very busy. Da demands on him, dey are unbelievable."

Her Fryingpanship, Millie, who had apparently been considering her words for some minutes, forged right on ahead. "Forgive a mere housekeeper for not knowing what's proper, but I wonder if the next time you do talk to His Holiness directly—it could be on the phone, you know, it doesn't have to be in person—but could you ask him something? For me? I'm not asking you to get back to me with what he says. Heavens, you'll probably never see the likes of me again. But just to ask him, one faithful Catholic to another."

"For a good daughter of da Church," said the bishop bureaucratically, "of course I will do what I canna when I canna. What is your, ah, question?"

"To the Holy Father, whom we pray for every day." Millie paused to run the words behind the back of her forehead one more time. Nodding her approval of the grammar, she gave utterance: "When we—'we' meaning the people of Los Angeles—needed an archbishop, the Vicar of Christ gave us Morley Fulbright; and when Archbishop Fulbright proved himself to be a nincompoop, and a dangerous one at that, the Supreme Pontiff promoted him to cardinal. So I ask you, 'What kind of a father would hand his son a stone when he asked him for some bread? Or a serpent when he asked for a fish? Or a scorpion when asked for an egg?'"

She was paraphrasing—effectively, I would say—the eleventh chapter of Saint Luke's Gospel, verses eleven and twelve. Rarely have I been more proud of our Millie. The truth be told, except for a few points of syntax, what she asked was exactly what I would have asked if I had thought to ask it.

> GARDENING TIPS: While it was actually the current
> Holy Father's predecessor who made our beloved
> Morley Fulbright an archbishop and then raised him
> to the College of Cardinals, the current Vicar of
> Christ had publicly announced his intention of
> continuing the policies of his precursor. Millie
> had chosen her words well. I was proud of her,
> albeit silently.
>
> —M.F.

Something reminiscent of an electrical arc from a Frankenstein movie not starring Boris Karloff flickered across the blackness of Sylvio Bonsignore's gaping pupils. It was the reflection of the bolt of lightning writhing across dear Millie's tempestuous eyes. This went on for several long seconds.

"I will see what I canna do," he said at last. I had expected anger or indignation, but should have known better. Sylvio Bonsignore was a lifelong diplomat. He could stare down a nuclear blast. Heck, he could stare down Cardinal Fulbright and send him fleeing all the way to Lompoc. He smiled, not convincingly, but appropriately. "Good day, Madam. Father Bapteesta. Meester Finny."

A moment later, after a swish of sash, a wave of amethyst, and the creak of the old wooden gate, we found ourselves debouched into the parking lot.

Father looked at Millie.

I looked at Millie.

It was a group hug moment, but Father and I decided to keep our teeth intact instead.

"So what was all that about?" asked the gardener, indicating the closed gate.

"Shall we go home?" asked Father, pointing to the car.

"To a kitchen full of clean dishes!" beamed Millie, who seldom beamed. "I can't wait—oh, yes I can. I need to stop at the bakery."

"The bakery?" I asked.

"You two have your little detours, I have mine," said she.

"Well, hey," said the gardener, "when you put it that way."

"Speaking of detours," said Father, "if you see photocopy shop, or even a big drugstore, I want to stop and make some copies of Ravenshorst's drawing of the artifact."

"Wasn't he not supposed to photograph it?" I asked.

"Correct," said he, "which is why he drew it; and nobody said I couldn't photocopy his rendering."

"What, may I ask," I asked, "do you need them for?"

"I don't know yet, but best to be prepared. In the immediate, I think I'd rather be carrying around copies on my person than Ravenshorst's originals."

"Just so long as I get to the bakery," said Millie.

"Will do," said I. "I think I can accommodate everyone's detours."

48

"YOU CALL THIS FRESH?" said Millie through gritted teeth, waving a loaf of extra-extra sourdough bread in a plastic bag in the face of the lady behind the glass counter.

"Is the clip on it yellow, Madam?" asked the lady, whose chiseled features and genteel mannerisms suggested ancestors who lived in mansions in Vermont.

Millie turned the loaf this way, then that, then peered at the clip that held the bag together. "It is."

"Then the answer is yes, Madam," said the lady, subtly pointing to a sign above the cash register.

<pre>
Monday: Blue
Tuesday: Green
Wednesday: —
Thursday: Red
Friday: White
Saturday: Yellow
Sunday: —
</pre>

I knew the lady as Mrs. Ampersand, and the situation was strange because it had always been yours truly who had come to this bakery at Millie's behest. It never would have occurred to me, invariably overcome on those missions by the malty sweet aroma of freshly baked carbohydrates, to question the freshness of anything in the establishment. But Millie, well, she was an oven-outcome scrutinizer in a class by herself.

"It doesn't feel fresh," insisted Millie, squeezing the poor thing like a cantaloupe.

"Extra-extra sourdough has a thick crust," answered Mrs. Ampersand, with a look that seemed to add, "Just like you."

"Pumpernickel," I mumbled without realizing it.

"What's that, Martin?" asked Father.

He and I were keeping out of trouble over by the cookie counter while Millie was enjoying herself in the bread section. Mr. Ampersand had just removed a slab of cookies from the oven—Danish sugar cookies, no less, still emitting wisps of buttery steam.

"What's what, Father?" I asked.

"Whatever you just said," said Father.

"Oh, I was just thinking about our visit to the Doily Sisters."

"Not that again."

"Yes, that again."

Something about Millie's exchange with Mrs. Ampersand had triggered something in the unpredictable contraption I playfully call my brain.

"Pumpernickel," Keating had said as he unwrapped the cellophane bag from around a loaf of hard, dark bread. *"Madam Mehitabelle's favorite. I bought it for her just the other day. Evening, actually, come to think of it."*

"Fresh?" I had asked.

"Of course, fresh. It would mean my head if I bought it even a day old."

Unpredictable, my brain. Did I mention flighty? Given to fanciful detours into uncharted frontiers. Still, I had the feeling that there was something significant it was trying to tell me. I just couldn't put my finger on it.

"Pumpernickel," I must have said again, because Father responded with:

"Are you suggesting that it was the pumpernickel Keating served you that made you ill and not the tea?"

"No," said I. "That would mean that Mrs. Ampersand was in on the conspiracy, and that's overreaching. Besides, I didn't eat any."

"So what are you saying?"

Having to account for the words coming out of my mouth—now there was a concept! Since I wasn't sure what was bothering me, I wasn't prepared to commit to anything more than, "I don't know."

"Well, you did say 'pumpernickel.'"

"I also said the ghost of a freewheeling Californio told me where to find the original site of Mission La Purisima."

"Which proved to be right."

"So did the flyer Millie found impaled on a cactus."

"How about your egg-sesame bread?" asked Millie of Mrs. Ampersand.

"Our specialty," answered the proprietrix.

"How fresh is it?"

Mrs. Ampersand sighed. "As fresh as everything else with today's clip on it. Anything that was baked yesterday has a white clip on it. We don't keep anything after that."

"You don't? What do you do with it?"

Mrs. Ampersand blew a strand of tangled gray hair away from her face. "What we don't sell to the local supermarkets, we give to the homeless shelter two blocks down."

"Oh," said Millie, conceding the point with a nod of approval. "Alright then. I'll take this loaf of extra-extra, and an egg-sesame."

"Very good, Ma'am," said Mrs. Ampersand.

"What are you waiting for?" asked Millie as she brushed past Father and me on her way to the door.

"Nothing, nothing," said the gardener.

49

OKAY, WE'RE FINALLY BACK HOME. Having parked in the rear lot next to Monsignor Havermeyer's RV, and having strolled past my room and our own private cemetery at the same time—they faced each other, and me a necropoliphobiac!—Father, Millie and I were approaching the kitchen on the mossy brick path between the rectory and the church.

"I can't wait," slavered Millie. She'd been humming and muttering all the way from the photocopy shop. "Imagine, all those dishes clean, and me away while they got that way. I know what Great-Aunt Carmella would say." She actually twirled her finger in the air like a lariat. "'Yippeeeee!'"

It think it was I who slowed first, but that's because I'm slow to begin with.

Then Father paused in his stride.

I thought it odd that the shades on the kitchen window were halfway down. It was peculiar because, to the best of my recollection, the window was equipped with curtains, but no shades. Stranger still, the upper half of the window was bright, while the bottom half was dark. Not blackly dark, but rather gray, and kind of hazy besides.

In her cowgirl enthusiasm, Millie didn't notice. She went stampeding obliviously ahead to the door.

"Millie—" cautioned Father.

"Wait—!" warned the gardener.

"Ta-dah!" cheered Millie as she grasped the knob and pulled. "Ready or not, clean dishes, here I—"

I'll never forget the sight of her startled shape against the open doorway, her hat with the two pears and three strawberries slightly askew, her shapeless purse still swinging from the crook of her elbow. From about eye-level up, everything was perfectly normal. The ceiling looked pretty much as it always had, badly stained and buckled in places. From eye-level down, there was a wall of whiteness. It had a soft buoyancy about it, and seemed to undulate slowly with a life of its own. Timing is everything, and as if on command, just as she finished her sentence—

"—come!"

—it poured in slow motion through the doorway, engulfing her in mounds of airy, cheerful bubbles.

There are moments in life when words truly fail. This was one of them. Father and I both opened our mouths to say something, but nothing, absolutely nothing germane presented itself for articulation.

We tried again but the realization repeated. What was there to do but silently wait to see just what Millie would do?

GARDENING TIPS: Though Father Baptist, in his previous life, had enjoyed the "happy misery of marriage"--that's what Dad used to call it, and he
loved Mom to distraction--as a homicide detective
I doubt Jack Lombard logged in much time in the
kitchen. From what I have gathered from the bits
and pieces he's revealed about that bygone phase
of his life, he and Christine had shared some old-
fashioned notions about the roles of men and
women.   Imagine that.
   Me, I'm a permanent bachelor in the indelible
sense. As a child with a marked tendency to shat-
ter things, even those marked "unbreakable," my
hours of helping in the kitchen were few and far
between indeed.   Mom used to say I was too smart
for my own good, whatever that had to do with it.
So I admit to being chore-challenged, a stranger
to the kitchen, too.
   Being men with functioning eyeballs, Father and
I perceived that the rectory kitchen was now
packed with suds. Our manly brains, however, did
not contain sufficient kitchen savvy to speculate
as to their cause. Given time to collect data,
surely the great priest detective, with the help
of his limping assistant, would surely have figured it all out, but time was the one thing we did
not have at that juncture.
   Oh, the joys of parish life!

                                                --M.F.

What Millie finally did surprised us both. Without a word, or even the slightest hint that something was wrong, she calmly and purpose-fully stepped through the doorway and disappeared.

"Father," said I in a startled whisper. "What do you—?"

I fell silent because I suddenly realized I was alone. Glancing around, I caught the shape of Father Baptist heading swiftly down the brick path toward the front of the rectory. Figuring he possessed the lion's share of brain matter between us, I grasped my cane with renewed determina-tion and followed. Anything was better than hanging around the kitchen door as it continued to sluggishly disgorge its sparkling river of airy cleanliness. Stiff as I was from all those hours of driving, I didn't catch up with him until he was through the front door, in his study, at his desk, and on the phone. As I came lumbering down the hallway I could see a wall of suds blocking the far end, the kitchen end. Fortunately the slow white wave hadn't yet reached the door of his study.

"I realize it's almost lunchtime," he was saying sternly as I entered, "but we've got an emergency over here."

As I made a "Who?" sign, a gritty little voice came yapping out of the receiver, wagging the coiled cord like a tail.

"Listen, Ernie," said Father, answering me without disrupting his train of thought, "this isn't my field of expertise. When we left early this morning she set it on automatic or whatever and when we came back just now—"

More yapping, more wagging.

"I tell you the kitchen is chin-deep in suds," said Father sternly, but with a twinkle in his eyes. "I don't know how or why."

Yap-yap-yap-yap-yap barked the King of Hotdogs.

"You bet I hold you responsible—"

Owoooooooooo!

"—and so will Millie."

Silence, then some pathetic canine whining, sniveling, and even some pawing and scratching.

"No, Martin and I have something important to attend to. I'll leave it to you and Some Guy to take care of things before I return, otherwise—"

There came a prolonged yowl followed by a decisive click. The coiled cord went limp.

"Excuse me, Father," said I as he cradled the receiver. "So much has been going on. What is the important thing we're attending to?"

"Didn't you see Roberto's truck parked out front?"

"No. I'll take your word for it. He's here to check the floor in the church, right?"

"I feel a pressing need to tend to that." His face was dead serious, except for his upturned lips. I think if I tried to make a face like that, I'd herniate something. "I'm happy to report that Ernie Corben and Some Guy are on their way."

I heaved my shoulders. It felt good, as well as conveyed my discomfiture. "And Millie?"

"I haven't heard a sound from the kitchen since Millie went in there."

"Spooky, huh?"

He shook his head. His expression remained serious as he pressed his fingers to his mouth, and then stifled a laugh behind them.

"What's so funny?" I asked.

Slowly, his fingers roved up to his eyes and stretched the skin of his cheeks back toward his ears, wiping away a bit of wetness—not tears of sorrow or joy, but of weariness.

It was a strain, but I tried to look serious as I said, "Or should I say 'hilarious'?"

"Martin," he said, shaking his head. "Perhaps you should check on Millie, just to make sure she hasn't fainted or suffocated." He clenched his jaw against the urge to chuckle. "Hilarious is right. I think it's just about the funniest thing imaginable, and yet my heart goes out to her. She's wanted this contraption for so long, and look what happens the first time she runs it when she finally gets it. A predictable woman she certainly is not. I can't imagine how she's going to deal with all this."

"Underneath all the wrath and clamor," said I, "she's a good soul, generous, and gratifyingly loyal. However she expresses her initial reaction, whether by punching into the kitchen walls with her bare hands and tying the pipes into knots, or by crushing your and my heads together—"

"Did I mention your predilection for hyperbole?"

"—in the end she'll not only come through intact, dragging us staggering behind, but the moment will come—maybe sooner, maybe later—the moment will come when she'll laugh about it. You'll see. As dear old Dad would say, 'She's one crusty broad, and a dem fine woman.'"

"Precisely, Martin, and that's why I don't want to infuriate her at this embarrassing moment. So please, use your cane to poke your way into the kitchen and make sure she's all right."

"Me? Oh, right, you don't want to infuriate her. Leave that to me."

"Assure her that she is loved, and that help is on the way."

"Right, sure. You can do me the same favor by summoning an ambulance straight away."

"You're hyperbolizing."

"I'll remind you of that when you see my head come rolling down the hallway. All right, all right. Assuming she's okay until 'that nice Mr. Corben' comes to salvage the situation, will I find you in the church?"

"There, or 'Peanuts.'"

"'Peanuts'?"

"Somehow I don't think lunch is big on Millie's mind at the moment."

"Probably not."

"I'll admit that it's starting to make inroads into mine."

"Okeydokey," said I, turning to leave. "See you shortly."

50

"THEY'RE OVER THERE," SAID GLORIA, the Hungarian waitress with mysterious eyes and bumper-car hips. Platters of food wobbled precariously in both of her hands, so she used her chin as a pointer. She winked, smacked her gum loudly and added, "Beebay."

Gloria called all her regular customers by one of four monikers: Toots (rhymes with "boots"), Snookums, Dingspring, or Beebay. These nicknames crossed gender lines, and once you were branded it was for life. I've yet to figure out what attributes merit which designation. Father and Theodora Turpin had long ago received the "Toots" appellation. Mrs. Turpin's husband, Tanner, and Clara Estelle Pounder shared the dubious honor of "Snookums." Curiously, Wanda Hemmingway, Danielle Parks, and the Tumblars were all "Dingspring," except for Pierre who earned the derivative "Dingdingspring." I'm the only one I've heard her call "Beebay," but I try not to make too much of it. I'm not sure I want to know what woman out there shares my beebayhood anyway.

The indicated table was a rounded triangle in the back corner near the fireplace in which fake cement logs were perpetually not consumed by gas flames. I could see Roberto at one end, and Monsignor Havermeyer at the other, but all in between were blocked by the familiar, gargantuan back of Mr. Gnocchi, the proprietor. He wasn't as big as Some Guy, who took all awards for sheer humongousness, but he was certainly intimidating in his own right.

"I mean it, Father," he was saying, or rather booming, as I approached. "I think everyone at Saint Paschal Baylon's is stark, raving mad, and Father Fargo is their maharishi. Why, last Maundy Thursday—you know that ceremony where the priest washes the feet of twelve laymen?"

"Of course," said Father's voice. I wasn't yet in a position where I could see him.

"It's pretty straight forward as ceremonies go," said Monsignor Havermeyer. "I don't see how it could be subject to much in the way of abuse."

"In the all-inclusive Nervous Ordeal," said a voice I recognized as Joel's, "at least seven of the washees would have to be women." He was a former seminarian, don't forget. He knew the modernist drill.

"Hah!" The back of Mr. Gnocchi's tailored jacket stretched to its elastic limit and contracted suddenly as he blurted that out. "I'll tell you about all-inclusive. Father Fargo made the lady lector do the washing in his place. Then he directed the twelve to wash another twelve, and they in turn another dozen. Would you believe by the time he was done everybody in the church that night—and I do mean everybody without a brain in their head, which was just about everybody—everyone was washing everyone else's feet! It became a freaking foot-washing orgy!"

A wave of chuckles went around the table as I lurched around Mr. Gnocchi and waved my cane in greeting to everyone. Seated on a bench seat around the far two sides of the table were, from left to right, Roberto Guadalupe, Spade, Duggo, Father Baptist, Joel Maruppa, Josef Maruppa, and Monsignor Havemeyer. Anticipating my arrival, they had arranged for a free-floating chair to be placed facing them from the near side. Sure, I'd have to eat around the elaborate assortment of shakers, cruets, squeeze bottles, and relish trays that had been shoved to that part of the table, but what the hey. I wasn't able to pull out the chair in order to seat myself just yet because the south slope of Mount Gnocchi was in the way, so I contented myself by standing and pretending not to be famished.

"Mr. Gnocchi," said I to the proprietor, glancing down and up and down at the chair by way of a hint, which he ignored, "you know where to go to avoid all that idiocy."

Tony Gnocchi, whose dad opened "Peanuts" the same year Pope John XXIII convened the Second Vatican Council—and with similar optimistic fanfare—gave me the same look he always gave me when I said that to him: incredulity. Mr. Gnocchi, who actually *was* nicknamed "Mount Gnocchi" by several occasional customers in black shirts with white ties who shared some of his facial characteristics, was rumored to be related to someone in the Mafia. A Roman Catholic from a grandfatherly line of Roman Catholics, he had yet to grace our little church across the street with his presence since Father Baptist took over. He had misgivings about us, and considering that many of our most outspoken parishioners invaded his banquet room every Sunday after Mass to engorge and bicker—Traditionalist pastimes: chomping and stomping—his suspicion was understandable. Instead, he braved the incessant horrors wrought by the liturgy committee at his own parish by relating them to Father Baptist and Monsignor Havermeyer every time they dined here. It had become a ritual that was, in liturgical committee terms, a local tradition. Equally traditional was the retort I had just delivered above. I'll repeat it here for effect: "Mr. Gnocchi, you know where to go to avoid all that idiocy."

"You're a fine one to speak of idiocy," replied he, breaking protocol by saying something entirely unexpected. His usual reply, you see, was, "There is idiocy, and there is idiocy."

I blinked and blinked again, a rare moment when my mouth disengaged from the yak center deep in my cerebral vortex. It was that look of amused revulsion he gave me that not only reconnected my speech circuits, but reminded me that my clothes were damp up to my armpits, and that clusters of soapsuds still huddled in various nooks and crannies all over me. The crackle in my right ear as I turned my head disclosed a sizable bubble colony perched on my shoulder.

"I—ahem—I can explain this," said I, my voice kicking in with an upward scoop like an electric drill after a power dip.

"No doubt," said Mr. Gnocchi doubtfully.

"No, really. Father, help me here. You told me to make sure Millie was all right, to assure her that she is loved and that help was on the way."

"¿Qué él está hablando? What's he talking about? Loved, hah? Yah? Yah! Hey, pass the salsa, would you? What kind of help?" said voices variously around the table. All but Roberto, who seemed to be absorbed in something he was writing on a piece of college-ruled paper.

"You had trouble with the washing machine?" asked Spade, pointing at me with a heaping, steaming spoonful of menudo. Some say that "Peanuts" menudo rivals "Panchitos" in the shadow of the San Gabriel Mission. I wouldn't know, because the thought of cow stomach on a spoon doesn't appeal to me, but obviously did to Spade. It occurred to me just then that I didn't know if Spade was his first, last, or nickname. Same with Duggo. Now was not the time to ask.

"You have a knack for understatement," said Monsignor Havermeyer to Spade. "Why do you think I'm here?"

"For breakfast and now for lunch," said Mr. Gnocchi. "Not that I'm complaining, you understand."

"Dishwashing machine," I clarified, airing the flaps of my jacket. "Millie just got a new one."

"Yes," said Monsignor Havermeyer. "I met the monster this morning when I went into the kitchen after Mass. I almost sprained an ankle on that tangle of hoses. It was rumbling something horrible."

"The dishwasher?" asked Joel.

"Yes," said the monsignor, setting his fork down on his plate. "Millie left a note on the refrigerator explaining that I was on my own meal-wise, but I almost didn't see it. I was busy backing out of the kitchen for fear of that thing exploding."

"You're exaggerating, of course," said Mr. Gnocchi.

"Hardly," said Havermeyer. "I admit I'm clueless about these labor-saving devices. I haven't washed a dish by hand since my childhood, nor by machine since the seminary. For all I knew it had some new-fangled high-torque motor or extra powerful jet-action water scrubber inside—but boy, was it making an awful sound. Scary. Pots and pans on the shelves, cups and plates in the cupboard, all of it rattling away, like it was all threatening to come down."

"Then what happened?" asked Joel.

The monsignor shrugged. "I came over here for breakfast, of course. I kid you not: it got worse. The ground around the rectory was actually shaking as I passed the kitchen on my way back to my camper about forty-five minutes later. Ask Roberto. He came running out of the church wondering what the heck was going on."

"It is true," said Roberto, looking up from his literary effort. "We thought an earthquake, maybe. Then we saw the suds. They were pushed up against the window. It was an evil sight."

Duggo and Spade nodded their agreement as Roberto returned his attention to the pen in his hand.

"Why didn't you just go into the kitchen and turn the darn thing off?" asked Joel.

Everyone at the table looked at him for a long, long moment.

"Bonk! Bonk!" cackled old Josef, making to bash his own head in with a spoon. "Millie! Yah!"

"Oh, right," said Joel, shrinking.

Mr. Gnocchi started grumbling something to himself. I thought I caught the words "woman," "fear of," and "unbelievable," but I wasn't sure.

"I spent the rest of the morning studying in my camper," said Monsignor. "By the time I broke for lunch, the ground was no longer shaking."

"The wash cycle," said Duggo. "It was over by then."

"Bzzzzzzzzzt!" agreed Old Josef, a couple of crumbs dribbling through the gaps in his smile. He knew enough about laborsaving devices to imitate them. "Yah. Yah."

"As I passed the kitchen on my way here," said Havermeyer, "I saw the soapsuds through the window. It was eerie, I tell you—completely outside my experience. I suppose I should have tried to do something, but I couldn't think of what. It being Millie's new appliance, I certainly didn't want to make matters worse."

We all nodded our profound understanding, except Mr. Gnocchi who was grumbling more and more condescendingly.

"So you fellows felt it, too?" asked Father, indicating Roberto, Duggo, and Spade.

"Sí, sí," they replied, nodding and nudging.

"We got an early start this morning," said Spade. "Right after morning Mass."

"We decided to see to the stone floor first," said Roberto, not looking up from his work. "The funeral isn't until Monday, and the floor, it is sinking now. Don't worry, we'll get the grave dug, too."

"Grave?" asked Mr. Gnocchi, nostrils slightly flared. At least the grumbling stopped. "Did you say 'grave'?"

"St. Philomena's does have a cemetery," said I. "You'd know that if you ever dropped by."

"It's for a priest," explained Father Baptist. "At least, there is evidence that the deceased was a priest. They haven't yet established his identity, and it's doubtful they ever will."

"By 'they' I assume you mean the police," said Mr. Gnocchi.

"That's right," said Father as he poured cream into his coffee. "The ecclesiastical authorities aren't being helpful, either, I'm afraid."

"Wonder of wonders," said Havermeyer.

"Spade and I will get the body right after lunch, Father," said Duggo, rubbing his hands together.

"I want to know more about the floor in the grotto," said Father, "but first, Martin, I assume your being here means the crisis in the kitchen has passed."

"Permit me to explain for the benefit of those who tuned in late," said I. "Gentlemen, when Father, Millie, and I got back from our errand to Lompoc, Millie walked right up to the kitchen door, opened it, walked inside, and disappeared."

"Into the suds?" gasped Spade, crossing himself.

"She just went on in?" asked Duggo, aghast.

"And was gone," said I, nodding my head while flicking suds from my sleeves. "Absorbed, dissolved, vanished from the face of the earth. That's why Father assigned me the task of leading the one-man safari into the foam jungle to find her."

"You waded into that?" asked the monsignor, mouth and eyes wide.

"Well, I had my trusty cane," said I, "so I wasn't completely blind. I covered my nose and mouth with a handkerchief. It took me a while, but I found her in the breakfast nook, a soggy cigarette in her hand, staring blankly ahead."

"Did she say anything?" asked Joel.

"Something about at least the kitchen being clean," said I.

"What did you do?" asked Havermeyer.

"As instructed," said I, "I informed said comatose housekeeptrix that she was loved."

"What did she say?" asked at least three voices at once.

"Nothing. She didn't acknowledge my presence until I assured her that sweet Ernie Corben and cuddly Some Guy were coming just as soon as they could."

"You know Ernie Corben?" asked Mount Gnocchi, alarmed and suspicious. *"The* Ernie Corben?"

"Hotdogs and all," said I.

"From my homicide days," said Father.

"Who—?" asked Roberto.

"They're the men who gave Millie the dishwasher," said I.

"Why?" asked Duggo.

"It's a long, long story," said I, "which is another way of saying I really don't know."

"Did she say anything else?" asked Havermeyer.

"Just one thing as I was leaving." I tried to imitate Millie's glare as I quoted her: "Suds!"

"Really," said Mr. Gnocchi as chuckles sputtered around the table. He looked at me as though some profound point had been made, or perhaps as though I were mad. It was hard to tell. Apparently having had his fill, he smiled disingenuously and said, "Father, Monsignor, Gentlemen, if you will excuse me." He vanished amidst the ruckus and roar of the restaurant like King Kong in his island jungle habitat.

"Have a seat," said Father.

"With pleasure," said yours truly, finally pulling out my chair. In moments the condiments had been redistributed around the table to make room for serious eating on my part.

"What's your gumption, Beebay?" purred Gloria into my ear a moment later. She reached around and deposited a clean set of silverware rolled in a red cloth napkin in front of me.

"What's the blue plate special?"

"For you, anything."

"Anything it is," said I, unrolling my eatingware.

"Living dangerously, are we?"

I indicated my companions with a wave of my hand. "Always."

"Wo-ho," said Joel.

"Bzzzzzzzzzt!" agreed Josef. "Yah."

"One dangerously anything," said Gloria, bumping my chair with a mischievous roll of her hip, "coming right up."

That playful bump almost made me swallow my tongue.

51

"SO," SAID FATHER AS I FINISHED SAYING GRACE under my breath. "Does your appearance here mean that the providers of the dishwasher have come to the rescue?"

"Precisely," said I, hefting the peppermill to see if it was full of corns. My salivary glands were uncertain how to prepare for whatever was coming. I looked around to see what my associates had been devouring. Roberto's empty plate—I'd recognize the footprint of a "Peanuts' Enchilada Ranchera Platter" anywhere—was shoved aside to make room for the sheet of paper he was scribbling on. It took me a second to realize he was translating the Spanish verse Father had photocopied between the bakery and home, the verse that had been hand-copied by Bishop Ravenshorst from the back of the famous artifact. I'd almost forgotten about that, but Father obviously hadn't. At Roberto's elbow Spade was just scraping the bottom of his tureen of cow stomach soup. Duggo, on the other hand, had braved the "Tostada Puttanesca," which was a strange and unstable amalgam of Mexican and Italian concepts of deliciousness. I'd tried it once and survived. Frankly, I was surprised Duggo had ordered it, and I wondered if he'd ever admit it to his relatives. The crumbs on Father's plate were likely the residue of a sandwich, probably turkey—the purplish, reddish smudge on the edge of his knife suggested cranberry sauce rather than catsup. Joel was still lapping up his cauldron of chili, and his grandfather was playing with his wide, shallow bowl of red cabbage soup. Monsignor Havermeyer had given up on his stack of buckwheat pancakes, soggy with butter and maple syrup.

"So?" asked Father.

"So?" I replied.

He sighed. "So what was the diagnosis?"

"What diagnosis?"

He sighed again. "The dishwasher, the suds up to here."

"Oh, that. It came down to an assumption on the part of the party of the first part when said party gave directions to the party of the second part. Said second party, not being familiar with the processes involved, acted according to what was familiar to her, which proved to be disastrous. In our increasingly technological environment, it's all too common."

"Eh?" asked Spade and Duggo.

"Eh!" agreed Josef. "Party!"

"Mr. Corben's parting instruction to Millie," I explained, "was to fill the machine with dishes, throw in the soap, and turn it on. There was something in there about presetting a delay—amazing what these appliances can do—so the machine didn't start until after we were gone. Everything would be washed and dried by the time we got back from Lompoc."

"And?" pressed Father and Monsignor in unison.

"And," said I, "Millie followed instructions. What she didn't know—and what Messrs. Corben and Guy neglected to tell her—is that dishwashing machines use soap that is specially formulated to clean without suds. She, on the other hand, used the same dishwashing detergent she squirts into the sink from a squeeze bottle, stuff that brags about its 'powerful sudsing action' on the label."

"Whew!" said Roberto.

"Not sure how much to use," I continued, "and probably doubtful of the claims of Mr. Corben, sweet little honey bunch that he is"—I scrunched my lips as I said those last seven words—"well, she shot in a couple of extra-long squirts. Probably half a bottle's worth."

"No wonder," said Joel, shaking his head and chuckling.

"I take it your mother has a dishwashing machine," said Father to Joel.

"Of course," said Joel. "I thought everybody did."

"So did Ernie Corben and Some Guy," said Father. "But Millie didn't know, and Martin and I certainly didn't."

"Don't new machines come with a sample of the kind of detergent the manufacturer recommends?" asked Joel. "You know, taped to the inside of the door?"

"I wouldn't know," said I. "I don't even know if the machine was actually new."

"From what you've told me about this Ernie Corben," said Havermeyer, "is it safe to assume the machine was procured legitimately?"

"I wouldn't have let him leave it on the premises," said Father, "if Ernie hadn't shown me the bill of sale. He actually looked insulted when I demanded to see it. Much as Millie wanted the thing, I wasn't about to allow stolen merchandise under our roof."

"So Messrs. Corben and Guy," said Havermeyer, "they did arrive, finally? I mean now, to the rescue?"

"They did," said I.

"So what did they do?" asked Joel.

"What they're still doing as we speak," said I. "They're taking the suds out in buckets."

"Where are they putting them?" asked Monsignor Havermeyer.

I heaved a shrug. Soapsuds crackled in my ear. "Outside. The garden's getting a good cleaning. The greenery may be spotty when it all dries, but those are the breaks. So, are we all caught up?"

"As far as the suds are concerned, it would seem so," said Father.

"But Martin," said Monsignor Havermeyer, "aren't you going to make one of your clever observations?"

"Excuse me, My Senior?" I asked in all innocence.

"You know, about the necessity of important information—like doctrines, dogmas, and dishwasher instructions—being preserved and conveyed in Latin, a language that practically defies misinterpretation."

"Now that you mention it, I wish I had."

"Now, Roberto," said Father, changing the subject, "what can you tell us about the subsiding floor in the church?"

"Uno momento, Padre," said Roberto Guadalupe, scowling at the sheet of paper in front of him. Renewing his grip on his pen, he finished the last line while mumbling to himself, "'...para rescatar almas en la oscuridad' ... Ah!" He carved the final word with finality. "There, it is done."

As he shoved the sheet across the table to Father Baptist, it struck me how different Roberto's accent was from Don Gusto's. It was hard to put my finger on. Was it a matter of place of origin, or perhaps century? Or perhaps that Don Gusto was just a figment of my imagination, even if he did show me the location of the original mission?

"Thank-you," said Father, glancing so casually at Roberto's effort before slipping it within the mysterious folds of his cassock that he almost had me convinced it was of little importance. It took me a second to reassemble the detritus in my brain to remember that he was under an obligation of discretion with respect to his errand for Cardinal Fulbright.

"In answer to your question," said Roberto, pulling a bowl of Peanuts' famous cornflake muffins toward himself, "the stones, they are sinking. There is no doubt. The only thing to do is pry them up to see why, and that is what we have been doing."

"It is difficult work," said Spade, rubbing his biceps.

"Not that he's complaining," said Duggo. "None of us are. It is an honor to work on the shrine of El Señor de los Temblores."

If they had been wearing hats, Roberto, Duggo, and Spade would have taken them off reverently just then.

"The what?" asked yours truly. My ethereal conversation with the vaporous Don Gusto that very morning came back to me against the background reverberation of the lowing of ghostly cows:

> "Ah. I have knelt een joor beeyooteeful leetle church many times as joo served Mass beside Padre Juan Bautista. I used to pray there long ago, too, when eet had another name."
>
> "You're talking about St. Philomena's?"
>
> "Sí, sí, when eet was an asistencia dedicated to El Señor de los Temblores."

When I have figments of imagination, I thought to myself, boy do I have figments!

"The statue on top of the big boulder in the grotto," explained Roberto reverently. "He is the Lord of the Earthquakes."

"You're sure of that?" asked Joel.

"Of course," said Roberto, more to his companions than to Father. They nodded in response.

"Didn't you know?" asked Spade.

Father pressed his palms against his temples. "I never thought to ask you."

"It isn't obvious to look at us," said Roberto significantly, rolling the tips of his enormous moustache, "but we three are men of many surprises."

"I'll remember that," said Father, resting his elbows on the table and his chin on his knuckles. "Martin, remind me to remember that."

"With Gusto," said I, then I asked, "What is an *asistencia*?" hoping I pronounced it correctly. I also hoped that Father caught the inference and made the connection.

"An extension of a mission," said Father after a couple of interrogative blinks. "Not a complete facility itself, but supported and staffed by friars a few miles from an established mission. Why?"

"Could St. Philomena's have been one?" I asked.

"Has someone suggested that recently?"

"Nobody in particular." I put a slight space between "no" and "body" as I said it.

He looked at me, puzzled. Then he smiled and mouthed, "Gusto."

"I was just wondering," said I, momentarily impressed, more so with his hint-taking talent than my thought-casting ability. I wiggled my eyes to indicate that others were present. "But lest the question gets sidetracked and therefore unanswered, let me repeat it. Could St. Philomena's have once been an *asistencia*? If so, to what mission?"

"Del Agua's closer than Los Angeles Mission, isn't it?" asked Joel.

"By several miles," agreed Havermeyer."

"It's possible," said Father, "but so far that's all it is. The rumor I've always heard, maintained by several elderly parishioners, is that it was originally a shrine. A chapel of wood was built on the site, but it burned to the ground, taking the early parish records with it. Our present stone structure is only the final phase of a complicated history."

"One good earthquake could bring on phase four," said Monsignor Havermeyer.

"Let's hope not," said Father.

"A shrine," said I. "A shrine dedicated to whom?"

"El Señor de los Temblores," said Roberto.

"'*Y he aquí que el velo del templo se rasgó en dos de arriba abajo,*'" said Spade. Something in the way he said it suggested it was a quote.

"'*Tembló a tierra y las piedras se partieron,*'" added Duggo, equally recitative.

"That's from the Bible, isn't it?" asked the gardener, perking up. "'El velo del templo' is 'the veil of the temple,' isn't it?"

"San Mateo," said Roberto. "Excuse me, Saint Matthew—"

"Chapter twenty-seven, verse fifty-one," said I, waxing scriptural. "'And behold the veil of the temple was rent in two from the top even to the bottom, and the earth quaked, and the rocks were rent.'"

"Leave it to Mr. Feeney," said Joel.

"Yah," agreed Old Josef, scraping at the last of his soup with his spoon. "Fee-nee!"

"Considering the seismic nature of California, it makes sense," said Father. "Mission La Purisima was destroyed by an earthquake in 1812. We walked amidst the rubble this morning."

"So what's making the church floor subside?" asked Joel.

"Don't blame Millie's dishwashing machine," said I. "It has only been wreaking havoc since this morning. Father and I discovered the subsidence in the church yesterday."

"What can you tell us?" asked Monsignor Havermeyer, leaning forward on his elbows.

"Not much," said Roberto with a shrug. "We started by removing the top layer of stones, one by one. The different shapes, they are—what is the word?"

"Irregular," suggested Duggo.

"Like the—¿Como se dice?—ah, the jigsaw puzzle," said Spade.

"We can't just pull them up and put them in the pile," said Roberto.

"We'd never be able to put them all back," said Duggo.

"So we carry them to the cemetery," said Spade. "We set them on the ground as they were in the floor."

"One layer at a time," said Roberto.

"How big an area are we talking here?" asked Father.

"The whole grotto floor," said Duggo.

"The whole grotto!" said Havermeyer. "How far down have you gone?"

"Five layers," said Spade.

"About three feet," said Duggo. "It is slow going."

"And you've no idea why the stones suddenly started settling," said Joel.

"That is right," said Roberto. "The mortar that has held them together has turned to sand."

"What could have caused that?" asked Father.

"Who knows?" said Roberto with a shrug.

"There were those tremors a few weeks ago," said the gardener helpfully.

"That's right," agreed Joel. "Just before Halloween."

"Yah," added Josef. "Wampyr, yah."

I began to say the word, "Bucky," but Father threw me a "Say no more!" glance. He zapped Joel and his grandfather with it, too, just as Gloria came up behind me and lowered a steaming platter of Hungarian goulash, stuffed peppers, and chicken paprikash onto my placemat.

"Enjoy," said she into my ear.

"Wow," said I. "I didn't realize how hungry I am."

"I did," said she.

"Whoa ho," said Joel.

"Ho," agreed Josef. "Yah."

"Um," said I, deciding which delicacy to attack first.

"Yum," corrected Gloria. In a matter of seconds she gathered all the dirty dishes from around the table and arranged them into two swaying, rattling towers. These she scooped up, one in the crook of each arm, and turned in the direction of the kitchen. Before she left she whispered, just loud enough for everyone to hear, "Beebay."

As Gloria sauntered through the swinging aluminum doors, the unmistakable rumble of amused males emanated from our table. Then, as if on cue, everyone wiped their mouths, set down their napkins, and looked to Father to say final Grace. He complied:

"We give Thee thanks, Almighty God, for these and all Thy benefits, which we have received from Thy Bounty through Christ Our Lord."

"Amen," said everyone but me, being as how I was still about to receive.

They gave me a look like tribesmen about to toss their good buddy into a sputtering fumarole to appease the volcano deity, then started heaving their way out from behind the table.

"My friends, my friends," said I, "why are you abandoning me?"

"G—l—o—r—i—a!"sang Joel as per the song by the sixties band, Them.

"Glorrrrria," trilled Roberto, Duggo, and Spade from a popular mariachi tune.

"*Gloria in excelsis Deo,*" intoned Monsignor Havermeyer from the Tridentine Mass.

"Bzzzzzzzzzzt!" croaked Old Josef, dragging his finger across his throat. "Yah!"

"You won't mind if I leave, too, will you?" asked Father, thoroughly amused with the antics of his companions.

"The least you can do is pay for my last meal," said I, plunging my fork into the larger of the two plump bell peppers.

"Done," said he. "I'm anxious to inspect their progress in the church, you understand."

"No problem. It's for moments like these that I carry a tattered paperback of *The Big Midget Murders* by Craig Rice in my jacket pocket."

"The lads are getting together this afternoon for drinks, then dinner," said Joel, patting my shoulder. "We've found a great new place. Want to join us?"

"Love to," said I, "but Father and I have a meeting with destiny." I was thinking of the note Father and I found at Willie "Skull" Kapps' shop: *The Saranac Lounge, Saturday afternoon, 5 o'clock.* Whatever that portended, it was fast approaching. "You go enjoy yourself."

I was just about to maneuver my fork into my mouth when a heavier hand landed on my shoulder. I could see the scarring out of the corner of my eye. "Monsignor Havermeyer," I acknowledged.

"Martin, I—"

"Don't mention it, Monsignor."

"Don't mention what?"

"I don't know. What were you going to say?"

"I was going to ask if you could drop by my camper when you're done here."

I set down my fork. "What's up, Mon Senior?"

"As per Father Baptist's admonition, I'm preparing myself to say a Requiem on Monday, just in case he's unavailable." The scar tissue over most of his face distorted whatever he was really thinking into an expression I'd rather not try to describe. "I've been struggling with the rubrics. You've been so helpful, I hate to ask, but I could use your guidance."

Initially the thought of me guiding Monsignor Havermeyer struck me as ludicrous, all the way to whacked. Then it hit me. What had Keating, the Doily Sisters' chauffeur, said that Monsignor Havermeyer had said? We were in the Doily kitchen at the time:

> *"He mentioned you in his sermon."* That was what Keating had said.
>
> *"No,"* had been my stunned reaction.
>
> *"Yes, indeed. Honestly, he went on at some length ... He said that the reason he was able to fill in for Father Baptist in his regrettable but unavoidable absence was that you had painstakingly rehearsed him in the language and rubrics of the Latin Mass. Is that so, Mr. Feeney?"*
>
> *"Well, yes,"* I had to admit, albeit unwillingly. It was a truly embarrassing moment, but it was about to get worse. *"I suppose I did give him a few pointers, but—"*
>
> *"You don't have to play humble with me, even if you're not Irish,"* he had countered, twitching and jigging as though he had joined the ranks of the Little People. Then came the clincher: *"The monsignor made it eminently clear that any parishioners who have maligned you for your deportment or demeanor should be ashamed of themselves, and that you are a treasure, albeit a crotchety, limping one."*

At least half a dozen clever comebacks presented themselves for the last sentence alone. Then I reminded myself that I hardly knew Keating and had no way of knowing the accuracy of his account. Furthermore, I did know Monsignor Havermeyer quite well, and his hunger for the

Latin Mass and all the Traditional Rituals pleased me deeply. Lastly, I looked fondly at the meal before me, recalling the words of the Grace I had said before it arrived.

"Of course, Monsignor," I said. "Give me a few minutes to wolf this down and I'll be right over."

"Don't make yourself sick."

"Not to worry," said I, hefting my fork again.

52

"MARTIN!" SAID THE GIANT SHADOW. It occluded the sun, the clouds, and the rest of the sky. My eyes were closed, but the shade fell upon my eyelids. In fact, it fell upon all of me. The temperature within the umbra dropped. I felt goose bumps on my arms.

"Hm?" I managed to mumble.

"Little Buddy, are you okay?" A bucket made a hollow plastic thud as it was dropped unceremoniously on the ground. A hunk of meat the size of a pot roast landed on my left shoulder and gave it a shove.

My head pivoted on its swivel, or words to that effect. I could have sworn I heard something rattling around in there. I tried to say, "Who wants to know?" but I'm sure that's not what came out.

"Hang on," said the Shadow, receding. "I'll get help."

Sunlight washed over me. I could tell by the way the earth shook as he stomped away that the familiar voice and slab of hand had belonged to none other than Some Guy. While it was reassuring to know he was around, and so considerately so, the matter didn't really penetrate the sludge pretending to be my brain just then.

Time passed. I know because my goose bumps subsided and fell into a collective snooze.

"Martin!" said Monsignor Havermeyer. It was an emphatic whisper, not a yell. It might as well have been a song, for all I cared.

His voice seemed to be close, and that T-bone steak resting on my right shoulder was probably his hand. Yes, that was confirmed when he used it to rock my shoulder on its squeaky hinges. This caused my eyes to spin around in their sockets behind my closed eyelids. Then I heard a strange sound, three quick sniffs, the third the loudest. What, was that him?

"Have you been drinking?" he hissed ever so softly. As he inhaled again, I could hear that he was looking around, suspicious, protective.

Pressing the tip of my tongue against the roof of my mouth just behind my front teeth, I made ready to say the word, "No," and I even intended to infuse it with a taken-aback what-me lilt.   But—hold on—what was that faint, sweet smell wafting away on the lazy afternoon breeze? Could that really be ... blueberry brandy? Almost gone. Almost, but not quite. And, just to confuse the issue further, I thought I heard, or thought I remembered hearing, the words of the Hundred-and-Twenty-Ninth Psalm from the Latin Vulgate. They sounded hollow and blurry, as if they were reverberating around the inside of a stone room—oh, not a mausoleum, please not that:

De profundis clamavi ad te Domine.
Domine exaudi vocem mean fiant aures ...

"Martin," insisted Monsignor Havermeyer.   The nudging of my shoulder became more jarring. My eyeballs were doing loop-the-loops when my eyelids suddenly popped involuntarily open, allowing Reality to come blasting into my consciousness as a swooshing spiral of blazing light.

"Gee," I managed to say.

The shaking ceased. My eyeballs stopped rolling around. The sound of a bird chirping in the overhanging branches penetrated my confusion. I was sitting on the wooden bench in the garden between the church and the rectory, the bench facing the statue of St. Thérèse the Little Flower. The surrounding bushes and shrubs were covered with clusters of quivering suds. That image alone was worth waking up to. It was only then that I realized I was waking up, and from a sleep into which I didn't remember falling. This was becoming a habit. "Gee," I said again. "Thirty-seven twenty four."

"What was that?" Havermeyer asked, easing himself onto the bench beside me. The creaky boards sagged under his additional weight.

"Genesis," said I. "'And they cast him into an old pit, where there was no water.'"

"I don't understand."

"Oh, and you think I do."

I closed my eyes and tried to reconstruct events. After leaving "Peanuts," Gloria's mammoth lunch special three-quarters consumed, my curiosity about the floor of the church burning intensely, I had crossed the street with the intention of entering the vestibule through the front door and from there going through the internal swinging doors to the nave. But just as I had hoisted myself up from the asphalt onto the curb with the help of my trusty cane and my usual outburst of grunting and grimacing, movement at the wrought-iron gate, the one leading to the garden, distracted me. I could have sworn that I saw a man pausing there to look at me before entering. What made it all the more strange was that he appeared to be an Indian dressed in the simple, loose-fitting white clothing of the indigenous Californians who learned horticulture and industry along with theology and metaphysics at the missions founded by the likes of Padre Fermin Lasuen at La Purisima. He had dark brown skin, shaggy black hair, and penetrating eyes. The clincher, of course, was the little burro accompanying him. It looked at me vacantly, yawned, and flexed its long, pointed ears in asymmetrical directions.

"Hey," I had sputtered, then gasped. "Profirio?"

All sorts of thoughts fluttered through my head at that moment. Surely if Profirio was here, Don Gusto must be close at hand, and I certainly wanted to ply him with several questions. The fact that I wanted to converse with a ghost hit me, hard. Amazing, wasn't it, the sorts of things I was beginning to take for granted? And I even knew the burro's name was Poca Roca!

A moment later, after a prolonged squeak and resounding clang of the metal gate, Don Gusto's servant and his little burro were gone. Seized with a sense of urgency, I heaved myself up the cement steps, opened the gate with another metallic squeal, and lumbered between the avocado and holly trees into the garden, which was now a wonderland of soft, cloudy mounds of soapsuds. There was no sign of Profirio, Poca Roca, or Don Gusto. There was, however, a gentle breeze heaving and shifting the mounds of foam all around. Thousands of bubbles, thus agitated, burst and regrouped into larger, wobbling spheres. The sizzle and crackle of millions of hilariously popping suds permeated the garden. The shuffling and settling of branches and froth somehow suggested the coy swishing of a shimmy dress. The unmistakable smell of blueberry brandy engulfed me. It was as though the air had become arms, wrapping themselves windily around me.

The airy arms engulfing me were immaterial, ethereal, hence their pressure did not crush me, but rather permeated me. The sensation was not weighty or compressive, but rather buoyant and expansive, and it conveyed a reassuring sense of affection, satisfaction, and even a touch of amusement. The heart from which this intimate expression of fondness flowed was unquestionably feminine. Her manner was gentle and sweet, fragranced with maternal encouragement and laced with girlish curiosity. I must be careful not to insinuate that she was "coming on" to me—no, not at all. Her embrace was as innocent as a kid sister's. But at the same time she was larger than life, precisely because she was beyond this life. For a grim and dour gardener, it was a heady experience indeed.

I opened my mouth to say the only word that came to mind, "Elza," but before I could give utterance the mood of the moment changed.

Feminine affection darkened to matronly apprehension. The ghostly arms squeezed me over-protectively, as if pulling me back before I could step off the curb at a dangerous intersection. Like the headstrong child that I was, and male besides, I struggled against her. I saw no danger, no cause for concern. Standing in a garden full of bubbles, what on earth was there for me to fear? Still, her grip was like vaporous iron: utterly insubstantial, thoroughly compelling. My lungs strained for breath.

"Hoo-boy!" I managed to say, as snapdragons on the fringe of my awareness began to sing. No, not flowers, not birds—piano keys. I recognized the tune my mother used to play on the family upright when my eyes had been level with the keys. It was an old Hungarian ditty, elevating yet melancholy, and it seemed to be coming from all around. Then I heard the words:

"Miseruntque in cisternam quae non habebat aquam ..."

That was definitely not Hungarian. No, it was Latin, and the verse was familiar to me:

"And they cast him into an old pit, where there was no water..."

"That's not Mom's song," I managed to say as I found myself sinking onto the wooden bench. I considered the wording of the Bible passage and asked, "Who him?"

The ethereal squeeze intensified. The simple tune on the piano became a storm of rolling arpeggios.

"Me him?" I gasped. "What pit? And what's so old about it?"

Whoa, even more pressure. The garden pulsated with two-handed chords as only Sergei Rachmaninoff used to perform. I remembered listening to Dad's old 1929 RCA 78 RPM recording of the maestro performing his own *Piano Concerto No. 2.* Double whoa!

> GARDENING TIPS: Sergei Rachmaninoff suffered from
> acromegaly, a deforming condition which, in his
> case, resulted in enlarged hands. This gave him a
> reach, and by extension a compositional stretch,
> that has left aspiring pianists sprawled in his
> dust ever since.
>
> —M.F.

"What?" I wheezed. "Not like The Apocalypse, seventeen eight: 'The beast, which thou sawest, was and is not, and shall come up out of the bottomless pit, and go into destruction—'"

The music exploded into something akin to the "Danse Sacrale" at the end of *The Rite of Spring*—the robust, four-fisted piano version, no less. I felt like a child being shaken by a frustrated parent.

"'Which of you shall have an ass fall into a pit,'" it seemed to raucously say, "'and will not immediately draw him out—?'"

"Ah," gasped I. "As in Luke fourteen five, condensed slightly for content. I take it I'm the ass—"

As if realizing she had overstepped, an apologetic breeze buffeted me. Back to the sweeping arpeggios, this time less tempestuous, more like waves breaking generously on the picturesque rocks, mushrooms of foam exploding gleefully. It was a little much. The mounds of Millie's first dishwashing experiment shivered and sizzled all around me, zillions of bubbles popping in the breeze redolent with blueberry brandy.

"So what are you trying to tell me?" I said as the music subsided back into the Hungarian ditty Mom used to play. The sudden *ritardando* and simultaneous *decrescendo* left me lightheaded.

No, beyond dizzy. I was sinking into unconsciousness.

Two things occurred to me as all of the above went away. First, the realization that I hadn't had the opportunity to test this spirit, nor that of Don Gusto, and certainly not Profirio—if I had indeed experienced them at all. I was the world's keenest cynic when it came to rumors of apparitions—and we heard about them all the time at Saint Philomena's, as evidenced by the flyer handed to me two days before outside Edison G. Winger's jewelry store proclaiming the visions of Quintana Morbo of New Orleans, the seer of Irwindale, who called herself the "Little Taper." The Apostle John warned in his First Epistle, chapter four: "Dearly beloved, believe not every spirit, but try the spirits if they be of God: because many false prophets are gone out into the world."

```
GARDENING TIPS: A warm-fuzzy feeling is not an
adequate test for a spirit, yet for many people,
thinking themselves worthily spiritual, it is more
than enough; which is why, perhaps not coinciden-
tally, the number of bona fide exorcisms is esca-
lating annually throughout the world. Beware what
you invite into your life.
    In this case, a ghost with piano chops was not
necessarily from Heaven, nor could I be sure it
was the same spirit I had encountered at the
"House of Illusions" a few weeks before, the
spirit who had saved my very life. I mean, she
sure seemed the same, but how much practical,
hands-on experience did I have under my belt when
it came to ghosts?
```

    All the above duly noted, I really, <u>really</u> liked
    that tune.

                                        --M.F.

The second thing that occurred to me was that, whatever or whoever had just visited me, the point of the exercise seemed to be a warning. Somewhere out there was a pit with no water in it, and I'm a dumb enough ass to fall in. Call me crazy, but somehow a hole to hide in seemed like a good idea just then. How long I sat there, slumped down on the bench like a transient, surrounded by mounds of crackling bubbles, I'm not sure.

The next thing I remember was being nudged awake by the Giant Shadow with a pot roast for a hand. "Hang on," he had said before stomping off, "I'll get help." Then came Monsignor Havermeyer with a gentler hand but a most disconcerting suspicion, "Have you been drinking?" It didn't end there, of course.

"Gracious me," intruded a new voice.

"Yes, you are, Mr. Folkstone," said I, followed by a prolonged exhale coupled with an attempt to straighten, look around, and take stock of the situation. The effort wasn't entirely successful.

"What on earth has happened here?" Mr. Folkstone was, of course, waving his arms at the foaming mounds all around. Though I called myself the gardener, he was the one who really took care of the grounds.

"Millie had a little problem with her new dishwashing machine," explained Monsignor Havermeyer, still seated on the bench beside me.

"A *little* problem?" said Mr. Folkstone, bewildered.

"I imagine it will all just pop itself away," said the Monsignor. "These suds, I mean."

"But Monsignor, it's soap!" cried the true groundskeeper. "Everything's going to be covered with residue."

"Nothing a good rain won't take care of," ventured the titular gardener.

"That will just draw it all into the ground," said Mr. F. "Down to the roots."

"Is that bad?" asked the monsignor.

Mr. Folkstone responded with a sound that combined elements of a growl, a huff, a smirk, and a shudder. "That depends. I must speak to Millie."

"She's kind of busy," said I.

"And so will I be," said Mr. Folkstone, in a rare moment of open annoyance. I think he may have even startled himself. "Excuse me."

As if to punctuate his outrage, he whirled around—and stomped right into the big, wide wall that was Some Guy, two foam-filled plastic buckets hanging from each of his gargantuan hands. For some inexplicable reason Mr. Guy had donned one of Millie's aprons, and all it did was cover his fly. As ridiculous as Some looked, he was still one huge feller to go stomping angrily into. Surprised, he dropped all four buckets, which banged, twirled, and rolled in a variety of directions, merrily spilling foam all over the mossy, green path and the ivy on either side. From where I sat I couldn't see Mr. Folkstone's face, just the back of his head as it tilted further, and further, and further back as he assessed the unbelievably horrendous turn his life had just taken.

"Dear, oh dear, oh dear," whimpered the poor, little man.

Some Guy, being a behemoth of the mild-mannered sort, merely gasped. His intake of breath lifted Fr. Folkstone's hair a good inch off his head—or was that just his wig slipping? Hard to tell from my angle. "Hey," said the giant, rubbing his tummy to make sure it was okay. "You should watch where you're going."

"My, my," stammered Mr. Folkstone. Then his voice rose into a shrill shriek. "You're absolutely right! I do so beg your pardon!"

Some Guy smiled kindly, which is to say goofily—to someone unfamiliar with his expressions it might have seemed hungrily. "Sure thing—" His acceptance of Mr. Folkstone's apology was itself interrupted by a bump from behind, two more buckets thudding on the ground, and some cross words from none other than Ernie Corben, the founder of the foamfest.

"Hey," said Ernie—I have deleted his curses. "Watch where you're goin'!"

"Okay," said Some Guy, still looking down at Mr. Folkstone with a look of mild puzzlement.

"Dear, oh dear, oh dear," sputtered Mr. F., his concern for his safety amplified considerably by the collision of events.

"I mean it," grumbled Ernie, still hidden from view behind Some Guy. He let loose with a few more words I'd rather not repeat, then added, "This is the last time I'm ever going to try to do something nice for somebody. I've never been so—"

"Ernie, watch your mouth," said a voice from even further behind. It was Millie, and she sounded as though she was capable of washing out said observed mouth with something bitterly antiseptic.

This was followed by a pause during which I thought I heard Mr. Corben mumble something akin to, "Dear, oh dear, oh dear," though somewhat more caustic and cacophonous. Some Guy kind of shrank, though for him it was ludicrous.

"And get out of my way," added Millie.

Ernie stepped to the left, coming into my view from behind Some Guy, who lumbered to the right, leaving poor Mr. Folkstone right in Millie's path. He shook so hard I thought he was going to separate in two and step to both sides at once. Instead, he backed up, tripped, and wound up squeezed between Monsignor Havermeyer and myself on the bench.

"Oomph," said he as he landed. "Dear, oh dear."

Next thing I knew, Millie was towering over us. She still had that soggy cigarette in her right hand. In her left she grasped a wineglass, half full of merlot, crowned with a head of soapsuds. She looked at me as she would a cockroach in her sink. "Summy said you were sick."

Summy? Some Guy, our very own biclops, was now *Summy?*

My world tilting, I looked up at my fate, then at the glass in her hand. "I appreciate your concern, Millie. You're most kind, but as you know, I've taken the pledge."

"That's okay," said she, absently flicking the butt and raising the glass to her lips. She lowered it, revealing a nose and upper lip coated with foam. This she wiped away with the back of her hand. "This wasn't for you."

"I think I may have fainted," said I, not wanting to try to explain Profirio, Poca Roca, and least of all Elza. "I'm still a little dizzy."

"Dear, oh dear, oh dear," mumbled Mr. Folkstone beside me.

"Am I missing something?" asked yet another voice.

"Father Baptist," said I, relieved to see him approaching from the side door of the church.

"Millie, Martin, Gentlemen," said he, coming among us.

"Father, Father, Father," replied the assembly.

"Well?" asked he.

"Mister Feeney will live," explained Millie, swirling the wine under the foam in her glass. "There will be no dinner this evening, for which I apologize. Now let's see, what else was there?"

"No need," said he after taking a half-second to look around and assess the situation. "To apologize, I mean. Martin and I can grab a bite at the hotel we'll be visiting shortly."

"Part of your investigation?" asked Havermeyer.

Father nodded. "Millie, I'm so sorry the maiden voyage of your new appliance went awry. Hopefully all future runs will be smooth and successful sailing."

"Surely they will," said Havermeyer, helpfully, rising from the bench.

"That's right," said Ernie Corben, uselessly.

"Uh-huh," agreed Summy, smiling sincerely.

Millie didn't seem to be paying attention. She was absorbed by the interplay of wine and foam in her glass.

"I'll buy you dinner at 'Peanuts,'" offered Havermeyer.

"By all means," said Father. "Better yet, take Millie to 'Darby's.' I'll phone Alan Ross and make a reservation before I leave."

"Excuse me," ventured Mr. Folkstone, wiping his face with a white handkerchief. He then waved it around as a vague pointer. "Regarding all these soapsuds. Might I ask what brand of dishwashing detergent was used to generate them? I need to know if it's safe for the plants."

"The bottle's under the sink," said she, holding her glass up to the light. "Help yourself."

"Oh, um, all right," said Mr. Folkstone, struggling to his feet. "If you will excuse me?"

Like a frail elf lost in a snowbound forest, he made his way between the oaks towering all around him. Some Guy even raised his branches to wave as Mr. F. disappeared through the kitchen door. Millie, lost in thought, turned and followed. Ernie and Summy noisily gathered up their buckets and did likewise.

"Martin," said Father, "we'd better be going."

"Oh?" Summoning my resolve for the task of rising to my feet, I said, "I'm sorry, Monsignor, that I haven't been of assistance to you as I'd promised."

The monsignor shrugged. "No help for it now."

"Perhaps I can come by later this evening."

I couldn't have been more mistaken.

53

"I THOUGHT YOU WANTED TO LEAVE right away," I said as I lumbered into Father's study. "What's keeping—?"

"You're sure," Father was saying into the telephone. He held up one finger, apparently indicating to me the number of minutes he wished me to wait.

He had come into the rectory to make that reservation at "Darby's" for Monsignor Havermeyer and Millie. When he didn't come out after ten minutes, I figured something was up.

"What's that?" he said into the receiver. "Oh, I just had what I thought was a flash of insight, but apparently I was mistaken. Sorry to have troubled you."

"No problem," the tiny voice said into his ear.

"Good night," said he, cradling the phone.

"Is 'Darby's' all filled up?" I asked.

"What?" said he, looking up at me. "Oh, no, Alan Ross was accommodating, as usual. I was just talking with Miss Wexler. Are you okay to drive, Martin?"

"Why shouldn't I be? Oh, you mean my fainting spell in the garden. I'm fine now."

"You're sure."

"Sure I'm sure."

"Was I imagining it, or did I smell blueberry brandy out there?"

"Monsignor Havermeyer noticed it, too."

"He said you were mumbling something about an old pit."

"Without water. I'll tell you about it in the car. What flash of insight, Father?"

Tired yet determined, he pushed himself up from the desk. "Oh, something that occurred to me when I saw the progress Roberto, Duggo and Spade have made in the church."

"I don't suppose there's time for me to take a gander before we leave."

"It will have to wait. We really need to be going."

"What occurred to you?" I asked as I followed him through the door and down the hall to the front door.

"Roberto and his men have indeed removed several layers of stones from the grotto floor. As I looked into the depression, I was reminded of Bishop Ravenshorst's excavation at the corner of El Barranco and La Colina."

"Ah yes, where the Ravine of Darkness meets the Hill of Slaughter and Foul Smells."

"The same." He paused at the front door, his hand on the knob. "Then I thought of Sybil's intersecting lines—"

"And you thought St. Philomena's might qualify as a dot on the wily bishop's real estate map." It was a little late to mention that I'd had a similar insight the night before as we left the barrio.

"That's right," said he. "As it so happens, we are nearly straddling one of the east-west lines—it misses us by five blocks—but the nearest intersection with a north-south line is several miles away."

"Don't tell me," I said. "The intersection of El Barranco and La Colina."

"That's right."

He opened the door. For half a second I thought I smelled blueberry brandy wafting in from outside. If nostrils could blink, mine would have. I took a deep sniff. Nothing—or rather, nothing reminiscent of sweet liqueur. The usual tang of soot and exhaust was certainly out there in full force, along with a faint, dishwashing liquid aftertaste.

"Wouldn't that have been something," I said as he closed the door behind us, "if your hunch had been right, I mean."

"Yes, wouldn't it—whatever he was looking for with such determination and at great cost being right under our feet all along. Alas, it's not going to be that easy."

He had no idea.

54

"THAT MUST BE IT," SAID FATHER as the Hotel Adirondack loomed blackly against the dimming orange and amber hues in the western sky. It was fifteen minutes after sunset, which is to say five o'clock on the dot. Curiously, we had passed within sight of it two mornings before when I drove Father west on Wilshire Boulevard to the coast before heading north to Camarillo. At that time my attention had been elsewhere. But now, as we veered off Wilshire onto Margaret Sheridan Drive, which headed briefly north for several blocks before swerving gracefully westward to approach the grand hotel's entrance head-on, it was hard to look away. My eyes were first drawn to that stylized "A" in a bas-relief circle above the entrance. It was perhaps thirty feet high, ornately seraphic, fanned from below by green and yellow floodlights. Behind it the central octagonal tower rose darkly, sphinx-like, a full seventeen stories, buttressed on both sides by less-tall-but-no-less-imposing shoulders, which descended into symmetrical extended claws on both sides of the expansive drive-up cul-de-sac. The effect, at least in my imaginative mind, was a gigantic, ravenous lion with an "A" for a nose, awaiting its prey. The stone beast was attended all around by rows and lanes of those tall, skinny, dare I say dorky-looking pine trees that architects and city planners once thought brought glamour to the arid desert that was the Los Angeles basin. Behind the hotel ascended the jagged escarpments that became Pacific Palisades before falling away into the ocean a half-mile beyond. A hundred balconied windows stared darkly down on us as we advanced, only a half dozen of them illuminated.

Had it only been the previous day, between our narrow escape from His Shrieking Cucumbership, Bishop Morell deQuet of New Bangor, and our foray amongst the ditzy frills and foul teas of the Doily Sisters, that Father had been examining a photograph of this very establishment?

"What are these dots?" he had asked.
"Excuse me?" I had responded.

> *"All over the façade of the building there's a motif of black dots. They're tiny in this picture, but they must be a foot or two in diameter. Maybe they're emblems—shields or something."*
>
> *"Beats me. I was just a kid the last time I was there. My mind was on other things."*
>
> *"The architect certainly made a point of using them. See? They accentuate every window, archway, turret, and rain gutter."* He had then compared the photograph to the card he'd found in Willie's shop. *"I wonder if there's any connection between them and the raised circles around the edge of this invitation."*
>
> I'd had to admit: *"This is where my value as a sidekick wanes."*

Well, there they were, coarse black dots all over the building. They were indeed two feet or so in diameter, and several inches thick. They seemed to be bolted to, or perhaps imbedded in the stone façade. This side of the hotel was draped in shadow, but it was also sprayed with floodlights planted at the base of the building among the shrubs. If not for the resulting hyperbolic arcs of startling light, the disks would not have stood out so. The designer must have had a thing for them, or whatever eccentric millionaire hired him to build his hotel.

"There're your dots," said I.

"Excuse me?" asked he.

"Dots. There."

"Ah, yes."

"All over the building."

"They certainly are."

"Now why am I getting the shivers?" As I steered the Jeep around and under the massive carport which lolled out of the front of the leonine edifice like a huge, hungry tongue, I braked to a stop beside a fountain that looked as though it hadn't passed water in decades. The regal lion, which had once spewed a perpetual gush from its marble maw, now gaped silent and parched. The blue tiles in the catch basin below were bone dry, crusted with algae long dead. Not to encourage those who would say that nausea seems to be my preoccupation throughout this story, but I realized with a start that the last time I had been here two of my pals had regurgitated copiously into this very fountain during the Queen's Dance, blending their spew with the lion's. It wasn't a pretty memory, but then few from high school are. "Suddenly, I'm feeling old," I said aloud, answering my own question.

"Suddenly?" said Father, a wee bit too amused.

"The last time I was here I was a teenager. This place looked a lot younger then."

"Well, if I may say so, you both aged gracefully."

"You may," said I, reaching for my cane, "but you'd be prevaricating."

"Hm-hm," he agreed a bit too readily. "Regarding your shivers, Martin, I was going to suggest that perhaps the place is haunted. Most old hotels are."

"That's a pleasant thought."

"Yes, isn't it? Considering."

"Considering what?"

"Considering some of the company you keep."

That last was a reference to the lively conversation we had enjoyed in the car on the way over. Our discussion had included such topics as Profirio, Poca Roca, blueberry brandy, dry pits, and dumb asses that fall in.

There was no doorman in sight, nor any sign directing or prohibiting parking that I could see. It wasn't as though there was a backup of autos delivering patrons who expected attention. I noticed that the exotic plants erupting from large decorative pots on both sides of the covered ramp hadn't been trimmed in a while, nor had cracks in the walkway been filled, nor missing tiles replaced. Indeed, I realized, mighty as it had no doubt been in its heyday, the Adirondack no longer attracted enough patrons to pay for the upkeep. I regarded her as an aged, formerly gorgeous movie star, with respect and sadness. And yes, the place certainly was haunted, if not by ectoplasmic specters, then at least by memories of vivid times when music was charming, women were elegant, and men didn't resent dressing up.

"Haunted, you say?" said I, turning off the ignition. "You think?"

"I'm not psychic," said Father. "While I lack your experience in these realms, I must say I'm getting a few tingles just looking at this place."

"We've gotta tell the Tumblars."

He laughed. "How did Pierre put it? 'No bar is worth going to unless it's older than we are.'"

"'Combined,'" I reminded him. "This place certainly fits the bill."

"Shall we?" asked he.

"We shall," said I, releasing my seatbelt. "It was so distracting, weaving through traffic, I forgot to press you about the floor."

"In the church?" said he, unsnapping his. "Yes, well, that's turning into quite an excavation."

"We seem to be encountering a lot of those lately."

"There are no coincidences, my Friend. Roberto was sparse with the details at lunch. It seems that beneath the grotto is a descending passageway—a stairway, actually. They found steps carved into the side of the enormous boulder upon which resides the Lord of the Earthquakes. How far down it goes is anyone's guess at this point. The stone that came loose under your weight was one of hundreds that were used to fill in the entire stairwell."

"Roberto said something about the mortar having turned to sand," said I.

"That's right," said Father. "And as you pointed out in the restaurant, we had that commotion just before Halloween. What a nightmare that was. The epicenter was our own cemetery. I wouldn't be surprised if those shockwaves started or accelerated a process of erosion from beneath. Let's hope the mortar holding our church together isn't similarly effected."

"You can say that again. Any idea what they'll find down there?"

"Many old churches have crypts beneath the sanctuary."

"Oh goodie, more dead bodies."

"Your favorite, I know, Martin. But that wouldn't explain why the chamber and stairway were packed with stones. I've really no idea what we'll find when they remove them all."

"Any idea what we'll find here?" I asked as I heaved myself out of the car.

"Only hunches, but I think a few pieces are going to fall into place tonight."

"To the Saranac Lounge, then."

I left the Cherokee there in the carport under a cupola supported by palatial columns. I caught a glimpse of a faded mosaic on the concave ceiling, something suggesting Roman chariots. The front doors to the hotel were marvelously balanced monoliths of solid glass with large brass handles. Beyond we found, not the lobby, but an ante-hallway that at first glance looked to be the length of a football field. This exaggerated sense of distance was due, I think, to the ceiling above, vaulted like a cathedral, and the rippled marble pillars supporting it all. These structures seemed to force the perspective. The stylized letter "A" was featured prominently atop every column, as were more of those dark metal disks imbedded in the arches between. This exaggerated corridor effectively drew us deep into the heart of the hotel.

Though I remembered being here years before, it only seemed vaguely familiar. Truly, my mind had been on other things back in high school.

The lobby, located at the hub of it all, was even more impressive, though aside from the desk clerk, an idle bellboy, and two elderly men snoozing in puffy chairs between potted palms near the elevators, we were the only ones there to appreciate it. It was a circular foyer, a breathtaking space, with high walls culminating in a domed ceiling several stories above. Illumination was provided by chandeliers of teakwood and crystal, suspended by long, ponderous chains from on high. The registration counter was at least fifty feet wide, made of polished granite long before Feng-shui facilitators decided such geological decorative statements were solidifying to the soul. A dozen of those incessant two-foot metallic "dots" were bolted across the front.

I hardly noticed them, my attention drawn instead to the series of gigantic paintings on the walls depicting in regal pigments a seemingly enchanting if convoluted story. The plot or theme was not obvious, though I assumed there had to be some unifying element. There were ten panels in all, flat so they protruded from the curved walls, mounted in elegant, ornate frames. Some of them showed signs of age, hairline cracks in the thick oil paints, water stains near the upper corners, soot around the edges. Nonetheless, they were once fresh, and they were still fascinating. The primary male characters in them had similar bone structure and facial characteristics, so I assumed them to be related.

Over there was an early nineteenth century naval battle in progress, or rather an American vessel, captained by a ferocious fellow, firing upon what looked to be fishing boats manned by very surprised and indignant fisherman. Two panels over, a dashing couple flailed as their horse-drawn carriage capsized on a picturesque street in old San Francisco. Three panels back, a medieval alchemist, hands clenched in divine gratitude, gazed in awe at something glowing brilliantly in a brick oven. On the opposite wall towered a man of considerable confidence and presence, his face radiant with pride, his right leg hitched up, foot planted triumphantly atop a stack of large, round, flat disks reminiscent of the "dots" all over the building. These paintings didn't make a lot of sense to me, but they were nonetheless intriguing. The extra-wide panel above the registration counter was another matter. There, a gruff-looking character in military dress, amidst stirring storm clouds and flapping banners, was presenting something to a man in a billowing cape, something I recognized only too well: the Cordova Rosary.

> GARDENING TIPS: In 1787 King Charles III of Spain
> and King Louis XVI of France jointly gifted the
> Cordova Rosary to the Del Agua Mission in Los An-
> geles in commemoration of its founding by Fathers
> Alonso Miranda and Jean Pierre de Chantal. The
> beads were as large as softballs, and the loop
> over thirty feet in diameter. The entire thing
> was made of brass and overlaid with gold. It was
> a stunning example of European art, royal generos-
> ity, and the enthusiastic missionary spirit of the
> time. As a piece of California history it had
> survived political upheaval, religious persecu-
> tion, and the ravages of time. It also proved it-
> self to be an efficient conductor of thousands of

```
volts of electricity in another story I told in
the aforementioned troublesome manuscript which
was to become immensely more troublesome before
the weekend was over.
                                        --M.F.
```

But first, as we strolled across this once-bustling foyer, the once-plush royal blue carpet now worn to the floorboards in places, we could hear the sound of gentlemanly laughter emanating from an archway to our right. The scrolled sign above announced THE CHAMPLAIN ROOM, and from what I could see, the chamber beyond was invitingly, charmingly maritime. The walls were made of weathered wood, some of it crusted with salt and barnacles. There were nets draped from stem to stern, with crabs and starfish dangling all over. Heat was provided by what looked to be an authentic galley stove, wood fire crackling in its belly, reminiscent of the range in the Doily Sisters' kitchen. Bittersweet Celtic drinking music emanated from speakers concealed in the bulkheads. It was turned down so low the flames in the stove were clearly audible—a radical departure from the blazing, pounding din typical in most bars these days. A sumptuous, buxom but oaken maiden, her solid blonde hair swirling all around her hand-carved shoulders, looked down benevolently from her perch overhanging the sumptuous bar. Much as I wanted to get a closer look and to see the gentlemen making merry within, our destination was THE SARANAC LOUNGE directly opposite. Yes, one good bar was not enough at the Adirondack, even in its decline.

Across the lobby, through an identical archway, was a watering hole with an equally inviting though entirely dissimilar ambiance. THE SARANAC LOUNGE was somber, dim, dominated by an opulent bar with backlit glass shelves cluttered with liquor bottles of every shape, color, and density. Here, too, the music—slow, sultry jazz—was turned way, way down. The patrons, perhaps two dozen in all, were huddled in pairs, their conversations subdued, their cigarettes smoldering in stylish ashtrays. The walls were of red brick, and the booths of red leather. Oil paintings of rustic lodges, snow-capped mountains, and serene lakes abounded, as did the framed autographed photos of Humphrey Bogart, Lauren Bacall, Peter Lorre, Claire Trevor, Craig Stevens, Lola Albright, on and on around the room. As with everything at the Adirondack, the elegance was threadbare, sort of like Father's cassock. I was musing along that very parallel as I followed him through the thick nicotine haze to the bar.

> GARDENING TIPS: Though California had become a de-
> cidedly anti-smoking state, the patrons of the
> Adirondack, in collusion with the management, had
> chosen to ignore the potential health hazard in
> favor of freedom of inhalation. I didn't know how
> long this flagrant practice of willful scofflaw
> had been going on, but I wholeheartedly endorsed
> it. If there had been a donation basket for the
> cause, and if I still smoked myself, I would have
> tossed in a few ciggies. If I smoked cigars I
> would have unwrapped one immediately. As it was I
> just savored the fumes.
>
>   --M.F.
>
> N.B.: It's not that I'm in favor of lung cancer,
> but rather that 1) being an Ultra-Realist, I know
> none of us is going to live forever, 2) it is God,
> not the AMA or even our city council, who decides
> when each of us has fulfilled our purpose and how
> we'll make an end, 3) the current no-smoking law
> applies even in bars, even if everyone present
> agrees they're willing to take the risk, and 4) I
> still don't understand how, according to the laws
> of our state, an adolescent girl can get an abor-
> tion without her parents' knowledge or consent
> while grownups can't smoke in any enclosed public
> place--an example of the ascendancy of reproduc-
> tive choice over respiratory rights. Don't get me
> started.

I couldn't help but be on the lookout for Keating. After all, he did say that it was the Doilys' custom to dine at the Blue Mountain Grill on Tuesday and Saturday evenings. How had he put it? *"Those are the quietest and noisiest nights respectively, customer-wise."* And hadn't he also praised the Saranac, where he hid while the old gals enjoyed themselves, as *"something out of an old, familiar movie"*? This being Saturday, the chances of bumping into him were therefore high, though I didn't see him anywhere at present.

Father Baptist stepped up to the bar and set his hands on the counter. The bartender looked through him, not bothered by his Roman collar and cassock in the least. He yawned like a man who had once been capable of surprise, but oh so long ago, and continued polishing a shot glass with a towel.

"Excuse me," said Father.

"Hm," answered the bartender.

"My friend and I would like some ginger ale."

"Hm."

"Saint Thomas," ventured Father's friend.

"'Blue label,' I suppose," sighed the man, "if I have it."

"How did you—?" said I, blinking back surprise.

"You look different tonight," said he, reaching for something behind the counter, "and you're early."

"Excuse me?" asked Father.

"Early for what?" said the gardener. "Different than what?"

"By several hours, and you know better than I," said the man. He gave us a second look and crinkled his brow. "Those getups—both of you. Toning it down this evening, I suppose."

"I don't follow you," said I. "We aren't regular customers, and this is how we always dress. I haven't been here in many years, and Father has never been, ever."

"Sure," said the man. Then he looked at us with an ounce more interest. I think he actually widened his eyes by a factor of zero point zero zero zero one. Then he narrowed them by twice as much. "You aren't Wobie and Slugger."

I looked at him with considerably more interest. "Were we supposed to be?"

"You usually are," said he with a suggestion of a shrug. "I mean, *they* usually are."

I admit that I was stumped, having no idea where this was going.

"So do you have it?" asked Father. "The ginger ale."

"Of course," said the bartender. "They throw a fit if I run out."

"Who throws a fit?" said I.

He sighed again and gave me a look that said, "That's all the explanation there's gonna be, Bub. Pick up the pieces of your shattered life." He scooped some crushed ice into a pair of tall glasses and set them on the bar. Then he produced two bottles of Saint Thomas, Salisbury, relieved them of their caps with a church key, and left them for us to pour. As he dropped the caps into a hollow receptacle behind the counter he said aloud, "They always insist on 1932 prices."

"Who do?" asked the gardener, pouring his precious ginger ale.

His eyebrows contorted as if trying to form the words: "Wobie and Slugger."

"And who are they?" I mouthed silently.

He responded with another "Don't go there" look as Father Baptist set a couple of coins on the counter. The bartender grimaced familiarly at the 1932 tip.

Father poured himself a glass of the finest ginger ale on the planet, paused as the foam subsided, and took a thoughtful sip. "I just may order this more often, Martin."

"Hm-hm," mumbled yours truly, my lips having dived beneath the foam in my glass. Just then my attention was diverted by a familiar sound that I couldn't quite place at first, a kind of soft chittering, like Rosary beads shifting in a nervous penitent's hands. There it was again, and it seemed to be coming from the farthest, darkest corner of the lounge.

"We'll be with those gentlemen over there," said Father, gathering up his glass and bottle.

"Sure," said the bartender, as if he cared.

To my swelling curiosity, Father steered me directly toward the sound in the corner. As we approached, the mumbling throughout the bar seemed to subside as one conversation emerged, not as the result of people noticing us, but of Father and myself changing our position relative to all the loquent sources. And what a conversation it was, the one in the corner:

"What dat you sayin'?" said Voice A amidst a flurry of little rattles.

"This is useless to me," replied Voice B, cold as granite.

"Whachoo mean, 'useless'? It what you say you seek. It what Ah find fo' you. What Ah get beat up and left to die fo'!"

"Nonetheless, it has been mutilated, and is therefore rendered worthless."

"Wort'less? It solid gold, Mon!"

"That is of no consequence."

"Solid gold? Even as toot'-fillah, Ah t'ink it wort' *some*t'in'."

"As a commodity, yes, but as what I am seeking, no."

Father paused in his approach, as if looking around for a table at which to sit. I assumed he didn't want to interrupt this conversation prematurely. I pretended to look around, too.

The owners of Voice A and Voice B were seated at a small, round table with their backs to us. My impression was that they were examining something between them, something they chose to hide from non-essential eyes. Voice A was wearing wrinkled, loose-fitting Caribbean linen. Voice B was attired in a tailored charcoal suit, and I caught sight of two ostentatious rings on his left hand, one gem deep purple, the other pale yellow.

"Dat was mah neck got risked, Mon," said Voice A, increasingly insistent. "Mo' den dat, Ah call in dah favah Ah cannot not no nevah repay!"

"That is not my concern," said voice B, not pausing to analyze his companion's multiple negatives.

"Ah find dah t'ing you seek!"

"'Finding' is a dangerous business, as you well know. You've been involved in it for as many years as I. You are therefore aware that the value of anything, from a diamond to a good woman—not to mention what is meant by 'good'—depends entirely on demand. I told you up front: I am not seeking this artifact for itself, but for the information it contains."

Voice A whined. "Mon: Ah find dah t'ing you seek! Ah come troo fo' you."

Voice B chuckled. "Not entirely through."

"Troo enough to 'spect to be paid. Gettin' it done got me landed in dah hospital, Mon."

"I will consider it."

"Aaaah—*dungbawbwa!*"

Between the dreadlocks that rattled like Rosary beads, the leathery black skin stretched thin over slender bones, those cross-cultural vocal mannerisms—not to mention the fact that I knew him well—I determined that Voice A belonged to Guillaume du Crane Cristal, also known as Willie "Skull" Kapps. Either his current accent was a contrivance, or the several others he frequently used certainly were. I have no idea to which dialect that last expletive belonged. His presence in this bar came as no surprise. We were here, after all, because of the note on Adirondack stationary that we found in his shop.

His companion, doubtless the author of the note, had a voice that was familiar, though not readily recognizable to me, but that granite-like bulge of jaw muscle under the ears could belong to none other than Roderick Roundhead, heir to the Roundhead Manhole Cover fortune. All things considered, it came as no surprise, his being involved.

"You dah head, big an' roun'," insisted Willie indignantly. "Whoa—*oogama boogama*—Ah am skeered witless. But word is 'Big an' Roun'' is honest mon. Honest. No mon get dat rep what ain't. So why you mess wit' Willie?"

Father Baptist took that as an opening. He stepped purposefully toward their table and said, "I'd like to know that myself." His clever and timely intrusion into the conversation was itself derailed by the sudden appearance of two bodyguards who, in that moody darkness, could have passed for living stone men from some hokey rocket-to-the-moon movie from the black-and-white Sci-Fi days. They didn't raise a hand. They simply shifted into our path, seemingly out of nowhere, like a sudden, inescapable rockslide. Their sheer igneous hugeness and quartzite stares were enough to deflate the courage of many a man, certainly one fidgety gardener, but not Father Baptist.

"They're okay," said Roderick Roundhead, not so much as glancing over his shoulder. "Father Baptist and Mister Feeney are expected."

Without a word, the boulders stepped adroitly, albeit tectonically, out of our way.

"Hey," exclaimed Willie, jumping up from the table, the bones and stones woven into his dreadlocks rattling noisily. "It Jack! Jack the Black, an' he back! An' Martin Mon. Watchoo doin' here?"

"My Friend," said Father, resting his left hand on Willie's shoulder while shaking hands with his right. "Martin and I are following clues, as usual."

"An' need mah help again, do you, Sleuth Mon?"

"To fill in a piece in a puzzle, yes. I'm glad to see you're fully recovered."

"T'anks to you," said Willie. "Yo' prayers is pow'ful mojo."

"Interesting company you're keeping these days," said Father, letting go of his rattling friend and facing the other man, who hadn't as yet turned to greet us. "Mr. Roundhead."

"Father Baptist," said the millionaire, folding his hands on the table. "You don't seem surprised that I was expecting you here."

"That I was surprised when I opened the package you sent me from Van Nuys goes without saying. Words fail."

Another round of "Auld Lang Syne" rolled through my head.

"I don't know what you're talking about," said Roundhead, "but I'm glad to learn that it arrived safely."

"As for being surprised that you were expecting me this evening," said Father, "to borrow an expression from one of your relatives: 'bushwa.' Surely you don't consider me so naïve as to believe that Ernie Corben and Some Guy have been hanging around my rectory because they have developed an adolescent affection for my housekeeper."

"Perhaps they have. But if you suspected, why did you phone them when that dishwasher malfunctioned?"

"They unleashed the beast upon us," said Father with an understated shrug. "They are obliged to clean up after it."

"I'll concede the point. Would it interest you that I know of your visit to the late Bishop Ravenshorst's piece of prized real estate? You know, the hole at the intersection of El Barranco Drive and La Colina Avenue."

"Messrs. Corben and Guy, I'll grant you, certainly weren't there."

"No, but Pedro San Marino was."

"Who?" asked the gardener.

"One of his informants, probably one of the onlookers," explained Father to me, then to him, "I don't think Officers Martel or Staplewhite would be the kind to sell you their services."

Mr. Roundhead sniffed. "You'd be amazed who is willing to sell me their services."

"Perhaps," said Father. "Everyone finds himself in need of money some time, and you're just the man to offer him some. I imagine your network to be extensive, permeating all strata of influence from the pistons of power to the grease pits beneath. It must be strange, living without any surprises whatsoever." Father flexed and clenched his fingers at his side. "This is becoming awkward. Since we're anticipated, perhaps we should join you. Martin?"

Father said the last while circling to the far side of the table and seating himself. He then pulled out a chair for me. With a few teeters above my per-stride average, I complied. As I came around I saw two empty pouches with ornate tasseled pull-strings sprawled on the deeply polished table. A ripple of the prickles trickled down my spine as I realized what I was looking at. Between the pouches lay two golden disks gleaming coldly in the blue darkness. The smaller disk was just the right size to nest snugly in the indentation in the center of the larger. Having glimpsed Bishop Ravenshorst's drawing in the rearview mirror on the way up to La Purisima, I readily recognized the golden disk that so concerned His Anxiousness the Cardinal.

My prickles sputtered and fizzled, however, at the sight of the smaller disk. As a much-sought key to an ancient puzzle, it was frankly disappointing. Oh, it was made of gold all right, but after all the buildup it just wasn't very impressive. It was engraved with nothing more illuminating or intriguing than a simple, stylized, bas-relief, equilateral Cross—no cryptic instructions, no arrows, no Corpus. While I valued the symbol for its basic Christian significance, I hardly saw how it could be the key to a mystery awaiting solution for centuries. In fact, from the angle of my chair, it was rendered by perspective into an unpretentious, even less convincing "X."

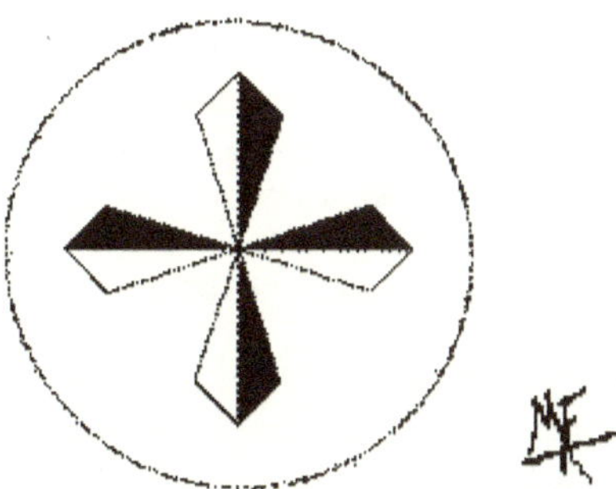

"Just what was I expecting?" I groaned under my breath as I settled my aching bones into a bent but passable sitting position.

From that angle I also got to see Roderick Roundhead straight on. He looked stern, rigid, angry—more so than when Father and I had first

met him in his sprawling mansion in the Hollywood Hills the previous
Monday. Now as then he struck me as a man with fewer years under
his belt than his position and reputation suggested. He didn't look a
day over forty-five. The cut of his suit was regal, his crop of dark hair
impeccably trimmed, his face meticulously shaved. He exuded a corona
of tension like a spring wound so tight it bulged menacingly, yet his
manners were calm, even, and deliberate. The green fire in his eyes
pierced the gloom, fierce and commanding. I found myself resenting
the fact that he hadn't so much as bothered to turn his head when we
arrived at his table, choosing to wait until we came around to sit in his
august presence.

"It isn't always money, of course, that lubricates the wheels," said
Father. "It's interesting that in all the time I've known Thurgood T.
Turnbuckle he never once mentioned you, let alone that he was related
to you by marriage."

"You know then," said Mr. Roundhead.

Ah, thought yours truly, apparently Threety isn't swift in his reports
to Roddy, or perhaps not entirely forthcoming.

"Even more interesting," continued Father, "is the fact that David
Smoley is still a seminarian, albeit technically. That is indeed a severe
price to pay for information."

"He'll never be a priest," said Roundhead. "I can assure you of that."

"Yet he thinks he still has a chance. That is the price of which I
spoke. Why continue to string him along? Surely he's lost his use-
fulness with respect to Monsignor Aspic."

"What makes you think that's his only service?"

"Who gave you the privilege of taking charge of his destiny?"

"Save the examination of conscience, Father. I'm not a penitent in
your confessional. In a time of spiritual upheaval, I do what must be
done. David Smoley is hardly an innocent. He's squarely in the thick
of things. If I may be so bold: so are you."

"Willie don' know what you talkin' 'bout," said Willie, reaching de-
jectedly for the small golden disk on the table. "Willie t'ink he take his
business someplace else."

Mr. Roundhead remained immovable, but Father's hand was faster
than Willie's. He snatched up the smaller disk and looked intently at
the pattern on the gleaming surface, then turned it over and examined
the back.

"Not so fast," said Father to Willie. "I once promised you, when I
returned it to your keeping, that I would never ask what was in that
pouch of yours."

"So much fo' dat," said Willie, slouching back in his chair.

"I don't remember saying anything about seeing for myself."

"Yo' aura, it be sparkin'," said Willie, shrugging begrudgingly. "As always."

Father winked at his friend and set down the small disk. Taking up the larger one, he turned to Mr. Roundhead. "So this is the copy of the papal artifact made for you by Edison Winger?"

"It is."

"I don't suppose you've got the original."

"No." Mr. Roundhead unfolded and refolded his hands. "That would be overreaching, even for me. This copy is all I wanted. Ask Winger. If he doesn't have it, he will answer to me for straying from instructions."

"I asked him the other day. He denied having it." Father was running his fingers around the outer edge of the disk, ignoring the scowl on Roundhead's face. He then explored the central depression, the home of the smaller disk. He pecked at the three indentations in the center of the crater with his pinkie nail. "Hm," he said at last. "I see the problem."

"Like Ah said," said Willie, splaying his fingers around his rattling head. "Sparkin'!"

"I'm not," said I. "Sparking, I mean. What is the problem?"

Father turned the larger disk so I could see the depression. "Remember the indentations indicated by Bishop Ravenshorst's drawing?"

"Oh yes," said I. "You assumed the small disk would have matching teeth to fit them."

I noticed Roderick Roundhead's eyebrows performing a double back flip at the mention of this. The gardener couldn't help enjoying a wee bit of satisfaction that Roddy's life was not entirely free from surprises after all.

"That's right," said Father, picking up the smaller disk and turning its back to me. "Apparently someone along the way removed them."

"Let me see that," said I, taking the small disk from him. Holding it with the Cross facing away from me, I rubbed the back with my thumbs. It was perfectly smooth. "Ah, that is a problem."

"Dah problem is dat he won' pay Willie," said Willie.

"The problem," said Roundhead sternly, "is that without the teeth that disk is useless to me."

Father overturned the larger disk and set it on the table so that the verse was facing up. "Do you understand what the smaller disk is supposed to reveal about the larger disk, assuming the teeth were still attached?"

"After all the trouble and expense you've caused me," said Roundhead, "do you really think I'd tell you?"

"That's an interesting question," observed Father, folding his hands on top of the verse.

"You suggested a moment ago that I live a life void of surprises," said Roundhead, pressing his palms against the surface of the table. "That borders on hyperbole, and I can't deny that you have produced a few."

"So what 'bout Willie?" asked Willie.

"I wouldn't worry, my Friend," said Father. "Wealthy and powerful he may be, but even Roderick Roundhead knows better than to tempt you to resort to one of your spells."

"He do?" squeaked Willie, peering at Mr. Roundhead, who was grimacing more than ever. Willie brightened at the sight. "Ah mean, he *do.*"

"He was just pulling your chain," said Father. "People in positions of power sometimes can't help themselves." He brightened, snapping his thumb and forefinger. "That reminds me, Willie. I owe you an apology."

"*You* do?"

"You discovered, did you not, when you returned from the hospital, that the front door to your establishment had not been repaired? It completely slipped my mind. Surely you deserved better than that from me. I should have called a locksmith, perhaps a carpenter, too. The place was wide open to invasion for days."

Willie shrugged, waved his spindly hands, then folded them on the table. "No problem, Jack."

"That's my point, actually," said Father. "Your confident lack of concern. You and I both know that nothing is missing." He turned his attention to Mr. Roundhead. "In fact, I'll wager the next round of drinks—no, add to that dinner with me and my undivided attention, at your expense, of course—that nothing whatsoever has been taken from his shop."

Roderick Roundhead flashed an intense look that said, "Did I hear you correctly?"

Wagering for beef, booze, and the pleasure of his own company struck me as out of character for Father Baptist, too. Something was up.

"Strange, is it not," said Father, "that there, dead center in the seediest part of town—yes, Martin, I know, in your esteemed literary opinion there is no seedy part of town—a neighborhood regarded as a 'red zone' by the police authorities, no one has entered and removed a single item. No one, not one."

"That was Willie," said I.

"Excuse me?" said Father.

"'There is no seedy part of town,'" I explained. "I got that line from Willie."

"You did?" asked Willie,

"You're sure of that, are you?" said Roderick Roundhead, that jaw muscle of his swollen to capacity.

"Yes," said I. "I even recorded it in one of my manuscri—"

"Not that," said Roundhead sternly. "I meant, are you sure, Father Baptist, that nothing has been removed from Willie's store?"

Father slammed his hand palm-down on the table. The gesture was not angry, but rather challenging. "You think I'd lightly wager an evening of my valuable time listening attentively to whatever you have to say to me, just for dinner and drinks?"

Roundhead's lips curled into a suggestion of a smile, then snapped back to expressionlessness.

"Where's your gaming spirit?" prodded Father. "The least you could do is add dessert to the wager, you know, something flashy and tableside like Baked Alaska."

Roundhead regarded Father with cold eyes, as if trying to penetrate the meaning behind the dare. "An inventory could take days. How would you suggest that we verify the matter one way or the other?"

"What have your extended eyes and ears reported? I'll take your word for it."

Suddenly, Roddy laughed uproariously. It was a genuinely charming laugh—not what I'd've expected from him at all—full-bodied and honest, if a tad pretentious. It was reminiscent of one of Pierre Bontemps' hearty guffaws. I was tempted to let down my guard a notch with respect to him—tempted to, I said, not decided to. His merriment went on for a bit, then subsided into a broad smile. "Why would I want to yammer at you for an evening? What would I possibly want to say to you that would take so long? You think too highly of yourself, Father. You need to confess your pride, that is, if you can find a priest in this archdiocese with the chutzpah to withstand the secrets of *your* heart. I know I'd sure be squeamish—but more so curious. No matter, to the point: everyone at this table knows why anyone who has survived that part of town would never set foot in Willie's shop while he was indisposed. They wouldn't want to stumble into some insidious hex-trap set by the infamous Guillaume du Crane Cristal. Even the Board of Public Health is reluctant to cite him for a dozen obvious violations."

"No surprise there," said Father, himself laughing. "Which of their inspectors in his right mind would knowingly cross the threshold of 'Wide Eye Do Dat?' let alone write up the proprietor for an infraction?"

Mr. Roundhead coughed into his fist, then resumed his hearty chuckling. "Tell me, Father: Mr. Kapps has never explained that 'Fortunes Untold' part to me. Has he to you?"

"Whoa, hol' on, Jack," intruded Willie.

"Don't worry," said Father. "I won't betray your secrets."

"Bettah not," said Mr. Kapps.

"So how about it?" said Father to Roundhead.

"This wager," said Roundhead to Father. "It is a test."

"It is what it is."

Mr. Roundhead's forehead went through some contortions that would even have impressed Monsignor Havermeyer. "All right. I win. I say that with a grain or two of salt. You know perfectly well that someone entered Willie's establishment and removed something without his permission. You probably have it with you: the message I left there arranging this very meeting."

"Discovered," said Father, producing the folded stationary with the distinctive "A" and all those little circles around the edge. "I guess I lose. Shall we remove ourselves to the famous Blue Mountain Grill? I understand your aunt Mehitabelle and her sister by marriage, Hortense, are regulars."

"By a happy coincidence, they happen to be there this evening," said Roundhead.

"Swell," said the gardener, massaging his sensitive tummy under the table. He also glanced around again, but no Keating.

"This being the Feast of the Commemoration of the Basilicas of Saints Peter and Paul," said Roundhead, "they are celebrating. At their age, any excuse, and all that. I'm afraid your wager has backfired on you, Father. Not only will you be treated to what I have to say, you'll have to endure everything they have to say as well."

"I shall be delighted," said Father. "Shall we proceed?"

"Excuse me," said I. "Father, Willie, Mr. Roundhead. I'm not particularly hungry at the moment, and I'd so like to explore this wonderful hotel. I trust you won't mind if I don't join you."

"I understand," said Father, winking at me so the others wouldn't see. "Perhaps I can prevail upon Mr. Roundhead further by asking him for a lift home. That would free you to leave when you wish."

"No problem," said Mr. Roundhead magnanimously. "I'll gladly oblige."

"Okay then," said I, amazed at how easily Father had slipped right into their circle like a greased eel through the eye of a needle ... or something like that. "I will bid you all goodnight."

"Willie be crushed to hear it," said Willie "Skull" Kapps, no doubt feeling as out of place as myself but figuring he might as well get a free meal out of the deal. "Yo' be missed, Martin Mon."

Even the infamous Guillaume du Crane Cristal had no idea how right he was.

55

FEELING EVER SO BLESSED for having been spared dinner with Mehitabelle and Hortense Doily, not to mention the ludicrous tableau of Roderick "Roddy" Roundhead spouting at the mouth while Father Baptist listened attentively, I made my way between the tables and out of the Saranac Lounge. My only regret was missing the opportunity to dine with Willie, having never had the pleasure. I thought I might catch sight of Keating pondering a tall glass of stout along the way, but he was nowhere to be seen.

"I trust you're having a pleasant evening, Sir," said a tall, gaunt man at the registration counter as I passed. His thin black hair was just long enough to be tucked behind his ears, and he wore small bifocals that slowly slid from the bridge of his nose to the tip during the following conversation. He did not smile, but nodded his head deferentially. There was a polished brass nameplate pinned to his jacket pocket: OSCAR LANGLEY, ASST. MANAGER.

"This place is fascinating," I said, genuinely enthused. "It must have an amazing history."

"You have no idea," said he, his face immobile, his voice monotone. His reserved detachment reminded me of the bartender back in the Saranac Lounge. The desk phone rang. He glanced at the flashing light on an attached panel, but ignored it. "Might I suggest a nightcap in the Champlain Room, Sir?"

Just then a burst of merriment erupted from within that very bar across the lobby. Strangely, some men were singing something to the tune of "It Don't Mean a Thing If It Ain't Got That Swing," but I could have sworn the words were in Latin: *"Nil significat nisi oscillat. Du vap, du vap, du vap, du vap, du vap, du vap, du vap, du vap!"*

"You certainly may," said I, intrigued, "but I left my car parked in your carport. I shouldn't have left it there so long. I'm going to move it to your parking lot. I assume it's around and behind."

"It's not a problem, Sir. We're not very busy this evening. You may as well leave it where it is, unless you'd care to spend the night."

"You know, that's almost a thought. Well, no, I'm expected at the homestead early tomorrow morning, and of course there's Sunday Mass. It would be something to arrange in the future, though."

"Very good, Sir."

The phone rang again. I could see the flash of light from the panel reflected off the wire rims of his spectacles. As he glanced down at it the second time I thought I caught his jaw muscles tighten, just enough to displace his ears ever so slightly.

"Do you need to get that?" I asked, helpfully.

"No, Sir. It's not for me."

"Oh, well then, did I say that this is one marvelous old hotel?"

"Words to that effect, Sir. Thank-you. It certainly is one of a kind."

"Would you believe the last time I was here was the night of my high school prom?"

"Really, Sir." I think he tried to smile, slightly. It was strained.

"I don't suppose I could see the Ticonderoga Ballroom?"

"I'm sorry, Sir. The ballroom is reserved this evening. The Hollywood Branch of the Theosophical Society."

"Oh, a lecture?"

"A group dancing lesson, I believe."

"Ah, well, maybe next time."

The phone rang a third time accompanied by the flashing light. It was mid-jingle when a mahogany door marked MANAGEMENT opened behind the clerk. A woman with batwing glasses, large pearl earrings, wearing a black sweater and dress leaned out. I couldn't see her name-tag, but from the pencils wedged over her left ear I assumed her to be an accountant. She sniffed, squinted, and pouted, "Oscar, the phone."

"It's Room 1953, Miss Giles."

"Oh." Her face fell, just a centimeter or two, but it definitely fell. "Never mind."

"Trouble with the phone?" asked yours truly as she withdrew, closing the door behind her with a solid click of the lock.

"Of a sort," said the clerk. "Room 1953 calls the front desk every day at precisely six o'clock on the dot."

"Is that a problem?"

His expression did not change, but he swallowed loudly. "Only that there is no room 1953 at the Adirondack—we only have seventeen floors in the main tower, twelve in the wings."

"Some sort of short circuit?"

"No doubt, Sir, but the technicians have been unable to locate it. There, you see? It has stopped." His jaw muscles and ears relaxed. "Is there anything more I can do for you?"

I couldn't think of anything, so I smiled, shook my head, and moved away.

Before heading for the Champlain Room, I paused to admire the large oil paintings around the lobby. One of the panels I hadn't noticed before depicted a wedding celebration in the courtyard of a charming hacienda. The bride was a dark-skinned beauty, her long hair trailing silk ribbons, her gown billowing and flowing behind. She proudly held the arm of a dashing pale fellow in a military uniform. It suddenly struck me that this was the same couple whose carriage would capsize some years later in San Francisco, the right front wheel having fallen through a hole in the pavement. I couldn't be sure without a closer look, but I suspected that this man also aged into the proud fellow on the other panel with his foot planted atop a stack of metallic disks. From there my eyes were drawn to the dozen similar disks bolted into the granite façade of the registration counter, and then to the disks mounted atop every pillar, decorating every archway, gracing every intersection of line inside and outside the building. The disks were all the same size, made of the same type of metal, but they had different patterns molded into their surfaces. Some were embellished with geometric configurations, some with interlocked rectangles or intertwined stars. I then recalled the invitation Father found at Willie's shop, the card with the stylized "A" for "Adirondack," the little embossed circles around the edge.

"What's with these disks?" I asked aloud. "Father called them 'dots.' Why do they permeate everything connected with this hotel — ?"

Why would Roderick Roundhead arrange to meet Willie "Skull" Kapps at this hotel in particular, the same establishment that housed the Blue Mountain Grill, the staff of which had presented the Doily Sisters with a set of engraved gravy boats. Who was Mehitabelle Doily but Roderick Roundhead's aunt? Why did it all come back to that bothersome name again and again?

I became dizzyingly aware of these circles everywhere, emblazoned on lampshades, engraved on all the glasses and ashtrays, molded into the handrails and picture frames, embossed on every pen and pencil. They were woven into the very fabric of the place like the clattering detritus in Willie's dreadlocks.

I can't honestly say whether it was my brain adding up the evidence and drawing a conclusion, or the simple action of my eyes focusing on the nearest disk, which happened to be mounted above an ornate drinking fountain set in a nearby wall. There it was, molded into the metal itself, the manufacturer of every metallic disk in the place:

ROUNDHEAD MANHOLE COVERS

Manhole covers!
Manhole covers!
I returned to the registration counter.
"Excuse me," said I.
"Yes, Sir," said Mr. Oscar Langley, who had not moved an inch since I'd left him.
"These metal disks all over the hotel."
"Yes, Sir."
"Are they — ?"

"Oh, yes," he said with the heroic patience of a man who had answered that very question a dozen times a day for the last dozen years. "The Adirondack, as the saying goes, is the hotel that manhole covers built."

I had an inkling that the saying was intended to be uttered with a tad more enthusiasm, but I wasn't about to press the point. My first thought was to ask to be directed to the Blue Mountain Grill so I could share this revelation with Father Baptist. My second thought was the image of Mehitabelle and Hortense fidgeting with their boas while their pompous nephew pummeled Father Baptist with his pretentious opinions and Guillaume du Crane Cristal suppressed the urge to turn them all, with the exception of himself and hopefully Father, into toads. My third thought was to continue on my interrupted journey to the maritime bar from which just then burst the welcoming sound of jovial, masculine laughter.

"Third time lucky," said yours truly, gripping my cane and lurching toward the Champlain Room.

56

"ONLY THE THIRD?" intruded a grating female voice before I could get there. "What happened the first two times?"

"Why Miss Crackerjack," said yours truly as I attempted to arrange my face into an expression not consistent with the annoyance I felt inside.

"Sweet man," said the producer of "Religion Regurgitated." Napolia Krackershak's breath was torrential with Drambuie and Chivas Regal. I mean, one good puff from this crusty gal could've toppled Hadrian's Wall. What I said before about her coming across as the kind of person who desperately needed advice on apparel but who would maul anyone who dared give it—well, it still applied. This time around she was wearing a silver jumpsuit with black fringes like string licorice dangling from every seam. Those extra thirty pounds had found release in this outfit, but in ways better left not described. Her gloved fingers did a little sashay up my tie, kicking high like a chorus girl in the midst of a frolicking encore. "I love it when you mispronounce my name."

"I hate it when a point gets missed," said I, stumbling a half-hobble back.

"Just so long as it's not the one I'm making," said she, advancing a step-and-a-half closer. "Fancy bumping into you here, of all places."

"Yessirree, Ma'am. Imagine that."

"I checked my horoscope this morning, Mr. Feeney. Would you believe I'm a Gemini?"

"Sure. I'm an Ultra-Realist myself."

"That means I have two faces, among other things."

"Well, nice bumping. If you will excuse me—"

"Wouldn't you know?" She performed a sultry knee dip, relished a rippling shiver, and gave herself a group hug. Almost as an afterthought, she whispered, "Just after you fled the makeup room, you dear man, and your priest friend shortly after that, a most succulent tidbit of exquisite information fell into my lap."

The fumes that burst from her mouth on every open vowel buffeted me. She had placed such a penetrating, almost condescending emphasis on "you dear man" that something deep in my ear canals shuddered. Wondering what interpretation she had applied to my explosive exit from the television station, I ventured to respond, "You don't say."

"I do say," slurred she. "It's about Monsignor Aspic. Look, Honeybunch, part of my job is sniffing out topics of interest for the show. I know they caught that Mercedes Sinclair guy, the nutcase who killed all those priests. I know you were present during the arrest, you and that retro-retro Father Baptist. The police think Aspic was Sinclair's most recent victim, but I know better."

"Who's your informant, Sheldon or Eira?"

"Be serious."

"Why?"

"Because this is important."

I couldn't help but harrumph. "Since when do all important things require seriousness? And since when can the term be connected in any way with Sheldon and Eira Levant? Speaking of which, why would you want to help locate Monsignor Aspic? He's worth more to you missing."

She winked at me and smacked her gum. "For the time being, sure, ratings are luscious. Sooner or later, though, he's going to surface, living or dead. Father Baptist will unquestionably be in on it, and I want his exclusive."

"For the Levants."

"Of course for them. I made them, and I sustain them, and that's how I take care of sweet, lovable me. What do you say?"

"I can't speak for Father Baptist. He's in the Blue Mountain Grill." I admit I enjoyed a brief, juicy daydream of the interaction between her and the Doily Sisters. Vinegar and oil. Heck, chlorine bleach and ammonia! Then I almost added, "Me, I'm for the Champlain Room," but decided that would sound like an invitation, so instead I just edged further away and stammered, "You'll have to ask him."

Undaunted, she crept inexorably closer. "What would you say, Mr. Feeney, if I told you that on the day he disappeared, Monsignor Aspic went to see an important media manipulator? We're talking a powerful man, the same one Cardinal Fulbright crawls to for help whenever we nasty media types report his booboos, which happens to be our job, don't you know?"

"A media manipulator," said I, glancing over my shoulder looking for obstacles to my rearward retreat. The last thing I wanted to do was sprawl backwards onto the floor at her feet. "I guess I'd say, 'Oh, really?'"

She pressed closer and closer and exhaled rocket fuel all over me. "I have it on good authority that your monsignor went to see the Wizard of Spin himself." She puffed herself up like a proud sea-lioness. "Willis P. Wedge."

"Oh him," said I with a dismissive wave of my hand. "Bendlebrain's left-hand man, or is it Cruiser's?"

She fluttered her eyelashes, momentarily perplexed. Then she pursed her lips into a pout. "I thought you'd be impressed."

"Impressed by something I already know?" said I. Then I snapped my fingers. "I get it. You've been following Father Baptist and me. You know we spoke with Mr. Wedge in his office two days ago."

"Not him and you," she breathed deeply. "You. I was following you. Not personally, naturally. I used my usual agency. When they phoned this evening with their up-to-the-minute report, I came here to see for myself."

"See what for yourself?"

"What I expected." She made to brush the dust from my shoulders, or was it suds residue? "As for Monsignor Aspic, I wouldn't put axing a troublemaker beyond the actuation potential of a control freak like Willy Wedge."

"Willy? Actuation potential?"

"There have been rumors," she said significantly.

"Rumors," said I obliviously.

"You know, annoyances who have disappeared."

"What are you suggesting?"

"Tell me. Is it true what I hear about Morell deQuet?"

"I've no idea, but I understand it's rampant. Just look around."

"Oh, you." There are few things in life worse than a woman with a chalkboard-scraping voice trying to sound meaningfully coy. "Sweetie," she said, eyelashes fluttering like befuddled moths, "you knew I meant Bishop deQuet."

"I knew nothing of the kind."

"Well, I did, and I did."

"If you say so."

"More than you know." She rested her right index finger against her lower lip. "Hasn't it occurred to you and your boss that Aspic's boss, Cardinal Fulbright, and deQuet's boss, Archbishop Mann, both hired Willy Boy to pick up their pieces? And there's toady-boy Aspic, right smack dab in the middle of a situation in which he could easily learn one too many things about where the skeletons are kept."

"Skeletons."

"Oh, come now." Napolia Krackershak repeated that knee-dip-with-rippling-shiver auto-hug routine. Then she did that wide open stare thing I described back at the TV station, followed by several quick blinks and a wayward glance. "It's no secret that Father Baptist is one of the cardinal's fix-it men. Don't look now, but some say he's the best there is."

I gave her a look that I hoped conveyed, "Hey, you retract that this instant!"

She just winked blearily back as if to say, "'Retract' ain't in my vocabulary, Sweetie Pie."

"I think we're done, Miss Krackershak," I said after a long-held breath.

"Suppose," she lolled, blinking all the blearier, "just suppose Monsignor Aspic in his capacity as recruiting officer, while checking Bishop deQuet's résumé, discovered that the good bishop is half-owner of a seedy little hotspot in Hollywood called 'Melvin di Milo's.' Regulars, according to my trustworthy, confidential source, affectionately call it 'Little Mel's Spanking Palace.'"

I admit I smiled at that one.

"Say," she said, arranging her face into a look of conspiratorial triumph. "Would you believe that Morell and Melvin went to the same seminary?"

"Hardly," I lied, backing away using my cane as a behind-me prodder. Thusly, I avoided knocking over a potted palm.

"Any harder to believe," she said, her voice rising in pitch, "than the nyah-nyah going around that Monsignor Aspic's brother was a flat out, real, live vampire?"

"Flat out," I said with a hint of derision. That was getting a little close for comfort, as was Napolia Krackershak in her liquidy, silvery, licoricey outfit. "I suppose there are no limits to what you'll do to add a few weeks of life to your show." Including, I added to myself, coming on to me like this.

"I do what I do with all my heart," said she, thinking she was being alluring. She was not.

"'For where thy treasure is, there is thy heart also,'" said I. Saint Matthew six twenty-one.

"You said it, Mister."

"So have you." There comes a point when there is nothing left to be said. Most people refuse to recognize it and keep on plodding. I chose to bail. "If you will excuse me, Miss Krackershak, my presence is required elsewhere."

As I turned away she just stood there looking gorgeous, or so she thought. She wasn't used to being dismissed, not by the likes of an innocuous bug like Martin Feeney. It occurred to me as I took the long way around the lobby to the Champlain Room that I had probably just made an enemy.

I thought of going all the way around the lobby again and reporting this encounter to Father Baptist, but decided it could wait until morning. It ended up waiting a bit longer, but let's not get ahead of ourselves.

57

"'LITERATURE IS THE EXPRESSION,'" read Pierre Bontemps from the notebook balanced in his open hand, "'through the artistic medium of words, of the dogmas of the Catholic Church, and that which is in any way out of harmony with these dogmas is not literature.'"

"Wow, whoa, what do you know!" exclaimed the other Tumblars severally.

"'Catholic dogma is merely the witness,'" continued Pierre, further down the page, "'under a special symbolism of the enduring facts of human nature and the universe.'"

"Where did you find that?" asked Jonathan Clubb.

Pierre turned back several pages. "'Hieroglyphics: Notes on the Ecstatic in Literature,' by Arthur Machen."

"That's definitely a keeper," said Edward Strypes Windham. That bird-of-prey crest over his nose fluttered its feathers. "Speaking of literature, Arthur, what was that you were saying about the cheer being wrong?"

"What cheer?" asked Joel Maruppa.

"You know," said Edward. "Our cheer. *The* cheer."

"Wrong?" persisted Joel. "How is it wrong?"

"Arthur?" insisted Edward.

"What're you saying?" asked Jonathan of Edward. "What's he saying?" he asked Joel.

"Arthur, dear chap," said Pierre, nudging the eldest Tumblar who had apparently fallen into a rambling snooze.

Arthur had phoned the rectory from Rome only two nights before, at half past four in the morning their time. Here he was at half past six in the evening, our time, with a polar flight and all the hustling and bustling that entails in between—not to mention the pretense of sleep in those narrow, angular seats the airlines so sadistically provide. Though formally attired, his clothes had that look of having just been unpacked from an over-stuffed suitcase. The nylon flight bag beside him suggested that he and they had just come from the airport.

"Wrong?" mumbled Arthur as his eyelids rolled back revealing bleary, red-ringed windows of his soul.

"What's this about the cheer being wrong?" insisted Joel. His perturbation was understandable, considering that he, being the last to join the troupe, had learned it from the rest of them.

"Oh, lyeccch!" sputtered Arthur, rubbing his eyes, smacking his lips, and swatting something from his tongue. "Sorry, Gentlemen, I have never been so jetlagged in all my life."

"Maybe we should take you home," said Jonathan.

"I'm fine," Arthur managed around a yawn. "If you don't mind me drifting in and out, I'd rather be here with you."

"You were saying," said Edward, "about our cheer."

"Being wrong," said Joel.

"Well," said Arthur, shifting himself erect in the seat and hooking his thumbs under his suspenders. "It's just that there was a fellow sitting next to me on the plane, a mumblesome old chap by the name of Stufflebeem, Professor Ichibod Stufflebeem. He was reading a book entitled *Verses* by H. Belloc, published in London in 1911. Naturally I engaged him in conversation. At some point I asked him if I might peruse his book, and he graciously obliged. Therein I found a poem called 'Heretics All.' The moment I read it I knew I had to bring it to your attention. Even with all that turbulence I managed to copy it onto the title page of Mr. Feeney's manuscript." Saying this, he unzipped the flight bag and produced a slab of photocopied sheets in a comb binder. This he peeled open and examined his handiwork. "I hope Sir Martin won't mind, I didn't have anything else to write on. You know how he can be."

"Do I ever," said Pierre. "Not to worry. I'll run you off a new first page at work on Monday. He'll never know the difference."

sions. I reported it in the very manuscript Arthur was holding in his hands:

                              * * *

     "'Where ever Catholic sun doth shine,'"
quoted Pierre, raising his glass.
     "'There's lots of laughter and good red
wine,'" chimed the others, rising to their
feet.
     "'At least I've always heard it so,'"
said Father.
     "'Benedicamus domino,'" said we all,
clinking our glasses together.
     "Hilaire Belloc," explained Pierre.
"Historian and poet."
                              * * *

   They had been spouting it for as long as I had
known them. Apparently they had never looked it
up . . . until now.

                                        --M.F.

"So how is it supposed to go?" asked Jonathan.

"Yes, Arthur," said Edward. "Do tell."

Arthur held the manuscript in both hands, squinting. "Ah," he said at last, "my writing's mangled, but I've got it. I'm not certain how to pronounce some of these names. Here goes:

> Heretics all, whoever you may be,
> In Tarbes or Nimes, or over the sea,
> You never shall have good words from me.
> *Caritas non conturbat me.*

"What was that last line?" asked Joel. "Latin, yes?"

"Professor Stufflebeem penciled in the translation," said Arthur, nodding. "It means 'Charity does not disturb me.' The second stanza is closest to what we've been saying:

> But Catholic men that live upon wine
> Are deep in the water, and frank, and fine;
> Wherever I travel I find it so,
> *Benedicamus Domino.*

"'Let us bless the Lord, '" translated Edward.

"Give the man a cigar," said Pierre.

Arthur continued:

> On childing women that are forlorn,
> And men that sweat in nothing but scorn:
> That is on all that ever were born,
> *Miserere Domine.*

"'Have mercy, O Lord,'" said Arthur, squinting at his own handwriting. "And finally:

> To my poor self on my deathbed,
> And all my dear companions dead,
> Because of the love that I bore them,
> *Dona Eis Requiem.*

"You should all recognize that last line from the *Dies Irae,*" said Arthur.

"Grant them rest," said everyone together.

"There you have it," said Arthur, setting the manuscript with uncertain hands on the table beside his drink. It looked like whiskey straight up, a mere fraction consumed. "Sorry Lads, I'm spent."

"So we've just been doing the second stanza," said Joel, "and wrong."

"Well," said Jonathan, "it certainly is different."

"I kind of like our way," said Edward.

"But it's wrong," said Joel.

"I suppose we could make adjustments," said Pierre, "or leave things the way they are."

"Something to ponder," mumbled Arthur, settling back in his seat.

"How did we get it so wrong?" said Joel, scowling.

"Who came up with it?" asked Edward.

All eyes turned to Pierre.

"Aha!" said the gardener under his breath as the cocktail waitress set a basket of extra-salty pretzels beside his elbow.

"Ahem!" said Pierre, rising to the occasion. He held up his empty glass and said, "To quote William Powell in *The Thin Man:* 'Ammunition?'"

"'Those were the good old days,'" said Arthur, wistfully furthering the scene from the movie.

"'Don't kid yourself,'" Pierre quoted Powell's response.

They all joined in: "*'These* are the good old days!'"

"Speaking of literature," said Edward to Pierre. "Mr. Feeney's manuscript. Any word from those publishers you gave it to?"

"Not a peep," said Pierre.

"Maybe you should give them a call," said Joel.

"Publishers, so I'm told, generally don't want to be pushed and prodded," said Pierre. "They're funny that way. But if I don't hear something in another week or so, I may give them a jingle."

"You read the manuscript on the plane," said Jonathan to Arthur. "What did you think of it?"

"Arthur?" asked Edward.

"Arthur?" asked Joel.

"He's asleep again," said Pierre. "Poor chap."

"So what did you think of it, Pierre?" asked Edward.

"Hi," greeted the waitress, disrupting the gardener's descent into voyeurism. Apparently she had been standing there waiting impatiently for several seconds. She fumbled with a small white cocktail napkin, but finally got it situated beside the pretzels. "Whuh cunnuh getcha?"

Riveted as he was to the conversation across the bar, it was with reluctance that the gardener looked up at her at all. She was young, probably just turned twenty-one, and slightly out of breath, as though she had barely made it to work to start her shift on time. This impression was reinforced by several strands of hair that had escaped capture in her ponytail dangling crookedly across her face—and the fact that her little plastic nametag, "CONNIE," was upside down. The way she was glancing around, perhaps she had reported for duty at the wrong bar. More than likely, this was her first day on the job. Unlike most cocktail waitresses in most of the lounges throughout the city, she was attired in a tasteful, modest black dress that covered her shoulders, concealed her décolletage, protected her derriere, and defended her fulcra. She also wore a charming blue apron with the familiar "A" embroidered on the front, with little decorative manhole covers trailing around the sash. Though she carried herself like a modern girl—which is to say, pretty much like a boy—her uniform transported her to a time before her time when women enjoyed walking like ladies. She was tangled in an anachronism, and he couldn't tell whether she was uncomfortable or clueless about it.

"I'd like a ginger ale, please," said he, a bit sheepishly, as if he had just been caught at something. "Saint Thomas, Salisbury. 'Blue label,' if you have it."

"Gee, um not shir. Ull hafta ask."

Deciding not to judge her harshly for her poor diction, she being a product of the modern miasma, he pointed in the direction of the barkeeper, who was wiping down the counter designed to suggest the wheel deck of an old frigate. The gardener couldn't help noticing that the bartender had cheeks that sagged like wet sandbags, and a sad, penetrating countenance to match.

"If he doesn't," said the gardener, "the fellow across the way in the Saranac Lounge does. I just came from there."

"Ull tellim," said she, jotting something down in her notebook and shoving it into a pocket in her apron. "Be back."

The gardener nodded at the notion as she left him and headed for the bartender. Grimacing at a sudden twinge of pain in his right hip, he returned his attention to the lads seated across the way.

Eavesdropping was new to him. It was not what he had intended as he strolled into the Champlain Room, having just discovered that the Adirondack Hotel was somehow connected with the Roundhead family. He had been mulling over this information as he entered the maritime ambience of the Champlain Room, drawn by the banter of friendly male voices within.

Upon entering the bar he had been confronted by two unexpected things. First, he heard his own name mentioned. The context was lost amidst the chuckles that followed. Secondly, he recognized the voice that had pronounced his name, as well as the larynxes that were laughing about it. Not believing in coincidences, the gardener marveled at the happenstance. Only two nights before, as the Knights of the Tumblar prepared to leave the rectory at the conclusion of their weekly meeting in Father's study, they had hinted about their recent discovery:

> *"Where are you fellows headed?"* the gardener had asked.
>
> *"There's a new place that's come to our attention,"* Edward had answered. *"Or rather, a very old place that we've only just learned about."*
>
> This was followed by Pierre's quip about no bar being worth their trouble unless it was older than they were. Then Father said:
>
> *"Do tell. As a policeman I used to know every hangout in town."*
>
> *"We'll report all when next we see you,"* promised Pierre. *"And now, lads, we must be off!"*
>
> They had all cheered *"Hurrah!"* except Jonathan, who had just been informed that his sweetheart, Stella, was being instructed in the opinions of St. Cyprian by Millie. This was two days before the coming of the suds.

Who would have thought that they had been talking about the Adirondack? Certainly not the gardener. In a city the size of Los Angeles, with so many millions of people and thousands of bars, it truly was something. So amazed was he that, for reasons he could not completely explain, he eased himself into a seat behind a table that was somewhat hidden from the Tumblars by a fishing net draped from the ceiling to the floor. He could peer between the webbing right at them, but since the light source was on their side, they could not readily see him unless they really looked, and why should they?

"If I may return to an earlier topic," Pierre was saying. "My editrix, Kahlúa Hummingbird, has suggested that I start a regular column in the *L. A. Artsy* called 'View from the Pew.' It's to be a weekly critique of sermons and worship services throughout our fair city."

"Worship services?" asked Joel.

"These days we must be at least ostensively interdenominational," explained Pierre. "The occasional Anglican or Presbyterian event will inevitably rear its head, but Kahlúa understands that the Catholic Church is my first concern. We need to get the ball rolling immediately. She figures that if word gets out among the clergy that they're being scrutinized—and by the same guy who blew the whistle on 'Fettuccini Cardinal Fulbright'—naturally they will all start buying the *Artsy* to see how they're doing."

"Sounds cockeyed to me," said Edward.

"No doubt," said Pierre, "but what isn't? Did I read you the article she wrote about my arrest and release earlier this week?"

"Twice," said Jonathan and Edward. Joel held up two fingers. Arthur was fast asleep.

"Amazing, isn't it," said Pierre, "how circs can change so in just a handful of days."

Just then Connie, the cocktail waitress with the inverted nametag, reached the counter where she engaged in subdued conversation with the bartender. He was shaking his head and pointing toward the archway. No doubt the Saint Thomas, Salisbury, as the gardener had suggested, was only to be had in the Saranac Lounge across the lobby. Her response was a protracted, deflating, victimized sigh. As she turned to commence the laborious, unfair, abysmal trek to the distant Saranac, she noticed the Tumblars. Her sad expression turned to joy as a light bulb clicked on above her head. The needs of the lads, representing the larger potential tip, took precedence over the imbibition of the lone gardener cowering behind the net. They were more dashing besides.

"What does this have to do with us?" Joel was asking.

"In the interest of saving time," said Pierre, "Madam Hummingbird has agreed to pay each of you twenty-five dollars for every church you research for me. In other words, you fellows go out for the next few weekends, attend the various Masses throughout the archdiocese, then

give me the details. I'll write the reviews as if I had been there myself—that's called journalistic license."

"I don't know," said Edward. "I really hate attending the Novus
Ordo—all that greeting and bleating. I avoid it if I can."

"As do we all," said Jonathan.

"But Gentlemen," said Pierre, "it's only for a few weekends. Tell
you what: you can go to the five-thirty Mass on Saturday afternoons.
Go to observe, not to attend. You can still go to Father Baptist's Tridentine Mass on Sundays. Come to think of it, this would be a great
excuse for us to check out some of the 'independent chapels' as well,
though they wouldn't have the Saturday afternoon option."

"You mean the ones run by independent priests," said Joel. "The
ones who have gone back to the Latin Mass without the cardinal's permission."

"My very thought," said Pierre.

"Or the SSPX," said Jonathan. "Don't they have a chapel somewhere?"

"It's in Vernon," said Edward. "I wouldn't mind checking them out."

"Perhaps we should consult the Code of Canon Law," said Joel, the
former seminarian, "to be sure of our ground. If their Mass is valid,
then there is no problem."

"If you have any question about their legitimacy," said Pierre, "you
could attend the early Mass at St. Philomena's on Sunday, and then
check out the noon Mass at the 'indie' afterwards. Come on, Lads. It's
not great money, but it's money to spend—no doubt on booze—plus
you'll be doing me an enormous favor I will be duty bound to repay.
What do you say?"

"Hi," interrupted Connie cheerfully, and a mite flirtatiously. "You
guys juscum frumma weddun ur sumthun?"

"Excuse me?" said Pierre, adjusting his cufflinks.

"Wull, jus lookit chu," said she. "A fyoonrul, maybe?"

"Why no, Miss," said Pierre. "We're just having a pleasant night
out."

"We always dress like this," said Edward.

"After six, anyway," said Joel.

"Gwan," she giggled. "Rully?"

"Arthur, old chap," said Edward, nudging the weary traveler. "Don't
we always dress like this in the evenings?"

"Wha—?" Arthur extricated himself from what was likely a satisfying dream in order to blink, smack his lips twice, and say obliviously,
"Why yes. Yes, of course."

"Shir," said she, skeptically. "No, rully. Arya headin' to a show ur
sumthun?"

"Okay, but you mustn't tell a soul," said Pierre, glancing around as if he were about to reveal a great secret. "The truth is, they only let us out once a year, on this very night."

"Letcha out?" said she, warily. "Whur frum?"

"It's kind of hard to explain," said Edward.

"That's right," agreed Joel. "Very hard."

"We're really not supposed to talk about it," said Jonathan to her, then to Pierre, "So you do the honors."

The gardener absently reached for a pretzel, wondering where this was leading.

"Before I tell you," said Pierre, beckoning her closer, "I'd like to order a round of Imperial Whiskey."

"Zatta bran?" asked she.

"*A* brand?" asked Edward. "Why it's *the* brand."

"It was Ed Wood's favorite," said Jonathan. "You've seen *Plan Nine from Outer Space,* haven't you?"

"Uuuuuh, no," said she, shrugging and shaking her head as if she'd always had better things to do.

"That's a shame," said Pierre. "He directed it."

"Who did?" asked Connie.

"Ed Wood," said Edward. "He also directed *Bride of the Atom,* but he peaked—wouldn't you Lads agree?—with *Plan Nine.*"

They rumbled their concurrence.

"Anyway," said Jonathan, "they stopped making it four decades ago."

"Makin' whut?" asked she, shaking her head some more.

"Why, Imperial Whiskey," said Joel.

"Barlow, your exceedingly knowledgeable and capable bartender, assured us," said Pierre, "that a truckload was recently found in the back of a truck buried in a landslide in Pacific Palisades. Imagine, it had been waiting there, aging all this time."

"Forty years in the bottle and underground besides," mused Arthur. "That would certainly take the edge off."

"This fine hotel bought the lot," said Pierre. "Ah, how I love the Adirondack!"

At the mention of his name, Barlow the somber bartender looked up from the counter he was absently polishing with a terrycloth towel. Somehow he managed to tug his facial muscles in such a way as to produce something akin to a knowing smile. The effect was somewhere between endearing and unsettling.

"Woodja like meeduh bring yuh thuh hole boddle?" asked Connie.

"That would make sense," said Arthur, "seeing as how our time is running short."

"Gotcha," said she. "Y'*arr* all goan sumplus speshull dooded up like that."

"Not at all," said Jonathan. "Our place is here."

"Uh doan geddit," said she, brushing one of those tangled strands away from her face.

"You were going to do the honors," said Jonathan to Pierre. It occurred to the listening gardener that they didn't know precisely where this was going, either.

"Ah well," said Pierre, tugging on the hem of his waistcoat for effect, "I suppose we can tell you: we're dead."

She gasped. Even the Tumblars fell momentarily silent. Barlow, eyebrows hitched high on his furrowed forehead, picked up a shot glass and started screwing the corner of the towel into it.

"Arthur here," said Pierre, patting the travel-weary Tumblar on the shoulder, "fell from a twelfth-story balcony during a New Year's Eve party back in '39."

"It was '29," corrected Arthur sleepily.

"Really?" said Pierre. "How time flies."

"It was a rough year," said Arthur.

"No doubt," commiserated Pierre.

"And I didn't exactly 'fall.'"

"We needn't go there, Old Chap. Now Edward, I'm sorry to say, committed suicide up on the tenth floor. What room was that?"

"I was so upset," admitted Edward, a melodramatic quiver in his voice. "Mumsie and Dadsy had just disinherited me."

"Whatever for?" asked Jonathan.

"Oh, the shame," sighed Edward, resting the back of his hand against his forehead. "Please don't press."

"When was that again?" asked Joel.

"I don't quite remember," whined Edward. "It was all so awful. I think the Germans invaded somebody-or-other the day before. I'm not sure."

"Jonathan and Joel, on the other hand, got themselves into a duel," said Pierre. "What was the lady's name?"

"Stella," said Jonathan, because for him there was no other woman.

"Stella," agreed Joel. "We drew pistols at twenty paces."

"Up on the roof," added Jonathan. "What a way to go."

"We both won," added Joel. "Therefore we both lost."

"Love and war," mused Jonathan with an exaggerated shrug. "All's fair? *Hah!*"

"An' wuddabow choo?" asked Connie, peering at Pierre as though he was about to change into a newt.

Pierre shuddered.

"It was a jealous husband," said Arthur, blocking his lips with his vertical index finger.

"Funny thing," said Pierre. "She wasn't his wife."

"It's all so complicated," said Jonathan.

"What isn't?" asked Edward.

"Anyway," said Joel, "they let us out once a year."

"Who they?" asked Connie, suppressing a shiver.

"We're not really supposed to say," said Joel. "You know how You-Know-Who can be."

"But it's always on the Eve of the Feast of Saint Mechtilde," said Pierre.

"She taught Saint Gertrude, you know," added Arthur. "We're not sure what the connection is to us, but there it is."

"And here we are," said Pierre.

"Yir kiddin," said Connie, nervously shoving her notepad into her apron pocket. She held onto her pen, though, almost as a defensive weapon.

"Surely you're aware that the Adirondack is haunted," said Pierre, oblivious to her unease.

"And not just by the likes of us," said Jonathan.

"We're small potatoes," said Joel.

"But loveable ones," said Edward.

"Y-yuh-you guys awr cuh-razy," stammered Connie, backing away.

"Undeniably," said Arthur.

"Certifiably," said Jonathan.

"Dead," concluded Pierre with a helpful but conclusive nod.

"Eek!" she squeaked. It was quite a shriek. All jerks and twitches, she scooted away from them, bumping an empty table, knocking into the rattling galley stove with its cheerful blaze—lucky she didn't burn herself—and then scuttling for the safety of the wise, old, dependable Barlow, whose face was still stretched into that sad, knowing smile.

"What's the problem?" he asked, setting down the shot glass and absently tossing the towel back over his shoulder.

"Those guys ovuh therr," said she, pointing to the Tumblars. "Didya heer whuh they said?"

Barlow craned his neck to look beyond her. He tilted his head to the left, then the right, then looked her square in the eyes. "What guys?"

The poor girl lost it. Too flabbergasted to scream, she scurried from the lounge, huffing and gasping frantically all the way. Tearing off her apron, she flung it away. More than one chair ended up on its side on the floor in her terrified wake.

The lads waited until she was out of sight before bursting into laughter.

"Barlow!" called Pierre.

"That was brilliant!" cheered the others. "Bravo!"

"Anything for patrons who prefer Imperial Whiskey," said the sad but smiling bartender, shrugging magnanimously. "Do you still want that bottle?"

"Do we!" said they all as one.

58

"YOU'LL HAVE TO EXCUSE ME," said Jonathan, rising unsteadily from his chair. "I'm off to the euphemism."

"I bet they have loo chains here," said Pierre.

"We'll await your report," said Edward.

The gardener watched as Jonathan strode across the lounge and through the archway to the lobby. He was considering his options. Should he get up, saunter over to their table, and reveal his presence? Would they realize he'd been listening at the keyhole, as it were? Perhaps the safest thing would be to slink away and forget the whole thing. But if he did that he'd never be able to include that last bit of cruel-if-playful buffoonery in his chronicles because they all knew he only wrote first-hand accounts. He was still contemplating his options several minutes later when another woman came up to his table.

"Sir," she said, somewhat reserved in her demeanor.

"Are you Connie's replacement?" I asked, noticing she didn't have a nametag, not even an upside-down one.

"I'm Toni," said she. "May I take your order?"

"Saint Thomas, Salisbury. 'Blue label,' if you have it."

She smiled, but it was from a long way off. She was an older woman than Connie. For that matter she was considerably older than me. Her makeup was applied with a heavy hand, reminding me somewhat of Eira Levant of "Religion Revisited." The rouge on her cheeks was way overstated, and her eyelashes were menacingly long, arced, and thoroughly tarred with mascara. Her lipstick was deep red, the edges uneven. I noticed that she was wearing a purple dress, the material woven in paisley patterns, with puffy sleeves and an old-fashioned doily around the collar. Apparently the only uniform required of the female staff at the Adirondack was the blue apron with the "A" flanked by cute little manhole covers—this she had secured around her narrow waist.

"A man who knows what he wants," said she, again with that distant smile.

"On rare occasions," I assured her.

I watched as she headed for the archway rather than toward Barlow. Perhaps she, having been around the block, knew the hotel kept its stash of premium ginger ale across the lobby in the Saranac Lounge. I also noted the fact that she walked with a bit of a limp. A well-concealed hobble, in fact. Being a limper myself, I could appreciate the artful way she redistributed her weight with each footfall to minimize the pain of whatever condition ailed her. Whatever it was, she was not going to let it limit her mobility. I imagined giving her a worthy tip.

I was absently nibbling another pretzel when I was accosted mid-swallow by an approaching, whispered male voice.

"Mister Feeney?"

"Jonathan?" said I, also whispering, not only surprised but absolutely flustered at being discovered by my young friend returning with his much-anticipated report from the loo front. "What are you doing here?"

"I could ask you the same question," said he, slipping into the chair across from me. "Whatever, this is absolutely fortuitous, bumping into you."

"Really? How so?"

He folded his hands on the edge of the table. Then he unfolded them and refolded them again. He took a moment to peer through the fishing net to see if the others had noticed him. They hadn't. "Are you aware that we're all here?" he asked at last.

I made a show of peeking through the netting. "I am now. Is something troubling you?"

"You can say that again."

Tempting as it was, I didn't. Instead I practiced Patience and waited for him to gather his thoughts into words.

"It's Stella," said he, repeating the hand routine. "You remember the other night, when you said Millie was reading St. Cyprian's *Treatises* to the girls?"

"It was a moment I'll not soon forget."

"Well, neither will Stella. You should have heard her last night. She says she's throwing away all her makeup, her jewelry, even the locket I gave her."

"Hm," said I, compressing my features into what I hoped was an expression of sincere, manly concern. "I gather she took it to heart."

"Totally, completely, irrevocably. She's even considering giving all her clothes to the poor and restocking from a thrift shop."

"Really." I wondered what her dad, Chief Montgomery "Bulldog" Billowack of phlegmatic fame, would have to say about that. Then I imagined Cheryl Farnsworth in her prison duds. I had to admit that for some women tatty clothes don't matter. Still, I could feel a touchy situation coming on.

"I don't know what to do," said he. Suddenly he placed his right hand on my left forearm. "Martin, many Saints gave away their goods and lived austere lives. Saint Rose of Lima uglified herself so as not to be a temptation to men who passed her on the street. I understand the principle, and I would never want to discourage Stella from any sort of spiritual advancement, not if that's what God is calling her to do."

"But you're not convinced that's the case."

"Well, no." He released my arm, shrugged, and folded his hands again. "I've been thinking that she and I, well, you know, that we'd maybe get married." He said it as though it was some kind of secret; as though everyone hadn't known from the moment those two had first met on the rectory steps. There was no "maybe" about it.

"And the thought of a shabby wife doesn't exactly appeal to you," said I.

"Stella, heck, she would be beautiful in sackcloth, but ..."

"I think this is one for Father Baptist."

"Yes, but you're the Bible expert. Surely there must be a verse to counteract this thing."

"To counteract St. Cyprian? Hm, that's a poser."

Just then Toni returned with my ginger ale. As she set it down on a cocktail napkin I started fishing for my wallet, but Jonathan intervened.

"Just put it on our tab," he told her.

"Those gentlemen?" asked she, pointing with her eyes.

"The same," said he.

"No problem," said Toni. Then as she turned to leave she winked, smiled conspiratorially, and said, "Hair of the dog."

"Thanks," said I, hefting the glass. As I drew it close I paused to appreciate the tickle of those wee wet darts against my face as tiny bubbles burst merrily all over the amber surface of my beverage. Then, when the rim was less than a centimeter from my lips, it occurred to me: *The hair of the dog.* Setting the glass down, I turned the thought over in my mind. When it reached medium rare I flipped it over again. Then I looked long and hard at Jonathan's face, specifically the inevitable dots of beard stubble that were making their appearance around the contours of his chin and jaw so late in the day. Yes, it definitely had possibilities.

"What're you looking at?" asked Jonathan, reshuffling his hands.

Taking up my glass, I rewarded myself with a long, slow swig. It was ice cold, just the way it should be.

"Well?" said he.

"I have a verse," said I. "It's not for Stella, it's for you. Leviticus nineteen, verse twenty-six—no, make that twenty-seven."

"What's it say?" That was the first sentence in our exchange that rose above a whisper.

"Patience," I told him, patting the air with my open palm to indicate the need to keep the volume down. "I'm giving you an assignment.

You follow it up and see if you don't think it'll work. This is an affair of the heart and I'm not competent to meddle in such things—"

"But you must!" So much for my attenuating gesticulations. "You simply must!"

"—except in the direst of circumstances. Hopefully you're not there just yet. So please: Patience. Keeping Leviticus in mind, go to the library and ponder the *Paedagogus* by St. Clement of Alexandria."

"The what?" Now that was an outburst.

The Tumblars turned in our direction.

Sighing, I spelled it for him. There was no point is whispering any longer. "I don't know St. Clement by chapter and verse, so you'll have to read the whole thing. It'll do you good, and I think you'll find a solution there. I don't dare say *the* solution—I still recommend Father Baptist for that—but it's certainly one possible solution, and one that I think you'll find easy to get behind."

"Who's that?" asked Edward.

"Someone's behind the net," said Joel.

"It's just Jonathan," said Pierre.

"Who's he with?" asked Edward.

"Don't pay attention to the man behind the curtain!" announced the gardener.

"What ho! It's Mr. Feeney! Hooray!" they cheered severally.

No help for it, I gripped my cane and struggled to my feet. Jonathan was already up and around the fishing net.

"Gentlemen," he proudly announced, "there are pull-chains in the loo!"

"Hurrah!" said Pierre. "This place keeps getting better by the minute! Mr. Feeney! Imagine meeting you here. Come join us!"

"Arthur," Jonathan was saying, shaking the eldest Tumblar. "Arthur, Old Bean. You've got the personal library we all envy. Sir Martin was just telling me about a book by St. Clement of Alexandria." He turned to me. "I'm sorry. What was it called?"

"*Paedagogus,*" said I, lumbering into their midst. "Also known as *The Pedagogue.*"

"That one," said Jonathan, shaking his friend all the harder. "Do you have it?"

Arthur, who didn't seem to mind being awakened yet again, so much did he enjoy the company of his noisy friends, blinked the flakes out of his eyes and said, "Why, of course. It's a classic. You're welcome to it."

"Oh, thank-you!" said Jonathan, grabbing Arthur by the shoulders and jostling him so hard his eyeballs rattled in their sockets. Then he turned to me and gave me the same shaking treatment. He meant well but my back reacted with a volley of snaps and pops. It cost me.

"So what brings you here?" asked Joel, jumping from his chair and offering it to me.

"Actually," said I, declining his offer, "I'm here with Father Baptist."

"Really," said Joel, graciously reseating himself.

"He's in the Blue Mountain Grill as we speak," said I. "He's dining with your friend Roderick Roundhead, his friend Willie Kapps, and somebody's something-or-others, the Doily Sisters."

"Really," marveled Pierre. "Did I hear right?"

"That's an eclectic assortment if there ever was one," observed Arthur. "I've read about Willie Kapps in your manuscript, of course, but who are the Doily Sisters? What's going on?"

"You might say that Father lost a bet," said I. "Albeit on purpose."

"Did he say the Doily Sisters?" asked Joel.

"The Doily Sisters!" said Pierre. "You mean—?"

"Yes," said I. "Mehitabelle and Hortense. They publish little-old-lady prayer books. They are nice enough old gals—"

"You met them, then."

"Monsignor Aspic visited them the day he disappeared. Father had some questions for them, but I don't think they were much help. I got vomitose after drinking some of their tea, which is why I bowed out of dinner with them this evening and wandered over here."

"Unfortunate," said Pierre. "Tell me, Martin, did—?"

"Shall we join them?" suggested Joel.

"That's a grand idea," said Edward.

"Sure," shrugged Arthur, apparently unconcerned where he fell asleep, so long as it was among his comrades.

"Do you think they'd mind?" asked Jonathan.

"I really can't say," said I. "As for me, it's been a long day. I think I'll be going home."

"Awwawwwh," they moaned, as if their happiness depended on my presence.

I didn't buy it for a second. They knew how I could be. I shook my head and set down my glass on their table. "You barstool theologians will be just fine without me."

"How will Father get home?" asked Joel.

"Mr. Roundhead offered to take him," said I. "But you're welcome to if you'd like. You gentlemen enjoy yourselves. I bid you goodnight."

"But you haven't finished your ginger ale," said Pierre.

"I've had enough," said I. The fact was that I was suddenly *very* tired. The image in my mind's eye of my lumpy little bed back at the rectory took on breathtaking proportions.

"Are you okay to drive?" asked Pierre.

"Sure," said I, not so sure.

"We should have Barlow send that bottle of Imperial over to the restaurant," said Edward.

"Good idea," said Pierre. "Hey, Barlow!"

They all turned to the bar, but the glum barkeeper wasn't there.

"Maybe he went somewhere to fetch it," said I.

"But he would have had to come past us," said Edward. "We would have seen him."

"Perhaps there's another door—?" said Pierre, rising.

They all got up and headed for the bar. Too tired to be interested, I nonetheless joined them in their short expedition.

"Something's fishy here," said Joel.

"Indeed," said Pierre.

The counter was U-shaped, with only one entrance through a lifting door at the far end next to the cash register. There was a terrycloth towel crumpled on a back ledge between several oversized bottles of deep-hued liqueur. A shot glass was resting on its side on the countertop, presumably the one Barlow had been cleaning with the towel. I noticed, albeit through billowing waves of weariness, that the inevitable bitter scent, that telltale tang of recently poured spirits was not hanging about the place. In fact, there was something eerily empty about the space, as if it had been untended and uninhabited for a long time.

"I don't get it," said Jonathan.

"I don't either," said Pierre.

"Excuse me, gentlemen," intruded an approaching male voice redolent with controlled disapproval. It belonged to a portly fellow in a black suit with a razor-thin black tie. He had a bulbous forehead, black-button eyes, and a pointed little chin. What hair he had had mostly faded from brown to gray, and it was shellacked to the periphery of his skull with a glistening layer of pomade. As a result, the sides of his head reflected more light than the hairless dome of his head. His voice was a tad high for the amount of authority he was assuming through it. "I'm Mr. Maxwell, the night manager. The Champlain Room is closed this evening. Wouldn't you be more comfortable in the Saranac Lounge?"

"Closed?" said Edward. "Did you say closed?"

"But we've been running up a tab in here for the better part of an hour," said Jonathan.

"Barlow just went to fetch us a fresh bottle of Imperial Whiskey," said Pierre.

"Barlow?" said Mr. Maxwell, a funny sort of tightness tugging at the edges of his face.

"Why, yes," said Pierre. "He is as excellent a bartender as we've ever had the pleasure to meet, and we've met quite a few."

"That may be, Sir. I'm glad to hear it. Nonetheless, the Champlain Room is closed."

"Wait a minute," said I, marveling that I was able to speak, so intense was my exhaustion. "Oscar, the fellow out at the registration desk. He suggested that I come in here when I came out of the Saranac Lounge."

"Hrm," grimaced Mr. Maxwell. "Perhaps Mr. Langley was having his little joke."

"He didn't seem very prone to levity," said I.

"Levity," said Mr. Maxwell, not amused. "I will have a word with him." I got the distinct impression that he'd had this conversation many times before, that such disciplinary chats with members of the staff were almost routine.

"Forgive me if I offend, Sir," said Arthur, blinking back his own drowsiness. "You're not making sense."

"Then I shall endeavor to be more clear," said Mr. Maxwell. "Our last bartender, Mr. Tendersmith, left unexpectedly a few days ago." The way he emphasized "last" suggested that the position was susceptible to turnover, and "unexpectedly" betokened a nervous breakdown or some such personal upheaval. This was my reading, anyway, as he continued, "Our standards being rather high, we've yet to find a suitable replacement. Until we do, the Champlain Room will remain closed. I would appreciate it—for insurance purposes, you understand—if you would kindly remove yourselves."

"And what about our bottle of Imperial?" asked Pierre.

"Perhaps Mr. Barlow was having his little joke as well," said Mr. Maxwell, again with that peculiar constriction around his face.

"Hold on," said Edward. "You mean Barlow isn't the bartender?"

"Not any more, Sir," said Mr. Maxwell.

"You mean he quit like Mr. Tendersmith?" asked Jonathan.

"Not precisely," said Mr. Maxwell.

"And what about our bottle of whiskey?" said Pierre.

"You did say Imperial," said Mr. Maxwell, skeptically. "I'll have to look in the storeroom. There isn't much call for it."

"Barlow said the hotel just bought a whole truckload," said Edward.

"Yes," said Jonathan. "It was found buried in a landslide or something."

"I should be quite surprised," said Mr. Maxwell, "if there is any of that left."

"Why?" asked Edward. "Has there been a sudden run on Imperial Whiskey?"

"You yourself said there isn't much call for it," said Joel. "Something's definitely fishy here."

"See here, my good man," said Pierre. "You have us at a disadvantage. What precisely is going on?"

"Yes," said the others severally. "Do explain."

The shimmer in Mr. Maxwell's eyes shifted from glacial ice to cold, hard steel. His ears moved back a full quarter inch on each side of his head. "Gentlemen, the truckload of Imperial you speak of was recovered some decades ago."

"What's that?" said Edward.

"It was after the heavy rains of 1956," said Mr. Maxwell. "The discovery was deemed fortuitous by my predecessor's predecessor, Mr. Anathoth, because it coincided with the premier of a movie by the director, Edward D. Wood, Jr."

"Ed Wood? Fifty-six!" said Edward, brightening amidst his confusion. "Lads, that would have been *Plan Nine from Outer Space!*"

"Gadzooks!" exclaimed Pierre. "The premier party was held here—at the Adirondack?"

"One of them," said Mr. Maxwell.

Jonathan looked perturbed. "But Barlow made it sound like, like—"

"That's right," said Edward, equally upset. "Just like—"

"And what's with Barlow?" asked Joel agitatedly. "If he doesn't work here anymore, what was he doing tending bar?"

"1956?" said Jonathan. "That would make him ... *ancient.*"

"He didn't seem anything near that old," said Edward.

"What is going on?" asked Pierre.

Mr. Maxwell face became as stone. "Gentlemen, I'm sorry to say that Mr. Barlow died, here at the hotel, in this very room, the night of the premier."

An eerie silence descended upon the Champlain Room. It wasn't just the cessation of voices, but of other sounds, too. The galley stove, which had been crackling and rumbling, filling the room with cheer and warmth, suddenly fell cold and silent. The melancholy Irish lament oozing from the ceiling speakers didn't fade or snap off with a click. It simply ceased in the middle of a metal-strung harpist's despondent riff. I think the thermometer fell a few degrees as well for good measure.

"Barlow—? How?" asked the Tumblars, looking around with wide eyes. "Why? You mean—? What happened?"

"I've already said more than I should," said Mr. Maxwell. "Gentlemen, I really must ask you to vacate this room. I'll look into the whiskey directly. Meanwhile, I'll have one of the staff escort you to the Grill."

With that he extended his arm toward the archway and all of us exited the bar.

59

"SO WHAT DO YOU THINK ABOUT THAT?" asked Arthur, flight bag in hand, as we reassembled in the lobby.

"I don't know what to think," said Joel.

"I do," said Pierre. Then he announced: "Obviously this grand old hotel has its ghosts!"

"Shh!" shushed Mr. Maxwell from behind the registration desk. After all, he had the reputation of the Adirondack to consider.

"Sorry," hissed Pierre in reply. "Just so you know, we think it's marvelous!"

Mr. Maxwell did not seem at all pleased. Nor did Oscar Langley, the improbable comic with the tight, deadpan face, who was standing, duly chastised, beside him.

This unsettling ghostly business suddenly reminded me of my own encounter with Don Gusto up at La Purisima, and then my blueberry brandy dream in the garden. It wasn't as though I hadn't been thinking about it, but rather that so many other things kept getting added to my cranial cement mixer. Small wonder, I told myself, I'm suddenly so tired. I patted my jacket pocket and found the fist-sized chunk of pebbles and mortar was still there. Gingerly, I removed it from my pocket and held it in the palm of my hand.

"You see this?" I asked, but none of the Tumblars took notice.

I wish I could better describe the varying looks of agitation, fear, and fascination that played upon their faces, but in truth I was preoccupied with the painful suppression of spacious yawns. The call of slumber was so intense I didn't really much care what they were feeling. I had just shoved the clump back into my pocket when the elevator doors squeaked open and a cute, smiling girl in a black dress and apron exactly like the one worn earlier by Connie stepped out. As she approached the Tumblars perked up considerably, especially as she waded into their midst.

"You gentlemen looking for the Blue Mountain Grill?" she asked. Her nametag was definitely right side up. "Hi, my name is Rikki."

"Hello, Rikki," said the Tumblars, breaking into chivalric smiles.

"Right this way," said she. "We'll be passing the Ticonderoga Ballroom and other items of interest along the way."

"You sure you won't join us?" said Pierre to me.

"Positive," said I, waving them on.

They all nodded and turned to follow Rikki, but Pierre held back.

"Are you sure you're okay to drive?" said he to me.

"Sure," said I, even less sure than before.

Maybe he wasn't sure, either.

He lingered to say, "I wanted to thank you for that lead regarding W. Warren Shufeld."

"Think nothing of it." Heck, I could hardly think, period.

"No, really, it's very interesting."

"We can discuss it tomorrow after Mass." Oh, the yearning to yawn.

"Okay," he said.

We started to turn away from each other, but something occurred to me. I almost hated to bring it up, my eyelids so wanting to close and be done with the day. But Pierre was a fellow Knight, and we were bound to help each other. "One more thing, Pierre. Last night Father and I were checking out an excavation at the corner of El Barranco Drive and La Colina Avenue. Do those street names mean anything to you?"

"They don't ring any bells."

"Well, we were told by a reliable source—"

"What kind of source?"

"A policeman. I doubt he'd want his name connected with this. He told us that El Barranco's full name used to be 'El Barranco de la Oscuridad.' I know my pronunciation is deplorable, but the English equivalent is 'The Ravine of Darkness.'"

Instantly Pierre produced his writing pad and pen in their silver case and started scribbling. "A name like that must have a history."

"My thought exactly," said I. "And I can top it."

"How much you want to bet?"

"Don't make this more difficult than it is, Pierre. The cross street was originally 'La Colina de las Mantazas y Olores Asquerosos.'" I'm not going to pretend that what came out of my mouth was precisely that.

"I'll find the spelling later." Pierre's pen was smoking. "Which means?"

"'The Hill of Something and Something Smells,' or something. Now you'd better rejoin the tour before they leave you behind."

"Thank-you, Sir Martin," said he, bowing. "I'll let you know if anything pans out."

"Enjoy." The yawn of all yawns finally came. It felt wonderful.

"Through that archway to our left is the Saranac Lounge," said their guide. "Humphrey Bogart and Lauren Bacall were regulars back in the glittering days of Tinseltown. Down this corridor we're going to pass . . ."

I stood watching them shrink into the marvelous, mysterious, alluring conundrum that was the Adirondack, wishing them well, and wondering how the heck I was going to make it home. For what seemed an hour, but was in reality only a half-second, I considered taking Oscar Langley up on his offer of a room for the night. Surely I hadn't the money in my withered wallet for such an escapade, and even if I had, no doubt I'd wind up in a room in which the wraith of some failed Hollywood starlet hanged herself from the rafters night after night after night.

"No help for it," I said. "It's back to St. Philomena's for me … if I can only make it to the car."

"Hey there," said a female voice.

"Toni," mumbled yours truly.

"You look like the dog that got wagged by its tail. Need some help to your car?"

"That would be nice, yes."

"This way."

I vaguely remember seeing the Jeep parked out front where I'd left it beside the dry fountain. Feelings of familiarity arose in my shrinking consciousness, as well as beckoning images in my imagination of the tiny parking lot behind St. Philomena's, the charm of the old brick church, and most of all the bumpy landscape of my bed. The image of myself curled up under the cozy covers chased all else away. I remember Toni guiding me to a car door. The handle was funny, not like the Jeep's, and the color was wrong. We didn't have a black car. And the door was all wrong, too. Who ever heard of a car door that opened upward?

I can't say exactly what happened then, other than I did, at long last, finally fall fast asleep.

Sunday, November Nineteenth

The Feast of Saint Mechtilde.
(Matilda von Hackeborn-Wippra,
1240 or 41 to 1298 AD).
Born to one of the most powerful
Thuringian families, her sister was the
Abbess Gertrude von Hackeborn.
At birth it was feared
that Matilda was too fragile to survive,
so the attendants ran for a priest
lest she die unbaptized.
After administering the primary Sacrament
—primary in the sense that it is the means
by which one gains access to the others,
for without it one cannot enter
the Catholic Church,
outside of which Salvation
is simply impossible—
the attending priest prophesied
that the child would become a
"saintly religious in whom God
will work many wonders."
Inspired by a visit to her sister who was a nun
in the Benedictine monastery of Rodardsdorf,
she pleaded at age seven to enter the alumnate.
Ten years later she took her vows
and became a nun.
While still very young the Abbess Gertrude
entrusted to her the direction of the choir.
Mechtilde held the office of *domna cantrix*,
the choir directress, her entire life.
Her holiness was rewarded with visitations
of Our Lord and Savior, Jesus Christ,

who called her His "nightingale."
She was also given responsibility
over the alumnate.
One of her charges was a five-year-old who would
not only join the monastery when she came of age,
but would become known as
St. Gertrude the Great
(not to be confused with the Abbess Gertrude,
mentioned above; see November 16th, her feast day).
Mechtilde was fifty years of age when she learned
that the two nuns in whom she had confided
her visions had been writing them down.
Gertrude, who would one day be called the Great,
had nearly finished a book about
Mechtilde's revelations.
Jesus' "nightingale" was troubled by this until
Christ appeared to her, holding in His hand
that very book, saying,
"All this has been committed to writing
by My Will and inspiration:
and, therefore you have no cause
to be troubled about it."
Furthermore, He expressed His desire
that the book be titled *Liber Speciale Gratiae,*
or *The Book of Special Grace.*
It was made available to the public
immediately after her death.
St. Gertrude the Great
said of her mentor, St. Mechtilde:
"Never has there arisen one like to her
in our monastery, nor, alas! I fear, will there
ever arise another such!"
Moreover, it is this author's opinion
(shared by the author of the article in the
Catholic Encyclopedia, from which he derived
most of this information)
that the character known as "Matilda"
in Dante's "Purgatorio" was based upon
our Blessed Mechtilde.
The book of her revelations,

popularized in Florence under the title,
La Laude di Donna Matelda,
would certainly have been known to Dante,
who was a man of his age
and no stranger to such popular works.
His "Purgatorio" was finished right at the time
when the book was making the rounds,
around 1315 AD.
St. Mechtilde, delight of Jesus
and mentor of St. Gertrude the Great,
pray for us!

1(60)

THIS BEING THE FIRST CHAPTER OF MY CONTRIBUTION TO THIS OPUS WHEREIN I OFFER EXPLANATION FOR MY INTRUSION INTO MR. FEENEY'S TALE, I AM RENDERED CONSCIOUS BY A PHONE CALL, AND IN WHICH MY EDITRIX ARRIVES IN HER STUNNING PINK MOTORCARRIAGE.

PIERRE BONTEMPS HERE.   Martin Feeney has asked me to write a chronicle of my experiences and observations of events that occurred on Sunday, November 19th, the Feast of Saint Mechtilde (see above).   He insists that his chronicles be first-hand accounts, free of forays into hearsay and unconfirmed rumor, a notion I appreciate but to which, as a journalist who relies on second-hand information for the meat of his articles, I have never subscribed. This will be a new adventure for me. I'm happy to oblige, though in fairness to myself and to my readers (I entertain a sneaking suspicion that there will some!) I would like to point out that, also in accordance with his wishes, as of the time of this writing I have not read any of his chapters leading up to this day nor what follows, even though I was present during some of the events described therein. He explained that he didn't want me to be influenced in any way by his slant on things.   That cannot be entirely avoided because I have read his manuscript, "The Endless Knot," which chronicles incidents that occurred the previous June, including, among other multitudinous happenings, the murder of four auxiliary bishops, the emergence of Fr. John Baptist as the "cop-turned-priest-turned-cop," and the assimilation of Joel Maruppa into the Order of Knights of the Tumblar. It comes as no surprise that Mr. Feeney has yet to ask what I thought of his portrayal of me in the story. He knows me too well to think that I would be offended. Surely one cannot be insulted by a mirror, only by the reflection therein; and, if I may descend to a colloquialism: he nailed me good. With but a few qualifications, his recollection of people and events closely coincides with my own, so why should I take issue with his depiction of me? His personal opinions and interpretations, which he peppers rampantly throughout, and to which he is certainly entitled, are precisely that: his personal opinions. Doubtless I shall incorporate a few of my own into the fabric of my tale. He did ask my opinion of his opus, however, and whether I might pass it on to any publishers if the opportunity presented itself. My critique was simple, direct, and forthcoming, since I thoroughly enjoyed the manuscript; but alas my staff position on the *L. A. Artsy* does not open many doors among "legitimate" publishers of books. I did manage to penetrate one publishing house, largely due to the fact that an acquaintance of mine was related to one of the owners, but they hadn't gotten back to me by the Sunday in question. Finally, I shall endeavor to keep all the people and place names consistent with his contrivances in order to perpetuate Mr. Feeney's device of setting his characters in a city that is entirely mythical but not allegorical. All that being said, I shall now begin my account.

∞ ∞ ∞

MY DAY BEGAN with a penetrating electronic trill. Unlike the primitive telephones throughout the rectory at St. Philomena's, mine is a mobile device with keys that blink when a call is coming in. It was nesting in its recharger on my nightstand. I looked at it sideways from my pillow for several chirrups before I realized I wasn't dreaming.

"Top of the morning," said I. "If it is, indeed, morning."

"It is, Pierre."

"Fr. Baptist?"

"Yes."

"Why oh why, Reverend Father, and then as how. How came my aching hangover to be so brutally jarred at this painful hour? That is to say, to what do I owe the pleasure of this call?"

"Excuse me for phoning so early, Pierre, but I'm concerned about Martin."

"Mr. Feeney? Why, so should we all be, considering all those dead clippings Mrs. Magillicuddy has been lavishing upon him, each for one of his, shall we say, humors."

"I'm serious, Pierre." His voice relayed the very fact.

"As shall I be." I rose to the task. "What is it, Father?"

"He's not here. He usually unlocks the church by 6:00 AM, but I found the doors still bolted at 7:00. Several parishioners were waiting outside. Mr. Folkstone came and got me."

"Did you check his room?"

"Of course. It's hard to say with all the stuff he's continually moving from his bed to his desk and back again, but it didn't look to me as though he'd slept there last night."

"Was his toothbrush wet?"

"I did used to be a detective, Pierre. The sink in his bathroom was bone dry. Worse, the Jeep Cherokee isn't parked out back."

"Hold it right there, Father," I said, thrusting myself up from my pillow and assuming a seated position. Ah, sitting up makes the blood rush from the brain. I work better on fumes. "You know, come to think of it, Mr. Feeney looked very tired when he made his farewells to us last night. He said he was going home, but is it possible he thought better of it and spent the night there?"

"Just before you I phoned the Adirondack. I spoke with Mr. Maxwell, the morning manager."

"Maxwell? But he's the night manager. I told you about him over dinner. He's the one who escorted me and the lads out of the Champlain Room last night."

"Nonetheless, he's on duty this morning. He assured me that no one named Feeney was registered there. He recognized Martin's description, but couldn't say when he left. I'm going to call Larry Taper and see if he could swing by the hotel on his way to Mass and wave his badge around. I got the impression that the staff there are a bit—"

"Weird."

"—on edge."

"Understandably. The lads and I told you about Mr. Barlow and Mr. Maxwell's attitude about the whole thing."

"From what I heard and saw there, characters like Mr. Barlow are not unique."

"Unlike the Adirondack, which is one interesting place, Father. We're thinking of making it our headquarters."

"Headquarters? You mean, for the Knights?"

"Ostensively. Most people wouldn't understand. We were thinking of a forum for public discussion. You know, like a book club—only nothing like. But what better place for gentlemen to congregate, say once a week, for the purpose of openly discussing the doctrines of the Catholic faith? We will not preach to those who don't want to hear. We will discuss theology among ourselves, as well as philosophy, history, art, and anything else as it pertains to our religion. A forum in a public place, but at a conversational volume level. Over drinks, naturally. Others are sure to be drawn in. Something Mr. Feeney said suggested the perfect name: The Institute for Barstool Theology."

"Barstool Theology? Actually, that's not original to Martin. Manly D. Mann, Archbishop of New Bangor, coined the term at a recent press conference. He was speaking pejoratively of Traditionalists."

"All the better. Manly the Mann, eh? The very man, that parasitic prelate of New Bangor. My editrix is getting persnickety, so I'll have to verify that those were his exact words before quoting him."

"Be my guest. Meanwhile, Pierre, I wonder if I might ask you to come here straight away. I know you usually attend the High Mass at ten-thirty, but I may need your help. It's seven-thirty now. I'll be saying the Low Mass at eight o'clock. Could you possibly make it?"

"At least by the Offertory, or my ancestor was not Pierre de la Visage Douleureus."

"See you then. God speed."

SPELUNKING SPINOFFS: If Martin Feeney is a gardener, then I'm a spelunker. Regarding his "gardening tips," I will grant that Mr. Feeney's device for inserting background information into his text is clever, although I think he misuses it at times as a means of interjecting unnecessary and often superfluous asides. Not that I blame him (I myself am finding the temptation all but overpowering). What he needs is a good editor—like me, for instance. But I stray from the immediate. We are crossing paths with a traditional Catholic discipline that begs clarification.

Every Catholic, even after Vatican II, is required to assist (i.e., to attend) a valid Mass in order to meet his Sunday Obligation. If the Mass be Tridentine, said obligation is fulfilled so long as he is present for the Offertory, the Consecration, and the Communion, all three of which occur during the second half of the liturgy.

I confess that I'm not entirely clear about the minimum requirements of the Novus Ordo for attendance. Participation, in the form of the crooning of insultingly inane songs, is expected, indeed demanded, throughout. Then there are special tasks reserved for divorcees, among them the "ministries" of greeting people at the door, liturgical dance on special feast days, and the melodramatic reading of misleading translations of Scripture from the pulpit. But, from what I've seen and heard, there are only two parts of the New Mass that seem to fulfill the Sunday Obligation (I understand that the National Conference of Bishops is seeking an alternate term that isn't so oppressive) while concurrently rendering the Mass valid. They are: the Collection and the Silly Handshake after the Our Father also known as the Sign of Piecemeal.

—P.B.

N.B.: For the record, I am writing my account on a computer. Much as I admire Mr. Feeney's tenacity with respect to his father's Underwood typewriter, I am incomprehensible without an active spell-checker.

Immediately, I pressed the "speed dial" function on the phone. The number I call more than any other is that of my boss, lady editor, and verbalism mentor, Kahlúa Hummingbird. Knowing she always lets her phone ring seven times before picking up, I slipped out of bed and onto my knees for my first obligation of the day:

Glory be to the Father, who hath created me.
Glory be to the Son, who hath redeemed me.
Glory be to the Holy Ghost, who hath sanctified me.
Blessed be the holy and united Trinity now and forever. Amen.

Normally this would be followed by the prayer of St. Alphonsus Liguori to the Blessed Virgin for preservation from mortal sin, as well as seven Aves for the Seven Dolors and a heartfelt greeting to my constant companion, my Guardian Angel. The situation being a potential emergency—a fellow Knight in trouble, no less!—I would attend to those morning prayers while in transit.

"Helly-oh-hooooo, Pierre!" greeted Madame Hummingbird into my ear halfway through the eighth ring.

"My dear woman, how did you know it's me?"

"Silly boy! You are the only man I know who would dare call me this early on a Sunday morning. So what's up?"

"Martin Feeney is missing."

"What do you mean, missing?"

"I mean Fr. Baptist just phoned to say that Mr. Feeney never came home last night. It might be nothing, but Father asked me to get over to St. Philomena's right away. I thought you might like to pick me up in your never-to-be-sufficiently-described-as-gaudy pink Cadillac and scout out the situation with me."

"Gaudy? You really think so?"

"It doesn't hold a candle to you, of course."

"Sweetie, you always know the right thing to say to please a girl. Be there in twenty."

That was just enough time to take a breakneck shower and grab a suit out of the closet. How she managed to do the female equivalent, a far more complex and mysterious process, and make the drive over in the same amount of time baffled me. But there she was, humming up to the curb as I came down the stairs from my apartment, my little *pied-à-terre* above the violin repair shop at the corner of Bodfish Avenue and Walker Drive until I become successful enough to move to a more spacious flat I have in mind over a tobacconist and an antiquarian book dealer on the next block.

"My, you look vibrant," I said as I slipped into the passenger seat.

"How else?" said she, plunging the accelerator to the floor.

My reply was left behind as we accelerated smoothly and powerfully beyond the speed of sound.

2(61)

THIS BEING THE SECOND CHAPTER, WHEREIN MY EMPLOYER AND I ARRIVE IN TIME FOR THE GENUFLECTION, WE LEARN WHAT LITTLE FR. BAPTIST KNOWS REGARDING MR. FEENEY'S DISAPPEARANCE, THE WIDOW POUNDER DEMONSTRATES HER PROFOUND GENEROSITY, MSGR. HAVERMEYER AND I STRIKE A BARGAIN, AND IN WHICH THE MONSIGNOR RECEIVES A REPRIMAND.

FIFTEEN MINUTES LATER we entered the nave of St. Philomena's just as Fr. Baptist was proclaiming as a matter of Faith that the Son of God entered into human history:

> Qui propter nos homines,
> et propter nostram salutem
> descendit de cælis.
> *Et incarnatus est de Spiritu Sancto*
> *ex Maria Virgine;*
> *et homo factus est.*

Though Madame Hummingbird and I were coming up the aisle, we fell to one knee on the spot at the *Incarnatus*. Father, of course, genuflected before the altar, as did the two hundred or so people in the pews. The reason for such reverence should be obvious from the meaning of the words. The Who, of course, is Our Lord and Savior, Jesus Christ:

> Who for us men,
> and for our salvation,
> came down from heaven;
> *and was incarnate by the Holy Ghost,*
> *of the Virgin Mary;*
> *and was made man.*

This obeisance takes place during the *Credo*, which immediately precedes the Offertory, so we had made it in time.

> *SPELUNKING SPINOFFS: Among the many liturgical reforms that followed the Second Vatican Council was the deletion of this fitting and rightful act of reverence from the New Mass, Christmas being the only exception, though most people forget even then. The misallette provided in the pews of modern Catholic churches suggests a bow, but it is universally neglected. One has to wonder how this innovation was perceived by anyone in spiritual authority as a step forward.*
>
> *As for me, in those rare circumstances when I am forced to attend the Novus Ordo, I make a point of genuflecting at the* Incarnatus, *then kneeling from the* Sanctus *("Holy, holy, holy") through to Holy Communion. In this way I at least avoid the Silly Handshake. Who cares if they think I'm antisocial or—bwah-hah-hah!—sanctimonious? The only effective method I know for avoiding the Collection is an attack of weak kidneys at the propitious moment. I cannot, in good faith, support a church that does not kneel before Almighty God.*
>
> *All the more reason for attending the tried-and-true Tridentine Mass, which is the only kind celebrated at St. Philomena's.*
>
> *—P.B.*

After Mass was concluded, Madame Humingbird and I headed around the outside of the church to the sacristy door. Fr. Baptist, who had removed his vestments, was corralled inside by Mrs. Clara Estelle Pounder. I must add that I was startled at the sheer weariness that hung from his eyes, cheeks, and jaw. His shoulders fell away from his neck at odd angles. I remembered noticing that he had appeared exhausted at the Knights' meeting Thursday evening, but I'd wager he hadn't slept since. He had rallied the night before at the Blue Mountain Grill, but it was catching up with him. It took a conscious act of will not to stare.

"I just had to tell you, Father," she was saying as I entered. Actually, the Widow Pounder doesn't just speak. Her pronunciation is to verbal communication as a blowtorch is to acetylene. "My sister, Priscilla, sent me this postcard. She's down in Central America, Father. Just look!"

In spite of all that must have been weighing on his mind, Father patiently accepted the card and gave it his attention. His eyes widened. Then he saw me.

"Pierre," he said. "So glad you could make it. Kahlúa, too. All the better. Here, take a look at this."

Mrs. Pounder gave me the wary look she always does. Then her face fell when Madame Hummingbird came in behind me. It may have been the fact that my employer's hat was an explosion of exotic feathers and tropical fronds that scraped against both sides of the doorway. Her dress, though certainly modest in design, was even more volatile in color than her headgear. Used as I am to her extravagant fashion statements, I hardly notice them anymore, but they tend to challenge the sensibilities of some of Father's flock.

"Why," said I, examining the glossy picture on the postcard, "this statue in—where is it? Columbia?— looks like the one in our grotto."

"El Señor de los Temblores," read Madame Hummingbird over my shoulder. The barbs from her hat poked the side of my face in three places. The Widow Pounder took a step back to avoid a similar fate.

"That confirms what Roberto Guadalupe told us," said Father as I returned the card to Mrs. Pounder's leather-gloved hand. "The Lord of the Earthquakes."

"It's one strange representation of Christ, don't you think?" said my boss, giving her perilous hat a good rattle.

"This is California," said I. "Land of countless seismic faults."

"'Without him was made nothing that was made,'" said Father. Then he smiled. "The Gospel according to St. John, chapter one. If Martin were here, he'd know the precise verse."

"I had hoped to say what I have next in private," said the widow to Father, though her eyes were squarely on me. "I can see that's not going to happen. Very well. I understand that dear Millie got a new dishwasher, and that subsequently there was a mishap due to her inexperience with such a vital modern convenience. More so, I was shocked to learn that it had been given to her by a hooligan."

"Hooligan?" asked Father.

"That's what she called him. Now don't misunderstand me. She said it affectionately."

"Excuse me, Mrs. Pounder," I inquired, "but how does one say 'hooligan' affectionately?"

Her eyes did some spelunking of their own, boring into me. "'That dear, sweet, generous hooligan,'" she said sternly, teeth clenched, apparently repeating Millie's account, "'who will be in my daily prayers for the rest of my days.'"

"Indeed," said I, stifling a smile. "Well, stranger things have happened."

"Actually," said Father, "I believe it was two hooligans."

Just then the ornate captain's clock on the sacristy wall, one of the Widow Pounder's many thoughtful gifts to St. Philomena's Church, chimed the third quarter after eight.

"As I was saying," said she, reaching into her ponderous purse. "I was appalled that it took an outsider to fill this need, a need I didn't realize until now. I usually chat with Millie in the garden, but this morning she invited me in for a peek at her new dishwasher. I've never seen her so proud and excited. Only then did I realize the deplorable lack of modern appliances in her kitchen. And the laundry room! I can't imagine how she manages. She's a Saint, our Millie."

"Why, that explains it, Honey," said Madame Hummingbird cheerfully.

Mrs. Pounder looked up from her purse and regarded my editrix like a bug on her windshield. "Excuse me?"

Kahlúa, God bless her, explained: "Saints do it the hard way, smilin'."

"Well, this saint needs some help," said Mrs. Pounder, returning her attention to the bowels of her handbag. After several moments of noisy scrounging, she found what she sought. She handed Fr. Baptist a business card. "This man just remodeled my kitchen. His work is excellent, all his workmen speak English, and his cost is reasonable. I want you to call him."

"I'm sorry," said Father, "there's no way we can afford—"

"Call him, have him over for a consultation with Millie, and when she is satisfied with his proposal, tell him to send the estimate and all subsequent bills to me."

"Mmmmm hm!" said Madame Hummingbird, twirling her necklace of genuine tiny orange starfish. "I so appreciate a lady who gets things done."

"I don't know what to say," said Father.

"Sure you do," said Mrs. Pounder, closing her purse with a snap. "Masses, plenty of them, for me and my dear departed husband."

SPELUNKING SPINOFFS: Historically, throughout the Age of Faith when Catholics took their religion at face value, i.e., as though it was the only vehicle through which they might save their souls, it was common to leave provisions in one's Last Will and Testament to pay for continued prayers on one's behalf. We find reference to this practice in a poem entitled "The Eve of St. Agnes" by John Keats (1795-1821):

> Numb were the Beadsman's fingers while he told
> His rosary, and while his frosted breath,
> Like pious incense from a censer old,
> Seemed taking flight for heaven, without a death,
> Past the sweet Virgin's picture, while his prayer he saith.

I mention this lest an uninformed reader take exception to Mrs. Pounder's businesslike expectations of prayers in exchange for donations.

—P.B.

With that, Clara Estelle Pounder made a hasty exit, as did the two altar boys who had been putting away their vestments and altar-serving accoutrements as hastily as reverence allowed, leaving Fr. Baptist, Kahlúa Hummingbird, and myself free to speak candidly.

"Any news about Mr. Feeney?" asked the lady editor and myself almost simultaneously.

"Not since I phoned you," said Father, hiding a yawn behind his left fist. "I did ask Lt. Taper to check things out at the Adirondack, but I haven't heard from him yet."

"Mr. Feeney's a big boy," said Madame Hummingbird. "Why are you both so up tight about him not coming home just this once?"

"'Just this once' is precisely the problem," said Father. "Martin is a man of self-imposed patterns. He is also thoroughly dependable. He knows I rely on him, so he is fastidious about making himself available and informing me when he is not. If prudence had dictated that he spend the night at the Adirondack or any other hotel, he would have phoned, or arranged for one of the staff to call to let me know."

"And a man like that is runnin' around free?" said she. "We gals have fallen down on the job!"

"Indeed," said Father.

"And where have you been hiding this Adirondack Hotel?" said she to me.

"It's been keeping its secrets without my help," said I. "Just north of Wilshire Boulevard about a half-mile shy of the coastal cliffs. The lads and I just learned of it a couple of days ago."

"Might I ask who told you about it?" asked Father.

"Why, Roderick Roundhead," said I.

"But of course. Who else to recommend a hotel adorned with manhole covers?"

"Manhole covers?" exclaimed Madame Hummingbird, eyes wide. "Did you say manhole covers?"

"There's an unobtrusive plaque in the lobby," said Father. "It says, 'The hotel that manhole covers built.' That's how the Roundheads made their fortune, and the Adirondack is where Roderick Roundhead arranged a meeting with Willie Kapps last night. I surmised a connection, and it presented itself in solid brass."

"Willie Kapps?" exclaimed Kahlúa. "Not Willie 'Skull' Kapps!"

"The same," said Father.

"Why, I haven't seen Skull in simply ages. Is he still ... you know?"

"I can't say," said Father, whatever he knew. "But yes, he's very much around. Now, down to business. I'm glad you both came. I'm going to need your—"

"Excuse me for interrupting, Father," said a voice from the open doorway. It was Msgr. Michael K. Havermeyer. "There's a call for you. It's Lt. Taper."

"What ho!" said I, or something of the sort.

"Any word of Martin?" asked Father as he ushered us out the door and through the garden.

"He said something about finding the Jeep," said the monsignor, bringing up the rear.

"Is that good?" asked Kahlúa.

"Can't say till I know more," said Father, already at the kitchen door.

Millie was not within when we hustled through, though her new dishwasher was prominently positioned in the middle of the floor.

"Wowie zowie," said Madame Hummingbird, running her hand over the top of the machine. "I gotta meet these hooligans. Where is dear Millie?"

"I've no idea," said Father.

"Perhaps in her room," suggested Msgr. Havermeyer.

"I'll go see," said she. "You fellas go on ahead. I get to be the angel that brings her the good news about her new kitchen."

So the men turned left into the hallway, and the rainbow on high heels headed to the right.

SPELUNKING SPINOFFS: It was the previous Monday when Lt. Taper and Sgt. Wickes intruded upon a party Arthur von Derschmidt was throwing in honor of his sister, Beth. The officers had been sent by Chief Billowack to bring me, Pierre Bontemps, in for questioning in relation to a murder investigation. Though I was overwhelmed by events, I do remember that my plight instigated an amicable bonding between my editrix and Fr. Baptist's housekeeper. It was unpredictable and unlikely, but moments of crisis can bring about amazing alliances.

> *Since Mr. Feeney has expressed his intention to write an account of the affairs surrounding the theft of the body of Saint Valeria, I will say no more about it here except to mention that I was still in the process of controlling my outrage at being arrested by men who should have known me better.*
>
> *—P.B.*

"Larry," said Fr. Baptist, snatching up the telephone resting on his desk in the study. "What did you find out?"

As Father listened intently to the barrage of information squawking out of the phone, Msgr. Havermeyer picked up a newspaper which he had apparently left open on Father's desk when Lt. Taper's call had interrupted him. Meanwhile I feigned interest in a quotation from J. R. R. Tolkien's *The Lord of the Rings* that Fr. Baptist keeps in a small frame on his desk, while noting well the article that had piqued the monsignor's interest. I had typeset it myself on one of the computers at the office. When Msgr. Havermeyer finished the article, he folded up the *Artsy* and tossed it onto an empty chair. At the same time, I retrieved the framed quotation from the desk. Finding the glass faintly smeared, I fogged it with my breath.

"I've been meaning to tell you," the monsignor stage-whispered to me. "You're truly quite a fellow, Monsieur Bontemps." His French pronunciation of my name was contrived, but I appreciated the attempt. He smiled as best he could, considering the fact that his face had been severely disfigured in an electrical fire the previous June. I suspect, though he hides it well, that he is in a great deal of pain. The involuntary twinge when he stretched his lips into too wide a smile just then was but one of many indicators.

"Whatever makes you say that, Monsignor?" said I, polishing the glass with my handkerchief. "Though of course I'm delighted that you think so."

"That whole St. Valeria thing. I'm disappointed in this article. It doesn't give much information."

"Father was specific about what he did and did not wish to see in print, which left less than a little. Even my editrix was intimidated."

"And who's this 'Tequila Sparrow, *Artsy* Staff Reporter,' who wrote it?"

"Kahlúa Hummingbird, naturally. Well, actually, in this case it's me impersonating her as she was busy ghost-writing two other articles before we went to press. Or is it spirits writing? Get it? Spirit writing, spirits writing ...?"

"I can't honestly say I find you as funny as you do, Pierre; but that's a limitation of mine, no doubt, not yours."

"You know, Monsignor, Sister Mary Banshee of the Comforting Rod and Staff always said I was overcome with my own humor. It's a shame I never outgrew the tendency, nor wanted to. Let's say we compromise: you don't have to pretend to laugh at my jokes, and I don't have to stay awake for your sermons."

"Huh-hah," he chuckled, inducing another painful twinge. "I suppose I deserve that."

I gave the glass a second breath treatment. "Returning to something you said a moment ago, Monsignor, that I am quite a fellow. At the risk of teasing hubris, I'm curious as to what, in your opinion, renders me so."

"Yes, well, what I meant to say is that I admire your pluck, you and your friends."

"Grand of you, Monsignor, but I must in all fairness confess that reports of our pluck have been grossly unsubstantiated."

"I hadn't a tenth your courage when I was your age, sad to say, nor your originality."

"Oh, we're original all right. Honestly, though, courage is something we find in a bottle."

"Alcohol may provide a boost, or an excuse, perhaps, but grace perfects nature. You can stop your artful dodging, young Dickens. I was at the airport, remember? I witnessed the result of your individual and collective efforts. I get chills thinking of the risks you all took. Pretending not to want to hear it doesn't fly. You can't con a con. May I suggest an alternate compromise: you go to work on your humility, while I pray for more faith and try to write better homilies."

"Humility is a tall order, Your Reverence, but I shall give it my all."

"Mine is no less imposing, Sir Pierre."

"I shall pray for your side of the bargain."

"And I yours."

"As for chills, Monsignor, just stick around. The Knights Tumblar have thrills in the works, shocks yet to come, cocktails to invent—"

"Be there as soon as I can," Fr. Baptist was concluding on the telephone. "Thanks, Larry."

"We'll have to postpone our compromises till another time," said I to my partner in prayer.

"So what did the lieutenant find out?" asked he of Father.

"The Jeep was found in the guests' lot in back," said Father, cradling the receiver. "It wasn't parked there by anyone on the staff. When Martin and I first arrived he left it in the carport in front of the hotel. He was with me until a little before six. Pierre, you said over dinner last night that he joined you and the Tumblars in the Champlain Room."

"That is so," said I. "At least until Mr. Maxwell informed us that the bar was closed, at which point Martin accompanied us to the lobby."

"Did you see him to the car?"

"No. We parted company near the reception desk. He headed for the front entrance, but I didn't actually accompany him that far."

"Strange, isn't it?" said Msgr. Havermeyer. "Msgr. Aspic disappeared while walking from his car to the television studio. Now Martin vanishes while walking to his car at the hotel."

"Are you suggesting they are connected?" asked Father.

"Aren't they?" said the monsignor with a feigned shrug. "What are the odds that two people known to you would disappear under similar circumstances within a few days of each other and not be somehow connected?"

"You know, Monsignor, you've been around Fr. Baptist too long," said I. "You're beginning to think like him."

"I take that as a compliment," said he. "So, Father, they are connected, yes?"

"It is obvious, as you suggest," said Father. "A parking lot and the carport of a hotel. Both places where a vehicle can pull up and drive away without attracting attention."

"But who moved the Jeep to the back lot?"

"Good question."

I returned Tolkien's framed quotation to its station between the statues of Sts. Thomas More and Anthony of Padua. "So," I asked, "what are you going to do?"

"I'm going to ask you and Kahlúa to accompany me to the Adirondack," said Father. "From there, she may go where she pleases. I have a spare set of keys, so we'll retrieve the Jeep. Larry said the books and materials I left on the back seat seem untouched, and I want to give them some of my attention. Pierre, if you wouldn't mind being my driver for the day, I could attend to the books while you take us places."

"I'm not properly attired for the part, Father," said I. "Do we have time for me to dash home for a quick change of apparel?"

"No."

"Will you be wanting champagne en route?"

"No."

"I see. We'll be roughing it. Will I get an exclusive for the *Artsy?*"

"I make no guarantees until I know what we're up against and who's involved."

"What about the first amendment?"

"I'm not impressed, not the way the courts have chosen to interpret it."

"Me neither. Okay, Father, you have editorial approval, and I'll be honored to act as temporary chauffeur, at least for today. Joel or one of the other lads will have to take over beyond that."

"Thank-you. Msgr. Havermeyer must prepare for the High Mass at ten-thirty. I need to fetch something from my room. Pierre, would you go find the ladies and solicit Miss Hummingbird's help with our transportation? She expressed interest in the Adirondack. Here's a chance for her to see the old place."

"I'll meet you at Madame's car," said I, easing myself in the direction of the door. "You can't miss it. It's parked across the street in front of Peanuts, and it's the only pink vehicle for miles."

"Good," said Father as I paused in the doorway.

"Happy hunting," said Monsignor.

"Sorry I'll miss your sermon," said I over my shoulder as I headed down the hallway.

"Now Monsignor, one more thing," I heard Father say. "I understand you've been giving homilies at weekday Masses."

"Oh. You heard."

"The Trad vine never fails, Monsignor. You know my policy."

"Yes, Father, but—"

"I realize it's your Mass, and you can do what you wish, but I'd like to review my rationale with you. It will only take a second."

"I feel like I'm in second grade again."

"'Whosoever therefore shall humble himself as this little child—'"

"I know, I know, even without Martin's help: 'he is the greater in the kingdom of heaven.'"

3(62)

CHAPTER THREE, WHEREIN JONATHAN REVEALS HIS PERILOUS STRATEGY WITH RESPECT TO HIS BELOVED, TRADOSAURS FREELY ROAM THE GARDEN, AND IN WHICH THREE MADEMOISELLES ARE CLEARLY NOT THEMSELVES.

HAVING NOT FOUND THE LADIES in Millie's room nor the kitchen, and certain they did not pass by Father's study in the interim, I decided they must be outside. It was a glorious Southern California morning, the sun hot and the air crisp. Parishioners were arriving early for Solemn High Mass. Some were already inside the church predisposing themselves, while others milled around outside, chatting away, enjoying the simple charm of the garden between the church and the rectory.

The first person I encountered as I exited the kitchen was none other than Jonathan Clubb, my friend and fellow Knight of the Tumblar. At first glance he looked his usual dashing self, the perpetual debonair romantic, attired in the charcoal suit that showed off his muscular shoulders to best advantage. But something in his demeanor belied all this, as did the furtive look in his eyes. Then, as I stepped closer, I said within myself, "Hair of the hound! Our Jonathan is so preoccupied with his heartthrob, Stella, that he plain forgot to shave this morning!"

As his friends all know, Jonathan has the most unfortunate, straggly, uneven, fast-growing facial hair of anyone in our acquaintance. This condition requires attention by razor at least twice a day, thrice for events that go past midnight. Stella, his sweetheart, in the spirit of interpersonal full disclosure, had been informed of his condition, but so far as I knew she had never seen it in full consequence. Sunday at Mass was, simply put, not the time! A sensitive yet savvy lass, she would be embarrassed—no, mortified—especially with all these acquaintances about. This unexpected conundrum presented me with two immediate problems: how was I to let him know without being indelicate, and then what was to be done about it?

"Good morning, Pierre," he said, shaking my hand. "What's this I hear about Mr. Feeney gone missing?"

"The Trad vine strikes again," said I. "Yes, it's official. Father Baptist phoned me early this morning to inquire if I might be his chauffeur today. Mr. Feeney apparently didn't make it to his car last night. Lt. Taper found the Cherokee parked behind the hotel."

"He looked awfully tired when we said our goodbyes in the lobby."

"I regret that I thought to see him to his car but didn't."

"Perhaps he decided he wasn't up to driving. Could he have taken a room for the night?"

"Apparently not."

"I suppose after our brush with Mr. Barlow, anything could happen there. Good Heavens, what can we do?"

"Father will be coming out in a moment. Perhaps he'll have assignments for us." I drew close to his ear. "In the meantime, dear chap, I don't know how to break this to you, but you forgot to shave this morning."

"I did not forget," said he, stroking his cheek self-consciously. "I neglected to do it on purpose."

I stepped back. "You're joking."

"No," said he, standing firm. "It was Mr. Feeney's idea."

"I don't get you. He told you not to shave?"

"He suggested that I read *The Pedagogue* by St. Clement of Alexandria."

"I remember you mentioning it to Arthur, but I'm not following you."

"Last night I complained to Mr. Feeney about the influence St. Cyprian is having on Stella. He recommended St. Clement. I borrowed Arthur's copy on the way home. I was up most of the night."

"Dear chap," I said, placing my hand on his shoulder. "Is this why you've been down in the dumps lately?"

"You've noticed then," he said, looking at his shoes.

"Hard not to. You've been keeping something close to the chest, but I had no idea it had to do with Stella. Why haven't you said something?"

"I did. To Mr. Feeney."

"But not to us?"

"I was hoping to avoid the ribbing you lads would give me about it."

"Come, come, Jonathan. Are we as heartless as all that?"

"You especially, Pierre."

"Zounds, but you cut me to the quick." I clutched at my heart to demonstrate the point. "I'm still not following you, but then I haven't read St. Clement. What does he have to do with your not shaving?"

"I'll explain later."

"But your beard, my Friend."

"Strategy," said he with an exaggerated wink. "Fire with fire. Look, here come Edward and Arthur."

"And Joel besides."

"Halloo," greeted Edward.

"Why Arthur," said I. "Grand to see you awake."

"Agreed," said he. Then his face widened into one of his famous smiles. "Jonathan! You *have* taken St. Clement to heart."

"I have indeed," said Jonathan. He stood tall, his chin forward, but his fingers were twitching.

"Jonathan," chortled Edward and Joel, both stroking their cheeks with their palms. "Dear chap, you forgot—"

"I didn't," protested Jonathan. "I neglected on purpose. It's all Mr. Feeney's doing, but I'll explain later. You'll just have to put up with me looking like *Fu Manchu* for a while."

"More like *Eegah!*" said Edward, demonstrating his interest in bad B movies from the fifties.

"Or *The Creeping Terror,*" opined Arthur, revealing his.

"So why are you lads all here so early?" I asked, not having to prove anything.

"Fr. Baptist phoned," said Edward. "He said he had a mission for us."

"Did he now?" said I. "And just what kind of a mission did he—"

"'Scuse me," intruded Patrick Railsback, the chief usher and collector of revenues during Mass. I have noted for some time that he never greets any of us Knights by name. "Word is going around that Mr. Feeney is missing."

"He's definitely not here," I agreed, "as far as I can tell."

Mr. Railsback cleared his throat knowingly. "Is it true that Fr. Baptist is working for the cardinal again?"

"Every diocesan priest answers to his bishop," said I.

"I mean another investigation," said he.

"You make it sound like it's voluntary on Father's part."

He glared at me with far more wariness than the Widow Pounder, with a little disgust mixed in for tang.

"Patrick," said another parishioner, Julius Caspar, coming up behind him. "It's been confirmed."

"Who by?" asked Railsback.

"Twigsy."

"Well," said Arthur. "If you got it from Argyle P. Twiggler, you certainly don't need to hear it from us."

"Twiggler," mused Edward as we proceeded down the brick path into the murmuring throng. "Isn't he the spider guy?"

"Not the one in the comic books," said Joel. "A different one."

"There they are," said Mrs. Theodora Turpin, who was approaching hurriedly, pulling her husband, Tanner, along with her.

"Yes, dear," said he. Mrs. Turpin tended to sprinkle herself with lots of talc, and a fair amount of it inevitably ended up dusting Mr. Turpin's arm and shoulder.

"We're looking for Fr. Baptist," said she to us.

"There are rumors, Mr. Bontemps," said he. "Rumors about Mr. Feeney."

"They say he's gone," said she.

"Missing, dear," corrected he. "Best to be specific."

"They're not the same?" said she.

"No, dear," said he. "Not at all."

"He's in the rectory," said I.

"Who is?" asked Mrs. Turpin.

"I believe he means Fr. Baptist," said Tanner Turpin.

"That is correct," said I. "He and Msgr. Havermeyer are discussing sermons."

"We simply must speak to him," said she. "Mustn't we?"

"Most assuredly, dear," said Tanner.

"He should be out soon," said I.

"He should get out more often," interrupted Mrs. Muriel Cladusky. "I tell him and tell him, but he don't listen."

"Who should?" asked Edward.

"Why, my Bennie," said Mrs. Cladusky. "Excuse me, Mr. Pierre. You all look the same to me. You are Mr. Pierre, aren't you?"

"I am indeed," I said, drawing her attention from Edward. "Pierre Bontemps, at your service."

"Well," she said, "I'm supposed to tell you that my friend, Millie, and her friend—what was her name, something like Colada Mockingbird?—they are in Mr. Feeney's room." All the while she poked me in the chest with her finger as if what she was saying was threatening.

"Really," I said, hiding all outward sign of pain. "Did they say why they went there?"

"No!" said she, again with the finger. "Did they say why you should go there? No! Did they ask me to go there? No! But you, you should get going there!"

"Their wish is my command, Mrs. Cladusky," I said, backing away from her. Rubbing my smarting chest, I turned toward the cemetery end of the property.

It was fortuitous that I stepped aside because just then Fr. Baptist and Msgr. Havermeyer emerged from the kitchen and came casually out into our midst.

"I understand that you've been influenced by the Novus Ordo, Monsignor," Father was saying, "but you must realize that the New Rite is entirely dependent on the personality of the priest. In the Old, however, everyone from priest to penitent is focused from minute one on God and God alone. Most people who attend weekday Mass here do so at the expense of breakfast or an unhurried drive to work. They don't need our frail wisdom blathered at them when all they want to do is receive Our Lord and be on their way."

"You're right, as usual," said Havermeyer, smiling as best he could at all the people who were reacting to their arrival in their midst.

Fr. Baptist, absorbed in his point, didn't seem to notice. "Besides," he continued, "it takes at least a week to prepare a good sermon, as you well know. Few of God's ministers are full of sufficient wisdom to impart twenty-minute's worth every single day. Most priests out there are, frankly, faking it. I'd loathe to be accused of such dereliction."

"There he is!" said Patrick Railsback, Julius Caspar, Theodora Turpin, and Muriel Cladusky—not to mention Edward, Jonathan, Arthur, and Joel—all at once.

"Indeed he is, Dear," said Tanner Turpin.

"What seems to be the trouble?" asked Father as the tsunami of questions gathered to crash upon him.

"Have you heard about this, Father?" insisted a young blonde woman, practically diving through the throng to get to him first. I had only seen her at St. Philomena's a couple of times, and I did not know her name. With the look of an eager, floppy puppy, she thrust a couple of stapled pages into his hand. The top sheet was bright yellow, and the second orange. I caught a glimpse of a drawing of the Blessed Virgin and the word Irwindale, but made no sense of it. "I've seen miracles there," she said, then took a second to catch her breath and gather her wits. "I'm not the only one from here. More and more are starting to go. You should come, too."

Father paused in mid-stride to accept the flyer and look at it for a moment. He did not look pleased, but she was too enthused with herself to notice. "Just the other day someone handed a copy of this flyer to Mr. Feeney. You say more and more of our parishioners are going there? I really must look into it."

"Good," said the young gal, looking positively validated. "Thank-you, Father. You won't ever regret it!"

"Now see here, Father, you've got to—" said Theodora Turpin and Patrick Railsback simultaneously. They looked at each other with a mixture of surprise and condescension.

"Go on, dear," said Mr. Tanner encouragingly. "Do definitely go on."

Much as I wanted to watch the ensuing entertainment, I had an errand to fulfill. Mr. Feeney's quarters are at the far end of the rectory, opposite the cemetery behind the church. It was there, near the first grave marker, that I happened upon three of the most self-conscious *mademoiselles* I'd ever seen in my life. They looked positively ill at ease—not at my approach, you understand. I was not the cause. Those discomfited looks were in advanced stages by the time I came along. What made their behavior all the more intriguing was the fact that they were all known to me personally—not equally, but well enough.

Wanda Hemmingway stood between the other two. Of the three, she seemed the most like herself. She had a pleasing complexion that didn't require much enhancement in front of a mirror. Her lipstick was soft in hue and lightly applied. Her hair was gathered into a short ponytail, and her outfit was decorated in bright floral colors. I didn't have to get close to detect the scent of patchouli, which is her favorite perfume. She is the first soprano in the choir, and would be singing beautifully during the High Mass. I felt a pang of regret that I would be missing it. But as to the immediate point, as I said, she seemed the most like herself. In fact, I got the distinct impression that she was struggling to make the point that she was, indeed, being herself. I might not have noticed except that she was flanked by females who were straining against the reins, as it were.

To Wanda's right stood Danielle Parks, our choir director. Danielle had applied her makeup with, shall we say, a heavier hand than usual. A weighty hand indeed. A welder's glove filled with buckshot comes to mind. Her lips were overstated, her rouge overindulged, and her hair too complicated. I'd never before seen her with extended eyelashes and fingernails. She had chosen large pearl earrings rather than the petite set she usually wore on Sundays. Her neckline was a tad steeper, her heels a half-inch taller, and her eyebrows a shade darker than was her custom. Everything about her was an exaggeration, not to the point of gaudiness, but to the point of being a point, though what that point might be was open to speculation.

I had known Danielle and Wanda much longer than Stella Billowack, but because she was Jonathan's beloved, I had seen much more of her lately, which was why her appearance surprised me the most. Like Wanda, she had never needed much touching up before facing the world. A hint of shadow, a stroke of lip-gloss, a fluff of the hair, and she was on her way. But not today. Not only was she not wearing any makeup whatsoever, she had somehow siphoned the sheen and body from her hair, the soft smoothness from her skin, the twinkle and luster from her eyes, and any trace of style from her clothing. She had gone from naturally beautiful to purposely frumpy.

There stood the three of them, not at all themselves, yet focused on no one but themselves. If ever I savored the temptation to say something gloriously chauvinistic, it was as I strolled nonchalantly by, bowing courteously while whistling Bernard Herrmann's theme from *The Day the Earth Stood Still*, and pressing on to Mr. Feeney's quarters in search of Mesdames Millie and Hummingbird.

4(63)

THE FOURTH CHAPTER, WHEREIN MR. FEENEY'S QUARTERS ARE INVADED BY TWO WOMEN ON A MISSION AND ONE RELUCTANT REPORTER.

"THERE YOU ARE, HONEYCHILE," said the latter, answering my knock. She peered beyond me at the three self-conscious enchantresses by the tombstone, shook her feathers and barbs, and yanked me inside. I was reminded of a moth getting too close to a Venus flytrap. "My, my," she said with both hands on her hips. "What is with those gals?"

"You noticed," I observed as I found myself deep within Mr. Feeney's private, secluded, currently invaded world.

"How could we not?" said Millie, who was leaning over Mr. Feeney's nightstand. Gingerly, she picked up a reliquary from its place next to the windup alarm clock. She mumbled something under her breath as she peered inside the little viewing window. "Empty," she said aloud with an equally audible sigh, setting it back down next to a gnarled object which seemed familiar but took me a moment to recognize: the charred, splintered, aspen handle of a walking stick shaped like a dragon's head—all that was left of a gift once presented to Mr. Feeney by the Knights Tumblar. (Long story there, which I knew Mr. Feeney to be in the throes of writing, and to which I'd been asked to contribute a few zingers.) Ignoring that oddity, Millie turned her attention to the nightstand drawer, pulling it open and frowning at the debris within.

"I honestly don't know," said I, looking around sheepishly. The place would have been crowded without the three of us adding to the clutter. I was not at all comfortable being there without Mr. Feeney present. "I wonder, though. Jonathan has been a bit preoccupied for the last three evenings. I should know. I was with him at the Adirondack. Thursday and Friday we stayed in the Saranac Lounge, then Saturday we moved to the Champlain Room, which we later learned was closed. The point being that I've never known our Jonathan to get progressively depressed during one of our famous four-day lost weekends. Would that I had paid more attention, or better still, asked what was wrong."

"No doubt you at least had a good time, eh, Sugar?" asked Madame Hummingbird, who seemed to be looking for something on Mr. Feeney's desk.

"Alas, that I cannot help," said I. "Being a man whose name is his destiny is a ponderous responsibility."

"Story of my life," said my editrix, opening and closing a drawer.

"You said the last three nights," said Millie, closing the nightstand drawer. "How's that a four-day weekend?"

"Counting this evening, of course," said I. "I must tell you, though: I can't get over the ambience of the place. The Adirondack, I mean. Why, when we were garrisoned in the Saranac Lounge, I kept expecting to turn and see Humphrey Bogart drinking in the corner with Lauren Bacall, or William Powell with Myrna Loy. There's a plaque over one booth that says, 'This was Jack Webb's favorite table.' And ladies, would you believe it? We saw a ghost last night!"

"You guys drink too much," said Millie. Her tone was stern, but the set of her lips was slightly askew, and her eyes were red and swollen.

"'Be this known to you, and with your ears receive my words,'" said I, quoting the second chapter of the Acts of the Apostles. "'For these are not drunk as you suppose, seeing it is but the third hour of the day.'" I'm no match for Mr. Feeney when it comes to scriptural recollection, but we Tumblars have made a point of memorizing verses that pertain to the consumption of alcohol. It's a matter of pride, spiritual enhancement, and occasionally self-defense.

"If Mr. Feeney was here he'd tell you the chapter and verse," said Millie as both of them turned their scrutiny toward the lopsided, teetering piles of books, notebooks, and loose papers collapsed together on the bed. "But that sounds like St. Peter just after the Holy Ghost stirred up the Apostles at Pentecost."

"Give the lady a bouquet of roses," said I.

"Wasn't it Evelyn Waugh who said," quoth Kahlúa, "'Beer commercials are so patriotic: Made the American Way. What does that have to do with America? Is that what America stands for? Feeling sluggish and urinating frequently?'"

Millie squeaked in spite of herself.

"Sounds like him," said I. "Of course, beer is of little interest to me, it being the beverage of choice of every nation that went the way of the Reformation. Now wine, that is the drink of the countries that held out."

"At least for a while," said Millie.

"By the way," said I, "not that it's any of my business, but you two ladies seem to be ransacking Mr. Feeney's apartment."

"We're not ransacking," said Madame Hummingbird, digging with her fingers to the bottom of one of the stacks and shifting it several inches in order to probe beneath.

"I didn't say that you were," said I, watching as several typed pages slipped to the floor.

"'Judge not,'" said Millie, likewise prodding amongst the wobbling stacks, "'that you may not be judged. For with what judgment you judge, you shall be judged.'"

"Somewhere in St. Matthew, and touché on the citation," said I. "In my own defense, however, I did say 'seem.' I am the first to insist that appearances may be deceiving, and second only to Fr. Baptist that words mean what they say. So are you going to tell me what you're doing in here, or am I to be left flailing around a potential occasion of sin? Wondering is not necessarily judging, the line of demarcation being imprecise, but I'm certainly doing it under the circs."

"Does he talk this way at the *Artsy?*" asked Millie of my editrix.

"Does he talk any other way anywhere?" answered my employer, ever loyal to her employees.

All the while they continued rummaging around and through and under the clutter. I cringed as papers got rearranged in the process, books got reordered in their columns, and bits and pieces kept slipping to the floor. Being a bachelor, researcher, and writer myself, I believed I understood Mr. Feeney's filing system. Not the specifics, of course, but the general rules. Items to which he referred the most were close to the top. Sources that were used less gradually sank to the bottom. The same rule also applied horizontally across the surface of the bed, though only Mr. Feeney would know which end was which. Loose pages, which were never numbered, followed similar guidelines albeit with complex subsets like dog-eared corners, paper clips for markers, and exclamation points scrawled across the top margins in dull graphite. I shuddered to think of the confusion to which Mr. Feeney was going to come home—assuming he came home.

"Very well," said I. "You two ladies aren't going to tell me why you're doing what you're doing. Would you perhaps be interested in what I'm doing here? My mission may not be clandestine, but it is—"

"What we're doing here is following Mr. Feeney's orders," said Millie gruffly (it might have been playfully, with her it's hard to tell sometimes).

"Really," said I. "He ordered you to go through his things?"

"In the event that something should happen to him, yes," said she. "Now don't you go getting all suspicious. It was while we was up at La Purisima—heavens, was it only yesterday?—he told me the most precious thing he had in the world was the chip from the Crown of Thorns that Bishop Xandaropolopolopolopolopolis gave him."

"Who did you say?" I asked, marveling at her extended mispronunciation.

"Oh, you know who I mean. Fr. Nicanor's something-or-other from Lebannon. I can't bring myself to call him Bishop Pip. Anyway, Mr. Feeney told me that if anything happened to him—Mr. Feeney, that is—he wanted me to make sure his relic didn't get lost or mislaid or forgotten."

"Are you saying he had some sort of premonition?"

She favored me with a penetrating, impenetrable glare. "He asked me not to repeat his reasons."

"Ah, well, then there's little to be said, at least about that," said I. "You're leaving me wondering, but no longer in danger of judging. For that I thank you. Oh, and I did come here with a purpose, a matter of some urgency, actually. Much as I hate to interrupt your fulfillment of Mr. Feeney's prudently salient and eerily timely request, Fr. Baptist has asked me to ask you, Madame Hummingbird, if you would do him the honor of driving him to the Adirondack Hotel. Myself included."

"Why me?" asked Kahlúa.

I shrugged. "You have a car, I suppose, and you've already been to Mass."

"What about me?" asked Millie. "I went to Mass, too."

"You don't own or drive a car," said I. "But of course you're welcome to come. The Adirondack is a place I think you would enjoy. In fact, if you wouldn't deem it a dereliction of duty, the two of you might like to try the Sunday brunch at the Blue Mountain Grill. That's the hotel's fine restaurant. Having dined there only last evening, I can highly recommend it."

Millie and Kahlúa suddenly stopped their prodding and looked at each other.

"I'm awful hungry, Sweetie," said Madame Hummingbird with a tropical wink and a swish of her fronds. "I've got some mad money saved up. I'll treat. How's by you?"

"But Mr. Feeney said," said Millie. "I still have to go through the clothes in his closet."

I had to intervene. If Mr. Feeney's clothing system was anything like my own, these women, through no fault of their own other than being female, would certainly reduce it to unrecoverable chaos in no time. "Ladies," I said, "even the authorities do not consider someone officially missing for seventy-two hours. I'm not questioning your good intentions—indeed, I applaud your unswerving reliability—but I'd give Mr. Feeney a little more time to prove himself truly missing before assaulting his privacy any further."

"Perhaps he's right," said Millie to Madame Hummingbird.

"Men are always right when it comes to food," said she to Millie.

"We can finish this later."

"Sure."

"Aren't you going to pick up what fell to the floor?" I asked as they squeezed by me.

"You did say it was urgent," said Millie over her shoulder as she twisted the doorknob.

"Yes, I did," I admitted, stooping to gather up Mr. Feeney's papers myself. "I did at that."

5(64)

THIS BEING THE FIFTH CHAPTER, WHEREIN FR. BAPTIST CHARGES THE TUMBLARS TO COMMENCE SPELUNKING, KAHLÚA HUMMINGBIRD HONKS HER HORN, AND IN WHICH MSGR. HAVERMEYER DELIVERS A DIRECT ORDER FROM HIS EMINENCE THE CARDINAL.

"GENTLEMEN, A WORD." said Fr. Baptist. Having extricated himself from the herd of Tradosaurus Rexes and Reginas (as Mr. Feeney calls them) in the garden, he had gathered Joel, Jonathan, Edward, myself, and Arthur into a huddle on the sidewalk in front of the church steps.

Madame and Millie were already across the street arranging themselves within Miss Hummingbird's pink carriage.

"I need your help," said Father.

"Then you shall have it, abundantly," said I.

"Whatever we can do," said Jonathan.

Father blinked twice at the sight of Jonathan's mutant facial growth, smiled furtively, but said nothing.

"You can count on us," said Arthur.

"At your service," said Edward and Joel.

"I'm going to give each of you something," said Father, producing several folded sheets of foolscap from a pocket in his cassock. "I must have your word that you will show it to no one, and I do mean no one. Jonathan, that includes Stella; Arthur, your sister, Beth; Pierre, not even Roderick Roundhead—especially not him."

I admit that brought me up short.

"What's going on?" asked everyone present, each in his own way.

"After we parted last evening I had an idea," said Father, unfolding the pages and handing one to each of us. "I copied these verses before I turned in last night. The first is an inscription from an artifact left in the cardinal's keeping by the Holy Father Himself during his visit to Los Angeles some years ago. My Spanish is deplorable, and I know none of you is proficient, but I provide it for reference."

We all examined the verse on the top half of the page. Fr. Baptist's handwriting is among the worst I've seen, but he had calmed his hand as best he could and painstakingly copied each word patiently and distinctly:

> Vuela, pequeña golondrina, de la cabeza extraña
> En tu camino hacia la casa de oro
> Que tu curso cruce sobre el arroyo de la vida
> Que fluye de la fuente a la vid
> Ahí donde y cuando son dichas las palabras sagradas
> Sobre la corona de espinas dentro de un altar de piedra
> Mientras que tres veintenas y quince manos debajo
> El tesoro sangra para rescatar almas en la oscuridad.

"It's Greek to me," said Joel and Edward almost simultaneously. They congratulated themselves on their timing by patting each other's backs.

"*'La casa de oro,'*" said Arthur. "Isn't there a Mexican restaurant with that name?"

"You're thinking of *El Toro de Oro,*" said Jonathan. "The Golden Bull."

"So *'casa de oro'* must be 'golden house,'" said Arthur.

"That's right," said Father. "Now, as you can see, beneath the fold is a translation provided by our own Roberto Guadalupe."

"Was this what he was working on at Peanuts yesterday?" asked Joel.

"Right again," said Father. "Now, Gentlemen, do take a look."

> Fly, little swallow, from the strange head
> On your way to the house of gold
> May your path cross over the stream of life
> That flows from the well to the vine
> Over where and when the sacred words are said
> Upon the crown of thorns within an altar of stone
> While three score and fifteen hands below
> The treasure bleeds to rescue souls in darkness.

"Intriguing imagery," said Arthur. "What does it mean?"

"I don't know," said Father. "From bits and pieces I've put together in and around so much else that's been going on, it would seem to be a set of directions."

"Directions to what?" asked Joel.

"It does say treasure," said Jonathan.

"But a treasure that bleeds," said Arthur. "What could that mean?"

"Maybe it's dangerous," said Edward. "You know, protected by booby traps."

"No, it's a good treasure," said Jonathan, smiling playfully. "It yearns to rescue souls."

"Over where and when," said Arthur, eyebrows furrowed. "What kind of construction is that?"

"What ho!" said I. "Could this be like 'The Musgrave Ritual'? You know: Sherlock Holmes."

"I wouldn't be surprised," said Father. He then reached into another part of his cassock and produced a photocopy which he unfolded and handed to Arthur. "This is a drawing of the artifact from which the verse was copied."

"What are all these symbols?" asked Arthur, turning the page around like a steering wheel as all of us pressed close.

"I'm not sure," said Father. "Perhaps part of the same puzzle, maybe something else entirely. It seems to be intrinsically connected with California, that much I can tell you."

"So you want us to try to figure this out?" asked Edward.

"In a word, yes," said Father. "I must caution you, however. I know of at least one man who was brutally beaten because he held a clue to the solution of this puzzle."

"Who was that?" asked Arthur.

"What clue?" asked Joel.

I was about to ask if he meant Monsieur Guillaume du Crane Cristal. Willie, as he called himself, had joined us for dinner at the Blue Mountain Grill the night before. His right eye and cheek had looked a bit swollen, and his recent stay in the hospital was mentioned in passing. For the most part he had said little during dinner, then slinked away when Roderick Roundhead took over the conversation and proceeded to expound on his opinions at great length.

Just then Kahlúa Hummingbird honked her horn. I had forgotten that she'd had it modified to make that charming but obnoxious *"Uhoogah!"* sound like an old jalopy.

"I haven't time," said Father. "So listen carefully. Pierre and I must go to the Adirondack to try to find a lead on what happened to Martin. I request that you pray for that intention at Mass shortly, and then that you put your digging skills to work. My attention has been somewhat divided. Perhaps your collective tunneling will unravel the riddle."

"California, eh?" said Edward. "I suppose we could all shoot over to the public library after Mass. You know, for reference materials."

"Better still," said Jonathan, "Arthur's place."

"Right," said Edward. "He's got tons of books."

"Well, a few pounds, anyway," said Arthur, humbly.

"Come on," said I. "Even the public library doesn't have a complete set of *The Writings of Fr. Junípero Serra.*"

"You have this?" asked Father, impressed.

"Just arrived," said Arthur proudly. "Excellent condition. It was delivered while I was in Rome. I might mention that I also have an unopened bottle of Sandeman port."

"Well, that settles it," said Edward, Jonathan, and Joel together.

Uhoooogah!

While all eyes momentarily darted to Madame Hummingbird's Cadillac, I stepped close to Jonathan's ear and whispered, "By the by, dear chap, have you seen Stella, or rather has she seen ...?"

His eyes darted about for a second as if he were expecting an attack from any direction, then he shook his head. "Not yet. Several people said they saw her around, but so far our paths haven't crossed."

"Whew," I said, patting him on his shoulder. "All I can say is—"

"Pierre and I will come by Arthur's later," said Father. "Gentlemen, to Mass. Pierre, we're off."

"Hang on, Father," called Msgr. Havermeyer from the top of the church stairs.

"Monsignor," said Father, "you should be vesting for Mass."

"Don't I know it." He came stiffly down the stairs, favoring his right leg. His injuries from that electrical fire apparently extended beyond his face and hands. "Just as I was about to head for the sacristy, the rectory phone rang. I went in, thinking it might be about Mr. Feeney."

"Was it?"

"It was Cardinal Fulbright."

"In what far-flung corner of the archdiocese does he want me to meet him this time?"

"He didn't say anything about meeting him." The monsignor, having gained the sidewalk, strutted over to Father and lowered his voice. "He told me to tell you that he wants you to return the books you removed from Bishop Ravenshorst's library."

"Did he?"

"He was adamant."

"What were his exact words?"

Havermeyer cleared his throat and gathered his face into a mighty scowl. "'Tell him to put the bloody books back where they damn well belong.' Yes, that's what he said. Then he went on at some length and amplitude about moral decay, of all things. He's never been much concerned about it before, so far as I know."

"Could he have been referring, not to the decline of ethics, but rather to His Lordship Morell deQuet, the bishop he's trying to woo to Los Angeles?"

"Ah, maybe so." The monsignor shrugged. "Morley was yelling so loud, it was hard to tell. Come to think of it, I've heard of deQuet. Isn't he from New Bangor?"

"That's right. I'm beginning to wonder why Bishop deQuet has taken such an intense interest in his friend's books."

"What friend?"

"The late Bishop Ravenshorst."

"Oh, so they knew each other, did they?"

Uhoooooooooooooogah!

"You must forgive me, Monsignor," said Father. "My transportation grows impatient."

"That's nothing compared to what will happen if you start Mass late," said Edward, drawing his index finger across his throat like a knife.

"That's right," said Jonathan, jerking his neck sideways as if he were being hanged. "A horrible death will come on swift wings if you keep them waiting."

"Trads — kept — waiting," said Arthur, as if he were reading a headline. "Bloodshed — ensues."

"Enough," said Father. "Pierre, shall we?"

"Godspeed," said Msgr. Havermeyer, turning to go back up the steps. "I'll be praying for your efforts during Mass."

"Here, here," said the Tumblars, waving and following.

"Ravenshorst's books," sighed Father, looking both ways before crossing the street. "Just what we need, another complication."

6(65)

CHAPTER THE SIXTH, WHEREIN I VIEW THE ADIRONDACK FOR THE FIRST TIME BY LIGHT OF DAY, FATHER BAPTIST AND I GAZE UPON THE PAINTINGS OF SEÑOR X, MR. MAXWELL IS NOT ENTHUSED, WE MEET UP WITH LT. TAPER, AND IN WHICH SOMETHING SIGNIFICANT IS MISSING FROM MR. FEENEY'S CAR.

"THIS SHOULD BE FINE," said Fr. Baptist as Madame Hummingbird glided her Cadillac to a halt beneath the massive carport at the entrance to the Adirondack Hotel. He was seated in the right rear passenger seat. "This is about where Martin parked our Jeep last night. Your car has an excellent ride, by the way."

"Mmmmm hm!" said our vibrant driver. "You know what they say about Kahlúa."

"The drink or the woman?" I asked from the left rear passenger seat.

"Same thing," said she. "Smooth."

"Also dark and rich, I hear," said Millie from the front passenger seat.

"You heard right," said Kahlúa. "I'm a little lean on rich right now, but otherwise my namesake is onnnnn target."

"I've never tried it."

"Then today is your day, Sweetie!"

"Would you believe the bartender at Musso and Frank's invented a drink in my lady editor's honor?" I asked as I unbuckled my seatbelt.

"Don't try it," said she.

"It's disgusting what that man added to a shot of Kahlúa," said my boss and I together, our tones and inflections perfectly matched.

Millie glanced at me over her shoulder, then at Kahlúa in front of me, a wry smile tugging at the edges of her lips.

Father and I got out before the ladies so we could open their doors for them. That gesture seemed to please them both immensely. The car was angled in beside an impressive fountain, or so it would have been if it hadn't run dry. The blue tiles in the basin were chalky with lime deposits and caked with ancient algae. A little bird fluttered to a landing in the parched mouth of the marble lion that reigned as the centerpiece.

Where water used to surge from this gaping mouth, a bird now pecked around a small patch of lichen that was growing there.

"Is that a swallow?" asked Millie.

"Probably a robin," said Father.

"Mr. Feeney showed me the nests the swallows build up at La Purisima." She caught herself talking about him as though he were deceased. She then sniffed, writhed her lips for half a second, took a deep breath, and continued. "Actually, it was so early it was too dark to see them up in the rafters, but he told me about them." She sniffed more deeply. "He also said he didn't think this caper involving Msgr. Aspic was interesting enough to write about. That was his word: caper." Millie sniffed so long, hard, and noisily I thought her sinuses were going to implode. "I suppose he's finding it interesting enough to write about now, seeing as how he's—he's—"

Ever so gently, Father touched Millie's arm. "You mustn't lose heart, nor give up hope."

"Never," she agreed, snorting with resolved finality. She wiped her nose with the back of her hand. "I've stuck it out with you, haven't I?"

"That you have," said Father appreciatively. "Let us say a prayer for our Martin, in hopes that he will be returned safely to us. In the name of the Father, and of the Son, and of the Holy Ghost. Amen."

The four of us signed ourselves, bowed our heads, and recited an Our Father, three Hail Marys, and one Glory Be. The robin flew away as we concluded with another Sign of the Cross.

"So, Honey," said Madame Hummingbird, curling my arm around hers. "Show us the works."

"Why certainly," said I. "Walk this way."

"No thanks," said she, mischievously. "I'll walk my way."

Did she.

SPELUNKING SPINOFFS: I do suspect that, as we drove up to the Adirondack that bright Sunday morning, the thrill that filled me at the sight of the old hotel was akin to the experience of Charles Piazzi Smyth, the Astronomer Royal of Scotland and Professor of Astronomy at Edinburgh University, when he, having traveled to Egypt to examine the Great Pyramid at Giza for himself in 1865, first saw the grandest of ancient stone monuments rising out of the desert on the outskirts of what is now urban Cairo. Like him, my mind was swimming with preconceptions. Because he had studied the speculations of John Taylor, Smyth already believed that the structure of the Great Pyramid had been designed, inspired, and directed by Almighty God, that its dimensions were based on the pyramid inch, that it embodied an elaborate and perfect system of measures and mathematical concepts, and that within its con-

structs was prophesied the history of mankind right up to the date of the Last Judgment. Not that I give credence to these exaggerated, misguided, and perhaps delusional projections, nor do I consider three evenings of cheerful imbibing in the lounges within the Adirondack to be on par with Professor Smyth's erudite expectations, but I do well recall the elation, the very exaltation that welled within me as we approached the grand hotel on Margaret Sheridan Drive that morning, and it is that experience of consuming adulation that I shared with the Astronomer Royal. She was moldering, no doubt about it, just as the Great Pyramid had seen better days, but she was ablaze with architectural taste and originality that had somehow fallen by the wayside, sodden with an underlying sense of aloof playfulness, awash with memories of a bygone era, and crawling with specters, both imagined and real. Gadzooks, even in her decline she was magnificent!

—P.B.

This was my first glimpse of the aged duchess in broad daylight. The hot white radiance of the morning sun was not kind to the old gal. The dry fountain was but a foretaste of what was to come. The crossbar of the "A" above the entrance was divided by a jagged vertical crack. In fact, there were cracks meandering all over the façade of the building. The painted trim of the balconies was peeled and faded. Those manhole covers all over the outside walls were red with rust, with streaks of iron oxide from decades of rain trailing beneath them, staining the stonework dried-blood brown. The shrubbery around the base of the building, so picturesque and exotic when illumined by the mellow glow of floodlights at night, was straggly, unkempt, and begging to be watered.

The front doors were slabs of glass that swiveled silently and elegantly at the slightest touch, but they were smeared with several days' worth of grime and fingerprints. The foyer beyond was a vaulted citadel with columns and arches on both sides. Every upright was crowned with a regal "A," while manhole covers accented the arches in between. Only in a place like the Adirondack could manhole covers be a fashion statement—and an elegant one at that! The carpet was deep pile, royal blue overlaid with hourglass patterns of green and gold, worn thin in the center with eons of foot traffic. I imagined movie stars and starlets, having emerged from their Bentleys and Packards, sauntering between the pillars to the tune of wistful groans, barking reporters, and flashing bulbs. Madame Hummingbird certainly would have fit in, as well as myself, if I may be so bold.

Millie gasped as we entered the lobby. I must admit it had taken some of my breath away the first time I saw it, too. At eye level it was round and spacious, with an impressive registration counter of dark, speckled granite directly across the way. Between here and there were several clusters of overstuffed chairs huddled around homey coffee tables, with potted palms and aromatic cedars dangling their foliage all around. One could imagine all sorts of dignitaries and personages taking advantage of this charming and inviting setting to read their morning newspapers. The eyes, however, were drawn upward by the lure of rustic wooden chandeliers suspended by chains from the domed ceiling far above. Between the hominess below and the loftiness above was a gallery of enormous oil paintings. The same hand had painted them all, as evidenced by the name displayed in the lower right corners: *Alejandro Xavier Alverado y San Pasqual,* the "X" being the most prominent feature of the artist's signature. From the intensity and drama of the style, it was obvious that the subjects of these paintings held great significance. The events portrayed were unknown to me, but some of the male characters bore a striking resemblance to my friend, Roderick Roundhead. I considered pointing this out to Fr. Baptist, but decided that he, being the celebrated sleuth, surely would have noticed as well.

"My, but you put in long hours," said I as we approached the registration counter.

"You again," said the stout man standing behind it. His face was shaped like an inverted teardrop, broad forehead and narrow chin, with deep-set eyes between. He was attired in the same black suit he had worn the night before, complete with a black silk tie half the width of his silver tie clip. He was bald on top, and what hair clung to the sides was the color of spent ashes, and it glistened with a suffocating application of setting gel. Several strands of hair had worked loose and dangled like unwound springs around his tight little ears.

"Yes indeed," said I. "You're going to be seeing a lot of us around here, methinks."

"How nice," said he in an unenthusiastic monotone.

"Kahlúa Hummingbird," I said grandly, "this is Mr. Maxwell. Mr. Maxwell, I've been raving about your fine hotel. Madame Hummingbird is the owner, publisher, and managing editor of the *L.A. Artsy.*"

"How beneficial for you, Madame," said he in the exact same tone.

"You better be nice to her," said Millie. I suspect she was trying to be funny. "She can make or break you, you know."

"Of course," said Mr. Maxwell, neither amused nor concerned.

"And this is Fr. John Baptist," said I. "We're here because—"

"Jack," interrupted Lt. Taper, coming toward us from the direction of the Saranac Lounge. He acknowledged Mesdames Kahlúa and Millie with a half smile, and me with a vague nod of the head.

I admit that the sight of the man who had arrested me charging toward us gave me a momentary chill, but I shook it off. That peril was behind me, and more important matters were afoot.

"I'm glad you're here," said the lieutenant.

"Have you found something more?" asked Father.

"'Fraid so. Or rather, it's what I haven't found."

"Show me."

"This way to the guest parking lot."

The manager didn't react at all to their departure. As the others followed Lt. Taper, I tarried for a moment. "Mr. Maxwell."

"Yes, sir."

"So how are your ghosts this morning?"

"Really, sir."

"Come on, my good man. Don't you find it fascinating?"

"That would not be my choice of adjective, sir."

"I'm sorry if I seem impertinent, but I have simply fallen under the spell of this wonderful old hotel. I'd like to learn more about its history."

"There is a library near the Ticonderoga Ballroom, sir. It is reserved for guests only, but it does contain books on the history of the hotel and the area."

"Guests, eh? How much is a room here?"

"If you need to ask, sir—"

"Ah, quite right. Still, I am fascinated. I don't suppose a press pass would suffice?"

"I think not, sir."

This did not deter me in the least, for I knew that if we Tumblars established ourselves in the magnificent bars it was only a matter of time before we would become part of the woodwork, and locked doors do not exist for regulars.

"Forgive my curiosity," said I, "but you were on duty last evening."

"I was indeed, sir."

"But here you are this morning."

"Miss Davenport, the morning manager, is … ill."

Quit more likely, thought I. "Um, do you have a high rate of turnover here? Among the staff, I mean."

He regarded me, inscrutably. "You should know, sir. You and your friends drove an inexperienced waitress from the premises only last night."

"Not so, not so, at least not entirely. We may have set up the young lady, but it was your Mr. Barlow who delivered the grand punch line."

"He does have that reputation, sir."

"I apologize if we contributed to your inconvenience."

"It's life at the Adirondack, if you'll excuse the double entendre."

"Excuse my lack of finesse, Mr. Maxwell, but will you be looking for a new morning manager? I ask because I know a couple of gentlemen who might be interested in the position."

"Really."

"Yes indeed."

"Tell them to contact Mr. Reinholz in Personnel. Cyril Reinholz. I understand a managerial position may be opening soon."

"Much appreciated, Mr. Maxwell. Thanks so much."

"Good day, sir."

I caught up with Lt. Taper and company as they were exiting the hotel through the door leading to the outdoor swimming pool. I must mention that, even with all the evidence of neglect, my appreciation for this fine old landmark from a bygone age mounted with every step, every encounter, and every view. Only the Adirondack would gently compel her patrons to stroll past a sumptuous swimming pool when going to or from the parking lot. A tropical lagoon, it was, complete with uproarious waterfalls—well, two of the three were not running this day. The pool was deep, completely tiled in indigo blue and sea green, with tropical shrubbery all around. The parking lot was achieved by following a gently meandering pathway of basaltic stones lined with spent tiki torches. The blacktop was, as was everything, poorly maintained. Serpentine cracks slithered all over the asphalt, and the painted lines which once delineated parking slots were so faded and eroded as to be rendered useless.

Nonetheless, there was the Jeep Cherokee that Mr. Feeney liked to drive so much. It had a metallic gold finish, which I believe they called "champagne" back in 1994 when the vehicle was assembled. A most charming color, in my opinion. The tailgate sagged with the weight of an oversized all-weather tire that matched the others in all things but tread wear. I noticed two other things about the car as we approached: the piles of books and scholarly papers heaped on the back seat, and the presence of dark, dusty residue on the handles and around the edges of the doors.

"You've been busy," said Fr. Baptist, indicating the handle on the driver's door.

"You trained me," said Lt. Taper.

"What is that?" asked Millie.

"I'd know fingerprinting powder anywhere," said Kahlúa.

"From your sordid past?" I asked her.

"From having my apartment burgled three times," said she.

"Jack here was my boss, you know," explained Taper. "Back when he ran Homicide. He taught me the benefit of keeping a fingerprint kit in my glove compartment. Not often, but sometimes the crime scene investigators get detained when evidence is in danger of corruption."

"This case isn't official," said Father. "Therefore there are no *crime sceners* on the way."

"I prefer calling them *'gators,* myself," said Taper, plucking one of his incisors with his thumbnail. "Sharp teeth."

"So did you find any prints?" asked Kahlúa, who was indulging in a close look at the door handle. As she turned her head her feathers and ferns brushed against the car. "Oops! Sorry, I didn't mean to wreck your evidence."

"You didn't," said Taper. "There are no prints."

"No prints?" asked Millie. "What does that mean?"

"That someone wiped the car free of them," said Father.

"That's right," said Taper, "and that worries me."

"Yes," said Father. "Me, too."

"Why?" asked Millie.

"Because," said Father, "it confirms that Martin did not move his car from the front of the hotel to here. Someone else did."

"Someone who knows what they're doing," said Taper.

"Or perhaps watches crime shows on TV," said Madame Hummingbird.

"Muriel and I have seen our share," said Millie. "I'd sure know enough to wipe off the handles and steering wheel if I'd just done something illegal with someone else's car."

"Pierre, what time did you leave here last night?" asked Father.

"You mean this morning," said I. "Around one."

"You weren't driving Kahlúa's Cadillac, were you?"

"No, I hitched a ride with Edward." I looked around more carefully, getting my bearings. "As a matter of fact, he and I saw those charming, witty Doily Sisters to their car over there, by that parking island with the Asian cactus. Their chauffeur, Keating, was waiting for them. He was seated behind the steering wheel, reading a book by the cabin light. I think there was another woman in the front passenger seat, but I'm not sure. It was an amazing car, by the way. A real classic. Father had already left with Mr. Roundhead, who I believe was driving a Porsche. Edward's van was just over there."

"Any chance the Jeep was parked here at the time you left?" asked Father.

"Hmm." I removed my monocle, exhaled upon it, and rubbed the results against my vest. "To tell you the truth, Father, I don't remember it being here, but I can't honestly say that it wasn't. My focus was elsewhere. Still, I do think that if it had been here it would have caught my attention, don't you?"

"That would depend," said he. "What were you so focused upon?"

"The moment. The conversation. The coolest of cars."

"How much had you had to drink?"

"Not enough not to see a car that was there, nor not to see a car that wasn't not."

"Huh?" gasped my editrix.

7(66)

CHAPTER NUMBER SEVEN, WHEREIN FATHER AND I PART COMPANY WITH LT. TAPER AND THE LADIES, I SPY SEVERAL INTERESTING PEOPLE EMERGING FROM THE ELEVATORS, FATHER NOTICES SOMETHING SIGNIFICANT IN ONE OF SEÑOR X'S PAINTINGS, AND IN WHICH MR. HECTOR UTURN WON'T TAKE NO FOR AN ANSWER.

"ENJOY THE BRUNCH," SAID FATHER to Millie and Madame Hummingbird. We were back in the lobby basking in Mr. Maxwell's disinterested scrutiny. "I wish we could join you, but Pierre and I have places to go. Larry, if you step on it you can still make Mass before the Credo."

"You sure you don't need me?" asked Lt. Taper, glancing at his watch.

"We need your prayers, as do you," said Father. "Pierre and I are going to rendezvous with the Tumblars at Arthur's apartment later. If you've a mind, why don't you meet us there?"

"Will do," said he. "And thanks."

"What for?"

"For not rubbing my nose in the arrest of Mercedes Sinclair."

"Oh yes, the man at Way True Life."

"He's fighting extradition to Louisiana as we speak. There's something of a feeding frenzy going on among all the states that want him. But he has an ironclad alibi for the evening Msgr. Aspic disappeared, and being in police custody, he certainly couldn't have had anything to do with whatever happened to Martin last night."

"Well, every door closed is a step forward in an investigation," said Father.

"But you already knew it. I should have … well, anyway, I must be off."

"God bless you, Larry," said Father. "May you make it to St. Philomena's in time. See you at Arthur's."

"I'll be there. You, too, Pierre, Ladies." With that, he was off.

"Well," said Father, rubbing his hands together.

"You won't be home for lunch, will you?" said Millie, her tone accusatory.

"Nor will you," said Father. "It's Sunday. Enjoy it."

"That will be the day. How can I? What about dinner?"

"'Be not therefore solicitous for dinner,'" said I, helpfully. "'For the dinner will be solicitous for itself.'"

"Nice, Pierre," said Kahlúa with an exaggerated wink. "But if you're trying to fill in for Mr. Feeney, you're not succeeding."

"His paraphrases may be lame," said Millie," but not that lame."

"A thousand pardons," said I, bowing obsequiously. "I should have known better than to try to limp in his moccasins."

"Anyway," said Millie, shrugging and looking at Kahlúa. "I guess I'm free then."

"Okay," said Madame Hummingbird, locking arms with Millie. "We gals is off to do untold damage to our girlish figgers."

"Enjoy," said I, waving as they made for the Blue Mountain Grill. In moments they were out of sight. Those ladies were hungry indeed.

"Now," said Father, patting his pockets. "Whoops. I neglected to bring my cell phone. Do you have yours with you, Pierre?"

"Much as my employer and taskmistress insists that I keep the one she provided on my person at all times, I'm afraid in rising so early today I was negligent."

"I won't tell. Ah, look. A phone booth. If you will excuse me a minute."

Yes, over by the elevator was an actual phone booth. Not just a metal telephonic unit bolted to the wall, but an old-fashioned closet with plush red leather interior, padded seat, overhead light, and elegant soundproof door with a small triangle of glass to see if it was occupied. It wasn't. Having read Mr. Feeney's manuscript, I knew it to be precisely the kind of phone booth that he would have appreciated.

While Father made his call in privacy, I amused myself by examining the magazines on a coffee table between two swanky chairs. He couldn't have been in there more than five minutes. During that time three interesting people stepped out of one of the three lobby elevators, though not simultaneously.

The first was a man that I'd never seen in person, but I recognized his face from the night Alan Ross, the owner of Darby's, badgered the Tumblars by insisting on tuning his big-screen TV to KLIE, making us suffer through promos for *Religion Revisited*. That was the night Msgr. Aspic disappeared. Actually, I knew the man's face better than that. Kahlúa Hummingbird kept his signed, framed photograph in her office. It was nailed to the wall in the corner a foot or so above her polished brass wastepaper basket. She enjoyed pummeling it with wads of crumpled paper en route to the dumpster. There's something about a man's picture so mockingly preserved that piques one's imagination.

SPELUNKING SPINOFFS: In a sunflower-seed-sized nutshell as told to me by Kahlúa Hummingbird, Sheldon and Eira Levant contacted my editor through their producer, a Ms. (with three z's) Napolia Krackershak, who invited her to interview them at their television production facility. Kahlúa thought it odd, but anything for the Artsy. *While the interview was in progress, Kahlúa noticed that Sheldon consulted his wristwatch every fifteen seconds, as if he were anticipating something. Sure enough, halfway through the exchange, her hosts received frantic word from their maid that Eira's precious miniature French poodle, Poopsie-Whoopsie, had somehow gotten itself entangled in an electrical extension cord at their palatial home in Malibu and was now fighting for its pupsy-whuspy life at a fashionable pet hospital in Santa Monica. Mrs. Levant left screaming, and Ms. Krackershak left with her, cooing and there-there-ing. This left Sheldon and Kahlúa alone in Napolia's control room. He actually tried to seduce her, right there on the audio/video console, all the while citing the names of notable women who had supposedly enjoyed the same fate. Kahlúa gave him a whack he wouldn't soon forget and left. The licentious worm actually sent her his autographed photo the next day signed "Anytime, anyplace, anywhere—Shel."*

—P.B.

Mr. Levant took five broad steps out of the carriage, looked around as though he owned the place, then strutted purposely to the registration desk. He was attired in loose-fitting beige pants, and a low-cut polo shirt designed to show off his puffy chest hair and the golden chain that hung from his turkey-skin neck.

While he was settling his bill with blustering abandon, the elevator deposited interesting person number two, an aging gal in a tighter-than-skintight silver outfit with black tassels. Her frizzled, unnaturally yellow hair was disheveled and her makeup worn away like paint in a sandstorm. She had the look about her of a cheap pillow that had been pounded every-which-way to accommodate a greasy man's sleeping posture. Her eyes darted around the lobby, and when they lighted on Mr. Levant they reacted by opening wide, blinking three times in rapid succession, and darting away. As gracefully as she could, which was negligible, she turned on her wobbly high heels and headed in the direction of the swimming pool, which was to say, the guest parking lot. Her body language suggested that she was making a quick getaway, hoping not to be noticed. The sprayed-on garment rendered the effort futile.

The third person of interest emerged just as Father Baptist came out of the classy phone booth. Without hesitation he marched straight for the registration counter where Mr. Levant was still vociferating eloquent at the clerk.

"Everything copasetic?" I asked Father.

"I just asked Sybil Wexler to join us at Arthur's," said Father, starting across the lobby.

"I hope she won't be bringing her partner with her."

"Tragg Halcomb? No chance of that. They're not partners anymore."

"Really."

"You have been out of touch, Pierre."

"You're absolutely right, Father. My recent incarceration as a guest of the police has left me completely cut off from—"

"Hold on," said Father, not to anyone in particular, least of all me. He looked up, then around, and then turned to gaze up at the largest oil painting in the lobby, the one above the registration counter. "Would you look at that?"

"You mean the Cordova Rosary?" said I, drawing up beside him. "Yes, I recognized that the first time I came through here."

"No, I mean that section over on the right, in the background."

I looked where he was pointing. Beyond the flapping banners in the foreground, punctuated by a flash of lighting above, a Mass was being celebrated outdoors on a makeshift altar. The priest whose back was three-quarters to us was a Franciscan, as evidenced by the brown cowl hanging over the back of his vestments. His chasuble was blue, the color the missionaries reserved for feast days of the Blessed Virgin Mary, of which there were many. The top of his head was shaved, leaving a hairy ring all the way around in the style of friars and monks of centuries past. The altar was a roughly hewn block of brownish-blue stone. On top rested a small altar cloth of white linen, its edges flailing in the storm. It was anchored by the weight of golden liturgical vessels: a chalice, a ciborium, and a sacred host resting on a round paten. On the side of the stone facing the priest, partially blocked by his body but revealed by a gust of wind whipping back his chasuble was a depiction of the crown of thorns worn by Jesus Christ at his crucifixion, life-size if the scale was accurate. The thorns were wickedly jagged, their stalks realistically twisted and gnarled, their tips blood red. Perhaps it was a trick of lighting or pigment, but I had the distinct impression that the thing was not supposed to be painted onto the stone, but was rather an illusion of the marbling within the stone itself.

"That verse I gave you and the lads," said Father. "Do you have it on you?"

"Of course," said I, retrieving it from my vest pocket and hurriedly unfolding it.

"Read the fifth and sixth lines, would you?"

"Let's see ..."

> Over where and when the sacred words are said
> Upon the crown of thorns within an altar of stone

"Could it be?" said Father, craning his neck.

"You mean there's a connection between this poem and that painting?" said I. "I thought you said this verse came from an artifact the Holy Father left with Cardinal Fulbright."

"That's right, a verse full of clues. We may have stumbled upon a key to one of them."

"So what does it mean?"

"I've no idea. But I can tell you one thing—"

"Whoa horses!" interrupted a deep, gruff voice. "It can't be, but it is! You're Fr. John Baptist, aren't you?"

Father's hand was suddenly engulfed by a gigantic paw. It belonged to the third person disgorged from the elevator. He had been waiting at the registration counter, impatiently grunting and glancing around the lobby while Mr. Levant blathered on obliviously at the desk clerk. Having spotted Father Baptist, he had come lunging toward us, appendage outstretched.

"I'm sorry," said Father as his arm was pumped up and down. "You have me at a disadvantage."

"Not at all, not at all," said the man with the paw. "My name's Uturn. Hector Uturn. I'm the president of A-T-A-C, you know, the Alliance of Traditional American Catholics, and I'm organizing the next West Coast Catholic Traditionalist Conference in December. It's been one problem after another. We were booked at the Hotel Merrimack, but we got bumped! Would you believe it? Just like that, after all the fliers had already gone out, the mailings, the posters, the newspaper ads, they refund our deposit and, well, anyway, that's why I'm here. And thank God the Ticonderoga Ballroom isn't reserved that weekend. If fact, they're offering us a great deal on rooms, too, so I think this is going to work out."

"Plus this place has atmosphere," said I.

"It really is going to work out," said he, apparently not hearing me.

"Excuse me, Mr. Uturn," said I, careful to pronounce his name as he had, without a "Y" at the beginning. "My name is Pierre Bontemps. I write for the *L. A. Artsy.* Have I understood you correctly? ATAC is going to hold its TradCon here at the Adirondack?" (I pronounced ATAC as "attack.")

"Absolutely!" said he, finally letting go of Father's hand. As he turned his head to look at me his smile slipped. "Who did you say you are?"

"Pierre Bontemps, at your service."

"Hey," said he, snapping his fingers. "You're the fettuccini guy."

"Well, I did write an article about—"

"What, you're a pal of the cardinal or something? Having lunch with him and all?"

"Excuse me. I never dined with—"

"Oh, I see, just to get the story. You did say you're a reporter."

"Yes I did, but—"

"The *Artsy*, you say."

"Yes, sir, that—"

"Well, whatever." He dismissed me easily and turned his sights on Father. "Fr. Baptist, it is just so darn good that I bumped into you. You are heaven-sent, Father. Heaven-sent."

"I don't understand," said Father.

"Fr. Path cancelled," said Mr. Uturn. "Would you fill in for him?"

"I'm no speaker," said Father, "and I'm not associated with your organization."

"You've heard of us, haven't you?"

"Yes, but all of it hearsay. But that's beside the point. As I said, I'm no speaker."

"I'm not asking you to give a talk. I want you to celebrate the Mass on Friday night, you know, to sort of kick off the whole shebang."

Father thought a moment and said, "I don't think so."

"And maybe Benediction later that evening. We're thinking of having Adoration in one of the suites throughout the weekend. Isn't that a great idea?"

"I wish you the best," said Father, "but at the moment Mr. Bontemps and I are late for a meeting of our own."

"But surely you'll do the Mass?"

"I'm sorry, I don't see—"

"Of course you don't. That's okay, I knew you'd do it."

"I didn't say that."

"You didn't have to. Thanks and thanks again."

With that, Mr. Hector Uturn spun around on his brown leather soles and hustled off in the direction of the registration counter. I had been so distracted by Father's exchange with him that I hadn't noticed when Mr. Levant had left. I thought to mention it, but just then Father provided me with an opening, and I never miss a chance to exercise my razor-sharp wit.

"What was that all about?" said Father, turning and heading toward the entrance foyer. "He wouldn't let my no be no."

"Don't look now, Father," said I, catching up and walking beside him. "You've just been ATAC-ed."

8(67)

THE EIGHTH CHAPTER, WHEREIN FATHER AND I VISIT A JEWELRY SHOP, FR. BAPTIST REAFFIRMS THAT THE PROPRIETOR IS CAPABLE OF DISHONESTY, SAID PROPRIETOR'S STORY DISAGREES WITH MR. ROUNDHEAD'S ON A SIGNIFICANT POINT, FATHER REVEALS THE CENTERPIECE, AND IN WHICH FATHER RETRIEVES THE CARDINAL'S ASHTRAY.

"THIS IS CERTAINLY A DISREPUTABLE looking establishment," said I as I steered the Jeep to a halt at an otherwise deserted curb in front of E. Winger's Fine Jewels and Settings. "Why, this isn't much more than a pawn shop."

"Less, I fear."

"So why are we stopping here?"

"The proprietor is an associate of your friend, Roderick Roundhead."

"Oh?"

"Yes: oh. I'm here to clear up something, and perhaps to pick up the cardinal's chalice."

"What chalice is that?"

"The one his mentor, Prof. Murkenstein, gave him."

"I've heard of it."

"Of course you have. Mr. Roundhead fouled it with his cigar. Surely he filled you in on that part of the St. Valeria episode. It's here being cleaned."

"As a matter of fact, he did, somewhat. I must say I can't imagine the cardinal leaving something which holds significance for him at such a place."

"He didn't," said Father, unbuckling his seatbelt. "Msgr. Aspic, to whom he consigned the chalice, did that."

"And why would he—?"

"Mr. Winger was recommended to both of them by Thurgood T. Turnbuckle at the behest of, wouldn't you know, Roderick Roundhead."

"I'm not following all this."

"Ah, speak of the devil. No time to explain it all now."

Just then a man carrying a cardboard carton turned the far corner and came slinking down the sidewalk toward us, apparently oblivious to our presence. Hefting up one knee on which to steady the box as he fumbled for his keys, his manner seemed furtive and skulking, even though he was entering his own shop.

"Coming?" asked Father, opening his car door.

"Of course," said I, complying.

"You again," said the proprietor as the front door rattled and banged shut behind us. He set the cardboard carton on the counter beside the cash register. "I'm closed."

"As you should be, it being Sunday," said Fr. Baptist.

"What do you want?"

"Since Msgr. Aspic has disappeared, I thought I might pick up His Eminence's property if it's ready."

"Whose?"

"Cardinal Fulbright. Msgr. Aspic left his chalice with you for cleaning."

"Oh, that. Yeah, it's ready." He retrieved it from a shelf and set it on the glass countertop. There was a bill affixed to the stem with loose twine. "There's no clerical discount."

"I didn't expect one," said Father. "I shall give the bill to the cardinal personally."

"Fat chance. It don't leave here not being paid for."

"You insult the cardinal."

"I'm crushed. You insulted me last time you were here by calling me a liar."

"But you were lying."

"You can go to blazes."

"Very well." Father turned as if to leave, winked at me, then faced Mr. Winger again. "Oh, by the way, I was dining with Mr. Roundhead last night."

"Who?"

"Don't be obtuse, Mr. Winger. You contacted Ernie Corben within minutes of my last visit."

"So what if I did?"

"He answers to Mr. Roundhead as, ultimately, do you. In the course of our conversation he confirmed what you denied, that you made him a copy of the golden artifact which Msgr. Aspic arranged to leave with you for that purpose."

"So?"

"So, Mr. Roundhead also assured me that you have the original."

"I don't. He has it."

"He says not."

"Then he's lying."

"That is unfortunate." Father dug around inside his cassock, producing a leather pouch. From this he removed an object wrapped in a black cloth. Resting it in his open left palm, he gently peeled away the cloth, revealing a golden disk, perhaps who inches in diameter. The surface was slightly convex, and was adorned with an engraved cross.

"Where did you get that?" exclaimed the proprietor, his eyes wide and avaricious.

"Really, Mr. Winger," said Father. "Why should I be forthcoming with you when you have been so cagey with me? I believe this piece fits into the center of the artifact you say you don't have. Projections on the bottom, I'm guessing, were designed to allow it to nest in only one position in the center of the larger disk. I'm not sure what that will mean, but I'd certainly like to test the theory."

"Well, you could if I had it," said Winger, glaring as Father gathered it in the black cloth, enclosed it in the pouch, and returned it to the pocket within his cassock. "But I don't."

"Then you will answer to Mr. Roundhead for straying from his instructions."

"What're you saying?"

"His words. You'll have to sort it all out with him. Well, Pierre, we'd best be going."

"Here," said Mr. Winger, handing Fr. Baptist the Murkenstein chalice.

Father looked at the horrid thing, surprised. "But you said—"

"On second thought, I'd rather get it out of my store. It's so hideous, it's bad for business."

"Well, at least we agree on one thing."

9(68)

CHAPTER NUMBER NINE, WHEREIN I HAVE A HEART-TO-HEART WITH ALMIGHTY GOD WHILE FATHER CATCHES UP ON HIS READING.

I SHALL HOP, SKIP, AND JUMP—or perhaps waltz—over most of the events of the next couple of hours because there were none to report—events, that is. There was, however, something of enormous import, to be sure, but it was a departure from my expectations of detective work.

Upon leaving Mr. Winger's shop on Sunset, we went up to Franklin, and turned north on Beachwood, the street seemingly aimed right at the famous Hollywood sign, and which I believe once served as a location during the filming of *Teenagers from Outer Space*. Then we turned left on a side street and right into a narrow driveway with a narrower gate, and suddenly I was parking the Jeep in a bricked area within the walls of an eighteenth century convent. According to a sign, it was in fact the Monastery of the Archangels, home of the cloistered Sisters of the Apparition of Mount Gargano. There were two other cars there, a bare-metal '63 Plymouth, and a late model Jaguar. This was obviously the visitors' parking lot.

"Since I've been ordered to return these books to where they belong, namely the late Bishop Ravenshorst's library," said he as we exited the Jeep, "I really must give them my attention for a while. Once returned I doubt I'll ever get near them again."

"Here?" I asked, skeptically.

"Well, it is quiet. It's unlikely that I'll be interrupted, and there is Perpetual Adoration in the chapel. You did make a deal with Msgr. Havermeyer."

"You mean about him working on his sermons."

"And you working on your humility."

"Oh, that."

"Yes: that. It's going to take me a good hour to go through all this stuff. Maybe more."

"I welcome the opportunity of course. What can be more important than having an eye-to-eye with my Creator? It isn't how I would have thought to spend my Sunday, but it is certainly fitting. But Father, are you sure I can't help you look for whatever it is that you're looking for?"

"I don't even know, Pierre. In fact, before I get started, I'm going to make a short visit in the chapel myself to pray for guidance." Which goes to show you just how different a detective our cop-turned-priest-turned-cop is from the norm. "Wait'll you see this," said he, leading me past a sign indicating the way. "Would that this could be the Tumblars' clubhouse *pro tem*. You lads could use more quiet time."

"You were here recently with Mr. Feeney?"

"Why, yes. Thursday, I believe. Why?"

"I was just wondering."

SPELUNKING SPINOFFS: Truly, to the Catholic, there is nothing more important than the Holy Eucharist. It is, after all, the Body, Blood, Soul, and Divinity of Our Lord and Savior, Jesus Christ. What human activity could possibly be more important than basking in the Real Presence? True, I had received the same in Holy Communion earlier that day, which is as close and intimate as it gets this side of the grave. But kneeling before the Blessed Sacrament—Creator and creature both exposed, as it were—that is a profoundly different experience.

Still, human frailty being what it is, the first thirty minutes of such a visit are invariably hard for me. I am as yet incapable of instant detachment from the world outside and all my connections to it. It takes a while for my attention to gradually narrow and focus, to get beyond all the things I have to say to all the things that don't require verbalization. Once beyond this hurdle, I invariably marvel at the effort it takes to turn off all the noise in my head. Then the words of St. Paul in his eighth chapter to the Romans take on a whole new meaning:

"For I am sure that neither death, nor life, nor angels, nor principalities, nor powers, nor things present, nor things to come, nor might, nor depth, nor any other creature, shall be able to separate us from the love of God, which is in Christ Jesus our Lord."

What did this have to do with looking for Mr. Feeney? Seemingly nothing, and yet, everything.

—P.B.

N.B.: Regarding mental agitation in circumstances like this, it was Fr. Leonard Feeney, MICM, who once said, "I'd rather be distracted before God than collected around anyone else."

I don't have to read Mr. Feeney's chapters to know that he will have described the chapel in detail. Suffice it to say that it was beautiful and peaceful, thoroughly conducive to mental prayer. More than a dozen faithful people came and went while I was there.

Father's visit to the chapel lasted only ten minutes. His every movement as he roused himself to leave conveyed reluctance to depart the sublime in order to deal with the material. His verbal rummaging out in the car lasted more than an hour more than he had predicted, but that was fine with me. My attention was beginning to wander again when he quietly returned and touched me on the shoulder.

"You and Mr. Feeney have been busy," said I, as I accelerated up the onramp onto the Hollywood Freeway. I felt enormously refreshed.

"You have no idea," said Father, straining to reach a volume from one of the swaying piles on the back seat. "Hang on, I've got to double-check something."

"Too bad we can't just photocopy the lot," said I. "Then you'd always have it for reference."

"That would be cost-prohibitive," said he, opening the book and scanning the table of contents.

"Ah, there is that," said I.

"Yes, there is."

"Would you mind if I asked you something? Not that I'm prying, you understand, Father, but that golden disk you showed Mr. Winger."

"What about it?" said he, in the tone of voice of a man who was absorbed in the pages of his book.

"It's news to me, as was Roderick's involvement with the artifact, and with Mr. Turnbuckle for that matter. This wasn't discussed over dinner last night."

"No, Pierre. That conversation occurred in the Saranac Lounge before dinner, no doubt while you and the Tumblars were in the Champlain Room."

"What was it that Roderick said in the Blue Mountain Grill about you losing a bet?"

"It was a ploy on my part to have dinner with him."

"Why not just invite him?"

"Because I wanted him to feel that he had the upper hand."

"But he didn't, of course, with you, not really."

"It's a matter of perspective."

"I see," I said. "The other evening at the Knights' meeting you told us of your trip to Camarillo to see the cardinal. You were summoned to investigate Msgr. Aspic's disappearance, and you said it was somehow connected to the man found in the mausoleum."

"Mm hmmm," he mumbled, turning a page.

"So where does that disk fit in?"

"Mm hmmm."

"You're not paying attention, are you?"

"Mm hmmm."

Presently he seemed satiated, at which point he began to shut the book. But as the pages fluttered closed something caught his attention, something in the upper corner of the inside cover. He rocked all the pages leftward and examined the inset of the back cover. "Good heavens," he said, half aloud. "Well, I'll be a ... words fail. How could I have missed that?"

"Missed what?" I asked, accelerating into a faster lane.

"Hang on," said he, reaching for another book from the back seat. Again he checked the inside covers, front and back. Then he grabbed another, and another, and another. One by one they ended up wedged on the floor around and on top of his feet. In a matter of minutes the level exceeded his knees. The file folders and sketches didn't seem to be part of this process. When only three books remained on the back seat, having been tossed there after inspection, he settled back in his seat. He exhaled, exhausted but elated. "I must be getting old."

"Aren't we all?" said I philosophically. "Especially when literally buried in books."

"To have missed something so obvious, I mean. I'm losing my touch."

"What did you miss?"

"The obvious."

"You said that."

"How far are we from St. Barbara's Chapel?"

"You know me and directions, Father. If I had been Columbus' navigator he would have discovered Antarctica."

"Perhaps that wouldn't have been so bad. Let me see. Have we passed the Vermont exit yet?"

"No. The last sign we passed said it was coming up in two and a half miles."

"Excellent."

"Excuse me, Father, but am I detecting some sort of newfound enthusiasm at the thought of obeying your lawful superior?"

"You might say that."

"But I thought—"

"So did I, but I was wrong."

"Oh."

"Pierre, I have a notion that things are going to start turning in our favor."

"What makes you think that, Father?"

"They had to sooner or later."

"Nothing like sound philosophical certainty upon which to hang one's hat, I always say. Not that I wish to intrude upon your thought processes, Father, but you seem to be more interested in those books than you are in finding Mr. Feeney."

"It may seem that way, but I assure you that Martin is my first priority."

"That Spanish verse Roberto translated for you. How is that connected with finding Mr. Feeney?"

"It's not, at least, not directly."

"Indirectly, then."

"We'll see."

"I'm beginning to understand why Mr. Feeney is so crotchety."

"I don't follow you."

"If you did, Mr. Feeney wouldn't be so crotchety."

"I'm definitely not following you, Pierre."

"Perhaps it's for the best."

10(69)

THE TENTH CHAPTER, WHEREIN FR. BAPTIST SOOTHES A SAVAGE HOUSEKEEPER, HE AND I VISIT AN IRATE BISHOP, AND IN WHICH THE BORROWED BOOKS ARE RESTORED TO THEIR RIGHTFUL OWNER.

"YOU!" EXCLAIMED THE TETCHY WOMAN who answered the rectory door at St. Barbara's Chapel.

"I'm sure the cardinal will love hearing from you again," said Father. He held up the few volumes he had extricated from the many in the car. "As before, I am here at his command. This is my associate, Monsieur Pierre Bontemps. I wonder if we might have the happiness of seeing His Lordship, Bishop deQuet?"

"'His Lordship,' now, is it?" said she with a haughty sneer. If she thought Fr. Baptist was groveling she surely mistook the man.

"Perhaps he prefers 'His Excellency,'" said Father.

"Not that I'm aware," scoffed she.

"Oh, well, in any case, I have come to return Bishop Ravenshorst's books to his library. I would leave them with you, except in light of Cardinal Fulbright's directive, I would prefer to see it through personally."

She glared at him challengingly, then at me dismissively, then suspiciously at the books in his hands. Her scowl seemed to go through several significant alterations as she assessed and reassessed the situation.

"You may come in," she said at last. "Wait here. I'll see if he'll see you."

"You are most kind," said Father. "Oh, before you go, would you mind if I asked you something?"

"I most certainly would," said she with a standoffish sniff.

"Madame," said Father gently but firmly. "Need I remind you that I am here at the direction of the Cardinal? I fully understand your feelings about Bishop Ravenshorst's possessions and my going through them."

"Stealing them, you mean."

"Let us say removing them. You obviously cared a great deal for Jeremiah Ravenshorst, and I know this intrusion into his affairs bothers you. But I have a job to do, a task His Eminence gave to me personally. Can we not try to work together?"

"Together?" she said suspiciously.

"At least, not at odds. I would prefer to tell the cardinal that you were a big help, rather than otherwise."

"Well, when you put it that way. What do you want to know?"

"I'm keenly aware of Bishop Ravenshorst's interest in the California Missions, especially the work he did regarding the Del Agua Mission."

Her face softened somewhat. "Yes, that project was so important to him."

"Indeed. I was just wondering if he made a point of visiting any of the other missions."

"You mean like San Juan Capistrano?" she said, almost wistfully. "Yes, he loved to visit when the swallows came. And San Gabriel. He took me there more than once."

"Really. What about the missions to the north? San Buenaventura, Santa Barbara?"

"Let me think. I believe he drove up to that one in the Danish town."

"Solvang?"

"That's right. Santa Ynez, I think it's called. He took the house staff to Solvang once. I got sick on butter cookies."

"There's another mission fairly close to there, near Solvang, but to the west, out toward Vandenberg Air Force Base."

"Oh, you mean La Purisima," she said.

"That's right. So he did go there?"

"Funny you should ask," said she. "I remember him saying that he had no interest in visiting La Purisima."

"Really."

"Yes. He said it was controlled by the State of California, and that they had renovated it, but he didn't consider it authentic."

"He never went to see for himself?"

"Not that I remember. Is it important?"

"I don't know," said Father. "Probably not. I was just there yesterday and I'd have to agree with him."

"Really?"

"It didn't seem authentic at all. I would have loved to see what he would have done with it."

That seemed to please her, or maybe puzzle her. I'm not sure. In any event, after a moment of shared appreciation for Jerry Ravenshorst's memory, she roused herself and said, "Well, I'd best be telling Morell you're here."

"Thank-you," said Father. "You've been most helpful."

"Excuse me, Father," said I after she had disappeared down a hallway. "Aren't you laying it on a little thick?"

"'Whatever can be done by smiling, you may rely on me to do.'"

"Is that Shakespeare?"

"No, Robert Bolt. *A Man for All Seasons.*"

"The play about St. Thomas More, the one Mr. Feeney is always quoting."

"The same."

"I pray I don't offend, Father, but I feel compelled to revisit an earlier point. Surely returning these books is not as important as investigating the disappearance of Mr. Feeney."

If Mr. Feeney were writing this chapter, he would probably say that Father favored me with a look that seemed to whisper, patient yet meaningfully, "Considering how long you've known me, Pierre, and all that we've been through, do you really think that anything short of my own salvation would take priority over my concern for my friend's safety?" But all he actually said was, "You think so?"

I confess that it would take the largest of Millie's spatulas to carve all the egg off my face at that moment. I knew this priest, both as confessor and mentor, and on some complex level, Friend. The Knights of the Tumblar would be an intriguing curiosity in a world gone mad, a jolly fun men's club at least, but they would not be duly knighted defenders of the Roman Catholic Faith if not for his effort and support. There are many things he has done for me and for my comrades, things about which Mr. Feeney has not written because he was not present or privy to them. In an age of doubt and imprecision, in which the smoke of Satan has billowed into the sanctuary to asphyxiate the hope of the faithful, Fr. Baptist has remained firm and resolute. He has stood up to one of the most powerful prelates in the world with nothing to back him but faith, an arthritic gardener, an irksome housekeeper, a disfigured monsignor, a murmuring congregation, and a whacked troop of castaways like the lads and myself. Who was I to question his priorities? To suggest that Martin Feeney's welfare, both physical and spiritual, were not paramount in his mind was, to put it mildly, insane.

"I beg your pardon," said I after a long silence. "I was completely out of place."

"Actually, I do understand," said he. "You must realize Pierre, that we stand at the intersection of several mysteries, one of historic proportions, another that now strikes my heart on several fronts. The Tolkien quotation you were kind enough to clean earlier today in my office says it all: 'Do we walk in legends or on the green earth in the daytime?'"

"'A man may do both,'" said I, answering for Aragorn. "'For not we but those who come after will make legends of our time.'"

"'The green earth, you say?'" we said together. "'That is a mighty matter of legend, though you tread it under the light of day!'"

"Consider this," said Father. "A dead man, most likely a priest, is found in an abandoned crypt. We don't know his identity, but evidence suggests he has been a prisoner for a long, long time—so long that no one remembers or cares when he first went missing.   He's wearing a crucifix once worn by my wife—"

"The one you gave Msgr. Aspic on Halloween."

"The same, except shortly thereafter the cardinal informs me that Msgr. Aspic has disappeared. The crucifix links them. It is reasonable to assume that the monsignor finds himself in the same predicament as the unidentified priest."

"A prisoner, you mean."

"Yes."

"But why?"

"I have no idea. If I'm correct in my assumption, then his life isn't in immediate danger, though according to the coroner's report he may have to get used to a diet of bread and water."

"Perish the thought. Do you think Mr. Feeney is in the same predicament? But he's not a priest."

"No, but if his abductor is the same, then his fate is likely the same. The matter of Christine's cross ties my heart in a knot to be sure. But on top of all this, Msgr. Aspic had in his possession an artifact left by the Holy Father himself in the care of Cardinal Fulbright. That artifact, I'm convinced, holds the key to a secret of monumental proportions. The cardinal, true to form, is interested in his reputation at the expense of all else, not in solving mysteries centuries old. Your friend, Roderick Roundhead, is hot on the trail of that very secret. It may be God's will that he find it, but then again it may not. In the midst of all this walking in legends, I must also tread on the green earth, which is itself a wonder."

"You're referring to your oath of obedience to the cardinal."

"In obeying the letter of his command, I find myself fulfilling the spirit of my ordination. I can't explain it all to you now for I don't yet have all the scattered pieces correctly assembled yet. It's quite a puzzle. Returning these books may be a tiny part of it all, but still a necessary one if I am to face Our Lord at the altar the next time I say Mass. On the other hand—"

"Bishop deQuet will see you now," said the housekeeper as she came strutting back into the entrance foyer.

We followed her down the hallway and through a series of rooms. She stood aside at what appeared to be a living room. It contained an opulent couch, an ornate coffee table, and the biggest television screen I'd ever seen mounted on the wall. It was bigger than Alan Ross's in the bar at Darby's. The bishop was seated deeply in the couch, luxuriating in a jade green silk kimono. He had olive skin that was closer to Greek green than the Kalamata variety.

"So, Fr. John Baptist," said he querulously, not rising but folding his thin arms rigidly across his chest. He planted his slippered heels on the edge of the table and began rocking his feet on them, splaying and slapping them together like a pair of prissy scissors. "So where is your wheelbarrow this time? Or is this young man here to do your legwork for you?"

I must say his voice had a shrill, nails-on-chalkboard quality to it, and he had a strange way of randomly inflecting his syllables. Some of his peaks almost made my eyes cross, leaving neon lime sparks around the periphery of my vision.

"The labor is mine, My Lord," said Father, stepping around the coffee table. He held three hardbound volumes horizontally in his hands. "Monsieur Bontemps is here to witness the carrying out of His Eminence's order."

"Bontemps, is it?" said the bishop, his foot scissoring quickening. "I've heard of you."

"My Lord," said I. "I can't imagine in what connection."

"Something to do with fettuccini," said he, vaguely.

"Couldn't be me. I'm a linguini man if I am anything."

"Of course you are," said he. "I was just—" Then his attention snapped to Fr. Baptist who set the books down on His Lordship's royal lap. "What's this?"

"By order of His Eminence, Morley Psalmellus Cardinal Fulbright, Archbishop of Los Angeles, I hereby—quote—'put the bloody books back where they damn well belong'—end quote."

"Just these three?" squeaked Bishop deQuet, examining the spines. "Why, this one is just a California state atlas, and this is a Spanish-English dictionary. The only one worth a damn is this history of El Camino Real."

"What?" said Father, taking the last mentioned book from His Lordship's slender hands. He opened the front cover and examined the inside. "Pardon my mistake. In my haste to obey my lawful superior, I included a volume that does not belong among the rest."

"What's that you're saying?"

"See for yourself," said Father, turning the book to show the bishop. "Right here on the inside cover."

I craned my neck to see what this was all about. Fortunately I do not actually need the monocle I sometimes wear. My eyesight is superlative. There it was, stamped by hand, and long ago as evidenced by the faded ink:

This book is the property of
The Sister Maria Luisa of Jesus Library
Msgr. Eugene Brassorie, Director

"What is this supposed to mean to me?" demanded the bishop. His erratic emphases growing wilder and his foot-flapping flappier as his agitation mounted. "Fr. Baptist, explain!"

"Gladly, Your Lordship."

"And stop calling me that."

"As you wish. It happens that all the books I borrowed from Bishop Ravenshorst's library, with the exception of those I have just handed to you, bear this same imprint."

"So?"

"So, it means your late and lamented friend borrowed all but these two volumes from his late and lamented friend, Eugene Brassorie, who was a monsignor at the time as well as pastor at St. Philomena's Catholic Church."

"It says nothing about St. Philomena's."

"No, but the Sister Maria Luisa of Jesus Library is on the premises. It is housed in a room next to the gardener's quarters."

"What difference does that make?" If Bishop deQuet had flapped his slippers any faster he would have taken off. "I shall call Morley immediately and get this straightened out."

"There's nothing to straighten out," said Father. "I purchased St. Philomena's with my own money several years ago. The library was specified in the sale. The books are legally mine."

"But I have need of them! My research—!"

"You are welcome to peruse them at St. Philomena's when the library is open."

"Open? When is it open?"

"You'll have to ask Msgr. Havermeyer. He's the new director of the library."

"No doubt one of your fellow bottom feeders. This is an outrage!"

"I wouldn't worry about it, Your Lordship," I chimed in. "He, like you, is on a first name basis with His Eminence the Cardinal."

"What did you say?" squealed the bishop.

"You will have to excuse us, Your Excellency," said Father. "There are important matters which require our attention."

That brought His Lordship to his feet, hands twitching, kimono flailing. "This is not acceptable!" Yikes! Those green spikes of his precipitous inflections were worse than Fr. Baptist's glares. "You do not seem to realize with whom you are dealing!"

"But I do," said Father. "I am dealing with Morell deQuet." The double entendre lingered in the air for several seconds. "Pierre, attend me."

And so I did, all the way to the front door, with moral decay yapping and threatening like a frenetic French poodle all the way.

11(70)

THE ELEVENTH CHAPTER, WHEREIN A GAP IN MY KNOWLEDGE IS ADDRESSED, A SECRET I'VE BEEN KEEPING IS REVEALED, AND IN WHICH FATHER AGREES TO KEEP IT HIDDEN.

"SO WHERE TO NOW?" I asked as I steered the Jeep through the slalom course between the cement mixers, construction equipment, building materials, and portable privies that peppered the parking area around St. Barbara's Chapel.

"Do you think you could find 7214 Villanova Terrace?"

"If it's near Antarctica, no problem. Anything north of the equator requires divining rods and three pints of basement-temp lager."

"Right, okay. 3rd Street is two blocks north of here."

"North?"

"Turn right, Pierre."

"Okay."

"Then left on 3rd. Take that westward—just follow it until I say otherwise."

"Done and done, Father. Now, may I ask I question?"

"What's at 7214 Villanova Terrace?"

"No, that will become apparent soon enough. I'm more interested in the Sister Maria Luisa of Jesus Library."

"Ah yes, well, I can't believe I didn't notice Msgr. Brassorie's name on the imprint in all those books." He pointed over his shoulder to the piles that had been restored to the back seat. "I mean, I saw it, but I didn't really see it."

"I know what you mean. Most of Arthur's books have imprints from various seminaries and convents that discarded them after Vatican II. After a while you stop noticing them."

"Exactly. Oddly enough, it wasn't Brassorie's name that caught my attention. It was the name Sister Maria Luisa."

"How so?"

"Pierre, are you not aware of the Dominican tertiary to whom was imparted knowledge of the life and death of St. Philomena from the Saint herself in 1833?"

"I'm sorry to admit that I am not, Father."

"Hm. I assumed, because of your considerable breadth of knowledge, that you certainly would have researched the patroness of our little parish."

"Perhaps I've been wandering in legends rather than walking on the green earth."

"Perhaps, or at least leaping the mile at the expense of the foot. Eucharistic miracles, which you have been researching, are not legends. They are proof and bedrock of the path we walk. Sometimes, however, we dwell on the lofty at the expense of the immediate. Every moment of our lives, every single one, is an opportunity for grace. How blind we are to that fact, with so much to distract us. In any case, at the next Knights meeting we must address the martyrdom of St. Philomena. The discovery of her tomb in 1802 presented something of a mystery at the time."

"Such as?"

"We'll deal with that Thursday evening at the rectory. Speaking of the immediate, turn right at the next intersection, then left at the second stop sign."

"Your wish is my command, Father."

After a swift series of twists and turns we arrived at an address I should have recognized if I hadn't been so preoccupied with the lofty at the expense of the immediate. It was a grand mansion in the old California style, complete with a front porch as wide as the house, a kind of eight-sided atrium in the southeast corner, and a beautiful statue of the Blessed Virgin Mary smiling upon a neatly-trimmed arrangement of red and white roses in the center of the front lawn.

"Father," I said, "now that we've arrived I realize I have been here before."

"Indeed," said he, glancing up at the house and then back at me. "Have you been writing prayer books and not told us?"

"Why do you ask that?"

"The owners are publishers. Their office in there is piled with manuscripts, novels mostly, but all they actually publish are standard—some would say classic—devotional books, the writings of the saints, solitary retreats, that sort of thing." He chuckled. "No, wait a minute. Let me guess. You took them a manuscript, didn't you?"

I began to sputter a reply, but he interrupted me. "Not yours—Martin's!"

"Guilty," I admitted. "One of the old gals is Rod's aunt, you see. I read him parts of Mr. Feeney's opus. I thought he might know someone. He's not much of a fiction man, but he found Mr. Feeney's turn of phrase amusing. He told me his aunt was a publisher. In fact, he phoned her by way of introduction."

"Roderick Roundhead. Well, that solves one mystery at least."

"What mystery is that, Father?"

"How Some Guy knew about Martin's novel."

"I'm not following you."

"No matter."

"Mr. Feeney would have you say, 'Few do.'"

Father shook his head, chortled knowingly, and straightened in his seat. "Roderick Roundhead. So he sent you to the Doily Sisters with Martin's manuscript."

"You say that as though he were playing a trick on me."

"Wasn't he? After all, Martin's book is hardly in their line."

"Perhaps, but they did agree to read it."

"Pierre, they read *everything* that's submitted to them, but they only publish what they already print."

"You're sure of that."

"Oh, most definitely. In my way I'm hoping to expand their catalog, but I'm not holding my breath."

"I don't follow you."

We locked eyes.

"Few do," we said together.

He pointed to the corner room with all the windows. "That's their office. Have you seen it?"

"Yes, briefly."

"It's piled with manuscripts that have been submitted for their consideration."

"They promised me they'd move Martin's manuscript to the front of the queue."

"No doubt they are ladies of their word—you being a debonair young man and 'Roddy' being, well, 'Roddy'—but the fact remains that they only publish what they print already. Your friend, Roderick, wasn't doing you any favors."

"I hope you're wrong about that, Father."

"I'm intrigued that you had this arrangement with the Doily Sisters and they didn't even hint at it over dinner last night, nor did they let on that they already knew you—nor you them, for that matter. It was quite an act all the way around."

"Easily explained," said I. "They were very twitchy about letting it be known that they were reading Martin's manuscript out of turn. They feared repercussions of the ferocious sort from the other submitters to whom they feel they owe something-or-other. Debonair I may be, Father, but it is Rod who holds sway. They agreed to read Mr. Feeney's pages out of turn on his say so, but they were uneasy about it. My sworn discretion was part of the deal."

"Well, it only goes to show you," said Father, opening his door and getting out of the car.

"What's that?" I asked, following suit.

"That even two sweet ditsy old ladies can keep a secret."

"Ditsy?"

"In a word. Shall we?"

"Can you, Father? Keep a secret?"

"Just watch."

12(71)

CHAPTER THE TWELFTH, WHEREIN TWO SWEET DITSY OLD LADIES AFFIRM THAT MY VOICE IS ROBUST, FR. BAPTIST LEAVES SOMETHING PRECIOUS TO HIM WITH THEM, AND IN WHICH I FIND SOMETHING MR. FEENEY INADVERTENTLY LEFT BEHIND.

"OH, HE REMEMBERED, didn't he, darling?" said Mrs. Mehitabelle Doily.

"Indeedy do, he did, sweetheart," answered Mrs. Hortense Doily.

"How could I forget?" said Fr. Baptist, handing them a little leather-bound book, about three and a half by two, and three-quarter inches thick. "This is a precious possession of mine."

"Why sweetheart," said Hortense, opening the little volume. "Look at all these wonderful prayers."

"Indeed, darling," said Mehitabelle. "Do I remember correctly, Father, that it contains the Mass in Latin and English?"

Father smiled and nodded. "As well as the epistle and gospel readings in English for all the Sundays and holy days of the year."

"And litanies," said Hortense, flipping the onionskin pages. "See: of the Blessed Virgin Mary, of the Holy Name of Jesus, and even for a Happy Death."

"Excuse me," I said. "May I ask what it is?"

"It's called *Garden of the Soul,*" said Father. "This copy was published in London around 1930, almost five hundred pages, a manual of frequently-used prayers small enough to fit in your shirt pocket. I thought these ladies would appreciate its compactness, utility, and density. I think you and the lads were indulging in a round of the 'Whiffenpoof Song' over at the piano when it came up last night."

"For the fifth time, sweetheart," said Hortense.

"Don't embellish, darling," said Mehitabelle. "It's unseemly."

"I am not embellishing, sweetheart. One round would have been quite enough. I'll allow a second chorus on account of youthful enthusiasm. But *five whole times*—even you'll agree Father, won't he, sweetheart?—it's disproportionate."

"I beg your pardon, Mrs. Doily," I said to Hortense, "but the lads and I always—"

"Youthful enthusiasm, I'll grant you," said Father, interrupting me with a firm pat on my shoulder. "I wish more young people today were so motivated."

"Motivation, my dear ladies," said I in my own defense, "according to Oscar Wilde's uncle's distant cousin, is the mother of—"

Father stopped me with another pat—more like a whack. "Yes," said he, smiling broadly. "So motivated."

"Perhaps, Fr. John," said Hortense. She looked me up and down as though I were one of her rosebushes that had grown crookedly. "You must admit—mustn't we, sweetheart?—that Mr. Bonbon has a ... ahem ... *robust* voice."

"I think everyone present last evening would agree with you, darling," said Mehitabelle.

"Thank you," said I, smiling graciously. No jolt from Father this time. "Thank you."

They were still keeping our secret, so was I, and Father wasn't letting on, either. Keating had been in and out of their office when I presented them with Mr. Feeney's manuscript. To some extent he was in on it, too. Secrets have a way of proliferating, don't you know.

We were gathered in the Doily Sisters' office, that octagonal room in the southeast corner of the house. Our hostesses were seated facing each other at a desk designed for just such an arrangement. The room was redolent with the smell of herbs and spices growing in elaborate window boxes, and heaped all around with hundreds of manuscripts.

"Keating," said Hortense. "Would you be so kind as to go to the kitchen and put on some water for tea?"

"Of course, Madame," said he, bowing graciously, albeit stiffly, and exiting the room. No doubt he had been with the family forever.

"It is with the greatest reticence," continued Father, "that I leave that book with you in the hope that you will consider reproducing it. I've no idea who might own the copyright, if there is one, and I know nothing about copyright law. That I'll leave to you. I simply think it's a marvelous little prayer book, one that a lot of traditional Catholics would enjoy owning. As that copy belonged to someone close to me who has departed this life, it is something I do not lend casually. I'll expect to come back for it in a day or two, if you don't mind."

"Your mother must have been a wonderful lady, Father," said Hortense.

"Why do you say that?" asked he.

"The way you said what you did just now," said Mehitabelle. "Your tone of voice, I mean. A man doesn't say that his brother or best friend 'departed this life.' He says 'he died.' Doesn't he, darling?"

"Sweetheart, my thought precisely," said Hortense. 'Well, kind of, sort of."

"There can be other women in a priest's life besides his mother," said Father.

"Not that many, I should think," said Mehitabelle. "What do you think, darling?"

"Oh, I should think not, sweetheart," said Hortense.

"Ah, look here," said Mehitabelle, nudging her sister and pointing to a bit of handwriting on the first page. Ah, whatever became of the fountain pen? "Who is Christine Maryvale, Father? That's the name inside."

"I'll never tell if you let anything happen to that book," said Father, consulting his watch. "Oh dear, I've lost track of the time. You must pardon me, ladies. I hate to say this, but Pierre and I have some pressing matters that require our attention. We'll have to forego the tea. Er, would you mind if I used your washroom before we leave?"

"Certainly-wertainly, that's what they're for," said Hortense. "Aren't they, sweetheart?"

"Don't be vulgar, darling," said Mehitabelle.

"Well, sweetheart, one can't help what they are for, can one?"

"Never mind, darling. Let's not pound the point, shall we? Surely Father John knows the way, or should I call Keating?"

"Madame?" queried the butler, who happened to be coming in again. "Am I needed?"

"Not by me," said Father, passing him in the doorway. "I was just coming to tell you that Pierre and I must forego the tea. Surely next time."

"As you say, Reverend Father," said the butler, watching Father exit the room. Then he turned to the ladies and said, "I came back to see if you would like me to prepare cucumber sandwiches to go with your tea."

"I wouldn't care for any, would you, darling?" said Mehitabelle.

"Nor I, sweetheart," said Hortense. "Not on an empty stomach."

"Very well," said Keating. "The water is on the stove. Perhaps I should wait here to see Father and Monsieur Bontemps out."

"Excellent," said both ladies simultaneously.

"Excuse me, Keating," said Mehitabelle. "Who is Monsieur Bontemps?"

"That would be me," said I.

"But your name is Mr. Bonbon," said Hortense. "Isn't it, sweetheart?"

"That's what he told us, darling," said Mehitabelle.

Just then I happened to see something on the carpet by one of the taloned feet of the double-sided writing desk. Realizing it would be difficult for anyone else in the room but me to fetch, I let out a hearty, "Hello, what's this?" and scooped it up. It was small enough to enclose within my right hand. I opened my fingers, revealing what appeared to be a small clump of mortar imbedded with irregular pebbles.

"Why, I don't have a notion what it is," said Mehitabelle. "Do you, darling?"

"Not the slightest, sweetheart," said Hortense. "It looks positively repugnant. What do you say, Keating?"

"Hm," said the butler, gingerly lifting it from my hand and bringing it close to his eyes. "I wonder, Mesdames, if it could belong to Mr. Feeney."

"Who?" asked Hortense.

"I think he means Marvin Spleeny, darling," said Mehitabelle. "Didn't he take a tumble right about here the other day?"

"I think you're right, sweetheart."

"Indeed, Mesdames," said Keating, offering it to them. They declined with fluttering fingers, so he handed it back to me. "We were showing him the priest hole behind the bookcase."

"Did you say a priest hole?" I asked, amazed. I'd no idea such things existed in California. Ireland and England after the Reformation, sure. But not here.

"Here, I'll show you," said he, stepping to a bookcase set in the wall. Placing his white-gloved hands upon the third shelf, he gave it a gentle push. There was a soft click in the wall, and whole set of shelves swerved forward a few inches. He then grasped the edge and gave it a tug, and the whole bookcase swung smoothly and silently open like the impressive door that it really was.

"Good heavens," I said. "Good, good heavens!"

Doubtless Mr. Feeney has described this marvelous mechanism in his account, so I will not tarry with the details. The wooden shelves and bunk bed within were coarsely made, incongruous with the superbly crafted swinging bookcase. The far wall was not a wall but a space, the head of a stairway descending into total darkness. Now *that* was interesting. I stepped to the edge and looked into the daunting depths.

"Not a mere hole, sweetheart," commented Hortense.

"No, darling, I should say a bit more than that," said Mehitabelle.

"More like a subway entrance," said I. They did not smile. "Mind if I go down?"

"Not at all, sir," said Keating, "but I got the distinct impression that Fr. John wishes to be on his way."

"Quite right," I said with a sigh.

Keating was just closing the bookshelf when Father strode back into the office.

"Ah," said Father. "I see you've discovered one of this house's secrets."

"Did you—?" I began to ask, pointing downward.

"Indeed I did," said he, "when Martin and I were here the other day. There's a beautiful chapel down there you must see, but not right now. We really must press on."

"Ladies," said I, turning to our hostesses. "I wonder if I might come again when there is more time to examine this exquisite treasure."

"Why certainly-wertainly," said Hortense. "You are welcome, isn't he, sweetheart?"

"Of course," said Mehitabelle. "Just so long as he doesn't favor us with a song, darling."

"And do give our regards to Mr. Feeney," said Keating.

That brought me up short. Father had not said anything to them about Mr. Feeney's disappearance. Figuring he must have had his reasons, I chose to go along with yet another secret. What was one more?

"Gladly, when I see him," I said to the ladies.

"Pierre, we must be off," said Father.

"Good day, Mesdames," said I. "And if I may say, by the tail of my great-aunt Regret who won the Derby—"

Wallop.

13(72)

CHAPTER THE THIRTEENTH, WHEREIN FATHER INTERVIEWS A LADY WITH VERY BAD TASTE, I MEET A LIVING LEGEND [SIC], I SCHMOOZE THE LEGEND'S EX-WIFE, AND IN WHICH I RECOGNIZE SOMEONE I HAD SEEN EARLIER THAT DAY.

"HEY THERE! DARN, I CAN'T call you handsome," screeched the woman seated behind an impressive audio/video console. She wasn't yelling, as far as I could tell. That was just the nature of her voice, poor woman, though I suspect she was not bothered by it in the least. It matched her apparel, which shrieked to high heaven, too. Imagine one of those balloon poodles the rent-a-clowns always make for kids at birthday parties. Now imagine it pumped up with way too much air, which begins to escape through the loosening knot on the tip of the thing's pinkly transparent, upturned nose, this irksome yowl amplified through a substantial PA system. Fortunately, her grating greeting was directed at Father, not myself. It might have shattered my monocle. "I was wondering," said she, deftly turning a glowing green potentiometer, "wondering when you'd be back."

"To ask more questions?" asked Father.

"Naw," she squawked around a wad of bright green chewing gum. The wad stood out all the more because her lips were painted fluorescent purple. "To get yourself on the show. I know: the lights, the excitement, the notoriety."

We were deep within the labyrinth that was KLIE, a subsidiary of Blink Broadcasting, Inc., as well as the home of *Religion Revisited*. This, too, was a retracing of the steps that Mr. Feeney and Fr. Baptist had already retraced in their pursuit of Msgr. Aspic. What had Msgr. Havermeyer said about not having my courage nor my originality when he was my age? So far this day the former had not been tapped, and the latter was out to lunch.

"The allure is so hard to resist," winked the lady with the gum. The mascara was caked so thickly on her eyelashes that they actually clicked.

"Not for me," said Father. "The last thing I want is more publicity."

"Oh yeah, sure," said she, flipping a big orange switch. "I've been doing some research on you." The image on her main monitor flickered, fluttered, and resolved to a stylized outline of a white dove with an olive branch in its beak against a red background. *"TCN,"* announced a jovial male voice as the dove dissolved into a sunrise, *"the Rapture Channel."* This was underscored with the bright yellow caption: *Caution: This Channel May be Suddenly Viewerless!*

"Uh oh," said Father as the screen flickered again, this time resolving to a picture of he himself and Mr. Feeney sitting at a large desk before a wall of fake bookshelves lined with two-dimensional volumes. An ersatz blaze crackled in the electric fireplace behind them.

"Aha," said Ms. Krackershak, winking with both eyes.

"Where did you get that?" asked Father.

"TCN is a rival," said she with an exaggerated, conspiratorial smile. She reached up to the fuzzy yellow flare-up she probably called a bouffant and gave it an ascending nudge with her cupped palm. "But I've got an in. T. Thurston Wallard was an associate producer when this was made. Now he's an executive producer, but I still call him Tee-Tee. Hee-hee!"

"TCN," said I a tad disparagingly. "The 'Totally Christian Network.'"

She stopped in mid gum-chaw, looked me up and down speculatively, and said, "Who are you again?"

"Tonight," blared my own—ahem—*robust* voice from the speakers above the console, *"we are featuring something absolutely, positively, irrevocably, unmistakably, undeniably new!"* I will admit to being startled, puzzled, and the truth be told, a tad delighted.

> *SPELUNKING SPINOFFS: Though I had played a part in this mad-cap production, I had never actually seen it. Father had intended it to be viewed in the bar at Darby's the previous June, but due to the misplaced aspirations of a cameraman at KROM named Steve Lambert who was also one of Father's parishioners, it had been spliced into TCN's broadcast signal. Mr. Feeney detailed the incident in "The Endless Knot." Because of this, added to the fact that it is a memorable Tumblar adventure, I pray that it will be published some day.*
>
> *—P.B.*

I answered her query regarding my identity by pointing to my golden throat, then to the speakers above her console, but her attention had already drifted back to Father. He did not look at all pleased as my introduction continued:

"The colossal Archdiocese of Los Angeles, California, the most humongous bishopric in the whole uncivilized world is proud to present: The Catholic Controversy, *with your host, Father John Baptist, or as we here at the Chancery affectionately call it,* The Slap Happy Bappy Latin Hour! *Tonight: Martin Feeney's rational reviews of local silly sermons—watch out Father Jay, your number is up—"*

"That's enough," said Father, reaching across the sea of buttons and knobs and sliders to flip the orange switch the other way. The picture zigzagged into oblivion, taking the sound with it. "If you'd done your homework thoroughly, Miss Krackershak, you would know that this was never intended for broadcast. It was merely my way of debunking an alibi—"

"Sure," said she, her voice like rusty nails on stainless steel. "Did you know DVDs of your little farce are selling for twenty-five bucks on the internet? I understand your diocesan seminary is one of the biggest customers."

"Good heavens. Miss Krackershak, I assure you—"

"So don't tell me you don't like publicity," said she, flipping the switch again.

"And now, here he is, the cop-turned-priest-turned-cop-turned-talk-show-host: Father Jooooooooooooohn—!"

Father Baptist was not amused. "Please—turn—that—off."

"How about down?" said she smugly, pulling a slide control toward her midriff. The sound level subsided to a mumble but the mouths on the screen kept moving vigorously.

"Off," said Father sternly.

She made a point of poising her hand over the fader for several heartbeats, then brought the level down to silence.

"I'll thank you to leave it that way," said he. "I'm here to ask you something."

"I don't answer questions from rude people."

"Come now, Miss Krackershak. You thrive on discourtesy. I need to know: did Msgr. Aspic show you his manuscript?"

"No, he didn't," said she. Her talons were poised, but she did not touch that control again. Perhaps she had other delights in her arsenal with which to bug him.

"Or any part of it?" he persisted. "An excerpt perhaps? A synopsis?"

"Nope. Not that he didn't offer, you understand, but we have a policy about unpublished—"

"How about Sheldon and Eira Levant?"

"How about them?"

"Miss Krackershak, this may be important."

"It's *Ms.* Krackershak." She popped her gum for emphasis. "One of our sponsors wants to see *you* on the show. I think his daughter's a fallen-away or something, or maybe he is. If you're trying to drive your fee up, you are probably succeeding. The funny thing is, I hope you get it. I could recommend a good agent—"

"All I want is to find Msgr. Aspic," said Father. "Whoever has him now has my associate."

She gave me a disdainful look. "What associate?"

"Martin Feeney," said he. "The man who was with me the last time I came here."

She looked back at Father. "Oh, you mean your friend with the, uh ..." She made a regurgitative motion with her mouth and hand, shrugged her bony shoulders, then returned her attention to the video monitor.

"The same," said Father.

"Well I'll be," said she, pointing to the talking head on her screen. "That's him!"

"Indeed," said Father, eyeing Mr. Feeney's animated silence.

"You say he's missing now, too?" This bit of information seemed to suddenly bring her up short, as if it had only just then sunk in. She pondered it uneasily, eyes darting furtively from side to side. Then, as if she had reached some sort of decision, she focused on Father again. "Missing," she said again.

"Yes. That isn't for broadcast."

"Like hell it isn't!"

"I'm serious."

"When it comes to my show, so am I. All other times, go figure."

"I can see it was a mistake to come here."

"Says you, Honey. What else do you want to know? I'm all ears."

Father cleared his throat, then tried again. "You said the ratings sky-rocketed when Msgr. Aspic didn't show up for your broadcast."

"You can say that again."

"How have they been since?"

"Down two tenths but that's still six points above where we were last week."

"So it would be safe to say that you have benefited from the monsignor's disappearance."

"Not in front of my attorney," intruded a male voice.

We all turned to see a face in the doorway. It was round with large eyes and a mouth simply made for a cheap cigar. A table-size sheet of plastic was tied under the chin and draped over the rest of his body. As he spoke, rivulets of pancake dust crumbled off his cheeks and slid down the tarp. I recognized him immediately, of course. I'd spotted him in the lobby of the Adirondack that very morning. His face hovered above Madame Hummingbird's wastebasket. Lately it had infested cheesy magazine racks as well.

"Sheldon Levant," scolded Ms. Krackershak. "The *living legend* himself. How many times have I told you not to come in here in full make-up? That powder plays havoc with the equipment."

"About as often as you tell me not to curse on the air," said Sheldon Levant. "But do I listen?"

"Only through keyholes," said she.

"HAH!" A plume of airy powder exploded from the folds of his face.

At his outburst, Ms. Krackershak opened her eyes wide, blinked three times in rapid succession, then turned away quickly, a blinking yellow light on the AV console demanded her attention. Something about that brief sequence of ocular activity caught my attention, reminding me of something … or someone. The memory was fleeting, like sparks in a fireplace.

"Father Baptist," said Sheldon Levant, celebrated co-host of *Religion Prevaricated,* "Thithero told me he saw you slink in here. I was hoping you'd reconsider coming onto our show."

"Thithero?" I mouthed silently.

"I haven't," said Father. "Slinked or reconsidered."

"A poor choice of words," agreed Mr. Levant. "But you should, you know. Reconsider, I mean. You have a lot to say, and a lot of folks are watching us these days, people yearning to learn the truth of things, or rather, the truth behind things, or at least somebody's version. Crackers, think of it. We can make Father here into a popular spiritual icon."

"That we could," said she. "The priest who gets things done."

"The priest who knows what the hell he's talking about," countered Sheldon. "Think of it, Father John. The cop-turned-priest-turned-star-of-the-airwaves. You could be the new Bishop Sheen!"

> *SPELUNKING SPINOFFS: Bishop Fulton J. Sheen was a popular Catholic evangelist from way back when. First he appeared on a radio show called* Catholic Hour, *then he upgraded to the now-defunct DuMont Television Network with a show called* Life is Worth Living. *It was broadcast opposite Milton Berle on Tuesday nights, and outshined "Uncle Miltie" in the ratings and even won an Emmy. The celebrated bishop actually referred to himself once as "Uncle Fultie."*
>
> *One of my favorite FJS quotes: "Who is going to save our Church? Not our bishops, not our priests and religious. It is up to you, the people. You have the minds, the eyes, the ears to save the Church. Your mission is to see that your priests act like priests, your bishops like bishops, and your religious act like religious." That was when he was an archbishop, and he was speaking to a Knights of Columbus meeting in 1972.*
>
> *—P.B.*

Sheldon rubbed his hands together under the tarp, an activity which produced a weird, rubbery noise. "Father, what we've done for your Mr. Aspic, we can do for you, too! When he turns up—we're holding positive thoughts in that regard, aren't we, Crackers?—anyway, when he does he's going to be giving his homilies to standing-room only assemblies. Count on it." He winked exaggeratedly. "Bank on it."

"A scary thought," said I.

Sheldon Levant's face froze in an attitude of icy glee. His eyes turned to me like synchronized anti-aircraft stations. "Just who are you, anyway?"

"Pierre Bontemps, at your service," said I. "I write for the—"

"Hey!" screeched Ms. Krackershak, slapping her knee. "I've finally placed you. You're the fettuccini guy."

"Oh, brother," said I under my breath. Then to her: "Fellow."

"Huh?"

"I prefer 'fellow.' I'm the fettuccini fellow."

"Whatever. You wrote that piece on Fulbright's pasta fetish."

"A preference, perhaps, hardly a fetish."

"Not by the time we're done with it. Who do you write for?"

"The *L. A. Artsy.*"

"Funny, I could've sworn I read it in the *South-Central Gutter.*"

"It's one of those bizarre things that happen in the newsprint world," said I, good-naturedly. Perhaps Fr. Baptist wasn't interested in publicity, but I certainly was. I turned on the charm.

"Is that what you call it?" said Ms. Krackershak, her sniff predictably morphing into a snort.

"An innocuous little story catches someone's attention," said I, pausing to smile knowingly. I emphasized my next sentence by pulling my handkerchief from my vest pocket in a dramatic arc. "Suddenly—by the intercession of St. Francis de Sales, Patron of the Press—it's syndicated."

"The *Artsy*," mused Ms. Krackershak. "We all gotta start somewhere."

My knowing look blossomed into camaraderie. "It's one of the little services I render to the world while I stock my mind." I then kicked my smile all the way up to appreciation. It was dangerous, I know, but I'm a Bontemps. I can handle myself.

"Maybe we should have him on the show," said Ms. Krackershak to Sheldon Levant, indicating me with a pointed pursing of her lips.

"I think I peaked with that," said I, pointing to my own face which had come up briefly on the video monitor. "But I'd always be willing to give it another shot."

"Interesting idea," said Mr. Levant. "If you like raw oysters."

"Excuse me?" I asked.

"Back to you, Father," said Mr. Levant. "I'm serious. What *Saturday Night Live* did for Fr. Guido Sarducci, we can do for you. Get this: you come on the show and sit *between* Eira and me, you know, like a friend of the family. We run clips from that show you did for TCN with you right there to answer our bewildered questions." He took a step closer. "After all, some of what you say in there is—well, come on, Father. But hey, I'm open even to close-minded people."

"I beg your pardon?" said Father and I together.

"Okay, not close-minded. Let's say you're ... *ecumenically challenged*. Not that that's a bad thing, not at all. We can use it. We can run with it. We can love you just the way you are. You'll get a certain amount of negative viewer reaction, of course, but that's gasoline on a fire in this business. Your very narrow-mindedness, coupled with your crime-solving reputation, heck—"

"Not to mention his zany colleagues," said I, indicating Arthur and Jonathan, who were now gracing the monitor screen, yapping and winking. If I remembered correctly, they were discussing curiosities in the fossil record that called the close-minded theory of evolution into question. "We helped. We work for booze, by the way. Cash is irrelevant."

"Says you," said Ms. Krackershak, eyeing me up and down, then winking significantly.

"Indeed," said I, winking right back, albeit insignificantly.

"Television is a visual medium," said Mr. Levant, trying to point to his eyes without success, his arms hampered by the plastic tarp. "It's amazing what you can get people to see, things they would never notice themselves. The TV screen gives reality a whole new meaning."

"Just imagine what Jesus would have done with television," said Ms. Krackershak.

"We already know," said Father. "He avoided it by two thousand years."

"Huh?" said Ms. Krackershak and Mr. Levant together.

"'Faith then cometh by hearing,'" said Father, tugging on his ear by way of demonstration, "'and hearing by the word of Christ.'"

"St. Paul's Epistle to the Romans," said I. I had a hunch that it was in chapter ten, but I didn't want to blunder just then.

"Sure, whatever," said Mr. Levant. "Quote the Bible all you want—even that Dooey version you push on that Slap Happy show—I can make you a household word, Father. Think of it. A household word."

"It's the Douay," said Father. "Douay-Rheims." He pronounced it with a French nasal blast. "The notion of popularity doesn't appeal to me, Mr. Levant."

"Sheldon, Father," said the man in the tarp. "Call me Sheldon. And if you're so reclusive, why are you celebrating the opening Mass at the A-T-A-C conference next month?"

"What?" Fr. Baptist glanced at me, surprised.

"Don't look now, Father," said I in a stage whisper. "You've been ATAC-ed."

"I told Mr. Uturn I was not interested in celebrating Mass at his conference," said Father.

"Really," said Mr. Levant. "That's not what he told me twenty minutes ago on the phone."

"Nor me," said Ms. Krackershak, her fingers hovering threateningly over her controls. "Hector's going to be on the show next week, you know. Maybe you'd care to join him on the air to discuss the matter?"

"I think not," said Father. Then he blinked as though he had just reviewed his conversation with Hector Uturn. "I would say most definitely not. Absolutely not."

"Ya hear that, Crackers?" asked Mr. Levant. "He's considering it."

"When did no stop being no?" asked Father.

"This is showbiz," said Ms. Krackershak. "There is no such thing as no."

"Except when you ask your producer for a raise," said Sheldon.

Napolia Krackershak opened her eyes wide at that remark, blinked three times in rapid succession, then turned her attention abruptly to someone standing in the doorway. There it was again, that ocular sequence again. Where, oh where, had I seen it before?

"Did I hear the magic word?" intruded a new female voice. This one belonged to a pouting little face that appeared around Mr. Levant's shoulder. She, too, was wearing a plastic tarp. Her face was a veritable Painted Desert of stratified powders and multicolored dust. It's amazing how the video camera in collusion with the cathode ray tube can turn something as desolate as that into smooth, healthy-looking skin, but that's the magic of television.

"Another country heard from," said Sheldon, squeaking beneath his tarp.

"Oh, good," said Father. "Mrs. Levant, you're here, too. Remember me? I'm Fr. John Baptist. There is something I came to ask you and your husband."

"I am no longer *Mrs.* Levant. Who—?" It took the dusty woman a moment to recognize the man in the cassock. "Not you! Sugar ruined my nose because of you!"

"That's not exactly how it happened, dearie," said Ms. Krackershak.

"You said at the last production meeting," whined the former Mrs. Levant like a little brat, "that we're not to concern ourselves with what really happens!"

"On the air, Honeykins," chuckled Sheldon. "She meant on the air. Not off-camera!"

"On or off camera, I don't want him here!" said his ex, trying but failing to raise her hand under her tarp to point at Father.

"Mrs. Levant, please," said Father. "I only want—"

"No, no, no, no, NO, NO, NO, NO, NO!!!" shrieked the banshee in the tarp almost as abrasively as her producer, Ms. Krackershak. "Absolutely, positively—"

"Eira Levant!" I broke in, adopting my best approximation of Tyrone Power. "I'm sorry, I didn't recognize you at first camouflaged under that unsightly, um, whatever it is." I indicated her makeup bib.

"Who—?" She turned her inverted teardrop face in my direction.

"My name is Bontemps, Madame," said I. "Pierre Bontemps. But what does a name matter when I am in the presence of the woman I have admired from afar for so long?"

"What—?" Her lips cavorted between a smile and a frown. Rivulets of fine powder cascaded from her cheeks.

"How many have been the hours that I have watched you on the TV screen, wrapping men around your finger, breaking hearts with abandon." I clutched my hands to my chest. "Would that it could be mine!"

"Your friend's got some screws sorely in need of tightening," said Mr. Levant to Father.

"And how," said Ms. Krackershak, eyeing me up and down. Her wily smile became appreciative.

"Pierre," said Father. "Perhaps—"

I cut him off with one of my "Here I come to save the day!" smiles, then turned my full attention back on Eira Levant. "Madame, spurn me if you must, for even a rebuff from you will make my day."

SPELUNKING SPINOFFS: Both of my parents were actors. They never got closer to Broadway than Seventh Street when they lived in New York, and when they moved to Los Angeles their prospects didn't get any better. Their story is one worth telling, but not here.

I mention them because Papa (emphasis on the second syllable) always used to say, "With regards to the fairer sex, Son: when in doubt, lay it on thick." Mamma's (ditto) addendum was invariably, "Mais oui, Kiddo, the thicker the better!"

These are maxims I have come to live by.

—P.B.

"Who did you say you are?" asked Eira Levant, making adjustments under her tarp.

"Oh, brother," said Mr. Levant, rolling his eyes.

"Pierre Bontemps, at your service," said I with an appropriate, that is to say, exaggerated bow. "I am but a struggling journalist who—"

"Who would do anything to get himself on our show," said Ms. Krackershak.

"I beg your pardon, but you wrong me," I said to the producer. Then I turned back to Mrs. Levant. "I am helping Fr. Baptist today because Mr. Feeney, his assistant, has been kidnapped."

"You don't say," said Eira Levant, struggling all the harder beneath the plastic.

"I do say," said I. "Father, what was the question you wanted to ask the illustrious and—dare I say it?— stunning Eira Levant and her, um, former husband?"

"Stunning?" gawked Mr. Levant.

"I should say so!" said Mrs. Levant, pulling the plastic every which way. Fortunately, it held.

"Oh, yes," said I before Father got the words past the expression on his face. "I've got it. Did either of you see or read any part of Msgr. Aspic's unpublished manuscript?"

"Oh, that," said Mr. Levant. "Yeah, I saw it—the cover, at least. He carried it in his briefcase and waved it around a lot, but as I told him: I—never—read—unpublished—stuff." He emphasized his last words with useless punches under the plastic. "I don't have time for freaking amateurs!"

"Never," sing-songed Ms. Krackershak. "Never, never, never."

"And what about you, Mrs. Levant?" I asked, or rather schmoozed—spreading it with an extra-wide butter knife.

She looked startled. "What about me?"

"Did you see Msgr. Aspic's manuscript?"

"See it?" she said, ceasing her flailing. "Why, I read it."

"The whole thing?" said Mr. Levant, eyes wide.

"Every single word," said his ex. "It was positively emanating."

"Excuse me?" said Ms. Krackershak and I together.

Mrs. Levant heaved a sigh and looked heavenward. "It was the second most inspirational book I've ever read. Not quite the first, you understand. That will always be *The Seventh Ray*. That made such sense to me! But the Monsignor's was close, and more entirely different from sweet, radiant Annie Bessant's wisdom than you can possibly imagine!"

"What on earth was it about?" asked her ex-husband.

"It isn't *about* anything," she said, shaking her little, brain-deprived head. "No, not about something, either. It is beyond mere meaning."

"So is ninety-nine percent of the bilge our *special guests* push on our show," said Sheldon. He set his head at a slight angle as though thinking it through, then straightened. "Eira, honey, you really got something out of it? You think other over-burdened under-bludgeoned divorcees will, too? Maybe we should give this thing another look."

"Some of us are serious about our work," said Eira, showing us her nostrils. "Msgr. Aspic certainly is about his visions."

"Visions," said Fr. Baptist.

"Well, sort of," said Mrs. Levant. "Windows to the future, you might say. Although there isn't much of it left, you know. It's all going to end, and all too soon."

"What is?" asked Sheldon.

"What is what?" asked Eira.

"What's going to end?"

"Why, the beginning, silly."

Mr. Levant gave her a "Small wonder we're divorced, Toots," look.

"For three days the world will be enshrouded in impenetrable light," said Eira Levant in a far-off voice. "The 'Luminosity of the Logos' he calls it."

"Is that a good thing or a bad thing, dearie?" asked Napolia Krackershak, rising from her console.

"Why, both of course," said Eira. "For most people, it will be utterly horrible. Just horrible. But for the few who heed the prophecy and prepare, it will act as a conduit into a prosthetic—I think that's the word, or is it prolific?—future."

"Really," said Sheldon Levant.

"Sort of," said Eira. "It's hard to know how much of it is definite and indefinite, but—"

"I think you're the one who's definitely indefinite," said Sheldon. "In fact, honey—"

"Behave, you two," said Ms. Karackershak. "You're giving Father here a skewed impression—"

"Not at all," said Father. "This is all very clarifying. Pierre, it's time to go."

"Oh, but you can't, not without," said Mrs. Levant. "I mean, but I thought—"

"Alas," said I to Mrs. Levant. "With or without, I must depart. Parting is debilitating, but I have promises to keep."

"And miles to go," said Father, "no time for sleep."

Mrs. Levant looked genuinely distressed. "You will be back, won't you, Mister, um—what did you say your name was?"

"Bontemps," I told her. "Pierre Bontemps, and I prefer Monsieur."

"The fettuccini fellow," said Ms. Krackershak with a smack of her lips and a pop of her gum. "Don't worry, Eira dear, he's been bitten. He'll be back."

"Bah!" scoffed Sheldon with a squeak of his paws under the tarp.

At the sound of Sheldon's derision, Napolia opened her eyes wide, rapid-fired her eyelashes thrice, then turned to Father Baptist. "Don't you forget, Father," she said. "There is an offer on the table."

Then it came to me. The woman who emerged from the elevator at the Adirondack shortly after Mr. Levant. The woman in the silver outfit. She had looked so different without makeup. But the eye-thing, that was unmistakable. She and Napolia Krackershak were one and the same! The wheels turned. She and Sheldon …? Naw. But then again: *This is showbiz. There is no such thing as no.*

"I'll leave it there," said Father. "Of course, if you'd like to work something out with Monsieur Bontemps, be my guest."

"You can reach me at the *Artsy,*" said I, bowing grandly.

"Don't bet on it, Bub," said Sheldon Levant.

As I straightened I blew Mrs. Levant a playful, disingenuous kiss.

She heaved a great sigh as Father and I turned and left.

"You, sir, are playing with fire," said he to me as we exited the building.

14(73)

CHAPTER FOURTEEN, WHEREIN THE KNIGHTS OF THE TUMBLAR COMPARE SHOVELS WITH FATHER BAPTIST.

"FJB & MF," SAID THE NOTE attached to Arthur's apartment door with a bright red thumbtack. *"Gone to Saranac Lounge to see our four-day lost weekend through to the bitter end!"* It was signed, *"JM, JC, ESW, & AvD."*

"Just like the lads," said I as I eased myself behind the steering wheel of the Jeep. "Traditionalists to the deepest strata imaginable, and at rock bottom prices!"

"I hope they took the pertinent books from Arthur's library with them," said Father, buckling his seatbelt.

"You can count on it," said I.

I was proved right, of course. Forty-five minutes later, when we made our way into the Saranac Lounge—the ultimate *noire* imbibition outpost in my experience—the lads were indeed sitting around several small round tables they had clustered together in the far corner. There were books spread open in front of each of them, with various drinking glasses standing guard within easy reach. The centermost table had been piled so high with musty old volumes that it resembled the Los Angeles skyline—well, it did after my fifth glass of champagne, anyway. Tendrils of smoke trickled upward from their cigars, mingling with a dense smoggy layer that hung a few feet beneath the ceiling throughout the lounge.

The bar itself was a work of art. Nowhere else had I seen such a grand assortment of alcoholic beverages, all those luscious, scrumptious, colorful liquids refracting the intense radiance from the tube lights behind the glass shelves on which they stood like armies in battle array, their labels poised as shields. A genre of music I call "stale bourbon and cigarette butt jazz" dripped forlornly from speakers hidden amidst the rafters, and oil paintings rendered in dark hues of rain-drenched streets in Old Hollywood whispered their mysterious stories from the walls. The empty spaces were filled with autographed photos of movie stars from films the likes of which will never be made again.

"Came the dawn," Arthur was saying as Father and I squeezed in amongst them. He set down his large gold-rimmed magnifying glass, the one he typically used to forestall eyestrain when reading old, faded books. In this instance he had been examining by bobbing candlelight the photocopy of Bishop Ravenshorst's drawing of the artifact that Fr.

Baptist had provided earlier that day. "Hello Father, Pierre. I was just saying that I think it's coming clear."

"Really," said Edward. "Would you mind de-obfuscating it for me?"

"Is that a word?" I asked playfully.

"His Grace, Jeremiah Ravenshorst was the archdiocesan historian," explained Arthur, rubbing his eyes with the thumb and index finger of his right hand. "At the risk of repetition, his forte was California history. The verse from the back of the artifact is in Spanish. What does that suggest to you?"

"Nothing in particular," said Edward, "but Father's the big detective, not me."

"Not you fellows, too," sighed Father. "I get enough of that from Martin."

"We're just filling in," Jonathan assured him, "until Mr. Feeney is restored to us."

I couldn't help but notice, even in the somber gloom of the Saranac Lounge, that Jonathan's beard had been growing horrifically throughout the day. He must have been consuming an abundance of protein of late. His straggled whiskers looked truly hideous. I couldn't help but stroke my own chin while looking at him questioningly. My interpretation of the enigmatic smile with which he responded to my gesture was inconclusive.

Another thing I noticed, now that I think about it, was Father reaching into the flap of his cassock and starting to produce something that looked like a rolled-up parchment. I thought I remembered it lolling around the back seat of the Jeep when all the books were crammed around Father's feet in the front. But before he pulled it all the way out—

"How about this," reasoned Arthur, blinking his eyes and taking up the photocopy again. "Nine of the symbol abbreviations begin with the letter S. Suppose it stands for *San* or *Santa.*"

"Martin thought it might stand for *Sanctus*," said Father, slipping the tube back into its hiding place. "But of course that's Latin. The verse is in Spanish, so it's a given that the initials around the front of the artifact are as well."

"San or Santa," said Joel. "As in Español for Saint?"

"Precisely," said Arthur, pointing to the drawing. "SJC: San Juan Capistrano."

"Came the dawn indeed," said Father. "SLO: San Luis Obispo. Well done, Arthur."

"SY," said I. "Santa Ynez."

"SG," said Jonathan. "San Gabriel."

"SB," prompted Arthur.

"San Buenaventura," said I.

"Close," said Arthur. "St. Thomas Aquinas' friend, I believe, is represented by SBV. SB must be—"

"Santa Barbara," said Edward and Joel together.

"Fortunately for us," said Father, "the Missions retained their Spanish names even though California became Anglicized."

"Bravo," said I, patting Sir Arthur on his broad back. "Um, but what about these initials that don't have S before them?"

"Not all the missions are named after saints," he replied. "NSR, for example—"

"I'm no good at crossword puzzles," said Jonathan.

"I'll give you a hint," said Arthur. "Porciuncula."

"Hold it," said I. "That rings a bell. N, S, R … Porcincula. It's almost like the *HMS Bounty,* only not. N, S, R … de los *Ahng*-heh-les de … Yes, of course: *Nuestra Señora Reina de los Angeles de Porciuncula.* NSR: Nuestra Señora Reina."

"Excellent, Pierre," said Father.

"The original Los Angeles Mission," said Joel. "The one near Olvera Street."

"I guess there wasn't room for Angels and Porciuncula," said Joel. "Even when reduced to initials."

"It's a small disk," said Arthur, "and whoever made it probably assumed that whoever possessed it would be familiar with its abbreviations."

"Excuse me," said Edward. "I understand how we get Los Angeles from Our Lady Queen of the Angels. What I'm not clear about is Porciuncula. That's not Spanish for porcupine, is it?"

"Hardly," said Father, smiling. "It's the name of a chapel in Italy. It's where the Crucifix of San Damiano spoke to St. Francis of Assisi."

"Really." Edward scratched his head. "Awfully long name for a mission, if you ask me."

"You'll have to blame Don Gaspar de Portola, the first governor of California," said Arthur. "When he and Fr. Junipero Serra came to what is now Los Angeles in 1769, that's the name he gave the little river running there, and the rest is history."

"Okay," said Jonathan. "That explains NSR. What were the other two? Without San or Santa, I mean."

"LPC and AV," said Arthur.

"Ah," said Joel. "Could AV be *Agua de la Vida* without the *de la*?"

"Of course," said I. *"La Misión del Agua de la Vida,* with which we are all familiar."

"The only way in is through!" cheered the lads, recapping my own battle cry from our escapade there the previous June.

"Mrs. Magillicuddy calls the grounds there 'Home,'" said Father, tugging his earlobe thoughtfully.

"That leaves LPC," said Edward. "What the heck is LPC?"

There was a moment of silence as we all pondered the possibilities.

"La Purisima Concepcion," said Arthur finally, unable to contain himself. "The largest of all the California Missions."

"Which harkens back to a significant document that was on Morley Fulbright's desk during the papal visit to Los Angeles two decades ago," said Father.

"What document was that?" asked Joel.

"The codicil by which Themolina Hubbard bequeathed the Chapel Hill Estate to the Archdiocese of Los Angeles," said Father. "I think it likely that papal advisors figured out the artifact's connection with the California Missions long ago."

"You really think so?" asked Jonathan.

"Whatever else may be going on in the Vatican," said Father, "the Holy Father sits at the hub of one of the greatest information networks of all time: the ecclesiastical grapevine. It was almost as fast as the internet centuries before anyone thought to harness electricity for communication purposes. Through it he has access to some of the world's keenest if not the holiest minds. My guess—no, more than a guess—is that all those interconnected human neurons figured out the Mission connection we just unraveled decades ago. There was, however, a hole in the center of their knowledge."

"How deep, would you say?" I asked.

"The hole?" said Father. "It might as well have been bottomless. Remember that the Del Agua Mission had fallen into such total disuse that its location, indeed its very existence, had become obscured by time and urbanization."

"That's right," said Arthur. "It had been written off by many authorities of Old California lore as a legend. The account of Padre Alonso Miranda and Pere Jean Pierre de Chantal meeting at a spring under an oak tree at the foot of a hill had sufficient fanciful overtones to render it suspect to certain cynical scholarly minds."

"Incidentally," I said, "Mr. Feeney tells that story in his manuscript."

"'The Endless Knot' strikes again," said Joel.

"That's right," said Arthur. "I wonder where he got his information."

"Probably from me, but let's not let our attention stray," said Father, pointing to the photocopy. "As I said, the very existence of the Del Agua Mission had come into question, but here on the disk that came into the Pope's possession we know not how or when, but which he and they were reasonably sure to be genuine, were the initials AV."

"Proving its existence," said Arthur.

"Yes," said Father. "But not its location."

"Is its location important?" asked Joel.

Father rubbed his forehead in thought. "It is conceivable that someone in high places had suspected that evidence of the mission built by Fathers Miranda and de Chantal was to be found on that valuable parcel of downtown land known as the Chapel Hill Estate. I doubt we'll ever know for sure, but it's not a big stretch. In any case, the announcement of the bequeathal was made public just before the papal visit. I think it likely that the Pope was already planning to bring the artifact to Los Angeles with him. The initials on the artifact confirmed the existence of the forgotten Del Agua Mission, and it was likely further investigation would prove it one way or another."

"So the Holy Father brought it himself," said I. "Why didn't he just send it along with a messenger, or the nuncio?"

"Good question," said Father. "He certainly didn't have to bring it himself. I think his interest was personal."

"As soon as Morley Fulbright had his talons on it," said Edward, "didn't he bring in a team of archeologists?"

"Indeed," said Father. "I wouldn't be surprised if the enlistment of their services had been suggested by His Holiness to the very Msgr. Jeremiah Ravenshorst who was subsequently and swiftly promoted to auxiliary bishop at the Holy Father's insistence."

"Excuse me," said Joel. "Maybe I'm missing something. Correct me if I'm wrong, but aren't there more Missions in California than you've got initials on that disk?"

"You're right, my Friend," said Arthur, tapping the drawing. "There are over twenty. But the initials here correspond with all of the Missions in Southern California."

"Inclusive?" asked Edward. "Are you sure?"

"I am," said Arthur. "Every one from San Diego in the south to San Luis Obispo to the north."

"Wait a minute," said Father. "North south. East west."

"What is it, Father?" asked Joel.

Fr. Baptist closed his eyes. His head moved this way and that as if he were looking at a complicated equation on a blackboard. "North south," he mumbled several times. "East west," several more times. Suddenly he opened his eyes. "Millie told me that Martin spoke to her about the swallow nests in the eaves. I wonder."

"What?" asked we all.

"I'll reserve comment for the nonce," said he.

"Aarrgghh!" we groaned.

"You can't do that, Father," said Joel.

"It's too cruel," said I.

"You'll live for a few minutes," said Father, smiling. "First I want to hear what you lads have made of the verse."

"Oh, that," said Arthur, setting down the photocopy of Ravenshorst's drawing and taking up the sheet with Father's handwritten copy of the words from the back of the artifact. "There, I'm afraid I'm stumped."

> Fly, little swallow, from the strange head
> On your way to the house of gold
> May your path cross over the stream of life
> That flows from the well to the vine
> Over where and when the sacred words are said
> Upon the crown of thorns within an altar of stone
> While three score and fifteen hands below
> The treasure bleeds to rescue souls in darkness.

"And when Arthur's stumped," said Jonathan.

"We're all stumped," said the troupe as one.

"Of course," said Arthur, "there's the obvious detail of the crown of thorns within the altar of stone."

"I take it you lads got a good look at the painting in the lobby," said I. "The one over the registration counter."

"That we did," said Joel and Edward together.

"Right," said Jonathan, "just as soon as Arthur dragged us all back here this afternoon to point it out to us."

"He noticed it last night," said Edward.

"It must have been during one of his lucid moments," said Joel with a chuckle.

"The blue chasuble worn by the friar in the painting caught my attention," explained Arthur. "I was keyed in because of the vestments you recently procured, Father. Mr. Feeney told us about them. You don't often see blue as a liturgical color."

"Ah, yes," said Father. "The vestments from Norman Slater's Studio Supply, late of St. Lucy's, care of Dennis Goodman."

"I was pretty zonked from jetlag last night," said Arthur. "When we first came through the lobby I was struck by the friar saying Mass in the storm, and again when we were expelled from the Champlain room I took further stock of Señor Alverado y San Pasqual's painting."

"You didn't say anything at the time," said Jonathan.

"I barely knew my own name at the time," said Arthur. "It registered, but only barely. In fact, when we started examining this verse at my apartment earlier this afternoon, the words leapt off the page at me, but I couldn't remember at first where I'd seen the image. I just got back from Rome. I thought perhaps I'd seen it there."

"You should have seen him wracking his brains," said Jonathan.

"It was truly heroic," said Joel.

"Inspiring," said Edward.

"Bosh," said Arthur. "But once I placed the image, I insisted that we come here and give it a good solid look."

"Not to mention completing our four-day drink-a-thon," said Jonathan.

"Men after my own heart," said I. "Truly these are the good old days."

"Well," said Father, "there is that. So what do you make of it? The stone altar, the crown of thorns?"

"Only this," said Arthur. "There's a treasure bleeding somewhere, whatever that means. It's buried three score and fifteen hands beneath the altar containing the crown of thorns."

"How long is a hand?" asked Father.

"Mine's seven inches from wrist to fingertip," said Arthur. "I've done the math. That would make the depth forty-three and three-quarters feet."

"'Scuse me, Old Bean," said I. "I'm something of a wishful equestrian, and as I understand it a horse's height is measured in hands. It's the width of the human hand, not the length."

"So what should it be?" asked Arthur, removing a pencil from his inside jacket pocket.

"Four inches," said I.

"Ah," said he, doodling the math on his paper napkin. "Three times twenty plus fifteen times four divided by twelve equals ... twenty-five feet."

"Is that how the Spaniards measured horses?" asked Joel.

"I've no idea," said Arthur and I together.

"Ah, precision," said Edward.

"How does a treasure bleed?" asked Jonathan.

"I keep thinking of an oil seep," said Joel. "There certainly are a lot of oil wells in Southern California, but who knows?"

"Father," I said, noticing that his attention was focused elsewhere. "Father? Have you figured it out?"

"It bleeds," he whispered faintly. Father blinked, then turned to me. "I was just thinking of something Cheryl Farnsworth said to Martin a couple of days ago."

"About wanting you to hear her confession?"

"No, something else. Don't mind me. What about the rest of the verse? Any insights?"

"Tons of ideas," said Jonathan. "But how can we tell if they're useful?"

"Are you sure of this translation, Father?" asked Arthur, tapping the page. "'Fly, little swallow.' Are we sure it's a swallow and not a robin or a dove? And 'from the strange head.' What could that possibly mean?"

"Deformed," suggested Jonathan. "What's that condition that enlarges the head?"

"You mean hydrocephaly?" I suggested.

Jonathan shrugged. "I do if that's what it's called."

"Was St. Ferdinand deformed?" asked Joel. "Or St. Louis, or St. John Capistrano?"

"Not that I've heard," said Father.

"Even so," said Arthur, "the swallow flies from the strange head to a house of gold."

"A gold mine?" suggested Edward.

"Or a refinery for gold ore?" said Jonathan.

"When was the California gold rush?" asked Joel.

"It began in 1848," said Arthur. "Does this artifact predate that?"

"I don't know," said Father.

"The last mission was founded in 1823," said Arthur, "so if the treasure is a hoard of gold—"

"Gentlemen," said I. "What are you talking about? The House of Gold—we say those words every day."

"That's right!" said Joel, smacking his forehead. "Why didn't I think of that?"

"Talk about not seeing the forest through the trees," said Jonathan.

"Or the rye through all the whiskey," said Arthur.

<u>SPELUNKING SPINOFFS</u>: The Litany of Loreto, which is one of several prayers we Knights of the Tumblar have agreed to pray daily as part of our devotional discipline, is a prayer that dates back to the twelfth century in Italy (there's even an Irish version that goes back to the eighth). It incorporates a long list of titles and attributes of the Blessed Virgin Mary. Allow me to reproduce just a small segment here for those who are unfamiliar with this grand celebration of Our Lady's many facets:

Mirror of justice,	pray for us.
Seat of wisdom,	pray for us.
Cause of our joy,	pray for us.
Spiritual vessel,	pray for us.
Vessel of honor,	pray for us.
Singular vessel of devotion,	pray for us.
Mystical rose,	pray for us.
Tower of David,	pray for us.
Tower of ivory,	pray for us.
House of gold,	pray for us.

Ark of the Covenant,	pray for us.
Gate of heaven,	pray for us.
Morning star,	pray for us.
Health of the sick,	pray for us.
Refuge of sinners,	pray for us.
Comforter of the afflicted,	pray for us.
Help of Christians,	pray for us.

A book could be written (some have been written) about each of these accolades, their meaning, history, and significance. Suffice it to say that just as the Holy of Holies in the Temple was lined with pure gold in order to be a fitting repository for the Ark of the Covenant which contained the Scrolls of Moses, the Blessed Virgin was immaculately conceived in order that she might be a fitting dwelling place for the Messiah whose coming was prophesied in those very scrolls. Alas, I must press on with my tale.

—P.B.

"So where are we?" said Arthur. "The swallow flies from the strange head to Our Blessed Mother?"

"Not exactly," said Father. "It says, 'Fly, little swallow.' It's not declarative, it's imperative—a series of instructions. In other words, 'To find the treasure that bleeds, first you fly from the strange head to the house of gold.'"

"We're the swallow?" asked Joel.

"So far as these instructions are concerned," said Father, "I believe so."

"That explains the fluttery feeling I've been getting," said Edward.

"Ouch," said Jonathan.

"Ouch," said Edward as Jonathan punched him playfully.

"And on the way," said I, attempting to push the exercise forward, "you will cross over the stream of life."

"Stream of life," repeated Arthur.

"Perhaps it's a river," said Edward. "If this has to do with Southern California, a veritable desert, it could be the Los Angeles River or the San Gabriel."

"Water in the desert," said Joel.

"Or could the stream of life be related to the water of life?" asked Arthur.

"The Del Agua Mission, you mean," said Father.

"I'm not sure," said Arthur. "The verse says 'May your path cross the stream of life.' I assume that means 'If you're correctly following these directions, your path *will* cross the stream of life.'"

"What path?" asked Joel.

"The one that starts at the strange head," said Jonathan, "and winds up at the house of gold."

"What if the starting point of the path, as well as its destination," proposed Father, "are to be found around among the missions designated on the artifact?"

"The strange head?" asked Joel.

"I don't know about the strange head," said Father, "but one of the missions indicated on the artifact could surely represent Our Blessed Mother as the House of Gold."

"You mean La Purisima," said Edward. "The one you and Mr. Feeney just visited."

"The same," said Father. "The Most Pure Conception."

"The Immaculate Conception," said Arthur. "House of Gold. That's very interesting."

"Hold on," said Edward. "It says, 'the stream of life that flows from the well to the vine.' Maybe the stream of life is, you know, like another path."

"A path from the well to the vine," mused Joel.

"Hey, Arthur," said Jonathan, scratching his ragged, hirsute chin. "Didn't you find something about a vine in connection with one of the missions?"

"Yes, as a matter of fact, now that you mention it," said Arthur, scratching his own opulently bearded chin. As Martin Feeney would say, the effect was not the same. "At the San Gabriel Mission there's a grapevine that was planted by the first friars. It's still alive and quite huge. That's how that mission supported itself: wine production."

"Maybe the stream of life runs," said Jonathan, "from Del Agua de la Vida to the winery at the San Gabriel Mission."

"That makes sense," said Joel.

"And the swallow's flight plan crosses it," said I.

"Crosses it," said Father, closing his eyes again. "North south. East west. Crosses it," he mumbled to himself. Then he opened his eyes and exclaimed, "Gentlemen: *crosses* it!"

"Yes?" we all said in a prolonged ascending tone.

Father reached into a pocket concealed within his cassock and pulled out a leather pouch with a tasseled pull string. It was the same pouch he had opened in the presence of Edison Winger in his jewelry shop. He loosened the cord, producing a small object wrapped in a dark cloth. This he unraveled, revealing the small golden disk that gleamed mystically in the dim light as he held it in his outstretched palm.

"This, gentlemen," said he, "is the piece that fits into the center of the artifact."

"Whoa," said Jonathan.

"Where did you get that?" asked Arthur.

"That's a long story," said Father. "Originally this disk had three teeth on its underside which matched the three indentations you see in the depressed area in the center of the drawing of the papal artifact, allowing it to nest one and only one way. Notice it is decorated on the front with the engraving of a cross. Nothing out of the ordinary there, not on a Spanish artifact. But what if the vertical and horizontal lines of the cross point to four missions around the perimeter of the artifact, denoting the beginning and ending of the two paths?"

"Deviously obvious," said I, "and oh so simple. Dare I say it, gentlemen? Where the paths cross, X marks the spot!"

"Originally," said Arthur. "You said originally, Father."

"Yes," said Father, turning the disk over for us to see. "Somewhere in its history the teeth were filed off, rendering the disk almost useless."

"Almost?" said Edward. "With the teeth gone, how is the damage not total?"

"The number of possibilities is narrowed," said Father. "Bishop Ravenshorst didn't have this disk in his possession. He correctly guessed that it would indicate which missions were connected to which in the verse. He may have surmised that it would be engraved with a cross, or crisscrossed arrows, or some other symbol, but he couldn't know for sure. It could have been a trident or two overlapping semicircles. This explains his interest in downtown real estate."

"Real estate," said Arthur. "Excuse me, Father. You've lost me."

"And when Arthur's lost," said Jonathan.

"We're all lost," said the troupe as one, except I inserted the word "helplessly."

"Not for long," said Father, pulling a sheet of computer paper out of another pocket in his cassock and unfolding it. "This, gentlemen, is a map of downtown Los Angeles, courtesy of Sybil Wexler. These dots represent properties that Bishop Ravenshorst purchased and quickly resold. In every case he arranged for geological testing. Core samples, to be precise, to a depth of thirty feet."

"You don't say," said I, peering closely at the map. "And what are these lines connecting the dots and running off the edge of the page?"

"A pattern discerned by Miss Wexler's computer program. Each property was located at the intersection of these lines. She couldn't figure out where the lines meant, but now I think I know."

"You mean the missions," said Arthur.

"Precisely," said Father. "The artifact had twelve missions around the rim. Bishop Ravenshorst knew from the verse on the back that intersecting paths connecting two pairs of them pinpointed the treasure. Unable to decipher all the clues in the verse regarding the pairs, and without the key to the puzzle—the center disk—he took the only course left to him. It was a costly method, but efficient in its way. He simply drew lines connecting all twelve missions to all the others—"

"And bought whatever was at the intersections!" said Edward.

"Good heavens," said Joel. "That must have taken an awful lot of money."

"And what if there was a high-rise where the lines crossed?" asked Jonathan.

"Real estate isn't always a matter of money," said Father. "Often it's a matter of manipulation, of wheeling and dealing. As I understand it without really understanding it, people in the know purchase property without much in the way of funds, then unload at a profit to buy and sell again. In any case, he sold each parcel as soon as he was convinced it wasn't the site of the treasure. I'm not sure at all what he was expecting to find, but when he didn't he sold the property and moved on. These dots only represent the sites he purchased downtown. I'll wager he bought quite a few properties between San Diego and San Luis Obispo. As for structures on the parcels, Miss Wexler said that there were some buildings involved, and even a parking lot under a freeway off-ramp. His latest project was at the corner of La Colina Ave. and El Barranco Drive. Martin and I visited the site Friday night."

I flashed on a moment the previous evening. Something Mr. Feeney had mentioned in the lobby, something I had written down. Something about dark ravines and foul smells. I patted my breast pocket to make sure my trusty notebook was still there. It was.

"Where once stood seven cottages," said Father, "there now gapes a hole thirty feet deep."

"Not just a core sample?" said Joel. "He must've hit pay dirt."

"Not necessarily," said Father. "The work was abandoned when he died. Nothing has come to light indicating that he found anything there, but that doesn't mean he didn't. We just don't know."

"He must have been sure before he dug it all up like that," said Jonathan.

"Or it was the last intersection," said Father. "Having exhausted all possibilities, perhaps he presumed that this had to be the right place and had it excavated."

"So he may or may not have found the bleeding treasure," said Arthur.

"I'd prefer to assume that he didn't," said Father.

"But if he exhausted all other possibilities," said Jonathan.

"We don't know that," said Father. "Maybe Bishop Ravenshorst missed something."

"Perhaps we should start over," said Edward.

"Without knowing what the strange head is, we don't know where to begin ourselves," said Joel.

"Granted," said Father. "Maybe we should try going at it another way. Tell me, what do we know about what we should expect to find where the two paths cross?"

"The stone altar, of course," said Arthur, "with the crown of thorn embedded within."

"We therefore need more information about the painting in the lobby," said Father. "It also depicts the Cordova Rosary, which we all know to be real."

"Another detail in Mr. Feeney's manuscript," said I.

"When the dust settles," said Jonathan, "I should think I'd like to read it."

"Me, too," said Edward.

"That can be arranged," said I. "For the nonce, might I suggest that I go to the front desk and see if I can dig up someone who knows something about the painting?"

"Excellent idea," said Father. "And by the way, gentlemen, this entire discussions remains our secret. I have taken you into my confidence, and that has proved fortuitous and rewarding. But I am bound by my oath of obedience to my lawful superior not to mention anything about the artifact to the police. By extension I am also binding you."

Moans went around the table. Mine was probably the loudest.

"Well," said I, rising to my feet after a protracted sigh. "I shall at least see what I can find out at the front desk."

"In the mean time," said Arthur, "we'll order another round."

"That will ensure my quick return," said I, heading for the exit.

15(74)

CHAPTER FIFTEEN, WHEREIN I, PIERRE BONTEMPS, ENCOUNTER TWO PAIRS OF PEOPLE AT THE ADIRONDACK, THE FIRST UNEXPECTED AND THE SECOND I SHOULD HAVE ANTICIPATED.

I SAID AT THE ONSET that I do not mind being a character in Mr. Feeney's fascinating novel. And I do mean fascinating. If ever there was proof that we really do not ever understand the people we think we know well, "The Endless Knot" surely provides it. I had no idea the man is in such constant agony. As I said further, his report is accurate as humanly possible and as far as I know. But his point of view is—how do I put this?—so very optimistic. You think I jest, but alas, alack, and Bill Bailey won't you please come home, I am deadly serious. If you, dear reader, are perusing these words, then these words have been *published*—proof that God indeed does have a sense of humor, a grand one indeed. If that is so, come to think of it, I have indeed become a character in a novel—in this case Sir Martin's current novel. Imagine the stalwart optimism it took to write such a book day after hurting day in the wee hours of the morning—that sure ain't pessimism. I have been speaking for myself in the last fourteen chapters, but you will have met me in the preceding chapters written by himself and therefore I have no doubt been introduced to you through his pained eyes. And I must say, as one of the principle characters trapped in this convoluted story, and as a friend of the author, the scene I'm about to relate to you could indeed have come from the perplexed mind of Martin Feeney. In fact, I'll admit the thought crossed my mind at the time: trapped in a novel not of my own choosing, but admittedly having a good time while I'm here.

∞ ∞ ∞

"Excuse me, Miss," I said to the young lady at the registration counter whose expression and demeanor could be accurately described as deadpan. "Do you happen to know anything about the painting hanging on the wall above you?"

"Painting?" said she, apparently disquieted by being called "Miss," the usual appellation no doubt being "'Scuse me."

"Above you," said I, pointing. "Up there."

"Nope," was her long-considered answer.

"Well, not that I'm in any way surprised," said I, empowering her to excel at being herself. "Is there anyone on duty who would, or who would know who would?"

"Would what?"

"Who would know about the painting."

"What painting?"

"Ah, what can I say? Is Mr. Maxwell on duty?"

"He's taking care of a disturbance on the third floor." She placed a slight, curious emphasis on the word disturbance, as if she had been instructed to use that word instead of one of her own preference. I know the drill because my lady editor is often suggesting words I'd rather not use.

"Well," I said. "Would you please tell him that Pierre Bontemps would appreciate it if he could seek me out in the Saranac Lounge when he gets back?"

"Who did you say?"

"Pierre Bontemps, at your service."

"Sure."

Somehow I wasn't convinced that she'd remember, but what's to be done? It occurred to me that I'd surely like to see a restroom, especially one with loo chains, so I made my merry way to said accommodation in the corridor that led to the Blue Mountain Grill. Marvels of hydrogravitational engineering, such are British commodes. Better still, there were real cloth towels neatly folded and piled beside the washbasins, no less. I exited the washroom with an air of aplomb, and who do you think I bumped into in the hallway?

At first I didn't recognized them, the one without his jade green silk kimono and lounging slippers, and the other without his customary red robes. Both were attired in clerical civvies: black shoes, pants, and shirts, with Roman collars ringing their throats. I should have spotted the former's amethyst ring, not to mention the other's sapphire ring, at first glance. Due to the unexpected nature of the encounter, a second glance was required.

"Your Eminence!" I blurted out as realization hit me. I'll admit for a nanosecond, perhaps two, I was taken aback, even a wee bit intimidated. Red ants perturb me. It passes quickly.

SPELUNKING SPINOFFS: As a journalist and a Catholic layman I have endured, pondered, prayed for, and railed against the antics of men such as these since I was old enough to realize that a generation of the faithful had been robbed of their rightful heritage. Such men have done the thieving. Then, to top it off, they perpetually brag in their pastoral letters about how wonderful everything has become in the Church since the "Spirit of Vatican II" started blowing around the world like a spiritual version of the Black Plague. Convents closed, parishes abandoned, dwindling seminaries disseminating heresy, nuns desiring to be priests, priests forcing themselves on innocent children, belief in the Real Presence held by a minority of adult Catholics—these have been the true fruits of Pope John XXIII's ill-conceived council. Any member of the hierarchy who insists publicly that these travesties are good things is, in fact, a fool or a liar. In person they could not help but be gorkier than their preceding reputations. The proof of this premise, ladies and gentlemen, is in the behavior.

—P.B.

"Your Eminence," I repeated, a little more forcefully, "a word if you please."

"What the—?" said Cardinal Morley Fulbright, Archbishop of Los Angeles. Accompanying him was none other than His Grace, Bishop Morell deQuet. Apparently they had been dining in the Grill. There were dots of French onion soup down the front of the cardinal's shirt barely but brownly visible against the dark background (they might have missed if his stomach hadn't provided such an expansive landing area). A smudge of purple-brown steak sauce marred the auxiliary from New Bangor's chinny-chin-chin. They stopped in their sacerdotal tracks. His Eminence and Its Grace looked from me to each other and back at me again. His Eminence's eyes, at first magisterial, narrowed in accusatory recognition as they zoomed in on my face. "You!"

"Me, Your Eminence?" said I, bowing.

"You're that Bawntemps fellow," said he. I write it as he pronounced it. "Peeyair Bawntemps."

"Your humble servant, Cardinal Foolbright," said I in return. I reached for his hand to kiss his ring.

"Go to the devil," said he, yanking it away.

"This man, this is the man," hissed Bishop deQuet, drawing close to His Eminence, eyes glaring at me. His percussive accents exploded greenly in the periphery of my vision. "He was with that scoundrel, Baptist!"

"This man," countered the cardinal in an ominous tone, pointing not at my heart but at my throat. "This man wrote the slanderous article about Paneno's."

"Begging your august pardon, Your Eminence," said I, bowing again. "There was no slander intended or implied. In fact, I understand business there has never been better since my little piece made the rounds. I fail to see how anything I wrote could have displeased you so."

"Displeased me?" he growled. Funny, but that revolting bump on his forehead seemed to glow red. It must have been a trick of the light. "Displeased me? Thanks to you, I can't dine at my favorite restaurant anymore, you erudite twit! I've had to content myself with bringing my guests to places such as this."

"You wound me, Your Eminence," said I, "more than words can convey. My article was inoffensive, innocuous, and in a word, kind. And as for this place, I can think of few places I'd rather wine and dine than the Adirondack. Darby's, of course, has a special place in my palate, but this hotel is so undeniably *noir*. It's haunted, you know."

"You see what I mean?" said deQuet, his hands slithering around each other like amorous snakes.

"You see what I have to put up with," said Fulbright. For another nanosecond I thought he might have been addressing me. Then I realized was speaking to his cucumbery companion. I couldn't resist saying, "Indeed," just as deQuest replied the same. The look they both gave me!

"However, if there is a lesson to be learned," said I, "it is that the removal of something we cherish from our lives can be devastating."

"What would you know about such things?" sneered Bishop deQuet.

"A great deal, actually," said I. "Something very precious to me has been stolen—worse, denigrated, stomped upon, and good-riddanced by perpetrators who held positions of authority and who were ensconced beyond the grasp of accountability."

"If that's the onset of a rant about the Tridentine Mass," said the cardinal, "you'll have to take that up with Pope Paul VI."

"No, Your Eminence, as unconscionable as that debacle was," said I, "I was recalling a time when Catholic laymen routinely regarded their bishops with pride. I was decrying the fact that the operating word has become embarrassment."

"Just who do you think you are?" said deQuet, his voice on the verge of squeaking.

"As I just explained, Your Grace," said I, blinking back flashes of green. "I'm one such layman."

"You fancy yourself a journalist, Mr. Bawntemps" said the cardinal, "but you're just a loathsome little troublemaker."

"Really, Cardinal Foolbright," said I. "Can someone who writes for the *Artsy* call himself a journalist? I'm but one voice crying in the wilderness, a forest rendered a wasteland by the likes of you. That you consider me a threat, well, I'm simply overwhelmed."

"You are a gnat on my windshield," said he.

"I am honored," said I. "No obstruction inconsequential, no inconvenience too small."

"So," said he, "you reveal your true colors."

"At least I am honest about them," said I.

"I advise you to watch your step, Peeyair Bawntemps," said he.

"Always, Cardinal Foolbright," said I. "May I have your blessing?"

"You'll have the toe of my boot if you don't get out of my way," said he. "I have warned Father Baptist to get you off my back. If you persist in writing your petulant articles, the weight of my wrath will fall upon him before it does you."

I admit that brought me up short. Placing myself on the chopping block is one thing, and one I would do willingly, but to endanger a good priest like Father Baptist, that is another matter.

Groping for words with which to brick up a reply, I barely stepped aside in time to avoid being trampled by His Eminence. Bishop deQuet gave me a "So there!" look over his angular shoulder as he shuffled by, all but clinging to his prospective lawful superior like a baby possum clutching its mother.

"Vade post me, Satana!" I said under my breath. *"Scandalum es mihi!"* Go behind me, Satan, thou art a scandal unto me! (Though I actually did know the Latin for this verse, I needed to look up the citation later: St. Matthew 16:23.) As I watched them waddle down the

hall, so caught up in their importance, another passage from the Bible rolled up and parked itself in the foreground of my imagination. Mr. Feeney had told me to look it up a couple of days before. It was almost spooky, how snugly it applied to the situation:

> Thou hast enlarged my steps under me; and my feet are not weakened. I will pursue after my enemies and overtake them, and I will not turn again until they are consumed.
>
> —Psalm 17:37-38

It occurred to me that Father Baptist would never want me to shirk my responsibilities, even if they brought peril to his doorstep. We are, after all, in this together. Still, try as I might, nothing truly useful came to mind in the way of a retort. So, gathering my resolve to prepare myself for a tumultuous future, I silently watched them strut angrily toward the archway leading to the front entrance. When they were out of sight I turned to head toward the Saranac Lounge when, lo and behold, I heard an outburst of female laughter emanating from the dark cave that was the Champlain Room. My male curiosity piqued, not to mention my fascination with whatever subtleties haunted the place, I veered in that direction. Before I reached the entryway, however, two women tangled arm-in-arm came lunging toward me out of the gloom.

"Ladies!" I said as we collided. "Did no one tell you that the Champlain Room is closed?"

"What do you mean, closed?" asked one.

"He's balmly, thatch what he is," said the other.

"That bar ish most definitely not closed," said the one, hooking her thumb over her shoulder.

"Itsh run by the nicest bartender in the whole world," said the other.

I have seen Madame Hummingbird "lit" on several occasions, but nothing like this. Likewise, I'd never seen Millie so much as kindled, but what can be said? These gals were thoroughly, blurrily inebriated, as in the habit of skunks.

"Well," said I, clapping my hands and rubbing them together. "Well, well, well."

"Been there," said Kahlúa.

"Done that," said Millie.

"Aha," said I. "Would you two ladies care to join us in the Saranac Lounge?"

"The where-anack?" asked Millie.

"I thought he said Sarah Mack," said Kahlúa.

"No, Lulu," said Millie. "I don't shink so."

"The other bar," I explained. "Father and the Tumblars are convened there as we speak."

"Oh, goodie," said Kahlúa. "We should have our tab sent over there. Let the men pick it up."

"That's the spirit," said I encouragingly. "This way, this way."

We proceeded to the Saranac Lounge much like contestants in a three-legged race, only there were three of us on our team, not two. In any case, I managed to herd the gals in a zigzagging course to the Tumblar encampment. Lo and behold, before I could say, "Look who I just bumped into in the lobby," Father and the lads were all on their feet in the presence of ladies.

"Millie," said Father. "Kahlúa. Have you been here all day?"

"So we have," said Kahlúa, suppressing a burp behind a clenched hand.

"Under a nice, cozy table," said Millie, smiling from ear to ear and waving her right arm in a wide arc. "I could get yoosht to thish place."

16(75)

CHAPTER SIXTEEN, WHEREIN I MAKE MY REPORT, THE STRANGE HEAD BECOMES FAMILIAR, ANOTHER UNEXPECTED PERSON MAKES HIS APPEARANCE AS DO TWO OTHERS WHO ARE NOT, AND IN WHICH FATHER GIVES US OUR ASSIGNMENTS.

"THE *NEW OXFORD REVIEW* you say?" asked Father.

"Yes, indeed," said I with an authoritative harrumph, rattling the computer printout in my hand. I had forgotten that it was in my jacket pocket, but discovered it when Joel asked me if I had a match. "At Mr. Feeney's suggestion, I did some checking into the background of one W. Warren Shufeld. No, I've no idea in what connection, but he's never steered me wrong yet. It took some valiant digging, but among other things, I came up with this article in the *NOR* called 'No Sane City' by a papal knight, no less, named Charles A. Coulombe." I spelled out the last name. "He's a Knight Commander in the Order of St. Sylvester."

"Cool ohm?" asked Millie, gripping the edge of the table lest she slide sideways. "What kind of a name is that?"

"Coulombe?" said Joel. "Isn't that a unit of electricity?"

"Coulombe," said Arthur, rubbing his temple. "Wasn't that the colonel who exposed Madame Blavatsky as a fraud?"

"No," said I. "It's Charles A. with a final E; not Charles Augustin de without the E, in whose honor the electrical Coulomb was named; nor Alexis without the E, who, with his wife Emma, figured so prominently in the *Hodgson Report*. I assume they're all related somewhere up the chute, but as to the point. Apparently, and historically, ours is not the only hunt for treasure hidden beneath the sedimentary sands of the Los Angeles Basin. Attend:

> One of the strange details in this story of American cults is the role of Southern California as headquarters to many cultist sects. Theosophy introduced many ideas of Hindus and Yogis into American thought in the nineteenth century, but at the beginning of the twentieth, one of the fractured strands took root in Point Loma. The region got a reputation as an occult land. Also locating there were Rosicrucians, various Aquarians, (yes, before the sixties), and different swamis. There was little opposition in the region from established churches, which were weaker in the west than elsewhere, and had always seemed to have lower local church membership and attendance. Some of the migrants to the west were invalids seeking healing by whatever method in the healthful weather. Practically, California real estate was cheap, so that imposing temples could be erected with relatively little cost. California law made establishing a new church very easy; a small filing fee, a couple of witnesses, and you were in business. Even occultist Aleister Crowley was appalled by the "amateurs" he saw peddling their beliefs around Los Angeles in 1918. H. L. Mencken explained that the "swamis, spiritualists, Christian Scientists, crystal-gazers, and the allied necromancer" swarmed to the area because "there were more morons collected in Los Angeles than any other place on earth."

"That explains it," said Jonathan as the sound of merriment rumbled around the table. "Los Angeles, I mean, and how someone like Cardinal Fulbright thrives here."

"More than you realize," said I. "I neglected to mention that I bumped into him and his protégé, Bishop deQuet, out in the lobby."

"When?" asked Father. His tone was at once surprised and concerned.

"Just a few minutes ago," said I, nonchalantly. "No need to panic, everyone. Last I saw, the dynamic duo were heading for the exit."

"You had words with him?" asked Father.

"Both of them, yes."

"And?"

"Not to worry, Father, I turned on the Bontemps charm."

"That's what worries me."

"But what does this have to do with the buried treasure?" asked Jonathan, pointing to the printout in my hand.

"I'm getting to it," said I. "I wanted to set the scene first. Allow me to continue. You'll get a kick out of this: 'Back then, this mindset—'"

"Back when?" asked Edward.

"Early twentieth century," I explained. "Your attention please:

> Back then, this mindset even showed itself as civic-mindedness, of a sort. Supposedly, Hopi legends told of a race of "Lizard people." These were said to have built three great underground cities near the Pacific Coast, 5000 years before us. One of these was underneath Los Angeles. In 1933, mining engineer W. Warren Shufeld won notoriety by claiming that the underground city beneath downtown L.A. was laid out in the shape of a lizard extending from what is now Dodger Stadium to the Central Library. The lizards had used special chemicals in tunneling through the bedrock, but in an end eerily prefiguring that of Superman's home planet of Krypton, had been destroyed by natural gas fires after escaping into their tunnels from a meteor shower. With his "radio X-ray" machine, Shufeld located the tunnels and a treasure room underneath downtown' s Fort Moore Hill. On February 21, 1933, the Los Angeles County Board of Supervisors approved a contract with Shufeld and his partners for them to drill. These latter were to bear all expenses, to leave the property in its original condition, and to share 50% of all discoveries and treasure with the city of L.A. The Board were reassured of the certainty of success by the visions of Pico Rivera psychic Edith Elden Robinson, who saw "a vast city ... in mammoth tunnels extending to the seashore." Having raised the necessary funds, Shufeld began drilling a 350-foot shaft. Unfortunately for the windfall expected by the City from this surefire success, work on the project was halted by fear of cave-ins. Shufeld vanished shortly thereafter.

"Holy bat cave, Batman," said Kahlúa, making goggles with her fingers and pressing them to her face.

"I was partial to Cat Woman myshelf," said Millie, resting her chin in her palm and her elbow on the edge of the table. "Julie Newmar—meowrrrr."

"So Martin suggested you look into Shufeld," said Father, speaking to me but glancing at the ladies.

"That's correct," said I. "He had a hunch, thought it might have some bearing on the case you were working on."

"I suppose it does," said Father. "In a Martin Feeney kind of way, at least. It was Sybil Wexler's computer, come to think of it, that made the initial suggestion. Did Martin have any other hunches?"

Suddenly I remembered the something I had jotted in my notebook. Digging it out and snapping it open, I looked at the last page of scribbles. "He did indeed," said I. "He told me to check out the history of a couple of streets, El Barranco Dr. and La Colina Ave., the intersection you mentioned a short while ago, but I haven't gotten to them yet."

"That should prove interesting," said Father. "Please let me know what you turn up."

"Mr. Feeney had that covered," said I. "He prefaced his hunches with a proviso that I run any and all results by you, Father, *en route* to print."

"Wise of him," said Father.

"So, may I? Go to print, I mean."

"I see no problem," said Father, "if you sit on it for a few months, then present the information as urban history, local color, that sort of thing. I admonish you, however, not to make any connection whatsoever to our artifact or our mission concerning it."

"I assume you mean ever."

"As in never."

I sighed long and hard, but to no avail.

"Never is an awfully long word," said Kahlúa, clutching her fists to her bosom. "Oooo, it makes my heart ache."

"That's strange," said Millie, her chin slipping out of her palm. "It's making my head ache."

"Never can do that, too," said Kahlúa, fluttering her fingers.

"Not never, Lulu," said Millie, rubbing her forehead with one hand and her tummy with the other. "It's the Manhattans made with Imperial Whiskey. Whew. By the way, Father, what was it the nuncio said about when the heart rules the head?"

"Funny you should mention that," said Father, regarding her calmly. "It's been rolling around in my head ever since he said it, and I don't even speak Italian: *È una cosa strana quando il cuore regola le teste*' —'It is a strange thing when the heart rules the head.'"

"Makes sense to me," said Jonathan knowingly.

"Was he referring to something in particular, Father?" asked Arthur.

"The curious thing," said Father, "was his choice of words throughout our conversation. For example, the way he spoke of Cardinal Fulbright's current unavailability. He said, 'Nor can you say where is your head, I mean, ah, your cardinal, I suppose?'"

"Sounds like his English is none too good," said Kahlúa.

"I think his English is excellent," said Millie. "On the other hand, you've got to love his pro-nuncio-ation!"

It took a moment for us to realize that Millie, our very Millie, had just cracked a joke. At first we didn't know how to react. I think I was the first to chuckle, though it may have been Joel. In any case, what began as an uncertain chortle became a resounding round of guffaws.

"Good show, my good woman," said I.

"I needed that," said Arthur.

"We all needed that," said Kahlúa, giving Millie a sideways hug.

Millie looked befuddled, and a mite ill at ease.

"Our Millie is astute," said Father. "His Lordship, Sylvio Bonsignore, is no bumpkin. He would not have been sent to the United States if his command of English wasn't profound. I believe he uses his accent to put people off their guard."

"But not you, Father," said I.

"No," he admitted. "Not me. As I was saying, he peppered the conversation with curious turns of phrase. When I touched on the rumor that he liked to visit Knott's Berry Farm, he said, 'Upon my head, it is strange indeed.'"

"Upon my head?" said Arthur. "What's so strange about that?"

"Nothing much by itself," said Father. "But, come to think of it, he used that word a lot. 'My head, it almost aches,' he said at one point in the conversation. 'To think that on every Feast of St. Joseph the celebrated California swallows descend upon a mission built by Spaniards and named after an obscure Italian Saint.'"

"What was he talking about?" asked Edward. "What obscure Italian saint?"

"San Juan Capistrano," said Father. "It was an odd thing for him to say on many levels. We were at the Mission San Fernando at the time."

"Well," said Joel, "the missionaries were Spanish, weren't they?"

"But St. Francis, the founder of their order, was Italian," said Arthur.

"That's what I mean," said Father. "And when I told him I would look into it, he said, 'Yes, you should keep it in your head—I mean, in your mind.'"

"Head again," said Kahlúa, pointing to hers.

"As in aching," said Millie, rubbing hers.

"Every time he said it," said Father, "he looked me straight in the eye. I half expected him to wink. I wonder why."

"Maybe it's an Italian thing," said Edward.

Suddenly Father Baptist straightened. Then he slapped both of his hands down on the table. "Pierre," he said forcefully. "How's your Italian?"

"Passable so far as wine lists," said I, taken aback. "Not much more."

"What's Italian for 'strange'?"

"Let me see. I think it's *strano.*"

"Strano. And how about for 'head'?"

"Head? *Testa,* if you mean the appendage atop your shoulders. *Capo* if you're talking about, say, the head of a family, or someone seated at the head of the table."

"Strano testa?" said Arthur. "Sounds like a medieval Italian poet."

"But *strano capo ...*" said Father. "... strange head ..."

"Don't the Italians usually put the noun before the adjective?" asked Joel.

Everyone looked at Father and said as one, "Capistrano!"

"So St. John Capistrano had a strange head?" asked Millie.

"No," said Father, smiling. "Capistrano was the town of his birth. Who knows why it was named that?"

"Actually, I'm no expert," said I. "But I'm pretty sure that *capi* is plural and *strano* is singular, so the name doesn't make sense even in Italian."

"But the nuncio," said Jonathan. "Why do you suppose—?"

"Cardinal Fulbright said the nuncio took inordinate interest in the artifact," said Father. "Apparently Bishop Bonsignore had a hunch of his own, or perhaps certain knowledge. It's funny really, how obvious he was being with me yesterday, and how obtuse I was at the time."

"But why should he coax you about it?" said Edward. "He's the papal nuncio. He deals with big fish. No offense, Father."

"None taken," said Father. "I'd much prefer being a little fish, but he did know exactly who I was. It was *he* who accosted *me.*"

"Methinks," said Arthur, rubbing his chin. "Better Father Baptist than Cardinal Fulbright."

"Doubtless the nuncio was thinking the same thing," said I.

"In the end, yes," said Father. "But the artifact was entrusted to Archbishop Fulbright years before he was elevated to the College of Cardinals."

"You mean," said I, "because Rome knew him to be the kind of man he is, the kind of men he knew—?"

"The kind of man," said Father, "who knew the kind of men who would find the missing disk with the solution to the puzzle."

"Albeit defaced," said Jonathan. "Or detoothed."

"The solution nonetheless," said Father.

"Is that why he was put in charge of the largest archdiocese on the planet?" said Joel, a mite angrily. Bear in mind he was an escapee from St. Joseph of Copertino Seminary. He had good reason to be riled.

"I'm not competent to answer for the whims of Rome," said Father, "or the Holy Father's choice of prelates."

"But now we can find the treasure, whatever it is," said Edward.

"That seems to be our destiny," said Father.

"Here we go, lads," said I, "walking in legends again."

"But in the immediate," said Father, "I'm more concerned about finding my friend, Martin, but that's a puzzle without clues, without a verse to unravel."

"Oh, my head," said Millie, holding hers. "Strange as it is. I wish the room would stop spinning."

"It ain't the room, dearie," said Kahlúa. "It's your eyeballs."

"Whatever's twirlin'," said Millie, rocking her head in her hands, "I just pray it doesn't go south."

"Honey," said Kahlúa, "if we were in my kitchen, I'd make you a Hummingdinger."

"What's that?" asked Edward and Jonathan.

"Gramma Hummingbird's instant hangover eradicator," said Kahlúa. "It's good for the ups and overs, too."

"Don't tell me," said I. "Worcestershire sauce, raw egg—"

"Pickle brine ... Cheyenne pepper ... gunpowder ..." mumbled Millie.

"Lordy, no, Pierre," said Kahlúa playfully. "Shame on you, Millie. That'd be a white man's potion for sure. Gramma's really worked. Let me think. I have the fresh juniper berries and jimson weed at home. But I'm fresh out of black cockerel—"

"Ah," said I. "That would be hard to find on a Sunday."

As various ahems and harrumphs rumbled around the table, I leaned toward Jonathan and whispered a question that had been festering in the back of my mind. "I say, did you and Stella ever connect at Mass this morning?"

"Strangely, no," he hissed in reply. "Several people mentioned noticing her, but somehow our paths never crossed. Hard to imagine, unless she was intentionally avoiding me."

"Hmm," was all I could think of mumbling in return.

"What I need," said Millie, slapping the table with both hands, " is another drink."

"Well," said Father, "there is that."

"But it doesn't cure nystagmus," said Arthur. "It just postpones it."

"Nystagmus?" said I. "Is that a word?"

"It is," said Arthur, smiling academically. "It means—"

"Hair of the dog," said Millie, looking around blurredly. "I need another Manhattan."

"I forget," said Joel. "What's in a Manhattan?"

"Sweet vermouth," said I, "whiskey and angostura bitters."

"Imperial Whiskey," corrected Millie. Suddenly her wavering eyes focused on something beyond our table, across the bar. A smile blossomed on her blurry face. "There he is," she said, heaving herself with a Herculean, or rather Amazonian effort, from her chair. "Just the man I want to see."

We turned to observe who had so roused her. I don't know about the others, but it took me several seconds of looking around the bar. There were patrons hunched at several tables, absorbed in their secrets. The bartender stood stoically behind the counter, gazing into eternity. My eyes must have brushed over the shape in the farthest corner several times before realizing it was a man, or seemed to be the shape of a man. It could have been a trick of combined shadows. His attention seemed riveted to a framed photograph on the wall. As I watched, he raised his right hand, slowly extended his fingers, and gingerly touched the glass. Darn if I didn't have the impression, from the position of his arm and hand, that he was reaching into the picture. I blinked twice. He was still there, but he was lowering his hand to his side.

"Yoo-hoo," called Millie. "Mr. Barlow!"

"Good heavens," said Arthur. "That *is* Barlow!"

"Barlow from last night?" gasped Jonathan.

"Whoa," said Edward.

"No," said Joel. "It's just a shadow."

"Hang on, Millie," said Father, but she was already swaggering across the room, bumping her way from table to table like a pinball.

Thinking of the bottle of Imperial that the ghostly keeper of the Champlain Room still owed us, I jumped up and strode quickly in that direction, attempting to catch up to Millie, but she was one determined woman.

"Mr. Barlow!" she called. "You hoo! I'm ailin' and you got the cure!"

"Look at that gal go!" laughed Kahlúa proudly.

I glanced at the solid bartender behind the counter, assuming that he'd be reacting to all this commotion, but all he could muster was a sigh of boredom, as if this happened all the time.

The shadowy Mr. Barlow reached for the picture again as we approached. By then Millie was blocking his hand from my sight, so I don't know about his fingers. I do know that he turned his head to look at us, that same expression on his face as when he had said, "What guys?" to the hapless cocktail waitress—serious yet amused all at once. But then, as we came up to him, he dissolved into a play of overlapping shadows, as if it had all been our imagination.

"Where'd he go?" insisted Millie.

We regarded the emptiness in moody silence.

"Oh darn," moaned Millie, sinking against me. "I was so hoping."

"There, there," I said, wrapping my brotherly arm around her shoulder. "We'll fix you up with the next best thing."

"There is no next best thing," said she.

"Pardon me," said Father, who had silently crept up behind us.

"Millie's okay," said I. "It was just our imagination."

"Yours and hers?" said he. "And mine as well? Perhaps, but perhaps … not …"

His voice trailed off as he stepped around us and examined the picture on the wall. It was a large black-and-white photograph, its impressive clarity and depth-of-field reminiscent of the work of Ansel Adams. In the foreground was a lean-to shack made of pine branches, its spindly roof buckling precariously under the weight of several feet of snow. The snow was heaped at odd angles against the trunks of the surrounding trees. In the distance rose the famous rock formation in Yosemite National Park known as Half Dome. I had seen many pictures of it, and even once taken a snapshot from a spot very near this one, but never quite like this. The facade of the giant precipice, even at this distance, was splattered and caked with ice and snow—unusual considering how vertical I knew it to be. For a second I thought I saw a human face looking at me, but when I looked again it was gone, or nearly gone. Yes, the way the snow had been tossed against the rock, apparently deposited there by high winds and unusual updrafts, it did take on hints of a face. There were the eyes, the nose, the mouth—almost impish in their expression.

My eyes were then drawn to a jagged inscription in the lower left corner, probably etched into the original negative: "After the freak blizzard of '67—H.D."

"Maybe Barlow used to vacation there," I suggested, albeit lamely.

"No," said Father, turning to me with a distinct glimmer in his eye. "He was telling me something."

"Oh? You? What?"

"Where what is lost is to be found."

"What? In Yosemite National Park?"

"No, Pierre. Someplace much closer to home than that." He stopped, blinked, and brought his hand up to his forehead. "Pumpernickel!" he exclaimed.

"Excuse me?" I asked.

"Something Martin called to my attention." With that he headed back to our table. I distinctly heard him say, "Thank you, Barlow," along the way.

A few minutes later we were all huddled tightly in our corner.

"So you're not going to tell us," Arthur was saying.

"Not until I'm sure," said Father.

"But we're your speleologists," said I.

"That's right," said Jonathan. "Whatever that is."

"Mr. Feeney would know," said Joel, "or he'd look it up."

"Meanwhile we'll guess from context," said Joel.

"Gentlemen," said Father, stretching his neck and adjusting his Roman collar. "I appreciate your desire to help. There is, in fact, something I want you to do for me."

"Anything," we all said, somewhat together. "You name it."

"First I'm going to repeat something to all of you," said Father. "No mention is to be made of anything to do with the artifact, the bleeding treasure, or our deciphering of the puzzle. That includes Larry Taper."

"Why do you feel you have to say that again?" asked Joel.

"Look who's coming to join us," said Father, rising from his chair yet again.

"Whew," said some of the lads, who likewise became upstanding as Lt. Taper and Officer Sybil Wexler approached.

"We're still outnumbered," said Kahlúa, nudging Millie with her elbow.

"Not really," sniggered Millie in return. "As long as there's one of us, we're never outnumbered."

"Now we're three."

"Heaven help 'em."

"Father, ladies, gentlemen," said Taper. Then he looked at me. "Pierre."

I confess the sight of him caused my chitterlings to bunch up again just a bit. This involuntary response wasn't as bad as with the cardinal and his crony, though, and passed more quickly. Since Larry Taper wasn't likely to move out of the state any time soon, I decided I really had to make getting beyond it a priority.

"Everyone," said Sybil Wexler by way of greeting, smiling inscrutably. The sight of her helped me to think past the past, just like that. I like that in a woman.

"Do join us," beckoned Father.

A moment later, two chairs having been whisked away from nearby vacant tables, we all seated ourselves and ordered another round of whatever we were having.

"We bumped into each other at St. Philomena's," explained Miss Wexler.

"Why did you go there?" asked Jonathan, self-consciously hiding the lower half of his face behind a napkin clenched in his hand.

"I went to Mass, of course," said Lt. Taper.

"You might say I went to observe," said Miss Wexler. "We compared notes afterwards and realized we both had invitations to the soirée at Mr. von Derschmidt's."

"I assume the note on Arthur's door brought you here," said Father.

"Of course," said Lt. Taper.

"And Sgt. Wickes?" asked Father.

"At the office filing reports. Somebody had to."

"I'd say you chose the better part."

"So would I," said Miss Wexler.

"I'm afraid this is our last drink," said Father.

"Last?" said the lads, almost as one. "Why, we haven't yet begun to imbibe!"

"No, you haven't," said Father. "but I've got an errand for you. You, too, Larry and Sybil, if you've a mind."

The two representatives of the Police Department looked at each other, shrugged, and nodded.

"What do you need?" asked Taper.

"Nothing particularly difficult," said Father. "Whose car did you come in?"

"Mine," said Sybil.

"Good," said Father. "Sybil, I'd like you to come with me."

"Where to?" she asked.

"That would be telling," said Father.

"What about me?" asked Taper.

"I'd like Arthur to drive you to Headquarters, retrieve your partner, and go to St. Philomena's. Pierre, please see your Madame Humming-bird and our dear Millie there in the Jeep Cherokee. Edward, you transport the Tumblars in your van."

"To St. Philomena's?" asked Arthur.

"No you don't," grumbled Millie. "I ain't fixin' dinner for a roaring horde like this."

"Roaring horde—us?" exclaimed Jonathan.

"I wouldn't ask it," said Father. "No, and I don't want you all jabbering in the rectory either. I want you in the church."

"What for?" we all asked in various inflections and tones.

"Why, to pray, of course," said Father. "Sybil and I have an errand to run. We'll need your prayerful support."

"Why don't we just go with you?" asked Joel.

"That's the ticket," said Edward.

"To give you our personal support," added Jonathan.

"Because what needs to be done can't be done by a herd," said Father.

"Then why not with one of us?" asked Arthur.

"Me, for instance?" said I.

"I repeat," said Father, smiling appreciatively. "For reasons I cannot explain at present, I believe Miss Wexler is the best choice."

"Well, Jack," said Larry, tucking in his shirt. "If you say so."

"You really shouldn't call him Jack, you know," said Millie. "His name is Father John Baptist."

"But we go back to before he became a priest," said Taper.

"All the more reason," said Millie.

"You tell 'im, sweetie," said Kahlúa.

"Okay," said Taper. "It's a hard habit to break, but I'll work on it."

"And we're all here to keep you on the straight and narrow," said Arthur.

"Just what I need," said Taper. "A support group."

"As for me," said Millie, glaring around the table, "I think you're all a bunch of scoundrels, but you love Our Blessed Mother, you keep Father on his toes, and you keep life at the rectory from getting dull." She slammed down her unfinished drink, a non-Imperial Manhattan. "I say let's get to the church as Father asks and pray our bloody guts out!"

"Hoorah!" said the lads.

17(76)

CHAPTER SEVENTEEN, WHEREIN THE BEST LAID PLANS OF PRIEST AND TUMBLARS AFT GANG AGLAY.

MILLIE WAS SLURRING THE WORDS to a song, one of my sultry favorites called "Sway," while Kahlúa was humming "The Night Has 1000 Eyes" as I herded the gals up the walkway from the alley parking lot, past the cemetery, toward the garden between the church and the rectory. Millie's insistence that we stop at three different liquor stores and one supermarket en route in a futile search for a bottle of Imperial Whiskey had slowed us down, so I was surprised to see the lads as well as Lt. Taper and Sgt. Wickes gathered outside the sacristy door.

"Pierre, ladies," said Arthur, "there you are."

"More or less," said I. "What's up? The lights are on within, so why are you all without?"

"Father Baptist neglected one detail," said Jonathan. "He didn't give us a key."

"Isn't Msgr. Havermeyer around?" I asked.

"No doubt that was Father's assumption," said Edward. "But alas, no. Joel checked his RV a half-hour ago."

"I took a peek inside," said Joel. "He wasn't there."

"Maybe he's in the church," said I.

"Yes, that's what we thought," said Lt. Taper.

"But we've pounded on all the doors," said Sgt. Wickes. "Not a peep."

"Is Roberto Guadalupe's truck still out front?" I asked.

"Yes," said Arthur. "I'm parked right behind it."

"That means Duggo and Spade are probably here, too," said Joel.

"But locked inside the church?" said I.

"That," said Arthur, "or they've all gone somewhere else.   That would explain the bolted door, the lack of response."

"They wouldn't all be at Peanuts, would they?" I asked.   "It's open till midnight."

"Thought of that, too," said Edward.   "No, I checked."

"No lights on in the rectory," said Joel.   "I don't suppose they're all hiding in there."

"Unlikely," said Lt. Taper.   "Millie, do you have a key to the church?"

"In my dishrag-and-hand-towel drawer," answered she, wiping her mouth with the back of her hand. "Second from the top to the right of the sink.   But it ain't there."

"Why not?" asked Sgt. Wickes.

"So long as he and his men's been workin' in the church," said Millie, "Father had me give it to Señor Guadalupe."

"So what should we do?" said Jonathan.

"You're not going to raid my refrigerator," said Millie.   She sing-songed it, albeit vaguely, more or less adhering to the melody of "Sway."

"Good for you," said Kahlúa to Millie, then to the rest of us, "What would Fr. Baptist want us to do?"

"Something wise and obvious, no doubt," said Millie, "and utterly impossible."

"When in doubts or certains," croaked an unexpected voice, "I always most ways sayses the Rosary, that bein' the most pleasin' prayer there is."

"Is that you, Mrs. Magillicuddy?" I asked.

"I am's I is," said she, "and so my Willum and I always have believed and did according-wise."

"Hey there, honeybunch," said Kahlúa, wrapping her arm around our homeless addition. Mrs. M. must have been huddled on the end of the bench, draped in shadow. Now she was the center of attention.

"You must be freezing," said Millie, joining in as the gals had their own little clucking huddle.

"Not's any more's I ain't," said Mrs. Magillicuddy.   "You's all too kind's, you are's."

"She's right, of course," said Arthur.   "Father told us to pray inside the church. No doubt he would want us to pray outside the church as the obvious alternative."

There followed a hubbub of agreement.

"Kneeling, sitting or standing, ladies and gentleman," said I.   "Let us begin."

We had gone through the Joyful Mysteries as well as the Sorrowful, when it fell to Jonathan to lead us in the first Glorious Mystery, the

Resurrection. Out of the corner of my ear I heard a car pull up in front of the church, one of the wheels scraping against the curb. I'm pretty sure I heard car doors open and close, but I may have just expected it vividly. In between the rhythms of the Hails Marys I thought I heard voices, indistinct, several of them, reverberating round from the front of the church. It struck me as odd that they didn't approach, they just stayed out front, rising and falling in a rhythm counter to our prayerful recitation.

In any case, Arthur had just begun the Third Glorious Mystery, the Descent of the Holy Ghost, when all our attentions were disrupted by a thunderous, churning, cranking then pounding sound. It rattled the church and trembled the ground.

"Good heavens," said several of us, looking around and then up.

SPELUNKING SPINOFFS: We all knew what it was, this ratcheting engagement of gears and counterweights, seemingly played at half speed. The old clock in the steeple, supposedly jammed and dormant, chose that moment to rouse itself from its chronometric coma in order to strike the beam where a bell once hung with a gigantic wooden mallet. The last time it had chimed was the evening of 31 October. As Mr. Feeney is currently writing an account of the events in which we participated on All Hallows Eve, I don't want to include any "spoilers" here.

—P.B.

N.B.: Mrs. Magillicuddy's accent is a mystery to me. I have attempted to utilize Mr. Feeney's arbitrary approach to writing her speech patterns. I make no guarantees that if you read her comments aloud as spelled and contracted here you will sound very much like her.

"What time is it?" asked Joel.

"Two minutes to midnight," said Arthur, consulting his watch. "It's a little early."

"Or twenty years late," said Edward. "Who's to say?"

"Well," said Jonathan, "perhaps we should continue with the Rosary."

"There's the ticket," said Edward. "Hey—what's that?"

"What's what?" asked Arthur.

"Don't you feel it?" said Edward.

"I thought I heard something in the church," said Jonathan.

"Yeah," said Joel. "Me, too."

Indeed, as the ground seemed to shift under our feet, a strange sound erupted from inside the building. It was an eerie mixture of syncopated bangs, scrapes, and bongs. My guess is that the wrought-iron chandeliers were set swaying by the movement of the earth until they began colliding with each other. That would account for the swirling metallic clangs that were hardly bells. Out of this high-pitched caterwauler grew a low-frequency growl that actually shook the ground.

"Earthquake," said Millie, stoically grabbing Kahlúa's arm.

"It's the big's one, it is!" gasped Mrs. Magillicuddy. "Hold's onto your teeth's!"

"You said it!" agreed my editrix. "Mmmmmm HM!"

Several of us knocked and nudged each other as we flailed to keep our balance. The rumble grew quickly in intensity, gave us all a good wobble, then stopped suddenly.

"Whoa," said Jonathan after several long, strained seconds of silence.

"And how," said Edward. "What have we awakened this time?"

"You felt it, too?" gasped Millie. "I thought it was all in my head."

"Just the backwards part, Honey," said Kahlúa.

"St. Philomena's," said Arthur. "Where the fun never stops."

Gradually we became aware of the city sounds around us again. We collectively took a deep breath and let it out slowly.

"I hope the church is okay," said Joel.

"Maybe we should get some flashlights and check," said Arthur. "At least we can have a look around the outside."

"Hold on," said Taper. "Didn't I hear a car pull up out front?"

"Yes," said Wickes. "Just before the, um, whatever that was. Maybe somebody's come back."

"First there was nobodies, there was's" said Mrs. Magillicuddy. "Now there's somebodies."

"I hear several pairs of footsteps," said Jonathan.

"Whoever it is," I said, "here they come."

18(77)

CHAPTER EIGHTEEN, WHEREIN I WRAP THINGS UP AND SAY MY PRAYERS.

AND THAT, LADIES AND GENTLEMEN, as they say, is pretty much that, at least so far as my contribution to the story. If nothing else, it fills in what Martin Feeney missed due to his mishap, and what the rest of us were doing in his absence. I can't say that the general flow of the day's events was all that compelling in the dramatic sense, but it had some splendid highpoints, at least for me.

I got to meet His Eminence Cardinal Fulbright for the second time. I think this is the one we'll both remember in the months to come. "Ah-hah! That's when everything started spiraling out of control and burst into flames" would be preferable to "I behaved my-self—(yawn!)—so nothing came of it." At least there would be forward motion. Of course, I can see myself changing my mind about that when things start descending and igniting.

The sycophantic Bishop de Quet I could well do without, but it seemed that his attachment to our rickety archdiocese was a done deal. One thing about the hierarchy: there is an endless supply of increasingly depraved candidates champing at their respective bits. One wonders where they all came from, and whose bright idea it was to elevate them in the first place. But I digress.

Having walked a few yards in his moccasins, I developed a keen appreciation for Mr. Feeney, for the function he performs in the slap-happy occult-thriller sitcom in which we find ourselves trapped. I better understand now what it's like to shuttle Father Baptist around, to be his faithful sidekick, if only for a day. *Kimo Sabe,* Tonto's name for the Lone Ranger, meant "trusty scout," after all. If I didn't have other plans for my life, I could see applying for the job. No pledge for me, however. No way, no how—at least, not until I've put a lot more mileage on this chassis.

The ultimate highpoint of my Sunday was, of course, receiving Holy Communion at Mass, in spite of the fact that my attention was somewhat diverted at the time. The penultimate moment occurred during my visit to the Adoration Chapel at the Monastery of the Archangels, equally preoccupied I'm afraid. These things go without saying, but it is always good to remind oneself what is truly important, regardless of one's feelings, stresses, and distractions at the time.

As for the event that I was sure to tell others about, over and over and over again, that had to be the sight of Mr. Barlow pointing to the photograph of Half Dome in the Saranac Lounge. To have seen the same ghost in two successive days in different rooms of the hotel, that seemed significant indeed. A paranormal investigator's dream, a Tumblar's way of life. It doesn't get better than this.

Would that I could continue my story through to the events of Monday morning, but I was asked to end my tale at midnight. This I have done, and will go no further.

Throughout the Feast of St. Mechtilde, I had the company of Father Baptist, Millie, and Kahlúa Hummingbird—no stranger investigative team has ever been conceived let alone assembled. The Knights Tumblar came and went and came. They are my trusted friends, tried by more than one fire, and no adventure would be complete, let alone worth the trouble, without them. I must add that praying in the garden with the likes of Lt. Taper and Sgt. Wickes did much to allay my disconcerting feelings toward them. After all, aren't we fortunate to have them more or less on our side?

Several days afterwards I borrowed that little book, *Garden of the Soul,* from Father after he retrieved it from the Doily sisters. Under Night Prayers I found the following gem, which I now recite, rain or fog, clear-headed or not, just before bed each night:

> O my Lord Jesus Christ, Judge of the living and the dead, before whom I must appear one day to give an exact account of my whole life, enlighten me, I beseech Thee, and give me an humble and contrite heart, that I may see wherein I have offended Thy infinite Majesty, and judge myself now with such a just severity, that then Thou mayest judge me with mercy and clemency.

The point of each and every day, after all, is to do all we can to save our souls. This day was but one step in my quest. I pray that yours may be equally beneficial.

TO BE CONTINUED ...

Sunday, November Nineteenth

The Feast of Saint Mechtilde,
a Benedictine nun,
who received revelations from God
which her student,
St. Gertrude the Great, recorded (1310 AD)

78

ME AGAIN. SIR MARTIN FEENEY. "Parcifal Remembered," and all that. I want to thank Pierre Bontemps for filling in a rather humongous blank in my story—as far as I was concerned, anyway. Now I shall again take up the baton, or rather the Underwood, and start clickety-clacking my way to the denouement. (Ding. Carriage return; crank-crank. Tab: new paragraph.)

You may remember that while the Tumblars headed for the Blue Mountain Grill where Father Baptist, Guillaume du Crane Cristal, Roderick Roundhead, and the unfathomable, unstoppable, unpreventable, and undeniably anti-anodyne Doily Sisters were dining, I was being escorted by an older woman, the waitress who called herself Toni, to the car parked in front of the hotel. I don't remember getting into it, traveling within it, or getting out of it. I just remember that the door handle seemed wrong, the door to which it was attached was wrong, and the paint-job was black, which was also wrong. Three wrongs certainly don't make a right, but I didn't object because I blacked out on my feet. The next thing I remembered was waking up in the dark.

Well, it wasn't entirely dark.

In fact, it was rather well lit.

It just took a few minutes for my eyes to adjust, and my brain to take it in.

Bear with me.

Rising slowly from the silent depths of utter blankness like an intoxicated sea tortoise on its back, flippers flapping in slow motion, breaking the surface with a surge of brackish foam, the thing that I call me opened my eyes. I saw black, and felt worse. My synapses, deprived of ocular input, turned their attention to a systems check of the rattletrap I call a body. The report was not encouraging. My limbs and torso felt crushed, stepped on by some colossal foot, the heel of which had given me an extra twist for good measure, as if to sneer, "Remember Martin that though art bug!"

"Speak Lord," I thought and may have whispered, "for your servant heareth."

An awful, aching sensation throbbed all over the back of my shoulders, my legs, everything that was not the front of me. "Aha," reasoned those aforementioned synapses, "we are laying on our back on a surface that sends mixed messages. It is soft to the touch, as our fingers and palms attest, yet it is nonetheless rigid overall, as our back and limbs are swearing to so vociferously."

This information was strange for two reasons. First, I never sleep on my back. My spine has deteriorated in such a way as to no longer be suited for such a normal human position, not even on a cozy mattress. The resulting cramps and residual pain the next day aren't worth it. Therefore, I reasoned, if I wasn't curled like a question mark on my side, then forces other than my own had left me in this pain-producing position. Second, knowing my bed to be lumpy and bumpy though nonetheless spongy, but sensing this substance on which I sprawled to be superficially soft but fundamentally unyielding, I realized I hadn't magically somnambulated myself all the way home and into my cozy little cot. No. I was definitely someplace else.

The nerves in my lower right leg sent a confused message to my slowly accelerating cerebellum. Something cold and heavy seemed to be encircling my ankle, weighing it down, squeezing it like an icy claw. That made no sense, so the hierarchy of my assembling thought processes set that poser aside and returned to the problem of sight and sound, and where the heck I was.

Looking straight ahead, which is to say straight up, lights began to emerge from the encompassing darkness. There were nine of them, yellow and wavering, arranged in a circle. After counting them twice to be sure, I thought about that for a minute. Eight lights in a ring please the eye with their symmetry, like the points of a compass. Twelve work well, too, like the face of a clock; and Our Blessed Mother is often depicted with a halo of twelve stars. I used to know the significance of the number, but somehow I'd forgotten. Anyway, in the immediate, there were nine of them spaced evenly but not pleasingly around some sort of wheel. Nine makes the circle restless somehow, off center, out of balance. The wheel seemed to be swaying ever so slightly, as if it were suspended from something above it, but my blurred vision couldn't yet see that far. It could very well have been me that was swaying, not the wheel, except that swaying requires elasticity, a quality my body finds challenging. Nonetheless, it looked familiar, eerily so, but my mind didn't want to deal with the implications, the Will preceding the Intellect and all that. So I closed my eyes and tried to regroup, albeit lazily.

Then I heard it.

The chilling, hollow rasping of heavy metal links dragged slowly and erratically over a thick rug. It was accompanied by agitated panting.

"Oh no," I may have mumbled, "I'm alone with a hungry beast. Mother always said I'd end this way. Dad never explained why."

Not wanting to know, I clenched my eyelids. Not knowing being worse, I forced them open again. The circle of throbbing lights had been replaced, or rather occluded by, of all things, a face. The hair was disheveled, the eyes crazed, and the skin glistened with perspiration.

"Feeney!" whispered the parched lips. The breath was unpleasant, reminiscent of the acrid expulsion of Trads fastidiously observing the "Black Fast" during Lent. "Feeney, are you awake?"

"I don't know," said I. "Am I?"

"Wake up." I felt the clutch of twitching fingers on my right arm, then my left, followed by a not-so-gentle tug. "You've got to get up."

"Ergrmph," I grunted as I was pulled painfully to a sitting position. From this new perspective I could see red carpeting around me. My pelvis and attached parts screamed at the change of position, as did my ribcage, all my creaking joints, and every single vertebra in my wartorn spine. The cream floating on top of the effect was the storm of electric arcs zapping and crackling all over the soles of my feet, concentrating between my toes. The pain wasn't burning, it was electrifying, and incredibly distracting. A wave of dizziness gushed through me, constricting my guts and spiraling my perspective. "Whoa cowboy. Where are we?"

"I don't know," hissed the face. The hands let go of my arms. "Good God, I've no idea. They're nuts, that's all I know. Stark raving mad, I tell you."

"Who?"

"Them! The ones that brought us here. You can't imagine what I've been through. It's unspeakable, unbelievable, un—"

"Excuse me," I managed to interject. "Who are you?"

"Feeney! Don't you recognize me? I'm Monsignor Aspic!"

"Oh dear," said I, as a sudden swelling plume of nausea ascended within me. "Oh, oh—uuuurrrrrgggllk!" Luckily I managed to direct what I will not name off to the right somewhere and not onto my lap.

"Ew!" he grimaced.

"Urp," I concurred, closing my eyes to the muck on the carpet, wondering why human nostrils weren't equipped with lids of their own.

"Now you've done it," said my twitchy companion.

I managed to pry one eye back open. "It's not as if I intended it just for your inconvenience, Monsignor." I gave him a penetrating cyclopean once-over. "You'll pardon me for saying this, and believe me I do see the irony, but you don't look well at all."

"Yes. I mean, no. I mean never mind me." As he shook his head, his pudgy cheeks, now drawn and sunken, waddled like empty hot water bottles. "They won't like it, what you've done there. They'll punish you for it. You'll see what I mean. They're merciless. I can't tell you how many days I haven't eaten. There are no windows here, and they took my wristwatch."

"Haven't eaten?" That sounded serious. I opened my other eye. A skyrocket of sizzling sparks exploded in my neck as I swiveled my head to look around. I only managed about an eighth turn. Less. Yellow embers swirled around the edges of my vision, leaving ghostly trails in their wake. This glimmering activity effectively short-circuited my peripheral vision, so I wasn't able to assess my surroundings just yet. Gingerly, I held out my left hand in front of me. Encountering nothing, I moved my outstretched arm slowly leftward. My fingers encountered something cold and hard. It moved slightly, rattling like a metal gate. Curiosity trumping pain, I managed to turn my head ever so slowly in that direction. I saw that, indeed, my hand was resting against a low-standing wrought-iron gate, one of an ornate pair that met in the middle. They were set between two sections of equally low-standing wooden guardrails. Hesitantly, I turned my head a bit further. Even on the best of days I can't rotate my noggin a full ninety degrees, and this was not one of them. I could turn enough to see three sources of light at some distance, but my distance vision was still blurred so I couldn't tell how far away they were. I could barely make out that the one in the center was round, and the two outer ones were rectangular. They radiated a mishmash of vague colors and shapes. My throat burned from regurgitation, but I managed to rasp, "Are those stained-glass windows?"

"Yes, but that's not daylight coming through. There are lamps behind the panes. I saw one of them refill the oil when they brought you in."

Whimsical, then foreboding images danced around the inside of my cranial cavity. "Them" as giant slugs, then noire gangsters, mad scientists, and finally Siamese twins who both looked like Warden Gladys Tracy. Did they drag me? Carry me? Heck if I didn't feel as though they had driven over me in their car.

His words finally penetrated. No watch, no sunlight, and no meals to break up the monotony. I grimaced at the thought. Wasn't there an episode of *The Twilight Zone* that went something like this? I was beginning, believe it or not, to feel sorry for the man. Better for him than for me.

"It's disconcerting, as you'll soon see," said he. "Can you tell me what day it is?"

I shut both eyes and retreated inside my skull. It was cramped in there. Good Heavens, he expected analytical thought. Oh well, no help for it. Maybe if I humored him a while he'd go away. Peeling my parched lips open I asked, "How long have I been here?"

"How should I know?" he growled. "I told you, I don't have a watch."

"Then how can you expect me to tell you anything about anything? I've been unconscious." I felt my wrist, knowing what I'd find. "They took mine, too, whoever they are. Yeow! And now I've got a headache."

"We're never going to get out of here."

"Don't say that."

"We're not, I tell you. There's no escape, none, ever."

"Don't go there, Monsignor."

"Why not? It's where I am!"

"Not so, not so." I swallowed a painful gob of nothing. "Here, I can tell you this: you went missing Wednesday evening. We traced your movements to—"

"We? Who we?"

"Excuse me?"

"Who traced my movements?" Something in his tone made me risk another peek. A glimmer of hope rippled erratically across his face. "You and, and, and—?"

I nodded encouragingly, opening my eyes all the way. "Father Baptist is the other 'who' in 'we.' Who else? The cardinal ordered him to find you."

His eyebrows fell sideways. "To find that golden disk, you mean. That's it, isn't it? Or that stinking chalice."

"Well, let us say your disappearance, for whatever reason, ignited a blaze of pastoral concern on the part of His Elegance, Cardinal Fulbright. He phoned the rectory the very evening you disappeared." I tried to make that sound reassuring. It didn't work. "One prevailing theory, I'll grant you, was that you were nabbed for the artifact, but Father Baptist didn't buy it."

"Oh? Why not?"

"I'm sorry but my mind isn't clear, not that it ever was, but—whew! Would you mind if I stopped thinking for a while?"

"You said one prevailing theory. There were others?"

"I asked nicely."

"I wasn't kidnapped for the artifact. It wasn't with me. I'd left it with a jeweler for appraisal."

"As well as that so-called chalice for cleaning. We know. The jeweler was Edison Winger."

"You know—? So you really were tracing my movements. Good. Good!" There was a pause as he mulled that over. I was about to let my ponderous eyelids slide on down again when he made a painful sound, something between a choke and a whimper. He brought his fretful face and malodorous breath close to mine and said accusingly, "Then why are you here?"

I glared back at him, unable to answer—a rare moment. I noticed the elbows of his black clerical jacket were frayed, and his black pants a mite ragged. His Roman collar was crooked, too. It was hard to believe that this was the same man I'd so often described as "perky." Out of a glaring lack of Charity on my part, I had never taken Conrad J. Aspic seriously, not as a priest nor a man. Now, like it or not, I was caught in the middle of the direst of circumstances with him. I marveled that events could have drawn us together like this.

I haven't mentioned the word "fear" yet, not because I was plucky or courageous, but simply because my thinking was still too fuzzy to have arrived there yet. My mind wasn't clear, but it was struggling to get there. The gravity of the situation, like a determined salmon, was struggling furiously against the current of my overtaxed body's craving to shut down. If the carpet had been deep pile I might have curled up on the spot. I thought to take in more of my surroundings, but the idea was met with outraged objections from every extremity, with the counter-threat of a tsunami of nausea from my stomach in particular. The electricity in my feet was easing a bit, but those yellow embers were still swirling around my peripheral vision, adding to my dizziness. No help for it, I had to close my eyes. I did so. It was that or add to the mess beside me.

"Feeney!" demanded the monsignor, angrily. "What in bloody blazes are you doing here?"

That question again, and with added color. Well, there was no help for it. I had to say something. "You might say I'm reconnoitering."

"In other words, Father Baptist doesn't know you're here."

"Or you might say that."

"Aaarrrggghhh!!"

That brought my eyes open again, albeit unwillingly. "Suit yourself."

He was twitching spasmodically. "You won't be so glib when they get through with you."

"They who?"

"*Them.*"

"Ah, and what do them want?"

"Want? They're out of their minds. They're—oh my God!"

The sound of muffled voices emanated from the direction of the windows that weren't windows. They were accompanied by the echoing sound of shoes on stone steps. A new source of light appeared, or rather a gaggle of little lights—a handheld candelabrum, judging by its erratic movements. The voices clarified as their owners entered through a doorway. There seemed to be several females and one male, all of them croaky with age.

"They're here," whimpered the monsignor.

79

AS I PEERED TO SEE WHO *THEY* WERE, I heard the monsignor skittering away. As he did so something segmented and metallic clattered noisily along with him. The scrape of soles against stone, the muddle of voices, and that creepy candelabrum came nearer and nearer. To every threatening approach there is an equal and opposite desire to flee. Since flight was not an option—heck, standing was not even an option yet—the best I could do was to turn my head to my right, away from the impending danger. Beyond the stain of my reeking expulsion, I saw three carpeted steps, then a little flat space, then a large block of marble, like a sarcophagus.

This was all too much. Another wave of nausea rippled crazily through me. Determined not to throw up again, I clamped my eyes shut and tried to calm my insides. This was not so much a head-in-the-sand approach to the situation as it may seem. The fact was that my body, with all its spasms, pains, and protesting joints, was not much use in a physical struggle. This was a time to summon wits, not brawn, and I was deficient in both. More than anything I needed not to puke just then. Therefore the best course was to lie in wait and not see. At least, that was all I could think to do at the time.

And there was that "fear" thing which—hoo-boy!—had just kicked in.

"I'll bet they've been listening," moaned the monsignor, huddled in a corner. "Oh no, oh no, oh dear God, no."

The footsteps clopped and scraped right on up to the metal gate and stopped. Some withered part of my brain realized that the floor must be bare stone beyond the gate and guardrail. The gaggle of voices also ceased. The monsignor's pleas grew tinier until they dribbled into silence. I thought I smelled several clashing scents: lavender was the most prominent, gardenia for sure, and something else I couldn't quite place. Probably mothballs.

Several seconds passed.

"There you are, Mister Spleeny," sing-songed a crinkled female voice. "Back to the land of the living!"

"Shhh, Darling," answered another voice, just as wrinkled and equally irritating. "Think of where we are."

"Oh, you're so right, Sweetheart. Shhh."

They continued to talk just as loudly as before.

"Dear me, have a look-see over there, Darling."

"We've made a mess, have we? Someone's going to have to clean it up."

They paused, as if nodding a rehearsed count, and warbled together, "Your Reverence."

"No!" whimpered Monsignor Aspic. "He did it. Make him, not me. No. Please!"

"Is that any way to accept an Opportunity for Grace?" chided the first voice, all gooey and shrill.

"We can see you need another attitude adjustment, Monsignor," said the other, beyond gooey to cloying.

"NooOOooOOoo!"

"Your Reverence! Think of where you are! Did I tell him, or did I tell him, Darling?"

A wave of prickles rippled all over me, the painful mass-eruption of ice-cold sweat from thousands of pores, a psycho-tectonic reaction induced by an unsettling realization. I forced my eyes open yet again, not as an overt act of courage so much as a capitulation to the dread of, and a sinking acceptance of, the inevitable. I gave my head a good shaking, an action which cracked my neck and enraged my headache, but which drove those swirling sparks away so I could see more clearly.

Yes, as my reader has already surmised—doubtless long before me—I was sitting on the carpeted floor at the foot of the altar in a chapel beneath a stately old early-California house at 7214 Villanova Terrace with a statue of the Blessed Virgin gracing the roses in the front and Harrigan Doily's ingenious velocipede, the uncelebrated "Half Dome," which only an old geezer named Rudyard can properly service, parked behind. There was Monsignor Aspic compressed in the corner, a heavy chain attached to his right ankle by a ponderous steel shackle. The chain meandered around a bit, overlapped itself twice, but eventually curled around the edge of the open sacristy door and disappeared into the darkness within. If that wasn't bad enough, I had a clear view of an identical implement clamped around my own lower extremity. In my unconscious reluctance to accept the true nature of the situation, I had ignored the sensation on my right ankle, not to mention the sight of the thing as I sat there on the floor. It summarized the situation all too well.

Mehitabelle and Hortense Doily were my hostesses. They were both wearing electric blue blouses, black skirts, and white feather boas. A ponderous string of azure stones hung around Mehitabelle's neck, and Hortense was apparently attempting to lengthen her earlobes with gigantic black pearls.

"Antoinette," said Hortense. "Would you be so kind?"

"Of course, Mum," said the woman who had introduced herself to me in the Champlain Room as Toni. She was wearing a different dress, this one black with white frills, with a matching housemaid's apron and hat with white ribbon tied under her chin. More striking was the complete absence of facial makeup this time around, a reversal of the heavy-handed application when we first met. Frankly, I thought she looked better this way, craggy wrinkles and all. The limp I had noticed in the Champlain Room seemed more pronounced down here, perhaps enhanced by the dungeon-like ambiance of the place. "I'll leave this bucket here, and I'll go fetch some washrags and carpet cleaner."

"Excellent," said Mehitabelle. "Keating, I think we could all do with a spot of tea, don't you agree, Darling?"

"I couldn't any more if I wanted to, Sweetheart," said Hortense.

"I'll see to it at once, Mesdames," said their old and stately butler. Imagine him being in on this, too. And to think that I had told him with my very own mouth where to snatch me:

"Are you familiar with the Adirondack?" he had asked me upstairs in the kitchen.

"My high school held our prom there, but I haven't been since," I had answered, and then, like the fly to the spider, fatefully continued: *"By sheer happenstance, Father and I are going to be meeting someone there tomorrow evening in the Saranac Lounge."*

"Ah, the Saranac," he had said, playing his part. *"That's where I sometimes retire while Mesdames dine. It's a lovely place to drink and think. It's like something out of an old, familiar movie. Tomorrow evening, you say. Well, perhaps our paths will cross."*

Cross indeed. Collided was more like it.

"Splendid," said Mehitabelle. "In the meantime, let us remember that His Reverence has prayed for Humility, and his plea has been answered, hasn't it, Darling?"

"Why, yes indeed it has, Sweetheart, and oh so generously, thanks to Mister Spleeny."

"Father Baptist will find us," I whispered to myself as Antoinette curtseyed and Keating bowed. They turned and headed back down the aisle between the pews, she petite and limping, he creaking but stately. Of all possible Opportunities for Grace, this got some kind of award. "Father must find us. He will figure out where we are, somehow. There is no doubt in my mind. Not a speck."

"Keating, be sure to bring seven, thirteen, and twenty-seven," called Mehitabelle, "and perhaps the forty-two."

"Yummy yums," hummed Hortense, anticipating the combination.

"Right away, Madam," said the butler as he and the maid reached the doorway beneath the stained glass windows. I watched as the bobbing candles disappeared up the dark steps.

On the other hand, I reminded myself, Father had been quick to dismiss my misgivings about these old biddies, even after I'd been poisoned by them in their house right before his eyes. He, the great cop-turned-priest-turned-cop, had been taken completely in. I mean: where was he when whatever it was happened to me happened? Dining with the rickety witches at the Adirondack, flattering them with his refined pastoral smiles, chortling at their ludicrous anecdotes, nodding and grimacing at their tales of woe. That's where!

Yes, I realized that sending my thoughts along this narrow, winding trail was the psychological equivalent of shooting myself in the foot, but the brain steers down whatever rocky roads it wishes. Often I find myself a backseat passenger in a high-speed chase.

"Mister Spleeny and we are going to have a nice little chat, aren't we, Sweetheart?" trilled half the voice of doom.

"The nicest, Darling," tweeted the other half. "I just know he's going to fit right in."

"Of course he will, Sweetheart. Of coursey-horsy he will."

I so wanted to curl up and disappear. The most I managed was to scratch the carpet with the metal clamp as I tried to bend my leg. A couple of links in the attached chain clunked heavily. The sound triggered a memory, a conversation at the county morgue ...

> *"Though it was unlikely that our John Doe was incarcerated in our penal system, there are indications that he was, nevertheless, a prisoner."* That had been Solomon Yung-sul Wong impersonating Boris Karloff playing an Oriental sleuth in a flickering old movie, or so it seemed from where I was sitting.
>
> *"Come again?"* said Father, playing himself.
>
> *"See for yourself,"* said John Holtsclaw, the mystical shaman, lifting a corner of the sheet. *"The scarring around the left ankle denotes continuous abrasion resulting in the buildup of a considerable layer of callus."*

> *"A shackle of some kind,"* surmised Father, leaning close.
> *"More than likely,"* agreed Holtsclaw.

"Oh dear," I may have said aloud as the ol' grey matter, revving as it gathered confidence in its newfound clarity, started doing what it does worst: thinking. What did the body of a man in a cassock found in Saint Valeria's niche in the mausoleum at New Golgotha Cemetery have in common with the likes of me? Not just with me, but with Monsignor Aspic? A shackled ankle, that's what, and steel chain dragging behind. Uh-oh, there was more:

> *"How do you suppose it got there?"* That had been me while driving up the coastal route to Camarillo. "There" referred to the neck of said dead body.
> *"The Crucifix?"* That was Father Baptist. Four tenths of a mile further, he had added thoughtfully, *"Millie said Monsignor Aspic wore it at the press conferences ... at least we know that Christine's Crucifix was in Monsignor Aspic's possession yesterday morning."*
> *"Yet somehow it wound up on an anonymous corpse."*
> *"Sealed in a crypt no less."*
> *"Saint Valeria's yet. What are the odds?"*
> *"Astronomical. Still, it did happen."*

Holes were still gaping in the tattered web of mystery in which we dangled. The solution in the form of two crazed old ladies hovered nearby like a couple of fat spiders considering their writhing prey. The mystery of Christine's Crucifix, no doubt, would soon be unraveled. But another problem elbowed all these considerations aside. The question presented itself: how long had that old man languished in this place, living on bread and water, dragging a chain from his ankle? The answer was forthcoming: until he was long forgotten, until his hair tuned white and his skin wrinkled, until asbestos fibers from this historic old house permeated his lungs, until he died of a zillion complications at a very, very, *very* old age.

"Come, come, Monsignor," twittered Hortense, "your little task awaits you."

"It has your name all over it," chirped Mehitabelle. "Doesn't it, Darling?"

"In doo-deedy-doo, it does-ditty-does, Sweetheart. Antoinette did leave the bucket, did she not?"

"B-b-buh-but, but, but,"sputtered His Reverence. "She hasn't come back with the rags and—"

"Idle hands are the devil's playthings," admonished Hortense. "Isn't that right, Sweetheart?"

"Ever so, Darling," agreed her sister. "Heavens, Monsignor, we mustn't let the devil get a foothold, must we not?"

"NoooOOOoooOOOooo!" whined Conrad J. Aspic.

"*'De profundus,'*" I shuddered to myself, quoting Psalm One Hundred Twenty-nine. "'Out of the depths I have cried to Thee, O Lord …'"

80

"YOU'LL HAVE TO DO BETTER THAN THAT, Your Reverence, won't he, Darling?"

"Yes, certainly wertainly, Sweetheart, he really willy woo."

"Errrgh," groaned yours twoowy—I mean truly. "I'm sorry, Monsignor, for your inconvenience."

"Inconvenience?" he seethed where he knelt beside my mess, then roared with eyeballs glaring, "You call cleaning up your—" He slapped the splattered, sopping carpet with his bare hands, sending unmentionable flecks flying. "—an *inconvenience?* Why you—!"

"Temper, temper!" chided Mehitabelle Doily.

"Remember your manners," added Hortense Doily.

"*Smile,* Your Reverence," they gushed together. "God loves you!"

The two old gals certainly enjoyed being themselves. I doubt they could possibly imagine how utterly irritating their incessant, tremulant banter could be. Or could they? Did they perhaps revel in it a bit too much?

Monsignor Aspic, glaring up at his tormentors, forced himself to a quaking halt. Ever so slowly, he splayed his lips revealing teeth riveted between his clenched jaws, then maneuvered his flared labial aperture in my direction. "You have to do what they say, Feeney," he jeered at me out of the side of his mouth. "You'll see."

GARDENING TIPS: Saint Julian was born in the third century in Cilicia, what is now Turkey. During the persecutions of the Christians, he debated a magistrate named Marcian, whom he infuriated with his keen insights and dogged adherence to the Catholic Faith. As a result, Julian was tortured in various excruciating ways, but nothing could

shake his resolve. Finally, he was condemned to a
most imaginatively wicked death: he was sewn up in
a sack with scorpions, serpents, and vipers, and
thrown into the sea. I mention this because some
Saints have left us remarkable examples of courage, fortitude, and unwavering determination.

I, Martin Feeney, had not been called to face
such torments. My captors were not heathens but
devout Catholics, for one thing, and they weren't
sheiks or warlords or magistrates, but batty octogenarian prayer book publishers!

If chronicling my adventures with Father Baptist
had not become my refuge in my lonely battle
against pain in the wee hours, if my embarrassing
predicament were not such an integral part of the
tale, and if the eventual outcome were not so remarkable, I would gladly forego this discomforting
episode altogether. I pray for my readers' understanding, though as they are about to see, it was
my very writing that got me into this mess in the
first place!

--M.F.

"You hush now, like a good monsignor," said Hortense, giving him
a knee-cracking mini-curtsey. "We need to discuss the situation with
Mister Spleeny. Your self-control is about to be rewarded, Your Reverence. Is that the right word, Sweetheart? 'Self-control,' I mean."

"As good as it gets," said Mehitabelle cheerfully. "What do you
think, Keating?"

"Most assuredly, Mesdames," said the indefatigable butler who, having brought in the infamous tea paraphernalia on a huge silver tray and
set it down on the bench of the Epistle-side front pew, was in the process of opening the metal gates. They groaned a lot like I felt, and clattered like my vertebrae as he hefted me up from my awkward position
on the floor at the foot of the altar—a surprisingly strong fellow, our
Keating—and rocked me onto a creaking metal folding chair which
Antoinette had carried in along with an armful of rags and a bottle of
something caustic and lemon-scented. Said chair was set on the uneven
stone floor just outside the wrought-iron gates, facing the pews. I was
startled by the clatter of my ankle chain when it made contact with the
stone floor.

"Here you go, Rev," said Antoinette, handing the monsignor the
cleaning things across the Communion rail. It was apparent that none
of these ladies dared violate the sanctity of the Sanctuary. Only Keating, being male, dared enter there. Ah, did I hear the sound of feminists

grinding their teeth? No, that was Monsignor Aspic clawing at the carpet. Antoinette curtseyed and added, "There. That should make things easier."

"Thank-you," shuddered the monsignor, his facial muscles twitching from the strain of maintaining that Joker-like smile. "Thank-you ever so much."

"There, you see?" said Mehitabelle, looking up from her witch's teapot, into which she was shoveling eye of newt and wing of bat from those silver boats courtesy of the staff at the Blue Mountain Grill. "Do you think he sees, Darling?"

"Of course he does, Sweetheart," said Hortense. "Doesn't-he wasn't-he?"

My eyes were on Mehitabelle, but I could almost hear the monsignor's rubbery neck squeakily swiveling as he nodded his exaggerated assurance that he definitely diddy-widdy-gumdrops see whatever it was he was supposed to. I'm afraid I had lost the drift by then, and I became even more distracted when Antoinette produced a can of aerosol spray from one of the deep pockets of her fluffy apron and with three swishing hisses added the smell of pine disinfectant to the jumble of noxious odors hanging in the air.

"I would say he does, Mesdames," said Keating, who had stepped aside and was now standing at attention awaiting further instructions.

"Antoinette," said Mehitabelle, extending a saucer with a steaming teacup rattling on top. "Would you be so kind as to serve our guest?"

"Of course, Mum," said she, accepting it, turning to me with another of her curtseys, and pressing it into my unwilling hands. "Hair of the dog," she said to me, followed by a sassy tisk-tisk out of the side of her mouth. For a microsecond she reminded me of Gloria at "Peanuts."

"I'd rather not, if you don't mind," said I, reaching it back to her. The liquid in the cup was yellowishly pale and smelled vaguely of overturned earth. My hand was shaking so much the cup danced precariously. I can't imagine how the steaming tea didn't end up scalding my fingers.

"But she does mind, Mister Spleeny," said Hortense as Antoinette backed away, refusing to take the cup and saucer from me. "As do I."

"The name is Feeney, if you please," said I, attempting to steady the saucer on my trembling knee. It just wobbled all the more. Fortunately the cup was less than half full. The ominous broth within wiggled around crazily. There was no way I could have bent down and set it on the floor, not with my back, so rattle it did through the conversation.

"Feeney, Spleeny," said Hortense gaily. "Whoever you are, we're very upset with you."

"All will be set right, Darling," said Mehitabelle, pouring herself and her sister-by-marriage their own special brews. "Antoinette, Dear, would you mind trotting upstairs and keeping an ear out for the doorbell and the phone?"

"Of course, Mum," said the maid. Her voice belied a touch of reluctance at leaving this hair-of-the-dog moment, but she treated her mistresses to another of her subservient dips and headed down the aisle. The echoes of her lopsided trot up the stairs reverberated in the stairwell a moment later. Old she was, short of fluidity but long in stamina.

"Best to be careful, isn't it, Darling?" said Mehitabelle. "You never know when someone may pay us a call."

"He is twitching so, Sweetheart," said Hortense, eyeing me as she seated herself in the Gospel-side front pew.

"We'll soon fix that," said Mehitabelle, settling beside her sister gracefully with a teacup in each hand. One she gave to Hortense, the other she held under her nose, savoring the aroma. Then she looked at me, long and hard, and said, "Must you jitter so, Mister Feeney?"

"I beg your pardon," I managed to utter with a shudder as various parts of my body jerked spasmodically. "My joints are unused to being stressed as they apparently were during cartage here. I assume your maid spiked my ginger ale at the hotel. A fine thing to do to a glass of blue label."

"All very necessary, we assure you," said Hortense. "Wasn't it, Sweetheart?"

"To be sure, Darling," said Mehitabelle, "but nonetheless crucial. Keating apprised us of Monsignor Hammer-Wire's sermon. Are you in pain, Mister Feeney?"

Seeing no reason to confirm the obvious, and indeed being in more agony than I could remember, I shuddered and cut to the chase: "Crucial to what?"

"It will calm your spasms," said Mehitabelle, drawing a circle with her teacup under her nose. The chase was apparently something she was in no hurry to cut to. "You really must have some."

"Why?" said I, swallowing hard because I had nothing in my mouth to swallow. "First it was ipecac, then knockout drops. What's it to be this time, hemlock?"

"He doesn't mean it, he doesn't understand," groveled Monsignor Aspic.

I should have been touched that he was sticking up for me, but I was preoccupied with a sudden, sinking pang of hopelessness. The spasm that rippled across my face at that moment was triggered by the jolting reprimand I was giving myself for daring to let my feelings drift so far south of the equator. I searched desperately for a north-moving oceanic storm on which to hitch a ride. There was none.

"Careful, Mister Spleeny," said Hortense, positively mewing. "You are teetering on the cusp of discourtesy."

"It would seem that I am a prisoner of yours," said I. By "yours" I meant "your discourtesy," but the subtlety was lost. My teeth were clenched, not in anger, but against a particularly excruciating spasm in my lower back.

"He certainly dashes to the point, doesn't he Darling?" said Mehitabelle after a long, noisy-but-elegant sip from her cup. Though just as bubbly, her voice took on a chill. "Be it ever so humble, along with everyone under its roof, this is now your home, Mister Feeney."

"As far as your chain can reach," said Hortense, equally sparkling but also frosting.

The temperature dropped. The teacup on my knee rattled all the more.

"You need sustenance," said Mehitabelle.

"Your throat must be parched," said Hortense. "I know mine would be after such a whoopsy."

"Darling, don't be vulgar."

"Well, what would you call it, Sweetheart?"

I wished she hadn't mentioned it, because suddenly the thought brought the sourness in my mouth to the fore. The good monsignor accented the point by slopping a whoopsy-soaked rag furiously into the metallic bucket.

"Allow me to point out, Sir," said Keating from on high, "that there is no running water down here. Except for the air which God Himself provides, all consumables come hither only through Mesdames' diligent generosity, which is contingent on your congenial cooperation."

"In other words, if I don't obey, and with a smile, I don't—" I was interrupted mid-snarl by the sudden realization of a grave implication. "No running water, you say? Then what about ...?"

Keating cleared his throat and lowered his tone. "At the risk of in-delicacy, Sir, you'll find the chamber pot through that door, in the sac-risty."

"You mean ...?"

"Precisely, Sir." His smile was almost devilish, or maybe it was just too Irish. I was so negatively agitated at the moment it was hard to tell. I was also Hungarian, don't forget, and an underlying absurdity suddenly hit me broadside. I couldn't help it. I actually started to laugh. It hurt my dry, bitter throat to do so, as well as my aching skeletal assemblage, but the guffaw erupted involuntarily.

"He finds it funny, does he, Sweetheart?" observed Hortense.

"Apparently so, Darling," acknowledged Mehtiabelle. "Would you care for a lump of sugar?"

"Dare I, Sweetheart?"

"Oh, live dangerously, Darling. Doctor Ferguson doesn't know what he's talking about. Now, what may I ask is so funny, Mister Feeney?"

"Nothing much," I said, regaining control of myself. "At the risk of further indelicacy, the thought of me and my arthritis trying to ... oh, never mind. Father Baptist always says there ain't no Humility without humiliation. So when are you going to tell me what I've ever done to either of you that has provoked you to treat me this way? Or Monsignor Aspic, for that matter?"

"That's what we've been trying to explain, Mister Spleeny, isn't it Sweetheart?"

"Precisely, Darling. As I started to say, Keating heard Monsignor Hammer-Wire's sermon the other day, the one in which he praised you for helping him to learn all the — what do you call them, Keating?"

"Rubrics, Madam," said the butler. "Mister Feeney here coached him in the rubrics of the Latin Mass."

"So?" asked the gardener.

"Why don't you try your tea?" asked Mehitabelle.

"Because I'd rather not," I answered.

"I assure you it will calm your nerves, ease the jitters. Brew twenty-seven is good for that."

"Right, like I'm going to trust you on matters of my physical comfort."

"Suit yourself, Mister Feeney, but you're not going to get anything else to drink or eat until you do."

"Is that a threat?"

"It's a fact, Sir," said Keating.

"Well," said I a tad brazenly, indicating the sacristy with my thumb. "All things considered, nothing in, nothing out."

"Don't be crude, Mister Feeney," said Mehitabelle.

"You're the ones without running water," said I. "I'm waiting for why I'm here."

"He's certainly discourteous, isn't he Sweetheart?" said Hortense.

"So was Father Albert, Darling, at first. You remember, don't you?"

"How he fussed and fretted, you mean, Sweetheart."

"Screamed, you mean, Darling. He yowled and bellowed. Why, he ranted for days."

"Men can be that way, I suppose, Sweetheart."

"Well, we've endured it before, Darling. We must simply persevere."

"To be sure, Sweetheart. How else are we going to have a decent Mass to attend?"

"Precisely, Darling. We must keep our focus."

"Indeedy do, Sweetheart."

"Excuse me," said I, having pieced one piece of the puzzle together. They had mentioned a Father Albert who had graciously been saying

Mass for them when Father Baptist and I had visited this very chapel. "Are you saying you kidnapped Father Albert, that you kept him prisoner down here, to say Mass for you?"

"Why, of course, young man," said Mehitabelle. "Haven't you been listening?"

"It was after that horrid council," said Hortense. "You know, when the rot set in."

"Don't be vulgar, Darling."

"But it did set in, Sweetheart. You know it did. It was awful. Father Albert was the pastor at Saints Felicitas and Perpetua, just down the street, at the bottom of the hill and two blocks to the right. Or is it to the left? By then Catholic churches were closing down willy-nilly. And to think Roddy's grandfather helped build the place back in—"

"Focus, Darling. Focus."

"Oh yes, Sweetheart. Thank-you, Dear. You see, Mister Spleeny, suddenly Father Albert went through some sort of diabolical change. We can't explain it any other way. And it wasn't just him, it was, well, all of them. Archbishop McInery, the one who blessed my Miraculous Medal on the first anniversary of his appointment to the archbishopric, he had just retired you see, although by then he had been elevated to cardinal, and his successor, that awful man, what was his name, Sweetheart?"

"It doesn't matter, Darling, they've all been so bad since then."

"Too true, Sweetheart, too true."

"Out went the Latin Mass, Mister Feeney, as you apparently remember. Lord knows we tried to adapt, didn't we Darling?"

"Indeed we did, Sweetheart. But it was so distasteful. It wasn't just abandoning the Latin, which was bad enough, of course. It was the whole thing: that dissonant folk music, the positively horrid translations, embarrassing sermons. It got worse and worse."

"Out went the statues, remember that, Darling?"

"And the Tabernacle was moved to a dark corner off to the side."

"And then they destroyed the altar."

"With jackhammers, Mister Spleeny. Can you imagine?"

"And the confessionals, Darling. You remember what became of them!"

"As if I want to tell my sins to a priest face-to-face, Sweetheart, and in a sitting room, yet! How can one confront one's sinfulness in a setting like that?"

"Not to mention that the furniture in there was so tasteless, Darling. Beyond tasteless. In fact, taste had nothing to do with it."

"And the chalice, Sweetheart. Remember when Father Albert threw it out—threw it out, Mister Spleeny, like an old clock or a cut of spoiled mutton, out into the trash with it—and started using a clay cup instead? A crooked, lumpy old thing—to hold Our Lord's Precious Blood!"

"And a cheap plate, not gold, not even decent porcelain, for Our Lord's Holy Body, Darling. Don't forget that."

"How can I, Sweetheart? How can I?"

"And then, Mister Feeney—I shudder to think of it—Father Albert hired workers to tear out the Communion rail. They came in one day when Hortense and I were praying before the Tabernacle, begging Our Lord to stop the desecration. They didn't bother to protect the marble floor or anything. They just pried it up with crowbars and carried it out—in—pieces—!"

"That Sunday at Mass, Father told us from now on we had to receive Our Lord standing, and not on our tongues, but—in—our—hands—!"

The old ladies had worked themselves up into such a lather they could no longer speak. They sat there, faces twisted painfully, tears flowing, shoulders heaving.

```
GARDENING TIPS: In spite of my predicament my
heart did go out to them -- no, not "all out," but
a wee bit, on one wafer-thin level.  I had endured
the same sorts of maniacal changes in the days
when St. Philomena's was a thriving parish with a
convent of nuns and an elementary school besides.
Many were the hours I had knelt before the Blessed
Sacrament which had been relegated to a corner,
begging for the travesties to cease.  Never will I
forget the day the pastor, Monsignor Brassorie,
ordered me to remove the Communion rail.  Oh yes,
I understood the plight of my jailers all too
well.
                                        --M.F.
```

"We talked to Father Albert about it," said Mehitabelle presently, dabbing her eyes with a delicate hankie. "Didn't we, Darling?"

"You mean we tried, Sweetheart," said Hortense, setting down her teacup on the bench and wiping her cheeks with the backs of her hands. If she had been wearing makeup she would have ruined her face. "But the more we pleaded, the more he laughed."

"That's what he did?" I asked. "He laughed at you?"

"Like a hyena," answered Mehitabelle.

"Or a jackal," added Hortense.

"We came home in such a state, didn't we, Darling?"

"Indeed we did, Sweetheart. Keating's papa, Keating Senior, listened to us wailing in the car all the way. He took it as hard as we did. Antoinette, too, when we told her at home. She was younger then, as were we all, and so devout even then."

"It was that evening while at dinner it came to us, wasn't it Darling?"

"Indeed it did, Sweetheart, like a thunderbolt."

"What came?" I asked.

"Why, the idea," said Mehitabelle.

"The inspiration," said Hortense.

"We knew about this chapel down here, of course, didn't we Darling?"

"Of course, Sweetheart. It was from the Old Days, long before our time, when the soldiers came."

"When the Americans stole California from Mexico. History repeats, Darling."

"Indeed it does, Sweetheart."

"Keating Senior understood—he was my Fillmore's papa's valet, don't forget."

"Only too well, the dear man—and my Roscoe's daddy's, too."

"It took him several months, didn't it Darling?—one and the same."

"At least, Sweetheart—of course, the very same."

"This chapel had been used as a wine cellar for years. But, with Antoinette's help, he managed to refurbish it into the worthy place of worship you now see."

"And you, Sweetheart, you found your great-aunt's diary in an old chest down here."

"Including her recipes for herbal teas, Darling."

"And I helped you with the herb gardens, Sweetheart."

"And when we were finally ready, Mister Feeney, we invited him in."

"Father Albert," I said.

"The very same," said Mehitabelle and Hortense together. They smiled at each other, proud of their accidental synchronization.

"Father Albert had abandoned his Roman collar," said Mehitabelle.

"And his cassock," added Hortsense. "In fact, his black clothes altogether."

"He had taken up jogging, remember Darling?"

"With horror, Sweetheart. Imagine a priest in those obscene bicycle shorts—shameless he was, and such knobby knees—trotting around the neighborhood like, like, I don't know what like."

"It was about noon, Darling, and Antoinette was tending the rhododendrons by the bougainvillea we used to have down near the curb. She invited 'Just call me Al' in for a spot of tea."

"Fortunately none of the neighbors noticed, Sweetheart. At least, no one ever said they'd seen anything."

"God was on our side, Darling, and as you said, Antoinette was younger then."

"And Father had become more man than priest, I'm afraid."

"Don't be vulgar, Darling."

"But he was, Sweetheart, and you know it. So did Antoinette, and she had no one to confess to but him, don't forget. But that was later. First we made him cozy comfy down here, didn't we?"

"We certainly did."

"And no one could hear him scream."

"Which he did, frightfully."

"Interminably."

"In the end, pointlessly."

"I don't understand," said I, shifting uncomfortably on my chair. It creaked in protest. "If he had gone bad, why did you snatch him?"

"I don't much like your tone, Mister Spleeny," said Hortense.

"But he's right, you know, Darling," said Mehitabelle. "We did, you know. Snatch him, I mean. You see, Mister Feeney, we knew he'd remember the right way to do things. He'd been properly trained in the seminary and had said the Latin Mass reverently for several years. He just needed a little incentive."

"Incentive," I said, moving my right ankle just enough to make my chain clatter on the floor.

"You know, Mister Spleeny," said Hortense. "It's the little things, like food and water."

"We simply told him," said Mehitabelle, "that if he'd say the Mass for us in Latin, we would supply these necessities. If he refused, why, we wouldn't."

Both ladies heaved their shoulders grandly and fluttered their eyelids innocently. It was quite a trick.

"I told you they're nuts," mumbled Monsignor Aspic, knocking his bucket angrily.

81

"SO IN ORDER TO SURVIVE THE STORM," said the gardener, "you ladies kidnapped a wayward priest and held him prisoner down here. I take it he settled down eventually."

"Indeedy do he did," said Hortense. "Oh, he was a challenge all right, but Keating Senior bought only the sturdiest chain."

"And with so many churches selling their Sacred Vessels to antique shops," said Mehitabelle, "we had a field day, didn't we Darling?"

"A super-duper spree, Sweetheart. We even found cassocks and vestments."

"Roddy donated a few very nice accoutrements, don't forget, Darling."

"Yes, but that was much, much later, Sweetheart."

"Oh, you are so right, Darling. It was years later to be sure."

"So Father Albert had no choice but to celebrate the Latin Mass for you," said I, trying to keep the wobbling canoe that was this conversation headed up stream.

"Every single day," said Hortense. "Right here in our own home."

"Funny thing, wasn't it, Darling?" said Mehitabelle. "How he felt compelled to vex us with one of his own horrid sermons in the middle of his first Mass for us. As if he had anything on St. John Marie Vianney, or St. Francis de Sales."

"So we gave him theirs to memorize, didn't we, Sweetheart? Their sermons, I mean. To guide his mouth, and thereby, it was hoped, to steer his mind."

"For starters, anyway, Darling. Remember how he squawked when we gave him *The Mysteries of Christianity,* and told him to explain it to us, chapter by chapter?"

"It was certainly over our heads, wasn't it, Sweetheart? But he did give it his best, seeing as how he wanted to eat and drink, albeit simply. It was still way over our heads, I'm afraid, but at least the difference was clearer."

"Um ... I'm not sure that made sense, Darling."

"Does it have to? In any case, by then he knew better, didn't he, Sweetheart? Or certainly should have."

"Ah well, some men take time to break, Darling. I know my Fillmore certainly wasn't easy."

"Nor was my Roscoe, Sweetheart." Hortense heaved a wistful sigh. "But we can't be wives without them, and there certainly can't be the Eucharist without priests."

"No truer words were ever said, Darling. But you know, I think *The Soul of the Apostolate* was Father Albert's turning point."

"I do think you've hit it on the proverbial head, Sweetheart. We gave it to him on his second anniversary with us. He didn't just memorize it, he—how would you put it, Sweetheart?"

"He absorbed it," suggested the gardener. "Internalized it."

They glared at him for a moment of blessed warble-free silence.

GARDENING TIPS: Matthias J. Scheeben's The Mysteries of Christianity is indeed a tough nut to crack -- way over the thing I playfully call my mind, but well worth the effort. The Soul of the Apos-

<u>tolate</u> was written by Dom Jean-Baptiste Chautard
(no relation to our beloved Father John Baptist,
but equally challenging, not to mention rewarding). I understand that His Holiness, Saint Pope
Pius X, kept a copy on his nightstand. Very good
reading.

                                        --M.F.

"From what me father, rest his soul, told me," ventured Keating, whom I'd almost forgotten was standing there, "Father Albert, up until that point, had been unwilling, most unwilling."

"But he changed," said I, thinking of my own reaction to Dom Chautard's work several years before, but more so of the golden high-lights in the hair of the man found in Saint Valeria's crypt. "Instead of acting like a priest in order to eat, he became the priest he should have been all along. In fact, I would say he became saintly."

"How would you know that, Sir?"

"I saw him—or at least, I saw his body."

The Doily Sisters gasped.

"And how is it that you came to see him, Sir?" asked Keating, stepping closer, clearly perturbed.

"I accompanied Father Baptist to New Golgotha Cemetery where you hid his body," said I, looking the butler right in the eyes. "I'll admit it was a brilliant hiding place, but timing, as they say, is everything. You had no way of knowing the police would release the crime scene before the plaster dried. They found Father Albert late Wednesday evening, only a few hours after you sealed him in Saint Valeria's crypt."

"Oh dear," said the sisters together.

"Me profoundest pardon, Mesdames," said Keating, bowing to them, "if by me ineptitude I have placed you in jeopardy."

The sisters were too busy holding their breath and ruffling their feathers to respond. Another moment of warble-free silence. I truly hated to break it.

"Excuse me," said I, shifting my weight painfully around on the metal chair. I can't sit in one position for long without my skeletal system raising a ruckus, which it was. "This is no monumental leap on my part, but I take it that when you lost your personal Latin Mass provider, you grabbed yourselves another. Might I ask why you selected Monsignor Aspic to fill the void?"

"We certainly didn't want to deprive the world of a *good* priest," said Mehitabelle, exhaling bravely.

"Certainly not," said Hortense, equally courageous. "That would have been greedy, and we wouldn't want selfishness on our consciences."

Monsignor Aspic grunted unintelligibly.

"Father Albert's health was failing," said Mehitabelle. "It was obvious, wasn't it, Darling?"

"Oh yes, Sweetheart," said Hortense. "It most certainly was. Keating Junior here, perceiving the inevitable, and being a brave soul, had been attending what they now call Mass at various parishes for some time. He was—what is the word I'm looking for, Sweetheart?"

"I believe the colloquialism is 'scoping out,' Darling."

"That's it. He was scoping them out."

"I compiled a list of possible candidates," said Keating. "A ponderous list it was, too, if I may say so, Sir."

"I can well imagine," said I.

"But when Monsignor Aspic came along," added he, "I knew we had our man."

"It was as if the clouds had opened, wasn't it Darling?" said Mehitabelle.

"Or the ground opened up, Sweetheart. I think it was more like that," countered Hortense, separating her hands and extending her fingers by way of illustration. Then she brought them together in a gentle clap. "In any case, our prayers were answered."

"We heard him on the radio, didn't we, Darling?"

"Oh my, yes, Sweetheart." Hortense fluttered her fingers. "The things he said."

"And then we watched him on the telly—what a horror that has become, don't you think? We so rarely watch it anymore. Monsignor seemed to fit right in. He was on the news a couple of times, making statements on behalf of the cardinal about—oh, awful things."

"Awful, awful, awful," chirped Hortense in an ascending major arpeggio. "And then there was that horrid show, Sweetheart, the one with that obnoxious married couple—or were they divorced? I suppose it doesn't matter, not these days. And then just the other morning—the morning of, wasn't it, Sweetheart?—Monsignor Plastic said that dear, sweet Saint Valeria had never, ever been here at the cathedral, that she was just a hoax!"

"Aspic," hissed His Reverence, squeezing a rag over the bucket, or so I gathered from the sounds he was making. "Conrad J. Asp—"

"Okay," I interrupted. I may have said it a little louder than I'd intended, but I had to stop this endless jibber-jabber. The high-pitched trill of their crackling voices penetrated my ears like darning needles. My body was twitching, my head was aching, my attention span was waning and my patience was preparing to fling itself from a precipice. "Okay!"

They looked at me, startled.

I looked back at them, not sure what to do. Naturally, I took the worst course imaginable. I opened my mouth and let more words come out. "Okay, I understand about Father Albert—not that I approve, but I do understand. I even understand why you picked Monsignor Aspic, which makes me wonder what Toni put in my ginger ale. What I don't understand—not at all—is me. What in Heaven's name do you want with me?"

"I should think that would be clear," said Mehitabelle. "Shouldn't it be, Darling?"

"As clear as holy water, Sweetheart," said Hortense.

"Then please, Ladies," said I. "Unclear it for me."

"He's trying to be clever, isn't he, Darling?"

"I think so, Sweetheart. But with his sort, it's sometimes hard to tell."

"My sort?" said I.

"Never mind," said Hortense, knowingly. "You tell him, Sweetheart."

"Tell him what, Darling?" said Mehitabelle.

"Why, why him, of course, Sweetheart."

"Oh yes, Darling. I'll be glad to, Mister Feeney. You see, we discovered in short order that His Reverence here received his seminary training—how do I put this?"

"After the rot set in, Sweetheart. You know it did."

"Very well, Darling, after the rot set in. He knows no Latin whatsoever. He's only said the Novus Ordo in English all his priestly life. Imagine that. He thinks Gregorian Chant is some sort of rockish group."

"He's never heard of St. Alphonsus Liguori, either. Don't forget that, Sweetheart."

"That's right, Darling, nor of St. John Chrysostom, St. Ambrose, Padre Pio, or just about anybody worth knowing about."

"If I may say so, Mesdames, Sir," said Keating. "His Reverence doesn't know a maniple from a chasuble, an amice from an alb, or a paten from a purificator."

"He doesn't know the Epistle side of the altar from the Gospel side either, does he, Sweetheart?"

"There is no Epistle or Gospel side in the New Rite," said I, wondering how Monsignor Aspic felt being talked about this way. "It's not as though it's entirely his fault—"

"That's exactly what I'm saying, Mister Spleeny," said Hortense. "He's clueless! Hopeless!"

"But," said Mehitabelle, "when Keating told us of Monsignor Hammer-Wire's sermon about you, Mister Feeney, we knew all was not lost."

My lips formed the word, "Oh," but the rest of me couldn't muster the enthusiasm to get behind it. A cold sweat meandered all over my body like a herd of lemurs in search of a cliff from which to fling themselves. So, I thought to myself, I have Monsignor Havermeyer to thank for this. I wonder if I'll ever get the opportunity to show him my appreciation personally.

Just then the now-familiar sound of Antoinette's shoes came scuttling down the stairs. Old as she was, she could move, and move she did awkwardly up the aisle toward us. She slipped into the pew behind her mistresses and bent down so her head was between theirs, her mouth level with their ears. Between the rattling of the cup and saucer on my knee, the squeak of my folding chair, and Monsignor Aspic scratching and scrubbing the carpet behind me, I couldn't make out what she whispered. Whatever it was, the sisters nodded to each other knowingly, then turned their attention back on me.

"Your tea has grown cold," said Mehitabelle. There was pressure in her voice.

"Antoinette, Dear," said Hortense. "Would you be so kind as to bring Mister Spleeny's cup hither for a warm-up?"

"Yes, Mum."

"No thank-you," said I, looking down at the tawny fluid in my cup. No sign of steam. I didn't engage in a tug-of-war with Antoinette over the saucer and cup as she sauntered around and took it from me, nor did I lean to peer around her as she handed it to Mehitabelle. I thought I heard the word "twenty-seven," but couldn't be sure. A moment later the cup was back on my knee, this time three-quarters full and steaming anew. In the replenishing it had acquired an added scent reminiscent of citrus rind, but unlike any orange or lemon in my experience.

"That's a dear," said Hortense, I'm not sure to whom.

Antoinette gave me a meaningful, wry smile, curtseyed, and withdrew hurriedly to the rear of the chapel. She proceeded back up the stairs, this time less noisily.

I looked at my wrist to check the time. A circle of pink skin looked back up at me, reminding me that they had taken my watch while I was unconscious. I wondered what else they had taken. Surreptitiously, I moved a hand to my right hip pocket and confirmed that my wallet was also gone. At least my Scapular was in place under my shirt behind my necktie, and the beads of my Rosary were nestled in my shirt pocket. I felt a moment of panic when I brushed my left hip pocket and didn't at first feel the expected lump there, the reliquary wrapped in black cloth in which resided the tiny chip from the Crown of Thorns.

An anxious shift of my center of gravity revealed that it was indeed in my pocket, just shifted deeper under my adipose folds than usual. Whew. Perhaps they had limited their confiscations to the obvious worldly items: pocket money, watch and wallet.

Still, I felt sure there was something missing. Shouldn't there be a hard lump in my jacket pocket, too? The throbbing between my temples increased two notches, but it did come back to me: the clump of stone and mortar Father Baptist had picked up at the original site of La Purisima. It bothered me immensely that it was missing, but I didn't deem this the appropriate moment for a discussion on the matter.

"As we were saying, Mister Spleeny," said Hortense with a voice heavier than before, "Monsignor needs a tutor. You will teach him."

"Yes, Mister Feeney, you will teach him," said Mehitabelle. Unlike her sister, who stressed the word "You," Mehitabelle's emphasis landed on "will."

"Hold it, hold it," I said aloud to them, wanting more than anything to grab my head, rattle it, and make them all go away. "Monsignor Havermeyer was a willing student. He was old enough to remember the Old Rite from his youth. The situation was entirely different."

"Monsignor Plastic may not have memories," said Mehitabelle, again with that disquieting chill in her voice, "but we can assure you that he'll be motivated."

"Oh yes," said Hortense, vocal temperature falling drastically. "He certainy wertainly will be."

"Well, I'm certainly wertainly not!" The words were mine, and they even surprised me a little, under the circs. "What do you take me for? A liturgical slave?"

"Shuh-shuh-*shush!*" came a ruptured pressure cooker behind me named Conrad "Plastic" Aspic. "Feeney! You don't want to cross them!"

"What if I don't *want* to teach you the rubrics, Monsignor?" said I, not bothering to traumatize my vertebrae by trying to look over my shoulder at him. Don't think I was being brave, whoa no. Rather, let's say the Doily Sisters were asking the impossible, and I had indeedily done exceeded my certainly-wertainly limit of sweetheart-darling chitter-chatter. More than anything, I needed a handful of aspirin and a tall glass of ice-cold milk. Not likely. But my mind had something to say, and I wasn't about to stop it. "Rubrics, Your Reverence, are the actions performed by the priest during Mass—the Old Mass. They require effort, profound enthusiasm, and meticulous attention to detail. Their purpose is to inspire reverence and awe on the part of the priest and those in attendance, as well as to preserve and protect the Doctrines of our Faith. There is an old Latin saying: *Legem credendi lex statuat supplicandi.* 'Let the law of prayer fix the law of faith.' In other words, 'How we pray is how we believe.' Clearly these concepts are beyond you, or rather beneath you. You don't really want to learn them, and doing so under duress is hardly sufficient. If you'll forgive my candor, the Lord commanded that we not cast our pearls before swine. Saint Matthew, chapter seven, verse six."

Actually, what came out was not quite so well put, but it was roughly equivalent. I've had time since to reconsider my words and rewrite them. The effect was the same, however, and the equal and opposite reaction was equally and oppositely brazen, appalling, and unexpected. While the words were spewing from my mouth, both of the Doily ladies puckered their age-fissured lips in Keating's direction. The butler responded with a terse bow and a couple of stiff steps to a dark corner. Back he came with a broom handle. Yes, a broom handle. He held it at one end and aimed it at me like Sister Agatha pointing to a botched math problem on the chalkboard. What was he going to do, poke me with it? It looked silly to me, but Monsignor Aspic proceeded to whine more pathetically than he had thus far, making sounds like a cross between a cowering peccary and a startled parrot. I could hear his ankle chain rattling and dragging on the carpet.

"So," said I, weary of the whole business, "now I get a beating."

"No, Sir," said Keating. "Incentive."

With that he thrust the broomstick, not at me, but at Monsignor Aspic. The end of the stick touched the monsignor's left leg. In that unexpected moment, several details imprinted themselves on my optic nerves. First, I heard the plastic rattle of a cheap electrical extension cord on the stone floor—okay, that would be my auditory nerves. Then I saw the light switch, the kind you find mounted behind small rectangular plastic panels next to doorways in houses everywhere and available at any hardware store, attached with carpenter screws to Keating's end of the stick like a trigger. Connected to the switch were several feet of ordinary electrical cord fastened to the broomstick with unevenly spaced staples. The cord made its way down the stick to my end—or rather Monsignor's Aspic's end—at which point one of the two copper-twine leads was frayed and splayed like a tiny broom. There was a small flash of brilliant blue-white light as this made contact with the sniveling monsignor, who gasped and yelped.

He had encountered this homemade persuader before.

Keating gave him another encounter, and another.

"Stop!" pleaded Aspic. "I didn't do anything! Stop it! Stop it!"

"Okay," I said, but was drowned out by the monsignor's entreaty. I said it, or rather barked it, much louder. "Okay! Don't hurt him anymore. Damn it, I'll do it!"

"What in the naughty word did he say, Sweetheart?" warbled Hortense.

"Precisely, Darling," answered Mehitabelle. "A naughty, naughty word. But it's a first step, and in the right direction. And now our guest will drink his tea, won't you Mister Feeney?"

I looked down at the chilling brew wavering around in the cup still balanced on my knee. There wasn't a doubt in my mind that further refusal on my part would result in additional voltage applied to Monsignor Aspic. They had me. Whatever opinion I held of the man, God's opinion of me was far more important. Besides, my mouth was terribly parched.

"You said earlier that you were upset with me," said I, raising the cup to my lips with shaky fingers. I took a sip. It tasted exactly like water in which earthworms and dead spiders had been steeping, or so I fancied. My lips tingled and my tongue writhed involuntarily as I swallowed. My next words were squeezed by a spasm in my throat. "You did poison me the other day, didn't you?"

"Only a little," said Mehitabelle.

"And as you deserved," said Hortense.

"Oh," said I, feeling the wicked broth descending in my esophagus like a rickety elevator. What had Cheryl said in her cell? *You will be swallowed by darkness.* Yes indeed. That gal had an uncanny sense of the future, and it was now. And then there was that ethereal encounter with Elza Maplewood Roundhead in the garden. *And they cast him into an old pit, where there was no water.* Only tea, and foul-tasting at that. *Which of you shall have an ass fall into a pit, and will not immediately draw him out—?* What had I responded? Oh yes: *Ah ... I take it I'm the ass—*

"Do finish your tea," said Mehitabelle.

"It will do you good," said Hortense.

"What the hey," I said, and downed the rest.

82

THE NEXT THING I KNEW, I was rising out of the depths of utter blackness like an inebriated sea tortoise again. The first time, breaking the brackish surface of consciousness had been an intriguing if befuddling adventure. The rerun lacked these qualities.

This time I found myself deposited on my side. While my bones were grateful, my aching head was not. The right half of my face was pressed into the carpet, so I could only pull my left eyelid up over my swollen eyeball. Not that it mattered, because again all I could see was murky darkness. My stomach was a slowly swirling gyre on Winky

Weatherby's animated weather map on a very, very bad day. I swallowed hard, then hard again, determined to keep the whoopsy down.

With Herculean, or rather platypusian effort, I managed to roll myself onto my back. My ribs, vertebrae, joints, and other assorted renegade components that had refused to enlist in the Martin Feeney United-We-Attempt-to-Stand Brigade, all protested vehemently. I waited a minute for the blood to seep back into the right side of my face, then peeled that eye open, too. The ring of nine kerosene lamps I expected to see above me was not there. I blinked twice. It was like dragging leather bags both ways over mounds of sand-sprinkled asphalt.

Finally the steel wool inside my eyes parted just enough to let in the light of a single bobbing flame a few feet above me, off to the right. It resolved into a candle in an old-fashioned brass holder with a finger ring for a handle. The angle was problematic, but I gathered that this precious source of light was resting on the edge of a wooden countertop of some kind. I could make out drawer handles descending toward me in a neat row. Above and beyond was the mottled ceiling, and there I noticed something that gave me pause. The material was stringy and sagging, the kind of asbestos-rich coating once used as an insulating material in old buildings. I recognized it because we had removed substantial amounts of it from some of the rooms at Saint Philomena's back when Monsignor Brassorie was the pastor. This explained the carcinogen that the coroners found in Father Albert's lungs. I wondered how long an exposure it took to cause irreparable damage to one's respiratory tissues. Perhaps I would find out.

Then came the all-too-familiar sound of heavy chain links chafing on soft carpet. It approached erratically from the darkness to my left.

"Feeney," rasped a voice.

"Monsignor ..." I rasped back. What was his name? It took a moment for the gears in my head to grind out a name to connect with the title. "... Plastic."

"Aspic," he hissed.

"... Of course. Sorry." I rolled my head away from him, only to dimly catch the outline of something round and open on the rug a few feet from me. It took my addled brain a moment to identity it as a quaint, elegant-in-its-lowly-way, antique chamber pot. I will not assault my reader with the embarrassing images that thrashed through my quaking mind at the sight of that thing. Given the choice of annoyances, I rotated my head back to face the man who, through every fault of his own, was responsible for my being in this mortifying predicament—the man who, being the only person within asking, would soon have to help steady unwieldy, arthritic me as I endured the double degradation of the other humiliation.

Ohohohoooo, I prayed within. Why this, Lord? Why me?? Just plain *why???*

"It's about time you woke up," said the monsignor, his voice angry, viciously so.

"Brew twenty-seven," I managed to say aloud. My tongue was gravelly, and my lips felt like deflated tires. "Sure calmed my nerves."

"Knocked you out, that's what it did."

I brought my right hand up to my face and examined it, or rather its silhouette against the yellow corona of candlelight. "Well, I'll be," I said, letting it drop limply to my side. "It really did ease the spasms." Something in that simple action caused some sort of chain-reaction in my spine, like a multi-car collision on the interstate. "Arg," I said through clenched teeth, "but not the pain."

"Good," said he, and I didn't think he was referring to my alleviated spasms.

"Where are we now?" I asked as my skeletal rattles subsided.

"You figure it out." Boy, was he testy.

Puffing my cheeks as I exhaled noisily, I blinked the flakes from my eyes, rolled my head, and looked around as best I could from my position on the floor. Wooden countertop, drawers, wooden closet over there, recessed wooden door with wrought-iron bolts, a pitcher and bowl on a table, religious images on the stone walls ... yes, it was probably, "The sacristy."

"Brilliant, Feeney."

"I don't much care for your tone, Monsignor."

"I don't much like cleaning up your puke with my bare hands."

"Well, there is that."

I focused my attention on the single candle, reminding myself of something Saint Paul wrote to the Romans:

> And we know that to them that love God, all things work together unto good, to such as, according to his purpose, are called to be saints.

Eight twenty-eight. Many were the times that Father Baptist and I had discussed the implications of the first fifteen words, let alone the latter twelve. In the light of this insight, nothing bad ever happens to the believer. Ever. Father invariably derived a sense of peace from the notion, whereas I inevitably got the shakes. Like now. So much for the effects of the tea.

"Yeah, there is that," huffed my fellow prisoner, kneeling beside me. He held his hands up to his face, sniffed loudly, then jerked them around behind his back. "Yick! This is unbelievable. They say I don't deserve any soap yet."

"I'm sorry, Monsignor," I managed to say, steering myself away from what I really wanted to say. "I had no idea, and I couldn't have helped it if I did."

"Just wait'll they turn that damn cattle prod on you. We'll see how you like it!"

"See here, there's no need to be—"

"You and the great detective," he said derisively. "Look at you. Where is the celebrated cop-turned-priest now, when you really need him?"

"Cop-turned-priest-turned-copping," I said offhandedly. "I imagine he's trying to find me."

"Yeah, right. Just like *you* found *me.*"

I shut my eyes and swallowed. It hurt. "Your point, Monsignor?"

"You—you Traditionalists are all alike. You think you're so superior."

I opened my eyes again. "I hardly see what—"

"So bloody superior." He morphed his voice into a shrill warble. "'We discovered that His Reverence received his training—how do I put this?—before the *rot* set in! You *know* it did, Sweetheart!'" Actually, his Doily impression wasn't bad. It made the nerves constrict behind my eyeballs. "'He thinks Gregorian Chant is a *rock* group! He's never heard of St. Alphonsus Chrysalis, or Padre Pizza, or *anybody* worth knowing about! Imagine that, Darling! He can't tell his mandible from a percolator!'"

"Don't hold back on my account," I mumbled under my breath, struggling to hoist myself up on my elbows. This made my tummy bulge, my funny bones teeter, and my common sense wonder why I had bothered to bend my body into this awkward, painful position. Oh yes, I think it had something to do with wanting to converse with eyes on a level. His *mandible* from a *percolator?* I couldn't make this up. I wasn't about to correct him on the details.

"You think you're so holy," said he, reverting to his own voice, "but you just use your religion to camouflage your intolerance. You think only Catholics—your kind of Catholics—go to Heaven, as if God is as narrow-minded as you are." He paused, scrunched his forehead into a knot, and puffed out his cheeks. "They taught us about you in the seminary. You embrace such beliefs because deep down you want to see people you don't like go to Hell. You just can't stand the idea that others have moved beyond where you sit in the midst of your spiritual constipation. It's people like you who flew planes into the World Trade Center. It's people like you who strap dynamite to themselves and blow up courthouses."

As I managed to claw to a sitting position on the floor, the Tit-for-Tat Division of my cerebral cortex proposed a nasty zinger to my Retort Supervisor who wholeheartedly approved, but before the comeback could be sent down to Larynx Operations, my Ethics Administrator made a quick search of the Epistle of Saint James, and found the following in the third chapter, beginning at verse six:

> And the tongue is a fire, a world of iniquity. The tongue is placed among our members, which defileth the whole body, and inflameth the wheel of our nativity, being set on fire by hell.
>
> For every nature of beasts, and of birds, and of serpents, and of the rest, is tamed, and hath been tamed, by the nature of man:
>
> But the tongue no man can tame, and unquiet evil, full of deadly poison.
>
> By it we bless God and the Father: and by it we curse men, who are made after the likeness of God.
>
> Out of the same mouth proceedeth blessing and cursing. My brethren, these things ought not so to be.

Darn. I hate Scriptural passages that were written specifically for me. After a few milliseconds of deliberation, said spiteful rejoinder was nixed by the whole chain of command simultaneously. Whew! Just in the nick of time, a sin was thus avoided that not only would have stained my soul, but which I would have had to eventually confess to the very man who had just accused me of fanaticism of the most maniacal sort.

"Begging your pardon, Monsignor," I finally said. "We're both in the same section of this prison: the inside. Adding to each other's discomfiture hardly makes sense."

"Discomfiture? You just arrived. That cattle prod was only the beginning!"

"Funny you should mention that," said I, cleverly trying to turn the conversation in another direction. "Interesting, isn't it?"

"What is?"

"That they used it on you to persuade me. What does that tell you?"

He rolled that around behind his cheeks a few times, raised his eyebrows as far as they would go, and blurted out, "That you Traditionalists stick together!"

I suppose I deserved that. Still, I wasn't going to take it lying down, well, lying down but not seriously, taking it, I mean.

"Thick as thieves," said I, wiggling my foot so my chain would rattle. "That's why I'm tethered to the same wall as you, to show their solidarity with me."

"Well … they're also stark, raving mad."

"Mad in the sense of angry, Monsignor, not insane."

He blinked at me, amazed. "What're you saying?"

"You wouldn't understand, I'm afraid. They were robbed, Your Reverence."

"What are you talking about? They're rich."

"It wasn't their money that was stolen. It was their religion, or rather, all the outward signs thereof. In that sense—yes, I admit it—I am on the same page with them."

"I knew it," he said smugly. "You bet your life you're on the same page with them."

"Monsignor," I said, shifting my legs to redistribute the cramps in them, "how would you like it if Cardinal Fulbright ordered you—ordered, mind you—to move the tabernacle in your church from the side chapel to the front and center of the sanctuary, then demanded that you start saying Mass facing it rather than the people?"

A strange look of puzzlement rippled all over his face and settled in his lips. "But that would undo all the liturgical advances since Vatican II."

"I repeat, you have been ordered. Your opinion is of no consequence. His Eminence then enjoins you to abandon every inspirational song you have enjoyed all your life in favor of music in a style you adamantly dislike. And those splats of molten metal on the walls you call the Stations of the Cross? They are replaced with realistic woodcarvings. Those stream-of-consciousness homilies you so love to give on Sundays? All gone. No more woolgathering in the podium, no more spontaneous theology. From now on, you are to instruct the congregation from the *Catechism of Trent,* the *Breviloquium* of St. Bonaventure, and the works of Dom Marmion. As if that weren't enough—"

"Good Heavens, Feeney! Haven't you been paying attention? That's exactly what's happened to me, except the order didn't come from the cardinal. It came from two little old troglodytes and their household staff!"

"Precisely my point," said I. "Now perhaps, if you'd open your heart a crack, you have a chance to understand the plight of the Trads."

"I attended Father Baptist's Mass, remember?" said he. "A couple of weeks ago. I heard his sermon. I mingled with your parishioners on the front steps afterwards. He—you—all—believe that non-Catholics go to Hell. How you live with yourselves, I can't imagine. Feeney, you're a fanatic, you and your whole bizarre gang of irate, obstinate, self-righteous castaways."

"Excuse me, Monsignor," said I. "You're blathering. True, the parishioners at St. Philomena's are angry, but not without cause. Obstinate? Stubborn? Pigheaded? How else does someone hold onto what is theirs when the hierarchy sworn to protect them becomes a self-applauding ring of liars, pilferers, burglars, and graffiti artists? I'll tell you this much: with all their observable faults, no one at St. Philomena's has ever hijacked a plane and steered it into an office building or dynamited a courthouse using themselves as a walking fuse. As for personal holiness, if Father Baptist doesn't find us, by luck of the one-straw draw, you'll become my confessor."

"I don't follow you."

"My confessor. You know, there used to be a ritual called the Sacrament of Penance. Not to worry. Our hostesses will want Absolution, and they'll want it administered a certain way, and now that you're their personal shriver, I can guarantee as the dawn precedes the day that I will shortly be instructing you in that very administration. You will not only get to hear their deepest, darkest transgressions, but mine as well. On that strangest of days, you will come to know just how holy I truly am and think myself to be."

"Or want me to think you are," said he.

"Lying to you about such things here and now would merely be a venial sin, Monsignor. Deceitfulness in the confessional as you suggest, on the other hand, is a mortal sin. I don't know how to break this to you, but the fate of my soul concerns me more than your impression of me. Anyway, when that time arrives you will be in a position to deny me Absolution if I have not convinced you of my sincerity. In the meantime, allow me to address your accusation of intolerance. I've been accused of that before, as if believing in something defined by the Church is the same as gleefully wishing damnation upon those who disagree. Trust me, I'd rather there were no Hell at all, but Jesus Himself declared that most people go there. My faults are too numerous for me to assume that I'm automatically among the minority who won't. But as for the impossibility of those outside the Catholic Church going to Heaven, that has been defined infallibly by three, count 'em, three different Popes. The Council of Trent declared that without the Catholic Faith it is impossible to please God."

GARDENING TIPS: Don't take my word for it. I invite interested readers to check out precisely what those Popes (Innocent III, Boniface VIII, and Eugene IV) declared in Henry Denzinger's _Enchiridion Symbolorum_, a.k.a. _The Sources of Catholic Dogma_, paragraphs 430, 468-69, and 714. The Council of Trent's Decree on Original Sin is to be found in the same volume, 787.

> As for the oft-neglected opinion of our Founder,
> Jesus Christ, check out Saint Matthew seven thir-
> teen and fourteen, and Saint Luke thirteen twenty-
> three and twenty-four.
>
>   --M.F.

I took a deep breath and continued. "I take no pleasure in this, Monsignor. Indeed, I shudder just to think of it. But it is my duty to believe it, so believe it I do, all the while praying that those flailing in the storm outside would come inside rather than perish. Great missionaries like Saint Francis Xavier and Blessed Junipero Serra believed it, or why would they have left their families to spend their lives spreading the Faith to the farthest regions of the planet?"

Monsignor Aspic's face just about turned itself inside out. It hurt to watch but was so fascinating. "If I had any doubt before, Feeney, you have put it to rest. You are out of your twisted mind, do you hear me?" He brought his right hand out from behind his back and pointed at me with a smelly index finger. "If I ever get out of here, I'll see that you and your whole parish of mentally crippled maniacs and religious bigots are gathered up and sealed in a rubber room for the rest of your miserable, inflexible, inconsequential lives!!"

As I glared at him with my facial muscles stretched into an expression of utter exasperation, my Tit-for-Tat Division generated a truly malicious comeback, the zinger of all zingers, the mother of rejoinders. But before it could be passed up the chain of command, the Ethics Administrator, also known as my Conscience, flipped back to the Epistle of James. This time to the second chapter, the second half of verse thirteen: "'And mercy exalteth itself above judgment.'"

> <u>GARDENING</u> <u>TIPS</u>: Not to belabor the point, but
> there is a lesson to be learned here propounded by
> many a Saint -- Thomas a\ Kempis, for example, in
> his opus, <u>The</u> <u>Imitation</u> <u>of</u> <u>Christ</u>:
>
>   * * *
>
> We blame little things in others and
> overlook great things in ourselves. We are
> quick enough in perceiving and weighing
> what we bear from others; but we think lit-
> tle of what others have to bear with us.
> He that should well and justly weigh his
> own dealings would find little cause to
> judge harshly of another.
>   * * *

```
Sigh.
```

```
                                    --M.F.
```

"Mercy exalteth itself," I hissed through gritted teeth. "So much for my judgment, which God knows I don't assume to be running on all cylinders." So, instead of letting my opponent have it with both barrels, I stifled the urge. It was not easy, the delectable poisonous dart being cocked and ready just behind my lips. Instead, I practiced self-control by stretching my lips into the semblance of a kindly smile. "Tell you what, Monsignor. I'll promise to only throw up on myself in the future, if you'll cool it with the invectives."

On most occasions refraining from sin, at least for me, leaves me feeling at a loss. By that I mean something I wanted to have or to do I haven't taken or done, so I feel deprived, even cheated, and then guilty for having thought of it in the first place. This proves that I am anything but truly holy, but also that I may be on the way. This was one of those rare occasions when the avoidance of sin paid off in the tangible immediate rather than the intangible, ethereal future, and in the most unanticipated way.

Monsignor Aspic looked at me long and hard, and then suddenly burst into tears.

"Monsignor?" I asked.

He didn't just sob or blubber. The man was heaving—big, deep, uneven draws of air followed by painful, irregular expulsions of misery. Tears flowed from his eyes as if from overturned barrels of seawater.

"Monsignor, it can't be as bad as all that."

"Can't it, Feeney? Can't it?" He barely got those words out as spasms gripped his chest. Swallowing hard, he grabbed my arm. "Feeney, they made me eat my manuscript! You hear me? They made me eat my bloody manuscript!"

83

"'THREE DAYS OF BRIGHTNESS'?" SAID I. "The whole thing?"

"The first five chapters so far," said the Monsignor between distressed lungfuls. "Sixty-seven pages. At this rate it will only take ..." His voice trailed off as he did the math. He swallowed hard, smacked his lips, rolled his eyes, and finally said, "Wait a minute. How did you know?"

"Me? Oh, you mean the title. Well, it's as I was telling you before—I mean before before." A wave of nausea rippled through me. True to my word, I pulled in my chin and looked straight ahead in case the ups-and-overs came up and over. Thankfully, they did not.

"Yes?" said the monsignor between his own heaves.

"Huh? Oh, sorry."

"You were saying—?"

"Perhaps I was showing off a bit, Monsignor. It's an incessant temptation for bumbling associates of great detectives. But yes, I saw your manuscript."

"Where—? How—?" He was really gasping for air.

"Father Baptist and I were retracing your movements, remember?"

"So you said, but—" He couldn't finish his sentence. The man needed distracting or he was going to suck his trachea inside out.

Did I mention my brain was aching? I doubted I would be much help to either of us, but I had to try. I tried to cross one leg over the other, but the chain made that awkward. I was still sitting on the floor, don't forget. The best I could do was to wiggle myself so my back was against the wooden drawers. One of the knobs dug into my right shoulder blade, but I decided that further shifting was only going to make it worse.

"On the day you vanished," I began, "your driver, David Smoley, drove you from your residence at St. Philip's to the Chancery, where you held a press conference. Seven in the morning, as I recall, which means you arrived at six-thirty. It is your tendency to show up a half-hour early."

His eyebrows did a little wormy dance as he took all that in, and his gasps ebbed to a low, labored wheeze. I thought I even caught a glimpse of appreciation in there for Father Baptist's thoroughness, perhaps a glimmer of hope. "That's right," he said. "Go on."

"You held a second press conference at the Del Agua Mission. Millie was not impressed with your comments about St. Valeria, by the way."

"Millie? Who's Millie?"

"Our housekeeper. You met her on Halloween. She watched you at Muriel Cladusky's."

"Muriel—?"

"Muriel Cladusky. She has a television. We don't have one at the rectory."

"You don't? Why not?"

"Father Baptist says he wants to get to Heaven. Anyway, you then visited Thurgood T. Turnbuckle at his residence, made a stop at a photocopy shop—forgive me if the name escapes me—then headed back to the Chancery where Cardinal Fulbright entrusted the papal artifact into your care."

"And that stinking chalice."

"The very one. From there you did a drive-thru at Bongo Burgers. The greasy wrappers were still in the back seat of your car. In all fairness to young Smoley, he said he intended to take your Mercedes to the carwash but Father Baptist insisted that he forego that."

Monsignor Aspic's face did a spasmodic dance at the second mention of his chauffeur, but let it pass.

"Then," I continued, "you had tea with a couple of sweet little-old-lady publishers who have since become our keepers and tormentors. I take it that was when you presented them with a copy of your manuscript?"

He expression turned queasy, and he began rubbing his upset tummy.

This being the very point from which I was attempting to distract him, I blundered forward. "That was just before you dropped said artifact and malodorous chalice at the establishment of Edison Winger—the golden disk for appraisal, the cup for fumigation. I understand Mister Turnbuckle recommended him."

That last bit of information only made it worse. He gripped his abdomen and produced a sound a frog might make as it was run over by a wheelbarrow. Perhaps he was experiencing a Saint Matthew six twenty-four moment—two masters, and all that.

"What then?" he grimaced.

"If I haven't forgotten something or gotten events out of sequence—you do lead one heck of a complicated life, at least compared to mine, except when Father and I are out retracing yours—anyway, that brings us to Way True Life Publishers, and your manuscript, 'Three Days of Brightness: How to Survive the End of the World.' I noted that your pen name is C. Jonas Aspic, without reference to your sacerdotal status."

"Yes, yes, yes!" Success. He let go of his stomach and began nodding his head.

"Let me see." I scratched my chin. "Oh, the proprietor's name was like your car: Mercedes. Mercedes Sinclair."

"That's right. He understood. He said my book had genuine potential."

I really should have thought it through before I replied: "Um, I hate to pop your bubble, Monsignor, but he wasn't interested in your book."

"What?!" I thought each of his eyebrows was going to collide with its opposite nostril on that one. "You don't know what you're talking about."

"Probably not, but he told Father Baptist he only wanted your title."

"My title?"

"He said he was going to add a word to it—I believe it was 'golden'—and paste the result on another manuscript by someone else who doesn't have your knack for titles."

"I don't believe it."

"I may be mistaken. There was a lot of confusion when the police showed up and arrested him right there in his office."

"Arrested him? For what?"

"Mr. Sinclair was a serial killer, wouldn't you know. He had a penchant for priests. How did someone there put it? Oh yes: 'the liberal, whacky, self-contradictory sort; the kind who write syrupy, self-involved memoirs about their personal spiritual pilgrimages.'"

I admit that was uncalled for, even if accurate. Words fail to convey what his eyebrows and nostrils did then, and the words that erupted from his mouth are not fit to repeat. I'll substitute something comparatively benign:

"You're full of hooey, Feeney."

"No doubt, Monsignor, but according to Lieutenant Taper, Mercedes Sinclair left a trail of mutilated clerics all the way from Washington DC to Glendale, Utah. The police found your manuscript in the storeroom at his office, and his explanations regarding his activities did not satisfy them. So they figured you to be his latest victim, your excoriated body as yet undiscovered. Father Baptist did his best to convince them otherwise, but without success. He was hampered by a gag order placed on him by your boss, Cardinal Fulbright."

"Do you mean the police are no longer looking for me?"

"Judging from their faces when they left, I'd say not—at least, not alive, and not with any enthusiasm."

"Well, that's just great." He repeated that several times as he began rocking like a child who had just been unfairly scolded.

"It could have been worse, Monsignor." Realizing I had done such a bad job of distracting the man that I couldn't remember what it was that I was supposedly distracting him from, I blundered unconfidently on. "Let's see," I said, rubbing my throbbing forehead. "Then it was off to the offices of Bendlebrain, Cruiser & Wedge for a round of public perception, crisis management, and tergiversation."

"You saw Willis P. Wedge?"

"The 'Wizard of Spin' himself. He confirmed that your disappearance was not a publicity stunt."

"Excuse me? Is that what you thought it was?"

"Me? Never. Nor did Father Baptist. Still, he had to be sure. Of course, taking the word of a man who keeps a picture of Antonio del Corro on his wall, well ..."

"Who?"

"Mr. Wedge claimed him as his ancestor by intention, philosophy, and objective—though not by blood."

"I'm not following you."

"It doesn't matter. Tergiversation—you gotta love it. Or at least, His Impenitence the Cardinal sure does. I just wonder how the average Catholic in the pew would feel, knowing how the money they toss into the basket is really being spent. I wonder about that a lot. Oh well, anyway, back to your movements. From BC&W, David Smoley drove you to the KLIE television station where he parked your car at the far end of the lot. Smoley stayed in the car while you got out, but you never made it to the celebrity entrance."

"What are you talking about?" His rocking ceased, but he began wagging his head wildly from side to side. "Smoley didn't take me to the television station."

That brought me up short. "He didn't?"

"No. He took me back to St. Philip's so I could get my sick call kit."

"Oh … That explains the glass vial Father Baptist found in the back seat. I'm confused. Why did you need a sick call kit?"

"Because someone was sick, of course."

"Of course. Someone at the television station?"

"Not the television station! I told you, Smoley didn't take me there."

"Sheldon and Eira Levant were expecting you, as was Napolia Crackerjack and a million—"

"That's Krackershak."

"Right, and a million adoring fans."

"Of course, but there was plenty of time, and I couldn't very well say no."

"Say no to whom, Monsignor?"

"To those Doily witches. Back up to when I gave them my manuscript. They told me they had a houseguest, an elderly priest, who was terribly ill, probably dying. They asked if I could give him Extreme Unction. I told them we don't call it that anymore. Then I advised them to call the pastor of his church, but they said this priest was from out of town. I suggested they call their own pastor, but they said he was playing golf. I told them I didn't have my sick call kit with me, that I'd have to go fetch it, and I wouldn't be able to return for several hours. I'd never done it, you see. Death makes me—you know—it's so upsetting. I was hoping they'd call another priest, but they were insistent, and I didn't want to offend them."

"No, of course not. Not if you were hoping they'd publish your book. Um—"

"What?"

"Isn't the proper procedure to query one publisher at a time, I mean, get their answer before submitting your manuscript to the next?"

"Is it? I wouldn't know."

"Oh. So let me see if I've got this straight. You went from the Chancery, via Bongo Burgers, to the Doily Sisters. After assuring them you would return with a sick call kit, you then pressed on to Edison Winger's, Way True Life Mutilators, the Wizard of Spin, then to Saint Phillip's for your sick call kit and back to the Doilys. It was there you administered the Last Rites—"

"You mean the Sacrament of the Sick."

"I actually mean Extreme Unction, but let's not belabor the point. So about this sick priest. Was he old—I mean very, *very* old—with lots of wrinkles and white, white hair with golden highlights?"

"I suppose."

"You suppose? Didn't you notice?"

"I had other things on my mind."

"Oh, of course. Your book, your appointment schedule, your appearance on 'Religion Revisited.'"

"Look, Feeney, I'd never administered the Sacrament of the Sick before. I hardly knew what to do. I was nervous, out of my element. My degrees were in management efficiency and organizational psychology. My skills are hardly pastoral."

"Didn't they instruct you in the seminary?"

"Just once, on one of those dummies they use to teach you CPR in first-aid classes."

"You're joking."

"No, I'm not. You can wipe that condescending smirk off your face, Feeney. They didn't stress it, so I didn't learn it. How was I to know?"

"I should think just being a Catholic ... Oh, never mind. I don't want to give any more credence to your negative perception of Traditionalists. Okay, so what about this very old priest? Was he the Father Albert they were talking about?"

"Yes, apparently. He was on the couch in the living room. I heard his Confession, and I started going through the motions of anointing him as best I could. He ended up telling me what to do. He was patient and even kind, and he seemed to know his end was imminent. I didn't even have holy water with me, and I didn't think to bring Holy Communion—"

At least you still call it that, thought the dizzy gardener, who then asked, "And the Crucifix?"

"Excuse me?"

"The Crucifix Father Baptist gave you on Halloween—black enamel Cross, golden Corpus, stainless steel chain."

"Oh. Yes, that was strange. When I first leaned over him he opened his eyes and focused on it. I was wearing it around my neck. He could hardly move, but he managed to reach up and touch it with his fingertips. It seemed to give him strength, so I transferred it from my neck to his. He was frail, so thin—weak."

At least you noticed that, I thought, and responded to it charitably. There's a spark of good in you despite your efforts to conceal it, Monsignor, and lo, it was repaid in kind. I then asked, "Then he told you what to do?"

"Sort of. Pointed, mostly. In the end, *he* blessed *me*. Hardly moved his hand, but I got the message."

"Then what?"

He sighed. "Then they invited me into their office, a room with lots of windows and tons of manuscripts, and offered me a cup of tea. They said they wanted to talk to me about my manuscript."

"And?"

"The next thing I knew, I was here—where ever this is."

"It's under their house. Deeper down than a mere basement."

"How do you know?"

"They brought Father and me down here—or rather there." I pointed to the closed door. "They gave us a guided tour."

"No."

"Yes. I assume you were locked away, here in the sacristy, at the time, drugged no doubt. Keating said he didn't have the key to the door."

"I wasn't drugged."

"No?"

"I've learned my lesson."

"The cattle prod?"

"Among other things. And Keating lied to you about the key. It's clipped to his suspenders."

My mind was inundated by vile possibilities at that moment, a surge that tripped a circuit breaker down in the basement of my cranial cavity. Then as the system rebooted it hit me, the memory of my own words exchanged with Father Baptist in the fragile safety of the Jeep as we drove toward Hollywood a few days before:

> *"Who besides the cardinal knew he was carrying it?"* Father had asked, the "it" referring to the papal artifact.
>
> *"David Smoley, you think?"* That was me, and the tone was a tad sarcastic. *"I don't trust him."*
>
> *"Neither do I. He's nervous, severely bruised, and probably dishonest. On the other hand, he lacks the stuff of overt criminal action."*

> *"You mean he'd more likely cover for an indiscretion than per-*
> *form one."*
> *"Something like that."*

Well, well, well, I chuckled to myself. David Smoley had more pluck than we thought. He was in on the kidnapping. But of course: Roderick Roundhead owned him. "Roddy" was Hortense Doily's dutiful nephew. He surely knew about their subterranean chapel. It was inconceivable that Roderick didn't know of his aunt and aunt-in-law's permanent houseguest down the hidden stairs. So David left the Doily house in the Mercedes. He needed to establish his story of the abduction, so he drove to the KLIE parking lot and must have placed a call on Monsignor Aspic's cell phone. *"See you at nine, but don't expect me to be very sharp after tonight."* That was a complete fabrication. David probably just hit "redial" and—yes, of course: the seventeen-second call to Bishop deQuet. What message had Morell left on Monsignor Aspic's answering machine?

> *Con*rad ... *"*Con*rad,* are you *there? Please* pick *up* if you *are.*
> This is *D.K.* You didn't *leave* a *mes*sage. I really *must* speak *with*
> you. ... *Please* call *me* back, hm? ... Con*rad? ..."*

You didn't leave a message. The bishop's answering machine probably had caller ID—yes, I've heard about such things—and he recognized Monsignor Aspic's number but found no verbal message. David Smoley just left a few seconds of silence. It was significant that he thought to do it, knowing that the position of a mobile phone is traceable. Was he sophisticated enough to come up with that? Naw. Which raised something to consider: Did David receive his instructions before, during, or after the sick call visit to the Doily Sisters?

My train of thought was interrupted just then by the grind of a key in the lock and the metallic growl of the latch on the door being lifted. This was followed by a wooden moan as said door opened slowly, revealing the figure of Keating, cattle prod in hand.

"Mister Feeney," he said with a slight bow. "Mesdames would like to have a word with you."

"Sure," I said jovially—a strained joviality, I'll admit, but a hearty attempt. "I hope they don't mind standing. There aren't any chairs in here."

"Fire and brimwater," said he with a wry smile. "You know very well, Mister Feeney, that they cannot enter the sanctuary, therefore they cannot come in here."

"What are you telling me, Keating?"

"You must come out to them, Sir."

"And if I don't want to?" I'll admit my joviality was slipping precariously.

"Don't even think it!" shrieked Monsignor Aspic. "Shut up, Feeney! I've had enough of that blasted broomstick. Keating, don't! Keep away from me!"

"I haven't moved an inch in your direction, Your Reverence," said Keating. "But as you can see, Mister Feeney, Monsignor Aspic does get the drift of the situation."

"I'll say this," said I, grunting and groaning to my feet. "Your methods are certainly effective."

"Thank-you, Sir."

"What about me?" whimpered Aspic.

"Please be so kind as to remain in here, Your Reverence," said Keating. "You might try praying, if I may be so bold."

84

"SO TELL US, MISTER FEENEY," said Mehitabelle Doily when we were seated as before, me folded in the unfolded metal chair, my keepers glaring at me from the front pew, Keating standing to one side, and Antoinette upstairs attending the phone and doorbell. "When you look at us, my sister and me, our maid, women in general, do you really wonder if we're—how do I say it, Darling?"

"With your eyes closed and teeth clenched, I'd imagine, Sweetheart," said Hortense, nodding sympathetically.

"You're right, of course, Darling." Mehitabelle actually scrunched her eyes, gritted her enamels, and ground out the words: "Mister Feeney, do you wonder if we're ... *ovulating?*"

A wallop on the side of my face from a hurling banana cream pie at that moment could not have surprised me as much. If I had made a list of questions they might ask me this time around, single-spaced and reaching all the way to the moon and back, this particular query would not be among them.

"I ... I beg your pardon?" I ventured.

They just glared at me. I glared right back. The question made no sense.

"Well?" they said together after close to a minute of perplexed aphonia on my part.

"I can't begin to imagine what you mean by asking me such a thing," I think I said, or words to that effect, maybe. I certainly couldn't remember ever looking at a woman and thinking such a thing, at least as an adult. I can't vouch for those hyper-hormonal adolescent years during which I thought a lot of things best jettisoned and forgotten. But even if I currently did think such things, I would certainly have bypassed Mehitabelle and Hortense, the nannies-turned-witches, and their maid-turned-kidnaptrix, Antoinette, on the basis of age. Nonetheless, topper of poppers, here was Mehitabelle asking me such a thing. What in Heaven's name was going on?

"It's right here in your book," said Hortense, holding up a handful of photocopied typewritten pages.

I blinked at least a dozen times. "Did you say my book?"

"It does say 'The Endless Knot' on the first page," said Mehitabelle, scrutinizing that sheet in particular.

"And 'by Martin Feeney' under that," said Hortense, pointing. "That must be your pseudonym, Mister Spleeny."

"Excuse me, Ladies," I said, fighting a sinking feeling that was permeating my being. "Might I ask how you came about having a copy of my manuscript?"

"That dashing young man, Pierre Bonbon. He gave us your manuscript to consider, didn't he, Darling?"

"That's absolutely right, Sweetheart. He even discreetly neglected to ask about it last night, Mister Spleeny, while you were already tucked away in the trunk of dearly departed Harrigan's Half Dome."

It took me a minute to process that.

"Just when did Mister Bonbon give it to us, Sweetheart?" asked Hortense.

"A week or so ago, wasn't it, Darling?" answered Mehitabelle. "He was so enthused about it—and it had Roddy's nod, to boot—so we read it that very night."

"We passed it back and forth, reading it aloud, didn't we Sweetheart?"

"That's the best way, Darling. You can't really tell about a book unless you read it aloud."

"As far as we got, anyway, Sweetheart."

"As much as we could stomach, in any case." Mehitabelle patted her sister's hand. "Why, by the time we got to the scene on the church steps after Sunday Mass, you were turning pale, Darling. Utterly pale."

"And your hands were clammy, Sweetheart," said Hortense with a shudder. "It was quite an ordeal ..."

I missed what they said next because I was drawn back in my imagination to a conversation held in the wee hours in the garden between the church and the rectory amidst the compelling fumes of *Lacrimae Christi:*

> *"In my case,"* Pierre had said, *"you were hoping I would use my influence as a journalist to persuade a couple of publishers to look at your opus with an open mind."*
>
> I had asked in reply, *"And did you?"*
>
> *"Did I what?"*
>
> *"Give it to a couple of open-minded publishers?"*
>
> *"A couple of publishers, yes. The openness of their minds remains to be seen. I haven't heard back from them yet."*
>
> *"Let me know when you do. I can add their rejection letters to my collection. It's impressive."*

A couple of publishers, yes. Yes, indeed. The image of my fingers enclosing Pierre's neck did intrude into the stream of my consciousness, but I banished it with a shake of my weary head.

"It's right here in Chapter 24," said Hortense, squinting at the page in her hands. Her craggy lips writhed in distaste as she uttered the forbidden words:

```
    Oh, what the heck?  Three strong women are more
than  equal  to  one  flighty  bishop,  aren't  they?
Appearing  at  the  ovulating  side  of  the  sanctuary
were  Mss.  Margaret  Dukes,  Madeline  Sugarman,  and
the  unsinkable  Stephanie  Fury  as  the  charcoal-clad
squad  of  extraordinary  Eucharistic  ministers.
They  more  than  filled  the  vacuum.   With  what  I
won't  say.   The  thought  occurred  to  me  that  they
might  do  a  rock  video  and  start  a  new  career  as
the "Altar Belles."
```

"Aren't you just a wee bit ashamed of yourself?" asked Mehitabelle, her voice a sneer from the bully at the top of the playground slide. "Three women you deem the 'Altar Belles'—bad enough that they're so Novus Ordo, but even so—when they gather at one end, that part of the church becomes the 'ovulating side'? Really, Mister Feeney."

"Begging your pardon, Ma'am," I said, the words and pages of my text whirling around inside my head. My Guardian Angel knew how hard I had worked on that description, and I didn't like it being misrepresented, especially by a certainly-wertainly Doily Sister! "You are misreading that paragraph. The 'ovulating side' is an extension of a metaphor which was introduced back in—ooh, my head—I think it was Chapter 8. A couple of paragraphs in, I believe."

Actually, it turned out to be the third and fourth paragraph of Chapter 9. Hortense having suffered through the hurried search, and after several false starts, endured even more unspeakable agony as she read aloud my description of St. Philip's Church:

```
    . . . we had just gone through a drive-thru for
lunch and Father was sipping a soft drink through
a straw.  We were passing by in the car when I
looked up and said, "Ah, that must be St. Fallo-
pia's."  Coke came out his nose.
    The anterior looked exactly like a biology text-
book frontal cross-section illustration of the hu-
man female reproduction facility—right down to the
bell-tower bulges which were dead ringers for ova-
ries.  I can't imagine anyone seeing the structure
and thinking otherwise, yet I've never heard any-
one else mention it.  One of our city's most glar-
ing and obviously cherished secrets.
```

"This is not amusing, is it, Darling?" said Mehitabelle when Hortense finally paused to take a few deep breaths.

"Not to my knowledge, no, Sweetheart," gasped Hortense.

"Good," sighed Mehitabelle. "For a moment there I was beginning to wonder."

"Don't you see?" I said, seeing as I did that they didn't. That's why my explanation came out as a series of questions: "Saint Philip's? Shaped like—well—like a woman's insides? Alternating ovulation? The Altar Belles were standing on the ovulating side?" I wrapped it up with two explanatory sentences: "It's not about them! It's about architecture!"

"Since when is architecture about ovulation?" asked Hortense.

"That was precisely my point," I said. "It shouldn't be, especially in the design of a church."

"Then why even mention it?" asked Mehitabelle.

"Because it's *there*," said I. "I draw my stories from life."

"Like many things in life," said Mehitabelle, "the matter is entirely inappropriate. Wouldn't you agree, Darling?"

"Inappropriate, Sweetheart," gasped Hortense. "My very word."

"Inappropriate," I huffed. "How?"

"I should think it would be obvious, wouldn't it Sweetheart?"

"Shouldn't it, Darling? Obviously."

"I'm afraid," said the cross-eyed gardener through gritted teeth, "you'll have to explain it to me."

"Very well," harrumphed Mehitabelle. Yes, harrumphed. Well, what passes for such in the high-pitched warble category. "This reference to a woman's … *fallopian tubes*. There: I said it."

"Better thee than me, Sweetheart," tittered Hortense.

"It's a *play* on fallopian tubes," I insisted. Or rather a play on an *allusion* to fallopian tubes."

"But," said Mehitabelle, "linked to ovaries, it is nonetheless a reference, isn't it, Darling?"

Hortense squinted at the pages in her hand. "As would be a—these are your very words, Mister Spleeny—'frontal cross-section illustration of the human female reproduction facility,' wouldn't you agree, Sweetheart?"

"It's entirely indecent, Darling. That is what it is."

"Excuse me, Ladies," said I. "Have you ever driven by there? Saint Philip's I mean. You tell me what the place looks like, if not just as I've written. There's a reason my friend and yours, Monsieur Bonbon, declined to attend a wedding there once. He's the sort who goes to such events in formal attire."

"I'm not a bit surprised," said Hortense. "Not the teeniest."

"That he didn't attend, Sweetheart?"

"That he would dress to the nines, Silly."

"The point," said I, "is that he refused to enter the front of a building wearing a tailcoat."

"Mister Feeney!" barked Mehitabelle.

"His very words, not mine," said I.

"Is that a double entendre?" said Hortense. "Are you trying to be clever?"

"It isn't working if you are," said Mehitabelle.

"Strange," said I. "I thought it worked perfectly. You are both reacting as though it did."

"We both have the good moral sense to be disgusted," said Mehitabelle. "If that's what you mean."

"Fine," said I. "But be disgusted with the church, not my description of it."

"Good Heavens, Sweetheart," said Hortense. "Mister Spleeny apparently feels it's appropriate to be inappropriate."

"But two wrongs don't make a right, Darling," said Mehitabelle.

"And inappropriateness, after all, Sweetheart, is inappropriate."

A pang of dizziness rippled through me. Writers, I've been told, need to develop thick skins about their work, otherwise they suffer severely when the inevitable critics start masticating their words. I had anticipated parts of my manuscript arousing ire and contention in some quarters—for which I even had a few snappy rebuttals prepared and waiting in my pocket—but not "Saint Fallopia," arguably the best punch line in the whole book!

"Excuse me, Ladies," I said, admittedly stiffly. "Just what is inappropriate about it?"

"Have you no sense of propriety?" growled Mehitabelle. "Such descriptions—how do I put this?—induce impure thoughts, especially in men."

"I don't know how to break it to you," said I, "but, much as we men may find you women alluring on ever so many levels, I would have to say that, with the exception of Hannibal Lecter, we are simply not aroused by thoughts of fallopian tubes and ovaries."

"What would you know about such things?" said Hortense.

"Well …" I began, thinking the answer obvious. Then I stopped. The look in their eyes left no room for doubt. I'd seen it many times on the faces of pugnacious parishioners on the church steps after Sunday Mass. This was not to be a discussion with minds at a level. The word "rational" did not apply. This was a reprimand without recourse, and Keating was indeed standing ready with that broomstick cattle prod contraption. "Hoo-boy!" was all I could think to say.

"Hannibal who?" mouthed Mehitabelle silently. It had been a stretch to think that these ladies would have been familiar with *The Silence of the Lambs* by Thomas Harris, or Anthony Hopkin's cinematic portrayal of the demented gourmet.

"You are deceiving yourself, Mister Spleeny, but not us," said Hortense, shuffling the pages in her hands. "Listen to your own words two paragraphs earlier:

```
    I can only hope that unsavory conclusions won't
be drawn regarding two men, albeit experienced in
the ways of the world and having left most of it
behind, who nonetheless shared the perception that
the church at the corner of Dominion and Delmonico
was shaped like . . . uh . . .
```

"That, Madam, is what is known as a literary device," I said. "It's called extending the build-up, delaying the punch line."

"Not so," said Mehitabelle, gingerly nudging her white hair with her palm. "It's called admitting that your thoughts are impure before revealing them. And how dare you draw a sweet, innocent priest like Father John into your insidious perceptions?"

Father Baptist? I thought. Sweet? Innocent? He was once the Chief of Homicide for Pete's sake!

Hortense took in a deep, quivering breath. "Not to mention your preoccupation with—dare I say it, Sweetheart?—the *occult.*"

Oh dear, I thought. The "O" word! Oh dear, oh dear, oh dear.

"'Wide eye do dat?'" read Hortense from a furiously clutched page. "'Fortunes untold, bones read, potions for all occasions … Guillaume du Crane Cristal, Proprietor.'"

"William of the Crystal Skull," translated Mehitabelle. "What kind of sorcery is that?"

"Is a crystal skull like a crystal ball, Sweetheart?" asked Hortense.

"Probably, Darling," said Mehitabelle, sighing unknowingly. "More than likely."

"You I can see cavorting with such a one, Mister Spleeny," said Hortense. "But Father John? Hardly."

"When you sup with the devil," said Mehitabelle, "it is best to use a long, long spoon."

"You two should know," said I, a tad impatiently. "You dined with him last night at the Blue Mountain Grill."

"What's that you say?" gasped Mehitabelle and Hortense together.

"The dark fellow with the rattling dreadlocks," said I. "Guillaume du Crane Cristal, also known as Willie 'Skull' Kapps."

"I thought he was Roddy's guest," said Hortense. "Wasn't he, Sweetheart?"

"That he was, Darling. That he certainly was."

"Your nephew sups with short spoons, apparently," said I.

"You have infected him with your wickedness," said Hortense, seething.

"On these filthy pages," said Mehitabelle, holding up a handful.

"I merely report what I see and hear," said I.

"Oh?" said Hortense. "Is that really *all* that you do? He thinks that, does he, Sweetheart?"

"Perhaps he believes it, Darling, but we know better, don't we?"

"He is devious, Sweetheart. Even that robust Mister Bonbon was taken in."

"Excuse me, Ladies," said I. "'The just is first accuser of himself.' Proverbs eighteen seventeen. Believe me, I accuse myself of many, many things in the confessional every other day. Like most of us, I tend to fudge in my examination of conscience, but—"

"Two Chapter 32s," said Mehitabelle, stopping me dead in my tracks. "That says it all, doesn't it, Darling?"

"It doesn't get more devious than that, Sweetheart," said Hortense.

"What are you talking about?" I asked, my mind racing until sparks spurted from my ears.

"You know good and well, Mister Spleeney," said Hortense. "No other chapter number in the book repeats. And if that's not enough to convince a jury, who ever heard of a book starting with Chapter Zero?"

"I beg your pardon," said I. "Convince a jury of what?"

"I actually thought the second one was a joke," said Mehitabelle.

"The second Chapter 32, you mean," said Hortense.

"The very one, Darling. In the second one the parishioners are bickering on Sunday morning in front of St. Philomena's after Mass. It breaks the flow of the story and makes Traditional Catholics look, well, like, like—"

"Disagreeable people, Sweetheart?"

"Roddy called them 'a pack of yapping Chihuahuas' last night, Darling."

"Oh, yes," said Hortense, hiding her chuckle behind her upturned hand. "I remember when he said that. Sweetheart, I told him to watch how many martinis he drank."

"I should say, Darling. He certainly watched himself drink a great many."

"I'm afraid I wasn't there," said I. "Let's see, that's right about when your maid was stuffing me into the trunk of your car, which, by the way, explains the throbbing throughout my body. I'd sure like to get a gander at her shoehorn! But please, if we may return to something before it slips away. I'm referring to the two Chapter 32s. You're not joking."

"Never about our work," said Mehitabelle. "Isn't that not so, Darling?"

"What about your tea?" said I. "What do you call lacing it with ipecac?"

"I would say 'fitting' under the circumstances," said Hortense. "Wouldn't you, Sweetheart?"

"Beyond 'fitting,' Darling," said Mehitabelle. "All the way to 'appropriate.' Consider it a mouth-washing from the stomach out, Mister Feeney."

"That's why you poisoned me?" I said, eyes no doubt wide. "To punish me? For my manuscript?"

"Someone certainly had to," said Hortense.

"What about 'Seek not revenge'?" said I. "Leviticus nineteen eighteen."

"'Thou shalt not hate thy brother in thy heart,'" replied Mehitabelle, "but reprove him openly, lest thou incur sin through him.' Verse seventeen."

"Consider yourself reproved, Mister Spleeny," said Hortense.

"Openly, Darling," said Mehitabelle.

Imagine me, Martin Feeney being scripturally one-upped by a couple of old geezerettes!

"Actually, Mister Spleeny," said Hortense gaily, "your tea was—'poisoned' seems too harsh a word, don't you think, Sweetheart?"

"I would say 'tainted,' Darling," said Mehitabelle.

"Excellent, excellent," said Hortense. "Your tea was 'tainted,' Mister Spleeny, because bad taste deserves to taste bad. I'm referring to your horrible book, of course."

"Plus," said Mehitabelle significantly, "you get a foretaste of what we can put in your drinking water, and that's all there is for you to drink. Isn't that right, Sweetheart?"

"Absolutely positively," said Hortense, gathering the pages in her hands and bringing them close to her face. "Now, lest it slip away—as you put it, Mister Feeney—regarding the repeated chapters numbers, I shall quote from the first Chapter 32:

```
"There are three criteria for becoming a Knight of
the Tumblar," Pierre was explaining to Joel Ma-
ruppa.  "The first, of course, is that you must be
a practicing Roman Catholic, upholding all that
the Church teaches, even those irksome things
which elude your present understanding."
```

"From there," said Hortense, looking up from the crumpled sheets, "it goes into the specifics of having a 'good time.'   It's a treatise on overindulgence of the worst possible kind, Sweetheart, if there ever was one."

"Men," said Mehitabelle disgustedly.

"I believe you have the second Chapter 32, Sweetheart," said Hortense.

"Ah," said Mehitabelle, scrutinizing a different handful of pages. "Yes, here we go. 'Chapter 32 …

```
   "You're walking on dangerous ground."  Mr. Turn-
buckle was standing on the steps in front of St.
Philomena's, his finger leveled at Father Bap-
tist's nose.  "How dare you accuse St. Thomas
Aquinas of error, and from the pulpit?"
```

Yes, I recognized both chapter beginnings. I should have checked the numbers when I proofed the last draft. It simply hadn't occurred to me. No more simple, honest, unimportant mistake could ever have been made by mortal man, and yet ...

"At first," said Hortense, "we thought the second Chapter 32 was a joke, all this nonsense about Traditionalists squabbling on the church steps."

"Surely you couldn't be serious about the awful things you said about Saint Thomas Aquinas," said Mehitabelle. "We used to publish a condensed large-print version of his *Summa*, didn't we, Darling?"

"Indeedy we did," agreed Hortense.

"As I recall," said I, "it was Father Baptist who was serious."

"And poor Threety," said Mehitabelle. "It's a crime how you portray him. Simply a crime, isn't it, Sweetheart?"

"I should say so," said Hortense. "'Arrogant know-it-all' indeed!"

"Are you saying he's not?" I asked. "Are you seriously saying that he's nothing like I portrayed him? I find that puzzling because I didn't use his real name!"

"We didn't read any further, did we, Darling?" said Mehitabelle.

"Not on your life, Sweetheart," said Hortense. "Two 32s was quite enough, thank-you."

"Hold it," said I. "Are you saying you didn't read the rest of the book?"

"We didn't have to," said Mehitabelle. "Did we, Darling?"

"Nor did we wish to," said Hortense. "In fact, Mister Spleeny, yours is the only manuscript we did not see through to the end, so horrible are the implications of the first thirty-two chapters—or should I say thirty-three?"

"Thirty-two equals thirty-three," said Mehitabelle. "Surely it's connected somehow to the Masonic Lodge."

"Or something equally deplorable, Sweetheart," said Hortesne. "'I know: maybe it's that 'diabolical disorientation' Roddy keeps talking about."

"You could be right, Darling. Things that aren't what they are pretending to be what they aren't, but numbers never lie."

```
GARDENING TIPS: Important announcement should I
ever have any readers: It was at that very moment
that I decided if I ever got out of there I would
absolutely positively insert two Chapter 64s in my
next book, for no other reason than orneriness.
Or could it be that I have an ulterior motive
about which I am unaware?  Does the truth have any
```

bearing whatsoever? Did Erle Stanley Gardner have
days like this?

—M.F.

"In any case, Mister Spleeny," said Mehitabelle, gathering her own pages and her sister's into a hefty bundle, "we must make sure that this manuscript of yours never sees the light of day."

Oh great, I thought. I have awakened in a Stephen King novel, and one I didn't like nearly as much as *The Shining*. "By all means," said I, almost beyond caring. After all there were several copies floating around out there somewhere. "Do you wish to grind it up to make brew eighty-six, burn it to heat the teapot, or is it to provide my daily requirement of fiber?"

"A chapter a day," said Mehitabelle.

"Perhaps two," said Hortense. "Yours are so much shorter than Monsignor Plastic's."

"Yum," grumbled the polymerized monsignor, peering around the edge of the sacristy doorway.

"Monsignor," said I over my shoulder. "Won't you join us for dinner?"

85

"KEATING, IT OCCURS TO ME," said I some time after that, "that I see no transformer on that zapper of yours. You realize that you could kill someone with household current like that."

"Don't," said Monsignor Aspic, who was now standing just within the sanctuary gates. It was quite a trick not getting our chains entangled, let me tell you.

"Don't what?" I asked.

"Call attention to it."

"It's already the center of attention, I would say."

"But you're not the one they keep electrocuting."

"So far," said I. "God help me, so far."

"I appreciate your concern, Sir," said Keating, wielder of the dreaded broomstick. "Can't say I truly understand the technology, but I have it on good authority that as long as the contact is restricted to the lower extremities, the current will go to ground through the feet. The danger is sending the current through the heart by contact with the torso. This is something I fastidiously avoid."

I thought of the nagging tingling in my feet and imagined how passing 117 volts through them would enhance the effect. It was only a matter of time before my keepers would require something of me that would necessitate the application of that broomstick to the lower extremities of my less-than-august personage.

"Keating," I said aloud, "I can only hope that you will not ask me to do something immoral, for I really don't think I could stand a jolt from your staff of obedience."

"Then let us hope, Sir," said he, "that we both agree on what is and isn't moral—"

I do so hope, I thought. I do, I do, I do.

"—or, more to the point, Sir," he continued, "what Mesdames decide."

There, I'll admit, my heart sank. I had experienced their concept of propriety and it turned out to be non-conducive to my creativity as an author. Criticism is one thing—any artist must expect that. Punishment was quite another, and torture was above and beyond, if anything ever was.

"So," chirped Mehitabelle. "Here we are, aren't we, Darling?"

"Yes indeedy," sang Hortense gaily. "Indeedy do we are, Sweetheart. Just one big happy family."

"Where is Antoinette, Darling?"

"She's keeping watch upstairs, Madam," said Keating.

"I beg your pardon," said I. "I'm not clear on the need for watch-keeping."

"We don't get many visitors these days," said Mehitabelle. "Do we, Darling?"

"Not nearly so many as we used to," sighed Hortense.

"But the callers we do get would be alarmed if our door or phone went unanswered, wouldn't they, Darling?"

"Precisely, Sweetheart."

Note my wording in the first sentence of this chapter: "some time after that." It's hard to describe the passing of time when you're in a room without windows, clock, or watch; when the gray Jell-o inside your skull is still jiggling from the aftershocks of brew twenty-seven; all the while feeling your bladder and bumper slowly imbuing, filling and swelling; and you're dreading the thought of that ankle-high potty in the sacristy so very, very much. Life slows to an over-cranked crawl and races with clenched talons all at once, and through a glass darkly to boot.

<u>GARDENING</u> <u>TIPS</u>: I must admit a lapse of conscious-
ness or at least certainty of continuity. After
the monsignor joined us in the previous chapter
but before he went ballistic in this one as you'll
soon see, I have a rippling recollection of tearing typewritten pages into narrow, supposedly
easy-to-chew strips and swallowing them, but the
inserting and chewing part I've forgotten. I'll
be referring to it up ahead a bit, and I remember
remembering it at the time, and the weight of the
awful cud in my stomach, but it's gone now. It's
what happens when brew twenty-seven arm-wrestles
with forty-two across the blood-brain barrier.

                                    --M.F.

Ah well, at some point some time later it was decided that, before the
ladies left us so we could get down to man's business, they very much
wanted Monsignor Aspic to give them Holy Communion. The late
Father Albert, don't forget, had left a supply of consecrated Hosts in the
chapel tabernacle, hence the burning sanctuary lamp. The Doily household all being Trads, they would never touch the Blessed Sacrament or
even the vessel containing It with their hands. That privilege, in the
old mindset, is reserved for the priest whose hands have been specifically anointed for that very purpose. How glad they were to have Monsignor Aspic in their midst, having not received the Supersubstantial
Bread—Saint Matthew six eleven—for several days. While a Tridentine
Mass was certainly beyond him for the present, Monsignor was at least
ordained, albeit via inferior rites, and could at the very least administer
the Sacrament. Since he did not as yet know the accompanying Latin
prayer—

    Corpus Domini nostri Jesu Christi custodiat animam tuam
in vitam aeternamm. Amen.

—the purloined gardener could say the words in his stead. The translation, by the by:

    May the Body of Our Lord Jesus Christ keep thy soul unto life
everlasting. Amen.

But first—and here's where they proceeded to stretch the monsignor's progressive spiritual elastic limit—they also decided that since we were all in this together, we might as well jointly make the Total Consecration to the Blessed Virgin Mary, as per the prescriptions of Saint Louis Marie de Montfort. We would say the prayers associated with this devotion as a pre-Communion meditation.

> <u>GARDENING</u> <u>TIPS</u>: The Total Consecration is a practice that involves thirty-three days of preparatory prayers which culminate on the thirty-fourth day with the supplicant willingly submitting himself as a slave to the Immaculate Heart of Mary. In the words of Saint de Montfort, from his magnum opus, <u>True</u> <u>Devotion</u> <u>to</u> <u>the</u> <u>Blessed</u> <u>Virgin</u> <u>Mary</u>:

> * * *

> This devotion consists, then, in giving ourselves entirely to Our Lady, in order to belong entirely to Jesus through her. We must give her (1) our body, with all its senses and its members; (2) our soul, with all its powers; (3) our exterior goods of fortune, whether present or to come; (4) our interior and spiritual goods, which are our merits and virtues, and our good works, past, present, and future. In a word, we must give her all we have in order of nature and in order of grace, and all that may become ours in the future, in the orders of nature, grace and glory; and this we must do without reserve of so much as one farthing, one hair, or one least good action; and we must do it also for all eternity; and we must do it, further, without pretending to, or hoping for, any other recompense for our offering and service except the honor of belonging to Jesus Christ through and in Mary—as though that sweet Mistress were not (as she always is) the most generous and the most grateful of creatures.

> * * *

>   This commitment, to put it mildly, is not to be
> entered into lightly, and certainly not under du-
> ress. The Doily Sisters, however, had their
> agenda. It was not novel to me, as I had so con-
> secrated myself years before and certainly didn't
> mind renewing my promises. But for Monsignor As-
> pic, this proved to be a bit over the top.
>
>   --M.F.

"First you must kneel," explained Mehitabelle to Monsignor Apsic.

"Kneel?" said the monsignor, aghast. "Me?"'

"I'd suggest in the center, Your Reverence," said I, pointing at the worn carpet draping the altar steps. "That's your spot. I'll kneel here at your side."

"And we'll use the Communion rail," said Hortense, indicating herself, her sister, and Keating. Antoinette was, alas, awaiting rings and knocks upstairs.

"Kneel?" said Monsignor, all the more incredulous. In modern smorgasbord Catholicism, kneeling before God was considered passé—beyond merely outmoded, all the way to unthinkable. Who are we here to worship, anyway? A wave of Keating's broomstick persuaded him to give it a shot. With heroic reluctance and epical self-defacement, he managed to settle himself onto his un-suppliant knees.

Here's where they really applied pressure.

"'During the first week,'" read Mehitabelle from an old, tattered book, "'we should offer up all our prayers and pious actions to ask for a knowledge of ourselves and contrition for our sins, and we should do this in a spirit of humility.'"

"What's she talking about?" grumbled the monsignor out of the side of his mouth.

"She's reading from Saint Louie Marie de Montfort," I whispered.

"'For that end we can, if we choose, meditate on our inward corruption,'" read Mehitabelle.

"'Inward corruption?'" scowled Monsignor.

"'We can look upon ourselves during these days as snails, crawling things, toads, swine, serpents, and unclean animals—'"

"Good Heavens, Feeney," hissed Aspic. He was actually beginning to quiver all over. "This is insane."

"Not so," said I. "This is Catholicism."

"'—or we can reflect on the three considerations of St. Bernard: the vileness of our origin, the dishonors of our present state, and our ending as food for worms. We should pray our Lord and the Holy Ghost to enlighten us—'"

"Vileness! Food for worms!?" rumbled Monsignor, who surely had never applied such words to his usually perky himself. I was reminded of a tremor I felt once when visiting Mount Lassen, a sleeping volcano in Northern California. The ol' magma was rising to the occasion. "What the Hell is she talking about?"

"Application," said I, whispering authoritatively.

"Application? Of what?"

"Saint John said it best, Monsignor. Twelve twenty-four and following: 'Amen, amen I say to you, unless the grain of wheat falling into the ground die, itself remaineth alone. But if it die it bringeth forth much fruit—'"

"This is unconscionable," grumbled he. "We've grown beyond this kind of unenlightened, masochistic self-flagellation."

"Maybe you have," said I. "We Trads, well, what can I say? We try to imitate canonized Saints figuring, well, they're canonized and all. We're funny that way."

"We'll say the Litanies afterwards as a Communion meditation," said Mehitabelle, closing her book. "Monsignor, please be so kind as to do the honors."

Shrugging as if disposing of a junkyard worth of dead weight, Monsignor Aspic rose to his feet and ascended the steps, his chain clinking sluggishly behind him. Gingerly, he turned the key which Keating had left in the ornate brass lock, and opened the tabernacle door. With trembling hands—trembling as it turned out, not with reverence, but mounting ire—he reached inside and withdrew a glistening golden ciborium. This much he knew to do.

Meanwhile I heaved myself up and lurched over to the little wooden stand near the Epistle side of the altar where I found a beautiful set of crystal cruets and, yes, a golden paten with a black enamel handle. The paten I retrieved and brought back to the foot of the altar steps.

> GARDENING TIPS: In the Old Rite, the altar boy -- in this case, me -- holds the paten, which is basically a golden plate, under the chin of each communicant. This is in case a smallest crumb should fall as the priest puts the Host on the recipient's tongue. Each crumb, you see, contains the entirety of the Body, Blood, Soul, and Divinity of Jesus Christ -- yes, just as much as the entire wafer, or a whole loaf, the sum being equal to any of its parts -- so great care must be taken lest the tiniest particle be lost, dropped, or stepped upon.
>
>   --M.F.

I'm going to share a secret with my readers, a secret known only to altar boys and priests: peoples' tongues are as distinct and unmistakable from one another as fingerprints. Some tongues are bloated and pompous, some are austere yet fidgety, others are wide and beneficent, or cocky and venturesome, while some are so shy the priest practically has to probe for them. In my time I've seen rattlesnakes, asps, sea serpents, moray eels, and even an elusive Nessie or two. Yes indeed, tongues extended to receive Our Lord have as much personality as their owners. You may laugh, but it's absolutely true.

I have no idea what Monsignor Aspic expected as he turned around, ciborium in hand. As far as I know he had no parish duties, so he didn't say public Masses or distribute Holy Communion regularly. In the average modern parish, the "priest-presider" can count on at least three "extraordinary Eucharistic ministers" for every communicant to hand out—and I do mean literally "hand out"—Communion. In this situation his only assistant was me, and I was strictly a paten-handler.

In fact, as he turned to face us, I dropped to my knees, placed the paten under my own chin, opened my mouth, and extended my—

"What are you doing?" he snarled at me.

"Excuse me?" I said, blinking up at him innocently. I know I sounded funny because my tongue was still extended.

"You shouldn't be kneeling to me."

"I'm not," said I. "I'm kneeling to receive Our Lord."

He grimaced as though he had just swallowed a good-sized cockroach, then said, "Get up."

"Begging your pardon, Monsignor," said I after retracting my tongue, "but this is the way we receive Holy Communion in the Tridentine Rite—on our knees, and on the tongue. You've attended, or rather observed Mass at Saint Philomena's. You know I'm not making this up."

"I'll not stand for it," he said sternly. Then he looked beyond me and his jaw dropped.

I didn't have to turn around to know that Mehitabelle, Hortense, and Keating had arranged themselves on their knees at the Communion rail. No doubt their tongues were still safely garaged within their mouths, but they were dying to come out writhing and wiggling. I could almost sympathize with Monsignor at that moment. The mental image was unnerving, to say the least.

"This is too much," said Apsic. "I'll get ... *saliva* on my fingers!"

"Not if you're careful," I whispered urgently up at him.

"No," he said, as his gears began to grind. "No, no, no."

"Monsignor," I hissed urgently, "this is hardly the time to draw a line in the sand."

"Your Reverence," said Mehitabelle. "Surely we realize you have adjustments to make, don't we, Darling?"

"We're not amateurs, are we, Sweetheart?" insisted Hortense. "Not when it comes to stubborn men."

"Under our roof," said Mehitabelle, "things are going to be done right, aren't they, Darling?"

"They most certainly-wertainly are," said Hortense. "Now be a good Monsignor and stop fidgeting. Rolling your eyes like that is unbecoming. My Roscoe made far more ferocious faces than that and only succeeded in wrinkling himself into a prune before his time. Besides, a little saliva isn't going to kill you."

"Don't be vulgar, Darling."

"But it won't, Sweetheart, and you know it won't."

Sometime during this round of banter Monsignor's mainspring—how do I put this?—sprang! Perhaps it was the thought of Doily saliva dripping from his fingers in long, gooey strands. Maybe the image of their insistent tongues reaching for him like squirming tentacles was just too much. Hey, let's not leave me out of the equation, either. Here I was, kneeling at his feet, my own maw gaping up at him. The sight of my crusted tongue writhing in the mirror above my bathroom sink has scared the flakes from my eyes on many a cold morning. Whatever caused him to snap, snap he did, with an almost audible sound:

Sproing-oing-oing-ng-ng-ng!

Suddenly his jaw muscles constricted, his earlobes undulated, and, spookiest of all, his eyes went glassy. There was a minute intake of air through his mouth, and then his nostrils seemed to blurt, "That's it!" He gripped the ciborium firmly, reminiscent of Millie with her largest frying pan, and raised it high. "I don't care what you do to me! I can't take it anymore!"

"Monsignor!" gasped Mehitabelle.

"Your Reverence!" pleaded Hortense.

"Careful there," warned Keating, rising from his knees and brandishing the prod.

"Dumdala bawbwa furkengah!" snarled the monsignor.

There was a stunned moment of frozen silence.

"Globilla morbillallaba bwabaw hort!" he persisted.

Ah, I thought. So this is *glossolalia*. Funny, Sheldon Levant's imitation in the PREPARATION room back at KLIE was completely different, and yet entirely the same. Gobbledygook. Millie was right, this wasn't "praying in the spirit," it was "braying under the influence"—in this case brought on by way too much cattle prodding and not enough nurturing and empowering.

While Monsignor's incoherent outburst did stop Keating in his zapping tracks for a couple of seconds, the novelty wore off almost immediately. Incredulity at the very thought set in. The butler resumed his advance with the broomstick.

"Gwilligamulbwabber!" roared the monsignor, clenching his fist about the stem of the ciborium. "If you touch me with that thing again I swear I'll throw this all the way across the chapel! *Gik lurgabawama furgle mumburga gikgik!* You don't like Communion in the hand? What about Hosts scattered all over the floor!?!?"

"Easy," said I, not knowing what else to say. Slowly I rose to my feet. "Easy, easy."

I could hear the rustling of dresses as the Doily Sisters rose from the Communion rail behind me.

"Monsignor Plastic," said Hortense, her voice strained with alarm. "You wouldn't! Would he, Sweetheart?"

"It's Aspic!" yelled the monsignor. "Conrad—Jonas—Aspic! And I'm not going to be your liturgical robot, not on your life! You want to go to an outmoded Mass? You've got a car, you've got a driver. Go to Father Baptist's church, or one of those half-witted independent chapels. But as for me, you're not going to make me do this. *Murglemum demina gok roggle skwirgle!* Latin is a dead language, just like you! There were reasons for Vatican II. You don't want to change with the times? Fine! Find yourselves a nice mausoleum and wall yourselves in!"

"Keating," warbled Hortense. "Do something, will you?"

"Monsignor, do please get a grip," said Keating, approaching with the prod.

"Back!" ordered Aspic, hefting the ciborium higher. "You keep that thing away from me!"

Keating halted his advance.

"Mister Spleeny," said Hortense.

"What?" I asked, not turning to look at her.

"You misunderstand," said she. "Keating, do please prod Mister Spleeny."

"Huh—?"

And prod he did, swiftly and directly. Just below and behind my right knee. Whatever I had imagined it might feel like was nothing compared to the actual experience. Simply put, the irksome tingles in my feet instantly became fierce, piercing daggers as the current found its way through the pathways of my nerves to ground. I'm pretty sure I made a sound, but I can't begin to describe it because, mercifully, I don't exactly remember it. The next thing I knew I was doubled over on the carpeted floor.

"Monsignor?" Mehitabelle was asking.

"What?" he answered.

"You see Mister Spleeny's peril," said Hortense.

"So?" rasped the plastic cleric.

"Aren't you the least bit—?" asked the sisters together.

"No!" he shouted. "Let Feeney see what it feels like. He certainly watched me squirm."

As if to prove some point which had escaped me, Keating jabbed me again, this time on my left calf. Somehow, after flailing around wildly, I ended up with my forehead pressed against the carpet and my ankle chain wrapped around my left wrist. Then, if that wasn't bad enough, I felt a spasm in my esophagus and an unexpected sound escaped me:

"Hick!"

I clutched at the carpet as my diaphragm was wracked with paroxysms. Just when you think your body has betrayed you as much as it possibly can, it invariably comes up with one more way to wrangle the self-respect out of you.

"Hick! Hick! Hick!"

Timing is everything! What could be more unwanted at a time like this than hiccups? No, I didn't want to consider the possibility because it was sure to manifest itself the moment I did.

"Keating?" asked Mehitabelle.

"Mister Spleeny?" asked Hortense.

"Yi!—*Hick! Hick!*—Yikes! Hey!—*Hick!*—Yeow!" That was me being zapped again and again and again, hiccupping all the while. It was hard to breath.

"Hah!" scoffed the impervious Monsignor Aspic above me, waving the ciborium this way and that like a drunken sailor. "See how you like it, Feeney!"

"Good Heavens!" trilled Mehitabelle.

"Keating!" warbled Hortense.

"Mon-SEEEEEEEN-yer!" I yelped as Keating applied the prod yet again. I was becoming delirious. *"Hick! Hick!*—Please!"

"Stay back, all of you!" yelled Monsignor Aspic. He extended his leg with the chain attached. "Let me out of this thing."

"Not on your life," said Mehitabelle.

"Absolutely not," insisted Hortense.

"Now!" screamed Aspic. *"Glomdillida womdillida!* Or you'll be picking up these Hosts all over the chapel. You want sacrilege? You'll get sacrilege!"

Keating applied the prod to my leg yet again. This time the shock unhinged something in my eyeballs. Suddenly, as far as I could see, the whole room was filled with brightly bouncing balls of Saint Elmo's Fire. They were everywhere. The pain in my feet was indescribable. The paroxysms in my esophagus were choking the life out of me. In a fleeting moment of befuddled bravura I actually considered lunging at Monsignor, probably knocking him down on the altar steps. The Consecrated Hosts would no doubt be dispersed all over the rug, but at least it would be a contained area—or so I rationalized in a moment of agony. I hesitated only because Keating zapped me yet again, which left me curled up on the rug, twitching and hiccupping—and because the thought of being the cause of such a calamitous sacrilege loomed large and damning at that moment.

I don't know where all of this would have led, and we'll never know, because just as Monsignor Aspic drew back his arm as if to throw the ciborium clanging and clattering down the center aisle, a bunch of unexpected sounds erupted from the door at the back of the chapel. Footfalls and voices were rumbling down the stairway, churning and echoing as they came.

"You mustn't!" cried Antoinette, who was descending the stairs amidst the clamor. "No! No! No! You mustn't!"

86

"YOU!" EXCLAIMED MONSIGNOR ASPIC.

"Father John!" exclaimed the Doilys in tremulous unison.

"Father Bap-*Hick!*" I exclaimed. "Officer Wex-*Hick!* How—? *Hick! Hick!* What—?"

"Martin," said he. "Are you all right?"

"That's not a gun, is it, Darling?" squeaked Mehitabelle, pointing to the weapon Sybil was pointing two-handed at the floor.

"Oh, Sweetheart, I do believe we're being invaded!" squealed Hortense. "Keating, do something!"

"Gladly," said Keating, grasping his broomstick like a WWI soldier brandishing a bayonet. I doubt it occurred to him how odd he looked to someone who didn't see the electrical cord trailing behind. "Um, might Mesdames have any suggestions?"

"I have one," said Sybil, her voice like steel. If I hadn't been hiccupping like a beached nautilus I might have appreciated how good she looked, even with a gun. "Turn that thing off," she said to Keating, "and set it down slowly. That's it." Apparently she saw the cord.

"You have some nerve, Young Lady," said Hortense. "Keating is our servant, isn't he, Sweetheart?"

"You've no right to tell him what to do, whoever you are," said Mehitabelle, "even if you do have a gun, does she, Darling?"

"I'm a police officer," said Sybil, "and I'm telling you all to keep your hands in plain sight. Martin, you didn't answer."

"Thanks for—*Hick!*—noticing," I winced. Of course I felt relief at the cavalry's arrival, but this potentially thrilling emotion was curtailed by my embarrassment at being unable to utter a complete sentence. "What—*Hick!*—can I tell you? I'm delighted to—*Hick!*—see you—*Hick!*—both of you."

By that time Father Baptist had come up to me and gripped me by the shoulders. "Am I glad to see you, Old Friend."

I tried to answer, but all that happened was involuntary contractions of my windpipe.

"Hold your breath," he suggested.

"Hmm—*Hk!*—mmm," I mumbled, trying to comply.

Meanwhile Monsignor Aspic just stood there clutching the ciborium portentously, eyes glaring, lips silently flapping his meaningless banter. He seemed to feel that he had the situation well under control.

"Better?" said Father to me.

After holding my breath longer than I thought I could, I exhaled tentatively, long and slow. My esophagus rippled threateningly, but settled down. The hiccups had abated. Whew.

"Martin?" asked Father. "Are you injured?"

"Just my pride," said I. "Well, my stomach too. I need to start using a more fibrous typing paper."

"What are you saying?"

"Remember Pierre telling us that he gave my manuscript to a couple of publishers? Well, here they are."

"So he told me earlier today." He pointed to the Doily Sisters, who were fidgeting frantically with their pearls and broaches. "You mean they made you—?"

"Page by page," said I. "More than a novel, it's a meal. If other critics adopted their methods, writing as a concept would vanish from the face of the earth—excepting authors on high-cellulose diets."

"Ahem," rumbled Monsignor Aspic.

"Oh," said Father Baptist, as if suddenly noticing him. He looked long and hard at the man brandishing the ciborium, assessing the situation, deciding how to deal with it. He finally said something. "Monsignor Aspic."

Conrad J. Aspic glanced from Father to the ciborium, then at me, then back at the ciborium. His facial muscles underwent a few embarrassed adjustments, then he slowly turned and gently placed the sacred vessel on the altar. "Father Baptist," he said a might unsteadily as he turned back to face him. "I can't tell you how good it is to see you—"

"I wouldn't trust him, Father—wouldn't you, Darling?" said Mehitabelle, pointing accusingly at Monsignor Plastic.

"Nor would I, Sweetheart," agreed Hortense. "Why, he said if he ever got out of here—"

"Quiet, you!" snapped the monsignor.

"Hush, you!" said Mehitabelle right back.

"He said," repeated Hortense, "if he ever got out of here he'd see that your parish of mentally crippled bigots and religious maniacs—I think that's accurate, Sweetheart."

"I do believe it is, Darling," said Mehitabelle.

"Where was I?" said Hortense. "Oh yes. He said he'd see that all those bigots and maniacs of yours would be committed to an asylum for the rest of their lives."

"Miserable," added the gardener, "inflexible, and inconsequential though they may be."

"This from a man," spat Aspic angrily pointing at me, perhaps desperately, "who said he didn't trust his own judgment, that it wasn't running on all cylinders!"

"Did you really say that?" asked Father.

"Would you believe me if I said so?" said Aspic.

"That does sound like me, doesn't it?" said I at the same time.

"Yes to both of you," said Father. "Monsignor Aspic, you've lost weight since I last saw you, and that was just a few days ago."

"You've no idea," said the monsignor, warming up to Father's concern. "He wasn't kidding about eating our manuscripts."

"How's your stomach taking that, Martin?" asked Father.

"Unhappily," said I. "But don't listen to it. It's delighted to see you for entirely other reasons."

"Oh?" said Father. "Such as?"

"Peristalsis," said I, "coupled with the fact that there's no running water down here. Speaking of which, Keating, unlock these shackles, will you? I'm not capable of dashing, but matters are pressing and I definitely need to crawl upstairs as soon as possible."

"No!" whined Mehitabelle as Keating reluctantly produced the key from his vest pocket. "You mustn't! Mustn't he, Darling?"

"Oh, what a world, what a world, Sweetheart," whimpered Hortense. "This day is simply not going our way."

"You can stop pointing that, that *cannon* at us, Miss," snarled Mehitabelle at Sybil Wexler, who held her gun steady, still aimed at the ground.

"So tell me, Martin," said Father, as Keating unlocked the shackle around my ankle. "Why did these dear, sweet ladies kidnap the two of you?"

"No, Father," said I firmly as that metal claw fell away. "You do your stuff. This is the part where you tell us what we're all doing down here, including yourself."

"Martin," said he, "I hardly think—"

"Yes indeed, Father," said Monsignor Aspic challengingly, a mite haughtily considering the circs. "This I'd like to hear."

"Actually, so would I," said Sybil. "This has been one weird day, and I'd like to get your take on it."

"You see, Father?" said I, feeling wobbly without my cane. "You really are trapped inside this novel. You may as well play your part."

"Feeney, don't you ever stop?" groaned Monsignor Aspic.

"Stop what, Your Reverence?" said I, innocently. Yes, I was thinking to myself as I teetered precariously on my aching legs and hips, I sure could use my cane. Then something deep within the labyrinthine ways of my insides growled menacingly. "Excuse me, one and all. I really do want to hear Father's summation of the situation, really I do, but first I need to attend to a personal matter."

"Might I suggest that we all convene in the living room?" said Father.

"Ordered around, Sweetheart!" whined Hortense.

"And in our own house, Darling," commiserated Mehitabelle. "What is the world coming to?"

"A bathroom," said I, lurching through the gates and down the aisle toward the doorway at the back of the chapel. It's amazing how you can expend the hyena's share of your energy by means of the desperate, awkward bending and flailing of your limbs, while your intense, concentrated focus is on another group of muscles entirely. "Excuse me, Ladies and Gentlemen. The world may go where it will, but I really, really need a bathroom."

"Hair of the dog," said Antoinette as I pushed past her.

87

"PUT IT DOWN, MONSIGNOR," Father was saying sternly as I lumbered into the living room about ten minutes later.

"But the police must be informed," Monsignor Aspic was answering, his hand still gripping the receiver of the antique telephone on the end table.

"That would be me," said Sybil Wexler. Somewhere along the way she must have holstered or pursed her gun. Her hands were on her hips.

"I don't see anyone in handcuffs," said Aspic.

"You can't be serious, Your Reverence," said Mehitabelle. "Can he, Darling?"

"I think he is, Sweetheart," said Hortense with a creaky shudder. "The cur."

The Doilys were huddled on the couch. Antoinette and Keating were posed near the pianoforte. Father was grandstanding near the fireplace, and Monsignor Aspic was hunched over the phone like a scavenger drooling at a bloated muskrat. Sybil Wexler, of course, was busy looking gorgeous, at least, as far as I was concerned. As out of place as I felt, a problem that had loomed so large minutes before was now on its way to the ocean, and frankly, I felt more relieved about that than my rescue from the dungeon below.

"Well?" said Monsignor insistently.

"Martin," said Father. "I see you survived."

"Love them loo chains," I mumbled to myself, but then I smiled and said aloud, "Love them loo chains."

Father looked at me with those unnerving eyes that seemed to whisper, piercing yet humbly, "Imagine what Jonas went through in the belly of the whale for three days, Martin—plumbing-wise," but what he actually said was, "Monsignor, please. Belay that."

Monsignor Aspic, face twitching as though he was about to bray in the spirit again, reluctantly lifted his hand from the telephone. "Father Baptist, these people kidnapped me," he said, the quaver in his voice angry and tight. "That's a federal offense. They forced me to eat my manuscript, subjected me to humiliating browbeating, and tormented me with some sort of electrical torture device. I believe the state would call that assault with a deadly weapon. I demand that they be arrested, prosecuted, tried and convicted—"

"One thing at a time, Monsignor," said Father.

"—and sent to prison for the rest of their miserable traditional lives!"

"You can't mean that," protested Mehitabelle. "He can't, can he, Darling?"

"I'm afraid he does, Sweetheart," sighed Hortense.

"Me oh my," rasped Mehitabelle. "Oh well: 'Blessed are they that suffer persecution for justice' sake.'"

"'Blessed are ye when they shall revile you and persecute you,'" agreed Hortense, "'and speak all that is evil against you—'"

"Shut up!" roared Aspic, apparently feeling that Saint Matthew five ten and eleven only applied to him. "Don't you dare quote—uh—" He paused, apparently put off with "Scripture" as a word and Saint Matthew as the author of his own Gospel. "—Bible stuff to me. You

Trads are all alike, but you're not going to get away with—with—*any* of this!"

"Monsignor," said Father. "I think—"

"No!" yelled Aspic. "You're one of them. You're going to protect them!"

"I believe I just effected your rescue from them," said Father. "I've been retracing your movements for four days at the cardinal's request."

"Don't give me that. Morley Fulbright is only interested in that stupid artifact."

"Perhaps. My interests, on the other hand—"

"I don't give a damn about your interests, Father. This is one time you're not going to—"

"Excuse me," said I, stepping closer. "I thought we agreed that we all wanted to hear Father's summation. Before we string these dear, sweet old ladies up by their feather boas—"

"*Mis*-ter Spleeny!" objected Mehitabelle.

"—and treat the maid and butler to a ride to the hoosegow on a certain broomstick—"

"Sir!" blinked Keating.

"Marvin!" pleaded Hortense, pressing a daintily frilled hankie to her nose.

"—I would like to know—" squeezed in yours truly.

"You would like to know," said Monsignor Aspic, with a scornful emphasis on "you." He put his hands on his once-pudgy now-sunken hips and grunted like a pompous peccary. "Who do you think you are, Feeney? Why you're nothing but a lazy, feigning, self-absorbed gardener with a big mouth who has convinced himself that he's the next Chesterton. But you're not."

"With the exception of the feigning," said I, "and any comparison to the creator of Father Brown, I agree with every word you say."

"You are incapable of coherent thought, Feeney."

"You'll forgive me for saying this, Monsignor—or not—but I have as much stake in this as you do. My carcass was in the soup pot right beside yours. My book was maligned and my pride mangled every bit as much as yours."

"Your pride," he said disdainfully.

I took a step closer. "Don't think I was unimpressed by your behavior when Keating turned his stick on me—"

Apparently he had forgotten about that. His eyes went wide and his sagging cheeks partially inflated. Perhaps he was working up to another outburst of blathering in tongues. I admit I kind of hoped he would, seeing as how Father Baptist had missed the show. I was disappointed, perhaps a bit irked—a bit?—when the best he could come up with was:

"You're twisting the facts, Feeney."

"I, Your Reverence? Well, fortunately there are witnesses."

"You can't mean them," said he, waving his hand at the gang of octogenarian culprits. "They're the perpetrators, and they're all batty."

"Am I hearing harassment on the basis of age?" I feigned wide-eyed surprise. "And from Cardinal Fulbright's own counselor?"

"Your opinion is irrelevant," said he. "You are irrelevant."

A pair of rusty clippers went *snap* inside this gardener's head. "No, Monsignor. You were the one who was about to scatter Our Lord's Body on the floor like so many pieces of silver."

"As a means of escape," said the monsignor, gruffly.

"For whatever reason," said I. "Because of that intended sacrilege, you lose all relevance, period." That had to be my best line of the evening, and of course I had to ruin it by losing my balance, and in doing so grabbing the edge of the end table stacked with Trad rags. It did not provide a secure purchase. Indeed, it tipped right over. Faded, brittle copies of *The Rambler, The Remainder,* and *The Tridentine Tribune* went every which way. I stood there looking at all the desperate, outraged verbiage at my feet. After all, I had also contemplated an act equally horrible. "Relevance," I whispered. Then I looked up at Father Baptist. "Well? Are you going to wow us with your brilliance, or are we just going to go to Bongo Burgers for a greasy burger and fries? Manuscript pages may be low in carbohydrates but miserable in the satisfaction department."

"Very well," said Father as Antoinette and Keating scurried to clean up the mess I had made.

"You encourage him," said Monsignor Aspic, his mouth twisted into a condescending snarl.

"I depend on him," said Father, "and from what I gather about what's been going on here, I agree with him. Were you really threatening to throw the Blessed Sacrament on the floor?"

"It was a threat. That's all that it was."

"Mighty impressive intimidation. I hope for your sake that's all it was."

"Who are you to question me?"

Father Baptist gave Monsignor Aspic a look that would take volumes to try to explain. "I'm the one who is restoring your life to you."

"I suppose that means I owe you something," said Aspic.

"That is for you to ponder," said Father. "But I do wonder how the cardinal is going to react when he hears my report."

"What report?"

"On your activities, Monsignor."

"My activities? These cranks kidnapped me because they saw me on 'Religion Rediscovered.' Any theological opinions I gave on that show were strictly in line with the cardinal's own—"

"I'm not referring to your kidnapping," said Father. "Nor to your threat of sacrilege. As you yourself just said, Cardinal Fulbright's primary concern was the papal artifact which he entrusted to your care. How you handled that—including your connection with Thurgood T. Turnbuckle and his to Roderick Roundhead—"

"Father John!" warbled Mehitabelle shrilly. "You watch how you talk about members of our family!"

Father Baptist smiled at her inscrutably. "I assure you that I only report the facts."

"What facts?" demanded Aspic, though confidence had drained somewhat from his tone.

"You did tell the cardinal when you accepted the artifact," said Father, "that you would take it to the jeweler—the one recommended by members of these ladies' family—the next day. As of this moment, the artifact is still unaccounted for."

"What are you talking about?" said the monsignor. "Surely Winger still has it."

"He says not," said Father.

"Then Roderick Roundhead—"

"Also says not. Meanwhile His Lordship Sylvio Bonsignore is circling."

"The vulture."

"Well, he's certainly watchful. He contacted me yesterday."

"You? Why would he—?"

"Just doing his job, I suppose. He knows more about that artifact than he lets on. In fact, well, we'll let that go for the nonce. There are other matters to consider. Tangential to the case—well, a good deal more relevant than that—is the circumstance of one David Smoley."

"You're right there," said Aspic, inflating his cheeks and taking a step forward. "Why, do you realize—"

"That he answers to Roderick Roundhead?" interrupted Father. "Yes, I'm aware of that. That you have treated him miserably since you discovered the deception when you visited the Turnbuckles? Again, yes. Consider how much sensitive, confidential information regarding the internal workings of the archdiocese made its way to Mr. Roundhead before these very ladies let the proverbial cat out of the bag."

"Oh dear, Darling," said Mehitabelle. "He knows."

"Oh double-dear, Sweetheart," answered Hortense. "What shall we do?"

"You'll rot in prison if I have anything to say about it," snapped Monsignor Aspic out of the side of his mouth. "That's what you'll do."

"Heavens!" cried Mehitabelle. "Father John, are you going to let that happen?"

"It's not his call," said Aspic, salivating cruelly.

"Perhaps not," said Father. "Still, Monsignor, I don't think you're suited to the quiet life."

That brought the monsignor up short. "What are you talking about?"

Father paused for a second and a half before replying, "The life that will be yours when Morley Fulbright banishes you to the farthest flung little toilet of a parish in the archdiocese—like the place he once threatened to send me. What he didn't realize at the time was that I would have been delighted to go there. God, I'm afraid, had other plans for me. Perhaps it will do you some good, though, come to think of it."

The monsignor didn't answer. He was too busy making noises like a rupturing pressure cooker.

"By the by," said Father, again to the Doily Sisters, "it's a safe bet that Roderick knew about your keeping Father Albert downstairs all these years. That was his name, wasn't it? You mentioned him the other day as the priest who had been saying Mass for you."

The Sisters nodded sadly.

"Roddy's more involved than that," I ventured to say. "Would you be surprised to learn that Monsignor Aspic wasn't abducted at the television station?"

"It happened here," said Father. It wasn't a question but a statement of fact.

"You knew?" I asked.

"I had an inkling," he answered, "hardly a suspicion, but no, I didn't know until now. David Smoley was in Roderick Roundhead's pay, shall we say, and—"

"You mean as an informant?" asked Sybil Wexler.

"Informant," said Father, "and perhaps sometimes more."

"How did you find out about that?" said Aspic, folding his arms, then refolding.

"One of your sponsors, shall we say, was present when it was disclosed to me," said Father, "so I may as well tell you as he. Mr. Turnbuckle's son, Biltmore, spilled the beans—if the ladies will pardon the expression."

Aspic exhaled loudly. I thought I heard the word "twit" in there somewhere.

"You've been treating David like dirt ever since," butt in the gardener, "if I may be so bold."

"You're still irrelevant as far as I'm concerned," said Aspic. I could almost see steam coming out of his ears. One of us was going to need counseling after this mess was over.

"Fine," said I. "That makes two of us. Let's let Father continue to impress us, shall we?"

"Gentlemen," said Father with a heroically patient nod. "As I was saying. David Smoley was not to be trusted, seeing how Roundhead had his strings clenched firmly in his hand. Excuse me for being so prolix, but I want to give my biographer some good zingers along the way."

"What biographer?" asked Aspic.

Father didn't so much as blink. "The holy water vial we found in your Mercedes suggested a recent sick call, Monsignor. No doubt the vial dropped out of your valise en route when you opened it at some point during your excursions that day."

Monsignor Aspic didn't say a word, but his expression practically screamed, "I will not admit that it wasn't in the sick call kit when I opened it at Father Albert's bedside. I won't, I won't, I won't."

"Finding Christine's Crucifix on Father Albert's body—"

"Whose?" asked Aspic.

"Christine," said Hortense with a wry smile. She dipped her hand into one of her puffy pockets and produced Father's copy of *Garden of the Soul*. I recognized his favorite little prayer book with the stained leather cover and frayed ribbon. I wondered how she got it. She opened the front cover and read the faded inscription penned inside. "Christine Maryvale."

"You should be a detective, Mrs. Doily," said Father, accepting the book from her.

"Wouldn't that be something, Darling?" said Mehitabelle, nudging her sister.

"Oh bosh, Sweetheart," giggled Hortense, puffing up like a pigeon.

"We should probably thank you, Father," said Mehitabelle, "for bringing that excellent little book to our attention. We intend to start making copyright inquiries tomorrow, don't we, Darling?"

"Oh yes indeedy do," said Hortense.

"That is indeed gratifying," said Father.

"Do you think Christine will be pleased?" asked Mehitabelle.

"I should think so," said Father, slipping his precious prayer book into the mysterious folds of his cassock. "I'd know her Crucifix any-where. I gave it to Monsignor Aspic several weeks ago. But there it was on the body of a dead priest, identity as yet unknown, a few days ago. It followed that the paths of Monsignor Aspic and the priest, living or dead, had recently intersected. Of all the calls he made last

Wednesday, this was the one most likely to have involved a sick call, I should think."

"I'm not sure I like the sound of that," said Mehitabelle. "Do you, Darling?"

"Not at all," said Hortense. "Not at ally-wally all."

"What I meant to say," said Father, "is that most of his stops were at businesses. This is a residence. A priest is far more likely to be called to a home than an office to administer Extreme Unction."

"Excuse me," said I. "You said you didn't know until now. That means you didn't know before you came here tonight. So what brought you here?"

"I think perhaps it was me fault," said Keating, rising to his full height to place a stack of retrieved newspapers back on the end table. "It must have been that piece of mortar."

"Piece of—?" asked Father.

"Mortar?" asked the gardener.

"When you came visiting earlier today with Monsieur Bontemps," said Keating to Father. "It was in Mesdames' office. While you were out of the room, Monsieur found a lump of mortar—or so I guess you'd call it—on the floor. It was so big, and there were pebbles imbedded in it."

As he said these words my hand went to the empty pocket where that piece of La Purisima should be.

"It must have dropped there when Antoinette and I carried Mister Feeney through to the chapel," said Keating. "Oddly enough, Mister Feeney had fallen down on that very spot a day or two before, so I assumed it to be his."

"Pierre did not mention it to me," said Father.

"He didn't?" I asked. My jaw creaked open a few notches.

"You know how Pierre is," said Father. "It must have slipped his mind. That chunk of mortar, you say? Yes, that would have given away the show, seeing as how Martin took his tumble here on Friday and we didn't visit La Purisima until Saturday. But no, I came here this evening because of something Mrs. Magillicuddy said Thursday night."

"Who?" asked several elderly people and Monsignor Aspic all at once.

"You mean what she said about—?" I began to say, but Father cut me off with one of his piercing laser beam looks.

"Mortar," I thought I heard him say to himself, not once but twice, but then he said aloud, "On second thought, Martin, Officer Wexler, we really should go."

"Whatever you say," said Sybil, relaxing her official stance. "It's past eleven, and I've got a big day tomorrow."

"What about tonight?" said Monsignor Aspic, eyes glaring. "What about now?"

"What *about* now?" asked Father.

"Well, aren't you going to arrest these people?" said the monsignor.

"Oh, must I?" said Sybil, calmly but laced with amusement.

"That would mean everything we've discussed becoming a matter of public record," said Father. "Your indiscretions as well as theirs."

"I'd hardly call kidnapping an indiscretion," said Aspic.

I couldn't help saying, "When compared to banishment to the farthest flung *twa-twa* of a parish in the archdiocese, surely Your Reverence sees the wisdom in letting it drop."

Father gave me an inscrutable look at my verbal substitution, but the Sisters looked pleased. A minor point, but there it is.

"Letting it drop?" said Aspic incredulously. "They tortured me. They—"

"I'm not denying their behavior was deplorable," said Father. "Certainly prosecutable. But the question we must ask is: what good will be served by placing the matter in the hands of the civil authorities? In addition to the disruption it would cause in our daily routines, it could easily become a media circus. Jacco Babs, the reporter for the *Times,* is no friend of mine, but he's got a nose for a good story. Just at a time when the Church is under fire for the improprieties of Her clergy, a story like this could wreak untold harm on several fronts."

"You'll know it'll be 'WHACKED TRADS TURN TO CANNIBALISM' before they're done," said I. 'FULBRIGHT SENDS CATSUP.'"

"Which is all the more reason that we should keep this whole matter 'in-house,'" said Father.

"You mean, just do nothing about it?" said Monsignor Aspic.

"I mean let's deal with it among ourselves," said Father. "I can promise you that from this day forward these ladies are going to have Keating drive them to St. Philomena's for daily Mass."

"Oh, but we couldn't, could we, Darling?" said Mehitabelle.

"Absolutely positively wositively not," said Hortense.

"And why is that?" asked Father.

"Dear me," said Hortense. "I completely forget why. How about you, Sweetheart?"

"I'm not sure that I ever knew, Darling," said Mehitabelle. "It must have been compelling, though, don't you think?"

"Trust me on this, Ladies," said Father. "You'll enjoy daily Mass at my little church. It's not exactly the good old days, but it's familiar. In return you'll give us your solemn promise not to kidnap any more priests."

"Wait a minute, Father," said Aspic. "That's it? They're made to attend Mass at your church?"

"And I delete certain irrelevant details from my report to the cardinal," said Father.

"This is blackmail," said Aspic.

"Well," said Father, "the only alternative I can see is giving you back to them."

"What?!" There was a moment of utter terror in Monsignor's eyes, followed by disbelief and consternation. "You wouldn't dare."

"Monsignor Aspic," said Father. "I am weary of archdiocesan politics; of the petty, self-serving concerns of my superiors; of heretics, pagans and charismatics dictating ecclesiastical policy; of being perceived as His Eminence's toady by members of my flock; and the list goes on at great length, I assure you. I'm in no mood for a police investigation, a court case, a lawsuit, or anything else. If pushed I will respond in ways that even I will regret, but to put it simply, I am fed up with you, with Cardinal Fulbright, and with everything remotely connected with Vatican II. Now can we please agree to let this pass, or do I go to the nearest telephone and wake up Jacco Babs?"

"Officer Wexler," said Aspic, turning to her. "I've heard about you. You're rash and insubordinate. Are you going along with him?"

"You seem to be standing quite alone in the middle of this," said Sybil. "Me, I'm just an apprentice watching a master." She wasn't looking at Monsignor Aspic when she said this, nor me, for that matter. When she did turn to face him, this is what she said. "I'll tell you what I do think, Monsignor. If it ever came to court, it would be your word against these two fine, upstanding publishers of prayer books, not to mention the famous cop-turned-priest, Father John Baptist. You're the one who babbles nonsense on television and claims it's the Holy Spirit giving utterance through you. On the other hand, it would assure the publication of your book and get you oodles of publicity—not necessarily favorable publicity, but you'd be a household word in no time. But the bottom line is this: my reputation does precede me. After the pending disciplinary hearing in a few days, I'll likely no longer be a police officer. Given that, I really would have no second thoughts about guiding you back downstairs at gunpoint so these people can shackle you up again."

The Doily Sisters seemed to rally at the notion. I'd describe Aspic's reaction as bristling.

"But," continued Sybil, "I couldn't do that to Mister Feeney, so you'd be on your own."

"I'd say your options are limited," said Father. "We can give you a ride to the Chancery, if you wish."

"I'll call a cab," said Monsignor Aspic, in the most disgusted, despondent voice imaginable.

"Hair of the dog," said Antoinette with a wry smile, producing my trusty cane from behind the loveseat and handing it to me with a curtsy.

"Hair of the dog," I agreed, thankfully resting my aching weight against it.

88

"TELL ME, SYBIL," said Father as we made our getaway in her Lexus. "How are you at geometry?"

"Abysmal," she answered. "But with this I am virtually knowledgeable. What do you need to know?"

"It involves the dots on the downtown map, the intersecting lines, what they mean."

"You mean you figured them out?"

"I believe so. I think this will interest you. How are you doing back there, Martin?"

"Feeling left out," said I. "Does this have anything to do with how you knew to look for me in the Doilys' dungeon?"

"No," said Father. "This is about the papal artifact, the puzzle it presents and its solution. Interested?"

"Oh, mildly. Um, didn't the cardinal forbid you from talking about the artifact with certain police types?"

"He didn't say anything about soon-not-to-be police types," said Father.

"Ah, there is that. I don't suppose you could meander near a Bongo Burgers as you're making your riveting unraveling speech?"

"You really eat those things?" Sybil asked over her shoulder.

"In a parish as poor as ours," said I, "you sometimes find yourself devouring things that are beneath your expectations. In this case, I happen to like Bongo's unique sludgy taste."

"Not if you're fasting before receiving Holy Communion," said Father.

"Am I?" I asked. "Oh. Okay." So we were on our way to Mass—unexpected, but there it was. This was one of those unsettling moments when the desire for a greasy hamburger, which we realize to be unhealthy and immediate, competes with the opportunity to receive Our Lord, which is a mighty and eternal matter indeed. I'm shamed to say that my initial reaction was actually disappointment. I had to actually step in and throttle myself: "Hey, you faithless idiot! What the heck are you thinking?"

Something I didn't mention and now must. As we exited the Doily house, making our getaway as it were—not that we were in the least bit of a hurry—Father had offhandedly said, "I've never driven a Lexus, Miss Wexler. Would you mind if I—?"

"Sure, Father," she responded with a delightful laugh. "I read somewhere that priests in Los Angeles are more likely to drive a Lexus than any other car."

"Not in my parish," said Father good-naturedly. "But as to my request, I should think it would be easier for you to utilize your computer if you're a passenger."

"Ah, so you just like me for my brains, literally both of them."

So there she sat with one of them on her lap, the sleek silver model she had used at "Paneno's." It made a whirr-click sound, the digital equivalent of a purr. "Your problem is geometrical?"

"That's right, but first—" said Father. His right shoulder hunched as he dug around inside the mysterious folds of his cassock, then he handed me what looked at first like a cardboard tube. "Martin, would you do the honors of unrolling that?"

It turned out to be a piece of parchment rolled together with a sheet of "onionskin." I recognized the latter as the sketch we had found on the corkboard in Bishop Ravenshorst's library, the pockmarked kid amazed that cornflakes can float—or was it an ectoplasmic entity with a serious fly problem?

The parchment turned out to be a map, a very old map, which had been rendered in colorful pigments by a long-dead cartographer:

"If you rotate the tracing and overlay it on top of the map," said Father, "I think you'll see what the late archdiocesan historian was after."

"I do indeed," said I. "The ghost had a mouth. No—I mean—the smeared splotches were not meteor craters, cities, volcanoes, or even squashed spiders. He was plotting the positions of the California Missions."

"Precisely," said Father. "Martin, your hunch was right about the S's on the disk. They do stand for *Sanctus,* or rather *San* and *Santa.* Now, Sybil, it's time for you to do your stuff. Imagine a line drawn from San Juan Capistrano to the Mission La Purisima at Lompoc."

"The lines on the map?" said she as a light bulb went on over her beautiful head. "They connect the missions?"

"I'm surprised your satellite network didn't figure that out," said he. "Don't tell me your super-system is agnostic."

"More likely my own search parameters were deficient."

"Allow me to help you to perfect them. You might want to render this on that contraption of yours."

"Contraption," she said, amused. "You said San Juan Capistrano and La Purisima." Her fingers wiggled and tapped silently on the keyboard surface. I leaned forward to watch her fingertips dancing on the illuminated dots.

"That's right," said he. "Now a second line, drawn from the San Gabriel Mission in the present city of San Gabriel, to the Del Agua Mission in the southwesternmost quarter of the area we call downtown."

"Gotcha." I could see the tiny image in her compact-size screen. It was impressively clear and sharply defined. Pale purplish light played on her face and hands.

"I'm willing to wager a dinner at Darby's," said Father, "that those two lines intersect at the corner of El Barranco and La Colina." There he was, wagering dinners again.

As she clicked a few keys the image zoomed into the barrio. "That's right," she said. "The site of Bishop Ravenshorst's last excavation."

"You're talking about the treasure in that Spanish verse," said I.

"Indeed," said he. "You've missed an important conversation or two."

"Timing is everything," said I. "So you're saying that Bishop Ravenshorst found the treasure."

"No," said Father. "He found nothing. He was looking in the wrong place. It must have been terribly disheartening to gaze upon a thirty-foot pit the size of the whole lot and still have nothing."

"I may be delirious from too little food or too much wastepaper," said I, "but if that's the solution to the puzzle, and that's where Ravenshorst looked, and the treasure wasn't there, then what gives? Did someone else solve the puzzle and get to it before him? Was it a hoax from the get-go?"

"No," said Father. "When can the right place not be the right place?"

"Ooohhh," I said. "No more brainteasers, please."

"Actually, Martin," said he, "I'm thinking of one of your new friends, the one you met up at the refurbished La Purisima."

"You mean Don Gusto," said I.

"That's the fellow. He told you that for years he had to tell the empty air that the mission wasn't originally here, it was over there."

"Why did he have to do that?" asked Sybil. "And who made him?"

"It's a long story," said Father. "For the moment let's take it at face value. His message was for you, Martin. His purpose was to call your attention to the change in location. Perchance your purpose is to draw my attention to the same thing."

"Okay," said I, bewildered, "so now that your attention has been duly drawn, what now?"

"Here's where the geometry comes in," said Father. "Sybil, what is the distance from San Juan Capistrano to La Purisima?"

"How accurate do I need to be?" asked she. "If you mean from bell tower to bell tower, it'll take some time to pull up ground plans for the missions. If you mean town to town, piece of cake."

"I don't think we have to be that exacting," said Father. "The old Spanish maps, like the one Martin is holding, were made long before the extensive geographical surveys of the mid-twentieth century."

"Well then," said Sybil, "I come up with 174 miles."

"Now," said Father, "how far is it from San Juan Capistrano to the point of intersection with the line between the San Gabriel and Del Agua Missions?"

"Hm," said she, grimacing. "Ah, 'X' marks the spot. Here it is: 113.1 miles."

"So the line goes on another ... 60.9 miles to La Purisima."

"That's right."

"Okay, here's the problem. Even though Bishop Ravenshorst was a historian, he forgot one important detail: Mission La Purisima was destroyed by an earthquake in 1812."

"And moved to a new location," said I, "five miles away."

"That being the case," said Father, "if we draw a line from San Juan Capistrano to the original site of La Purisima, taking into account that disparity of five miles, how far does that shift the point of intersection on the line between the San Gabriel and Del Agua Missions?"

"Hm," said Sybil as letters and lines materialized on her screen. "Let's change that to 'F' marks the spot. AF is to FB as AE is to EC ..."

"While she's working on that, Father," said I, "you said something about Mrs. Magillicuddy back at the Doily house—"

"Got it," said Sybil.

"That was quick," said Father.

"Timing is everything," I mumbled to myself.

"Martin, see?" said she, holding up her little silver contraption. "Bear in mind that this chart is skewed because a right triangle 174 miles long and 5 wide would be a narrow geometric figure indeed. This diagram just shows the ratios of the distances involved."

"Of course," said I, as though what she had said made perfect sense to me.

"In answer to your question, Father," said Sybil, "if Bishop Ravenshorst had taken into account that the site of La Purisma had changed, he would have dug a hole about 1.75 miles closer to the Del Agua Mission. Of course, whoever formulated this puzzle was using maps of the time, so the distances involved are rough estimates anyway. Considering the margin for error he might have dug it between two and two-and-a-half miles closer to the Del Agua Mission."

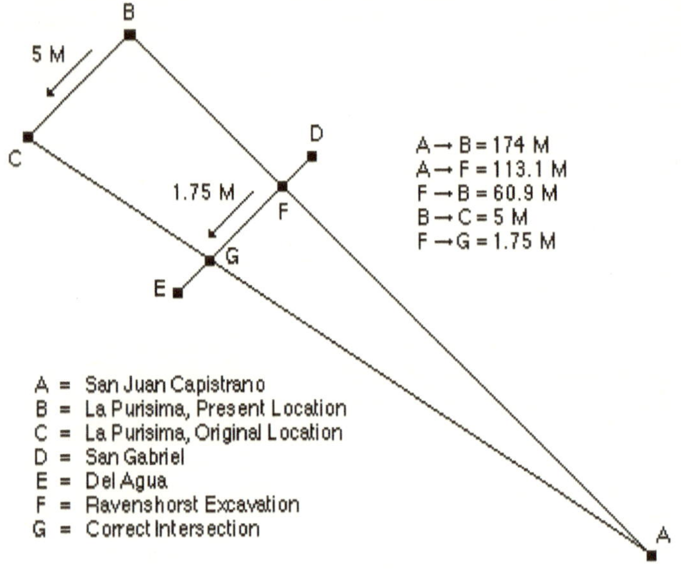

"And where might that be?" asked Father.

"I think you already know," said she.

"It seems obvious to me," said he, "even without all that geometry."

"I understand that it could never be," said she, "but I could sure use you for a partner when I go private."

"As you say, it could never be. But if it could, I'd seriously consider it."

Me, I tried humming Mrs. Magillicuddy to the tune of "Row, Row, Row Your Boat," but kept coming up three syllables short—yes, just like with *disjecta membra*. Funny how that works.

"What's that you're humming, Martin?" asked Father as he made a wide turn onto Hoover Avenue.

"Oh nothing," I said. "Nothing."

90

WHICH BRINGS US to the last few minutes of my exciting Sunday, which was all but a tiddly-widdly prequel to the events that were about to transpire right after midnight.

Father Baptist, a teeny bit out of practice, actually scraped the curb with the front tire as he guided the Lexus to a stop in front of St. Philomena's Church. Sybil seemed more amused than annoyed by his vehicular clumsiness.

Don't get me wrong, the Lexus is a fine car, surely built for the comfort of the average traveler. Nonetheless, my spine is not average, and unfolding it from the question-mark shape it had assumed in the rear passenger seat, especially after the jostles it had received in the last twenty-four hours, well, let's just say that getting out of the car was a blessing and a curse. Standing upright, once I had maneuvered my feet onto the ground, was a task achieved in excruciating stages. Father and Sybil, being average travelers, physically anyway, had no problem getting out of the car and even enjoying a good stretch.

"Shall we?" said Father, stepping up onto the curb.

"You're the boss," said Sybil.

"Hopefully everyone is here," said he.

"Like who?" asked yours truly, ascending from the gutter to the sidewalk with teetering difficulty.

"Like me," said an unexpected voice.

Out of the shadow of the archway in the front of the church lunged a shape. It was too dark to make out details, the nearest streetlamp being too dirty to produce much light and our assailant being clothed in black, but I distinctly heard the metallic hollow clank of a large gun being cocked. He stood his ground halfway down the church steps.

"All of you stay calm," said the voice, which was anything but. "Don't move and you won't get hurt."

"What do you want?" asked Sybil, her hands moving slowly to her sides.

"Shut up, sister," snapped the man, his voice cracking.

Rather than argue the point, Officer Wexler complied. The man ignored me and turned his attention on Father Baptist.

"I want the center thingy," he said.

"The what?" asked Father.

"Don't play stupid. You said it only fits one way into the bigger disk."

The tremor in the man's voice sounded familiar. I wondered who this man was and when Father had taken him into his confidence. What had Father said back at the Doily ranch? *You've missed an important con-*

versation or two. No kidding. Still, there was something about the man, his movements and mannerisms, that sparked my sluggish synapses. As he slowly descended the rest of the steps, it dawned on me who he was.

Father cleared his throat and said, "I believe I said it had been designed for that purpose."

"So give it to me," said the man angrily, approaching. "I want to put it in its place."

"It won't work, Mr. Winger," said Father.

"Why the Hell not?"

"I neglected to mention that someone—I've no idea who or when—someone filed the teeth off the back."

"Don't give me that."

"I assure you it's useless."

"I don't believe you," said the jeweler, stepping close enough for us to see him.

Father rolled his shoulders. "You trusted me enough to give me the cardinal's chalice without—"

"That glorified ashtray? Who cares? I saw the inscription on the back of the disk. I got myself a Spanish dictionary. This is about a bloody treasure, and I want it!"

"A treasure that bleeds, Mr. Winger, not—"

"Shut up! Just shut up, and give it to me. Take it out slowly. Don't try anything."

"So you did keep the papal artifact," said Father, otherwise motionless. "Do you have it with you?"

"What?"

"You do, don't you?"

"Just give me the thingy," said Mr. Winger. The quivering barrel of his gun gleamed shakily in the dim light. "Hand it over or I'll—"

Timing is everything. Just then a cranking, grinding sound emanated from the church. It was mechanical, unlubricated, and very, very loud. Talk about a *deus ex machina* moment. Mr. Winger's jaw fell open, then snapped shut as we were buffeted by twelve unevenly spaced repercussions, like cannon fire without the gunpowder. The hinges on the front doors of the church actually rattled.

```
GARDENING TIPS: Regulars at St. Philomena's were
familiar with the clock in the tower.  It had a
history too long and convoluted to tell here.
Suffice it to say that every now and then, without
apparent rhyme or reason, the mechanism struck
twelve.  The piston or striker or whatever it's
```

called didn't have a bell to beat upon because
that fell from its perch during the Whittier
Earthquake of 1987. The beam that it once hung
from received the blows in its stead.
     That being said, I can't help but think that
on this occasion our beloved parish church had an
announcement to make. This thunderous barrage was
a kind of fanfare. Perhaps I'm romanticizing.
I'll let my reader be the judge a few chapters
hence.

                                        --M.F.

"What the heck was that?" asked Sybil as the pounding abruptly ceased.

"That would be the old clock in our steeple," said Father.

"Wow," said she. "Your neighbors must really appreciate that."

"It's creepy, I'll grant you," said I. "Like something out of an old ghost story."

"It's certainly annoying—" said she.

"Shut up!" barked Mr. Winger, regrouping his fingers around the handle of his gun. "What's with you people?"

Where to begin? thought the gardener. But before he could open his mouth to do some real damage, a new and unfamiliar sound suddenly came clanging out of the church. It was eerily metallic and rattling, not mechanical but intricately rhythmic—or should I say polyrhythmic. I thought of the dozens of ways different clocks will strike the time all at once in a clock shop. Then rusty hubcaps, garbage can lids, and Millie's new dishwasher rolling around together inside a gigantic cement mixer came to mind—but then, I have that kind of imagination.

"What the Hell?" gasped Mr. Winger.

"Hardly that," said Father, as the cacophony within the building seemed to broaden into a low roar and spread to the ground, as if the subway to Hell was roaring by beneath our feet. The sidewalk heaved and shuddered.

I'd like to take credit for what happened next, but in truth it was entirely accidental. I suppose I could pretend that a rocking earth straightens everything out for a crooked man like me, but that isn't actually the case. I have enough trouble keeping vertical at the best of times, but during an earthquake all bets are off. Fearing what another fall would do to my throbbing bones, especially on this cement surface, I made matters worse by flailing my arms every which way in an attempt to keep my balance. My cane being clutched in my left hand, it went every which way, too, and so it was that the rubber tip hit Edison Winger's right temple. An unintelligible sound burst from his lips and his fingers involuntarily splayed. He and his weapon hit the pavement at about the same instant. Officer Wexler, who had been poised for any opportunity which might present itself, dropped to a crouch beside him. She shook her head to indicate that he was safely unconscious.

"Good work, Martin," said Father as the quake suddenly ceased.

"Gorsh," said the gardener, grateful to be leaning on his cane again.

"Well, well. Look what we have here," said the soon-not-to-be police officer, after a cursory search of the soon-to-be-booked jeweler's pockets.

"The papal artifact," said Father as she handed him the sandwich-size leather pouch. He loosened the tasseled cord and peeked inside. "Words fail to express how good it feels to be done with yet another of the cardinal's errands."

"I can't wait to see you hand him yet another bill," I said. "Perhaps you should hire a collection agency for the fees he owes you."

"One thing at a time," said Father, slipping the pouch within the mysterious folds of his cassock. "We have things to attend to inside. What should we do with Mr. Winger?"

"I'll cuff him to that," said Sybil, indicating the gate through which I'd recently seen the ghosts of Profirio and Poca Roca disappear.

"Good idea," said Father.

Together they dragged the unconscious jeweler to the suggested tethering station. Quick as a blink Sybil had Winger's arms inserted through the bars and his wrists handcuffed.

"Excellent," said Father, straightening. "Now to more important matters."

Monday, November Twentieth

**The Feast of Saint Felix of Valois,
co-founder along with Saint John of Matha
of the Trinitarian Order whose purpose
was to rescue Christian slaves from the Mohammedans
in Spain and North Africa (1212 AD).**

91

IT'S HARD TO DESCRIBE WHAT I FELT as Father Baptist, Sybil Wexler, and I entered the garden through the front gate. In the last four days I had been many places and seen many things, from mausoleum to dungeon, downtown to countryside, photocopy shop to corporate office, from morgue to mission to mansion. I had encountered the rich, the poor, the angry, the mad, the thick, the ethereal, the powerfully positioned, and the pathetically put-upon. Still, I figured, all that had to be leading up to something. Passing between the leather-leafed avocado tree and the finger-zinger leaves of the holly bush, we came upon a group of people huddled in the garden. It was deadly dark, that gloom imposed from above that sometimes descends in the middle of the night in Los Angeles—the City of Angels is a reclaimed desert, don't forget. The dim light from the clock on the stove, refracted by the uneven glass of the kitchen window, gave their faces an eerie amber glow as they turned at our approach. Their apparent ghoulishness was further enhanced by the inky blue light emanating from the stained-glass windows on the side of the church which played upon the backs of their heads and shoulders. The chandeliers within the building were still reeling and rocking a bit from the earthquake, so the garden was alive with dancing shadows and writhing vegetation. Honestly, Folks, this is all my poor stomach needed.

It took me a few moments to realize who was present. The Tumblars, of course, were always a welcome sight in their formalwear, whether in the blazing foyer of a grand hotel or the parish garden in the dead of night. A stalwart police presence can be reassuring in said deadness of night in the heart of the city, and Lieutenant Taper and Sergeant Wickes were almost family. Millie was always appreciated in moments of hunger or self-castigation, Kahlúa at times of, well, whenever, and Mrs. Magillicuddy could be counted on for a handful of dead weeds and a backhanded compliment. Such wonderful characters, but all mixed together at once? What were they doing here?

It was a surrealistic moment if there ever was one as they turned their various expectant, troubled eyes in our direction. Not only did I feel as though I'd been here before—small wonder, there—but everyone in this gloomy but heartwarming diorama was actually someone I got along with pretty well. I hadn't realized how much I'd missed them during my brief sojourn in the Belly of the Doily.

"Father Baptist?" asked Pierre. "Is that you?"

"Indeed," said Father, "and look who's—"

"Why, it's Mister Feeney!" cried Arthur.

"Hoorah!" cheered the Knights of the Tumblar. "Sir Martin!"

"Grand to have you back!" said Pierre loudest of all.

"Why?" asked Mrs. Magillicuddy. "Had's the old grouch been's away, has he?"

I had a very, very, very strange thought: Is this what it's going to be like in Heaven?

"I assume you all heard the clock strike," said Father.

"Our very own beastie in the tower," agreed Pierre.

"And the earthquake," said Arthur. "Don't forget the earthquake."

"Not likely," said Father. "In fact, I don't think—"

"You're alive!" said Millie almost accusingly after peering long and hard at me. She seemed out of focus somehow. "Pierre was right. Wasn't he, Lulu?"

"Right about what?" I asked.

"Don't worry, we didn't finish," said Kahlúa. "We didn't find it."

"Finish what?" I asked. "Find what?"

"We left everything just as you left it," said Millie.

"Not a paper out of place," said Kahlúa.

Pierre coughed significantly.

"Oh?" said I, my heart sinking from its rightful place behind my sternum to a new position next to my throbbing stomach. It rebounded to fitful attention at the ensuing question:

"Where have you been, Mister Feeney?" asked Arthur and Edward.

"Mister Feeney?" asked Joel, after several seconds of silence.

"Mmmmm-hm Martin?" prodded Kahlúa, after several seconds more.

"Oh, there and back again," said I with a shaky wave of my cane. "A very dark and dreary 'there,' and it's good to be home."

"There!?" said Mrs. Magillicuddy knowingly, hugging herself through a fit of shudders. "I know's a things or two's about *there*. Was Lou Costello after you's, too?"

"Maybe so," said I. "The critics had their field day, that's for sure."

"I should imagine we'll all get to read the sordid tale in manuscript form," said Father, "or do you still maintain, Martin, that the events of the last few days really weren't worth writing about?"

"Every moment in your service is worth writing about," said I. "At least, to keep my fingers nimble. Telling this tale, however, would be an act of humility that is beyond me."

"Don't plant suggestions in your confessor's head," said Father. "That would be an excellent penance: the meticulous exposition of every detail of the last several days."

"I can always switch to Monsignor Havermeyer's confessional," said I. "And from what I hear, he thinks I'm a real treasure. Where is he, by the way? And why are you all here?"

"Monsignor Mike?" said Jonathan. I couldn't see him, but his voice seemed to be coming from behind Arthur and Pierre. "We've been looking for him since we got here."

"Father told us all to come here to pray," said Arthur.

"Pray?" said I.

"We were concerned about you, Sir Martin," said Joel.

"If something happened to you," said Edward, "who would write the Tumblar chronicles?"

"What about me?" said Pierre.

"I repeat," said Edward.

"I repeat," said I. "Pray?"

"Father's orders," said Arthur.

"Isn't that what's a church's is for?" mumbled Mrs. Magillicuddy.

"But the door was locked," said Jonathan. "None of us has the key."

"The lights are on," said Father, nodding at the stained glass windows.

"Señor Guadalupe's truck is parked out front," said Sybil.

"No sign of him or his men, either," said Joel.

"Nor of Monsignor Havermeyer?" said I.

"We checked his RV," said Edward. "Across the street, too."

"Perhaps he's making a sick call," said Father. "Few other things would cause him to leave the place unattended."

Thankfully the chandeliers within the church had just about rocked themselves out. The swirling blue light show calmed to a placid, slowly surging, azure glow.

"I hope the church is okay," said Joel. "That was quite a trembler."

"It's a wonder she's still standing," said Father. "The microcosm reflects the macrocosm."

"So where have you been?" said Pierre, lunging forward and seizing my hand.

"Yes," said they all, suddenly enthused. "What happened? Where were you?"

"Well," said I, blinking back a wave of hunger-induced dizziness, "the truth be told, I was attending a symposium of sorts. The topic was 'Writers in Inanity.'"

"Inanity?" asked Pierre, playfully. "Is that a word?"

"Inanely so," I shrugged. "A panel of judges—two publishers of some renown, as a matter of fact—were comparing the unpublished works of myself and none other than C. Jonas Aspic."

"Favorably?" asked Joel.

"Not favorably, no," said I.

"Negatively then," said Arthur.

"They frowned a lot," said I, "at both of us."

"Both of you?" asked Joel.

"Pretty much equally," I admitted. "You begin to see why writing about this would be embarrassing."

"You mean—?" said Edward.

"You're telling us—?" said Jonathan.

"You were with Monsignor Aspic?" said Arthur.

"Eating our words," said I, rubbing my aching tummy. "I kid you not."

"With or without catsup and mustard," said Millie. "That's what I'd like to know."

"I'd have mine blackened," said Kahlúa.

"Raw's best," said Mrs. Magillicuddy. "You can't beat's what's raw's, as I always says."

"Did you say publishers?" asked Pierre.

"I did," said I. "The two you gave my manuscript to."

"Wait a minute," said Jonathan, still in the back somewhere. "Pierre, didn't you say you gave it to—?"

"The Doily Sisters?" said other Knights severally. I could feel blood rushing to my head as realization dawned and the derisive chuckles commenced. "The Doily Sisters! You were held prisoner and made to eat your words by *the Doily Sisters?*"

"Who happen to be experts in vile, foamy potions that are soluble in tea," said I in my own unsupportable defense. "Their maid's talents include slipping knockout drops into drinks in public bars. Her name is Antoinette. Be glad you fellows weren't targeted that evening—"

"Toni?" asked Pierre. "You mean she was the one—? That's why you became so fatigued?"

"The same," said I. "And yes."

"He's got a point," said Joel. "We were drinking in the same bar."

"Not to mention their butler," said I. "His proficiency with a homemade cattle prod is legendary among the priest hole set."

"You're not joking," said Arthur.

"Never about pain," said I.

Their smirks were shifting but not fading. My heart began to slip from its perch again.

"Hold on, Martin," said Lieutenant Taper, folding his arms authoritatively. "You were drugged and abducted?"

"By the Doily Sisters, no less," kidded Joel and Jonathan, no point prodded too much.

"You did say 'held prisoner,'" added Taper. "Against your will."

"Yes," I cringed.

"That's called kidnapping," said Sergeant Wickes. "I think we'd better—"

"Leave it to the Feds," said Father. "Or better yet, just leave it alone."

"But Jack," said Taper. "I can't just—"

"Trust me on this, Gentlemen," said Father firmly. "Lesson learned, yes?"

"Pierre," said I pointedly. "Some time—but not right now—you must explain to me the thinking processes that led to your giving my mystery novel to a couple of hyper-twitchy prayer book publishers, not that you had any idea what crimes they were perpetrating in their basement, but still, I want to hear about those processes."

"So would I, Honey," said Kahlúa Hummingbird, looking at her assistant editor slyly. "What wuz you thinkin'?"

"Madam, I assure you," said Pierre, spinning to face her. "I solemnly assure you—"

"That reminds me," said I, tapping him on the shoulder. "I think you have something of mine. Something you picked up yesterday in the Doily Sisters' office."

"What? Oh, quite right," replied Pierre, reaching into his pocket as he completed his pirouette facing me. "Yes. It was this chunk of mortar. Mister Keating said it must have fallen out of your pocket when you tripped and fell."

"My humiliation quotient just keeps climbing," said I, accepting the piece of La Purisima from him. "I did take a tumble in their office, but that was on Friday. I couldn't have dropped this then. It didn't come into my possession until Saturday morning when the cardinal summoned Father Baptist up to Lompoc. It could only have fallen out of my pocket when I was being maneuvered through there—God knowest how—when I was unconscious."

"Oh," said Pierre. Then his eyes opened wide as the time line fell into place in his head. "Oh, I say! The 'priest hole'! Were you being kept down those stairs?"

"You saw them?" asked Father.

"Why yes, Father," said Pierre. "Keating showed me the swiveling bookcase when you left the room. Pretty bold of him, don't you think?"

"Not really," said Father. "I had already expressed my need to leave presently. It was unlikely that I'd have agreed to a tour just then."

"Even so," said Pierre. "It was a risk."

"Not really," said I. "More than likely we were locked safely away in the sacristy—me drugged and Monsignor Aspic cowed into silence. Speaking of the sacristy, why don't you use your key, Father? I'd just as soon move on to another topic."

"Mister Feeney!" said Millie. Funny, she looked blurry.

"Yes?" said I, though my attention was on Father's hand as he reached into the mysterious folds of his cassock.

"Just Mister Feeney!" said Millie again. Lunging forward, she threw her muscular arms around my neck. She smelled of stale whiskey. It wasn't exactly a greeting card moment.

"Millie," I tried to say through a collapsed windpipe. "Millie—"

"There there, Sugar," said Madam Hummingbird as she helped disentangle our over-enthused housekeeper from the crushed broccoli that was me.

Just then there came a loud, hollow, metallic click from the side door of the church. We all turned as the latch lifted and the knob rotated. The warm glow of candles and high-hung chandeliers burst into the garden as the door swung inward. There was something odd about the light, though. It seemed gritty somehow, as though permeated with suspended particles like afternoon sunlight on the desert after a windstorm. The doorway was filled with the unmistakable silhouette of—

"Monsignor Havermeyer!" said several of the lads.

"Mikey!" I thought I heard Millie say.

"Who's there?" said the startled monsignor, glaring out into the darkness.

"Never fear," said Pierre. "We are all your friends!"

"Well, some of them at least," said Millie. "That is to say, a fine, upstanding churchman like you, surely you've probably got other acquaintances—"

"But all of us here's," said Mrs. Magillicuddy, "well, we's at least's all's friendly toward ya, an' ain't it the so's."

"It so is," agreed Millie.

"Honey, that's my line," said Kahlúa, regarding Millie appreciatively.

Our beloved housekeeper responded with a resounding burp.

"Why, Honey," said Kahlúa. "That's a ditto for sure."

The monsignor took a step forward. I realized, as the ghostly light played on his head and shoulders, that he was covered with fine, gray powder. His hair was caked and chalky. As his eyebrows went up flakes of dirt trickled down his face. I was reminded of Tanner Turpin, one of our steadfast parishioners, when his wife, Theodora, overdoses herself with talc and most of it ends up on him. It also reminded me of the Levants in their powder-puff room. I shook my head to clear it.

"My Senior," I said, taking a step toward him. "What has happened to you?"

"Why, the most amazing thing," he said. "I was down there with—" He leaned forward, peering at me. "Feeney? Martin!!" Suddenly he lunged forward and, heedless of my protests, wrapped his arms around me. Neither he nor I are huggy fellows, especially he, so the moment fell into the awkward category. Worse, puffs of fine powder billowed around us, reminding me of when Dad used to clean the ashes out of the backyard incinerator—that was back when backyard incinerators were legal in Los Angeles, back in the days before the terms "smog" and "environmental concern" bumped into each other at some highfalutin cocktail party. "You're back!" he laughed. "You're safe!"

"More or less," I said as my head rattled. "What, may I ask again, has happened to you?"

Releasing me, he stepped back. He looked at all the residue he had deposited on me, then down at himself. "Happened?" he said, looking around. "Happened! Father Baptist! Millie! Lieutenant, Sergeant, Officer! Miss Hummingbird! And dear Mrs. Magillicuddy. All you dapper Knights! The most extraordinary thing has happened! Simply the most—most—"

Suddenly he was seized by a fit of coughing.

He was joined by a chorus of sneezes. It took me a moment to realize they were coming from behind him, back inside the church. The gritty light pouring through the door was disturbed by approaching, lumbering shadows.

"Hola, out there," said Roberto Guadalupe, emerging from the church. Duggo and Spade came on his heels. Their steps were uneven, as if they were dizzy or confused, or perhaps inebriated. Fine dust wafted from their shoulders and hair.

"Greetings," said Father Baptist. "You fellows have been busy."

Spade sputtered something through the red handkerchief he had cupped over his mouth. Duggo cleared his throat and upchucked something in Spanish that ended in "milagro," or at least sounded like it to my ears. Having once seen *The Milagro Beanfield War* at a Saturday matinee I knew it meant "miracle," but I was hampered from further comprehension by the fact that whenever Roberto and his men slipped into their native tongue all my gringo ears heard was "Blah-blah-blamos, muchachos. Blah-blah-blah-blamos."

"What have you done to my church?" asked Father, looking them up and down, then peering at the dirty light pouring through the doorway.

"What you wanted, Padre," said Roberto with a heave of his innocent shoulders. "The stones from the grotto floor, we remove them. We find a stairway. We keep removing the rocks, the stairway it go down, down, down, winding around the big boulder. It end at a wall made of granite stones. It made no sense, such a passageway ending at a blank wall."

"We think," said Duggo, "something important must be behind."

"The stones were not held with mortar," said Duggo. "Just fit together, just like the stones in the stairwell."

"Perfectly," said Spade.

"Each stone was—what is the word?" said Roberto.

"Strange shape," said Duggo. "All crooked."

"Many are the angles," said Spade.

"Wedged so tight," said Roberto, "we could not pry one out, not one."

"It was most impressive," agreed Monsignor Havermeyer. "Like an intricate three-dimensional jigsaw puzzle—amazingly complicated shapes, yet the wall surface was perfectly flat. The backs of the stones were interlocked, impossible to remove."

"I'm confused," said I, "and not the first time. If the wall is perfectly flat and you were unable to pry out a single stone, how do you know how complicated they were behind?"

"I assumed you wouldn't mind, Father," said Havermeyer. "I told them to go ahead and use a sledgehammer."

"I might have suggested waiting," said Father.

"Oh," said the monsignor sheepishly. "Well, anyway, as it turned out, the decision was out of our hands."

"Duggo was about to take the first swing," said Roberto.

"But suddenly the old clock," said Duggo, "it start to strike. Pow! Pow! Pow!"

"Then the earth," said Spade, "it start to shake!"

"Oooh," said Kahlúa Hummingbird. "Just like in the movies."

"What movies?" asked Millie.

"Abbot's and Costello's movies," suggested Mrs. Magillicuddy.

"El Señor de los Temblores," said Duggo and Spade, crossing themselves.

"He opened the wall," said Roberto. "The stones fell away, just like that."

"The wall fell apart?" asked Father.

"As quickly as you or I can open a door," said Havermeyer. "One second it was a wall, the next a pile of odd-shaped rocks."

"And gobs of dust," said Spade.

"Plumes of it," said Havermeyer.

"Oh," said I, my question finally answered.

"What lay beyond?" asked Pierre, just as Spade sneezed explosively.

"Pardon?" asked the monsignor.

"What was beyond the blasted wall?" said everybody, though some used slightly different expressions.

"Amazingly, we found our way through the rubble," said Monsignor Havermeyer.

"I look inside with the flashlight," said Roberto. "The dust, it was too thick to see. The air, hard to breathe."

"I thought it best to get some fresh air and let the dust settle," said Monsignor Havermeyer.

"I have some lanterns in the truck," said Duggo, trotting toward the front gate. "Be right back."

"Good," said Father after him. "I'm anxious to go down there."

"Excuse me, Father," said I. "Not that I'd want to change your style or adjust your timing, but shouldn't this be where you impress the heck out of us by telling us what's down there before we go and see for ourselves?"

"Mister Feeney!" objected Millie.

"I knew it," said Pierre. "We're all trapped in another of Mister Feeney's novels!"

"What an odd thing to say," said Kahlúa.

"It's an odd place to be," said Pierre.

"He's kidding, of course," said Edward.

"Don't be too sure," said Joel.

"It would explain a lot of things," said Jonathan.

"Sure, sure," said I dubiously. Then I shrugged. "Trapped or not, kidding or not. Whatever. I would prefer it if Father would explain."

Father laughed. "I'm hardly in a position to write your denouement for you, Martin, tempting as that may be." He then fell silent. His protestations to the contrary, I felt sure he was about to thrill us with one of his fascinating summations. We all held our breath and waited.

And waited.

"Well?" asked the gardener.

"Precisely," said Father. "It is well." He peered around, giving each one present a nod of approval. "However, I think we can safely assume that those who from all ages were meant to be here at this moment are present."

"Huh?" grumbled yours truly. Between the vacancies in my head and the groaning emptiness of my stomach, combined with the frustration of the moment, I was beginning to long for my lumpy bed. As I understood it, Father himself had arranged for everyone to be here who was here. Ah, perhaps there had been others invited who didn't make it. I made a note to corner Pierre at the earliest opportunity and squeeze out of him a detailed synopsis of the events I had missed, his having been asked by Father Baptist to fill the void when I vanished. I found Father's choice of number-two chauffeur, a writer like myself, though of a different sort, significant. Could it be that he simply made sure that events would get chronicled without interruption by an experienced writer? Naw. Not him. No way.

"Here comes Duggo," said Arthur, as Roberto's trusty assistant came trotting back at the same clip as when he'd departed, puffs of dust still trailing from his clothes.

"Need any help?" offered Joel, who didn't mind getting dirty.

"No, gracias," said Duggo, drawing to a halt. He clutched three large kerosene lanterns in each of his fists. He had two more hooked on his belt. "Padre Baptiste, did you know there is a man handcuffed to the gate?"

"Yes," said Father. "Did he say anything?"

"He was—*¿Como se dice?*—out like the light."

"Speaking of lights," said Lieutenant Taper, "will those be enough?"

"I think so," said Roberto. "There are also the electric lamps already in the stairway. Give us a few minutes to get them hung, make sure it's safe." He tapped Spade on the shoulder as if to say, *"Vamanos."*

"How long is a few minutes?" asked Pierre.

"Perhaps fifteen minutes, no more."

The assembly groaned, the Tumblars the loudest.

"Time enough for a Rosary," said Father happily. "Then we'll see what there is to see."

"Just what my stomach needs," I grumbled to myself. Of course, on one level, a Rosary is the sublimest of prayers. On another, grrrrrrrr.

"Usted no creerá sus ojos, Padre," said Duggo over his shoulder as he entered the church.

"Excuse me?" said Millie.

"Your eyes, *Señora,*" said Roberto with a parting wave. "You will not believe them."

92

WHATEVER THEY BELIEVED as we entered the church, my eyes first had to adjust to the grit in the air. The light sources throughout the nave of the building, electric bulbs in the chandeliers as well as the bobbing flames of votive candles in their wrought-iron racks, were blurred and encircled with gray-brown haloes. Stationary shafts of light from strategically positioned spotlights, aimed at some of our more prominent statues, were overlaid with gyres of slowly swirling particles. The place smelled of ground stone and powdered iron. It was dreamy yet reeked of violence, like a smoldering battlefield bathed in morning light after a night of fierce combat.

Bear in mind we were in the Sacred Presence, so all the following discourse was subdued.

"When all this dust settles," said Father as we followed him to the center of the church, "we're going to have some cleaning up to do."

"Don't look at me," grumbled Millie as we genuflected severally. "Oh!"

She was startled by the sight of a casket positioned at the front of the center aisle on one of those accordion-folding brass coffin carts. It was a simple wooden affair with economical metal hardware, not yet draped with flowers nor pall. Like everything else in the church it was covered with a fine layer of powder.

"Who might this be?" asked Pierre.

"I believe his name was Father Albert," said Father Baptist.

"Late of Saints Felicitas and Perpetua Parish," added yours truly.

Father Baptist gave me one of those "Really?" looks, to which I responded with an "Uh-huh" nod.

"Is he perhaps the priest from the mausoleum?" asked Arthur.

"Wait a minute," said Sergeant Wickes. "Not the one we found in Saint Valeria's—?"

"The same," said Father. "Not to worry, Sergeant, no one claimed the body so I obliged. It's the least I could do. I'm not even sure if Albert is his first or last name. My guess is first because the Doilys presumed to call me 'Father John.'"

"Such informality among Traditionalists," commented Sybil. "Odd, isn't it?"

"Not really," said Arthur. "The truly modernized would just call him 'John.'"

"Or worse," said Pierre, "'Johnny B.'"

"I read Solomon Yung-sul Wong's report," said Lieutenant Taper.

"The victim was held prisoner for a slew of years," said Sergeant Taper.

"Jack," said Taper, "are you telling us he—like Martin here and Monsignor Aspic—?"

"That's right," said Father. "He was a prisoner of the Doily Sisters."

"How did you figure that out, Father?" asked Jonathan. "And how did you know to look for Mister Feeney there?"

"Precisely!" said I, for that had been my question from the start. I was going to say something more—hardly in a position to write my denouement for me indeed!—but I became distracted by the fact that I couldn't find Jonathan's eyes to lock onto when I said it.

"Why is he here?" asked Sybil, which derailed the discussion completely.

"As a priest he deserves a Requiem," said Monsignor Havermeyer.

"In the middle of the night?" said Lieutenant Taper.

"At morning Mass," said Father.

"Somebody better get a feather duster," said Millie, scowling at the powdered surface.

"I'll say, a whole team of dust mops," said Kahlúa. "Otherwise your parishioners are gonna get their clothes filthy when they sit down."

"Surely, Lads, we will rise to the occasion," said Pierre, always glad to volunteer his friends.

"Sure we will," said the Lads, albeit sluggishly.

"After you, Pierre," said Edward.

Just then Spade and Duggo appeared at the mouth of the grotto. They beckoned for us to follow them below.

"In me old parish way in the back when's, when's I was just's a girl," said Mrs. Magillicuddy. "Saint Ambrose, it was. We had dances, we did's, in's the church basement."

Well, I thought, there is that.

"Shall we?" suggested Father.

We proceeded to the mouth of the grotto, out of which mushrooms of dust were still gushing in slow motion. Being the most polite of the bunch, not to mention the slowest and most lumbering, I brought up the rear. As a result, I didn't see what everyone else saw. I just perceived a wall of black tailcoats with Kahlúa's feathers flailing above.

"Land's sakes!" I heard Mrs. Magillicuddy exclaim from the front of the throng. "Pardon's me outburst, Faddah, but the grotto! It's—it's—"

"Not exactly gone," said Millie.

"An' not exactly here, either," said Kahlúa.

"Wow," said Joel. "Double wow."

"Is it safe?" asked Edward.

"As safe as God allows," said Duggo.

"Come," said Roberto from somewhere below. "Come, come. You will see."

I heard clopping steps, the sound of shoes on stone stairs. The group inched forward. Then their heads began to sink in metered swoops. Finally I came up to the edge and beheld the stairway that hadn't been there two days before. It was hard to see through all the descending people, but light was coming from below, the yellow-white light of bare hundred-watt bulbs strung from electrical wire. The suspended dust was thicker down there. I noticed, as I pulled a crumpled hankie from my pocket to cover my nose and mouth, that others were doing likewise.

Realizing I'd need both hands to proceed, I took a deep breath, wedged the handkerchief in my shirt pocket, and steadied myself with one hand on my cane and the other against the side of the boulder out of which the stairs had been hewn. Down and down it went, curling to the right, ever to the right, until we had gone round three-quarters of a turn. This deposited us on a flat floor of dark, rectangular stones. Again, with me lumbering behind and the others blocking my sight, my view of things was limited. I didn't realize we were stepping through a gaping archway where a wall had been until we were already beyond and I became aware of the sprawl of irregularly shaped stones around us—the impenetrable wall that had crumbled during the earthquake. After that everyone spread out and I began to see more and more of where we were.

It was a sub-sanctuary, a chapel beneath the sanctuary in the church above. The chamber was rectangular—that is, it had four corners. The walls, however, were noticeably concave which, along with a ceiling that was slightly arched, gave the place a sense of expansion. Kerosene lamps with their somber yellow glow had been hastily hung around the periphery, giving the place the ambiance of an archeological dig in a 1930s mummy movie. There was a very old, fascinatingly ornate wooden altar. It reminded me of the rough yet reverent altar at the San Gabriel Mission about twenty miles away. I estimated it to be just about below the main altar in the sanctuary above, and oriented the same way. Shriveled candles stood in ornate metal holders, about half burned-down the last time they were extinguished many years before, waiting all this time to be lit again, to give the rest of their all to God. The soles of our shoes made a considerable clatter on the floor, which was an intricate mosaic of multicolored tiles. With so many walking all over it I couldn't discern the pattern.

"Oooweeooo," whispered Kahlúa in a spooky low voice, her marble eyes rolling around in their wondrous sockets. "What have we here?"

"What's this chamber for?" asked Sybil Wexler.

"It was often the practice when erecting a church," answered Father Baptist, "to build a room beneath the sanctuary. As you can see, it makes an excellent crypt."

It was only then that I espied the facing stones on about a dozen nameplates on the wall opposite the altar. The names were definitely Spanish, and I saw no dates later than the mid-nineteenth century. My heart and stomach got themselves entangled among my intestines at the sight.

"Necropoliphobia," I whispered to myself. "Above ground, now below ground—you gotta love it."

"It also provides a chapel," continued Father, "where a priest might say a private Mass while a public Mass is in progress in the church above."

"Why not just concelebrate?" asked Sybil.

"You know the term?" asked Monsignor Havermeyer.

"I watched a Mass on television a couple of days ago," said she. "I came across it by accident. There were three priests saying Mass together. The commentator used the word several times."

"Was this sacerdotal trio clapping their hands and having a grand time?" asked Joel.

"Did they sing 'Somewhere Over the Rainbow' instead of the Our Father?" asked Edward.

"Concelebration is one of the earmarks of the New Order," explained Pierre. "The more priests they have concelebrating, the more extraordinary Eucharistic ministers are required to distribute Holy Communion."

"Am I missing a joke here?" asked Sybil.

"It depends on what you consider funny," said Father. "Suffice it to say no, they didn't concelebrate in those days, and only ordained priests distributed Holy Communion. You see, according to Saint Thomas Aquinas and others, only the priest who consecrates should distribute because—"

"Whoa," said Sergeant Wickes. "Would you look at that."

He was pointing at something large and obvious, but which I hadn't seen until everyone spread out around it. It was a solid block of coarsely hewn stone, about six feet wide, three and a half tall, and three deep—about the same dimensions as the altar. Mostly brown and gray-blue, it was speckled with tiny flecks of silvery minerals, and its many brittle edges and contours glistened glassily under the glare of the bare light bulbs. As I moved around to the side facing the altar my insides entangled themselves further, for there, imbedded within the fabric of the stone, was a representation of the Crown of Thorns. No, "representation" is the wrong word. It implies an artist, but this image had not been rendered by human hands. As I looked closer and closer I could see the interwoven ring of twigs and fiendish, jagged thorns, the tips shimmering as if dipped in fresh blood. It seemed to be three-dimensional, as if held suspended in a glass case; yet the stone in which it floated was opaque. Clearly it was one of the most amazing things I had ever seen, but let's not sell the night short. There was more to come.

Suddenly I felt a burning sensation, very much like I had experienced the previous Friday morning during Mass. I gripped my pocket, gathering the contents away from my skin. It was as if the chip from the actual Crown of Thorns bequeathed to me by Bishop Xandaronolopolis of Lebanon was responding to the image in the stone.

"Oh my God!" I heard Arthur say, as though he was miles away.

"Me oh mine oh my!" said Mrs. Magillicuddy, equally distant.

"Is that what I think it is?" asked Edward.

"What do you think it is?" asked Sybil Wexler.

"Pienso que es un milagro," said Spade. There was that "milagro" word again.

"La corona!" Duggo was hissing. In this reverberatory chamber his voice sounded like a set of those melon-sized maracas. *"La corona de espinas dentro de un altar de piedra!"*

"The crown of thorns within an altar of stone," said Roberto, translating.

"The verse!" said Joel.

"The painting at the hotel!" said Pierre.

"What painting?" asked Millie.

"Over the registration desk," said Pierre. "It shows this very stone being used as an altar for Mass. It was outside, though, with a terrific storm thundering all around."

The verse I assumed was the one Roberto had been translating at "Peanuts," but I hadn't been graced with a look at his efforts. I remembered the paintings at the Adirondack, but nothing about this strange altar, if that's what it was. My attention was distracted at the moment by the burning sensation in my pocket. "Dear Jesus," I mumbled to myself, still clutching the relic through the fabric. "Have mercy on me, a sinner."

"There's a declivity here," said Father, tracing a rectangular depression on the top of the stone with his fingers. "Looks to be the right size for an altar stone. Yes, I'd say this is a *bona fide* altar."

"Amazing," Monsignor Havermeyer was saying. "Do you suppose the Crown within is the work of an artisan?"

"I'm no geologist," said Pierre, "but I'd bet my monocle that image was formed when the stone was made."

"Hrmph," snorted Sergeant Wickes, ever the arm's-length skeptic. "I've seen geodes containing crystals that looked like carved images. It's quite possible this image was made as various minerals cooled at different temperatures."

"Either way," said Sybil Wexler skeptically, "it's uncanny."

"As you said, Pierre," said Arthur, "in the painting this stone was on a battlefield. I wonder how it got down here."

"From the marks on the floor," said Father, pointing to the scratches on the tiles, "I'd say it came the same way we did: down the grotto stairs, probably on wooden slats."

"Whew," said Joel. "That would have been quite a chore."

"Then it was walled in," said Lieutenant Taper, who had fallen to a crouch. "But from what the monsignor told us, the wall had to be constructed from inside."

"It sure took some planning," said Havermeyer. "The wall, I mean, the way the pieces fit so intricately together. This was no hasty project."

"I see what you mean," said Taper. "A lot of thought and consideration went into the execution of such a wall."

"So what happened to them?" asked Edward. "The men who built it, I mean?"

With a sudden feeling of foreboding and a flurry of footfalls on the tiled floor, we all looked around the chamber. Nope, no skeletons sprawled on the floor or propped in the corner. That was a relief.

"Find something, Jack?" asked Lieutenant Taper as the clatter died down.

"The answer, I think," said Father, whose perusal had drawn him to the Gospel-side wall. He was fingering the mortar between the stones as he said, "I think our concealers outdid themselves. They not only built the wall at the base of the stairs from within, they built this wall over here the same way."

"What do you suppose is beyond that?" asked Joel.

"If I've got my bearings right," said Father, "the rectory is about seventy-five feet in this direction. I wouldn't be surprised if there's a connecting passageway."

A snippet of a conversation between Father and myself three days before flickered through my muddled memory. It had taken place in the grotto just after I'd lost my balance:

"Martin," he had said as he crouched to examine the stone floor. *"I think the floor is subsiding."*

"That's odd," his profoundly observant gardener had replied.

"There are no records, unfortunately, but I suspect this archway, wall, and floor were part of an earlier structure."

"I thought this building replaced a wooden chapel."

"Yes, but the chapel was built on the site of a shrine. You can see the difference in the masonry here, the size and shape of the stones, the chunky mortar."

The gardener, as if to prove his observational profundity, had then suggested, *"Reminiscent of the fireplace in your study, don't you think?"*

"You may be right, my Friend," answered Father, as if to pat his sidekick encouragingly on the head.

"Don't that beat all," Kahlúa Hummingbird was saying. "We've got us our very own catacomb!"

"Perhaps," said Father. "Our little church certainly is proving to have a provocative history."

"You're not thinking of busting it down and breaking into my basement!" growled Millie. "I'm not gonna clean up the mess!"

"No need to fear," said Father. "At least, not in the immediate. We've got a more important matter pressing."

"Like what?" asked a gaggle of voices.

"Like that," said Father, pointing.

All eyes turned to something set upon the wooden altar, something positioned in front of the tabernacle. Because of the placement of the electric lights and the resulting crisscross of shadows, it had been virtually hidden in plain sight. It was about two-and-a-half feet tall. The once-royal-red material draped over it was rotted and crumbling, but still held together by hearty threads of gold that permeated the fabric.

"Is this, like maybe, you know, considered a sanctuary?" asked Kahlúa Hummingbird as Father approached the altar. "I mean, are us girls allowed—?"

Father paused, thought a moment, and said quietly and gently, "I appreciate your sense of propriety. While I sincerely believe that you are all meant to be present, until I am sure as to the nature of what is here, I suggest that only the monsignor and I approach."

We backed away as Monsignor Havermeyer, his face quavering with a wondrous mixture of pride, humility, and awe, moved to Father's side. Together they advanced to the altar, and guided by a mutually-held reverence, sank to their knees before it. For once I was in a position to see what was happening, standing as I was, directly behind them, with my back to the stone containing the mysterious thorny crown. Perhaps some of the sacerdotal reverence had rubbed off on me, so often had I participated at Mass as an altar boy, because I found myself, with clenched teeth and trembling cane, descending upon my aching knees. I sensed the others following suit. From that position I could see the golden base of the object protruding beneath the deteriorating cover. There was an ornate oval setting with an inscription. It was a word of only five letters, but it took several seconds for my bleary eyes to decipher them:

LLULL

"Llull?" whispered Pierre, who without my realizing it, had fallen to his knees beside me to the right.

"Good Heavens!" gasped Arthur, who I assumed was on the other side of Pierre.

"What's the matter?" asked Millie, somewhere to my left.

"What is it?" hissed several voices behind and around the stone.

"I've seen the name, this spelling, before," said Arthur.

"Who is it?" hissed the chorus of voices again.

"Blessed Raymond Lully," said Arthur. "He spoke Catalan, and that's how he spelled his name."

"Catalan?" asked Sybil Wexler.

"A Romance language related to Provençal in Southern France," said Arthur. "The language Our Lady spoke to Saint Bernadette at Lourdes."

"So that's a reliquary?" asked Jonathan, who was kneeling to my immediate left.

"I don't think so," whispered Arthur as Father Baptist and Monsignor Havermeyer rose to their feet. "This is something different."

"But it apparently belonged to Raymond Lully," said Pierre.

"I wonder how it made its way here," said Arthur.

I'm sorry to interrupt the flow here, but in spite of the enormity of the moment, I was distracted by the discovery of Jonathan next to me. For some time now I had been hearing his disembodied voice without seeing his face. My neck cracked painfully as I turned to look at him. An involuntary gasp escaped me at the sight of the Neanderthal Man kneeling beside me. I think my jaw opened and closed several times as our conversation in the bar came back to me. It seemed like centuries before and involved the writings of Sts. Cyprian and Clement of Alexandria. No way had I imagined what a hairy monster I had aroused in the cause of Love. A gasp from the others snapped my attention and my head back to the matter at hand on the altar. During that moment of distraction Father and Monsignor had untied the cords that held the cover in place. The rotting cloth had parted and fallen away.

"Heavens," gasped Monsignor Havermeyer, falling back onto his knees.

"My Lord and my God," whispered Father, likewise descending.

"It's sure is pritsy, it's is," marveled Mrs. Magillicuddy. "I wish's my Willum was here's to see it's, I does ... whatever it's is."

Words so often fail. All I can do is try. From its overall shape I had suspected it was a monstrance like the one I described at the Monastery of the Archangels, but this was unlike any such vessel I had seen before. It was a masterpiece of craftsmanship, meticulously executed by talented European hands that had long since crumbled into dust. As with most ostensoria, magnificent shards of jewel-studded gold and silver radiated from the center, but the stellar vortex was occupied, not by a round window, but by something reminiscent of an hourglass. The upper glass chamber, circular in front but thin in depth, contained a large round Host, five or so inches in diameter, pure and white as snow. This upper compartment narrowed to a thin throat beneath the Sacred Bread, then expanded to a slightly larger, bulbous chamber below. The glass of both chambers was crystal clear except for a faint yellow-brown line encircling the lower chamber two-thirds from the bottom, as if it had once held a liquid that had left a stain.

If I were as holy as my Patron Saint, I would have been unaware of the throbbing in my knees. But, being the food for worms that I am, in very few minutes I was aware of little else. It was with great relief that I watched Father rise to his full height. Monsignor Havermeyer, following his lead, genuflected, and then accompanied him back through the rubble of the crumbled wall to the base of the grotto stairway. The rest of us did likewise.

"Father," asked we all in various ways, "what is that, that, whatever it is?"

He hushed us with a wave of his hand. "Ladies, gentlemen," he said in a soft voice with a firm tone. "If my surmises are correct, we have all been invited by Providence to witness a miracle."

This was met with a flurry of excited, quizzical whispers, which he silenced by raising his right index finger to his lips.

"The puzzle on the back of the papal artifact comes clear," he said. "The flight path of the swallow and the course of the river intersect here. Yes, right here at our beloved St. Philomena's, where many years ago a battle was fought, as the painting at the Adirondack attests. Above us, where a church now stands, the Padre Alonso Miranda and Pere Jean Pierre de Chantal established an *asistencia,* a extension of their Del Agua Mission. Perhaps it was already a shrine dedicated to the Lord of the Earthquakes, or maybe that came about as the *asistencia* fell into disuse—that we'll have to investigate later. Somewhere along the line, that marvelous stone altar which seems to contain a holograph of the Crown of Thorns was brought down here, along with a monstrance which has some connection with Blessed Raymond Lully. This, too, will be the focus of later investigation. Arthur, you're hired."

"At your service," said Arthur. "Gladly."

"Masses were said upon it," said Father, "apparently in the open air."

"And this crypt was constructed beneath," said Edward. "Three score and fifteen hands below."

"We'll measure to make sure," said Father, "but yes, probably so."

"Then at some point," said Lieutenant Taper, "the keepers of the shrine decided to hide the altar down here."

"Probably when the Americanos invaded," said Monsignor Havermeyer. "You think so, Roberto?"

"This I do not know," said Mr. Guadalupe.

"I think yes," said Duggo.

"I can see I'm going to be very, very busy," said Arthur, sighing good-naturedly. "But what about the treasure that bleeds?"

"I think I have that figured out," said Father.

"Well don't keep us hangin' from the rafters," said Kahlúa Hummingbird. "Lead us to it."

"You've already seen it," said Father. "But the treasure bleeds only under specific circumstances."

"Ah," said Pierre. "When the sacred words are said—"

"Upon the crown of thorns within an altar of stone," said the Jonanderthal Man—hey, I could swear I'd seen his picture in books.

"So all you have to do is celebrate Mass—?" said Joel.

"And the bread in that monstrance will bleed?" concluded Sergeant Wickes, albeit derisively. "I've heard some strange things—"

"Not so fast," said Lieutenant Taper. "I've read about such things."

"Sure," said the sergeant, "and every other week someone finds Jesus' face in a tortilla."

"Much as I dislike making it sound like a clinical experiment," said Father, "the fact is that Father Albert is going to have a Requiem. I don't know if the Consecration must occur on the stone altar down here or whether the altar above will do—somehow I tend to think it doesn't matter, Transubstantiation being, well, Transubstantiation. Still, if you Tumblars wouldn't mind carrying the casket down the stairs—"

"We will be honored," said Edward.

"Indeed," said Pierre. "Lads, let's get to it."

"We'll need a sixth pallbearer," said Arthur.

"Be glad to," offered Lieutenant Taper.

"You would," said his partner.

"Be prepared to eat your hat," said Taper.

"I don't wear one."

"Your words, then."

"Monsignor," said Father, "would you like to do the honors, or shall I?"

"Let's haggle about that on our way upstairs to fetch our vestments and accoutrements," said Havermeyer.

"Roberto," said Father, "did you get a grave dug out back?"

"Dios mios," answered Mr. Guadalupe. "We did not."

"Not to worry," said Father. "I wouldn't be surprised if there's a niche waiting for Father Albert down here. See if you can find it."

"What about ush?" asked Millie.

"Honey," said Kahlúa, "this is where we get ourselves properly disposed."

"Disposed away," said Mrs. Magillicuddy. "Now where's in tarnation's green earth is my Rosary?"

93

HOW DOES ONE DESCRIBE the indescribable? As best as one can.

It took an excruciating hour to get ready, what with Father and Monsignor procuring black vestments and altar vessels, Larry Taper and the Tumblars lugging down Father Albert's casket and cart, Kahlúa and Millie fetching the altar linens and coverings, Duggo and Spade getting wooden folding chairs from the storage room in the rectory, Roberto probing the rear wall for an unoccupied burial niche—successfully, as it turned out—and Mrs. Magillicuddy reciting fifteen decades of the Rosary aloud as only she can mispronounce the prayers. Father gave me the task of retrieving an altar stone from the desk drawer in his study, the same altar stone that a man named Norman Slater, proprietor of "Norman's Studio Supply" entrusted to him a week ago Saturday during our first case involving Cardinal Fulbright's Murkenstein chalice. It was an arduous task, ascending and descending the grotto stairs again, but it distracted me from the quivering whimpering of my imploded stomach.

Well, I suppose that hunger is its own distraction.

Father Baptist insisted that the kerosene lamps be extinguished and all illumination be via the burning of beeswax candles. Candlesticks were placed on both sides of both altars, and several more were spaced around the room. Duggo and Spade took the news good-naturedly that we had all decided to kneel throughout the Mass rather than sit on the chairs they had provided. When I said "we had all decided" I meant that everyone else but me, including Mrs. Magillicuddy, had so resolved and I was shamed into concurring. The folding chairs were relegated to the rear corners.

Oh yes, there was one final element. Father Baptist hustled back up the stairs one more time. He came back with a simple golden Chalice which he kept secreted behind a loose stone in the church. The Chalice had a grand history and a name: *Le San Pres'que Grall.*

In any case, having left the monstrance where it had waited for so many years, Monsignor Havermeyer celebrated Mass at the stone altar facing the wooden altar. Blessed Raymond's monstrance was in his line of sight, though his attention was riveted on the matter before him. Father Baptist acted as deacon at his side. What coin they tossed or candlestick they had spun to see who did what I do not know. We, the ragtag congregation, were situated between the two altars facing Blessed Raymond's monstrance. Father Albert's coffin was in our midst, but that's the way of funerals—as well as one more loop of barbwire wrapped around my stomach.

> <u>GARDENING</u> <u>TIPS</u>: It may seem odd to attend Mass with the priest behind, but that's actually how St. Peter's in Rome is arranged, or was before the Novus Ordo was promulgated. Back in the day, the Pope celebrated Mass facing east with the congregation in front of him likewise facing east -- away from him. Proof that the Church in Her wisdom never intended that the congregation and the celebrant face each other.
>
> --M.F.

There's nothing quite like a traditional Requiem Mass to sober one up, and it seemed to have that very effect on our dear Millie. As for me, I held my breath through the Prayers at the Foot of the Altar—yes, even if there's no stairs that's what this introductory ritual is called. I started taking little gasps during the reading of the Epistle and Gospel. By the Preface and into the Canon I was breathing more or less normally. But come the Consecration, I was back in oxygen-depravation mode. I had certainly heard of Eucharistic Miracles for years, but they always happened in an unpretentious village in an unpronounceable province of an unfamiliar foreign country. This was about to happen right here, at our very own St. Philomena's in front of our very eyes. And of course, no matter the stamp of Blessed Raymond Lully on the monstrance or the stains on the glass receptacle, no matter all the hoopla over the artifact and its puzzle, there was always the nagging doubt that this time, perhaps because of creepy me being there, the miracle wouldn't happen. But it had to happen, we were all sure of it. Of course we were.

My heart seemed to stop, or at least the blood-flow to my brain was temporarily derailed, when the moment arrived. Monsignor Havermeyer leaned over the host grasped between his thumbs and forefingers, and whispered the Sacred Words:

HOC EST ENIM CORPUS MEUM.

For this is my Body.

A red blemish appeared on the Host in the monstrance, or rather burst from its white center, and began spreading downward. I was reminded of the time Father took a bullet in his right shoulder, only there was no jostle of impact, just the eruption of blood. The moment was too intense for gasps or exclamations. As Father rang the bells and Monsignor elevated the Bread of Life, a thousand drops of scalding sweat popped out of my scalp all at once. I suspect everyone present experienced some analogous reaction.

As the pulsing overtones of the bells died away, silence reigned except for faint, wispy hisses as Monsignor Havermeyer, his attention riveted on the miracle taking place in his very hands, sibilated the words that transformed ordinary wine into the Precious Blood of Christ:

HIC EST ENIM CALIX SANGUINUS MEI,
NOVI ET ÆTERNI TESTAMENTI:
MYSTERIUM FIDEI:
QUI PRO VOBIS ET PRO MULTIS
EFFUNDETUR IN REMISSIONEM PECCATORUM.

For this is the chalice of my Blood,
of the new and eternal testament:
the mystery of faith:
which shall be shed for you and for many
unto remission of sins.

My own blood pounded in my temples as I watched the glistening crimson fluid ooze from the Host in the monstrance. Having saturated the lower half of the Host, it began pouring in undulating dribbles into the lower chamber of the hourglass. The liquid glistened mysteriously in the candlelight as it pooled and rose within its glass prison. Monsignor Havermeyer completed the formula thus:

HÆC QUOTIESCUMQUE FECERITIS,
IN MEI MEMORIAM FACIETIS.

> *As often as ye shall do these things,*
> *ye shall do them in memory of me.*

With that he genuflected and elevated the chalice, Father rang the bells again, and the blood in the monstrance churned and bubbled like lava in a caldera. Suddenly it struck me. Raymond Lully was alive when the thirteenth century gave way to the fourteenth. Whether he had been present when this marvel first occurred, or It had been bleeding for centuries in that hourglass and he had simply arranged for its encasement, I did not know. Whatever the circumstances, the Blood of Christ had been gushing and gathering in that ostensorium for many, many years. Somehow, sometime, it had been transported halfway around the world to this far-flung outpost of the Catholic Faith. I seemed to recall that Blessed Junipero Serra had been buried in the Mission San Carlos Borromeo at Carmel-by-the-Sea with a relic of Blessed Lully on his chest. Perhaps he or one of his fellow missionaries had carted the monstrance to California. Most likely the Host had bled down here in the dark every time Father Baptist and all his predecessors celebrated Mass above, whether in the church or the shrine or in the open air. And here I was—me, Martin Feeney, an incompetent gardener and a worthless sinner—kneeling among these good people, about to receive the Body, Blood, Soul and Divinity of Christ on my tongue at the hand of Monsignor Havermeyer, and it would be the same Body, Blood, Soul and Divinity that bled away in that monstrance, and that the Apostles consumed at the Last Supper, and that Faithful Catholics would consume until the end of time. My chest, my skull, my very being was gripped with a severe case of the crushing humbles.

How true it was, and how earnestly my words commingled with Monsignor Havermeyer's as he said:

DOMINE, NON SUM DIGNUS,
UT INTRES SUB TECTUM MEUM:
SED TANTUM DIC VERBO, ET SANABITUR ANIMA MEA.

> *Lord, I am not worthy*
> *that thou shouldst enter under my roof:*
> *say but the word, and my soul shall be healed.*

94

IT WAS NEARLY FOUR A.M. when Pierre knocked on my door.

"You barely made it up the grotto stairs after Mass," he whispered as I pulled it open. "I was surprised to see your light on."

"Pain trumps fatigue," I answered with a wince and a grimace. "Come on in."

"I thought maybe you'd collapsed, sprawled across your bed, and to heck with the lights. Oh—I didn't realize."

"Not to worry. Ignore the priest upon my mattress. Unlike me, Father can sleep through earthquakes, monsoons, and presidential elections."

Pierre dropped his whisper to a faint hiss. "Does he often sleep in your room?"

"First time."

"And what happened to your books? They were all over the bed yesterday."

"On the chair behind you. Father offered to help me move them so I could lie down. I had an idea I wanted to pound out at the typewriter before I hit the sack, and he offered to test the bedsprings. He read for a few minutes from my copy of *Eucharistic Miracles* by Joan Carroll Cruz, refreshing his awesome memory, no doubt. He then said he wanted to think for a minute and that the clacking of my keys was soothing—a notion I found odd but what the hey. Next thing I knew I had reworked and hopefully improved my account of our first encounter with Lucius T. Portifoy at the 'House of Illusions,' and Father was bonding with Peter, James, and John in Gethsemane. Say—how did you know about the books on my bed?"

"It's complicated."

"Pierre."

"Okay, if you must know. Yesterday morning Father needed a lift to the Adirondack—you having gone missing and all—and knowing that my editrix had a car, sent me to fetch her. She and Millie were in here—"

"Here? Kahlúa and Millie? What the devil were they—?"

"Sorry, Old Top. Surely you noticed the disarray. They were on a mission, you see. Millie said you said that if anything happened to you she was to make sure your relic of the Crown of Thorns was secure."

"What? Yesterday was Sunday, right? I was snatched, what, Saturday night. Why, I'd only been missing a few hours—"

"Don't pop a vessel, Dear Chap. Remember your blood pressure."

"My veins are withstanding the strain, thank-you. I guess I asked for it, but I can't help feeling invaded."

"Look at it this way: you now know how seriously Millie takes your requests."

"If I ever have an estate I'll be sure to make her the executrix. And what was Kahlúa doing in here with her?"

"They've become attached at the hip, methinks."

"Oh great, Siamese busybodies. I guess that explains why Millie brought me a snack an hour ago—a plate of fried chicken, grits, and black-eyed peas. That's a first, too. Say, have you and the lads finished cleaning up the church?"

"Hardly." Pierre patted his coat sleeves. I did not appreciate the powder that puffed off of them in my close quarters. "It will take weeks. Mainly we dusted off the pews and kneelers so the morning congregants won't ruin their clothes. Would that the dust would vanish the same way the Blood in the monstrance did as Monsignor Havermeyer said *'Ite, missa est.'*"

"Is that when it happened? I wasn't looking."

"Just like that. Suddenly the Host was pure white and the Blood was gone."

"I wonder if it's been doing that all along."

"What do you mean?"

"All these years when Mass has been said on the altar in the church. I mean, surely the miracle isn't dependent on Mass being said on the stone altar."

"You're right. Blessed Lully never came to California, and clearly the monstrance belonged to him. It wouldn't have been fashioned as it was if the Host hadn't been bleeding already, probably whenever Mass was said near it."

"So has everyone gone home?" I asked around a yawn.

"The lads, yes," said Pierre. "I didn't notice when Taper and Wickes left. Officer Wexler is curled up on the bench in the garden, and Mrs. Magillicuddy is huddled beside her. Haven't seen my editrix for a while, and Millie's light is off."

"I guess that accounts for everyone," I nodded.

"There's something you could fill me in on," said Pierre. "I understand that our Jonathan is having his first relational crisis with his beloved Stella. Apparently she's been negatively influenced by Millie's recitation of Saint Cyprian."

"So he told me."

"Yesterday he shows up for High Mass unshaven. When I pointed out this embarrassing oversight, he laid the responsibility at your feet. He said you had suggested that he peruse *The Pedagogue* by Saint

Clement of Alexandria. Your strategy he described as 'Fire with fire.' That's a quote."

"I suppose I am guilty, though I'm not sure of precisely what. Trads have a knack for finding something in a Saint's writings that bolsters some itch they can't scratch. You know how Father harps on viewing all such things in context. I confess I don't know the circumstances under which St. Cyprian wrote *Treatises*. Apparently the women were out of control and needed reeling in. How scrupulously his admonitions apply to us today in our culture, I don't know. I told Jonathan this was one for Father Baptist, but he insisted."

"So what did St. Clement have to say?"

"It's been a while," said I, clearing my throat, "but to the best of my recollection, it goes something like this:

> How womanly it is for one who is a man to comb himself and shave himself with a razor, for the sake of fine effect, and to arrange his hair at the mirror, shave his cheeks, pluck hairs out of them, and smooth them! ... For God wished women to be smooth and to rejoice in their locks alone growing spontaneously, as a horse in his mane. But He adorned man like the lions, with a beard, and endowed him as an attribute of manhood, with a hairy chest—a sign of strength and rule.

"Whoa ho!" exclaimed Pierre. "That explains our Jonathan's behavior."

"And I think he'll win points with this part:

> This, then, is the mark of a man, the beard. By this, he is seen to be a man. It is older than Eve. It is the token of the superior nature ... It is therefore unholy to desecrate the symbol of manhood, hairiness.

"Oh, my dear Martin," said Pierre, positively beside himself. "I do believe you have provided hairy young Jonathan with a brilliant stratagem—an imposing counter-weapon to be sure—and no doubt unleashed the winds of war!"

By this point in the conversation I really wanted to sit down, but as there was only the squeaky chair at the writing desk, I didn't want to seem impolite. Fortified with Millie's wee-hour snack, I bravely pressed on. "What about the grotto?"

"Oh, that," sighed Pierre, reluctant to return to the green earth. "Ah well, Señor Guadalupe blocked off the entrance with sawhorses and duct tape. Father Baptist is going to make an announcement from the pulpit, warning everyone not to go in there for the time being. I imagine the stairway will have to be reinforced and handrails put in. I can't imagine how it will ever be made wheelchair accessible."

"Wheelchair—? What are you talking about, Pierre?"

"Pilgrims, Sir Martin. Surely Saint Philomena's will become a great shrine. People will come from miles around to see the Treasure that Bleeds."

"Get real, Pierre. This is Los Angeles. As Sergeant Wickes pointed out, people will flock to a taco stand where the cook finds the face of Jesus on a tortilla. Do you want hordes of gullible miracle chasers and snake-oil peddlers invading our peaceful haven here?"

"Hmm. You have a point there, Mister Feeney. There are more morons collected here than any other place on earth. H. L. Mencken said so."

"Well, there you have it."

"So what do you think Father will do about the, uh, the miracle under the church?"

"No doubt he'll leave it be," said an unexpected voice.

"Father Baptist," said Pierre and myself.

The lumpy mattress squeaked as Father heaved himself to a sitting position. "'Give not that which is holy to dogs; neither cast ye your pearls before swine, lest perhaps they trample them under their feet, and turning upon you, they tear you.'"

"Saint Matthew," said the gardener. "Seven six."

"Then you're not going public with this," said Pierre.

Father shook his head, smacked his dry lips, and blinked flakes from his eyes. "Much as I'd like to stoke your ambitions and increase the circulation of the *Artsy*, Pierre, I meant what I said down below after Mass. First off, we don't know what we have here. A miracle, yes, but where did it come from? What is its history? Secondly, an ecclesiastical investigation would draw Cardinal Fulbright's gaze upon us in ways that we've been spared thus far."

"And thirdly?" coaxed yours truly. "There has to be a thirdly."

Father glanced at me, then swung himself off the bed and rose to an upright position. "Who was it who said, 'God in His omnipotence could not give more, in His wisdom He knew not how to give more, in His riches He had not more to give, than the Eucharist.'"

"Sounds like St. Augustine," said Pierre.

"Bravo," said Father. "The Eucharist itself is the greatest gift we have. A bleeding Host is not a greater miracle. It is merely a compelling confirmation of the hidden Reality. I'm not denying that such phenomena can bolster our Faith, but I'm not inclined to cater to the marvel-mongers. Not at this point in time, in any case."

"So it'll just be our secret," I mused. "Just us three, and Millie and Kahlúa and Mrs. Magillicuddy and Sybil Wexler and Lieutenant Taper—"

"And Sergeant Wickes," said Pierre with a chuckle. "Surely he can keep it under his hat."

"And the Tumblars," said I. "Let's see, did we leave anyone out?"

"I admit it will take a considerable collective self-restraint," said Father. "Everyone who was meant to see the miracle did. Of this we can be sure. Let us hope they will live up to the responsibility."

"They should," said I. "The oath of secrecy you made everyone take, gathered around the altar of stone, well—"

"I should think it would be sufficiently intimidating," said Pierre.

"I was going to say," said I, "that I won't even record it in my memoirs."

"That intimidating," said Father. "Well, then let's hope everyone else takes it as seriously. By the way, Pierre, you didn't finish your story."

"Excuse me?" said Pierre.

"Thursday evening at the Knights' meeting when you graced us with a synopsis of the sacrilegious behavior of one Oswald Misler, you left out the best part."

"Did I?" Pierre adjusted his monocle. "What could be better than the floor falling away and the Sir Oswald clinging to the edge of the altar for dear life?"

"The fact," said Father, "that when he begged the priest to remove the large Host from his mouth it was found to be bleeding."

"The Host? You don't say."

"I do say."

"Bleeding."

"Profusely. It was placed in a silver monstrance. So many pilgrims came to venerate the miraculous bleeding Host that a large church was built around the original altar. Emperors and archdukes were among the supplicants."

"I can't believe I missed that," said Pierre. "I gleaned my part of the story from a pilgrim tour website on the Internet. I should have looked into good Catholic sources—and to think I might have solved the riddle of the bleeding treasure."

"Well, at least you understood the significance of the 'house of gold.'"

"That I did." Pierre patted himself on the head. "That I did."

"I assume you're talking about the verse from the back of the artifact," said I, taking up my cane and shifting some of my weary weight onto it.

"Indeed," said Father. "I'm not above kicking myself for missing the significance of the treasure that bleeds. Only last week I was reading *The Holy Sacrifice of the Mass* by Fr. Michael Müller while I was working on my sermon. The book began with the story of the Church of the Holy Cross."

"Twelfth century," interjected the gardener who had transformed Father's illegible scribbling into ten typed pages. "Augsburg, Germany. A certain woman, after receiving Holy Communion at Mass, removed the Host from her mouth and took it home. She somehow coated it all over with wax and kept it for years."

"Why do you suppose she did that?" asked Pierre.

"I hold the hope," said Father, "that it was misplaced zeal, that she genuinely cherished the Eucharist and therefore wanted to have It close. Perhaps, like most of us, she felt her needs were special, that her concerns superceded propriety."

"Maybe she was inordinately self-involved," said I.

"Or just plain bonkers," suggested Pierre.

"Alas," said Father, "none of us knows, and Fr. Müller didn't say, so let us be charitable and hope for the best."

"Whatever," said I. "Guilt began to gnaw at her, until finally she was compelled to confess what she had done to a priest."

"He immediately retrieved the homemade reliquary and tried to open it," said Father. "But instead of the Host inside the wax, he discovered—"

"Raw flesh," said I. "It was placed in a crystal vase and returned to the Church of the Cross where it resides, blood-red and intact, to this day. A medical team examined it and found it to be the cross-section of a human heart. They said it shouldn't have survived incorrupt in its non-airtight receptacle, but there it was."

"Many have been healed," said Father, "by praying before the Host of Augsburg. Eight centuries it's been there, yet few today have heard of it."

"Or would believe it if they did," said Pierre. "Would that we could all afford a road tour of these and other wonders."

"But why should we," noted the gardener, "considering we ourselves are now on the miracle map?"

"This site has been on the map since before we were born," said Father. "Fortunately it has been hidden, and hidden it shall remain—"

He was interrupted by a fierce trilling sound.

"Father," said Pierre.

"Oh," said Father, surprised to find a cell phone lurking within the mysterious concourses of his cassock. "I retrieved this from my desk before Mass."

"The send button," said Pierre. "The one with the little telephone icon on it."

"Hello," said Father, tossing him a "As if I didn't know" glance. "Oh, why yes, My Lord. How did you get this number? *I* don't even know this number … Oh?"

"Who?" asked Pierre.

"A bishop, obviously," said I, clasping my hands behind my back. "Father's well-connected, you know."

"Right away, Your Lordship," said Father, clicking off the device like a pro.

"So what's up?" I asked.

"That was the nuncio," said Father. "He's a man of surprising … resources."

"How so?" said Pierre, his journalistic nerve piqued.

"This is definitely not for publication," said Father. "No, don't stick out your lower lip like that and look like a wounded puppy. This is 'in the family.' Martin, do you remember when Sylvio Bonsignore joined us at the San Fernando Mission? He kept working the words 'strange' and 'head' into his sentences."

"Now that you mention it," said I with a nod, though I must confess the memory was rather sketchy.

"He was feeding me information," said Father, "and if you fellows want to know why, he's in my study."

"You mean he—?" asked Pierre.

"That's where he just called me from." Father looked as though he'd just guzzled two pots of Millie's boiled-down-to-tar coffee. "Let's go."

95

"FATHER BAPTEESTA," SAID SYLVIO BONSIGNORE as we bounded into Father's den. Onlookers probably would not have described my hobbling as bounding, but inside I was a raging, if careworn, basset hound with a burst of enthusiasm. What little enthusiasm that might be, it vaporized altogether when I saw that His Lordship was seated in my favorite chair! Father, having knelt and kissed the bishop's ring, moved directly to his favorite chair behind his desk. Pierre, having followed suit, positioned himself in front of my favorite chair's twin. This left me with the seat Monsignor Havermeyer would have favored by default if he had been with us. I know, I know, a trivial matter, but it was nonetheless distracting. "Not wanting to awaken your, ah, gracious housekeeper, I took da liberty of entering t'roo da kitchen door," said the nuncio, smiling with an excess of teeth to match his fingers. "My, ah, chauffeur weel return for me shortly."

"My house is your house," said Father. "Do you mind if my friends join us?"

"Monsieur Bontemps I know by reputation," said the bishop with a twinkle in his eyes. "I weel trust him if you weel, Father, provided he swear never to repeat or report dat which is spoken in dis room tonight. Meester Feeney, you are not obliged to kiss my ring. I can see you are inna pain."

"Not in the least, My Lord," said I. "But I appreciate the reprieve—"

"Provided," he added with a raised finger, "you swear dat when you work dees conversation into one of youra stories you report da facts accurately in dat, ah, mythical City of Los Angeles of yours. Don't looka so surprised. From what I 'ave read of your knotty book, it is—how do you say it?—ah, si: it is a hoot."

"My Lord, what can I say?" said I, or at least so I tried. Actually nothing came out of my mouth but an inarticulate rasp. I wondered if he had read as far as the Saint Fallopia joke.

Pierre suppressed a protest at the uneven distribution of conditions regarding our inclusion in the conversation. I would have sympathized with him, but at that moment I was pondering how the papal nuncio might have heard of my writing efforts, as he had alluded to at the San Fernando Mission, let alone obtained and read my unpublished manuscript as he had just now disclosed.

"Perhaps I have too much time onna my hands," admitted the bishop with a conspiratorial wink. He patted Pierre's arm as the Tumblar seated himself. "Strange, is it not, Monsieur Bontemps, dat Cardinal Fulbright has not been seen at 'Paneno's' of late?"

"We all play our parts," said Pierre, smiling knowingly.

"To what do we owe the honor of your visit, My Lord?" asked Father, opening a drawer and dredging up his briar pipe.

"Much has happened dis night," said the nuncio, settling back into my chair. "Da Treasure, it did bleed, did it not?"

"Indeed," said Father, stuffing his pipe thoughtfully.

"And how," said Pierre, producing a cigar. He held it out to the bishop, who declined.

"And da Crown of Thorns in da altar of stone," said Sylvio Bonsignore, his smile expansive, "it resides beneath your beautiful church?"

"Three score and fifteen hands below," said Pierre as he clipped off the end of the cigar.

"How did you know—?" I asked both of them.

"Shall we say," said the bishop, "that da eyes of Rome—or rather, ah, some of dem—'ave been watching, waiting to see if da legend were true."

"Then you knew it was here all along," said Father, striking a match.

"Let us say dat I so hoped," said the nuncio. "As did others."

"'It is a strange thing when the heart rules the head,'" said Father, drawing the flame into the bowl of his pipe. Smoke erupted from it and his mouth and nose. "You knew that San Juan Capistrano was the starting point."

"Si, si. I also arranged for your Meester Weellie Kappsa to procure da, ah, da centerpiece. "

"How did you manage that?" asked Father.

The nuncio rolled his eyes under those overhanging shrubberies that served as his eyebrows and laughed. "It was hoped dat you, Father Bapteesta, would succeed where Bishop Ravenshorst did not. I am likewise satisfied dat da miracle resides on your private property."

And not in Morley Fulbright's clutches, thought the gardener.

"I hope it weel stay datta way," added the bishop.

"Then you're not going to take it with you?" asked Pierre, accepting Father's match.

"Heavens, no," said the nuncio, laughing again. He inhaled deeply of the smoke swirling around him. "It is precisely where it belongs: in safe hands."

"I don't know what to say," said Father, easing back in his chair.

"No doubt it weel come to you when I have gone." I got the impression that the nuncio had said all that he had come to say, but just then he fished around in the magisterial folds of his cassock and produced a small piece of folded paper which he handed to Father Baptist. "Please be so kind as to give dis to Arthur von Derschmidt. We have observed his recent travels with … enthusiasm."

"And what is it?" asked Father.

"Something dat weel, ah, interest him," said the nuncio. "You may look at it if you like. By da way, something you should know: da trail to da men who injured your friend, Meester Weellie Kappsa, it leads to da Flying Saint."

"Saint Joseph of Copertino?" said Father.

"Dis conversation 'as never occurred," said Sylvio Bonsignore, rising regally from my seat. "Except, perhaps, in Meester Feeney's Los Angeles."

That being said, Father accompanied the papal nuncio down the hallway to the front door, Pierre and yours truly following behind. It was truly surprising, at least for me, when Father opened said door and there, standing on the stoop with his hand poised to knock, was none other than Roderick Roundhead.

"I have come for His Lordship," said the man manhole covers built.

"My ride," explained His Lordship.

"Indeed," said Father. He looked at me with those eyes that seemed to whisper, fatigued yet sparkling, "Well, Martin, this explains a few things," but all he actually said around the pipe clenched in his teeth was, "Mr. Roundhead, a moment if you please."

> GARDENING TIPS: For one thing, at least for me, it explained how Bishop Bonsignore knew the number of Father Baptist's cell phone: Ernie Corben gave him the phone a week before; Ernie worked for Roderick Roundhead; and Roddy gave the nuncio rides in his limo, no doubt discussing such matters. Small world.
>
> It also explained how the nuncio obtained a copy of my manuscript. I should be sending out demands for royalties.
>
> —M.F.

"Here?" asked the millionaire.

"I shall wait in da car," said Bishop Bonsignore. "I bid you good evening."

"Good night, Your Lordship," said Father. Then, as the nuncio descended the stairs and crossed the sidewalk to the stretch limo waiting there, he turned his attention to the richest man for miles. "Please be sure to give my regards to your Aunt Hortense. She and Mehitabelle are considering reprinting a prayer book I recommended to them. I imagine she has already contacted you about Monsignor Aspic."

Roundhead remained silent and stern, not the slightest bit intimidated or defensive.

"I'll not beat around the bush," said Father. "I can't prove your involvement, but even you should have known that drawing Mister Feeney into the situation would provoke my—"

"I admit," said Roundhead, "that suggesting to Pierre that he take Mister Feeney's manuscript to Horty and Hitty was ... farfetched." His facial musculature pulled into a tenth of a smile on the last word.

"I'd call it malicious at least," said Pierre, adjusting his monocle, "and at worst, cruel."

"And that's all you're going to admit," said Father scornfully.

Pierre cleared his throat while Roundhead heaved his shoulders all of three millimeters.

Father outdid both of them in the throat clearing and shrugging department. "Be advised that this changes matters."

"What matters?" asked Roundhead, smile gone.

"All that matters. You may be beyond the law, but you are not above rebuke."

"Spare me your sermons, Father. The nuncio has a plane to catch and I promised to get him to the airport on time. I make it a rule never to disappoint a Prince of the Church."

"But her lesser servants, the bushwa, they are expendable." Father placed a hand on my shoulder. "And their servants' servants are even more at risk."

Roundhead's jaw muscles rippled. "I will hardly admit knowledge of the good monsignor's troubles: allegedly kidnapped by my aunts, the Doily Sisters." His million-dollar grimace conveyed disdain beyond mere derision. "Do you really think any sane police investigator would believe them capable of such acts of outrageous, criminal behavior? Sounds to me like some wild plot your dramatist gardener would concoct. But let's—just as an impromptu exercise in frivolous speculation—let's suppose that I have been, in fact, in on the whole thing. I can easily buy the monsignor's silent cooperation with the promise of a book contract, and he's the cardinal archbishop's right-hand man to boot. That leaves your gardener to face alone a world desensitized to scandals involving the Church, to tell a crazy story about the Church's own spokesman that even he won't confirm. To extend the speculative exercise a frivolous step further, I only learned of Mister Feeney's, shall we say, predicament a short while ago when my aunt phoned me in a panic. I assure you I was taken completely by surprise."

"So you didn't know about their designs on Mister Feeney," said Father, removing his hand from my shoulder.

Mr. Roundhead sniffed. "You, Father, had just left the premises, your over-imaginative partner and a discredited policewoman in tow. A curious situation, to be sure. I should think that it would seem to some that Mister Feeney's true purpose is to draw attention to his spooky, twisted manuscript; and this at the expense of the reputation of two venerable, if admittedly tipsy, old women—sweet, elderly ladies who would gleefully swat a fly but would certainly not form a kidnapping ring. And should he complain anyway, loud enough to attract media attention, I can think of several of your parishioners who would be only too glad to whisper their dark suspicions regarding Mister Feeney to an eager and sympathetic correspondent from a major network. While such things are easy for me to arrange, the opportunity to appear on national television does not present itself every day to the average angry Traditionalist."

"The plane," said Father, his tone cold.

"Right," said Roundhead. He stopped himself in mid-turn. "Be advised, I took the liberty of removing the trash from your doorstep."

"Trash?" asked the twisted dramatist. It's true: my insides were considerably intertwined at that moment. The body reacts like that when your ego has been kicked in the *solar plexus*. I figured I was due for a break.

"Edison Winger," said Roundhead offhandedly. He dug into the outside pocket of his overcoat and produced a set of handcuffs. They gleamed in the gloom. "I understand the clock is ticking with respect to Officer Wexler's tenure with the police force, but she may need these yet."

"She has to account for them, in any case," said Father. "Thank-you."

"And," said Roundhead, parting the front of his overcoat and digging something else out of an inside pocket—a familiar leather pouch as it turned out. "Bishop Bonsignore insists that I hand this over to you. Mister Winger had this on him. It was manifestly against orders for him to keep the artifact. He was to have given it to you along with that hideous chalice. That would have been the end of that storyline at least. For this prolongation he now has a penalty levied against him, a kind of reparation tax if you will. In any case, you can now be twice the hero when you go riding into Morley Fulbright's current hiding place on your noble white steed. He happens to be staying in the northeast penthouse at the Adirondack, though it's likely he'll be moving to his next hideout later this morning. Checkout time is eleven."

> GARDENING TIPS: Did you catch that reference to a
> storyline? I can't help but wonder if that was a
> reveal on his part. He knew about me. Surely he
> knew that, God permitting, I would write about
> this one day. Could it be that he was beginning
> to perceive himself as a potential character in
> one of my books? Could he have been trying to
> write his own part, as it were, assuming I would
> allow him to get away with it? Now this is truly
> getting spooky and twisted!
>
> —M.F.

"One can't help but wonder," said Father, accepting the pouch, "the involvement of the papal nuncio in all this."

"It goes without saying that he is unaware of the, uh, subterranean activities of my aunts," said Roundhead. "His head is tangled in artifacts and ecclesiastical politics. I find his insistence that you be the caretaker of the Treasure to be troublesome. I could protect It better than you, but as I said—"

"You make it a rule never to disappoint a Prince of the Church," said Pierre.

Roderick actually held up his right hand, snapped his ringed fingers—he really had that snap down, by the way, like bamboo sticks—and actually pointed at Pierre. Surely I'd seen that gesture in a black-and-white movie in which the streets are wet and the streetlights poorly maintained. "Don't be perturbed," he said to the Tumblar. "We all play our parts."

Pierre suppressed a cough.

"I honestly had no idea how it would go, Pierre," said Mr. Roundhead, his voice strangely low, almost conspiratorial. "Sending you to my aunts was, to put it plainly, a practical joke I meant to play on them." His sudden candor took me completely by surprise, but Father Baptist just luxuriated in a prosperous plume of smoke. "We Roundheads are consummate pranksters. I assure you it never occurred to me that they might take Mister Feeney into the umbra of their hospitality."

"But you did know about Monsignor Aspic," said Father.

"Guilty," he said, "but protected as stated before. Look, Father, I've no wish to strong-arm you, of all people. But blood, as they say, is thicker than water. I will protect my own, and don't think for a moment I won't."

"And Father Albert," said Father after executing a perfect ring within a ring. "Surely you knew about him."

"Yes, but not until he had been their prisoner for some time."

"They mentioned your participation in the refurbishing of their chapel," said Father.

"At the time," said Roundhead, voice still low but lips smiling, "I was only too glad to help them with the restoration. I thought they were doing it for sentimental, hopefully devotional reasons. I had no idea that Father Albert was locked away in the sacristy."

"But one day," prompted Father.

"But one day," deferred Mr. Roundhead, "they invited me over, all atwitter. It was the anniversary of their double wedding, you see, and they told me they'd found a priest to say a Tridentine Mass. They pulled me downstairs ever so dangerously in their excitement. They had done such a magnificent job of restoring that chapel. Indeed, it had never looked like that in all its history. And there we were, kneeling in the front pew, our little family mouthing our devotions together … when the sacristy door opened, and out came Father Albert, dragging a chain behind him!"

Pierre let out a snigger.

I must admit I saw the humor of the scenario. It was like something out of *Arsenic and Old Lace*. What do you do when you discover that your sweet, twiddly aunts are sweet but raving lunatics?

Even Father was smiling around the pipe clenched between his teeth. He removed the smoldering implement and said, "You're telling us the truth."

"I couldn't make it up," said Roderick. I use his first name here for human he had become. "It was the weirdest moment of my life. 'What is the meaning of this?' I demanded then and there. 'Shush!' they replied. 'Didn't your parents teach you never to talk during Mass?'"

"I'm sure it was quite an explanation after the Last Gospel," said Pierre after a long drag on his log.

"To be sure," said Roderick. "That was the night I got most of these gray hairs. Naturally I told them this was unconscionable, that we had to restore Father Albert to his rightful life, that I would probably exhaust our fortune paying off the powers that be. Oddly, it was Father Albert who would have no part of it. He stood there in full vestments, that chain trailing off behind him, insisting that he be allowed to stay. He wanted no part of the world he had left behind, that he considered the shackle on his ankle a bracelet of honor. I tell you—Father, Pierre, Martin—he told me he had saved his soul down there. Imagine that. It's like that verse St. Thomas More wrote in his Psalter in the Tower of London. 'Give me the Grace, O Lord ... to think my greatest enemies my best friends—'"

"'For the brethren of Joseph," cut in the gardener, "'could never have done him so much good with their love and favor as they did him with their malice and hatred.'"

"That's right, Martin," said Roderick. "You quote it in your story. That's why it comes to mind."

"So you've read it, too," said I.

"I must say," said he with a wink. "I like the Saint Fallopia joke."

"Your aunts sure didn't," said I, rubbing my poor tummy.

"I knew they wouldn't," said he.

"Did you know about the cattle prod?" I asked pointedly.

"Cattle prod?" asked Roderick innocently.

"Hi yo Keating," said I.

"You're joking."

"Never about cattle prods."

"So Father Albert chose to stay," said Father thoughtfully. "That says a lot. It's as I suspected. Our Father Albert had a right to his Requiem. Since he wanted to stay below the world from which he had been saved, it is fitting that he's resting in another part of the same shrine."

"The Lord of the Earthquakes," said Roderick. "St. Philomena's has quite a history."

"As does the Treasure that Bleeds," said Father.

"I can help you with that," said Roderick. "But not tonight. The b—"

"Bishop's plane," said Father, Pierre, and myself as one.

"Right," said Roderick. "And Martin, don't be cross at the way I spoke earlier."

"I'm not cross," said I.

"You look cross," said Pierre.

"I'm crotchety," said I. "But no more than usual. I suppose I should be grateful that my manuscript is getting so much use. As a practical joke, now that's one purpose I hadn't imagined. But what the hey, at least it's getting read. Publishing is just a technicality."

"I wouldn't want you to think I'm trying to buy you off," said Roderick, "but I do think I could persuade a publisher or two to give your manuscript a look."

"They've probably already rejected it," said I, thinking of my collection of rejection letters. It is impressive.

"Then perhaps I can encourage them to give it a second look," said Roderick. "No promises. Frankly, I think it's too Catholic to be accepted by any of the major houses. Who knows? Maybe someone should start a new publishing company."

"Now you are trying to buy me off," said the gardener. "Father, I assume you want to go wake up the cardinal. That worked best last time, catching him when he's not running on all cylinders."

"Good idea," said Roderick. "The old bat is blind at sunrise."

"Then good morning, Mister Roundhead," said Father. "Oh, dare I ask just when you learned of your aunts' plans to replace Father Albert with Monsignor Aspic?"

"Better that you don't," said Roderick. "But do bear in mind that what transformed Father Albert might have done likewise to Monsignor Aspic."

"Believe me," said Father. "There was a moment when I was sorely tempted to leave the monsignor in their keeping. But alas, I couldn't. On some level, Father Albert knew he had gone sour and wanted to redeem himself. I don't think Monsignor Aspic perceives that he has done anything amiss. Indeed, he is thoroughly pleased with himself, or so he'd like to believe. He has no devotional roots to return to, no past to make up for. For better or worse, Monsignor Aspic's path is out there in the world Father Albert was happy to leave behind. Heaven help us, but that's where he belongs."

"Perhaps," said Roderick. "We're certainly going to find out."

"Something I'd like to know," said Father. "What is to become of David Smoley? I ask because he was in on the kidnapping of Monsignor Aspic, and I doubt very much that he would have done that on his own."

"Don't be too sure," said Roderick.

"David never met the Doilys," said Father. "Monsignor Aspic always left him in the car after his secret was out. In a family as chatty as yours, your aunts knew all about him. Perhaps they were even aware of the punitive treatment he was receiving from the monsignor. Even so, how would they have contacted him, and why would they have trusted him with their deepest secret?"

"They are resourceful gals," said Roderick, chortling with pride. "I wouldn't put any of it past them."

"Incidentally," I butted in. "Something I figured out while I was, uh, in my predicament: after leaving Monsignor Aspic with the Doily Sisters, David drove to the TV station and used the monsignor's phone. Maybe he just hit 'redial,' or maybe he knew Bishop deQuet's number—he may have even known the bishop was going to be out. I think he left a silent message on the bishop's answering machine, which probably had caller ID—"

"Which explains the message deQuet subsequently left on Aspic's answering machine," said Father, not missing a beat. "'*You didn't leave a message.*' Very good, Martin."

"Ah, shucks."

Father turned his sights on Roderick. "You don't seriously expect me to believe that you didn't instruct David to drive away after Monsignor Aspic went into your aunts' house on a sick call. Surely his subsequent actions, driving to the television station and placing a call from the monsignor's cell phone, that sort of shrewdness is clearly beyond him."

"You'd be surprised about David Smoley," said Roderick. "There's more than you know pent up in that kid. In a strange way, his participation in the kidnapping is his coming out party. He might just be on the verge of starting to grow up."

"But growing up into what?" said the gardener, clearly not buying any of it. "Father, we took David's behavior as the result of perpetual anxiety—well, it was certainly that, but on top of that, perhaps it was just that he was a very bad liar."

"You may be right," said Roderick. "Be that as it may, I think I can find a place for David Smoley. It will take time to convince him once and for all that he doesn't have a vocation, but in time he will understand. I'll see that he gets work suited to his character."

"You mean a taster at a chocolate cake factory?" said I.

"I'm afraid I haven't met the fellow," said Pierre. "Sounds like you've been using him, Old Chap. How are you going to use him in the future?"

"Now don't take that tone with me," said Roderick, but he was smiling. "I have to look out for my soul, too. I needed to know some things that he was in a position to see and hear. Even after Monsignor Aspic learned that David answered to me, he was still privy to certain things that were useful. Monsignor Aspic may be on a leash at the moment, but he's in a position to make David's life even more hellish. He could assign the poor kid to some disreputable priest who's not in jail only because he changes his name and his parish as regularly as his socks."

"That would be awful," said Father.

"So trust me to soften Monsignor Aspic's temper," said Roderick. "I'll see that he gets the necessary strokes and distractions until I can wean David away from under his nose."

"You tread treacherous waters," said Father.

"On that somber note, I bid you all good night."

96

"WAS I DREAMING, PIERRE," ASKED FATHER BAPTIST as he set his pipe in the ashtray on his desk, "or did I hear you say that Sybil Wexler is sleeping in the garden?"

"I did indeed," said Pierre, likewise setting down his cigar. "She's using Mrs. Magillicuddy for a pillow."

"And Kahlúa left in her ostentatious Cadillac?"

"Be sure to say that when she can hear it," said Pierre. "I assume so. It's not out front. I looked when we were on the porch."

"So you're stuck," said Father. "Would you mind watching the fort until I return? Make sure Monsignor Havermeyer is up in time for Mass, that sort of thing."

"I suppose," said Pierre, "though I was hoping you'd give me a lift home so I could at least shower before reporting to work an hour late."

"I'll square it with Kahlúa," said Father. "She'll want an exclusive."

"But you're not going to let her print anything about anything that's been going on," said Pierre.

"Something else will come along," said Father. "It always does. So you'll stay?"

"Yes, under protest, but yes."

"Come, Martin."

We let ourselves out through the kitchen door, but instead of turning left toward the back parking lot, Father turned right toward the garden.

"I have some explaining to do," whispered Father to me. "You'll want to hear this."

"Oh goodie," said I.

We found Sybil Wexler, as foretold, curled up on the bench facing Saint Thérèse the Little Flower. She made such a beautiful question mark. The way her gorgeous fulcra were folded, it frankly took my breath away. And, as also foretold, Sybil's head was resting in dear Mrs. Magillicuddy's lap.

"Shhh," hushed the old woman as we approached.

"Good evening," whispered Father, stooping to a crouch beside her. "I hope you're not uncomfortable."

"Me's?" she rasped. "Ah, you're joshin', Faddah. Her head's as light's as a feather's, it is. Reminds me of my Nell."

"Nell?" asked Father.

"She was sweetness itself, she was," said the old woman dreamily, gently stroking Sybil's hair. "And so is this one's, Faddah. Do let me take her home's with me."

"That's up to her," smiled Father. "Say, I want to talk to you about Lou Costello. You're going to be seeing more of him, right here at St. Philomena's."

"Oh dears," she gasped. "But he's comin' for me in that hearse!"

"That explains it," said Father. "You saw the big black car at the Del Agua Mission, didn't you? The one with Lou Costello as a nun on the side."

"That's right's," said she. "That's right's. I'm old and shriveled up's, don't's I know's it, but I don't want to goes just yet."

Lou Costello, I mouthed silently as a memory from the dining nook wavered behind my eyes.

> *"But then I saw's the hearse."* She had said that through the open window.
>
> *"Hearse?"* asked Father.
>
> *"Parked with all the other cars, it was,"* said she with a mighty sniff. *"Cold shivers, it gave's me, it did's. I thoughts to me self's, 'Uh-oh, he's a'comin' for you, you old crumpet.' I mean's, I asks you, Faddah, why would Lou Costello become a nun? And why would's he comes after me? So's I hidey-tailed it out of there."*
>
> *"I beg your pardon?"* asked Father.
>
> *"I was always so sad, I was, when Abbot 'n' Costello broke up, they did's. But I ask's you, would the nuns take's that cute li'l Lou into their convent? And why's was he's after me's?"*

"The Half Dome insignia on the side of the Doilys' car," said Father to me, shattering my reverie.

"I remember it," said I after a couple of recuperative blinks. "When did you see it?"

"I had two opportunities to go into their kitchen," said Father. "Once when you were ill, and the second time when I used the washroom when Pierre was with me. I saw it both times, and I noticed the recognizable symbol often connected with Yosemite National Park."

"Ah, yes," said Mrs. Magillicuddy. "Me Willum and me used to go there when we's was young, we was."

"Were you perhaps there during the freak blizzard of 1967?" asked Father.

"I'll say we was!" said she, rocking Sybil's head in the process. "Brrrr! It was colder than cold's, it was."

"That was the year updrafts deposited snow on the sheer face of Half Dome," said Father. "There's a photograph of it in the Saranac Lounge, Martin. Some people thought they saw a face on the mountain. Some—my own dad among them—claimed it looked like Lou Costello."

"And with the gentle sloped part of the mountain behind—" said I.

"The veil of a nun," said Father.

Something skittered in the ivy.

I thought it was Father starting to laugh, and I almost started to join him. But then I realized it was just a lizard and he was only smiling. Thank Heaven I hadn't heaved up a belly laugh.

"But Mrs. Magillicuddy," said Father. "That car is not a hearse. It's owned by a couple of sweet old ladies who are going to start attending Mass here at St. Philomena's. There's nothing to be afraid of. Lou Costello is not coming for you, at least, not to take you away. He just wants to say hello."

"Are you sure's?" asked Mrs. Magillicuddy. "You wouldn't be foolin' an old woman, would ya?"

"I would not," said Father, patting her knee. "And I couldn't fool you if I wanted to, and you know it. Now, I want you to do a favor for me."

"Anything, Faddah."

"When Sybil wakes I'd like you to give these bracelets to her. She's a police officer, you know."

"No," said the old woman incredulously.

"Yes, indeed. And these are hers. Now Martin and I must be going. Right, Martin?"

"Anything you say, Father," said I. "By the way, Mrs. Magillicuddy, Sybil said this was to be a big day for her. Give her my best wishes, will you?"

"I'll remembers, I wills," said she, "an' I'll see that she does."

As we passed the statue of St. Joseph, the Patron of Departing Souls, I ventured, "Father, is that how you figured out where I was? You saw the picture at the Adirondack?"

"That's right," said he. "Believe it or not, Barlow pointed it out."

"Barlow. Wait a minute. He's the barroom ghost."

"That's right. You can ask Pierre. We all saw him pointing to a photo in the Saranac Lounge. When I got to where he'd been standing he was gone, and there was the picture of Half Dome after the blizzard of '67."

"Are you saying I owe my release from the Doily dungeon to a, a—"

"Yes," said Father. "Barlow, it seems, had a purpose to fulfill as well."

"I feel like I'm becoming a ghost magnet."

"You may have something there," said Father seriously. "Elza, Don Gusto, and now Barlow—each one's Purgatory somehow connected with you. Could it be that we have the makings of a mystic in our midst?"

"Could it be that you've been hitting the *Lacrimae Christi* and not telling me?"

"Does it bother you, Martin?"

"Doesn't it you?"

"I revel in it," said Father. "Think of the things you and I have seen. What marvelous times we live in!"

"I was thinking I understand why you didn't do a big reveal to everyone about how you solved the kidnapping."

"I reveal to those who need to know what they need to know."

"Right, sure."

"Martin, I don't need to grandstand. You wanted me to explain everything earlier outside the church. I could have said much, but there was no point."

"Well, how about filling in a few gaps for your chronicler?"

"Fair enough," said Father as we were passing the cemetery. "There was also the pumpernickel."

"Excuse me?" said I, hobbling to his left to put him between me and the gravestones.

"Keating said the clip on the pumpernickel was red."

"He did? Oh yes, come to think of it—"

"The day we first visited the Doily Sisters—Thursday—while you were helping Keating in the kitchen, the ladies told me that on the day Monsignor Aspic visited them—Wednesday—they had hair appointments, and that they had sent out Keating to purchase bread that evening. He couldn't have. They don't bake bread on Wednesdays at the Tory Hill Bakery. While they were serving us our tea—yes, the brew that caused you such gastric distress—Keating mentioned the red clip on the pumpernickel, assuring the ladies that it was fresh."

"That's right," said I. "I saw it when he was preparing the tray in the kitchen."

"He had to buy the bread that very morning—Thursday—or else it was a week old."

"He told me Mehitabelle fed bread older than two days to the birds."

"Hence it was a lie," said Father. "A seemingly small one, but one in which they had all agreed."

"Amazing that you caught it."

"How can you say that? It was you who drew my attention to it when we were in the bakery."

"I did?"

"To the pumpernickel, anyway."

"Ah well, you said I'd make a fine detective. Even, it turns out, on the subconscious level."

"So if the Doily Sisters and their butler were in on a collective lie—"

"Then they could have plotted together to poison me!"

"Uh, yes. Actually I was going to say their collective lie revolved around the time of Monsignor Aspic's disappearance, and their 'hearse' had been seen by Mrs. Magillicuddy at the Del Agua Mission when he held a press conference there. They had been following him, I think, or at least Keating had been. The pieces started coming together, and just in the nick of time as it turned out. I'd hate to think what Monsignor Aspic would have done if my arrival had been delayed by so much as a minute."

"Just how much of this do you intend to tell Cardinal Fulbright?"

"As little as possible, my Friend. The less he knows I know, the better."

97

"WHAT THE DEVIL DO YOU WANT?" roared Morley Fulbright.

"A few minutes of your time, Your Eminence," said Father.

We were standing on the balcony of the cardinal's penthouse suite at the Adirondack. From here we could see the megalopolis of Los Angeles sprawling like a drunken wildebeest before the rising sun. The cardinal was wrapped around with a puffy, silken, ocean blue bathrobe.

He was holding a saucer and cup of coffee in his left hand, and with his right he was massaging the bump on his forehead.

"I anticipated your wanting to see me immediately," explained Father, digging around in his cassock. He produced the leather pouch with the yellow tassels. "I have retrieved the papal artifact, as you wished." Without waiting for the cardinal to respond, he untied the noose and slipped the golden disk into his palm. "There it is, Your Eminence."

Morley's right hand flashed out, snatched the disk, and brought it close to his bloodshot eyes. "Good," he said at last. "Very good. A little late, but better than never."

"I don't understand," said Father.

"The nuncio left a few minutes ago on a flight to Seattle," said Fulbright gruffly. "He left a message to that effect at the Chancery. Naturally he didn't say when he'd be back to annoy me again."

Now you can grace your favorite table at "Paneno's," Your Gracelessness, thought the gardener, and that's all the gratitude you can muster?

"Martin," said Father, motioning to me.

I blinked, then I blinked again. "Oh," I said, producing the hideous Murkenstein chalice. Father had made me carry the damn thing as an act of humility. Now he made me hand it to the cardinal as an act of further debasement. Food for worms, indeed.

Morley looked at the disk in his right hand, the coffee in his left, then at Father, then at the chalice in my hand. He handed the disk to Father and grabbed the Murkenmug from me.

"I'm not going to let this out of my sight again," he said, brandishing it like a club.

"And the artifact?" asked Father, slipping it back into the pouch.

"I'll keep that in the wall safe in my own chambers from now on," said Fulbright. "Next time Sylvio Bonsignore drops in, I'll serve him crackers on it."

"That I'd like to see," said Father. "By the way, has Monsignor Aspic made an appearance?"

"I don't know. Has he?"

"I believe you will find him back at work when you return to the Chancery. That is where you're going, is it not?"

"I should say so. The place falls apart when I'm away for a few days."

"I don't suppose it would do any good to discuss my fees," said Father.

"It would not," said the cardinal. "You will have to take that up with Monsignor Aspic."

"I was afraid you would say that."

And that, as they say, was that. The ride down the elevator lacked the sense of triumph I had come to expect after round-up meetings with the cardinal. A landslide of weariness seemed to have descended upon Father as the doors rolled open revealing the marvelous lobby with its sumptuous chairs, lazy palms, and fascinating paintings. At this hour on a Monday, the place was deserted. Well, not quite. There was Mr. Maxwell at the registration counter, his hair glistening under a thick layer of pomade. And there, too, was none other than Edward Strypes Windham, standing before him with a look of confident determination, his bird-of-prey eyebrows perched at the crest of his long, resolute nose.

"I understand there's a position open," the dapper Tumblar was saying. "I'm here to see Mr. Reinholz, Mr. Cyril Reinholz. Monsieur Bontemps said he would be expecting me."

"I shall see if he's in his office," said Mr. Maxwell with all the enthusiasm of a mannequin.

Seeing that Mr. Windham was conducting business, I refrained from hailing him. Instead, I followed Father Baptist toward the hallway leading to the entrance where the Jeep was waiting, hopefully with doors that opened correctly, side to side.

Tuesday, November Twenty-first

The Feast of the Presentation
of the Blessed Virgin Mary by
Her Parents, Saints Joachim and Anne,
in the Temple at Jerusalem (13 BC)

∞ Early Evening Epilogue ∞

98

"ABOUT FIFTY MILES EAST OF HERE," said Father Baptist, "there's an interesting formation on the south-facing slope of a mountain. You can see it from Highway 18 as you drive toward Lake Arrowhead. It's more than twelve hundred feet tall, over four hundred feet wide, and covers seven and a half acres. It's visible for miles. The white settlers called it the 'Ace of Spades,' but the Indians saw it as an arrowhead pointing down to the hot mineral springs below. The lake is named after it."

"And your point?" asked the gardener.

"No one doubts that, as remarkable as it may appear, as clear and symmetrical as it is, it is a natural formation. What forces did God utilize when that mountain was made to create that image for all to see?"

"It's nice to know that once in a while God winks at us through His Creation."

"So why is it so hard to believe that He could fashion the image of the Crown of Thorns in a stone, He without whom was made nothing that was made?"

"Saint John one three. For some, like Sergeant Wickes, it's terribly hard."

"It's good to have you back, Martin. Should I assume that's a bottle of *Lacrimae Christi* under your jacket? I hope so because I'm tired of holding these glasses under my cassock so they won't clink."

"As you say, Father, it's good to be back."

"'For as Jonas was in the whale's belly three days and three nights,'" said Father.

"Saint Matthew twelve forty," said I. "But it wasn't really three days."

"It wasn't the belly of a whale, either."

"Well, there is that."

Yes, at long last, we were back in our peaceful garden. The sun had set, and Millie had stuffed us with dinner and gone out with Muriel, swearing on her Aunt Carmella's pot roast pan as she departed that she would not breathe a word to her best friend about the you-know-what down in the you-know-where. All that was dessert to the twelve-hour sleep Father had enjoyed before that. Me, I got some serious typing done. Sybil Wexler and Mrs. Magillicuddy had long since moved on. I wondered if the old gal had persuaded the girl who reminded her of her Nell to go visit her gingerbread house in the forest on the grounds of the Del Agua Mission. Perhaps Father and I would be following breadcrumbs by day's end, but then again, Sybil Wexler could take care of herself.

"You don't sound entirely at ease," said Father, holding out the glasses for sustenance. "You're destroying that cork."

"Not at all," said I as the thing finally came out. "The crumbs add 'chew' to the wine—several whole grades above 'bite,' 'fruitiness' and 'nuttiness' in connoisseurs' parlance. It's an L.A. thing."

"That mythical city of yours," sighed Father.

"Don't knock it till you've lived there a few years. It's become my home from home."

"The poet builds castles in the sky."

"And the fool gardener goes and lives in them—but I wouldn't call them castles in the sky. More like cardboard boxes under a freeway overpass."

"Be they ever so humble, and no doubt comfortable—you still don't seem relaxed."

"You try living in cardboard boxes and see how relaxed you are."

"You're spilling the wine."

"You're moving the glasses."

"Come on, Martin. Something's on your mind."

I managed to get enough of the stuff into our glasses for a taste. It always struck my tongue as bitter but my throat as comforting.

"Good Heavens," I caught myself. "We haven't toasted Our Lady."

"To She Who is our Life, our Sweetness, and our Hope," said Father, touching his glass to mine. This was good because my hand would have had a hard time finding his just then. He regarded me as he took a slow, grateful sip. After a minute of silent savoring, he finally inquired, "So what's up?"

I took another sip and regarded the wine rocking around in my glass. "… Purgatory, if you must know."

"What about Purgatory?"

"Don Gusto talking to the air for years?" said I, waving my glass around vaguely. "What was the point? To tell me the mission had moved. Millie found the flyer, didn't she?"

"Yes, but she wouldn't have spoken up about it on her own."

"But you might have found it where she left it on the kitchen table, and you being the great detective, you would have pieced it together."

"Perhaps, perhaps not. I might have set my coffee down on it and never noticed. I'm not the genius you suppose me to be, but it seems to me that from all ages God knew that the way to get us up there so I'd get a good look at it was to plant a bee in your bonnet—excuse me, a cocklebur in your sock. I needed to get it firmly impressed in my mind, and that visit to the ruins accomplished that. I'm still amazed that Bishop Jeremiah Ravenshorst, may he rest in peace, got so immersed in the fever of his quest that he neglected to take into account the change of sites of the greatest of the missions. He had his blind spots, as do I."

"Still, it seems overkill to me, making poor Don Gusto yack at the empty air year after year after year."

"I'm not saying that was his only reason for being, but it certainly was one of them. Maybe he needed a lesson in humility, he is in Purgatory after all."

"I wonder how many years Barlow has been pointing at the photograph in the Saranac Lounge."

"I have a feeling Edward will become an expert on Adirondack lore in no time. I suspect he'll tell us it's been going on for years."

"Years and years," said I.

"Martin, you're trembling."

"Naw, it's just another earthquake. *El Señor de los Temblores,* and all that."

"Martin."

"We joked earlier about me being a ghost magnet, but you know I'm no mystic. I'm colorblind at the blue end of the spectrum, yet they are somehow connected to me."

"I believe it was you who first made the effort to connect with Elza."

"Yes, but I didn't expect her to serenade me on the piano."

"Perhaps not," he chuckled. But then he gathered me into his eyes. "You take them seriously—not as the object of a quasi-scientific ghost hunt, nor as the confirmation of self-aggrandizing aspirations of psychic powers, but as souls languishing in the purifying fires of Purgatory. You pray for them, and most important, you don't pat yourself on the back for being special. Dare I say that's what makes you … never mind. Surely this isn't what's troubling you."

" … Okay, it's about Don Gusto. Last night I had a dream that he came into my bedroom. I was seated at my typewriter copying some verses from Jeremiah that I thought touched on my predicament when I was a guest at the second happiest place on earth, Doilyland."

"And what verses were those?"

"Chapter twenty, verses seven and nine."

"What about eight?"

"Outshone by ten and resolved by eleven. Look, it was a dream. Only in the REM state would I compare myself to a great prophet, even in one of his frustrated moments. I think it was triggered by the threatening scenario Roderick Roundhead painted yesterday morning about what would happen if I spoke up about his aunts' shenanigans. He as much as said some of our parishioners would turn on me—"

"And that bothers you."

"Right."

"After all you've done for them."

"Well …"

"Surely they owe you more than they do me."

"I said it was a dream."

"So what did Señor Gusto have to say?"

"Nothing. He placed his left hand on my open Bible and raised his right hand like he was taking an oath. Other than that he just stood there smiling."

"That's it?"

"Then he disappeared just like he did at the mission. Everything faded except his eyes and the gap in his smile. Then he blinked and his eyes were gone. The hole was the last to go."

"Really."

"Then I woke up. Surprise, surprise, I had fallen asleep before the typewriter with my Bible open beside me. It was open to Jeremiah."

"And?"

"And there was a handprint scorched on the pages of my Bible."

"I'd very much like to see that."

"I've got it here but it's too dark to see clearly."

"I thought I smelled something charred."

"Anyway, that explains my jitters."

"Hmm."

The city hummed around us. Yes, and many of the hummers were, in fact, morons. They were drowned out by harrumphs of all the geniuses who comprised the rest of the chorus. It occurred to me that every spiritual icon of the twentieth century spent at least some time in the City of Angels, from Aleister Crowley to L. Ron Hubbard to

Krishnamurti to Pope John Paul II. Was it the morons or the geniuses that brought them here? Or was it something deeper, something literally within the very ground that drew them here like metal to magnetite?

"By the by," I ventured, "what was the nuncio's message for Arthur?"

"Ah, just a quotation from a fragment of the diary of Padre Alonso Miranda. Until the site of the actual Del Agua Mission was discovered the document was considered to be of dubious authenticity, but now it's enjoying newfound interest."

"Why should it concern Arthur?"

"It refers to the stone altar, actually. Since St. Philomena's was originally an *asistencia* of the Del Agua Mission, Padre Miranda had something to do with the establishment of the Shrine of Our Lord of the Earthquakes. Apparently the stone altar was here long before the Europeans discovered it and realized its significance."

"So what does the fragment say?"

"I'm quoting: 'Even the pagans we first encountered here reverenced the stone. Eerily, they named it 'The Headdress of Agony.'"

"They saw it as a crown, then."

"Indeed."

"That's awesome, Father. Really it is."

"How it came to be here is open to speculation. I'm no geologist, but it sure doesn't look like it came from around here. That the Indians already revered it is significant. I wonder if the site of Saint Philomena's had a pagan past before a Catholic one."

"I wonder who else is buried down there with Father Albert. Oddly, that reminds me. What about Christine's Crucifix?"

"I have it here," said Father.

"So you decided not to bury it with Father Albert."

"Precisely the opposite. After an admittedly tough round of soul searching, I decided it belonged around his neck and instructed Roberto to arrange it so. Yet, and this he swore on his mother's grave to be true, when he finished the internment he found the Crucifix resting on the stone altar. He could think of no recourse but to give it to me."

"Wow. It must yet have a purpose to serve up here in the light of day."

"Or in the dark of night, as the case may be. I must also add that Roberto admitted that he was exhausted from a long day of strenuous labor. He couldn't swear, even on the place where he buried his pet cat, that he had positively placed the Crucifix inside the coffin. You know sometimes you can have a task so clearly in your mind that you think you've done it—"

"But you haven't," said I. "Story of my life."

"So rather than add to Roberto's tasks, I decided the Crucifix will stay with me for the time being."

"I'm glad."

A squirrel came scampering out of the tree, coming to a screeching halt at the base of the cement birdbath. The light from the clock on the stove in the kitchen gleamed in its apprehensive round eyes. If it had held out a nutshell I might have obliged with a bit of wine, but as it was I poured it into our glasses. My hands had calmed down. The squirrel fluttered its tail a few times, then vanished into the ivy.

"By the way," said Father, "was it you who suggested that Jonathan consult *The Pedagogue* by St. Clement of Alexandria?"

"Um, yes. First I suggested Leviticus nineteen twenty-seven: 'Nor shall you cut your hair round-wise: nor shave your beard.'"

"And what did you intend to accomplish by introducing Jonathan to these references?"

"I suppose I was supplying him with ammunition."

"That you did."

"Even before the Leviticus I told him to consult you, really I did. But you were occupied and he was adamant."

"And you were brilliant," said Father, chuckling, then laughing outright. "So far as I know, Stella and Jonathan have yet to meet face-to-face. Still, if I get the chance, I may try to dissuade Jonathan from this course. She'll see it as reprisal, and my sense is that she can hurt him more than he can hurt her."

"Hoo-boy. I resign as advisor to the lovelorn."

"Of course, they may just laugh themselves half to death and get on with their courtship. Let's hope that's the outcome."

"Right."

"Otherwise there will be two more parishioners who'd love to talk to a nationally-syndicated newscaster about you."

"Ouch."

The squirrel reappeared from the undergrowth, wiggled its nose at us inscrutably, and then tore back up the tree from which it had come in the first place. I celebrated his homecoming by pouring more of the comforting tears.

"So," I said, "are there any other loose ends before we move on to our next adventure?"

"I can think of one. I need to visit Cheryl Farnsworth. Perhaps I should call and make an appointment. Did you say Warden Tracy prefers to be called Gladys?"

"Ahem. As I recall, she prefers to be called Warden Tracy."

"I'm intrigued by Miss Farnsworth's foreknowledge of events. And now she wants to return to the Sacraments. This is when being a priest is worth it."

"I can imagine, and that's all that I can do," said I.

The rumble of the chorus of morons and geniuses all around us seemed to grow louder. I thought about all those millions of people going about their tasks, so deeply distracted by the chaos of their lives. Then I thought of the few I had seen at the Adoration Chapel at the Monastery of the Archangels, where geniuses and morons turned their attention to the Point of their existence. As long as there were outposts like that, oases of Faith in the wilderness, then certainly there was Hope. And now Saint Philomena's—our sweet, crumbling, little Saint Philomena's!—was home to a fascinating miracle. As Father had reminded us, a bleeding Host is not a greater miracle than the Holy Eucharist that we receive at Mass. It is merely a compelling confirmation of the hidden Reality. And what a Reality!

"Wine's almost finished," said Father. "Just enough for a final toast."

"How wine flies," sighed the gardener. "Perhaps I should fetch another bottle."

"I think not, Martin. Actually, I was wondering if you had plans for this evening."

"Other than finishing off this bottle, no."

"Well I've got an idea. Instead of turning in, let's do something unexpected. Let's go on a lark."

"A lark."

"You know, something you'd appreciate. Something whacky. On one level it will be most amusing. On another, tragic—that will fulfill your need for pathos. Who knows? Perhaps we'll find ourselves in another of your adventures."

"Ah ha. A lark. And where precisely is this whacky, amusing, tragic, pathetic bird to be found?"

"I was thinking of that flier someone handed you outside Edison Winger's shop the other day.

"Our Lady of Irwindale?"

"It has come to my attention that some of our parishioners are going there to see the apparition. Some of them are getting rather wrapped up in it, as I understand it. I was thinking I'd like to go and see for myself. Sound intriguing?"

"I would have used another word, but okay."

"You don't sound enthused."

"I could fake it, but I'm too crotchety. No, but seriously, where you go I go. Surely it could fill a page or two in the ol' chronicles."

"There's always room for more castles in the sky, eh?" said Father.

"And cardboard boxes," said I. "Never underestimate the lure of the ordinary."

"Nor the Reality of the Supernatural," said Father, raising his glass. "I'd like to toast Don Gusto, his servant Profirio, and your friend, Elza. May their souls and all the souls of the Faithful Departed through the Mercy of God rest in peace."

"Amen," said I, knocking his glass and finishing mine.

He set down his empty wineglass on the bench. Reluctantly, I followed suit. I listened for the bray of a burro or the tinkle of piano keys but heard none. I sniffed the air for a whiff of sage or the tickle of blueberry brandy. Nothing.

"Well," said Father, rubbing his hands together. "Let us embark on another adventure."

"An adventure in a rock quarry," I said skeptically.

"Exactly."

"You said the other day that you'd want to go in disguise."

"Quite right. I must see to that at once."

"You really are serious."

"Definitely."

"Okay," I sighed. "You go do what you gotta do. I'll wait here."

"Excellent," said he, gathering up the empties. "I won't be long."

I closed my eyes and listened as he entered the rectory through the kitchen door. His footfalls circled around Millie's dishwasher and meandered into the bowels of the rickety building. I rested my hand on the Bible beside me on the bench. Ah, the bitter smell of the charred pages reached my nostrils. It wasn't blueberry brandy, but it was something I could touch. While it wouldn't prove anything to a stiff-necked skeptic, it confirmed all I needed to know.

"Yes," I mused aloud. "From mausoleum to dungeon, from photocopy shop to corporate office, from morgue to mission to mansion. The rich, the poor, the angry, the mad, the powerful and the put-upon. Just when you think you've seen it all ... the rock quarry of Our Lady of Irwindale!"

There was a plop in the ivy.

I didn't have to open my eyes to know that the little stone bird had fallen from his insecure perch on the rim of the cement birdbath.

"You are so right, my Friend," said I, raising my eyelids and wishing I had seen where he had fallen.

It's a long way down and who knows what's lurking in that ivy, but I'd do it a thousand times for that little lump of stone. Wouldn't you know, I found him almost immediately. As I struggled to my feet, I looked down at the thing in my hand.

"All right?" I asked.

I do believe I could almost see him wink, wiggle his formless wing, and say, "'S'all right!"

The End

—Init: August 15, 2002
The Feast of the Assumption

—Finis: November 8, 2006
The Feast of the Four Crowned Martyrs of Pannonia;
Saint Godfrey (a.k.a. Geoffrey) of France;
also of Blessed John Duns Scotus who held the title
Doctor of the Immaculate Conception at Oxford;
and, coincidentally,
the birthday of my friend Charles A. Coulombe.
Happy birthday, Charles!

Rock Haven.

Half Dome
"After the freak blizzard of '67—H.D."
The Saranac Lounge, Hotel Adirondack.

NOTES: